The ARSENAL

The ARSENAL

Slaves Among Us

Kenneth Whaley

Library of Congress Control Number: 2007903640
ISBN: Hardcover 978-1-4257-8553-6
Softcover 978-1-4257-8547-5

This book was printed in the United States of America.

To order additional copies of this book, contact:
Xlibris Corporation
1-888-795-4274
www.Xlibris.com
Orders@Xlibris.com
36923

MY HEART FELT THANKS TO

CONNIE,

BARBARA,

And

RUSS

FOR THEIR CONTNUED, UNFALTERING,
ASSISTANCE AND SUPPORT

ALSO

I WANT TO THANK GREG BAIN FOR HIS COUNSEL
AND ART WORK ON THE FRONT COVER.

Chapter One

"This is not a fake call! No, I'm not drunk! Will you just listen for a minute? All I'm trying to do . . . Well the only way you're going to find out is to come over here and see for yourself. You know where I am? That's right. No, I'm not going anywhere, I'll be right here."

Lost in thought for a moment, Leon, standing in the dimly lit hallway of the Bartlett Hotel, pauses before placing the receiver back on the hook, then turns toward his room. A fixture hangs, giving off enough light to expose the need of new paint, fresh wallpaper, and carpet. The floor creaks under his weight as he walks.

He notices the door across the hall from his room is cracked enough to allow an eye to peer through. It closes. His right hand catches the knob to his room, two more steps and he is safely back in his rented space.

He glances at the bed with a rumpled bedspread, and then crosses the room to a mirrored vanity. A hand on the top rung and a twist of his wrist turns the only straight-back chair in the room to face the mirror. He sits, places his elbows on the dresser, puts his head in his hands, leans forward, and looks at the mirror before him. He sucks in a long breath of air via his nose, then blows it out through his puffed jaws and rounded lips.

"God, how did this happen? Where has the time gone? I'm tired, and I feel as old as dirt."

Leon, at five feet eleven inches tall, weighs one hundred and seventy pounds with a medium frame. He has not shaved or bathed for three days. Lines in his face and his graying unkempt hair, make him seem deeply distressed. His partially open faded tan shirt tucked in at the waist of his wrinkled pants, and a pair of old scuffed Western-style boots complete his apparel. A chain holding a gold cross around his neck is easily seen. A shave, a haircut, a hot bath, decent food, and a long sleep might make him look and feel human again.

His body shakes when his mind snaps back to the reality of his life.

"They'll be here any minute now," he says to himself in a whisper as he has all night. "How should I tell them?" A pause, his mind turns. "Will they believe me? Hell, I can't prove any of this. I've got to stop second-guessing myself, I've got to tell them.

"They'll probably not believe a word I say, and blame it all on me." His mind is spinning now, "I shouldn't have called them. Damn! Damn! Damn!"

Almost in a panic, he is on his feet, ranting out loud, "What'll I do now? I should have left and let them figure things out for themselves. I can't change anything by myself. Where did everybody go?"

He strides toward the window of his room, his thoughts becoming a blur.

"I have to get away! Get out of here! Have to leave!" his voice echoes off the walls spurring him on. Four long steps to the door and he will be gone. His hand grabs the knob. One quick twist . . .

BAM! BAM! BAM!

"Leon, you in there . . . ? This is Chief Durrell Turner. You called me a little bit ago. Open up . . ."

Startled, the half-crazed man reacts instinctually; his hand moves from the knob to the key in the lock and gives it a turn.

"I know you're in there, Leon. I heard talking, and I know you just locked the door. Now open up!"

BAM! BAM! BAM! BAM! The thumps on the door are more rapid and insistent.

No response.

"Dammit, man! Open the door!

"Aw, to hell with it. Before I kick this door in, run downstairs and see if Vern has another key," the chief orders his Deputy Raymond Marcum.

As Durrell waits for Marc to bring the key back, he tries the door again, and then bends down for a look through the keyhole. The key in the hole on the other side has blocked any view of the room.

Marc returns.

"Put a little piece of your chewing gum on the end of that key. See if you can put it in the hole and turn the key on the other side so we can push it out." the chief calmly instructs his deputy.

Marc does as he is told, and after playing around with it for a minute, he succeeds. The key falls to the floor on the other side of the door.

A quick turn of the key on their side, and the lawman opens the door with a little push of his hand. He stands and looks inside to determine his next move.

The eye peeking through the cracked door across the hall is not missing a thing.

"Careful going in, he might have a gun," the senior officer cautions.

The first man through the open door is Chief Turner, his arm stretched straight, gun in hand, swinging side to side, not knowing what to expect. Deputy Ray Marcum moves directly behind him to stand back to back with his boss. The chief turns to the right toward the bed while Marcum turns to the right toward the window.

"There's no one here."

"You're right about that."

"Check under the bed, Marc. There's nowhere else to hide."

Carefully, the deputy moves to the bed, bends down on one knee, and with the barrel of his gun, carefully pushes back the hanging bedspread. Cautiously, he lowers his head to look.

"He's not here," he offers with a silent sigh of relief.

"That doesn't surprise me much. But I don't understand how we heard a voice, and heard the door lock, if he wasn't in here. I figured he was just playing around when he called. I'll check with—"

Marc cuts the chief off, motioning at the rumpled bed with the barrel of his gun. "You better look at this."

Silence falls over the room as DT moves to the bed, his eyes find the object barely showing beneath the bedspread.

"Are those toes?"

"Yeah, they sure are," the deputy assures. "Could this be Leon under here?" He continues with a "we gotcha now" manner in his voice. Then, with a smirk of a grin on his face, he pokes at the toes with his gun.

"Get up, Leon, we got you," he orders. "Get up."

The bedspread lays still.

"Pull it back. Let's see what we've got here. Be ready, we don't know what might happen," the chief warns.

With his gun in his right hand, Marc nervously picks up the bedspread from the head of the bed with his left hand and pulls it down. He stops when he uncovers dark brown hair and the face of a woman.

"Keep going," DT urges.

His deputy pulls the blanket off and tosses it onto the floor.

"It's a woman!" he exclaims. "Looks like she's dead."

Chief Turner bends over the bed to put the first two fingers of his left hand on the woman's temple, at the same time holstering his gun.

"No pulse," he calmly mutters as his fingers move to the side of the woman's neck. "Nope, no heartbeat that I can tell. I don't know where Leon got off to, but we sure as hell got us a dead body, just like he said." Hc turns to his deputy.

"Don't touch anything else. We have to get the sheriff and the coroner over here. Go downstairs and have Vern shut this place up. Leon just might still be here in the building somewhere. Go back to the office and call the sheriff. Tell him what we've got here, and ask him to call the coroner. Don't touch the phone on the wall out there in the hall, there might be prints on it, and don't use the phone downstairs. I don't want this getting out all over town any sooner than it has to. And here, take this key back to Vern. Now get going, I'll need you back here," the police chief commands.

"Do you think she was killed?" Marc asks.

"I don't know," he responds. "The coroner can tell us that when he gets here. But we have to assume she was until we know for sure. Now, get going and get back here; and don't tell anybody about any of this."

"Okay, I'll be right back. I'll tell Vern," the excited deputy says as he leaves through the open door.

Since things are secure for the moment, Chief Turner turns his attention to making himself aware of all the facts at hand. The furniture is sparse with just a four-poster bed, an old overstuffed chair, a vanity dresser with a three-foot-wide round mirror attached to the top, and a straight-back wooden chair. There are no closets in the room. The one window overlooks a straight drop to the first floor ground, then with a slight slope it goes on another fifteen feet to a creek bed of pebbles and sand. The window is painted shut and looks like it hasn't been opened for years.

He notices the sewer drain from the hotel running out to the creek where it dumps into the water. It starts from under the building somewhere, so a man could not use it to slide down from the second floor. The electric wire coming to the building is too far away from the window to be reached. It's obvious nobody left this room through this window.

"The bathroom's down the hall," he mutters to himself as he moves to the bed.

"I know I heard a man's voice in here, and I know someone locked that door just before we came in. But where could he have gone to?"

He looks down at the body on the bed, letting his eyes scan the scene.

She appears to be in her late twenties. Clad in a rumpled white blouse tucked in the waist of a dark blue straight skirt, she's lying on her right side and stomach, her face on the pillow with her shoulder-length dark brown hair lying loosely about her face and neck.

"Looks like she just went to sleep," he muses.

Her shoes are lying on the floor. He looks for stockings or socks, but finds nothing.

"The body's cold, she's been dead a while. No marks I can see. Nice looking woman, damn shame. I wonder what happened here? No sign of a fight, no evidence of a man ever being here," he puzzles, "I'd better check the bathroom and knock on the rest of the doors up here to see if anybody knows anything."

Entering the hallway he notices the eye peering through the ajar door across the way.

"I'll be back to talk to you, Mavis, just as soon as I check the rest of these rooms."

All it takes is a glance into the bathroom to discover there is nobody hiding there. He checks the knobs and knocks on each door, working his way back to Mavis's room. All the doors are locked, and no one responds to his inquiry.

"They're all gone for the day. They won't be back for a while," Mavis advises from the now open doorway of her room.

"Are all these rooms occupied?" the chief asks.

"Yes, they're all rented out," she replies.

"Are you all right? Everything okay?" he asks, walking toward her.

"Open your door all the way so I can see inside. I need to be sure there's no one else in there with you," he instructs firmly.

She opens the door, but keeps both hands on the edge of it and walks backward.

"Move over to the middle of the room," he demands.

He rests his hand on the butt of his gun, and then pushes the door back against the wall with his foot. Two steps inside is all he needs to see that everything is what it seems to be, no Leon.

"Did you see everything that's gone on across the hall? Anything you can tell me?" he asks.

"Well, I saw a man, who was talking on the phone, walk back to his room and close the door. Then I heard him talking real loud in there. The next thing I know, you and Marc show up. That's all I know," she insists.

"What did he say?"

"He kept telling somebody he shouldn't have called. Said he'd be blamed for it no matter what."

"What did he look like?"

"He was about six feet tall. Had on a button-up-type white shirt and a pair of tan pants. Oh yes, he had on cowboy boots. You know, like they wear out West, and a cross on a gold chain around his neck."

"Did you see a woman with him when he got here?"

"I've not seen a woman at all."

"I'd appreciate it if you'd take the time to write down everything you saw, and sign it. I'll need it for my records. Thanks, Mavis, I appreciate your help," he says and turns for the door.

"I sure will. Would you like a cup of coffee? I've got a fresh pot."

Mavis Greenley has lived in this one room for years. A two-burner hotplate sets on the table, which allows her to cook when she feels like it. She never married, says she has never found a man that had any interest in her, or her in him. She makes everyone's business her own, and that being the case, not much goes on around this end of town that Mavis does not see or hear about. Her whole life is peering from her window, or through a partially cracked door. She is fifty-five years old, sort of frumpy, and a bit overweight. She works at the five and ten store a block down the street.

Chief Turner has always felt that Mavis would like to get him alone. And since he doesn't see her that way, nor need the gossip it would cause, there is no chance of her luring him with a cup of coffee, or anything else, to stay in her room.

"Can't right now, Mavis . . . too much going on I have to take care of. But thanks anyway," he says over his shoulder. "Stay in your room until this is over. Okay?"

"Surely, DT . . . anything you say."

He turns toward the head of the stairs, glances through the doorway at the woman lying on the bed, changes his direction, enters the room, and takes one more look around. He picks the key up from the floor, closes the door, and locks it. Key in hand, he descends the stairs to the lobby.

"Vern, did you lock the place up like Marc asked you to?" he inquires of the desk clerk.

Vern Whitman is a thin balding man, fifty-seven years old, with a good amount of nervous energy. His movements are quick, to the point of being jerky. The lack of clutter, along with the apparent organization at the front desk, attests to Vern's need for order within his life. His pants and shirt are neatly pressed. Wire rim reading glasses set on the tip of his nose, allowing him to peer over them at things a distance away. Rumors in town have Vern and Mavis wrapped up in an affair that has been going on for years.

"Yep, I did, nobody has come in or gone out," he replies.

"Did you see the man and woman in 204 when they checked in?"

"I didn't, but I went home about six o'clock last night. I see here where he checked in at about seven thirty. Betty Marie was on the desk till midnight, so she must have seen him. There's no mention of a woman on the register. Here . . . see for yourself," Vern righteously states as he spins the register around on the desk.

Chief Turner walks over to the desk and looks down.

"I see you write in this blank space here how many people check in at one time. There's nothing in the blank beside Leon's name. Does that mean he was by himself when he got here?"

"I guess so. That's the way we do it," the daytime desk clerk explains.

"I'll need to talk to Betty Marie, but don't bother her right now. I'll stop over at her house later on," the police officer advises.

"Marc said there's a dead woman up there, is that right?" Vern asks.

Before DT can answer, he hears Marc's voice at the door wanting to be let inside.

"They're on the way. What'll we do now?" the deputy asks, obviously caught up in the mystery of it all.

"I want you to check everywhere downstairs to see if you can find our missing man. He's about six feet tall wearing a white shirt and tan pants. If you find anybody you don't know, hold them and find me. And keep your eyes open, we don't know what this man might do," Mr. Turner advises.

As Marc turns away to begin his search, the leader of the investigation, once again, puts his focus on Vern.

"Were you here about forty-five minutes ago?" He asks.

"Yep." Vern is quick to reply.

"That phone upstairs in the hall is hooked up through your switchboard down here, isn't it?" DT's question is more like a statement of fact. Without letting Vern answer, he continues, "And that being the case, you would have to put a call through for anyone using it. Am I right?"

"Yep, I sure did," Vern offers, with a look of "where's this headed?"

The chief's expression turns serious; his forehead scowls.

"Did you stay on the line to hear what was said?" his voice matches the look on his face.

"Now, DT, you know I'm not allowed to do that. Mr. Bartlett could fire me for sure for doing that," the nervous clerk quivers.

"I need to know that someone else heard what I heard, that's all, Vern. I won't bring you in on this unless I just have to. Now answer me, did you hear what was said?"

"I heard every word," he answers flatly. "I heard him tell you there was a dead woman there in his room, that he didn't kill her, and that he would tell you all about it when you got here."

Now more relaxed, Durrell insists, "Take a piece of paper and write down everything you remember was said by him and me, and sign it at the bottom. If we don't find this guy, I'll need it to prove he was even here.

"I won't use it unless I just have to," DT's redundancy is calming to the edgy man's nerves.

"One more thing, you'd better call Mr. Bartlett and let him know what's going on," the chief speaks as he slips the key to room 204 into his pants pocket and walks toward the front door.

"I will. I will do that," Vern affirms as he watches the law turn the key to open the outside door.

"I'm going outside to look around a bit. If I'm not back when the sheriff and the doc get here, call my office and have Billy get me on my car radio. Come over here and lock this door behind me. Nobody in, nobody out. Got it?"

"Yes, sir, I surely will." The response is quick and positive.

About a dozen of the town's people have gathered outside to greet the chief when he opens the door and steps out onto the sidewalk. He knows they are curious about the small commotion. He holds up his hands and speaks.

"I'll tell you all about what's going on later. Right now, I have my job to do. So, thanks for your understanding."

Durrell Turner is six feet two inches tall and weighs two hundred pounds. He is a young-looking forty-five-year-old with his jet black hair and narrow mustache. He is dressed, as usual, in jeans with a dark blue shirt. Patches on his shoulders, and a badge pinned to his left breast pocket, clearly indicate he is the chief of police of Bartlettsville. His other breast pocket holds his cigarettes and sunglasses. The peace officer's utility belt carries his handcuffs, a leather pouch for extra ammunition, and a holster with a hammer strap containing his Colt revolver. The two-inch heels of his shined black boots make him taller, and look more forceful. His overall appearance is one of the man in charge, a man with the ability to back up anything he says.

He steps off the porch and walks to his car. The black 1947 sedan is decorated with a single light on top. The word POLICE is painted down both sides with white paint, and a long steel antenna extends upward from the rear bumper. As he slides behind the wheel, his stomach growls, letting him know he has not eaten anything yet today.

Raymond Marcum, Marc to most people, starts searching the first floor of the hotel just as his boss asked him to do. DT's full-time deputy is twenty-eight years old, measures six feet in height, and weighs in at two hundred thirty pounds. He keeps fit for his job, so along with his large-boned frame, he is a handful in a fight. His blond hair short in a burr cut, a round face, big dark blue eyes, and a wide mouth, all give him a look of youth and innocence. People who know him realize he has a great tenacity for his job and takes it very seriously. His garb is similar to DT's, except the badge he wears has the word "deputy" across it.

Marc looks at the large octagon-shaped wooden clock on the wall behind the front desk before as he starts down the hall to check the rooms.

"It's ten after nine. This day is sure off to one hell of a start," he says to himself.

At each door, he knocks then waits a few seconds before he calls out, "This is Deputy Marcum, open up."

People answer their doors dressed in all sorts of getups. Robes and underwear seem to be the dress of the morning. One thing all of the occupants have in common is their questioning look when they see him in the hallway.

"What's going on, Marc?" he hears in one form or another at every door.

It takes time, but he is able to check every room on the first floor. There is no trace of Leon.

"Let me have the keys to the cellar and the storage room doors," He demands of Vern as he walks up to the front desk.

"Now, Marc, I can't do that. I don't have a key to fit either of those two doors," Vern explains.

"I have to get in there. You heard DT, I have to look everywhere. Where are the keys?" he asks, disappointed at the desk clerk's response.

"As I say, I don't really know. I just called Mr. Bartlett, he's on his way over here, and maybe he knows where they are. Nobody ever goes in there. The doors are always locked, been that way for years."

"Hand me that lost and found box you've got back there. I seem to remember some keys in there. Won't hurt to try."

The deputy dumps the contents of the box on the desk and begins to search through the clutter of assorted items, finally coming up with three keys.

"Ha!" he comments. "Let's see if any of these will work."

As Vern picks up the mess just created for him, the officer walks down the hall to the storage room. The first key he tries fits.

He moves inside to discover old paperwork piled on top of boxes of who knows what. Just a lot of junk and dust. He closes and locks the door as he leaves.

The cellar is next.

At the lobby, Vern is unlocking the door to let the sheriff and Mr. Bartlett inside.

"I'm Sheriff Collins, Vern, do you remember me?"

"I surely do, Sheriff. Morning, Mr. Bartlett," Vern acknowledges.

"Doc Edwards is right behind me, so leave the door open," the sheriff commands.

"What's going on here?" poses Jefferson Lee Bartlett, the only living relative of a long list of Bartletts, the village founders.

The sheriff is about to answer when he hears Doc Edwards's voice.

"Morning, Mr. Bartlett. Morning, Sheriff, Vern. I got here as quick as I could. I hear we have a body, is that right?" Doc asks.

"That's about all I know, Doc. Where is she, Vern? We might as well get started," the officer pushes on.

Vern is just about to hang up the phone, when he hears the question.

"Thanks, Billy, tell him right away."

"The dead woman is upstairs in 204, Sheriff. You going to wait on DT, he'll be right here?"

"No, we should move right along here. We'll catch him up when he gets here," Doc reasons.

"Well then, you better take this key with you. I'm pretty sure he locked that door, because I saw him have a key in his hand when he came downstairs." The organized desk clerk extends his hand.

"Thanks," the sheriff says. "We'll be upstairs, so send him up when he gets here."

DT's car radio cracks with the static of an incoming message. "Chief, this is Billy. You there? Over."

He grabs the microphone, and puts it close to his mouth. "Go ahead, Billy."

"Vern just called and said the sheriff is at the hotel. Over."

"Thanks, I'm on my way there now," DT answers and drops the mike on the seat beside him.

Marc puts the second of the three keys in the lock of the cellar door. It turns.

"How about that? It's my lucky day," he mutters and pulls the door toward himself exposing the stairway leading down.

The steps are not much more than a ladder nailed at the top, the side rails resting on the mud and stone floor below.

"I wonder if these will hold me?" He thinks before putting his right foot on the top one, being very careful. It is only about six feet to the cellar floor, but a fall like that could break something.

"It's sort of spooky looking, I'd best be aware." he thinks, and loosens his gun in its holster.

DT walks into the lobby about to ask Vern about the open front door, when he hears Marc shouting at the top of his lungs, clamoring up the cellar stairs. He runs down the hall toward the lobby, and yells again.

"Oh my God! Bodies! There're bodies down there in the cellar!"

"What?" Durrell yells back.

"DT, I went down in the cellar to check it out just like you said, and I found some bodies. Probably eight or ten of them, all laid out in boxes. Come on, I'll show you," Marc pants with excitement.

"Man, oh man, this day is full of surprises. What's going to happen next?" the chief exclaims just before he hears a voice he knows to be Doc's.

"I can tell you it's not going to be long before you find out, because I've got another little piece of news."

The chief, speechless and braced for the unexpected, turns to see Doc standing at the bottom of the stairs.

"You know the body of the dead woman you said is upstairs in 204? Well, sir . . . she's gone . . . she's not there."

Chapter Two

She steps from the doorway out onto the wooden porch leaving the screen door to slam behind her. The bright sun has the world lit up so that everything looks alive.

It's the year 1855, a Saturday morning, and her world is aglow. The air is so sweet to her nose she wants to chew it up and swallow it. Spring is here. She's so happy her legs want to jump, hop, and skip instead of walk. The porch steps creak under her weight as she steps to the ground on her way to the barn.

She looks up to see a cloudless blue sky, listens to the birds calling to each other, and watches clucking chickens as they peck at the ground.

"I love today. I want it to never end," she sings to herself.

Her name is Sheree (Shur-ee) and she's ten years old. She has long dark brown hair that hangs down to the center of her back. Her mama curls it on the sides in the front, and lets the rest hang straight. But today she's going to ride Pooch, her horse, so her hair is gathered up into a pony tail; held tight with a piece of yellow ribbon, leaving the curls hang down in the front on both sides. Skirts and dresses are all right, but she would rather wear pants, like she is today. Her mama says she's beautiful no matter what she wears.

She loves her mama. One reason is she fixes her breakfast and fusses over her to make sure she's dressed right with clean clothes. They talk about things Sheree likes to do, like riding Pooch, and playing with her dog, Peaches. Mama hugs her a lot and tells her how much she loves her. It makes a ten-year-old feel good about herself.

"I feel free. I like being me." The song continues in her mind.

She doesn't see her daddy all that much, mostly on the weekends. He travels a lot, so he's gone for days and weeks at a time. He has business friends come to see him a lot, sometimes they stay overnight. Some of them stay over the weekends. They go into the den, close the doors, and have long meetings. She doesn't know what they have to talk about that takes so much time, but she wonders about it.

Daddy gave her Pooch for her last birthday. She knows he loves her, and she loves him too, but she wishes they could be together more, to talk the way she and Mama do. She has a sister, Charlotte, her age, and a brother, Robert, seven years older. People say she and her sister look a lot alike, and that's so, except Charlotte's hair is black and her skin is darker.

Robert goes to school in Philadelphia, so he's not around except for holidays and the summer months. Charlotte goes to regular school, but Sheree doesn't. Her mother says she's special, and that's why she's tutored at home. Her mama says she has been reading since she was two years old. Sheree has no friends so her books keep her busy, and they let her learn about new places, places she's never been.

Well, that is not quite true. She does have one friend Daddy and Mama do not know about. It's a secret. His name is Randall, but she calls him Randy. He lives on the next farm over called Der Bote. She met him last summer when she was out riding Pooch. Now they're best friends. He even kissed her once and asked if she would be his girlfriend. It was only a peck on the cheek, but it meant a lot to her. Now she has a secret boyfriend.

They tell each other everything, sworn to be kept secret, of course. They meet as often as they can by a big weeping willow tree that marks the edge of their adjoining land. A fence is nailed to the side of the tree, showing that it belongs to her family's farm.

They both know they'll meet there, if they can, no later than ten thirty in the morning on Saturdays, and three thirty in the afternoon on Tuesdays and Thursdays. When they get to the willow, they wait about fifteen minutes. If the other one doesn't show up by then, they leave. They can't tell their folks about their friendship because their parents have forbidden them to talk to their neighbors on that side of their farms. It's always been this way. Both have asked why they can't be friendly, but the parents just say, "Do what you're told, and stay away from those people."

She hears the screen door slam, then her mama's voice, "Sheree, you be careful with that horse and don't run him. You stay on our property, and don't be gone all day. Do you hear me, honey?"

Her mama thinks she's too little to ride Pooch, but her daddy says to let her have some fun.

She looks back over her shoulder. "I hear you, Mama. I won't be gone all that long. I'll be careful."

She turns back toward the barn to see Jim, their around-the-house hand, dressed in an old faded blue print long-sleeved shirt, jeans, and boots, leading Pooch out through the barn door with the reins in his right hand.

"I got him all ready for you, honey," he says as she walks up to them.

He reaches out with his free hand, while pulling Pooch's head the other direction with the reins.

"Now, don't let him see this carrot," he whispers. "Take it and give it to him after I give you the reins. Your daddy says Pooch will know the carrot is from you that way. And don't forget, don't tease him with it because that'll make him so he won't trust you."

"Okay, Jim, I know . . . I won't. Thanks for remembering the carrot." She takes the reins from him.

Pooch turns his head and nuzzles against hers. She offers him the carrot, which he gladly takes from her fingers with his velvety soft lips. She hears him crunching as she takes a couple of steps to his side.

Jim is standing there with the fingers of both hands locked together, making a place for her to put her foot. In it goes, and he lifts up as she swings her leg over Pooch's back. She's in the saddle.

"I can get on by myself, but Jim likes to help me," she thinks, but never says anything to hurt his feelings.

"There you go, honey. Now be careful. Pooch wouldn't do anything to hurt you, but you know he's young and full of pep. It's up to you to let him know who's boss if he gets to acting up. You listen to your mama and don't run him. There's lots of time for that after you grow up a little more."

As Jim is talking, she pulls the reins gently to the left and nudges her horse's sides with the heels of her boots.

"I'll be careful, Jim," she grins with thanks.

Pooch responds by turning left and starts to walk away from the barn. She sees her mama standing, watching all that is going on.

"Mama is beautiful standing there with her long green dress almost touching the ground." Sheree notices and gives her a big smile.

She blows a kiss and then leaves the barnyard with Pooch at a walk so all can see she is being very careful. She and her horse are on their own.

As soon as they get out of sight of the house, she nudges Pooch's sides again. He starts to trot. He loves to gallop, so she nudges him again.

"I don't want to miss Randy," she thinks to herself as they gallop along. She can tell Pooch is happy to get out in the open; she can feel his strength through her legs and hips as he moves. The breeze on her face makes her feel like she's flying, and the sound of Pooch's hooves on the ground gives her the urge. Another gentle nudge and he's running.

Randall Stoker's thoughts are on meeting his best friend as he walks toward their secret meeting place. He can see her smiling face and hear her voice in his head, paying little notice to the remnants of last years weeds and briars scratching at his pants with every step he takes.

"Gosh, I hope she's coming today," he quietly mutters. "I have to get back before somebody sees I'm gone and comes looking for me. I sure hope she's there."

His clubfoot causes some difficulty, especially with all the rocks and furrows covered over with grass and weeds the way they are. But his mind is set on getting to the tree as fast as he can. Stumbling occasionally is part of his life, he accepts it for what it is, and doesn't let it slow him down. He's been up since five thirty this morning, and had a breakfast of pancakes with molasses and a lot of cool milk. He ate a big stack for a boy of twelve years old, knowing he'll get nothing else until his noon meal. The daily chores started right after breakfast, so he worked hard and fast to get ahead. Now he has some time to meet his friend.

Randall is the son of Jacob and Alberta Mae Stoker. He has two older sisters and a set of twin brothers younger than him. That makes up the family. They all work for Colonel Charles Housler on his farm Der Bote. Alberta Mae cooks for the colonel and his wife, Selma, as her main job. She also helps with the cleaning of the main house and tends to the large vegetable garden just out in the back.

Randall's family lives in a four-room house about a hundred yards behind the Housler family home. His mama keeps it shining inside and out. It's small, but it has wooden floors. There is not much furniture, which is okay, since there is little room for it. There's always the smell of fresh-baked bread in the air. Nothing fancy, but it's a loving home for a poor family.

Jacob Stoker's job is the driver of the other seven hands. They labor hard every day starting before sun up until almost dark, six days a week, to keep up with the work of a producing farm and stable. The children of the families do whatever they can to help. The hands all live in two-room huts about a quarter of a mile west of the main house. They all have shed roofs and dirt floors. It's a simple life, one they were born into with little knowledge of change in the future.

Randall can see the top of the willow tree now as he starts the climb up a rolling hill a few hundred feet from the fence where they will meet. His breathing speeds up and gets a bit more labored as he climbs. As he walks faster and faster, the anticipation of seeing his friend gets stronger and stronger. He can see the fence now.

"She's not here." A little sense of sadness creeps into his being. "She'll be here, I just know she'll be here," runs through his mind.

He climbs the white board fence to sit on the top edge of the third board, close to a post so he can steady himself, facing the direction his friend will come. Still catching his breath, he waits.

After a few minutes, which seems like hours to him, the sound of a horse's hooves beating the ground reaches his ears.

"I'll bet that's her. I'll bet that's Sheree. She'll be here in a minute," he swells up a little inside and is just about to jump off the fence to run to meet her when another thought crosses his mind.

"What if it's not Sheree? What if it's someone else? If they catch me here, I'll be in big trouble." He slides toward the tree along the top board of the fence until he is partially hidden beneath the drooping willow branches. Now, he'll wait right here until he's sure it's her.

His heart starts to pound when he hears the horse's hooves splashing through the water of the small creek, just over the little rise about sixty yards from where he's perched. As the horse climbs and crests the bank of the creek, he can see it is his awaited friend.

"Yeah! Yeah!" he yells.

She's leaning up over Pooch's neck with her hair flying behind her, almost as if someone's chasing her. Her horse is running all out, his passenger hanging on.

She can feel the cool water splashing up from Pooch's hooves. It feels like a spring rain, almost stinging as it hits her face and arms. Both are getting drenched.

She can see the top of the willow tree as they start up the opposite bank of the creek. Her horse is really moving; he leaps up the incline. She can see the willow tree, but does not see Ran—.

Something's wrong! Pooch is falling forward! She's leaning way back over his hindquarters, the reins still in her hands. With Pooch's head already down, she's pulling him down even farther.

The horse starts to roll frontward. She feels her body snap back up straight and continue forward, leaving the saddle, flying over Pooch's buried head. The leather reins slide out of her grip as she flies through the air, burning her hands and fingers.

Randall jumps off the fence at the same time Pooch makes a loud whining screaming sound. He jerks up to see the horse's head drop toward the ground, then roll up under his own feet. He also sees Sheree leave the saddle, flying through the air ten feet off the ground. With his eyes on her, he hears the horse slam to the ground, letting out a sound as if he groaned and belched at the same time.

"I've got to get my arms out in front of me before I hit the ground, can't do it! No time!" Thoughts flash through Sheree's mind, but everything's happening too quickly for the young girl to react.

The arc of her flight lands her some thirty feet ahead of Pooch. She hits the ground face first, which pushes her head back toward her shoulder blades. The speed she's moving causes her to flip over, her feet up in the air, making her land on her back, then bounce twice before sliding to a stop. Her body lies still, limp on the short grass, with her arms stretched out above her head, lifeless in appearance.

Randall notices Pooch, lying on his side with his head raised a little off the ground, snorting and blowing, trying to catch his breath. His deep guttural noises show he's in pain and misery, making no attempt to get up.

He runs as fast as he can to Sheree's still body only to stop a few feet away to creep up, hoping for the best, but knowing the worst has happened.

Her face, spattered with blood, eyes open, is lying on it's left side, but pointed up a little. Her neck is tilted in a twisted way that makes him cringe and pull away.

"I'm all right, Randy. Help me get up. I'll be okay . . . ," he doesn't hear me. "I'm all right, Randy. Help me up. I can't get up by myself," she speaks in her mind, but there is nothing coming from her mouth.

"Oh my God! No! No . . . !" The sight of his friend lying there is more than he can bear. He drops to his knees in a daze, tears flood down his face.

After a few seconds he regains his composure, realizing he's kneeling on the grass beside his girlfriend. The scene of the horse falling and her flying through the air slams him back into full awareness of what has just happened. He stands up and prays that what he saw and remembers is not real, but the terrible cold truth is still there. Sheree and Pooch, both lying on the ground, make no movements or sounds, except for the horse's heavy panting.

"I've got to get help! I've got to run and get help fast!" he takes off and starts climbing the fence, then realizes that if he runs home to tell his parents, he'll be in big trouble. Sheree's parents will be after him too. He can feel Sheree's life draining away as he stands there trying to decide what to do next.

"Randy, I'm alive! Can't you hear me! I can't move at all, but I can hear and even see straight ahead! Don't leave me Randy! Stay here with me!" The young girl's screams go unheard.

He turns when he hears Pooch stir behind him.

"He's trying to get back on his feet. Maybe he's okay enough that I can send him home," the desperate boy says out loud. "When they see him come home without Sheree, they'll come looking for her. That'll bring the help we need."

He runs to Pooch's side and picks up the reins. His daddy has taught him about horses, so he pulls on the reins to encourage the animal to stand.

The injured horse rolls back and rocks forward with a lunge. He's able to get his front legs folded up under himself. Another half twisting, half lunge head first, and his rear legs are in position. Two big snorts and up he comes on his rear feet. Then he pushes himself to a full standing position with his front legs and dances around a little, stabilizing his footing. Randall, still holding the reins, pats him on the neck and rubs the top of his head with his hand.

"You look okay." Thinking to himself, he walks around and around leading the animal with the reins, watching his legs for signs of an injury. "All I see is a little cut there on your shoulder."

Satisfied, he turns Pooch to face the direction of the house, drapes the reins over the saddle horn, and smacks him on his hindquarter yelling, "Go home, Pooch, go home!"

The horse seems to understand the urgency of getting help and takes off running full speed toward the house, showing no signs of the fall.

Knowing he can't leave Sheree unguarded until help arrives, and that he can't be seen when the help gets there, he ponders what his next move should be. He bends down next to his best friend and says, "Don't worry, I'm not leaving you until some help gets here. I'm going to climb up in the willow and wait. They won't see me there, and I'll keep watch over you."

He walks to the fence and climbs to the top board. Standing on it makes it possible for him to reach a branch and hoist himself up to lie on a bough of the tree. He gets into a position that allows him to see his girlfriend and any help when it gets there.

Still he ponders. "Maybe I should run home. What if Pooch doesn't make it? If I do I'll have to leave her by herself, and I'll be in big trouble when they find out where I've been." He decides to wait.

A few minutes pass before his emotions build up to the point where he can't stand to be idle . . . he has to help his friend. Down he slides to put his feet on the edge of the top board of the fence, but when he lets go of the limb above he's a bit off balance. His choices are to fall off backward, or jump to the ground forward. Instinct pushes him forward. When he lands his clubfoot is pushed more to the inside causing his bad ankle to buckle under his weight. Pain shoots up through his leg like a hot poker. But without hesitation, he shivers down a good breath, then continues to Sheree's side to kneel down over her.

"I'm still here," he says softly. "I wish I could do something for you. I sent Pooch home after some help. I think he's okay."

"I love you. Please don't go away. I don't know what I'll do if you do. Please don't die. I need you to stay here. Can you hear me?"

Carefully and gently he bends down over his best friend and presses his lips to hers.

"I can hear you. I can see you when you get in front of me. I love you too. I'm not going to die. I'm okay. Oh, Randy, I wish you could hear me. I'll never forget this kiss."

It seems longer than the thirty minutes that have passed when the young farm boy hears the hoofbeats of at least two horses coming toward him. He has to hide in the willow, but running on his injured ankle causes severe pain to shoot up his leg with every step, slowing him down. A knot forming in the back of his neck presents fear that creeps down his spine, fear he will not make it to the tree in time.

The horses keep coming, closer and closer.

He's at the fence and climbing as fast as he can. A grab for the limb, a push with his feet off the top fence rail will put him where he needs to be. If he misses the limb, he'll fall. Up he goes, his fingers wrap around the branch to get a solid grasp. A swing back one time and a shift of his weight propels him upon the limb, a split second before two riders loom up over the bank of the creek, headed directly toward him. He knows they're farmhands by the clothes they wear and the way they look.

A long deep breath . . . what a relief he feels knowing his friend will get the help she so desperately needs.

"Horses. I hear horses. Closer, they're coming closer. I hear voices. Voices yelling." Sheree strains to look and see in the periphery of her sight.

"Here she is! She's over here! We found her!"

The horses' hooves clop to a stop.

"Footsteps are running toward me. They're here. Now maybe they'll help me get up. I'll be fine if they just help me up," she mistakenly believes.

"Oh my Lord, honey, what's done happened to you? Can you hear me? Are you alive?" She hears Jim's voice rambling excitedly.

"I'm alive, I can hear you!" she shouts in vain. "They don't hear me."

"She looks hurt real bad. Her eyes are open, but she's not moving them around," Jim yells.

She hears another horse come in at a gallop, then a set of quick footsteps coming toward her.

"Sheree, can you hear me?" her daddy's voice is calm and reassuring.

"I can hear you, Daddy. Please hear me!" she screams unheard, feeling the terror of what is happening.

John Anderson picks her arm up by the wrist. "She has a pulse . . . steady and strong. She's alive. Her eyes are open, but she's not conscious. We need to get her to the doctor as fast as we can," he places both her arms by her sides.

Down on one knee beside his daughter, he turns at the waist to face the other two men.

"Josh," he addresses the other farmhand who arrived with Jim, "Go back to the house . . . tell Mrs. Anderson we found her. Bring her and a wagon back here right away."

"Jim, you stay here with Sheree. When Mrs. Anderson gets here with the wagon, take her to the guesthouse. It's closer to here and to town than the main house. You both stay there with them until I get back with Doc Shaw."

"Be careful how you handle her. She's still alive, but there's no telling how bad she's hurt. Don't fold her up when you put her on the wagon, and don't move her any more than necessary."

"Now, Josh, go on, get going," Mr. Anderson directs the two farmhands.

Sheree hears footsteps in the grass, then horses leaving in a hurry.

"I can feel Jim sitting on the ground next to me. He's taking my right hand in his, and putting his other hand on top. He's singing low and softly stroking my hand." Church hymns are some of her favorite music to hear, especially when Jim sings them. It settles her down.

They wait.

"At last . . . I hear the rattling of a wagon coming toward us. I know Mama's on the wagon with Josh, and probably one or two other farmhands, brought along just in case," the young girl thinks.

The wagon stops just short of where she lies in the grass. She hears the rustle of clothes moving and knows for sure, her mama has arrived.

"Your mama is here, honey. We're going to take good care of you, don't be afraid. Dr. Shaw is going to meet us at the guesthouse. I want to hug you, but I'd better not until we know what all is hurt." June Anderson feels her daughter's pain.

She bends low, putting her face close to her child's lips feeling for a hint of breath. Then she places her fingers on her temple looking for a pulse.

"Why are your eyes open? Usually people's eyes stay open and fixed when they're dead. You're alive. Your breathing and pulse is good and strong," the worried mother wonders to herself.

"We're going to pick you up now, and put you on the back of the wagon. I hope we don't cause you more pain. So, are you ready? Here goes," June warns and cautions, as if she knows her daughter can hear.

Sheree feels herself moving up, some bouncing around, then the hard wood of the wagon bed against her back. She doesn't know it, but her mama has laid a folded quilt on the boards as a cushion.

"Okay, Josh, try to stay off the big bumps and holes. Let me get situated under her, then let's get her over to the guesthouse," the worried mother commands as she lifts her ten-year-old up enough to slide her legs under, so she can lay the girl's head in her lap.

"I love the smell of Mama's perfume." Sheree notices as she watches a gentle kiss being placed on her forehead.

She can see her mama's face wet with tears. Her eyes look full of pain and worry. The wagon jerks as the horses take the slack out of the harnesses.

"Please don't worry, Mama, I'm okay. I'll be all right. I'm sorry I ran Pooch when you told me not to. I'm so sorry," the injured girl tries to relate. "Something must be wrong with me, but I don't feel like I'm hurt anywhere. Why can't I talk out loud?"

Randall watches the whole rescue from his perch in the willow. After everyone leaves, he climbs down, glad things worked out the way they have. Sheree is safe now.

"I'd better get back home. They're looking for me by now, I just know it," he whispers to himself. "I sure wish I could go with her to see how she is. But I can't, I got to go home."

He forces himself to place one foot in front of the other. Every step he takes is painful, and moves him farther from his friend. After a few minutes, he stops. "I got to know how she is. I'll take what I got coming when I get home, but I got to know."

He turns in his tracks and heads back. He knows where the guesthouse is because, once, he and Sheree went there to see it. He'll not follow the way the wagon went, though. He can cut off some distance by cutting through places where the wagon can't go. Truth is, he will probably be there before them.

The ride to the guesthouse is slow because they don't want the wagon to bounce around any more than necessary. No one has said a word until, finally, they stop. Then Josh asks.

"Do you want Jim and me to take her in the house, Ms. Anderson? Where are we going to take her to in there?" Concern can be heard in his voice.

"I think we'll just put her on the couch in the parlor, Josh. It'll be easier on her that way," her mother responds, dismissing the idea of taking her upstairs to a bedroom.

Sheree feels herself floating along in Josh's arms. When they enter, she can smell the stale musty odor of a house that needs to be aired out. She can see just bits and pieces of things they pass on their way to the parlor. The soft cushions feel good against her back when they lay her down carefully.

Her mama appears directly in front of her.

"Honey, you just lie still now. We're all through jostling you around. Dr. Shaw should be here soon. Try to stay awake if you can," June sits on the floor beside the couch and pats her arm, just to let her know she's there.

"Jim, you and Josh go out on the porch and watch for John and the doctor," the worried mother instructs, giving them something to do.

They wait.

"They're here, Ms. Anderson, they're coming real fast," Jim shouts from the front porch as he watches Doc's buggy, a wagon, and three horseback riders arrive.

John Anderson and Doc Shaw arrive with three other men. They're talking back and forth when they hurry into the room.

"I don't recognize their voices but they're different, so I can kind of keep track of who's talking. I think one of the voices is a man who comes to our house to talk to Daddy." The injured child tries to understand, and grasp the situation.

Suddenly she sees Dr. Shaw's face.

"What in the world have you done to yourself, Sheree? Let me look you over. I'll be as careful as I can," he assures.

Doc gently examines her saying "Um-huh. Um-huh." He looks into her eyes, nose, and ears, and then feels her neck, arms, legs, and tummy. He sits her up, examines her back, and listens with his stethoscope.

"Well, folks," he reports. "I don't find anything seriously wrong with her. Just some small cuts on her face and arms, bruises on her shoulders and thighs. Things you'd probably expect from a fall off a horse. She's hit her head kind of hard, but except for some sore spots, I think she'll wake up and be okay. A little time will do the trick. She'll be just fine in a few days. She's one lucky little girl, it could be a lot worse."

"What about her eyes? Should they be open like that, Doc?" June asks.

"I've seen it before with a whack on the head like she's had. I don't imagine she can see anything. My experience tells me it's nothing to worry about."

"Now, as I said on the way out here, the Sanders's are expecting me over at their place, their daughter's down sick. If you need me for anything, come and get me over there. I left some supplies so you can clean up the cuts she has. If you don't mind, you can tend to those."

"Walk me out, will you, John?" he concludes.

"Thank you very, very much, Doc," Sheree hears her daddy say. "I appreciate your coming all the way out here to check her out."

"Me too, Doctor," her mama announces at the same time she begins to wipe her daughter's wounds with alcohol. "I can't thank you enough."

Those in the parlor hear the door close as Dr. Shaw and John walk out onto the porch.

"Here's a bottle of medicinc. If she wakes up and feels uncomfortable, give her a spoonful. It'll ease the pain and make her sleep. Now don't you two worry, I'm sure she'll be fine in a couple of days," Doc says as he hands the bottle to the concerned father. Jim and Josh appear around the corner of the house leading Doc's freshly watered horse pulling the buggy after him.

"Doc's gone," John relates as he comes back inside.

"I was just about to take a look at your daughter for myself, John," one of the three men who came with him says.

"All right," Sheree hears her daddy say.

He shines a light right into her right eye, and then her left one. He holds her wrist to take her pulse.

"I think we can stay with our plan, John, but we should move it up."

"She's in a comatose state right now. Probably caused by the bump to her head. I'd like to get her back to our laboratory where we can run some tests. I don't think this condition will last, so we should complete our business together a bit sooner than we expected."

"You mean you want to take her now? Today?" June blurts out.

"Yes, that's right," the man insists, "This is a perfect opportunity. You can tell a story that's mostly true; she died due to her injuries from the accident. We won't get a better opportunity than this, John?"

"Whoa, just a minute, I agree with my wife. We have four more years with our daughter, and by damned we want them," Mr. Anderson declares.

"She's progressed mentally a lot farther than we expected at this age. To wait much longer will lessen our effectiveness with her training. We must do this today," the man insists more firmly.

"But I haven't had a chance to say goodbye," June clutches at her child on the couch.

"What if I said we've changed our minds, we're not giving her up?" John tests the water.

"I'm not here to threaten you, but you know the Company. The people there can get mean if they take the notion. Now, I know you don't want their wrath coming down on your entire family. Think about this sensibly for a minute. The older she gets, the harder it will be for you to give her up. It could be a horrible separation for her as well as you. This way it will be a clean break, she won't have to suffer leaving you behind. She'll bounce back faster at this age too. The time is right to do this now."

"Yes, I see your point. We can do this today, if we must, but we thought we'd have more time. This isn't supposed to happen for several more years. You've taken us by surprise," Mr. Anderson states.

"Yes, well, as I said, this is the perfect situation. No one will question her disappearance," the man repeats.

The girl on the couch hears her daddy conclude, "We've followed the plan as it was laid out so far. If we must, we can do this today."

"Good." The man likes what he hears.

"You've agreed . . . you'll not try to see her again."

"That's right. Let's do it now, before I change my mind," John says with a defiant tone.

"Okay . . . here's the rest of your money. This ends it between your family and the Company as long as you don't try to go back on the agreement," the man explains.

Sheree feels the weight of her mother as she throws herself across her.

"I'm so dreadfully sorry, Sheree," she sobs. "I thought we'd have more time. I'm so, so sorry. We'll all burn in hell for what we're doing here today. I hope someday you'll be able to forgive me for what I've done. I know I'll never forgive myself."

"Now, now, June . . . we knew this day was coming. It's best to leave as quickly as we can," John explains as he pulls his wife away from their daughter.

Sobbing, completely out of control, she painfully pleads.

"I'll miss you forever, my sweet cherished daughter. I'll love you always."

Another one of the men that came with Sheree's daddy says, "Here's how we'll handle it. You two go on outside and tell your hands that your daughter has died, and take them home with you. We'll take care of everything here."

"What about the doctor?" the first man says. "He thinks the child is going to be fine."

"Yeah, let's not forget him," the second man continues. "You'll need to tell him the same as you do your farmhands. She took a turn for the worse, and died."

The injured ten-year-old girl lies on the couch, hearing every word being said.

"Are they really going to leave me here with these strange men? Will I never see my mama and daddy again, ever?"

"I don't want to do this! Mama! Daddy! Take me with you! Don't leave me here! Don't go without me! I'll be good! I'll do everything you say! Just keep me here. Please! Please, don't leave me here!" her young voice pleads within her head.

She hears her mother say, "Goodbye, Sheree, darling, we love you and always will."

The door closes.

Outside on the porch, John is faced with the first telling of a heart-wrenching lie.

"Josh, you take my horse. I'm going to ride with Mrs. Anderson."

He helps the heartbroken, sobbing, obviously miserable woman aboard the wagon, then he climbs up and remains standing.

"Our daughter has died today of her injuries from the accident. There's nothing more we can do for now. I'll return later today to take care of things. These kind gentlemen have agreed to stay here, with Sheree, until I get back." John's words stick in his throat. Forcing them makes his voice sound strained and broken. With tears rolling down his cheeks, and the look of his wife, anyone would believe Sheree is dead.

"Let's get back home and let everyone know what's gone on here. I need to get Mrs. Anderson settled down too."

His words are not heard by June. Her mind is in a daze, not thinking, just hurting. She feels as if her head is being squeezed in a giant vice. The pressure is almost unbearable. Her baby is gone.

Back inside, those remaining wait for the commotion to settle down. A few minutes pass, then the wagon rolls away, everything gets quiet.

One of the men left in the room with Sheree speaks.

"Okay, they're gone. Let's get moving. She might come out of this anytime. I have some ether with me, so if she starts stirring around we can use it."

"What's ether for? What are they going to do with me?" The frightened child worries.

"What's that?" one man says with a startled voice.

"What are you talking about?" the other two wonder.

"I thought I saw someone looking through that window over there," he warns.

"You'd better go check it out. We don't need anybody snooping around."

Outside, Randall has been peering through the window and saw everything. Although he couldn't hear it all, he has pieced some of it together. But now they've seen him.

"Hide! But where! There's no time to think about it! Hide now!"

In a panic, he looks around for a place, but everything is too far away. Not even a tree is close enough to hide behind before the man will come around the corner of the house and see him. The well—can he make it to the well?

Back inside the house, decisions are being made.

"See that cedar chest over there in the corner? Let's put her in there so nobody sees her with us. Block the lid open a little so she can get some air."

"I'm floating again. They're laying me in the chest. Help! Help! Don't do this to me! I don't want to go with you! Let me out of here!" She screams uselessly.

The blankets they left in the chest are soft to her skin. Darkness settles in as the lid closes.

She jostles back and forth in her small prison when they move it. She feels the jolt, and hears it hit the wagon bed with a bump.

"Someone please help me! Help me please! I'm here in this box. Help!" she continues to plead quietly.

Randall clings to the top face board with just his fingers showing as he hangs down inside the well out in back of the guesthouse. His toes grip the stone wall below to help a little, but his position is not at all secure.

"Lord, don't let him see my fingers," the youngster prays.

He hears footsteps coming closer, they faintly echo in the hollowness of the circular stone wall. His glance down shows the water glistening about six feet below.

"If I slip off this board, the splash will make that man find me for sure. I have to hang on." Randall agonizes to himself.

He keeps his face close to the stone and his eyes shut. His heart is pounding so loud he's afraid the man will hear it.

"Chad, you see anybody back there?" one of the men out in front of the house calls to the one now standing at the top of the well, not a foot from the tips of Randall's fingers.

"Not yet, but give me a minute or two." The man's voice sounds like he's looking straight down at the top of the young boy's head.

His heart leaps. He can't help it, he has to peek. As he looks up slowly, carefully, he sees the man's bearded face. All he has to do is look down.

Randall feels the increasing need to get a better grip with his fingers. They're getting tired and seem to be slipping.

"Go away. Go away," he chants to himself.

The man is in no hurry to leave.

"Chad, come on. We're leaving." He's called from the front of the house again.

"I'll be right there," he yells back, clears his throat, leans over the well, and spits, just missing the top of the boy's head, then turns and walks away.

"My fingers are slipping," Randall screams silently to himself. "I can't hold on any longer."

If looking down from above, one could see his fingers creep to the edge of the board and disappear. His toes slip off the stones of the wall. Down he goes.

The shiny liquid below resounds with a loud *splash* followed by waves bouncing off the walls to slosh back and forth in the narrow space.

Randall, expecting to be submerged, realizes the water is only a couple of feet deep. He's lying on his back propped up against the wall, his head above the water.

Convinced the man above has heard the loud splash, his eyes are open as wide as his mouth as he looks up at the round opening exposing the blue sky, waiting for a bearded face to appear.

Stay still. He has to stay completely still. Not a muscle moves. The water is almost cold; it moves back and forth settling down. The well stinks like wet dirt and moss mixed with stale air. It gets brighter as the wall ascends, but where he's lying it's pitch black. The next minute seems like an hour.

"He's not coming back. He must not have heard the splash," he tells himself very quietly. "As soon as it's safe I'm getting out of here, and I'm going home."

After a bit of time, he decides to climb out, only to find the walls this far down are slippery with damp moss. Try and try as he does, he's unable to get a grip or a toe hold on anything to lift himself up. There's nothing down there to use to aid his escape. He decides to try to jump up higher to see if he can find a grip, somewhere, to get himself started.

His first jump provides no encouragement when his fingers slide off, bringing a fist full of moss with them. The water he's standing in and his sprained ankle don't help matters since they retard the upward force he's able to muster. His second try is no better than his first, and this time when coming down, he slips on the muddy bottom and falls backward with all the weight of his body. He instinctively braces for a collision, but instead finds himself falling through the wall, out of the water, to land on his back on muddy but fairly dry ground. It's so dark, it's impossible to see where he has landed. He feels around to discover a hole in the wall. It's above the water level, but lower than the area of the wall he has so frantically searched. His first move is to put a foot on the bottom edge of the hole and try to bounce upward to get a grip. Still with no luck, he's unable to keep his balance. After several tries, he deems it impossible.

With his options running out, he decides to see how deep this hole goes into the wall. He creeps on his hands and knees, feeling blindly out in front of himself, trying to locate the back wall. At first, he moves a foot, then three, then ten.

"This must be a tunnel. I wonder where it goes?" the young Stoker boy says out loud. "I have to follow it, I've got no other choice."

He continues to creep along, feeling carefully with his hands, unable to see a thing. The shallow mud on the floor squishes between his fingers as he crawls. After proceeding for a few minutes, he comes to a place where the tunnel takes a sharp turn to the right. He's about to turn and keep going, but a wisp of moving air hits his face. He backs up a couple of feet and stops to see if he feels it there. Nothing. There has to be another tunnel or opening connected here somewhere. He decides to move forward again, this time feeling straight ahead instead of around the corner. Aha! There is another tunnel, straight ahead.

"Which one should I take?" he ponders. "I don't know my directions because I got all turned around back there in the well. If I'm headed to the house from the well, then I should go straight. But if I'm not headed for the house, hmmmm, maybe if I take the turn, I'll be headed for the house. Either one of these tunnels could be a dead end too. I think I'll stick with the tunnel from the well and go straight. If I have to, I can always come back here and take the turn."

Suddenly, he hears what sounds like the patter of small feet in mud. A surge of adrenaline goes through his body when something, maybe a good-sized animal, hits his leg and keeps on going.

"Something's in here with me. I have to get moving and stay moving," he says loudly, as if to scare away whatever it was.

Now he moves at a much faster pace, taking the chance he'll bump his head, fall into another well, or tangle with something. After another hundred feet he arrives at what seems to be a wooden door. His hands move all the way around it, but it gives him no clue about how it should open. Maybe a strong shove will work.

He puts his shoulder up against the wooden structure as best he can with the small amount of space he has to work in, then, with all his strength, pushes. The door gives away. The noise of objects falling, glass breaking, metal banging, and heavy things thudding to the floor breaks the silence. He squeezes his head though the small space he has created to discover a dimly lit room.

Chapter Three

The guesthouse was the family home on the farm adjoining the Andersons' before John's father bought the land to enlarge his holdings. It sets about a mile toward town from the Andersons' home. The rolling hills between the Andersons' and this house obscures one's properties from the other. The guesthouse isn't used on a regular basis, so when needed, they have it opened up and aired out. It's completely furnished and outfitted to make it livable.

Christine Junelle Anderson is a loving, warm person. She's been called June since her childhood, hardly ever hearing her first name as an adult. She's a woman of medium size, at five feet six inches tall. Her breasts are large in comparison to her narrow waist and rounded hips. She keeps her dark brown hair up in a bun during the day to keep it out of the way. When she lets it down, it hangs a little below her shoulders. Dark eyebrows enhance her bright green eyes. Smooth high cheekbones flatter her somewhat wide nose. Her lips are a bit thicker than average and rest together to form an unintentional hint of a smile, lending to the dimples that appear on each side of her face when she speaks. Her presence is one of poise, strength, and considerable beauty. The clothes and jewelry she wears emit a condition of wealth in the family. The perfect wife for an upcoming, energetic entrepreneur with political ambitions, namely, John Anderson.

Appearances are deceiving though. In reality, June's whole life is wrapped up in her husband. Her feelings of herself are self-doubt and insecurity. She uses her husband's strength and energy to portray the person she believes others need her to be. Secretly she would like to be a mother living with her children on a small farm with enough to get by, not having all the pressures and worries that go along with the life she's leading. Her family is her happiness.

The wagon stops in front of the Andersons' home, beckoning all the workers and their families to stop whatever they're doing and begin to gather in front of the horses. They're aware of the accident, but do not yet know the outcome.

"I must inform you," John says as he stands up in the wagon, "that our daughter, Sheree, has passed away. Injuries caused by the accident has taken our baby away from us. I'm sorry, I can't continue to talk about it right now.

"Jim and Josh can give you more of the details.

"Right now, I need to get Mrs. Anderson into the house. I know your prayers will be with us. I'll let you all know later about the service. And I'll appreciate it if you don't go to the guesthouse for a few days. I'm sure you understand.

"Jim, I need to talk to you after I get Mrs. Anderson settled in the house."

Having said that, John climbs down off the wagon then helps his wife to the ground. With their arms around each other's waist, she lays her head on his upper arm as they walk up the front porch steps, across the porch, and into the house.

"Where's Charlotte?" he asks, as he eases the screen door closed behind them.

"She went to pick strawberries with Mona Jean. She must not be back yet," she responds. "You'd better get word to Robert, John. I don't know if he'll be able to get home in time for the service, but I want him here anyway."

They carry the facade of Sheree's demise with them as if it's gospel.

"I need to go back to the guesthouse to be sure everything is handled. I'll go on to town from there and get a wire off to him," John replies solemnly. "I know he'll get here as quickly as he can."

"Do you want something to drink?" he asks his wife as they walk through the hallway from the porch. "I'm going to pour a very large glass of bourbon for myself."

She doesn't respond as they separate from each other when they enter the living room. He walks to a small round table covered with a white lacy cloth that hangs down almost to the floor. He picks up a glass decanter, removes the glass stopper, and pours whiskey into a glass. She walks slowly across the room and slumps down into a large overstuffed chair.

With the glass of whiskey to his lips, he turns toward his wife to hear her say.

"John, I want my baby back! I want her back now!"

"We can't do that. You know we agreed to give her up. You know how these people are, they won't understand. They won't give her back to us."

"I don't care. We can do something. I can't stand thinking of her being alone. I don't know what they'll do to her. She must be frightfully afraid. She's hurt, John, she's not even conscious. They won't take care of her like I would. What will she think when she wakes up and finds herself in a strange place? I won't be there to help her understand. She's just a little girl. She'll need me and I won't be there for her. I can't do this . . . I won't," she sobs.

He looks at her with disbelieving eyes.

She glares back.

"Don't you understand? I'm her mother," she insists with a loud voice. "How can you—her father—not feel the way I do? You act like you don't care at all." She becomes more hysterical as each thought comes through her lips.

"You've known about this for a long time, June. We made this agreement with these people shortly after Sheree was born. She's special, honey, we can't give her all she'll need. I'm talking about opportunity. Think about the possibilities she'll have to further her life. There's no limits to what she might do." He turns around to refill his empty glass.

"Besides that, they gave us a considerable amount of money when we needed it. Remember? We have to keep up our part of the agreement. I won't try to get Sheree back. It wouldn't do any good anyway." His tone is matter-of-fact and firm.

"Well, I know something can be done. I'll give the money back. I'll go to the Marshal. I'll tell them, and the law will get Sheree back," she cries, getting louder.

He sets his glass down, turns, and steps to the front of the chair where his wife is sitting, gets down on his knees, puts his hands on her shoulders, and shakes her gently, as he speaks firmly.

"Listen to me. You're going to do no such thing. There's too much involved here. I can't let you do that. What can I do to make you understand? I'm not able to get her back. Give it a little time—wait until morning. This whole thing will look a lot different in the morning.

"You need to settle down, honey. We have two other children to think of. If you start talking about all that's gone on, you and I both will likely wind up in prison. What'll happen to Robert and Charlotte? Do this for us . . . for them," John says with a tear creeping down his left cheek.

"Wait until tomorrow! You want me to wait? You want me to wait when I know my baby is getting farther away from me every minute? Well, I'm not waiting! I'm going after her right now! You can come with me, or you can go straight to hell!" She pushes her husband away with the force of a demon, jumps up out of the chair, and runs for the door.

John, surprised by his wife's actions, struggles to gain his balance, falls backward, and rolls almost completely over before he's able to get on his feet to go after her. She's nearly at the door to the porch before he can get a hand on her. He grabs an arm and jerks her to a stop. As she spins sideways from the force of her momentum, he puts his arms around her waist, picks her up off the floor, and drags her back into the living room, kicking, fighting, and screaming, to throw her forcefully down into the same chair she has just vacated. As he lets go, she turns a quarter turn in the air. While turning, she clenches her right hand into a fist, swings, and finds his left eye with a resounding smack.

He reacts without thinking and raises his right hand above his left shoulder intending to backhand her across the face. She screams thinking she's about to receive a sharp blow. But he catches himself just before letting go and stands there, his arm raised, looking down at his quivering wife.

"My God, what am I doing? June, I am so sorry . . . I'll never forgive myself if I hurt you. I can't do this. I won't try to stop you again. If you must go, then go. Just understand what you'll be doing to us and our family before you start something we can't stop. Is that what you want? Do you want to punish yourself and everybody else around you for what we've done?"

"You don't love her, John, not like I do," she sobs. "You couldn't love her and be the way you are right now. How can you stand there, with no feelings at all, and tell me I'm wrong, that I have to let her go?"

"I have deep feelings for Sheree too, honey. I know you wouldn't say such things if you weren't so upset. Try to recall back ten years ago when we made our agreement to give her to the Company. Remember? We did it to save this farm and hundreds of other people. At the time, we couldn't do anything else. Remember? We grieved over our decision before agreeing to do it. We went ahead with it because we both knew then, as well as now, we don't have the knowledge or the resources to give Sheree everything she's going to need as she gets older. They do. They can handle her. We'll never be able to control her. Don't you remember?

"Think of the hundreds of lives we've changed over the last ten years, all because we made the right decision. You will certainly be an angel in heaven for the sacrifices you made then and now. No one has ever made a more noble decision. We must not change our minds now, honey. We'll get past this, we'll continue to help people and change lives. We still have the rest of our family, and thanks to the Company, our farm. Try to think back to our reasons, our commitment for doing this in the first place. If we throw it all away now, we'll lose everything we've gained. You know, and I know, we'll not get her back either way. Please try. Wait until morning,"John pleads with tears dripping from his chin.

"Oh, John, I'm sorry I hit you. I didn't mean to, but I don't understand, I have never understood. I've gone along with things since we've been married that, to me, just weren't right. Because I love you so much, I've done things for you that turn my stomach to think about. I still love you, but I can't do it any more. This is killing me. Can't you see that? It's been going on too long. It's just too much, I have to find some peace. I'm begging you. Help me." She turns her face away.

"Well . . . going to the marshal won't get Sheree back. It'll just stir up a lot of things that neither you nor I want people to know about. People around here will probably hang the both of us," he finishes firmly to emphasize his point.

"How in the world will I ever live with myself if I let this happen? You're going to have to tell me and show me how, because I don't know. Can you make me understand—make me see the good part in what we're doing? You have to help me or I'll go insane. I just know it," she mournfully begs.

"Let me try, honey, Lord knows I can't live without you. I need you as much as you need me," he continues to plead.

"Let me get you a glass of wine. Sip it and relax in this chair for a few minutes. You'll feel better. Will you do that . . . for me?"

"I will. I'll try," she replies. "I just don't know what anyone can do to make me feel any better."

As John turns to get the wine, his mind races to find a solution to his wife's hysteria.

"There's no reasoning with her right now," he tells himself. "She needs something to calm her down."

Then he recalls the small bottle of medicine Dr. Shaw gave him for Sheree. Keeping his back to his distraught wife, he takes the bottle from his pants pocket, removes the stopper, and tips it up allowing a more than generous ration of the red medicine to flow into a wineglass. With that accomplished, he fills the rest of the glass with red wine, sets the wine bottle down, reseals, and slips the small medicine bottle back into his pocket, then swirls the mixture with his finger.

When he returns to his wife, he drags a footstool along with him. After handing her the glass, he sits on the stool, and intently watches as his partner in life takes the glass and raises it up to put her lips to the rim.

"Go ahead, honey, take a good drink. You'll feel better in a few minutes."

Hearing that, she takes two large swallows, then lowers the glass to her lap. She sucks in a long breath, sinks farther into the chair, and blows it out through her open mouth, hoping for some sort of relief.

"Go ahead, finish that off and I'll let you rest," he assures her.

She raises the glass and with several swallows empties it completely.

He takes her left hand in his and sits looking at the woman he loves. After many minutes pass, and knowing June is asleep from exhaustion as well as the wine, he says out loud, "I'm so sorry about all of this. You deserve better than me. I swear, I'll make it up to you somehow. I don't know how or when, but I promise, I will."

He lays her hand gently back on her lap, takes the empty glass, and stands up.

"She'll sleep for quite a while. I'll go to town and send a wire to Robert. Then I'll stop by the guesthouse. I need to find Doc Shaw and let him know about all of this too," he says under his breath, then walks out of the room.

Jim is standing at the edge of the porch with his arm stretched out above his head, leaning on the post, waiting for Mr. Anderson to come out of the house.

"You want me to ride along with you, Mr. Anderson? Maybe I can help with something somehow," he asks. "You know we all feel real bad about what happened. We love you all. We'll do anything we can for you and Mrs. Anderson."

"I know, Jim. We appreciate it too. But right now, some things need to be done that I have to do myself."

"Mrs. Anderson is asleep in the living room. If she wakes up, tell her I went in to town to send a wire to Robert. I'll be back as soon as I can. And sort of keep an eye on her for me. She's taking this pretty hard, and I'll feel better knowing that you'll be here while I'm gone. Try to keep her here at the house."

"Come here for a minute," John directs as he turns back into the house.

Jim follows.

"Here's the money I promised you'd get when Sheree went away," he says.

"No, sir, Mr. Anderson. I don't want it this way. That money will do me no good with the blood of that little girl on it," Jim replies.

"I don't want to hear it, Jim. You've earned this money over the last ten years, not just today. Here, take it, and be careful how you spend it. People won't be used to seeing you with this much. So, just be careful," John pushes the wad of bills into his hand.

This time he accepts it, and quickly stuffs it into his front pants pocket.

"Now . . . I want you to handle my daughter's death with your family and all our hands. Tell them you'll let them know when the service will be. Tell them there will be no work done on this farm for the rest of the day after the service. Let them know I don't want this to be known by anybody outside of our farm. We'll bury her at our family graveyard. It'll be a small service. Can you handle all that for me?"

"Yes, sir, I can, and I'm glad you trust me to do it."

"Make up a marker for her grave, too. Something simple with her name on it, and today's date. I appreciate it, Jim, thanks," John concludes.

"Yes, sir."

"Oh yeah, one other thing. I don't like asking because it's my place to do it, but Charlotte hasn't come home yet. We think she's off somewhere with Mona Jean, picking strawberries. She knows nothing about the death of her sister. Will you keep her busy with something until I get back, or until Mrs. Anderson wakes up? I just think she should be told of this by her mother or me."

"I will, Mr. Anderson, I'll make sure nobody else here tells her anything," Jim responds. "And don't you worry about nothing, I'll take care of all we talked about here today."

"Thanks again," John repeats.

June's husband walks to the wagon where his horse is tied, mounts up, pulls the reins to the right, and with a little kick from the heels of his boots, he's off at a trot to fulfill his responsibilities.

Meantime, at Der Bote.

Randall Stoker's thoughts are divided between trying to understand everything he saw at the guesthouse and the big trouble he's facing when he gets home. Being soaked to the skin, and mud from head to toe, isn't going to help him explain where he's been. Besides that, he told no one he was going anywhere. His mama's probably frantic, thinking the worst. His daddy will act like he's crazy about the chores not being done. But the boy knows that's not the real reason he'll be angry. It'll be because he's upset his mama.

"Am I going to make up a story, am I going to lie? Or am I going to tell the truth? Am I going lie to them., or . . . can I tell 'em the truth?

"Why did they put Sheree in that box? They said to tell everybody she's dead, but that's not so. It doesn't make sense. Mr. Anderson told everybody out there she's dead, and it just isn't so. I was listening at the corner of the house and heard Mr. Anderson say Sheree is dead and they were leaving her there for these three men to take care of. She wasn't in the house anywhere when I got in there from the tunnel, I checked all over. They must have taken her away on that wagon they had."

He keeps pondering back and forth over the questions in his mind. This twelve-year-old boy knows what he's seen and heard isn't right. Something's going on and he's unable to get the straight of it all. He feels he owes his best friend more than he's able to give. But what can he do? Who can he tell? Who will believe him . . . a young boy?

The water squishes around his toes in his shoes as he crests the last small hill before he can see his home. He, as yet, hasn't decided what he'll say to his parents.

His mama and daddy are standing about fifty feet apart in the barnyard. Both see and start toward him at the same time. Panic courses through his small body.

"I'm going to get it now." Speaking out loud makes it a grim reality.

"Where you been child!?" His mama's voice comes loud and forcefully.

"We've been looking for you for the best part of this day. You get on over here, your daddy wants to talk to you, now!" she takes him by the arm and pulls him along, headed straight for his father.

"You gave us a scare child. I sure hope you've got a good reason for being gone all this time. Your daddy's really mad at you."

Jacob Stoker stands silently, watching his wife drag his son toward him. Alberta Mae lets him go with a shove that makes him fall against his father.

"You're wet to the skin, son, mud from head to toe. Where have you been all day? What have you been doing? And this better be good," his father looks down with scorn in his eyes.

"I went over to the neighbor's creek to play, and I fell in." Randall trembles, "I've been trying to dry off before I came home. I'll do my chores now and get caught up. I won't do it again. I'm sorry, Daddy, Mama."

"Are you telling us the truth, Randall?" His mother questions sternly.

Before he can answer, his daddy interjects.

"Is this the best you can do, boy? I know you're fibbing to me. Now, I want you to try again, and this time you cut out the lies and tell me the truth."

Jacob starts to remove the belt from his pants.

"Go ahead, boy, and if it's not the truth this time, you'll make me use this belt. Do you hear what I am saying to you, child?" his father demands.

The twelve-year-old boy, on the ground, sitting on his legs, looks up at his daddy.

"If I tell you, you'll beat me for sure, Daddy. Please don't beat me. If I tell you the truth, you won't believe me. You'll think I'm lying, and you'll beat me."

Mr. Stoker looks down at this small boy at his feet, begging him not to whip him, and is lost for words. He loves his son; the words he's hearing sear into his heart. His son is at his feet so afraid he's shivering.

"What were you doing over at the Andersons' other house? Sadie saw you sneaking around the outside when she was coming home with supplies from town. I waited a while, but when you didn't come home, I went over there looking for you. I couldn't find hide nor hair of you, and that was quite a while ago. Now, you'd better tell me the truth, or things are going to get rough for you. You try again, and this time I'd better believe it."

Fear is being pumped through Randall's body with every heartbeat. He feels sick to his stomach. Beginning to cry, he blurts out.

"I can't, Daddy. You won't believe me anyhow. Please don't beat me, I won't ever do it again, I promise." Tears roll down his cheeks.

Alberta Mae bends over and takes her son in her arms.

"Your daddy isn't going to beat you. He just wants the straight of it all." She kisses him gently through the tears on his cheek.

"Let's do this. Go get some dry clothes on, then finish up your chores. Supper will be ready by that time, and you can eat."

"I want you to think about what you need to tell us, and after we get the dishes cleaned up, we'll all sit down and talk this out." Alberta Mae's voice is calmly reassuring.

"Don't be afraid, child. Nobody's going to beat you. Now, you get moving so you'll be ready for supper."

As soon as he's out of earshot, Alberta Mae says to Jacob, "We need to find out what he was doing over there and where he's been all this time, honey. He'll never tell us if we stay mean with him."

"Sadie says there were two wagons, a buggy, and at least three saddled horses outside that house. She says she could only see two folk outside there. I know he can tell us something about what was going on," Alberta Mae explains.

"I know you're right, Alberta Mae. I just don't know how much I want to hear about what's going on over there. On the one hand, I want to know; but on the other hand, I sure don't want to get things all stirred up again. I guess I'd rather just not know and let things be as they are."

Jacob Stoker's words are heard by his wife, but the curious woman's instincts will never let this pass over. Not without some sort of explanation.

John Anderson sees Doc Shaw's buggy as his horse trots up to the front of Cole Sanders's place. He dismounts and turns to tie his reins to the hitching post when Doc opens the door and comes out of the house.

The sun is warm and bright, prompting Doc to raise his left hand up to his forehead to shade his eyes, then step off the porch.

"Something more wrong, John?" he asks, genuinely concerned.

"You might say that, Doc. I need to talk to you for a minute. Can we go out by the barn?"

They walk slowly, side by side.

The medical man's rumpled black three piece suit shows dust scattered here and there on his shoulders, arms, and legs. His vest has five of the seven buttons closed, with his shirt open at the collar. A gentle breeze moves his gray hair across the top of his balding head. An ever-present pipe protruding from the right corner of his mouth allows him to speak, but only with his teeth clenched together.

"The Company took Sheree, Doc. They said it was the perfect setup to take her. I let them do it. They gave me the rest of the money. It's all over. They've got her."

"Is that why they were with you when you came to my office?" Doc asks, "They're not from around here, are they?"

"No, they just got into town this morning. They were sitting out on the porch of the hotel and saw me when I came in to get you. I know two of them, they've been out to the farm before. They came over and asked what was going on, so I told them about the accident as we walked to your office. They said they were coming out to the farm tomorrow anyway, so when they asked if they could ride along with us back to the guesthouse, I didn't think much of it. From there on there wasn't much said," John gets his good friend informed.

"They're a few years early, aren't they?" Doc asks, looking his friend straight in the eyes.

"Yes, that's true. But if you think about it, they're probably right. We can say she died because of the accident, and if somebody asks, you can say she died after you left her alive at the guesthouse. Once we have the funeral service, it'll be over. No one will ever question it."

"How's June holding up? She looked like hell back at the house. Is she going to make it through this okay?" Doc poses.

"I had to give her some of the medicine you gave me for Sheree to settle her down. She's asleep right now. It's going to be hard on her, but I think she'll be fine. I'm going to town from here to wire Robert. When June gets Charlotte and Robert close to her for a few days, I think she'll be okay."

"That's good. As soon as I can leave here, I'll get a coffin from town and make like I'm picking up her body. I'll line up Reverend Raymond while I'm at it. Is she supposed to be at your guesthouse?" Doc looks into John's face waiting for answers.

"Yes, she's supposed to be at the guesthouse. But I'd rather not involve the reverend in this unless we just have to."

"I want this to be a small service with just those people there that knows something has happened to Sheree. If we do anything more, we'll be begging people to ask questions."

"Yes, I suppose you're right," the doctor confirms, then ponders.

"We shouldn't wait too long for the service then. Are you going to try to get Robert here for it?"

"I don't see how. It'll take him at least three days, maybe five, to get here. I think that's too long, don't you?" John questions.

"Yeah, you're right. Might as well have it right away then. Let's say tomorrow afternoon at two o'clock. Will that do for you? Since tomorrow's Sunday, the Reverend will understand why we didn't involve him—if and when he finds out about it," Doc thinks ahead.

"Yes, that'll do fine. It's settled then. Thanks, Doc. I appreciate what you're doing."

John moves closer to his longtime friend.

"Here's your share of the rest of the money. This should square us up. Thanks, you don't know how much your friendship means to me."

Mr. Anderson turns and walks toward his horse.

"Just a minute, one last thing. Are we having the service at your family graveyard?" Doc asks, his hand still in his pocket clutching the wad of money.

John turns his head and nods yes, mounts up, and heads toward town.

Although he's sure that Sheree is no longer at the guesthouse, he doesn't want to go and find them still there. And yet, he's uneasy deep down, hoping he doesn't see them in town. There's no need to test himself. Sheree's gone, and that's that. Besides, he hopes to never again have the occasion to see or deal with anyone from the Company.

Johnathan Adams Anderson's look makes quite an impression. He's six feet three inches tall and weighs one hundred eighty-five pounds. His jet black hair matches his well groomed, rather thick, mustache. Gray eyes that have a soft look about them allows him to look directly at you without making you feel uncomfortable. His thin handsome face lends itself to his broad shouldered, trim, yet muscular body. His boots are always shined, his hair always trimmed just at his ears, but left long enough to lay two inches down the collar of his shirt in the back. His sideburns are trimmed even with the bottom of his ears and are about an inch and a half wide at the bottom. He's well educated with college degrees in law and political science. He's well known for his interests in politics, and is often tapped for his opinions by the elects of the state. It's rumored he will attempt to secure an office in the state congress at the next upcoming election.

His horse stops in front of the telegraph office, which also serves the United States postal service. He dismounts and steps up onto the board porch.

"Afternoon, John. What you doing in town this time of day?" asks the short, thin, bald man from behind the counter. His area is closed off from the rest of the room with counter space. Behind him, up against the wall, are rows of small boxes with letters and pieces of paper protruding here and there.

"Good afternoon, Virg, I need to send Robert a wire. Can we get that off today?"

"You bet we can. The lines were down this morning for about three hours, but they must have fixed it, it's working now. Just write down here on this pad what you want to say, and I'll get it off right away, before something else happens," Virgil says.

John takes the pad and pencil, then thinks a moment to decide exactly how he'll tell his son to come home. The pencil moves. When finished, he raises his head and hands the pad back to the telegraph operator.

"Let's see here," Virgil reads. "To Robert Anderson, in care of State College, Philadelphia, Pennsylvania. Dear Robert, we need your presence at home immediately. Will explain when you get here. Wire back arrival plans. Signed, your father, John Anderson."

"That'll be, let's see . . . fifteen cents. I'll get it off right away."

"Thanks, Virg. I appreciate it," John says as he hands over the money. "I'll come into town late tomorrow afternoon to get his reply. No need for you to send anybody out to the farm."

"Okay, if that's the way you want it, that's the way we will do it."

Mr. Anderson turns, walks out the door, and down the steps. Noticing two men across the street, he raises his hand and nods. The men both nod back.

It's getting late in the afternoon when John arrives at the guesthouse. The air is cool, and smells pure and clean. He's beginning to feel better about the situation and himself. Casually, he looks around outside, expecting nothing in particular, just looking. When he steps onto the front porch, however, he notices muddy footprints that appear to come from inside the house.

His immediate instinct pulls him to follow them. After a glance around to be sure Sheree and the men are gone, he trails the tracks to the open cellar door lying back on its hinges on the floor. He walks to the opening knowing someone has discovered the tunnel leading to the well. The size of the footprints tell him the intruder is a child or a small woman. Cautiously, he peers down through the opening in the floor.

He descends taking each step of the ladder carefully. Once below the floor, he can see by the dim fading light that the tunnel is exposed. The shelving that hides the hole in the wall has been pushed over on it's face. Everything setting on the shelves has fallen and lies scattered on the floor. As fast as he can, as though someone is going to see the opening, he lifts and pushes the shelving back into place, covering the hole completely. He picks up and puts most of the items back on the shelves where they belong. The broken pieces he pushes aside with the side of his foot. Then, using an old broom that's been left there for that purpose, he brushes away the scrape marks caused by the sliding of the shelving, and any footprints.

"Whoever it was is gone now," he mutters to himself, and turns to climb the ladder.

Once upstairs, he closes the open trap door and positions the oval braided rug to conceal it as intended, then walks through the kitchen looking for a bucket and mop. He pushes the screen door open to the porch where he spots a bucket, with a mop stuck in it, setting on the ground next to a rain barrel. After submerging the bucket into the barrel filling it partially, he grabs the mop and returns inside.

Cleaning up the muddy tracks leads him upstairs and through the hallway. There are no tracks into the rooms.

"They must have been looking for something. There's bits of mud all over down here and upstairs," he thinks to as he descends from the second floor.

"I'll finish up down here and get the porch, then I have to get back to the house. Charlotte's probably back by now, and if June wakes up before I get home, I'm not sure she can handle telling her by herself."

Chapter Four

"Where am I? I must have cried myself to sleep. Darn, I still can't move. Can you hear me out there? I'm the same as I was, no one can hear me. I can't cry anymore. They don't want me. They've given me away to someone else. Why, what did I do? Don't they love me any more?" Sheree tries to understand while her mind races from one thought to another.

"Who are these people? What's going to happen to me? Where are they taking me? Why am I in this box? Why am I unable to move or talk? What will they do to me? I need to swallow, but I can't. It's hard to breathe in here, not enough air.

"Wait. Wait. I'm probably scaring myself. If I settle down I'll be able to breathe better. I should be more grown up, how would I act if I was fifteen? Hmm, I need to put all of this in order. I need to make a plan. So, what do I know for sure?

"I know Mama and Daddy aren't coming after me. They sold me. The only way I'll find out why is to escape and go back home. How can I get away?

"Well . . . I'm not able to move, so there's not much I can do right now. First, I need to get over whatever has happened to me, then I can make a plan to get away. I need to stay calm, do whatever they say, and wait my chance. One thing at a time.

"I feel better now. I know I'll get back home, Mama and Daddy will forgive me, and everything will be all right again.

"They're probably angry with me because I ran Pooch. That's what's wrong. I know they'll forgive me when I tell them how sorry I am, and that I won't ever do it again. I won't ride Pooch for a month, or even a year, if that's what they want.

"Poor Randy . . . he doesn't know I'm still alive. Mama and Daddy are going to tell everyone I died. He'll think I'm dead, and then he'll forget about me too. I hope I can get back home before he forgets me. He'll probably find another girlfriend, maybe even my sister, she's a lot like me.

"I shouldn't think like this. I should keep thinking that I'm going to get away and get back home. I sure hope Pooch is okay? Will Mama and Daddy punish him? It's not his fault, it's mine. I shouldn't have ran him. I'm going home. I am.

"I can't see much through the space in the lid of this box. If I could turn just a little bit, I could see a lot better. But I can't. It looks dark outside. I can almost hear those men talking, but the wagon wheels make too much noise to hear it all. Let me see if I can put some of it together."

"Tomorrow noon . . . a train . . . can't be late . . . keep moving . . . need to eat . . . let me drive a while . . . fresh horses . . . Betty and Crystal . . . laughing . . ." the men banter off and on.

"I don't know what all this means, I just want to be home. I miss my home," the ten-year-old lets her mind drift off into wistfulness.

Time passes at Der Bote.

Randall Stoker is walking toward the water basin that sets on a small shelf, which is nailed to the house, just around the corner from the front porch. He's finished his chores, and is about to wash up for supper. There's already water in the basin. Soap is lying on the shelf, and a towel is hanging looped through a ring of steel attached to the side of the house with nails, so it will swivel up and down. He's splashing water on his face to rinse off the soap when the front screen door opens, and he hears his name.

"Randall? Randall? Do you hear me, child?" his mother calls out. "Your supper's ready on the table. Hurry now, everybody's ready to eat but you."

He leans around the corner. "I'm here, Mama, I'll be right there. I sure am hungry."

"Then get yourself in here; things are getting cold."

The young boy sits down at the supper table and looks around. He feels a little uncomfortable due to all that's gone on today. He expects to be questioned and may be yelled at by everybody here. But not so, the food is passed to him as if nothing's happened. Everybody's talking to each other like normal. The twins are picking at each other too, like they always do. Daddy even gives him a little smile.

"Mama's cooking has never tasted this good," he says to himself while in the process of swallowing a big mouthful of mashed potatoes and gravy.

"Can somebody pass me one of Mama's good biscuits please?"

Alberta Mae picks up the biscuits, walks around the table, and lets him pick one right out of the pan.

"You eat all you can hold, honey. We got plenty," she gives him a little hug with her free arm, sets the biscuits down where he can reach them, and returns to her seat.

The rest of the dinner is as usual. Whenever Mama bakes anything for the big house's table, she always makes enough for her family's table too. Tonight's dessert is strawberry cake, topped with whipped cream.

Randall eats like this is his last meal. He's the last one up from the table, thinking his mama and daddy wants him to stay right there. Finally, she says to him.

"Go on out on the porch. Your daddy has a harness to mend, and the girls and I need to get this kitchen cleaned up. We'll all have our talk after that. Now, don't you worry, all we're going to do is talk. Okay?"

"Okay, Mama? I'll be just outside."

At the next farm over from Der Bote, John Anderson rides up to his home just at sunset. The shadows from the house, barn, and trees are long, lying across the short grass. Jim is there to take the reins when he climbs down from his mount.

"I'll take care of your horse, Mr. Anderson."

"Thanks, Jim. Has Mrs. Anderson been up yet or is she still asleep?"

“Well, sir, it’s like this. Ms. Charlotte came home and woke her up from her sleep. There was a lot of crying coming from in the house. Then Mrs. Anderson came out with a gun and went straight into the barn. I’ve not seen her since, and I’m not going in that barn as long as she has that gun in there with her.”

“What about Charlotte? Has she been out of the house since my wife went into the barn?” John asks.

“Not that I’ve seen.”

“Stay here, Jim. I’m going to see what she’s doing in there with that gun.”

“Yes, sir, I can do that well enough,” the concerned hand replies.

John walks at a fast pace to the large opening of the barn doors. He peers in cautiously to see his wife sitting on a bale of hay in the dim light, holding the rifle across her lap. Not wanting to startle her, he speaks from the doorway.

“June, are you all right, honey? I’m coming in to be with you.” A little feeling of discomfort accompanies him as he enters and moves toward his wife.

“What are you doing with that rifle? Will you give it to me?” he asks.

She holds the gun out sideways with both hands, “Take it, I can’t do it anyhow.”

“What are you trying to do? You’re not thinking of hurting yourself, are you?”

“No,” she begins tersely. “I wanted to kill this damned horse. He’s been nothing but a worry for me since the day you gave him to Sheree. And now, look at what’s happened. It’s because he threw her off that she got hurt, and now she’s gone from me forever. I can’t stand knowing he’s still here. He’s alive. He’s okay, and my daughter’s gone forever.”

“I see. I’ll get him off this farm within a week. Think about this for a minute or two if you can. Maybe it’ll help a little. Pooch came home to let us know Sheree needed help. I think he loved our daughter the way only an animal can love a person. I don’t think he’d do anything to hurt her on his own. This whole thing must have been a terrible accident,” John’s words leave his lips with a tone of consolation.

“Charlotte came home, John, and well . . . I must have fallen asleep, because I didn’t hear her come into the house. She woke me up to show me the strawberries she picked.”

A pause that lasts fifteen seconds.

“I had to tell her, I had to tell her about her sister. Do you know what she said? Do you know what your daughter said?” She starts to weep, and pauses to pull a jerky breath through a stuffy nose.

“She said, ‘Can I have Pooch now, Mama? Sheree doesn’t need him now, so he should be mine. I should have got him instead of her anyway. He should have been mine all along.’ How could she say such a thing? How can she feel that way about her sister?” June’s tears flow steadily down her face.

After drying her eyes and nose with a hanky, she looks at the floor for a moment, then turns her face toward her husband.

“I’ve been sitting here asking myself these questions over and over.

“Am I the only person on this farm that has any feelings for our daughter? Is there no one else that gives a damn that she’s gone? What in the world have I done to cause such feelings toward Sheree? Have I ignored Charlotte to the point that she hates me and resents her sister?

"I just can't swallow it. From this day forward, every time I see Pooch I'll be reminded not only of Sheree, but that our daughter, Charlotte, couldn't care less that her sister's gone. And now, Robert will be home in a few days. Will he feel the way Charlotte does? Will he honestly despise me too? I'm terrified that he'll hate me and say things, spiteful things, things that will turn us against each other.

"What about our son, John? Robert's almost full grown. What will you tell him? Are you going to lie to him as well? Of his two sisters, Robert is closest to Sheree. He might have a few more questions than you expect. What do you think he'll do if he finds out about all that's happened. He will never forgive us? Will he ever forgive me?

"Charlotte's so indifferent she cares nothing about our family, and Robert will probably leave, never to return.

"And you, John . . . Sheree's gone; and all you want to think about is the cover up so no one will question anything that's happened.

"Have you honestly thought about it . . . about me? You're all wrapped up with the money and the politics of it all. You hardly know I'm around anymore.

"I'll say this to you, if it comes to pass that all I've said comes true. I'll leave you. You'll never see me again. I could not possibly be any more miserable than I am at this moment? And you don't care!" she shouts.

"You don't give a damn about anybody but yourself. Yourself and what the future holds for you." She sags and sobs, her shoulders slump.

"You stay right where you are," he commands quietly. "I'll be back in a minute."

He takes a lantern off a nail in the post over June's head, raises the glass and lights it with a match he strikes by slicing his thumbnail across its head. After hanging the lantern back on the nail, he walks to the double doors of the barn.

"Jim!" he yells.

Jim, who is still standing outside with the horses reins in his hand, moves toward the open doors.

"See those two buckets there by the trough. Fill them with water and bring them to me?" Mr. Anderson wants to stay where he can keep an eye on his wife.

"Yes, sir," he responds. As he turns to get the buckets, he drops the reins to the ground.

John glances back and forth at June while watching Jim fill the containers.

A couple of scoops at the trough, then his hand brings the buckets, water sloshing over the sides, and sets them on the ground in front of his boss.

"This is going to take a little while. You might as well go home to your family until I can get this all worked out. Thanks."

"What about your horse?"

"Put him around back under the lean-to for the night. And here, put this rifle by the door there on the porch," John instructs, "I don't want Mrs. Anderson to see it any more tonight."

June's husband picks up the two buckets and carries them toward her. He sets them down and returns to close the barn doors, then walks back to his wife.

"I can't let you hurt this way, honey. We need to have this out here and now. If we're not able to come to some sort of an understanding, well . . . then we'll cross that bridge of doom when we get to it."

He gets up close to her face, puts the fingers of his left hand under her chin and lifts her head so she has to look at him.

"Have I ever, and I mean ever, during our marriage not supported you, and been there for you? You know I've always been there, no matter what. I've listened to you howl and bellyache, now you're about to get off your righteous perch and listen to me." He turns to the side, picks up a bucket of water and dumps it straight down over her head.

Sputtering and gasping from the surprise and the cool water, she cries, "What are you doing? Why did you do tha—?"

He cuts her off before she can finish.

"Shut up and listen for a change," he demands.

June's eyes are wide open with surprise, her sobbing stops.

"You—yes, I said you. You're the cause of this whole mess we're in right now. Eleven years ago, I did what I had to do to save your good name. I spent a fortune over a year and a half to keep people quiet, to keep them loyal to us. It took every dime I had and all I could borrow. The farm was mortgaged for more than it was worth, and was about to be taken away because we couldn't keep up with the payments.

"You were, oh so willing back then to make amends, you were ready to sign a pact with the devil himself, just to keep the life you had. You were so sorry for your adulterous affair, you were willing to promise me anything, because you needed me to stay and clean up your mess.

"Well, I did . . . I did it by any means I could, and I almost lost this farm in the process. This farm . . . this land . . . this land that has been in our family since it was gifted to my grandfather by the president of the United States. I know you remember what this farm has meant to so many people for so long. You put it all in jeopardy.

"And I know you remember what we had to do to keep it? Think back to the day the babies were born? Remember? I know you do. Sheree was stillborn. They thought she was dead and laid her aside. An hour later, a doctor noticed she hadn't changed color and took another look. That's when he found a faint heartbeat. We were intent on saving our daughter, so they called in the best men they could find. To hell with the expense, we wanted her to live.

"It was determined that she has a condition where she can lapse into a state of being almost dead, yet still be alive. Well, one of these doctors they called in was from the Company. He knew exactly what to do. He knew how to save our daughter, but it came with a price.

"He could bring that beautiful child back to us if we would promise to give her to the Company when she turned fourteen. They would pay all our debts, no matter who we owed, no matter the amount. They would pay off our farm, and let us keep it. They would pay us seventy thousand dollars in cash, on top of all of that, spaced out evenly over the next fourteen years? And they gave us the first five thousand dollars right then."

"But, John, I—" June tries to interrupt.

"I said to shut up and listen. Now listen.

"I didn't want any part of this whole thing, and you know that's true. But we had to make a decision quickly. We did what we had to do. You agreed to do it. I didn't force you. I told you we'd figure another way out of our woes. But you reasoned that it was better to have Sheree for fourteen years, than not at all. You also saw a quick fix for all of our problems, all that money."

"I admit it—it was a way out for me too. I could keep the farm, along with all it has stood for, and further my political career with the money.

"But June, listen to me . . . I would never have done any of it had you not agreed. And I wouldn't have went along with it at all if I didn't love you as I do. It broke my heart to discover the affair you were wrapped up in, but I just couldn't let you go. I had no reason to go on without you, and that's the real reason I agreed to do all this. I couldn't stand the thought of losing you.

"And now, here we are, I still love you as I did back then, only more.

"I love Sheree just as much as you do. One of us, though, has always had to take care of business before anything else. That has been me. I hurt inside the same as you, yearning for our daughter. But I know there's nothing I can do to get her back. Anything I do will only cause suspicion and probably dredge up this whole ugly series of events again. I know you don't want that to happen. I also know you want our children to grow up knowing you and me as they believe we are right now. They never need to know what you and I are capable of doing. If we tell them about this mess, they'll never get over it.

"I don't agree with you that Charlotte's only thoughts and feelings toward Sheree are vindictive. And Robert adores you. You've allowed yourself to succumb to your innermost thoughts and fears, and let them take over your mind. Both of our children will grieve for Sheree in their own way. They'll miss her, perhaps not the same way you or I will, but they'll miss her.

"Telling those children the truth will do nothing but turn them against us both. It'll scar them for life. That's not the wise thing to do, and you know it.

"If you'll let me, I'll grieve with you, but I'm unable to let it out right now. I must keep my mind to the task at hand. It'll take a few days, maybe a week. But only then, when the details are finished, will I be able to let my true feelings out. I'll need you then, June, even more than I do at this moment.

"Can I count on you, honey? Can we continue to play the hand we've dealt ourselves? We need to stand together. This whole mess will start to settle down in a few weeks, and I need to know that I can depend on you. What's it going to be? Are we in this together as we've always been? I need your answer, you must tell me now."

In the meantime, over at the Stoker home.

Randall sits on the porch, with his feet resting on the top of the first step, his elbows on his knees, and his face in his hands, waiting for his life to end.

Jacob is walking from the tack shed toward him. As he reaches the steps, he puts his open hand on top of his son's head, rubs it, and continues into the house. His daddy's touch makes the boy grin on the inside. It makes him feel a whole lot more relaxed.

In short order, his mama swings the door open and steps out onto the porch with her husband right behind. They each grab a straight-back chair and drag them together so they're about three feet away from the frightened lad, and face him as he turns around.

"Now, we're all settled down, and we want to hear the exact truth. There's not anything so bad that you can't tell your mama and daddy. You talk, and we'll listen," Alberta Mae says.

Randall made up his mind to tell the truth at that very moment. He knows it's the only way he can help Sheree, if at all.

"Well, here goes," he says to himself.

"I made friends with the girl next door, her name's Sheree. We've been friends for over a year now. We had it made up to meet at the willow this morning. Only, when she was coming up the creek bank on her horse Pooch, he slipped on the mud and threw her off up into the air. She got hurt real bad when she landed, so I sent her horse home after some help. I figured they'd come when he got there without her in the saddle. When her daddy and some hands came there, they took her away on a wagon to their guesthouse. I just wanted to know how she was, so I went on over there to find out . . .

Back at the Anderson farm . . . inside the barn.

"Me, righteous . . . me, on a perch? You . . . the king of control! You . . . the answer for everything—man! I see you remember everything about how I was back then. What about you? Have you forgotten your part in all of this?" June spits venom at her husband, in response to his onslaught and final question.

"You've conveniently forgotten your part in this, haven't you?

"The reason I allowed myself to get caught up in an affair was that you were never around. You were always off somewhere, at a political meeting, or commanding the moves of the people all over the county. You were never home. You were never there for me as you said."

"I did the best I could," John tries to interrupt her tirade.

"Oh shut up, John. You had your say and now I'm going to give you your answer.

"You do not recall, do you? I would never have been pregnant in the first place if not for you! Remember? You're damned right you do. You were drunk out of your mind, and crazy with agony from learning about my so-called affair. You forced him to have sex with me. You forced me to have sex with that man!

"Believe me, I loathe the day that happened. I only did it to keep you. I did it for us. I would never have considered having a physical relationship with him otherwise. You made that happen, and now the only way you can forgive yourself is to deny it ever happened.

"Well, it happened all right. Those babies prove it every day of their lives.

"Yes, you cleaned up the mess, but it wasn't just for me. You cleaned it up for yourself as well. I don't know if you would have done it just for me.

"You want an answer? The one you must have right now?" she says, her narrowed green eyes glaring fury into his.

Off the hay bale she jumps, grabs the rope handle of the second bucket of water, lifts it up over his head, and dumps the entire content. His head and shoulders are completely drenched in water.

Not all of it soaks into John, however. A good amount of it splashes back at her, causing her face and the front of her dress to get another dousing.

The truth of the matter is still being explained at the Stoker home.

"And so, when I pushed away the shelves, I saw I was in a cellar. There wasn't much light, but I could see a ladder and figured there must be a door there in the floor. So, I climbed up and pushed it open. When I climbed up there, I knew I was inside Sheree's guesthouse. I looked all over the for her, but she wasn't there. Then I came home.

"And that's the whole truth of it. Please forgive me, Mama, please forgive me, Daddy. I know I did wrong, and I swear I won't do it again."

Jacob and Alberta Mae just sit there, first looking at each other, then at Randall, then at each other again.

"Son," Jacob starts, "there's an awful lot I can't tell you right now, maybe when you are older. But I want you to promise me and your mama that you won't go back to that farm for any reason.

"Will you promise us that?"

"Yes, sir. I won't ever go back there again. I don't want to," the young man assures.

"Something else, honey," Alberta Mae looks at her son knowingly. "I sense that you like that little girl a whole lot, and I know you'd like to find out what happened to her and why. But that's best left to your daddy and me to find out. We'll see what we can do. No promises, you understand. But we'll try."

"Thanks a lot, Mama. I love both of you. I've got the best Mama and Daddy in the whole world."

Almost together, Jacob and Alberta Mae say, "We love you too, son."

"You should go on to bed now, my boy," his father says. "No need to talk about this any more tonight."

Randall gets up and walks into the house, allowing the screen door to slam behind him.

"That child," Alberta Mae softly relates to her husband, "he's got such a good heart."

"We've got some serious talking to do, Alberta Mae," Jacob says, ignoring her comment.

"I know we do, but it'll keep until the morning. We'll be rested and better able to know what to do. It's a shame about their little girl, Sheree."

Things have cooled things off a little at the Andersons' barn.

John and June stand there, soaked with the water from the buckets. He feels the cool liquid searching its way through his clothing to his skin, running down his body, then over his legs, filling up his boots.

June is looking at her husband's eyes wide open with surprise, at the same time sputtering from the water that splashed back on her face.

"Do I have your attention now? Will you listen to me?" she says, unable to stop a small grin as it crosses her lips. Her voice softens as they look at each other, standing in the barn, completely soaked.

His face lights up with a smile when she speaks.

"I just realized that you brought that extra bucket of water knowing what I would do if you pushed me hard enough. You know me too well, John Anderson, all too well. You know I'll do anything, whatever it takes, to keep us and our family together.

"Don't expect me to ask for your forgiveness for anything I've said. It's all true—what you said to me—and me to you. We don't need to take it back."

She steps toward him at the same time he steps closer to her. Their arms find their way around each other and slowly pull their bodies together. He pulls himself away just enough to put his right hand under her chin and gently pull it up toward his face. He continues to look into her eyes and carefully bends down to tenderly kiss her lips.

"John, I adore you. You know I do. You are the most noble man I have ever known in my life. You've lived your life for others, and your plans are to do the same in the future. I don't know what makes you love me the way you do. But I'm glad I don't, for if I did, I'd probably find a way to destroy it," she coos.

"Oh, my darling June," John whispers, "I love you more now than I've loved you since we met. I don't want to live without you. I can go on in life no matter what if I still have you, if I know you're still here with me.

"You think you offer so little to me and those around you. You're so wrong—so, so wrong. Half the men in this county would change places with me in a second, just so they could look at you across the breakfast table in the morning. Among your wonderful traits, you have a tender loving heart. You love very easily, and that's a gift you gladly give to all those around you. You get hurt more because of it, but it seems that hurt just causes you to love more.

"Of course, you do know I married you for the sex. You are aware of that, are you not?" he compliments and toys with her.

"I'm really glad to hear that, because you're exactly what I need right now," she whispers, and their lips come together again.

Their passion heightens as their mouths open slightly, allowing their tongues to caress.

Deeper and deeper, as their bodies press more and more tightly together, lips part allowing their breaths to become heavy and fast. He picks her up in his arms, carries her to an empty stall, and lays her down gently in the clean, sweet-smelling straw. While embracing they kiss again, with John lying on top, his arms supporting most of his weight.

"I love you so much. Hold me. Take me," she whispers between gasps for breath.

He rises to his knees and begins to remove his water-soaked shirt. She impatiently watches him struggle with the buttons. This is taking too long, she can't wait. Her hands go up to grab a side each, then she pulls sideways, in opposite directions, with all her might. Buttons tear loose flying everywhere; the shirt is wide open exposing his bare chest.

That's all she needs to start removing her own clothes. He fusses with his wet boots and pants, while she unhooks her dress down the back. She has the same problem with the long wet sleeves, causing him to stop his own efforts to help her. Finally, the dress slides off her arms, and she's able to push it down over her hips, over her legs, and off her feet.

The light from the lantern is dim but bright enough for him to see the tempting curves of his wife's body when she removes her underwear. He stops to drink in her loveliness. Lust builds fiercely within his body and mind. He slips out of the rest of his wet clothes and moves toward his bride as she lies back, down on the straw. Their nude bodies entwine and give in to their starving animalistic desires.

This day has been exhausting for them both. The closeness and the sex relieves some of the stress burdening both their minds. Once they've taken their fill of each other, they settle closely into the straw on the floor of the stall, and relax. The spattering of rain drops on the metal roof lulls them to sleep. The lantern continues to burn under the watchful eye of an undetected rooster, who has taken a perch upon the wall of the stall where they lie.

Chapter Five

A soft rain continues through the night, giving the ground a good soaking. The pattering of the droplets on the roof of the barn, at the Anderson farm, creates a symphony of calm and restfulness. Mr. and Mrs. Anderson sleep peacefully in the straw below. They've not stirred.

Daybreak brings the large rooster to life on his roost atop the stable wall. He flutters his wings, leaves his perch, lands on the floor of the barn, and begins strutting around, pecking at the dirt floor.

The two doors of the haymow that swing outward to rest against the front of the barn have been left open allowing the early morning light to start chasing the interior darkness away. The rooster, trapped on the lower floor since the main doors were closed last night, cocks an eye at the oncoming light. He flaps his wings furiously, which moves him into the air in a rather awkward circular flight, but still he finds his way to the haymow above. He lands in the hay and straw and struts in a zigzag fashion toward the open doors. After taking a look around, his head jerking back and forth, side to side, he spreads his wings as if he's going to fly out into the barnyard from the second story opening. Instead, his neck stretches up and out as far as he can.

Cock-a-doodle-do! Cock-a-doodle-do!

A pause of five seconds.

Cock-a-doodle-do! Cock-a-doodle-do!

The morning sun makes its first appearance with streaks of bright light coming up from the horizon. The beginning of a new day is at hand. The rooster's commotion awakens June. Startled for a second, she sits up not knowing where she is. A glance around at her surroundings brings it all back. She turns her head to see her husband lying on his back, just starting to stir. That's her cue to roll over and lay her nude body against his. She places a soft kiss on his lips causing him to flutter his eyes open.

"John," she whispers, "you'd better get up and get dressed. Someone's banging on the door."

"What?" he questions. "I didn't hear anything."

"Well they did, and you're lying here naked. You know the door isn't locked, they can come right on in here anytime they want to. I'm already dressed, so it's okay with me."

He throws her off his chest and sits up at the same time. As soon as she lands in the straw next to him, he can see that she's naked too.

"Very funny," he says, acting as though he's upset. "Let's see how you like this."

As he lunges at her, she rolls over and tries to crawl away. He reaches, grabs the calf of her leg, and pulls her back. She slides easily on the straw and turns over to face him at the same time. Now on his knees, he looks down. The straw in her hair, and a look of "what's going to happen next" on her angelic innocent face is all it takes. He settles down on top of her, his bare chest against her soft breasts. Without a sound, their eyes meet and their lips come together. Their bodies give in to their lustful minds without further concern of the unlocked barn door.

Afterward, they lie panting in the straw.

"John . . . honey . . . we'd better get up and get dressed before one of the children wanders in here. I can't believe we did this in the barn, not once, but twice," she says as she stands up.

"Let's see if we can make it three," her husband says as he reaches out for her hand.

"Not today, we have too much to do—to get through," she reminds.

"I know, that's been on my mind too. How do you feel about it this morning?"

"Some better, I suppose. I know you're right with what you say. It's really hard for me to accept, but I will. It'll take some time, though. That darling little face is on my mind all the time," his wife responds.

"You mean . . . even when we . . . ?"

"No, no, no, not then," she assures him. "I used your body last night, sweetheart. Do you hate me for it? You were like a sedative for me."

"Hate you? I've never loved you more in my life. I needed you too, you know. I'll be here for you anytime you want me. How do you feel about right now?"

"I think I hear someone coming. Get dressed," she replies, teasing her man.

Together, they search through the hay and straw trying to locate their clothes, which are still wet. Then in the loose sense of the word, they get dressed. John pours water from his boots. There's no sense in tying every bow and buttoning every button when it's all going to be done over again in a few minutes. They each take a barn door and push them open, then walk out together, hand in hand.

After taking time to take a bath and get into some clean dry clothes, they descend the stairs to the first floor. Someone hears them coming, causing a voice to ring out from the kitchen.

"Mr. Anderson, Mrs. Anderson, Ms. Charlotte is in here in the kitchen with me having her breakfast this morning. Do you want me to set the table in the dining room, or do you want to come on in here and eat your breakfast with her?" Belle, the Andersons' housemaid and cook, asks.

"There's no sense in making another mess, Belle. We'll have our breakfast with Charlotte," June responds, as she and her husband enter the kitchen.

"I'm having eggs and sausages. What are you going to have?" their daughter chimes.

"I think I'll have some toast and coffee, Belle," Mama Anderson answers.

"How are you this morning, dear?" she asks her daughter. "Did you sleep well last night?"

"All right, I guess. I went into your room last night, and you and Daddy weren't there. I looked all over for you and couldn't find you anywhere. Belle told me this morning you were out in the barn. Did you stay in the barn all night?" the youngster asks.

John looks at his wife and grins a little. "The truth is, honey, we kept Pooch company last night? He was restless . . . missing your sister, I suppose."

"Why were you looking for us, were you afraid?" Her mother is concerned.

"No, Mama, I just wanted to tell you that I'm sorry for what I said yesterday. I didn't mean it. Will you forgive me? I miss Sheree a lot. Is she gone forever? Won't she ever come back?" Tears roll down the young girl's cheeks.

John watches as emotion takes over his wife's face. A lump grows in his throat as his daughter reaches out for her mother. To his surprise, June almost runs, picks the ten-year-old up from her seat—as if she's a feather—and gives her a mighty hug. The girl wraps her legs and arms around her mama, then they both begin to cry and speak at the same time.

"There is nothing to forgive you for."

"I am so sorry, Mama."

"I miss her too."

"I'll be here for you, honey."

"I hurt inside, Mama . . ."

"Me too."

"Can I see her again?"

"No, sweetheart, Sheree's gone. We're going to have a service for her so we can say goodbye."

Silence falls over the kitchen as the two embrace in tears.

"Belle, I think I'll have some hotcakes with my eggs and sausage," John orders, as he wipes the water from his eyes with his fingers, and swallows the lump in his throat. "I have an appetite all of a sudden."

The three of them sit at the kitchen table eating their breakfasts, while John relates the plans for Sheree's funeral. They're just finishing when Jim appears at the back door.

"I need to show you something, Mr. Anderson," he says.

"What is it?" the elder Anderson asks.

"I best show you, sir. I don't rightly know what to make of it," their household hand and farm driver replies.

"I'll be right there. Let me swallow the rest of this coffee."

As they walk toward the barn, John inquires, "Will you take Josh to our family cemetery and dig a grave for Sheree? If you don't think you're up to it, have Josh take someone else. Dig it next to my father's—her granddaddy. Tell everyone the service will be held at two o'clock this afternoon."

"Yes, sir, Mr. Anderson. Josh and me, we'll dig that grave for Ms. Sheree. We will be honored that you want us to do it," he says grimly.

"Well now, what is it you want me to see?" John asks, as they walk up to the barn doors. The thought of June's underwear being tossed everywhere last night, darts through his mind.

"Well, I took your horse around to the lean-to last night, and put him in there for the night, just like you said. I brushed him down a little, and fed him some grain. But with all that was going on, I didn't get to feed Pooch or tend to him at all after all the running he did—it just slipped my mind. And since you and Mrs. Anderson had the doors shut on the barn, I didn't want to bother you none. So, I just waited to do it this morning. Well, sir, after I put his grain bag on I started to brush him down, I noticed something that made me think something must have happened to make Pooch throw Ms. Sheree," he relates as they walk up to the stall where the animal is standing.

He opens the stall door and walks in ahead of John, and pats the horse on his forehead as he crosses in front of him.

"See here . . . right here, about three inches above his left front leg. Looks like he's been stabbed with something. Maybe he fell down when he threw Ms. Sheree off. Maybe something stuck in him then, but this sure wasn't there when they left here yesterday."

"Let me see," John says, bending over as Jim steps out of the way.

"This horse has been shot. I've seen enough gunshot wounds to know one." He puts his fingers on the wound to see if he can feel the shot. Pooch rears his head, snorts, and stomps his feet. "We have to get that shot out of there. If we don't, the wound will fester, or worse than that, he could get lead poisoning. We sure don't want that. Good job, Jim. Another couple of days of healing and we might never have seen it. I'm going to the house to get some alcohol and a knife. While I am gone, lay him down on his right side. I'll be right back."

"If he's willing, I'm willing," the horse's experienced hand responds.

When John returns, he sees that Jim has been successful with getting the horse to lie down. He's squatted down beside Pooch, rubbing the horse's head.

"I found some long nosed pliers and salve while I was at it. I brought some clean rags too. I'm going to sterilize this knife blade with some alcohol, then, I need you to get down and lay your body across his neck, up close to his head. Put this rag over his eyes," John orders quietly so as not to scare the horse.

"I hope he'll allow us to do this. If he starts to fight and get upset, move out of the way. We might have to tie him to get this job done."

John knows they're no match for the strength of a horse. He also knows that if he goes about this slowly and deliberately, there's a good chance Pooch will put up with it.

Mr. Anderson kneels down behind Pooch's left front leg, then carefully places his left hand an inch above the wound.

"Easy does it. You ready?" he says calmly.

"Yep."

He takes the knife point to the wound knowing he'll have to scrape off the dried blood and scabbing before he can get the pliers into the skin and flesh. Pooch snorts and pants, as he tries to throw his head, but he doesn't try to break away from them.

"I'm going in." John's voice is almost a whisper.

Jim feels Pooch's head wanting to come up, and hears his breathing become heavy and faster. He makes a sound of pain, almost like a bass toned suppressed whinny. The horse still doesn't try to get loose. It's almost as if he knows the shot has to be removed, and that it will soon be over.

"I can feel it . . . hold on . . . just a little more. I have the pliers around it. I'm going to pull it out. Get ready . . ."

Pooch lets out a mixed snort and scream, and jerks, almost throwing Jim off his neck.

"I have it," John says triumphantly.

"Hold him just a minute more while I put some of this salve in this hole."

"Okay, let him up, I think he'll be fine. And that's thanks to you, Jim. You did a great job. He knows you. I don't think he would have allowed me to hold him down like that." The man with the knife in his hand explains to his helper.

As soon as the blindfold is taken away from his eyes and the weight off his neck, the horse gets to his feet. Jim gets in front of him to pat and rub his head and say, "Good boy. Good boy."

"Look at this piece of lead that was in him. I've never seen anything like it before? Have you?" John sounds puzzled.

Jim takes the bloody object from his boss's hand. It's more than a quarter of an inch in diameter, and well over an inch and a half long. It tapers along its length to a point where it's mushroomed from the force of the impact.

"My Lord. I've never seen anything like this before. What kind of gun would shoot something like this?" Jim agrees.

"I don't know for sure, but I have some ideas." John follows up, "Let's not tell anyone about this. I'm not sure of what's happened here, so I need some time to consider the possibilities. I don't want to upset Mrs. Anderson any more than she is already, so we'll keep this to ourselves for the present."

"Yes, sir," Jim agrees totally.

Meanwhile, still in the clutches of her abductors, Sheree bounces along in the cedar chest the three men procured from the guesthouse.

Daybreak is starting. She can see a faint light through the opening of the box. It's been a long night. They stopped just once, that was when they had to relieve themselves. Still unable to move at all, she doesn't feel any different than she did last night.

"Wait a minute, the wagon has stopped. I hear voices, other wagons. We must be going through a town," she realizes.

"Chad, you and Nate get off here. See if you can find a place that will wrap up something to eat, and get a pot of coffee, then bring it over to the station. I'm about to starve. I'll take our package on over there and wait. Hurry up now," Sheree hears the man she thinks is her daddy's friend say.

The wagon jerks; they're moving again.

"We're in a town for sure. People are talking everywhere. If only I could yell out loud. When the wagon isn't moving, I can hear most of anything being said around it. I wonder why I'm not hungry, and I'm not thirsty either. That's good, I suppose. These men haven't given any thought that I might need the privy, or be hungry, or thirsty.

"We've stopped again." The young girl senses.

"What time is the train due in? Is it on time?" She hears the man on the wagon say.

"The station must be a train depot. And it sounds like we're meeting a train. Where are they taking me?"

"Yep, she's on time for a change. Should be here about eleven this morning," a different man replies.

"Okay, if I put this here box on the dock until we can load it?" the man on the wagon asks.

"Sure. What you got in there? I'll make up a waybill on it," the depot man offers.

"That's not necessary. This is going on a private car coming in with the train," the man on the wagon explains.

"Well here, let me help you set it up here on the platform."

"That's all right. I can get it myself. It looks heavier than it is." The wagon driver wants no one close to the cedar chest.

"No trouble at all, mister. That's a good-size box for one man to handle," the depot man insists.

"I can tell by his voice, he's really close to the wagon."

"Just be real careful. I don't want to drop it or anything; and don't touch it until I get down there." The wagon shakes as the driver climbs down to the ground. "I'll slide it back, then you get the back end off the wagon," the driver says.

Sheree feels the chest moving.

"Wait just a minute. What's this?" She hears the depot man say.

The bright light burns her eyes because she's unable to close them.

"That hurts? But wait—the lid's open!"

"He has to be able to see me—he's found me!" she yells to herself.

In the meantime at the Stokers' house, at the back of the main house on the Housler farm, Der Bote . . .

"Can we do something today to find out about Sheree, Daddy?" Randall talks as he stuffs his mouth with breakfast grits.

"Son, we have to be real careful as to how we go about that. As far as we know, they don't know you saw or heard anything. If we just up and go over there and start asking questions, they'll be sure to think we know something. I don't want them to start asking questions. They'll figure out it was you, and then I don't know what we'd do. I need to think on it for a spell yet."

"Your daddy's right," Alberta Mae supports her husband. "You need to hold your britches until we think it through. We can't be the cause of stirring up trouble. The colonel won't like that, and besides, it's none of our business when you get right down to it. Finish your breakfast children, you all have chores; and, Randall, you don't go anywhere near that farm. Do you hear me, child? I'm not fooling with you."

"Yes, Mama."

"We'll talk about this again at the end of our day," Jacob informs his wife and son.

At the same time, not too far away, at the Anderson farm.

"John, is there something wrong?" June asks from the porch as he walks toward the house. "I noticed you took some salve and bandages to the barn."

"Nothing to worry your pretty little head about. Jim found a place on Pooch's leg, so we put some salve on it. We don't want it to get festered," he explains, not wanting to let her know about the gunshot wound.

"That's good. I just wondered."

"Listen, honey, as much as I don't want to go, I think I should let the colonel know something about the funeral service. He is our neighbor and involved in all this too."

"Must I go too?"

"I don't think that's necessary, but once I tell them, you should expect them to show up at the service. You'll have to deal with them then."

"I know. If I can just get through this day," June agrees.

"We will. We must. We'll get through it together: you, Charlotte, and me," her husband speaks with certainty.

"I think I'll have Jim saddle my horse and go over there now. Will you be all right while I am gone?"

"I'll be fine. Go ahead, get it done."

"Just so you're aware, Jim and Josh are going over to our cemetery to take care of things there."

"That's fine," she says, as she reaches for the rifle left leaning against the house last night, "I'll put this where it belongs."

"I won't be gone long," he says, as he turns back toward the barn.

Back to the train depot, where the cedar chest is being loaded onto the freight platform.

"What the hell are you doing? Close that lid now? There's nothing in this box that concerns you? Get away from here!" the wagon driver yells at the station master.

"Sorry . . . there was a bit of a blanket sticking out from under the lid. I just put it back, that's all. Simmer down, I didn't see in there. Like you say, none of my business."

"All right then, grab that end. Set it up there under the shade of the roof."

"He didn't see me. Darn, the lid's closed tight now. There's no light in here at all, and that means no air can get in here either. How long can I breathe with the air that's in here now? Am I going to die in here?" Sheree's mind whirls with more unanswered questions.

She feels the chest hit the wooden floor of the platform and then slide some distance. There are a few muffled words, but nothing she can make out.

"Dear Lord, please let them remember I need air in here to breathe. Amen."

Time passes.

"It seems like forever since they closed this lid down on me. It's really warm in here, too. I don't seem to be having any trouble breathing, but I need to keep myself settled down, the air will last longer if I do. Maybe the depot man did see me. Maybe he's off telling someone about me right now.

"Dear Lord, please make it so. Let the depot man tell somebody I'm in this box. Amen. I wish I could hear what's going on out there. If they put me on a train, how will I ever get back home? I won't know where I am. I won't know which way to go. I'll just find a sheriff when I get free, that's what I'll do. A sheriff will know how to get me back home. I'll just wait my chance. I'll get away from these people . . . I will.

"Dear God, please help me get away from these people. Amen.

"I hear hissing, hissing and puffing. The train must be here.

"Oh no! Don't put me on that train? I've never been on a train before.

"I wonder where it's going? I want out of this box. When are they ever going to get me out of this box? Dear Lord, please, please, get me out of this box. Amen.

"This chest is moving again. They must be putting me on that train." Sheree's thoughts continue to run rampant. She feels the bangs and jerks as the box is roughly handled for a few minutes.

"It's bright. They've opened the lid, I can feel the cool air against my face and hands. I smell—cigar smoke? And wait . . . Mama's perfume? She's here, Mama's here!

"Oh, thank you, Lord." The young Anderson girl believes she's been saved.

"Here she is, boss, this is Sheree Anderson. I don't know what's so special about her. She looks just like any other young girl to me," the wagon driver comments.

"How did it go? Were there any significant problems that I need to be concerned about?" a man with a deep, smooth, bass voice requests.

"Well, she came along yesterday morning just the way you said she would. She was riding a horse, though. So, Chad had to shoot it. The thing is, the horse no sooner hit the ground than some young boy came running up to the girl, who was lying on the ground, and he just stayed there. We didn't want to get anybody else wrapped up in this, so we waited to see what was going to happen. The girl was just lying on the ground in the same shape she's in now. Finally, her dad showed up with a couple of farmhands. He left one of them there with the girl and sent the other one off at a run. The father mounted up and took off at a dead run too, we figured to town to get a doctor. So, we took off in that direction too. We got there a just minute ahead of him. He headed straight for the doctor's office."

"I've met John Anderson several times before, so I asked if we could ride along with him and the doctor back to the farm. As it worked out, the girl is in some sort of unconscious state. The doctor said she'll be okay in a couple of days. I thought it was best that we take her right then instead of waiting. So, we paid off Anderson with the money you gave us, and here we are."

"What about the boy? Did you kill the horse?"

"No, the boy got the horse up and sent him home to get the help that showed up. The boy climbed up into a willow tree and hid until Anderson showed up. Then we left for town. I don't know what happened to him after that."

"I don't understand you. You might have killed this little girl. A fall from a horse can be dangerous. And now, there's a boy that saw what went on out there. Your orders were to locate the girl, tell the parents the Company needed to take her immediately, and give them the final payment. Nothing in those orders required gunplay. You, sir, are a fool. I don't like loose ends. You go back there and make sure nobody is coming to look for her, and I mean nobody. Do you understand?"

"Yes, but I don't think we should show our faces around there for a while, boss. I think we should just leave it be, the way it is," the wagon driver expresses.

"Well, maybe you're right. Stay around here for a few days. Then, if no one shows up looking or asking questions, come back to the office. I have another job for you. But I'm warning you right now, one more idiotic stunt, and you'll suffer dire consequences.

"Now, get out of my sight," the deep voice growls.

The men grumble but make no further comments. They leave and close the door to the rail car behind them.

"Sally, close these curtains." The deep voice is calm and smooth again. "I want to get a good look at our new disciple. Hello, young lady, I know you're unable to see me, however, in some cases your condition will allow you to hear me. My name is Dr. Ernst Valdamere. I'm a physician with a special education giving me the knowledge to help you. I mean you no harm. I'm here to assist you through your next few days."

He leans down in front of Sheree. She can see him. He looks a little scary with very bushy gray and black eyebrows. Various long hairs stick out in all directions. His beard is bushy too, and his hair looks all mixed up. A pair of glasses sets out on the end of his wide bubble nose, enabling his dark blue eyes to look out over the top of them. His lips are thick and make different shapes when he talks, revealing his dark yellowed teeth.

"He believes I can hear him, but he thinks I can't see him. I'll not let him know any different. I'll just stay calm and listen. Perhaps he'll give me the chance I need to get away. Who's Sally? I can still smell Mama's perfume. Come on, get in front of me, Mama, so I can see you. I know you're there.

"He's shining a light into my eyes. I wish he'd stop that. All I can see for a while after they do that are orange and yellow dots, with white spots."

"Yes, she's in there all right. Sally, come around to the side of this chest. I have something that will bring her back to us. Yes, that's good, stand right there," the base voice booms, "Sheree . . . that's your name, is it not? I'm going to let you sniff something. It's going to cause your nostrils to burn a little, then you'll start to feel warm all over. Don't be alarmed, that's normal. You'll slowly regain your senses and be able to move."

"Are you ready? Sally, put your hands on her shoulders just in case she wants to get up too fast."

"Oh my? It does burn, but more than a little. Ooooo . . . I feel like a fire has started in my stomach. It's spreading out all over my whole body, down my arms into my hands. It feels like my fingers could explode from within when it reaches the ends. My legs feel the same way too, and it's going up my neck to my head. Such a feeling, none like I've ever had before. It's in my head. I want it to stop, but I don't want it to stop. It feels . . . soooooo good. Oh—ohooo!

"It's stopped. I can move my eyes, and head. Where's Mama? I can't sit up, she's holding me down. Aahhh, I can see her now that I've rolled my head up and backward. Wait a minute. It's her, she smells like Mama, but she's not."

"Well, well, you're back with us, Sheree," the doctor says. "Would you like to sit up and get out of this chest? Come on, we'll help you. Hold on to Sally, she'll get you to a chair where you can sit for a few minutes to get your faculties back. Here we go now. This is good, up you come."

"It feels so good to move again. I'm a little wobbly and short of breath, but I feel good. My neck and shoulder hurts, and my face stings a little in places too." Their young prisoner senses without complaint.

"Sally is beautiful. She has long bright red hair that lies on her shoulders and down her back. A barrette on each side holds it away from her face. Her lipstick is as red as her hair, and rouge, applied with great care, adorns her cheek bones. Her long medium brown dress is perfectly pressed and fitted. I like her, she's wonderful."

"Lean on me, honey. Don't be afraid, you're safe here with us." Sally's lips smile as she speaks.

"She smells just like my mama, and she's gentle and squeezes me tight so I don't fall. Gently, carefully, she lowers me into a chair, allowing me to lie back to catch my breath."

"Are you thirsty?" she says. "Abraham, bring this lady something cool to drink."

In just seconds, a dark-skinned, gray-haired old man, dressed in a black suit, brings her a large glass of lemonade. Her hand shakes when she takes it from him.

"Drink slowly, dear, there's plenty more where that came from. Do you need some help holding the glass?" Sally says sweetly.

She shakes her head no.

"Mmmm? I've never tasted anything this good. It's cool going down my throat."

"You can call me Ernie, if you like, Sheree, all my best friends do. Abraham is fixing us some food, but that's going to take a few minutes, so let's talk while we wait."

"I want my mama. I want to go home. I can feel my eyes welling up for a good cry, but they don't know it. I'm going to control myself, wait for a chance, then I'm gone." She tells herself.

"Go ahead, you dear child, cry, get it out of your system. Let it all out." Ernie is more intuitive than she thought.

"He's right, Sheree. You have every right to be furious and angry. Cry—scream if you feel like it. Here, hit me hard, fight with me. It'll make you feel better," Sally encourages as she moves in front of her and kneels on the floor.

That's all it takes to bring the young girl's emotions to the surface.

"I'm scared. I have no family, no friends, no one cares about me. My mama and daddy have given me away. What's going to happen to me? I don't know what I did that was so bad. Is it because I ran Pooch? Does Mama and Daddy hate me for it?" Her voice is very loud now, tears fall off her chin, her nose leaks down over her lips.

"I have to get out of here," she screams, pushes Sally backward onto the floor, and runs for the railroad car door. Surprised that nobody chases her, she soon realizes the door is locked; she then sinks to the floor facing the door with her hand still on the knob. She hasn't the strength, or the will, to fight any more. At least not right now.

Sally's at her side, bending down and putting her arms around her.

"I want to be your friend, Sheree, if you'll let me. I give you my word, no harm will come to you. This same thing happened to me when I was fourteen years old. Believe me when I say, I know how you feel.

"Please, let me help you up," she says.

Her words, for some reason, have a calming effect on the troubled child. She needs someone, and she needs her right now.

Sheree gets to her feet as her new friend puts her arms around her and pulls her to her breast. Sally is so gentle and soft, and smells just like her mama. She lays her head on the red-haired woman's chest and cries. Little by little, Ms. Anderson starts to feel better. She walks back to the chair with her friend, in each other's arms.

As she sits down, the youngster looks around for Ernie. He's sitting at the table ready to eat. A long white bib is tucked in his collar and draped down over his lap. He's very portly. She hadn't noticed before, but he's almost as big around as he is tall.

Seeing him there, as he is, looks funny to her, so when he says, "I'm ready for something to eat, how about you?" she can't stop a smile.

"Good, let Sally help you to sit over here. The three of us can have a nice chat with our breakfast. I'll explain to you what has happened and what you can expect."

She sits at the table to see the food is already there. Scrambled eggs, bacon, sausage, fried grits, biscuits, jelly, apple butter, apple juice, and a large chocolate cake. She looks up to be sure both Ernie and Sally are there with her. They're smiling, fixing their plates, getting ready to eat. Sally reaches and takes Sheree's plate.

"I'm not sure what all you like, but I'll give you some of everything to start. From there, you can help yourself. How's that?" she says, with a twinkle in her voice.

"That's fine," Sheree hears herself agreeing.

Nothing is said for the next minute or so, until Sally sets a plate loaded with food in front of her.

"Abraham, bring this young lady some milk," says Ernie.

They all begin to eat. Abraham brings the milk.

"I love milk. I'll eat and listen. I'm not supposed to talk with my mouth full anyway." The unsettled child decides within herself.

"Should you have questions as I go along, please stop me and ask them. I'll do my best to give you the answers," Ernie instructs with a smile.

In the intervening time, the morning wears on back at the farms.

John reins his horse to a stop in front of the home of Colonel Charles Housler. After dismounting, he notices his horse's hooves and lower legs are wet and muddy.

"That was a good rain last night," he thinks to himself. "Jim and Josh are probably busy digging the grave by now. The ground should be softer today."

The house is a stately colonial-style mansion having a verandah reaching all the way from front to back, down the one side. Seven large round sculpted pillars support the roof. The front of the house has a much smaller porch, however, and that roof is supported with two pillars of the same shape and size as those on the verandah. The second story uses the roofs of both the porch and verandah to become elevated porches, without roofs themselves. Both of the second floor porches have wooden banisters with a balustrade carved in the same design as the support pillars below. Double doors with small paned glass windows open out from the house onto all of the areas, where seating and tables make up the furniture. Everything is painted bright white. It's a large house, with twenty-one rooms.

John uses the bright brass knocker to rap three times, then turns to look out over the fields as he waits.

The door opens.

"Good morning, sir. Welcome to Der Bote. How may I help you?" asks an older, properly dressed butler.

"I'd like a few minutes with Colonel Housler, if I may. My name is John Anderson," he answers and requests.

"Step in, Mr. Anderson. I'll announce you. Please wait here," the butler advises with great dignity.

"Morning, John. What brings you here so early in the day? Come on into the library. Sachel, bring us some coffee." The colonel appears and waves his arm at his guest in a "follow me" manner.

No one speaks until they are in the library, and sitting on two large red leather chairs facing each other, with a small short square table between them.

"I have some terrible news, Charles," John begins, noting the colonel's face is turning a pasty white. "We're going to bury our daughter, Sheree, at two o'clock this afternoon. June and I were wondering if you and Selma would come to the service?"

"What happened? How did she die?" the colonel rushes to inquire.

"She's not actually dead," John stops speaking when Sachel walks through the open door into the room.

"Thank you, Sachel. Put it here on the table. We'll pour it ourselves," Mr. Housler instructs his butler. "Close the door on your way out."

As soon as the door is closed, the colonel looks straight into John's eyes. "What? What in the world happened?"

"The Company took her. She was involved in an accident with her horse. He threw her and rendered her unconscious. Benny was in town when I went to get Doc. He and two of his cohorts followed us back to our guesthouse. After Doc examined her and said she'd be all right, Benny handed me a stack of cash and said they were taking her, and not waiting until she's fourteen. He said it was a perfect situation, that no one would question her disappearance. It was all over before I could come up with a strong argument.

"Honestly though, I think he's right," John continues and supports the decision. "I know this sounds cold, but the longer she was with us, the more difficult the parting would be. June's having a lot of trouble with it. Everything's upset at our place."

"My God, I can understand that. So, this is a mock service to cover her disappearance, I imagine. Of course we'll be there. Two o'clock this afternoon, you say?" the colonel confirms. "Is there anything at all we can do?"

"Thanks, Charles, it'll mean a lot to June and me, and no . . . there's nothing left to do. The service is going to be simple, just to put an end to it," Mr. Anderson replies.

"Is Doc totally aware of the situation?" queries the colonel.

"He is now. He wasn't there when Benny made his play. I caught up to him later in the day and explained the whole thing. He's bringing an empty coffin to bury. The grave is being dug as we speak. I have your money, Charles," John blurts, as he stands to get his hand into his pants pocket.

"I know what you are going to say, but I want you to take it, I'll have it no other way. You've kept our agreement, and the money is due you." Mr. Housler's visitor lays a stack of bills on the table beside the coffee service.

"I'm not going to fight over it. However, I still believe you should use it for another purpose, and you know what that is. I don't need the money. Why don't you put it where it 'll do some good, to help somebody."

"You know I can't to do that. It's too risky in my position. I think we're getting close to reaching our goals, and people would likely ask questions not realizing what they're doing. The risk is just too great."

"I know, you're right, of course," the colonel agrees. "It's still a damn shame."

"One last thing, Charles; I came by our guesthouse last evening on my way back from town. The front door was wide open and there were muddy footprints all over the house. The worst part of it is the bookcase was moved and the tunnel door was wide open. Someone knows about the tunnel. I noticed that the general direction of the tracks would lead me here to your place. I tried to follow them, but they faded out.

"They were too small for a man, could have been made by a woman or an older child. Have you heard anything or seen anybody?"

"Not a thing. But I'll ask some of my folks, maybe they've seen something. I'll let you know when I see you this afternoon."

"Well then, I'll see you later this afternoon. Please give Selma my thanks. Tell her, there's not going to be a problem with her being there. If she gets too uncomfortable, you can bring her back home." John offers his good-byes.

"I think she'll be okay with it, but I'll explain it to her anyway. We'll be there," Colonel Housler states. "I'll walk you out."

As soon as John rides away, headed back toward his farm, the colonel walks leisurely around the side of the house toward the home of Jacob and Alberta Mae. He sees Jacob working to remove a broken wheel from their black surrey. As he walks up he says, "Morning, Jacob. Do you think you'll have a wheel back on the carriage in time to use it early this afternoon?"

"Good morning, sir." Jacob looks up from his work to acknowledge the colonel.

"Yes, sir, it'll be ready for you. I got another wheel in the barn to put on here."

"Good. Say Jacob, while I am talking with you, have you heard or seen anything suspicious around here yesterday or yet today? According to Mr. Anderson, someone was in his guesthouse last night, leaving muddy tracks all over. He thinks whoever it was might have came this way. He says the tracks were made by a woman or a good-sized child.

"Do you know anything about it?"

Chapter Six

"How's your food, Sheree, is it good?" Ernie asks.

She nods yes.

"As I was saying," he continues, "I can only repeat what I've been told, but I'll do my best to explain. When you were born, it was apparent to those close to you that you were more than a normal child. A representative of the Company was present to offer your parents an opportunity—an opportunity, which would provide the education and environment, leading to a life you would otherwise never experience. Further, at that time, you needed immediate medical attention that your parents were unable to provide. In other words, you would not be here today, should your parents have elected to reject the Company's offer.

"Do you understand so far, any questions?"

"Yes. Who's the Company?" Sheree speaks up, even though she has promised herself she wouldn't. It just came out.

"Please bear with me a while longer, you'll better understand as we go along. You were born with a special gift. Only a few people in the whole world have it. The instructors at the Company will explain your gift in detail when you start your lessons. You are, also, blessed with an almost total recall of everything you see. Your studies at the Company will be extensive. Your ability to think and to reason will be measured. You'll meet special people, such as you, from all over the world. You'll see their abilities for yourself. Then, later on, after you have completed the majority of your studies, when you've grown up some, you'll be given various assignments. Am I making myself clear?"

No response.

"We're taking you to a place of secrecy. Once there, after you get settled in a bit, you'll begin learning many new things, some you'll find unbelievable. You'll have everything you need? Clothing, food, friends, a home, everything. Your training will take quite a while, probably five or six years. Your instructors will explain it all with much greater detail, so for now, please believe me when I say no harm will come to you. The Company will do everything necessary to keep you comfortable.

"We'll be on this train for at least another day before we arrive at our next destination. Sally and I will be here with you throughout our trip.

"Any questions of either Sally or me?"

Sheree nods her head yes.

"Will my mama and daddy come to visit me?"

"That's the hard part, honey," Sally begins. "We must break all our ties with your family. You'll probably never see any of them again. Bernie's right, though, you're going to make many new friends at the Company. As I said, I've been through most of what you're experiencing, and I've found many new friends. They've become as dear to me as family. You'll be with those who understand you the way you are. You'll not be alone."

"What about Randy and Pooch?" the Anderson child goes on.

Sally looks to her cohort.

"We don't know Randy and Pooch. Who are they?" he puzzles.

"Randy's my boyfriend and Pooch's my horse. Are they all right? Randy will wonder where I am. Pooch and I fell down. Is he okay? I heard that man say he shot him."

"I'm sure they're both just fine," Sally says. "We have word that your horse went to get help for you after your fall? As for Randy, he'll remember you and you'll remember him. But as I said, the hard part is to understand that you'll not see him again."

"Am I a prisoner? Will I have to live in a little room with bars on the windows, all by myself?" They don't know it, but she sort of likes the feeling of captivity. She'll have plenty of time to plan her escape. It'll be her against all of them.

"No, no, sweetheart, it won't be that way. It'll be almost like living at home. It's a very large place with plenty of room to run, explore, or be by yourself, if that's what you want. I won't lie to you, though, you won't be allowed to leave. But I doubt very much that you'll want to once you get settled into the exciting life that awaits you.

"Is there anything you would like to add to that Sally?" Bernie finishes.

"It's not a scary place at all. It's bright and beautiful. Just wait until you meet the others who are already there. You'll feel very comfortable." Sally adds, "I felt the way you're feeling now when I first arrived. But it took me only two days to adjust. Since then, I've been happy and have never wanted for anything. The Company will be very good to you. You'll see."

"Okay, we've covered most of it. Sally's going to arrange a hot bath for you. When you're finished, she'll have some new clean clothes for you to wear. That'll make you feel much better. She'll also show you where you'll sleep. After that, you can explore this railroad car from top to bottom, from end to end. Wouldn't you like to do that?" Bernie explains with a smile.

"Will I have to give the clothes back? All of my clothes are at home. I don't have any." Sheree misses her possessions.

"All of the clothes I'm going to show you are yours to keep. And just think, you'll get a lot more of them when we get there. You'll have new dresses, skirts, shoes, hats, things to put in your hair; perfume, stockings, underwear, everything you can imagine. And do you know the best part? You can decide which you'd like to keep and those will be yours forever. You can pick them out for yourself," Sally explains brightly.

Back at Der Bote.

Jacob turns his dark face to look directly at the colonel, something he has never done until now. Colonel Housler senses something has happened, a feeling that he knows something about the incident at the Andersons' guesthouse.

"I hope by now you know you can tell me anything that's on your mind Jacob. You know full well I think of you as family. Is there something we should talk about?"

"You kind of got me by surprise, Mr. Colonel. I wasn't expecting you to ask me that. The truth is, I was thinking as to how to go about asking for your help. You see, my boy, Randall, came home last night all wet and mud from head to toe, and told me and Alberta Mae a story about falling down into that well by Mr. Andersons' guesthouse. He couldn't get out no other way, so he found a tunnel that took him inside the guesthouse. We scolded him real good for it. He won't be bothering around there again." Jacob's face shows how he feels about what happened.

"I see . . . but how can I help you?" The colonel fishes for more information.

"Well, sir, Randall says he's made friends with a little girl over there. He saw her get thrown off her horse and get hurt. Her mama took her to their guesthouse, and that's why he went there in the first place. He's asked me if I can find out how she is? You suppose you could find out something for me? It would mean a lot to him." Jacob feels he's a taking a serious chance by admitting his son's guilt.

"You do remember the children are not to associate with the Andersons, right?"

"Yes, sir, I know . . . and the children know that too. Randall made a mistake by doing what he done." Jacob recalls his place and turns his head away.

"I need to think about this for a while, Jacob. Get the surrey fixed, then come to the kitchen of the main house. Have Alberta Mae tell me when you get there. We'll decide exactly how we're going to handle this. We might have a situation on our hands."

"Yes, sir," Randy's daddy replies, as Mr. Housler walks away.

John Anderson is returning to his farm from Der Bote.

As his horse walks up to the hitching rail at the front of his home, he notices Jim and Josh about to enter the tool shed with digging tools laid across their shoulders. He speaks loud enough for them to hear.

"Are you finished with your job? Did you put it next to her grandfather?"

They turn to look.

"Yes, sir," Jim calls back, "we got it all took care of."

"Good work. I'd like to leave here no later then one o'clock. The service will start at two. I'd like to be there a little early to welcome all those who attend."

"Yes, sir," Josh continues, "we'll have the buggy out front ready to go."

"I'm back, June," John shouts as he enters the house. "Where are you, honey?"

"I'm upstairs, getting Charlotte dressed for the service, we'll be down soon. Have a cup of coffee and rest a while before you change your clothes."

The colonel, Selma, Jacob, and Alberta Mae meet in the kitchen at Der Bote.

The Houslers are sitting at one end of the large kitchen table when Jacob enters through the back door. Alberta Mae turns from her work at the stove to greet him.

"We're all just waiting for you, honey," she says. "Can I get you something?"

"Some coffee will do just fine." He quietly answers as he stops, pulls off his hat, and holds it in front of his chest with both hands.

His wife pours some steaming coffee into a large brown mug, and walks to the table with the pot in her hand. She sets it down on a trivet, slides a chair away from the table, sits down, then turns to her husband.

"Well, come on over here and sit yourself down. Quit acting that way. The colonel and Ms. Selma aren't going to bite you."

As Jacob sits down across the table from his wife, the colonel begins.

"I've explained to Selma, and Alberta Mae, about our conversation, Jacob. They know all that we know. Now . . . relax and be yourself, you don't need to keep up a pretense while you're in this house. Do you understand?" Without waiting for an answer, the colonel continues.

"I've been told that the Andersons' daughter, Sheree, died yesterday as a result of injuries from an accident. I believe that will answer your son's question. Her funeral service will be held this afternoon at two o'clock.

"Mrs. Housler and I have been requested to attend. However, I believe we should all attend. By that, I mean all of us, including the children. It will show our support for the Anderson family, as well as allow Randall to see his friend buried. I would hope that will settle his mind once and for all." The colonel says, first looking at Alberta Mae, then at Jacob.

"Are you sure you should go, Ms. Selma? Are you up to it?" Alberta Mae asks.

"I must go," she responds. "It's been over ten years since I last saw her. It's time."

"Jacob, are you here to agree with us? Do you have something to add, something else to say?" The colonel's remarks are direct to the point, but the inflection in his voice lets Jacob know it's his way of giving him a chance to speak.

"Is there more to this story than is being said here in this kitchen?" Jacob is just as blunt with the colonel.

"There's always more to the story, I think we all know that. But we all decided a long time ago that the fewer people who know the entire story, the better off we'll all be. Don't ask for more, Jacob. The less you know the better you'll sleep at night." Selma's reply to his question brings a few seconds of silence at the table.

"Anything else? Selma? Jacob? Alberta Mae?" A pause between each name brings no response.

"It is settled then." He remarks as he gets to his feet, and reaches his hand into his right front pants pocket. When he pulls it out he's holding a small stack of paper money.

"This is that last of it, there'll be no more. Since Sheree's gone, the agreement is finished—paid off," he says and lays the money on the table in front of Jacob and Alberta Mae. "There's quite a sum here. Be careful how you use it. Don't let anyone know you have it. Personally, I'm glad it's over," he finishes.

They both look at the money, then at each other. She reaches out, picks up the bills with her right hand and slips them into her apron pocket as she gets up from the table.

"We thank you, sir. We've made up a plan for this money here and most of the rest you've gave us over the years. It's been put away to be spent later on, when it'll do the most good for the children. We thank you again. Your dinner will be on the table in thirty minutes, so get yourselves ready," she says, almost dancing to the stove.

"Honey, you round up everybody and tell them where we're going this afternoon, and get our children ready to eat. I'll bring the food to the house as soon as I get everything laid out here. We'll all be ready to leave at the same time you and the missus are, Colonel. Yes, sir, we'll all be ready to go." Alberta Mae gets organized.

Jacob rises from his seat and sticks out his empty hand to the colonel.

"Look at me, Jacob."

The colonel takes his hand in his, puts his other hand on top of them, looks his friend straight in the eyes and says, "You're a good man, Jacob Stoker. I hope one day to be able to let the world know how we feel about you and your family. Until then, just be assured that you all are our family. I pray that the children you're raising will grow to be the true Americans you and Alberta Mae are today. As long as Selma or I am alive, no harm will come to you ever again, I pledge this to you."

A tear rolls down Jacob's face, while a sniffle is to be heard from his wife, busy at the stove.

The Andersons and their hands are at the family graveyard.

"You both did a fine job with the grave," John says to Jim and Josh, as he looks around at the preparation for the burial of his daughter's casket. "You could put a few of those boards, stacked over there, down over some of the mud and water. People will need a place to stand and be out of it."

They get right to it, placing boards as instructed.

"Here comes Doc now, June. We arrived just in time." John is happy with the timing.

He looks around and sees Charlotte standing by herself, at the edge of the cemetery, not knowing what to do or how to act. She appears lost.

He approaches her, then bends down to say quietly in her ear. "Why not go over and stand with the other children until the ceremonies start, honey."

She nods her head yes and moves quickly to her friends, all standing away from the grown-ups. They whisper to each other, and watch as Doc's wagon, carrying a coffin, arrives. The horses' hooves and the wagon's wheels leave a trail in the soft moist dirt.

"Afternoon, Doc," John says somberly.

"Yes, sir, it is that," he responds and climbs down off the wagon.

"Will you boys give me a hand with this? I set it on a couple of heavy boards, one at the head and one at the foot, so we'd have a place to put our fingers and get a grip on it. Wait, though. Before we move it, take these two pieces of rope and lay them across the grave on either side. Spread them out a little. We can use them to let the casket down into the grave after the service. Lay these boards here crossways to support it until we're ready."

"All the folks from Der Bote are coming," June blurts out as the men set the coffin on the boards above the freshly dug grave.

"Oh my God," she says to herself. "Selma's coming with them."

She feels a flush come over her face and turns away so it will not be seen by those already present. Her heart is pounding.

"Will I be able to face her? What will we say? It's been so long. I have to be strong and not let on at all. I wonder what's going on in her mind?" All these thoughts, along with deep, long suppressed feelings, creep through her being.

As the group gets nearer, she can see that Selma has her head bent down, looking at the ground. She decides to wait to see how things work out, and not approach her yet. With that thought, her eyes on the ground, she turns her back toward them, and takes a position beside the coffin at the head of the open grave, with her husband.

The Housler and Stoker families arrive, meet the Andersons and their workers, and pass warm greetings around freely. They've not seen each other for years. The reunion brings tears to some eyes, with hardy handshakes and hugs among them all.

On the other hand, June and Selma offer no notice of each other. Instead, they make certain there is no opportunity for their eyes to meet.

"I believe we're all present," John, with a voice loud enough for all to hear, announces. Silence falls over the graveyard. He continues.

"June, Charlotte, and I, thank you all for coming to support us at this grievous time. Our son Robert is making his way home from Philadelphia, so he couldn't be here today. Please include him in your prayers."

"John, I stopped by the telegraph office on my way out here. I thought if Robert answered your wire I might save you a trip in to town later. Sure enough, it was there, so I brought it with me." Doc approaches with the telegram in his outstretched hand.

Robert's father takes the piece of paper and opens it up.

"I'll read to you what our son has to say."

"Coming home immediately. No need to meet me. Will arrive by horseback in a few days. Love, your son, Robert."

"It seems he'll be here by the middle of the week." John folds the paper, puts it in the breast pocket of his coat, and continues.

"If you will all please gather around, we shall begin the service."

Standing at the head of the grave beside his wife, John watches as some twenty-five people position themselves around Sheree's coffin. Seeing that everyone is settled, he begins.

"Lord, we are all gathered here today to say goodbye to Sheree, our daughter, sister, and friend . . ."

June has no interest in the words coming from John's mouth. She knows Sheree's not in the coffin and can't find it in herself to be a serious part of this service. Her thoughts are being controlled by the woman standing less than fifteen feet from her. It's as if they are communicating while neither have acknowledged the presence of the other.

Slowly, deliberately, she raises her head enough to see Selma. At the same time, as if June had called her name, the woman she hasn't seen or spoken to for years, jerks her head up and their eyes lock together.

June gasps for air, feeling her knees start to give under her weight, the blood draining from her head. Her heart is pounding. Unable to look away, she knows Selma has the same feelings by the expression on her face. Both manage a small smile and a hello formed with mute lips, unseen by the solemn group around them.

"She looks so good. She's not aged at all," June says to herself as she steals another look, feeling more confident. "I must find a way to talk with her alone after the service. There are so many questions needing answers. I strongly sense she has the same feelings. Perhaps we can walk together back to our home afterward. If we lag behind a bit, we can speak with some privacy. How can John or the colonel object to that? I'll not ask permission, I'll just do it. Her eyes still look into my soul, after ten years."

Selma thinks after the first glance, "She's more beautiful today than she was ten years ago. I miss hearing her voice and watching her face as she speaks. I've always known her true feelings by the looks on her face. I can tell she wants to talk as much as I do. I'll stay out of it and let her work it out. I know her well enough, she will."

"I can't help seeing June look at you, and you her," the colonel whispers to Selma with his lips close to her ear, "I don't know what emotion you're feeling, but you're about to crush my hand."

"Oh my God," she thinks, trying not to show emotion, "I forgot he was holding my hand. What's going on in his mind now, do you suppose? Well, that which is done is done, I can't change it now. It's best just to let it go and see if he says anything more about it." Thoughts rage through her mind as she numbly removes her hand from his.

The next fifteen minutes are filled with glowing remarks that represent Sheree as the perfect child. Prayers are said for her as well as for all in attendance Everyone standing around the open grave is solemn, a few are softly sobbing. Not so with June and Selma. Since they both know the coffin contains no body, their thoughts are on each other, and on memories of a time a decade ago.

John's last, and fairly loud "Amen" snaps them both back to the present and the realization that the service has finished.

"If you all can come back to our home, you'll find refreshments, and something a bit stronger, if you've a mind and taste for it. Unless you have a need to be somewhere else this afternoon, my family and I will be glad for your company. It's Sunday and I know there is a lot of catching up to do. A little later, in plenty time for you all to get back to your home before dark, we'll enjoy a nice supper, carefully prepared by Belle. So, please come with us, as we return home now."

John and June are the first to walk through the gate of the graveyard, and stand just outside to give a handshake or hug to one and all as they exit. Four of the hands stay back to finish the job of burying the coffin. Doc waits with them while the rest climb aboard several wagons or mount horses for the trip to the Andersons' home.

"John, I believe I'll walk back with Selma," June informs her husband.

"Do you think you should?" he asks quickly, his face sober and grim as he looks at her.

"I think I must," she replies.

"I respect that thought, but don't linger too long behind us. I might come looking for you. We have guests." His eyes are narrow and serious. He knows he must give his wife the space she needs, but he has a feeling of dread in his heart and stomach.

June takes several steps toward Selma to get her attention. She's standing beside the colonel, watching for a signal.

When she sees June start to approach, she tugs on the her husband's arm and pulls his face close to hers. June is unable to hear what's being said, but it takes only a few seconds. The colonel nods his head indicting he understands. Then Selma walks directly to greet her friend face to face.

John walks back into the graveyard to be sure Doc is planning to come to the house and spend some time this afternoon. He tries to keep his steps on the various boards previously laid out on the ground. Others who have stepped on the boards left wet, somewhat muddy, tracks. One draws his attention.

"That's an unusual footprint there. It turns in from the heel and is more like the side of the foot is being used. Where have I seen that before? Wait a minute, these are the same tracks I saw on the porch of the guesthouse. Whoever it was is here now with this group of people."

"Doc, you're coming to the house, aren't you?" Sheree's daddy asks as he approaches.

"I sure am. It's a slow day for me, and I can use a good home cooked meal."

"Great, I need to talk with you when we get the chance. See you there."

Selma and June stand looking at each other, saying nothing, waiting for the group to leave. They gaze, taking in the features of each other's face. A quiet smile appears around and in their eyes when, at last, they meet. A sense of serenity engulfs them both as they stand, not speaking, letting that feeling take over the moment.

"They're gone," Selma whispers, breaking the silence.

June turns to see the last of the people disappear over the first rise in the terrain. The only sounds are that of a bird flapping it's wings as it leaves a tree in the graveyard, the sound of shovels sliding into the soil, an occasional grunt as a heavy soil is lifted, and that of the dirt hitting the top of the coffin in the grave.

"You all come to the house when you are finished, okay?" June's voice is louder than she intends. "I must get control of myself," she thinks as she hears them answer "Yes, ma'am."

Selma takes June by her left hand to turn her on the path toward home. June, feeling Selma's hand in hers, decides to keep it there. They both start walking toward the house, hands swinging back and forth like school pals.

"John would have a cow if he saw us right now, you know that. I could tell by the way he looked at me back there," June says.

"Charles would probably wring my neck," replies Selma, as she looks back over her shoulder. When she turns her head to the front she says, "We're out of their sight, front and back."

They stop and turn to look at each other.

"A little hug is in order?" June states in the form of a question, "May I?"

"May you? If you don't, I'll make you," Selma erupts bluntly.

Their hands part, allowing them to slowly, carefully, put their arms around each other. Breast to breast they can sense each other's heartbeat. Their bodies are filled with feelings of memories, togetherness, and wholeness; urges that only women who have loved each other for years can understand.

June relaxes her arms and allows her friend to pull away just enough to see the yearning in her eyes. Slowly, deliberately, they press their lips together. They have found each other again.

Selma suddenly draws a quick breath through her nose with a snort, and pulls herself from June, shoving her away.

"What's wrong?" she pleads.

"I hear a wagon coming, it's probably Doc," Selma whispers, "We can't let him see us like this. Quickly now, collect yourself."

June takes two deep gulps of air and blows them out forcibly through rounded lips in an effort to catch her breath and settle her feelings. She runs her fingers along the sides of her head, through her hair, just as the wagon comes up over the crest of the small hill that has been providing privacy for their long over due encounter. They both stand looking, waiting for the wagon to arrive and come to a stop.

"Can I offer you ladies a lift to the house?" Doc unassumingly and cheerfully asks, "I promise I'll not interfere with your gab session."

"Well, Doc, that will be lovely," Selma accepts for the both of them. She steps to the wagon, puts her foot on the front wheel axle hub, and reaches up for Doc's hand. He easily pulls her up so she can step over the sideboard and turn to sit beside him on the seat.

"You're next, June. Just a minute I'll jump down and give you a hand," he says.

"Hardly," June's voice is insistent. "Slide over, here I come."

With one foot on the axle hub, she shoves with her other leg from the ground. At the same time, she reaches for a hand above her that isn't there. She's about to fall backward when Doc jumps up from his seat, reaches across Selma, bumping her hard, and grabs June's hand. Selma's legs roll up as she falls over the backless seat, catching Doc in the side with her feet, pulling him over with her. He keeps the grip he has on June, making him pull with a mighty force as he continues into the back of the wagon, falling on top of Selma. June finds herself flying up over the sideboard, and before she knows what's happening, or has a chance to correct her direction, she piles on top of them both. All three are momentarily dazed and roll around aimlessly, trying to gain a grip on composure. The women work to get their dresses pushed down to cover their exposure. They look at each other and start laughing, point fingers and laugh again. The rest of the trip to the house is a pleasant ride.

Later in the afternoon, John corners Doc and explains the incident of the tracks in the guesthouse, the open floor door to the cellar, and the storage shelf setting away from the wall exposing the tunnel. He then ties the footprints at the guesthouse with those at the graveyard.

"I don't know who it is, Doc, but I do know that person is here with us right now. We need to learn who it is and determine the extent of our exposure."

"I see what you mean," the doctor confirms. "I assume you believe it's someone from Der Bote. I mean, since you know all of your own people. That right?"

"Yes, I believe it is."

"It shouldn't be too hard to take them one at a time and see if we can match up the facts with the person. You start over there, and I'll start over there. We can meet back here in ten minutes and compare notes. Then we'll have the mystery solved." The medical man says like there's nothing to it.

It's a beautiful afternoon for a gathering outside at the Anderson home. The spring sun is warm and the breeze fragrant with appearing blossoms adorning the fruit trees and bushes. The voices of all those present mix with their occasional laughter, and children shout as they chase after each other around and through the tables being set up for the planned supper. Two of the hands are building a fire beneath a large iron pot hanging from a chain hooked to a tripod. Beef stew is on the menu. The scene is one of friendship, the tempo is that of relaxation.

"Well John, it all boils down to this," Doc explains. "It has to be a boy named Randall, the son of a hand of Charles Housler. He has a clubfoot. That's the reason for the odd footprint you saw. He looks to be about eleven or twelve years old."

"Point him out," John orders.

"That's him over there, standing by his mother. I believe her name is Alberta Mae." Doc's words find John's ears with an understanding tone. "What's our next move?"

"I don't want to start anything here and now. The situation might grow and get out of control. I'll speak with the colonel tomorrow or the day after. I want to be present when the boy is approached. I'd like to learn what all he knows and thinks. What needs to be done can be determined from there. I'll keep you informed, Doc. Thanks, I appreciate your help."

Chapter Seven

"I can tell by the gray look outside the windows it's starting to get daylight. Where am I? Everything feels strange to me. Oh, now I remember. My God, I'm on a train headed for a place called the Company. I'm a prisoner of either the Company, or Ernie and Sally, maybe both. Regardless, I can't get away. I must do as they say . . . follow their orders. Although, I do feel safe. I'll snuggle down under my covers and pretend I'm still asleep. We're supposed to get there today, wherever there is. Sally and I searched this railroad car all over yesterday, but we didn't find anything interesting. I like all of my new clothes. Sally says I'm going to get more when we get there. I'm not tired any more, and I don't feel like lying here. I want to do something. Uh Oh? Someone's coming." Sheree thinks as the last day of her trip begins.

"Are you awake?" It's Sally's voice.

Sheree rolls over to prop herself up on one elbow.

"It is time to get up. We're there. Get dressed, after a bit of breakfast, we can get out of this stuffy, cigar smoke filled, railroad car. How does that fit your fancy?" she says.

Their carriage passes many new buildings with lots of people milling everywhere, keeping the young girl occupied. It turns off the main road onto a private lane. She knows because they went through a large gate that a man closed after they passed. There's a big house, or building of some kind ahead. It's larger than any building she's ever seen in her life. They stop right at the front door, which opens as they arrive. A man in a black suit comes out and opens the door of the carriage. Ernie gets out first, then he helps Sally. Now he's holding out his hand to Sheree.

"Come my dear, let's take a look at your new home." His voice is still deep and sort of scary, but she now knows that's just the way it is, so he seems pleasant to her.

They go inside through the open door.

"Wow? This is a huge place. Hallways go everywhere from this big room we're standing in. Stairways on either side go up to another floor. Everything I see seems to be made of polished stone. A great big bright chandelier is hanging from chain that's hooked to the ceiling, which is very high." The ten-year-old says to herself, craning her neck trying to take it all in.

"That chandelier is made of crystal, Sheree. It's very expensive. Isn't it beautiful?" Sally asks.

"It really is beautiful," she hears herself saying.

At that moment, a man appears from behind a closed door and motions them to follow.

"Come this way. We've been expecting you. I'll show you where you can place your things," he speaks.

They follow him down a long hallway, up a set of stairs to another hallway, and then they turn right, then left, then right. It seems this building must go on forever. They keep going and going. Finally, their leader stops in front of an open door.

"Welcome to your new home, miss. This will be your room for the time being. After you have been processed and go through orientation, you will be assigned permanent quarters," he says.

"I know he doesn't really mean I'm welcome, he has to say that. He has to say that to everybody that comes here. He's not fooling me," she confidently confides to herself.

Ernie and Sally go into the room; she follows, carefully.

"This isn't so bad, it's pretty in here. It's nothing like a jail or a prison. Nice and soft." She tells herself as she sits on the bed.

There are no windows, and the only light is provided by the gas lights on the walls. She can hear the faint hissing of the gas as it surges from the pipes below the flames.

"Do you think you'll be comfortable here for a few days, honey? You won't be here in your room all that much. You'll be busy getting to know all about your new adventure," Sally poses.

The youngster nods yes.

"Are you going to stay with me, Sally?" Her words seem to come out before she thinks them.

"No, I'll not be able to do that. They want you all to themselves, but, you'll be fine. Don't be afraid. You'll see, no harm will come to you. I'll be back in a few days to keep an eye on you. You'll see a lot of me for the next several years. We can become great friends. We'll stay with you today until they're ready for your first meeting. That's when they'll explain everything to you. You'll meet a few other young people who are here for their first day too."

Sheree sits on the bed waiting. For what, she's not so sure.

"Oh, they're here already," Ernie exclaims. "Leave your things, they'll be safe."

A student walks into her room. He's not much older than her, and a nice-looking young man, she notices.

"Your name is Sheree, right? Please follow me."

"Wait, I want to say goodbye to Sally."

They put their arms around each other and hug for a few seconds, then Ernie gently pulls her away and turns her toward the young man.

"My name is Sparrow." He leaves the room, obviously expecting her to follow.

"I know it's different than a name you would expect to hear. You'll learn all about that in a few minutes. We're glad to have you here with us, and I mean that. We'll be able to talk from time to time. Anyway, we're here. Please go in and sit anywhere you like." He motions with his hands.

Sheree feels lost since she failed to keep track of how they arrived here. Listening to the interesting words of Sparrow took her mind off their route.

The door is open so she enters to see five wooden chairs setting in a semicircle. They have a straight-back with an armrest on the right side that gets bigger as it goes out to the front until it's at least a twelve inches wide. He said to take any chair. She elects to sit on the one at the far right side, so she can see the doorway without turning around. So far, she's the only one here.

A large blackboard, with names of birds and flowers printed on it, is attached to the front wall. The floor is wood polished to a high shine. There are large windows on the left side of the room, allowing plenty of light to flood through. Someone's coming. It's a young girl with blond hair, probably a little older than Sheree, a little shorter in stature.

"She looks friendly enough, but she just glanced at me, and she's going to take a seat on the farthest chair, facing me," the first to arrive in the room takes note.

"Some other people come through the doorway, three boys. One of them looks at both the girls and smiles. Neither smiles back, but lowers their heads. The boys are all about the same age, about sixteen. They walk around to the front of the chairs and sit down. The one that smiled sits next to Sheree. She steals a good look at him.

"He's good looking, and he seems to have a friendly space around him. I might need a friend to help me get out of here," she thinks.

A door at the front, beside the black board, opens allowing a man to walk into the room. He positions himself behind a table centered in front of their chairs, so he's able to look directly at them. He brings a leather case, which he opens to remove a short stack of papers. He places them both on the table, lifts his head as if to acknowledge they are there, then looks at the blond girl, without saying a word.

Now he's looking at the boy next to her the same way. They look back at him, saying nothing either. Now he's looking at the boy in the center of the group.

"One more, then he'll be looking at me. He's looking at me now. I'll not even blink, I'll look him right in the eye," the daughter of June Anderson thinks to herself.

He's a slender man, with a weak build. They all wear the same sort of clothes around here. He's dressed in a black suit, has a gray mustache and a gray beard that's just on his chin. It's about three inches long and comes to a point at the end. His wire-rimmed spectacles set far down on the end of his nose. He's looking over the top of them at her. His forehead has several age wrinkles, although he does have a full head of gray hair parted down the middle and combed to either side. At last, he looks down at his papers. Then, after a few seconds, he raises up again.

"Good morning, my name is Mr. Vaughn. I wish to welcome each of you to the Company. I'll be talking with you, informing you as to what you might expect while you're here. As I am sure you are all curious, we'll take all the time necessary to answer your questions. First things first, however. We need to know each other's names. Since you already know mine, we need to know yours. If you'll look at the blackboard, you'll see a list of birds and flowers. I want you to select one that appeals to you."

"Girls pick a flower, and boys pick a bird. I'll give you exactly one minute to make your selection. Once a name has been made and given to me, it cannot be used again, so, have a second choice in mind in case someone before you takes your first choice. Any questions? No? Your time begins now."

"Oh my, let me see . . . hmm, okay, I'll pick the rose and the lilly. I hope I get the rose." Sheree selects those familiar to her.

"Time's up. The lady on the end, what's your choice?"

"He's not pointing at me, she gets first pick. Darn. Oh well, I don't mind. I like both of my choices. Perhaps she won't pick the rose anyway."

"I choose the rose," the blond girl replies.

"That's okay, I'll select the lilly," Ms. Anderson decides.

He points to the boy sitting beside the blond girl. "Next."

"Falcon."

"Hawk."

"Eagle."

"Lilly," Sheree proudly calls out.

"Are you all satisfied with your choices?" No responses, just nods.

"Good. From this point on, the name you have just chosen will be your new name. The name you have used up until now must be forgotten. You are now, Rose, Falcon, Hawk, Eagle, and Lilly," he points to each of them as he speaks.

"Is that understood? That's now your name, get used to it. You'll not hear your birth name again. Anyone addressing you from this point on will use your new name."

The boy next to Sheree raises his right arm.

"Yes, Eagle, you have a question?" Mr. Vaughn patiently inquires.

"Yes, Mr. Vaughn, shall we continue to use our last name?"

"Good question. No, you shall not. From this time on, your name will be the one you chose. You no longer have a last name."

"I know you want an explanation as to why you've been taken away from your families and brought here to the Company. I think it best that we explain a few things about the Company before we get going on that. The Company is a name for an organization that works secretly throughout the world in a effort to maintain the economies of all nations. It is our job to obtain information about the nations that will enable us to offer our assistance to the entire world. The governments of the nations know little about us. We make every effort to keep our existence and our intentions a secret. Our organization, the Company, is controlled by the wealthiest men alive. It is our goal to control all of the currency of the world. We work to balance out the wealth, the power, of the world."

The boy beside Rose raises his arm.

"You have a question, Falcon?"

"Who are these immensely wealthy men?"

"No one can be certain. The vast number of different companies, varied jobs, and levels of people, make it impossible to trace them down and identify them. I understand, however, there are at least fifty of them. By them, I mean families of people. The bloodline is followed, so the fortunes of each family are passed on to the next generation, and so on. Those who have made a serious attempt to determine the identities of these men have all been discovered and dealt with long before they uncovered much. These powerful men are located in various places. I understand they meet twice a year to discuss the progress that has been made with their plan.

"To continue on, as for your place within the Company, each of you has an ability or talent that has set you apart from a normal citizen. Although you were probably not aware of it, you've been tested over the past several years to determine your mental capacities. I can tell you that you are all of the genius quality. You each, also, possess a physical attribute that further sets you apart from all others. As an example, Lilly here, is capable of feigning death. Her heartbeat, breathing, and overall appearance, could indicate she has expired. Her complete system slows down to the degree it cannot be ascertained without special equipment. While in that state of suspended life, she will not age, which means her total lifetime on earth could be unlimited."

"Wow, I didn't know that. That's me he is talking about," Sheree beams silently.

"Eagle has the ability to understand the thoughts of other people. The ability to feel their feelings simply by looking at them and touching them."

"Hawk's talent is speed. He will probably become the fastest human being on the face of this earth. His mind works the same way. Before his training is complete, he will be able to digest a six-hundred-page book in just two and a half hours, and quote it word for word afterward."

"Falcon's contribution to the group is logic. He can predict the result of almost anything as long as he has all the pertaining facts. When he's finished with his training, he'll be able to predict the results of wars, games, scientific projects, love affairs, the toss of a coin, and so on. He'll be accurate with his predictions ninety-four out of every one hundred times."

"And lastly, Rose. I have saved Rose for last as I want her to give us a little demonstration. Stand up, Rose, and show us."

"Which shall I show you, Mr. Vaughn? My face? My color? My hair?" she asks.

"Change your color, Rose," he replies. "Watch closely now, everyone."

"I can't believe my own eyes. Her fair-colored skin is turning red. It's getting brighter and brighter. She looks as though she has a really bad sunburn."

"That's fine. You can relax now and return to your normal color," Mr. Vaughn says with a chuckle. "You may sit down."

"Rose has the ability to somewhat change the features of her face and her hair. She can also change her appearance by looking thinner or heavier."

"You see, you all have a special talent which will, in time, be used to further the endeavors of the Company. Future training will allow each of you to expand your understanding and the use of your talent, as well as control it. Our experts will explain it more fully as you go through the process of settling into your new life."

"All of your needs will be attended to by our staff. If there is something you feel you require, ask the staff member assigned to you. If it's at all possible, your wishes will be granted. You'll be given a small manual when you leave this room. In it you'll find such things as a map of our facilities, the times food will be served and where, and certain rules. Most of them are common sense, but we expect you will respect them. Rule number one, however, I would like to explain with clarity right now. You are not permitted outside the confines of our walls."

"If you're discovered outside these walls without proper authorization, you'll be punished. The punishment will be isolation for the first violation, as long as you're returned here without leaving the immediate area. Each violation after that will be dealt with more severely. Should you leave our grounds and we're not able to locate you for a period of twenty-four hours, a dispatch will be sent to your homelands with orders to locate and kill your mother and father immediately. Should we not be able to locate you for a period of two weeks, your brothers, sisters, aunts, uncles, nieces, nephews, and other family members will be eliminated at a rate of one per week, until you return."

"Do any of you not understand what I've just said?"

"A cold chill just went down my back. It's like he's talking about me. He must have somehow found out I'm going to try to get away. I don't want him to hurt my mama or daddy, or anybody, though. He's looking at us one at a time again. We're all shaking our heads that we understand. I must not think about escaping just now. I have to find out how he knows my mind. He said Eagle can read people's minds, so, I should stay away from him. I have to be very careful. Is there anyone I can trust?" Lilly starts to see the reality of her situation. She is a prisoner, it's just that her cell is larger than most.

At the Anderson farm, we hear the elders speaking.

"When do you expect Robert to arrive, John?" June's question reaches his ears as he pulls his boot snug against his left foot.

"I think no later than Wednesday," he replies. "I noticed you and Selma spent some time together yesterday afternoon. What did you find to talk about all that time?"

"Yes, well . . . you know I've not seen her for more than ten years, and the children, the same. There's a lot of catching up to do."

"Is anything going on, June?" his question stings her ears.

"That's all over. It never came up. Besides, we're older now, much more mature in our ways. Stop your worrying, nothing is happening between us. Can't Selma and I just be friends?"

"That's fine, as long as it stays that way. You know how crazy I was before. I don't want anything like that to happen again. I think, at my age, I couldn't accept it again. Unless there's good reason, I won't mention it again," he's not comfortable knowing his wife is reunited with the wife of his next door neighbor, not at all.

"If I'm going to keep a close eye on their relationship, I'll need some help," he thinks to himself.

"I'm going to see the colonel this morning, are you coming with me?" He hopes she will decline but feels he must ask.

"I think not. I want to spend some time with Charlotte. You should too, you know," she states with a voice of insinuation.

"I plan to take some time when Robert arrives and spend it with you and the children. Maybe a month or so. How does that sound?" he counters using his most reassuring voice.

"Let's hope you'll be able to do that," she responds, feeling he'll be pulled away to satisfy other duties.

John travels to Der Bote to meet with his old friend and colleague, Colonel Charles Housler.

"Good morning, Mr. Anderson," Sachel cheerily quips after opening the door to see John.

"Welcome to Der Bote. I want to thank you and your missus for your hospitality yesterday. How can I help you, sir?"

"I would like a few words with the colonel . . . if possible."

"Certainly, sir, let me locate him for you. Would you like to wait in the library?"

"Thank you, Sachel," John calmly says, and turns to walk into the appointed room.

No sooner has he sat down than he hears the colonel.

"Hello, John. Nice morning, isn't it? Let's move you out onto the verandah. It's nice out there this time of day. I've asked Sachel to bring us coffee and a piece of Alberta Mae's custard pie. What brings you all the way over here today? It must be important, something we couldn't talk about last afternoon," the colonel acts concerned.

"It's nothing that can't wait, but it's on my mind, and as you say, it's a nice morning for a ride. So, here I am."

Sachel appears with a tray of coffee and pie and sets it down on a white wicker table located between the white chairs, where the men have seated themselves. He doesn't linger and turns away to disappear through the open double doors.

"I'm concerned about our wives, Charles," John says.

The colonel knows this is serious, John has just called him Charles. He does that only when he speaks of things he would rather not.

"You mean their relationship," the colonel states.

"I do," John answers, "June tells me nothing's going on between them. But Doc told me he saw them holding hands yesterday afternoon, just before he picked them up with his wagon and brought them home. He said they were walking hand in hand and went out of his sight over the crest of the hill, just this side of the graveyard. When he finally got to his wagon and trailed after them, he found them standing too close together to be having just a conversation. He said their actions led him to believe there was more going on before he was able to see them."

"Did he question them?" The colonel is curious.

"No, he didn't. He said he felt it wasn't his place. He did get them onto the wagon and brought them home."

"Damn, what do you think we should do?" the colonel implores.

"I think we should keep our eyes open and get a keen sense of what to look for between them. If something is going to start up again, I want positive proof before I do anything. Let's confide in one another and watch for any suspicious acts on their part. Then we can decide what to do."

"I don't know what I'll do if they start up. Selma and those children are my life, John. I just don't know." The colonel bows his head and turns away as he speaks.

"You know I feel the same way, Charles. Perhaps it'll all blow over if we give it a chance." He chooses his words and emphasizes carefully.

"I doubt it, and you doubt it, but what else is there to do? We'll do nothing now, as you say. I'll make myself aware of her comings and goings, and listen carefully to all she says. If anything is going on, it'll show itself. I'll keep you informed of anything I suspect. Now . . . what else is on your mind?" The colonel wants to talk no further about their wives.

Realizing that his friend is upset, John also believes a change of subject is a good idea.

"You will recall our conversation yesterday morning concerning my guesthouse and the tracks. The cellar door was open and the bookcase covering the tunnel was slid out away from the wall?" His statement comes out in the form of a question.

"Yesterday at the service, I noticed those same footprints on a board in the graveyard. The footprints had an odd character to them, in that, one of them was turned toward the other. It appeared to be more the side of a foot, rather than flat, like you would expect. I saw similar tracks on the front porch of the guesthouse. I believe the tracks were made by Randall, Jacob's son. Help me with this, Colonel, can you tell me anything you've determined since our conversation yesterday morning?" He stops and waits for a response.

The colonel turns back to face Mr. Anderson as he listens. When John stops speaking, a pause seems in order.

Selma's husband picks up a cup and takes a sip of hot coffee. June's husband watches intently.

"I can tell you that you and Doc are exactly correct. Jacob related the circumstances to me just after you left for home. With all that was going on yesterday, I thought it best to withhold the information for a better time. My plan was to come to your home tomorrow and let you know then. I'm sorry about that—" John cuts him off.

"Don't concern yourself with that, but we might have another problem. It's possible that Randall saw and heard enough to realize Sheree is still alive. He could know that the coffin didn't contain her body. If that's the case, what must be going through his mind? How strongly does he feel about what he knows? What might he do with the information? These are all questions that we should, perhaps, address."

"Jacob said nothing about that. As far as I know, he and his wife believe Sheree's in that coffin. At first thought, I can understand the need to control the situation, however, to do that we must assume that Randall has seen or heard it all. And we must further assume that he'll attempt to do something with the information."

Mr. Housler takes in a deep breath and lets it out slowly through an open mouth. He pauses to think. John is about to speak when, unknowingly, the colonel begins again.

“No, no, I believe we should do absolutely nothing about this, either. If we attempt to pry for information, we’ll only escalate the problem. Jacob assures me that he has spoken to Randall, and the boy understands he’s not to go near your place in the future. I honestly believe we should just leave it at that.” As he finishes speaking, he raises his cup to his lips for another sip of coffee, and looks over the top edge for a response.

“I’m sure you’re correct with your thinking. It appears I might have been a bit too anxious with the situation. I’ll bow to your wisdom.” John feels an apology is in order.

“Good, I’m glad we agree. Try that coffee and pie, you’ll find it excellent,” Charles urges his visitor to relax and enjoy the surroundings. A few seconds pass as John forks a bite of the custard pie into his mouth. The colonel watches as John smacks his lips and goes for another bite, then nods his head.

“I have word of a group coming through Thursday, this week. Are you in a position to give me a hand with them?” he comments thoughtfully.

“How many?” John asks, as his eyes quickly come in contact with the colonel’s.

“It could be as many as twenty. I can’t be sure, though. If we prepare for that many, we’ll not be caught by surprise.” Mr. Housler points out.

“I’ll be ready,” his comrade says quietly. “Any idea who’s with them, bringing them through?”

“Not for sure, but it’s probably Marty Schoener. Does it make a difference?”

“I suppose not. Marty’s a good man. I’m just curious. Any idea of the time yet?”

“No, not yet, it’s a bit early on. It’ll probably be shortly after dark, but I’ll let you know for sure as soon as I know. There’s nothing special in this group. Just keep an eye out for the normal things.”

“I’ll have everything ready,” John assures. “Is there any more of this pie?”

We return to the Anderson farm.

June feels exceptionally cheerful and full of life this morning, and she likes it that John isn’t here to notice. As she runs a brush through Charlotte’s hair, her mind is reliving the time she was with Selma yesterday.

“Not so hard, Mama.”

“I’m sorry, honey, I’ll be more careful.”

“I wonder if she’s thinking of me as I am of her. I don’t know if I can wait until Thursday to see her again. I can’t believe it, we’re back together again after more than ten years. I’m so happy I want to scream. But I must keep myself calm, because if John suspects anything at all, I’ll not be able to get away to meet her. Everything must go on as if nothing has changed. And why shouldn’t it, after all, nothing has . . . yet.

Chapter Eight

Time marches on at the Company's compound. Sheree, oops, that is to say, Lilly, is struggling to adapt to her new surroundings, trying to fit in.

"It's Wednesday already, and I've been here going on my second day now. I've never been so busy in my whole life. There's not been one minute for me to try to figure out a plan to get out of here. It's just one thing after another.

"Sally said I'm supposed to get all new clothes. Hrumph! The only clothes I have are black pants and white shirts, except for my underwear. Everybody dresses alike here. The boys and the girls are all the same way, black pants and white tops. I don't think I'll need new clothes anyway. There's no reason, or enough time for that matter, to wear them. It's get up at 5 AM, eat breakfast, and start classes that last all morning. Dinner is at noon, classes again until 3 PM, then exercise until 6 PM. Supper follows that, then it's study for next day's classes, and to bed by eight. I'm ready for bed by then, believe me, I am ready.

"We have fun exercising. I'm learning to dance ballet and ballroom style. Horseshoes—we play horseshoes. I never. They're also teaching us to run and jump up in the air, then roll forward, without getting hurt. We did cartwheels yesterday. I have to learn to bend over backward, put my hands on the ground, then throw my feet over so I can stand up straight. I don't know if I'll ever be able to do it, but they say I'll learn.

"There must be at least fifty students here. Some of them are older, eighteen or so. I've seen some of them riding, so there must be horses. Some of them even carry guns, the boys and the girls. Everyone is nice to me. They're always asking if I have everything I need, and they make sure no one is left by themselves, anytime.

"We're supposed to move into our real rooms by Friday. I'll get a room all my own. I get to choose the color of the walls and everything. Maybe I'll get my new clothes then.

"I thought this place would be scary, like a prison, but it's not anything like that. I don't feel afraid. Truth be told, I'm sort of having fun. I know, though, I must find a way out of here. But I have to be very careful even thinking about it. I don't want them to hurt Mama and Daddy. I'll find a way, it might take a few days, or even a week, but I'll plan something."

"Good morning, Lilly. Are you ready to go to breakfast?"

"Good morning, yes, I'm ready to go, just let me tie this shoelace."

Randall, Sheree's boyfriend from home, frets and ponders as he does his chores.

"They can have a service for Sheree if they want to, but I sure know she wasn't in that box. I don't know what's going on, and I don't know what to do about it even if I did. Nobody's going to tell me anything. To them, I'm just a kid who doesn't know any better. Sheree is my best friend, and I can't just do nothing. I have to try. If I go over to the guesthouse and look around some more, maybe I can find out something. That's what I'll do. The first chance I get, I'll go on over there after dark and see what I can find."

Colonel Housler looks across the breakfast table at his wife Selma.

"I'll not be available tomorrow evening for a while, honey. I have some business to handle, but I should be home before midnight," he says with a reassuring voice.

"I don't want to know," she responds. Whatever it is will keep him busy, away from the house for a few hours tomorrow evening; and for her purposes, that's perfect.

"You know how I feel about business matters. Take your time and don't concern yourself with me. I think Alberta Mae and I will lay out my new dress. I already have the material." Selma is gleaming on the inside. She and June made a plan on Sunday to meet Thursday shortly after dark at the willow tree bordering their farms. This is grand.

"What time do you plan to leave? Should we have supper a little earlier than usual?" This is the one last thing she needs to know.

"No, I'll leave shortly after supper," he answers, and notices her to be especially gleeful today.

"I'd best speak with Alberta Mae before I leave tomorrow evening, and ask her to keep an eye on my lovely wife while I'm gone," he schemes to himself.

The morning is getting started at the Anderson farm.

"John, get yourself out of that bed, it's almost seven o'clock. Today is the day Robert's coming home, I just know it." June's voice sings out through their bedroom.

"Let's be ready for him. I'm going to ask Belle to prepare all his favorite foods. I want to welcome my son home properly."

"Now, don't get your hopes up too high, sweetheart. There's no sure way to know when he'll arrive here," her husband says, as he raises his head to look at his wife.

He feels quite jubilant himself, although, for some reason he hasn't pinpointed why. He feels leery about letting it out in the open.

"I was out a little later than I planned last night. Business in town took longer than I figured. I tried not to wake you when I got home. I was asleep before my head hit my pillow."

"I felt you get in bed, but I had no idea what time it was. No wonder I was able to get up and get dressed without waking you. Are you coming down for breakfast, or shall I have Belle watch for you a little later?" June asks, her face bright with a smile.

"I'll be down in about fifteen minutes. Will you wait? We can eat together," John suggests.

"And oh, before it slips my mind . . . business is going to keep me away for a few hours Thursday evening. I'll do my best to get back early."

Hearing his words strikes a spot in June's stomach, causing a pleasant burning sensation. It's as if her meeting with Selma is meant to be. She squirms a little, then composes herself to answer without letting anything show.

"I'll wait for you downstairs. Don't be too long," she replies with a bit of music in her voice.

With that, she turns and walks from their bedroom to the head of the stairs. A quick glance around to be sure no one is watching, then she picks up the front of her long dress and bounces down the steps, two and three at a time. At the bottom, she looks around again, throws her arms into the air, and lets out a whispered scream.

John and June have finished eating and are enjoying another cup of coffee when they hear Jim's voice at the same time he jumps onto the back porch.

"We got a rider coming. No way to tell who it is though, still too far away."

She jumps up. "It's Robert, John. He's home."

He's on her heels as she runs out through the back door, jumps to the ground from the porch, and tears around the house. Jim is not far behind them. She stops when she reaches the hitching post, and puts her hand up to shade her eyes.

"I don't see him."

The words no sooner leave her lips than a horse and rider appear, coming up the rise about two hundred yards away.

"I think it is him," she clamors.

"Now, now, honey . . . it could be anybody. We can't tell for sure from this distance." John holds back his own excitement.

He's also watching his mate as she stands, bouncing up and down with expectation, straining her eyes to be the first to recognize their son. He's not seen her this excited for a long time. He thinks to himself how beautiful she is with her heart so involved in the emotion of the moment.

"It is! It is him!" she yells, and takes off running toward the approaching rider.

John and Jim hold their spot at the hitching rail and watch her run, hair flying, arms waving in the air, her dress swinging above her knees. The rider stops and slides to the ground from his saddle. He runs, pulling his horse after him, to meet his mother. She jumps the last three feet in the air to slam into her son, hugging and kissing, almost knocking him over backward. The horse, startled, rears its head and lets out a snort, flapping it lips.

"It is so good to see you, Robert! Welcome home!" she yells in his ear.

"It's great to see you too, Mama! You look wonderful!" he exclaims with excitement, trying to push her mouth away from his ear before she yells again.

"So do you, son. You get more handsome the older you get. I need to pinch myself to be sure this is not a dream. You're home. You're home."

They hug again, then turn to walk, an arm around each other, leading the horse, toward John and Jim. As they approach, his daddy puts his hand out. Robert takes it and pulls his father to him for a good strong hug and a few pats on the back.

"Welcome home, son. I'm glad you made it safe and sound."

"Me too . . . I'm just as glad to be here." He releases his grip to pull away and extend his hand out to a longtime friend.

Jim extends his hand out as well and steps forward, looking a bit shy.

"Come here and give me a hug," Robert exclaims, as he grabs the man's hand at the same time putting his other arm around him. Their farmhand responds likewise, and they are again good friends who have been a long time separated.

"Where is everybody? Where are the girls?" Robert poses with anticipation.

"Well, Charlotte is upstairs in her room, Belle is in the barn looking for eggs, and everyone else is off working to keep this farm going," John says intending to keep going, but his Son interrupts.

"Where's Sheree?" he asks, still full of excitement from being at home.

"Are you hungry?" his mama asks. "You're probably worn out too."

"Where's Sheree, Daddy? Is something wrong? Is she ill?"

"Let's go into the house. We have some terrible news."

"Is she all right? I knew something terrible had happened when I received your wire. You didn't say why you needed me home so urgently. I've been worried sick ever since. What's happened to Sheree? Tell me. Tell me now!" he demands.

"I think it's best if we go inside, Robert. I'll explain it all in the house," John's words only cause a belly full of fear for the young man.

"Oh my God, she's dead," he says bowing his head as he doubles over, holding his stomach with both hands.

"Let's help him into the kitchen, Jim," June says. "We can give him some coffee and settle him down."

They get on either side of the grief-stricken young man. With his arms over their shoulders and their arms around his waist, they walk to the rear of the house to enter the kitchen through the back door. They place him down on a chair at the large table. June grabs a cup from a peg below the cupboard and fills it with coffee, then sets it down in front of her son as John starts to speak.

"There was an accident. Sheree was thrown from her horse last Saturday. Her injuries resulted in her death. We held a service for her this past Sunday. She's been placed beside her granddaddy in the family cemetery." His words are solemn.

"We brought Doc out to look at her as soon as we could after the accident. He thought she would be okay. She was unconscious, though, and passed away soon after he left. She never woke up. I'm sorry, I should have put it in my wire, but I just couldn't bring myself to do it."

As his father speaks, Robert crosses his arms on the table and lays his face down on them. When John finishes and things fall quiet, he raises his head. Tears are flowing down his face to drip off his chin.

"What happened? How did she fall off the horse? Was it Pooch?" he tearfully asks, at the same time using his left forearm to wipe his face with his sleeve.

"Yes, it was Pooch. He came home without her to get help. I thought I would die when I saw that empty saddle. I told her before she left to be careful and not to run that horse. I've told her and told her, have I not, John?" June says, looking for support.

She starts crying along with her son. Not because of Sheree's death; she knows that's a lie. It's because he feels so much pain.

"John—Robert must know the truth," she blurts out, kneeling down beside him. "He must have some solace."

Their son looks first at his mother, then his father. A look of disbelief has taken over his sadness.

"What—what are you talking about?" he demands.

"Jim, I'm sorry, will you leave us alone for a while. This is likely to get a little messy. There's no sense in you getting involved. Thanks," John says knowing he is, once again, trapped by his wife's soft heart.

Knowing his son as he does, he's not going to be able to put this off. But where does he start? One thing will lead to another. Robert's not stupid. He'll ask more questions, and those answers will lead to more questions.

He pulls a chair from table, back away from, but facing the two of them, and sits down as they both watch his every move. He waits for Jim to go out on to the porch.

"Tell him, June. I don't think I can," John knows that she fully expects him to explain just enough to give Robert comfort from the grief, and is depending on him to find a way to stop short of a full confession.

"She has put me in this position for the last time. Let's see how she works it out for a change," he muses to himself, certain there is no explanation, other than the whole truth, that will satisfy his boy now.

"I'm not good at this sort of thing. You know that. You tell him," she demands.

John sits quietly with his arms crossed over his chest.

Robert waits as long as he can. Unable to contain himself any longer, he stands up and takes control of the floor.

"What's going on here? I'm part of this family, and I deserve an honest answer."

Silence in the kitchen. If stress had a foul odor, the stench would burn your nose.

Young Mr. Anderson gets his good looks from both his parents. His height, at six feet three inches, comes from his daddy, and his soft green eyes from his mama. His quick tongue and calculating mind is a meld from them both. One thing that is surely his own is his claim to relentless tenacity. He will accomplish that which he sets his mind to do, come hell or high water, and those in the kitchen know it.

He walks as if in thought to the stove, the air heavy with guilt and expectation. Then with all he can muster, he lifts his right hand, clenches a fist, and slams it down on the hot metal stove top with a force that shakes everything in the kitchen. Pots and pans hanging on the wall clang against each other, dishes in the cupboard rattle, and the hot pot bounces off on to the floor splashing coffee all over.

"Now, I'm going to get some answers. One of you is going to tell me straight out. Do you understand?" he screams, using every bit of air in his lungs.

"You treat me like I'm some little child," he says in a somewhat softer manner.

"I want you to start at the beginning and tell me everything. But before you do, I have something to tell you. I've dropped out of school, and I'm home to stay. I'm almost eighteen years old, and I'm going to be a complete part of this family. I'm a man, dammit. Treat me like one." His voice is back to normal, although, he's still a little short of breath.

"Let me get you started with your explanation," he continues.

"Do you realize that when you both were so angry with each other ten years ago, I was seven years old. Not a small child who would forget everything he had heard or seen. I know it all firsthand. I saw how you caught Mama in bed with Selma Housler," he says, glaring at this father.

"I was there, I heard everything. I saw how you forced them both to have sex with Jacob Stoker, that very night, in that very bed, upstairs. Mama and Mrs. Housler didn't want to do it, but you forced them, Daddy," he accuses, pointing his finger.

"You were drunk out of your mind. Jacob was just waiting on the front porch for Mrs. Housler, to take her home. He had no idea what was happening when you ran downstairs, pulled him back to the bedroom, and made him have sex with Mama and Mrs. Housler. They were screaming so loud it hurt my ears.

"Jacob begged you to let him leave. He got on his knees and put his arms around your legs and begged you. But you beat him with your belt, Daddy. You beat Jacob into having sex with Mama. You kept screaming, 'Have sex with a man if you want it, you whore. I must not be good enough for you, let's see if he can satisfy you!'

"You wouldn't let Mrs. Housler leave before she watched Jacob and Mama together. You kept asking her, 'Do you see what you've made me do? Do you see?' Then every few seconds, you'd hit Jacob with your belt and yell, 'Harder, harder, I want her to remember this night!' When you thought Mama had enough, you made Mrs. Housler get on the bed and forced Jacob to do the same thing to her. By the time Jacob finished with Mrs. Housler, you were huddled in the corner on the floor by the dresser, mumbling to your drunken self.

"Mama and Mrs. Housler got dressed, as did Jacob, and they all went downstairs. Jacob was so numb, he didn't utter a word. I heard the wagon leave.

"In a few minutes, Mama came back upstairs and stood in the doorway of the bedroom, looking at you huddled in a ball on the floor. That's when she said the only thing stopping her from killing you was what it would do to me. I still remember it all after ten years, word for word. I could tell from the look on her face, she wanted to kill you. She looked at you so cold, so full of scorn, I expected her to do it.

"Do you think I don't remember the rest of it?"

"No more Robert, please," June breaks in, her arms outstretched to her son.

"Sorry, Mama, you're going to hear it all, both of you." He needs to empty his mind of this pent-up memory.

"As I grew up, I understood better all that happened that night. Jacob got Mama pregnant. The both of you decided to stay together, not as man and wife, just together, for the sake of all concerned. Slowly, over the next nine months, you started being civil, and I think, in your own way, you forgave each other, but probably not yourselves. When it came time for the baby to be born, Mama got really ill, so you took her to Atlanta, to the medical facility there. I have no firsthand knowledge as to what happened there, but I pieced it together from what I overheard later."

He stops for a moment to get the cup of coffee from the table. After putting it to his lips for a sip, he swallows and starts again.

"You gave birth to five babies, Mama—five babies. You thought you were going to have one, but you had five. One of them died as it was being born; I think it was a girl. But you still had two girls and two boys. You and the babies were at the medical facility for several weeks. When you finally came home with the four of them, you arranged a meeting with Mr. and Mrs. Housler, and the Stokers. You all went into the library and talked, I listened at the door. You all decided that Jacob and Alberta Mae should take the two boys because of the dark color of their skin. You would keep the girls due to their lighter skin. Everything could be explained a lot easier that way. The Housler's would help Jacob and Alberta Mae raise the boys as their own. You all agreed that the Houslers couldn't keep them as their own, even with her skin being dark too, since it was well known she couldn't have a child.

"I heard about the Company, but not much. I feared then, as I do now, that a secret accord was reached between you and them before you came home from Atlanta. Shortly after this all happened, you sent me off to school. I've always felt you did it to keep me quiet. You sent me away so I'd forget. Well . . . it hasn't worked out that way. As you've heard, I haven't forgotten, and I'm home to stay. So, believe me, I'm going to have the answers I deserve.

"And, oh yes, Daddy," June and John thought he was finished, but there, he starts again, "you should be aware that I know all about your business, so don't try to avoid a complete explanation of this further involvement, and how it's added to your already complicated lives.

"I love and respect you both, and I believe you did the best you could, probably better than anyone could expect with the same circumstances. But now, your oldest child, your only son, stands here today asking—no, begging you to let him finally be a true part of this family. I'll support your needs, but I mean to know everything." He slouches onto a chair.

The kitchen is totally silent. The tears, that were flowing a short few minutes ago, are no more. John and June sit on their chairs sober and agape. Never have they heard such truth from anyone.

John's emotions jump from a feeling of total exposure, to a strong admiration for his son, and finally to heavy, guilt laden embarrassment. He understands that an apology for his actions is irrelevant to Robert. His son wants the respect he has rightfully deserved and craved for years. How does a man go about that? How does a father tell his boy he will do everything possible to be the daddy he deserves? He would speak, but the muscles in his throat and jowls are so tight from fighting back emotion, he's rendered dumb. He sits on his chair, unable to say a word.

June can't believe the clear understanding Robert has of that traumatic evening ten years ago. She recalls the whole incident through his eyes and ears. Now stunned, frozen in her pose, she stares at her first-born. To this point, she has never given into the fact that he witnessed the whole ugly scene. Unable to think otherwise, she had believed he was asleep in his room. How did a small boy live his whole life with this knowledge, by himself, away from home, with not a soul to support him? She feels she has forsaken him totally, for herself and John. How could a mother, any mother, do this to her innocent young child? It's unforgivable. Now, here he is, a courageously strong man, home at last, and all he wants is to finally be a part of the family that sent him away.

She feels light headed as the blood drains from her face. Her head starts to spin. Faraway voices are calling her name. Helpless, she lets her consciousness slip away, vaguely aware of a pair of strong arms catching her before she falls.

Robert picks her up. To her, his voice sounds as if his mouth is muffled.

"Where shall I put her, Daddy?"

"On the soft chair in the living room, I'll bring a cool cloth. Be careful with her."

He carries his mother toward the living room, while John grabs a dish towel and soaks it with cool water from the pump. He dashes after them, stopping to fill a small snifter with brandy before approaching the chair where June is sitting, with her son kneeling in front of her.

"I think she just fainted. Let me have that towel." Robert is quite collected and calm. "Is that brandy for you or Mama?"

He's serious with his question, but John sees the humor in it and almost chuckles out loud.

"It's for your mother. Here, see if she can take a little sip. It should bring some color back in to her face."

The young man lays the cool cloth on her forehead and speaks softly, "I'm so sorry. Can you hear me? Are you all right?"

The words she hears are sounding much clearer than a few minutes ago. She feels her strength mustering and she's able to open her eyes.

"Here, take a little sip of this brandy. It'll make you feel better." He puts the small snifter to her lips.

Just the aroma entering her nostrils as it rises from the glass brings the blood back to her head. With two short sniffs, June's entire body jerks, she's then capable of sitting upright in the chair, her eyes still searching for a place to focus.

"She's back with us," Robert says with certainty.

"I believe she is. Are you feeling better, honey?" her husband encourages.

"Will the two of you quit fussing over me. Dear Lord, have neither of you witnessed a lady swoon before? I'm fine." Her response is indicative of her embarrassment.

"I will take a swallow of that brandy, however."

"Perhaps, we should discontinue this discussion for a while." John's words are delivered as a statement, but all there take it as a question.

June speaks up as soon as she can clear her mouth of the brandy without choking.

"I would rather have my say right now—if you both agree."

She feels the liquor warming her throat and stomach as it goes down. When neither of the men object, she takes another small sip from the glass, sets it on a table at the right side of the chair, and looks first at John and then Robert.

"Your mother is not the woman you think she is. I'm deeply concerned that you'll have no respect for me at all after you hear what I have to say."

She turns to pick up the glass of brandy and drains the last of it over her tongue. She again sets the glass on the table and rises to her feet. Her words come as she starts to pace slowly across the room.

"Before I met your father, I worked in a brothel in New Orleans. I lived there with sixteen other women. My previous life was difficult. My family consisted of a vagabond mother of Irish descent and a local Indian from the bayou. I am truly a bastard child. I know nothing of my father, not even his name. My mother left me when I was fifteen years of age to run away with a tar from a slave hulk. I had nowhere to go, nowhere to live, no means of supporting myself. I agreed to work at the brothel as their maid and cleaning woman, since there was no other apparent way to survive. I honestly don't know how long I assisted them there while they did the devil's work. I cooked and cleaned, washed the soiled bedding, emptied the night pots of all the rooms at least twice a day, and whatever else needed doing. I do know I'm here today because the women of that house took me in and cared for me. They protected me from the perils of an almost lawless atmosphere."

She pauses when she reaches the chair she sat in a few minutes earlier, to pick up the empty brandy snifter and hold it out toward John.

"Will you fill this up for me, honey?"

He silently takes the glass and turns to get the decanter.

She continues to pace quietly from the chair across the room and back to accept the freshened snifter from her husband's hand.

"The women there didn't allow me to get involved with the work they did for the men who came there for the sex. But I wanted to earn enough money to get away from that life. The only way I could do that was to get involved with the men. After squabbling with the women for a while, I finally explained that I would either work there with them or at another house nearby. They finally gave in to my demands and had it set up for me to start the work on the upcoming Saturday evening." June stops to take a mouthful of the brandy and a breath.

"As it happened, shortly after supper that evening, I dressed myself with the old worn-out garments the women gave me; I had none of my own. I straightened up my room and went downstairs to find a likely spot to sit, to wait for a man. The way it works—" Robert interrupts to set her straight.

"I know how it works, Mama. You can skip that part," he insists.

"At your age too. My, my," she continues.

"Well, out of all those women, there were just three of us left, when in walked the most handsome boy I had ever seen. Obviously, he was from a family with resources; so sure of himself—somewhat aloof—but kind with his words and manners.

"My heart did a little flip and I'm sure it must have stopped, because it didn't start again until I took a breath. I knew the moment I saw him. I fell in love before he noticed I was in the room. The earlier words of warning from the other women echoed in my head. Do not allow yourself to be taken in by a man's looks or his money. He's here for just one thing. When it's finished, when he's had his fill, he'll leave nothing of himself behind, and be gone.

"Surprisingly to me, he didn't hesitate to make a decision between the three of us, but walked directly to me and reached out. I took his hand and stood up. Not knowing what to say, I turned and led him up the stairs to my room. My heart was pounding. I was wondering if every man I took to my room would make me feel the same way. Regardless, I knew I had to do what he wanted if I was ever to be free to have a different life.

“Once we were alone and I started taking off my clothes . . .”

“Mama,” Robert requests.

“I’m sorry. Anyway after we finished doing what he came there to do, I became a bit upset. Not toward him I insisted, it was just that I had done the deed. He knew it was my first time, he told me so. He also asked me why I was doing that kind of work. When I told him my story, he took my hand and said—” She stops and looks at her husband. “Do you remember?”

“As if it were yesterday,” he says, “I said, ‘do you believe in love at first sight?’”

“It was you?” Robert’s question is blurted out with surprise.

“It was, and is,” she answers. “His words took the strength right out of my legs. I could hardly stand up. I looked at him, and he looked at me. At that moment, I knew—as did he—we should be together. He took me from there that very evening. Keep in mind now, there was little privacy inside that house. All those other men and the women there noticed him and me, and what we were doing. There was a bit of a commotion when I announced I was leaving, so that drew attention to us too.

“Nonetheless, your daddy took me away with him, all the way to Richmond, where he provided us with a nice little three-room place. We posed as man and wife, and lived there for over a year, getting to know each other, and falling more deeply in love. He was constantly traveling from Richmond to his parents, home and back, trying to find a way to bring me into his life. Realize that back then, people’s reputations and their place in life was greatly more coveted then than they are today. We had to be very careful.

“Your father, at last, had all the arrangements in place and took me home with him to announce our engagement. We were married two months later. His mother and father accepted me as one of their own. We stayed right here in this house with them. Eleven months later, we were blessed with you.”

“Your grandparents never knew the truth about me, it never came up. I loved them very much, and wished many times you could have had more time with them. They were such fine people, and they cherished you. You had just turned two years old when it all started. Two men came to this house to talk with your daddy. You see, they both were customers at the bordello the night we met. They had firsthand knowledge of everything. They came for—what else—money. Money to stop them from telling everything they knew. We couldn’t allow them to ruin so many lives. We could have stood up against them if it was just us, but the shadow would fall upon John’s parents, and scandalize them as well. Those terrible men had plans to embellish the facts to make everything seem worse then it truly was. So, we paid them.

“I’m sure it’s no surprise when I tell you they continued wanting money after that. The amounts getting larger each time. We gave them everything we had and could borrow. When your grandparents died, they passed their worth to us. Within three years, those men had taken it all. Finally, we borrowed against this farm, and we gave them all of it to protect our name. Your father worked night and day trying to make ends meet. He was gone most of the time. That left me here alone, to cope with the problems of running this farm. We had borrowed money from all of our close friends. The Houslers, Dr. Shaw,

Mr. Olson at the bank, I could go on and on. They all came to our rescue and gave us all they could, not knowing the whole truth to our dilemma.

"I'm unable to tell you how I felt about all of this. It was all due to my background. None of this would have happened to this family if not for me. I was ready to do away with myself. I hadn't mentioned it to your daddy. He was doing everything he could and didn't need to hear that from me. I couldn't eat or sleep. I even avoided you, Robert. If it was not for Belle, you would have starved to death. I put up a good facade when your father was home, but as soon as he left, it all started again. I was making plans to end it all, when one morning Selma stopped by for coffee. I needed someone, anyone, so badly, I took her into my trust and divulged my intentions. I was surprised to learn that she too had been living a life of loneliness. We needed each other if we were to continue our lives.

"Your daddy started drinking to help himself from day to day. It became a nasty habit. His gentleness left him and he became miserable. That caused him to drink more.

"That horrible night, Selma came over so we could trade our clothes back and forth. With no money to buy new, we thought the change would be good for us both. She brought a pile of clothes with her. When we both started changing clothes, modesty left our minds. Well, one thing led to another, and then another, and before we knew it, we were on the bed with each other. And that's when John showed up at the door, falling down drunk. When he saw us that way, he went crazy, screaming and yelling. You obviously know the rest of what happened that night.

"Selma and I needed to be close to someone that night. Our men wanted no part of us, so we turned to each other. I'm not proud of it. But I'm not going to apologize for an act that wasn't planned. It just happened. If the circumstances had been different for either of us, I'm sure it wouldn't have happened. Until this past Sunday, I hadn't seen or spoken to Selma since the day they took my two boys to Der Bote."

She pauses to take another swallow from her glass of brandy.

"I believe this experience has been more taxing for me than I thought. Would you mind if I took leave to lie down for a few minutes? I'm suddenly exhausted. Mind you now, the brandy I've drunk has nothing to do with this. Please forgive me," she says with a little smile on her lips and a bit of orneriness in her eyes.

"I think you should, honey," John enforces her thinking. "You relax for a little while. Robert and I will be just fine. We'll wake you for dinner if need be."

June leaves the room headed upstairs.

"Can we go on with this? I'd like to get everything out in the open as quickly as possible." Robert isn't about to let this drop until he gets a complete understanding of the situation.

"Certainly, I now believe we need to do this," John begins.

"Everything your mother said is true. She passed lightly over some areas, but there was no lack of truth in what she said."

He rises from the love seat where he has been posed listening to his wife, walks to the table holding the remnants of her glass of brandy, and picks it up.

"No sense wasting this. Would you like something?"

"No, no, it's too early for me," Robert explains, holding the palms of both hands up to his father. "You go right ahead, though."

John takes a mouthful of the remaining brandy and sits down into the chair his wife has just vacated. He takes a moment to collect his thoughts while the younger Anderson sits patiently on a straight-back wooden chair, watching. He begins speaking again.

"You know, a man doesn't know what he's truly capable of doing until he's put in a position he sees no way to get clear from. Those two men continued to pressure us for money until there was no more. I had no way to keep them quiet any longer. So the colonel, your mother, Doc Shaw, and I made a plan. It was simple enough. I'd lure the both of them out here to our guesthouse on the pretense of giving them more money. Once they were in the house, we'd do away with them, and Doc would see to their remains.

"I never imagined how difficult it would be to kill another human being, or how long it can take a human body to die. It took the four of us to handle those two men, but we did it, then Doc took the bodies as we planned. We shall all be judged by the almighty when that day comes. That, of course, ended our predicament. However, we still owed everybody money. I couldn't see how we could possibly repay such a staggering sum."

Robert is sitting on the edge of his chair, his mouth open. "I had no idea, no idea at all. You had no choice, Daddy. You did the right thing, I assure you."

"Thank you for that, my boy, at times it eats at me. I'll never get that scene out of my mind. It was such a brutal thing to do. I don't think I could do it again.

"To continue," John starts again, "when I took your mama to the Atlanta hospital to give birth to the baby, I had thirty-five dollars to my name, and I spent half of that to get there. When the doctors examined her and discovered it was going to be a multiple birth, I was exasperated. June was having a hard time of it. So, I was worried about her and did not have money to pay for what might need to be done. And then to find out we were going to get several little people to feed and take care of. Hell, I didn't know how we were going to care for one baby, let alone several."

"They weren't sure if they could save your mother or any of the babies. They had to cut her belly to get them. You were right when you said you heard there were five. The first one was a girl. They took her away immediately and worked to get the others out and get them to breathe on their own. Three did just fine, but one, Sheree, looked just like the first one. We all thought she was dead too. It so happened one of the doctors noticed Sheree's color didn't change. She stayed pink and didn't turn the dark bluish color of the first baby. Seeing that, he called in another doctor, one from the Company. After an hour of carefully examining Sheree, he told us she could be kept alive, but it would be expensive. He asked us if we wanted him to save her."

"We told him we had no money. At that point, he asked the others to leave the room, and that's when he presented us with an opportunity. He would save Sheree, pay off all our outstanding indebtedness, including the charges of the hospital, and give us a large amount of cash to spend as we saw fit. And for all that, he wanted just one thing."

"What did he want?" Robert's voice is drenched with anticipation.

"He wanted Sheree, Robert. He would wait until she turned fourteen years of age, but at that time, we had to present her to the Company, never to see her again. We had one hour to make our decision. What else could we do? If we didn't agree, Sheree would die. If we agreed, she would be taken from us at age fourteen. So, after a soul-searching hour, we agreed."

"But where is she now? She's just ten, we still have four more years. I know in my heart she's not dead. Tell me now," the only pure Anderson son pleads.

"The accident with the horse is true. But Sheree didn't die, she was left in a coma. The Company felt it was a perfect opportunity for them to step in and take her. No one would question her death, because of the accident. They took her, son. The grave is empty, but Sheree still isn't with us. Now we've lost her forever."

"What will the Company do with her? Where will they take her? Is there a way we can convince them to give her back?" Robert fires questions rapidly.

"I have no idea where they'll take her, or for what purpose they want her. I do believe they'll take proper care of her. I have to believe that. We signed papers granting her to them, and times being as they are, those papers will probably stand up under scrutiny. I don't know of a way to get her back. I'm not sure, for that matter, that I can contact the Company at all," John feels the weight of the whole thing all over again.

"You feel then, she's in no immediate danger?"

"Let me say that I believe no physical harm will come to her. They seem to be interested in an ability she has to appear to be dead when she's not. It's a condition of her brain. Some sort of a nerve derangement only a few people are born with. They believe they can control it with chemicals. They explained to us that without the proper care, she could possibly lose her mind at an early adult age."

"I can plainly see you and Mama had no choice but to accept their proposal. Don't harbor blame for that decision. What else could you do? You did the right thing." His son's support bolsters John's courage.

"The pressure the two of you have been pinned under seems to me to be tremendous. It's been a great burden. You'll not regret bringing me into the family, I'll be here for you and Mama. I'll not let you down, I swear it."

John feels a fresh strength stirring deep inside his body as he hears his son's words. He knows he means everything he's saying. He's grown into a strong, intelligent, family committed, man. It's good to have him home. His love for his boy has never been greater than at this moment.

"Let's see if we can get Belle to brew a pot of coffee, then we'll talk about business."

Chapter Nine

As Belle pours coffee for the two Anderson men, John realizes it's time to give his son a complete explanation of his father, fill him in on the expected problems ahead.

"It's time to share my mind and put Robert in a position to understand me and my purposes. He can help with the many details, and we'll be able to offer each other another opinion when needed. I'll have more time to be a better husband and father, too." John knows his son lacks maturity and the knowledge that goes with it, but the words running through his mind give him an eerie sense of relief.

"I must!" he says out loud, unintentionally.

"What did you say?" his curious son asks.

"Aw, I was just thinking how good it is to have you home, and how wonderful it feels to be the father of such a fine young man. Are you sure you want to take on the involvements of this family, and all that goes into making a life in this part of the country?"

"Yes, sir, I do. I know I'm young and I have a lot to learn. But I have no ties to sever anywhere. So, I'll devote myself entirely to it, and I'll earn your trust if you'll give me the chance." The young man's voice is calm, his words are delivered with certainty.

The back screen door creaks as Belle leaves the kitchen; she knows when to leave menfolk alone.

John nods his head yes. "Good, I'll do my best to inform you as quickly as I can. First things first, though. You must realize that the only other person you can fully trust is me, and me you. We'll endanger our causes, and each other, if we break that trust. Do you understand?" John looks at him directly and pauses.

"It's you and me, Daddy, all the way." His words soothe the older man's soul.

Robert feels he's home at last, knowing he will learn his purpose shortly. His father's trust means everything to him. His legs want to bounce up and down as he sits at the table. Anticipation is eating him up.

"Do you recall your mother's explanation of Sheree's accident with Pooch?" John continues without waiting for a response. "Well, the day after the accident, Jim found a wound above Pooch's left front leg. I dug a bullet out of it, at least I think it's a bullet. Pooch fell with Sheree because someone shot him. Take a look at this." John takes the object from his pocket and hands it over. "Ever seen anything like this?"

Robert reaches and accepts the long metal object and turns it over in his hands. "Yes, I have. This is a new type of long rifle bullet that's being made in Europe. It fits a new kind of rifle. As you know, the ones we have are made with the barrel smooth on the inside, and use round bullets. They're only accurate to up to a hundred yards on a calm day. These new ones have a twisting groove inside, they will shoot this bullet accurate up to four hundred yards. Another thing, loading one of our military guns takes almost forty-five seconds, but these new ones take less than twenty. I had no idea they are available around here yet."

John's jaw drops as he takes in his son's words. To say he's caught by surprise with Robert's knowledge of this strange bullet, is an understatement.

"See here," he leans forward to explain.

"The front's tapered to a finer point to cut through the air. The back's hollowed out to accept more of the thrust as the powder explodes. The hollow also expands to the barrel's insides, sealing the force of the explosion behind it. That makes it come out of the muzzle a lot faster. Who do you suppose has a rifle like that around here? There can't be too many of them. It's sort of like leaving your name behind to shoot something and leave this bullet to be found."

"I don't know for certain, but my gut tells me it's the Company. Three of their men were in town when I went after Doc for your sister. I know one of them named Benny. He's been here any number of times. Even had supper with us. I don't know him well, but he seems to be their errand boy. I didn't recognize the other two, although one of them looked familiar. Their names are Chad and Nate. It was no coincidence they were in town that day; Benny had the money with him to make their final payment."

"What payment's that?" Robert interrupts.

"It was part of the agreement we made when we committed to give up Sheree. They paid just as they said they would, all of our existing debts, and gave us money to spend right then. They, also, agreed to give us money each year until she reached fourteen. The money he gave me was for the last four years they figured they owed.

"I believe they were here to take Sheree, regardless, one way or another. I wonder if they shot Pooch. But then, why didn't they just collect Sheree from the accident site and take her with them," John tries to understand.

"It seems to me they probably realized they would leave too many loose ends. You and Mama would ask a lot of questions, and would search high and low for Sheree, probably forever. This way it's over. Six months from now, nobody will question anything that happened. It seems risky, though, to shoot a horse out from under a person. People get killed all the time from falling off a horse. If that's what they did, their reasoning needs to be adjusted," Robert's offers his opinion.

"I can see a lot of truth in what you say, but, there's more to consider. Sheree's accident happened at the willow, we took her to the guesthouse from there. The whole arrangement for the Company to take her was talked about right there. Later that day I found muddy footprints all over inside the guesthouse. It's possible someone else was there and overheard everything. I traced down the footprints and learned they belong to Jacob's oldest son, Randall. I've not yet approached him, but I did ask the colonel to keep a watchful eye on the boy.

"I know Randall. He must be twelve or thirteen by now."

"I identified his tracks by his bad foot," John's statement allows him to follow another path of conversation.

"We have some business to handle tomorrow evening, and I'd like you to take part in it. You'll better understand the rest of the problem after that. Another thing, I'd like you to become familiar with the work here on the farm. As you know, our income is earned by raising tobacco. Jim drives the rest of the help, while I oversee it all. I have an income from my political ties as well. With the money we've been receiving each year from the Company, we've been able to accumulate and set aside a considerable sum.

"You're going to need money of your own to get along. I'm not sure what you might expect, but certainly, there's enough to provide for us all. Perhaps it's too soon to impose all this upon you?" John's statement comes out as a question.

"Whatever you think. It makes little difference to me how we work that out. I know Belle and Mama will feed me and give me a place to sleep. That's all I really need right now, and like I said, I want to know it all."

At Der Bote, Randall is busy cleaning out the horse stalls of the main stable. He's trying to come up with a plan to get back to the Andersons' guesthouse without getting caught. "There's no sure way to do it," he mutters to himself. "I just have to make up my mind as to when, and then do it. I best do it after everybody's asleep. I can slip out my bedroom window, do all I need to do, and be back before anybody knows I'm gone. Mama never checks on us after we go to bed. I'll do it tomorrow night, as early as I can get away. Maybe I'll find something they left behind when they took Sheree. I sure hope so. I'm going to need a match or two to light a lamp or something once I get there. I'll get them from the kitchen today and hide them under my pillow. If I was smart, I'd take a change of clothes and hide them outside somewhere, maybe here in the barn. Aww fiddle, I won't need them, I'm just going to walk over there and back. That's it then, I'm going tomorrow evening."

Selma and Alberta Mae are sitting at the kitchen table talking about the new dress they are about to start cutting from the material spread out, in front of them.

"This cloth will make you a fine dress, Ms. Selma," Alberta Mae says. "It shore is beautiful. I'm going to hold on to the scraps for quilting. The colors are real bright, so they'll fit right in with what I've already got started. You don't mind do you?"

"Of course not, plan on using all you want. Can I ask?" Selma thinks better of what she is about to say, and stops in midsentence.

Alberta Mae raises her eyes up away from the material to look her straight in the face. "Honey, you can ask me anything, you know that. What is it you want?"

"I'm afraid I'll upset you, and I really don't want to do that. I have a favor to ask of you, but no . . . I'd better not. It isn't fair to you. I don't want to hurt you." Selma's voice is quiet and caring.

"You let me worry about that, Ms. Selma. You know I'll do anything I can for you." She isn't going to let this drop. Her curiosity has peaked, "What is it you want?"

Selma allows her thoughts to overcome her tight lips and empties her mind with one burst of words. "I want to meet June Anderson tomorrow evening, and I've told the colonel that you and I are going to work on this dress while he's gone out on business.

He'll be upset if he learns I'm meeting her. So, if he asks you later about tomorrow night, will you tell him I spent the evening with you?

"I'm not planning anything with June, so don't be concerned with that. We just need to talk for a while, nothing else. I've not forgotten the mess she and I caused before, and I know the part you had to play in it all. It's still fresh in my mind. Nothing like that will ever happen again. I know it's a lot to ask, so if you think you shouldn't do it, I'll understand completely."

"Funny thing, Ms. Selma, the colonel, just earlier this morning, asked me to keep an eye on you tomorrow evening while he's out. I wondered what was going on, and now I know. I want to thank you for trusting me to tell me the truth. Now don't you worry your pretty little head none, Alberta Mae will handle the colonel, and your secret is safe with me." Her words are delivered with a big warm smile.

"I can't thank you enough." Selma is assured and drops her head as a hint of a smile appears on her face. She feels like a small child who has just been relieved of a punishment. "I love you, Alberta Mae."

Thursday's supper time creeps into this Appalachia valley of rolling hills. The sun casts shadows that keep getting longer as the day progresses. The silence of darkness will bring an end to another day of labor for those who use their brawn to keep the farms producing. Workers can be seen walking from the fields toward their homes. They give off a weary appearance, scuffing their feet as they walk, their tools in their hands or resting on a shoulder being held in place by one arm draped over the handle. Tired and hungry, they've put in a good day's work, now it's time to rest and be with their families. Heat from fireplaces and stoves will be welcomed this cool evening. All is peaceful and serene.

"That was another fine meal," the colonel comments to Alberta Mae as he sips his coffee and prepares to put a match to the cigar in his other hand.

"That's good to hear. Will you be needing me for anything else right now?" she responds. "If not, I'm going to go feed my family and me."

"You go right ahead, we have everything we need. I'll clear the table when we're finished here," Selma encourages.

"Okay then, I'll just gather up what I need and head on home. I'll be back after while, though, to help with your dress. I shouldn't be gone for more than an hour or so." The cook's comment was meant for the colonel's ears.

Colonel Charles Housler is a stout-looking man. His thinning gray hair is combed back on the top and sides, and hangs over the back collar of his shirt some four inches. He has heavy eyebrows of thick gray hair with longer shoots sticking out here and there to curl on the ends. His reading glasses set on a strong narrow nose that spreads as it protrudes over his lips. His nostrils contain the same thick hair as his eyebrows, and although he tries, he's unable to keep it trimmed so it's not noticeable. A mustache that lays on his upper lip is kept reasonably short, except he lets it grow longer on the sides enabling it to be twisted at the ends. His lips are heavy and normally express no hint of a smile. A square jaw and a goatee for a gray beard gives him the look of a true colonel. The truth of the matter is, the title of colonel was given to him by the governor of the state as an honor in appreciation for services rendered. He has no military history at all.

"I love you very much you know."

The colonel's words catch Selma off guard. She raises her head a little and looks at him out of the corner of her eyes.

"I'm aware I've not been much of a husband to you, physically or emotionally, lately."

She doesn't move, just sits quietly.

"It's getting so I don't know what to say," he continues, "I feel that I'm not being fair with you, and I'm concerned that you'll learn to despise me, if you haven't already. I want you to know that I'm trying to find my way back to you. It's on my mind most of the time. I don't seem to be able to put the words together to explain clearly the way I feel. Every morning I pray I'll understand myself more, and be able to relate better to you that day."

Now Selma has turned and faces her husband, hanging on every word. He pauses to puff his cigar. This is obviously difficult for him to do. The strain on his face is evidence that there is more to be said.

"And," she pries.

"I'm very worried that you'll leave me to be with June," he says, his voice breaking a little. "I couldn't stand losing you."

"All these years, and you have never forgiven me," she starts. "The only thing wrong with our relationship is the one thing you'll never get over. Your pride, your damn stupid pride. John has forgiven June, and they're getting on with their lives. We can too, but you'll never let it happen. Do you really care about me, or are you actually afraid I'll find someone else, leave you, and put you in a position that makes you look like a fool? Charles, I'm not entirely to blame for what happened that night. Where were you when I needed you? Were you out fooling around with other women, or maybe another man? You know, when a woman senses her man doesn't find her attractive any more, all sorts of things run through her mind. You haven't laid a hand on me for over twelve years. Do you realize that? For me, the truly sad part of it all is, I don't think there is, or ever has been, another woman. What does that leave to consider? Not much, does it?

"Am I supposed to pity you and take your head to my breast to console you? Is that what you want? Do you want me to swear that I still love you, and there isn't anyone else, never has been, and never will be?" Her words sting like the tip of a whip in the colonel's ears.

"Is this what I deserve from you, Selma, after all I've done for you? Where would you be today if it weren't for me? You would probably be living in a dirt floor shack somewhere, with ten screaming children running around. Have you forgotten where you came from?" her husband throws a punch.

"No, I've not forgotten, and I can tell, neither have you. Is that what this is all about? Are you ashamed of me, of my roots? I can't change who I am. I can't change where I came from. My God, I never dreamed you've had those regrets about us, about me, about my heritage. You knew all about me before we married. And here I've thought all along it was what I did. If not the incident with June, then something else." She stops speaking and puts her face in her hands, unable to look at him any more.

"I'm unable to continue with this right now. I can tell you this, however. It's not what you think. I'm leaving now, I'll be back later tonight. I'm sorry I upset you." With that he gets up from the table, puts on his coat and leaves through the back door.

Selma rises from her chair and begins clearing the dishes from the table. Tears roll down her face as her mind spins with old thoughts and feelings. Alone, hopelessness overcomes her, causing a familiar weakness to pull her back down onto the chair.

"After all these years, what do I have to show for it?" she says out loud. "I have no children, though no fault of my own. He doesn't want children. I have no social life, no friends, no relatives near here. Everything we have belongs to him. I never have money of my own. He wouldn't take me to town, or allow me to go with someone else to shop anyway. I'm a prisoner in this house.

"He's ashamed, and thinks he's better than me because of my color. He doesn't want to be seen with me. I'm married to a bigot who acts like he doesn't know it.

"Times being what they are, what chance do I have of changing him? He can probably do whatever he wants with me, and there's not much I can do about it. He tells me I'm a free woman. Free to do what? The cold truth is, I'm nothing more than a wedded slave to him. I'm so glad to have a friend like June back. I need to be with her tonight. She must be there, she just must."

"Are you all right, Ms. Selma?" Alberta Mae's words startle her out of the thought-produced state she occupies. "You look like you just lost your best friend. What happened while I was gone? Did the colonel abuse you, child?"

"I'm okay. We had a disagreement, that's all. I'll tell you all about it later. Your caring means more to me then I can say, Alberta Mae. No matter what happens, don't give up on me. I'm going to need you more than ever, but right now, I have to leave to meet with June." She grabs a shawl from the hall tree, drapes it over her shoulders, and leaves through the back door.

Alberta Mae stands, mouth agape, and watches her disappear off the back porch as the screen door slams shut.

At the Anderson home, John is saying goodbye as he and Robert prepare to leave for the evening.

"I'm not sure when we'll return this evening, honey, but it shouldn't be too late. Don't worry, Robert will take good care of me." He shows a big teethy grin to June and Charlotte as he speaks.

June steps up close to him and starts picking lint from his coat as she says, "Oh, I'm sure no trouble with find either of you as long as you're with one another. Take your time and enjoy being together. Charlotte and I will find something domestic to do while you're out changing the world. Don't worry about us, we'll be just fine."

"Good, come on, son, we need to get a move on to be there on time."

Robert follows his father out through the front door, and down the steps. He turns right toward the barn, but turns back when his daddy says. "We'll not be using the horses tonight. They'll just be in our way."

"Where we going?"

"We're going to meet with the colonel and twenty or twenty-five of his friends, at the northeast end of his lake, near the spring that feeds it. It'll all explain itself when we meet them. Come on now, we best not keep them waiting."

June watches from inside the front door screen until her men disappear in the shadows of the coming darkness. She looks at the sky for the light of the moon to note there is none, then walks the hallway back to the dining room with her mind contemplating an excuse to leave the house to meet Selma. Charlotte's cheery voice greets her as she turns to enter the room.

"What are we women going to do now that the men are gone, Mama?" Her face is one big smile as she waits for an answer.

"Well . . . I've been craving some of Bell's pecan chocolate fudge. I believe there's plenty of pecans left in that bag we received last fall from Atlanta. You won't mind shelling some of them for us will you, honey."

"That sounds good, I'll go get them. I'll do it on the back porch so the mess won't be in the house. Are you going to help me?"

"I have a splitting headache. Do you mind if I lie down an hour or so? I'm sure I'll be fine after that."

"That's okay, I can do it by myself. You go lie down.'

"Thanks for understanding, I'll ask Belle to start the recipe. Careful now, don't spill those pecans all over the kitchen floor before you get them out on the porch," June calls after Charlotte, who is already on the move to start her part of the candy making process. June follows her into the kitchen to see Belle finishing up the supper dishes. She picks up a towel, then a supper plate, and begins wiping it dry.

"I need your help for a while this evening, Belle. I'd like you to make some chocolate fudge. Charlotte is going to crack and shell some pecans. I've explained to her that I have a headache and need to lie down for a while. I'll appreciate it if you can keep her busy for the evening. I'm going to close my bedroom door and wish not to be disturbed. The excitement of Robert coming home, and all, has completely tuckered me out. Do you mind?"

"No, ma'am, that'll be just fine. I like spending time with your daughter. She's quite a child you know."

"Good then, thanks. John and Robert will be out until late, so when she tires out, just send her to bed."

"Yes, ma'am," Belle agrees.

As soon as Charlotte's mother enters the bedroom, she closes the door, turns up the lamp, then takes off her dress and petticoat. She dons a long-sleeve shirt, riding pants, and boots. She puts her hair up tight in a ball on the back of her head, grabs a chore jacket from the clothes tree, slips her arms through the sleeves, and throws the collar upon her shoulders, not bothering to button the front. A puff from her lips snuffs the lamp. She opens the door, peers out momentarily, creeps quietly through the hallway, down the stairs, and out the front door, closing it softly. She's on her way to meet Selma at the willow tree.

At Der Bote, Randall is lying on the bed beside his twin brothers, fully dressed, waiting for complete darkness. Finally, it's time. Carefully, so as not to shake the bed, he sits up and listens for sleeping sounds coming from the twins just inches away. Satisfied, he inches off the edge of the bed, creeps to the partially open window, silently slides it up, and squeezes through head first. As his body slips over the windowsill, he puts his hands down to catch his weight and lowers himself to the ground. He gets to his feet, turns, and is on his way to the Andersons' farm, but he doesn't see the farm dog, a large collie, that has positioned itself at the corner of the house, waiting for him to get closer. When close enough, the dog lets out a deep, growling, snarling, bark, and lunges at him. Startled, Randall loses his balance, awkwardly stumbles sideways, and lands on his back. The large dog is on top of him before he stops falling. The boy instinctively grabs the animal by the throat with both hands and rolls to his left, causing the collie to fall off him and land on it's side. With a loud whisper he shouts.

"It's me, Queenie. Stop it. It's me." The dog immediately starts licking his face. "Good girl. Now go on back to the barn. Go on—git."

Because of the commotion, the boy, sitting on the ground, pauses, expecting someone in the house to check on the noise. When no one responds, he rises and turns to walk away, almost falling over Queenie as she starts rubbing against his legs. He tries to make the dog stay at home, but thinking he's playing, she won't, and yaps at him. This isn't working at all, and the noise will eventually bring someone to settle things down. So, together, they head toward the Andersons' guesthouse.

Selma arrives first at the willow tree, climbs the board fence, perches herself on top with her heels resting on the upper edge of the middle board, and faces the direction she knows June will come. Carefully maintaining her balance, she rearranges her shawl to cover more of her body. The night air is quite cool. Everything is dead quiet. She can hear her own heart beat. The sun has disappeared over the horizon snuffing what little light that was left of the day. It's dark, but once her eyes adjust, she's able to see her hand when she extends her arm. Anything lurking in the shadows, however, is completely hidden. Thinking she hears footsteps, she turns her head so both ears can collect sound from that direction. Nothing.

"Might have been an animal of some sort," she thinks. Ten minutes go by, no June. Suddenly, something big, with a wide wing span, swings down from the willow just missing her head. She lets out a short scream as she fights to keep her balance on the fence.

"What in the world was that?" she says loudly, her heart pounding, as she instinctively shrinks down to lower her center of gravity.

"I don't know, but it almost hit me. It must have been an owl judging by it's size." Another voice replies, not fifteen feet from her. Startled again, she blurts out loud enough to break the silence for quite some distance in all directions.

"June, is that you? I'm bound to be frightened to my grave tonight."

"Yes, it's me. Can you quiet down? Someone might hear you."

"Oh, thank goodness. It's spooky out here tonight. I've been waiting for a while, and I guess I'm a little jumpy. I'm so glad you're here. I need to talk with you." Selma's voice is almost a whisper now.

"I've had a terrible time finding you in this dark," June explains why she's late. "I finally found the fence and turned to my left to follow it, then that thing almost hit me in the head. I had no idea we were that close to each other. I almost fainted when you screamed."

"Obviously, I didn't know you were there either. There was still a little light when I got here, so I didn't have a problem."

"Did you have any trouble getting away from the house?" Mrs. Anderson wonders.

"No, it was easy. Charles and I had a few nasty words for each other after supper so, he went his way, and I mine. How about you?"

"I suppose not. Actually, I'm at home right now, in my bedroom sleeping off a headache. John's out somewhere with Robert doing who knows what."

"Robert's home then?" Selma notices.

"Yes, he arrived Tuesday mid-morning. What a homecoming. It was terrible. He asked about Sheree and wouldn't let up until we told him everything, and I mean everything. I told him things about my past that I could hardly remember myself. He was so insistent and quick with his questions, as well as his understanding, there was nothing else to do."

"Did he ask about you and me?" Mrs. Housler questions, thinking there would be no reason for him to do so.

"Well, no, he didn't ask. He told us all about that night. He was right there and saw the whole thing. There was nothing more for us to tell him. He knew more about it than I remembered. It was so horrible, I fainted dead away.

"Oh no, can today get any worse? He hates me, doesn't he, for getting you involved that way? I'm so sorry that you had to go through it all again. My life is such a shamble, and now to find I've brought all this down on you."

"Shush girl. It's not your fault. I don't want you taking the blame upon yourself like that. It happened. We were both there, and we both did it. If circumstance were the same, I'd do it again. A little more discretely, of course, but I'd do it again." She chuckles. "Besides . . . Robert has accepted it completely. He really understands and blames his father. Can you believe it? He truly places the blame on John, and has forgiven him. You and I are the innocent victims of a roaring drunk."

"He really doesn't despise me at all? He knows what we were doing?" The woman from Der Bote is amazed.

"He knows and completely respects you, and me. He understands we were driven to do what we did. The hardest part for him was the violence that poured from his father. I'm sure he believes Jacob is a Saint."

"Does he know about the babies, too?"

"His memory was a little sketchy since a lot of what was said and went on was outside of his eyes and ears. But he knew enough to ask the right questions. I had to lie down for a while, well the truth is, I had a couple of drinks and had to sleep it off. John told me later that he had explained the whole thing, the Company and all. He told him about our agreement to give up Sheree, the entire mess. Robert says he's dropped out of school to stay at home and help us handle the farm. John seems to feel that it makes sense to give him his head and see. At this point, it really makes no big difference to me, I'm just glad to have him home."

"I'm so glad your life is finally coming together. You deserve it if anyone does. You've been through enough for one person, and it's about time things change for you and your family. I'm happy for you." Unable to hold back any longer, Selma breaks down in tears.

In the dark, near the lake on Der Bote.

"I can barely see where we're going. Another five minutes and we'll be feeling our way around with our toes. We should have brought a lantern," Robert comments as he and his father tromp along.

"We're almost there. Quiet now, no more noise than necessary," John cautions.

Robert is recalling his younger life on this farm. He doesn't remember it being this far to the lake at Der Bote. He takes a deep breath of the cool, clean, fresh air, and lets it out through his nose. He swam in this lake with the workers' children when he was small. The water was always clear and sweet. The lake is spring fed and drains at the opposite end into a small creek. The same creek that meanders across the Anderson farm to eventually meet up with a much larger creek, that runs through town, about ten miles away. He can picture the surface of the lake, it must cover some five acres. Kidney shaped, the bank at the far end is covered with low growing bushes, with water reeds and lilies spreading out into the water some twenty feet. A large sycamore tree grows on the edge of the bank at the center of the inside curve. He remembers how, as a child, he climbed the tree to jump off a large limb that extended out over the water.

At last he's able to see the water. It glistens with a dark murky depth of calmness, so still not a ripple can be seen.

"Here, we'll wait here," his father whispers as he squats down to sit on his heels.

Robert doesn't reply. From here on he's a spectator, to what he isn't sure. He knows he's ready to find out about anything that's this shrouded with secrecy.

"Watch over there toward those lilies," John breathes, holding out his arm pointing a finger.

Not knowing what to expect, not wanting to miss a thing, Robert keeps his eyes on that spot. The few minutes that pass seem like twenty before the glow of a light, probably a match, shines for a few seconds, and dies. He hears a match come to life with the scrape of his daddy's thumbnail. John holds it up over his head for a few seconds then lowers it to his mouth and extinguishes it with a puff of breath. Robert notes how eerie he appears with the light of the match briefly illuminating and shadowing his face.

"Sit still and don't say anything. We've got company coming our way."

A few seconds pass before movement is detected near the spot where the light of the match appeared on the other side of the lake. There seems to be a lot of people moving toward them. The closer they get, the more Robert realizes there must be at least twenty in the group. They stop about a hundred feet away, except for one who moves fast, directly toward where he and his daddy wait. John stands up.

"That you, Marty?" he says with a low voice.

"Yeah, John, it's me. You got somebody with you?" the voice whispers back.

"It's my son, Robert," John explains as he walks toward the man.

"Oh yeah . . . well, I was expecting you to be alone, had me going there for a minute. We heard you walk up, but we waited a while. You know, being careful and all."

"Sorry, I had no way of letting you know. Robert just got home on Tuesday from school. He's going to start helping out, so I wanted him to get this experience tonight," John apologizes.

"I trust you, John. I figure you know what you're doing. I've got twenty-three with me. Fifteen men and eight women," Marty divulges.

The two men stand close together so their voices do not carry far.

"Let's get a count so you can give me the money and sign for them. You know I don't like to wait around any longer than I have to. No sense taking chances."

"I understand completely. Is the colonel with you?" Mr. Anderson asks.

"Yeah, he's there with them."

John doesn't reply, but walks toward the group, and motions for Robert to follow. Marty turns and joins them. The colonel walks out from the group toward them.

"Colonel, you get a twenty-three count? Fifteen male, eight female?" John inquires.

"That's right. All healthy, hungry, and tired," the colonel confirms.

"How many started out with you, Marty?" John needs to know if any were lost along the way.

"Just the twenty-three you see here. I understand the original group totaled twenty-seven. Four dropped off due to sickness and their age. Too old to make the trip, I'm told."

"Any trouble at all that you know about?" the questions keep coming, "Anything suspicious to you?"

"What are you looking for, John? Has there been an incident?"

"Not really, I saw two new faces in town five days ago. They seemed to want to look me over, but were friendly enough. They were dressed like farmhands. Maybe I'm being too careful, but they looked more like the coat and tie type to me. Just struck me odd, that's all."

"I've seen nothing of them my friend. My part of the trip has been quiet and uneventful. I'll keep my eyes open for those two though," Marty assures.

John turns and reaches out his hand at the same time Marty passes him some papers, then turns around allowing John to use his back as a support while signing the documents.

When they're finished, he turns back to face Mr. Anderson. He accepts an envelope, folds it in half, sticks it in his left breast pocket, and says, "Let's get together the next time you get close to my home. I miss our talks. I hear you might get a stab at the top job around here. That right?"

"There's some talk about it, but no one's made me an offer as yet. If they offer it to me, you know I'll take it. That's what I'm all about. I know I can do some real good for this state from that position," John relates.

"We're talking governor, right?" Marty counters.

"That's what they tell me. If I get the call, I'll get word to you right away. I'll probably be looking for a backer or two. You interested?" John pitches back at him.

"You bet I am. I'll drop everything to help you campaign. Just let me know."

"You'd better take your own advice and get out of here. It's up to us now. Thanks for bringing them through. Say hello for June and me to your missus." John relates as he grips the hand of his friend.

Marty walks away along the edge of the lake, shakes the colonel's hand and gives him a pat on the back as he passes. He waves to the twenty-three people and they wave back. John and Robert walk up to the colonel.

"We had better get a move on," he says. "Are we splitting up like we've done before?"

"I think it's best, Colonel. The smaller the crowd, the less noise, right?" John suggests. "I'll take twelve, you take eleven; let them decide how to split up."

As the colonel walks toward the group, Robert is unable to hold back any longer, "Are they slaves? Are they on the run?"

"Yes, son, they are."

"Where we taking them?" he's quick to ask.

"The colonel is taking his group directly to our guesthouse. We'll take our group out past the willow. There we'll rest for an hour. Then we'll go the rest of the way and meet them there. That'll give him time to get his group inside the house and get settled before we get there. We can't have people milling around outside."

"What do we do then?"

"I'll explain more later. Right now, we need to get these folks to the willow? We'll follow the creek. That way, if we spot trouble, we can hide down behind the banks until it blows over. I want you out in front about a hundred yards. Keep your eyes and ears open. Don't take anything for granted, be suspicious of everything. Your job is to keep the rest of us from getting caught off guard. Now go, get your head start. We'll be right behind you.

Robert doesn't reply, he just starts walking toward the creek bank. The feelings of importance and belonging build up inside him. He knows his daddy took a chance just bringing him along unannounced. It shows that he has a lot of say about what happened here tonight.

"I never thought Daddy's business was anything like this. I wonder where these people are headed? What are we going to do with all of them at the guesthouse? I'll just have to wait and see." His questions are many and the answers are few, at least for the moment. He looks back to see if the group is coming, but can't see a thing in the dark.

"How can I stay a hundred yards ahead of them when I don't know where they are in the first place," he muses. "I guess it won't make any difference unless there's trouble. And if there is, I'll go back looking for them. I'll just get to the willow first and wait there.

Not too far away, there's more movement in the darkness. Randall is keeping a steady pace as he walks with Queenie at his side. His clubfoot is bothersome from the fall a few days ago, and the uneven land isn't helping anything. He's found his way to the wagon road leading from the Andersons' main house to the guesthouse, thinking it will be easier walking. A good decision, it's a lot easier not having to deal with all the briars, weeds, and the rutted surface of the ground. He can see the lights inside the Anderson home as he looks back over his shoulder.

"Won't be long now until we get there, Queenie," he says to his dog, "I'm sort of glad you came along with me, it's mighty dark out here tonight."

He reaches out to pat the collie on the head, but the darkness and his sudden movement startles her, she growls and pulls away. Quickly though, she sees her mistake and makes up by pushing her nose into his hand for a lick.

Another fifteen minutes, at a steady gait, brings the pair to the front porch steps of the dark spooky house. Stillness fills the quiet of the surroundings. Queenie sits on the ground next to Randall, both surveying the layout. So many dark shadows could hide anything or anybody. He feels more secure with the collie at his side. She would notice if something was lurking in those dark places, or, at least, he feels he must believe that if he's going to continue with his plan.

"I hope the door's not locked," he whispers to the dog. "If it is, I'll have to go through a window or something. We need to get inside and find us a lamp, or a candle, or something.

A few steps and they're on the front porch standing in front of the door. He reaches out to the knob and gives it a turn. The door opens. Now all they need is a light.

It's even darker inside the house. The only way to locate anything is to feel around. His hand touches what he believes to be a table. Carefully, he searches the surface for a lamp, and, aha, he finds one. A scratch of one of his matches on the wood floor and a touch of it to the wick sends light in all directions.

"Okay, now we can get to looking around Queenie. You let me know if you hear anything, all right." The dog prances, her toenails tapping on the wooden floor.

"Let's start upstairs and work our way down," he says and proceeds up the stairs. He walks to the end of the hallway and enters the last room on the right. He sets the lamp on a dresser and begins opening drawers, looking under the furniture, patting the bed, then a wooden box setting in the corner catches his eye.

The two women at the willow tree are caught up in conversation. June can see that her friend is deeply hurt, and approaches the fence as Selma slides to the ground.

"I'm sorry, honey, here I am thinking only of myself, when all the while you're very upset," June's voice is consoling, "What's wrong, what did he say to upset you so?"

Selma puts her arms around her friend and lays her head on her shoulder, sobbing, "Oh, June, I'm so tired of my life; I don't want to live any more. There's no way to solve anything that's going on. You're the only person that would miss me if I wasn't here. He doesn't care how he hurts me. He probably wishes me dead. I'm stranded in a world by myself, going through the motions every day, trying not to notice everyone's indifference toward me. No one knows me, I mean the real me, not even you, sweet June. It's too hard, too lonely—I'm too insecure. I'm actually thinking about killing myself. Not for the pity of others, I know there will be none of that. I badly need some peace in my heart, and I know of no any other way. You know the worst part? I'm afraid I'll do it. I'm actually afraid of what I might do if I'm alone." Selma can hardly breathe, her sobbing and crying are well beyond controllable at this point.

"My word, I had no idea. You poor dear. What can I do? How can I help?" June doesn't expect an answer to her questions, since her friend is so broken up.

"I can tell you one thing. You'll not be alone until we can decide what needs to be done to get you through this. Come on, I'm taking you home with me." The words no more than leave her lips.

"Who's there? Is someone there?" A loud whisper reaches their ears.

"Shussssh, Selma, someone's out there," June quietly warns her friend, and puts her hand over her mouth to stop the sobbing.

Selma's cries stop as if she's ceased breathing. The voice comes through the darkness again, this time a little more than a whisper.

"Is someone there? What are you doing here?"

"Oh no," June whispers into Selma's ear, "that sounds like Robert. What's he doing here? We can't let him find us together. Let's get out of here right now, before he walks in on us. If we stay in the shadows, maybe he won't see us. Come on, we'll go to my house."

Robert is following the creek bank as he nears the willow. The women must hide within a few yards of him, and let him get past before they can go on. They stoop down to the ground and make themselves as small as possible as Robert feels his way along, not thirty feet away. They keep their faces down and covered with Selma's shawl. They hold their breath and remain absolutely still. If he looks to the right he will surely see them. Once he gets far enough past, with his back toward them, they can steal away without being noticed. The next sixty seconds are vital to their secrecy.

When the young Mr. Anderson gets as close to them as he can before he starts moving away, he stops.

"That smells like perfume, must be blossoms around here close." He tells himself, and continues toward the willow. He sneaks up to the fence, crouching low, carefully placing each foot as he moves.

"I could swear I heard crying over here. I've heard stories about how quiet can make a person hear things that aren't there, but this is a first for me." He leans on the fence with both hands, his arms out straight, and listens. Nothing.

The two women slip away in the darkness, headed home.

"All I do now is wait here. They can't be all that far behind me. He thinks and looks down between his arms at the ground. A white patch catches his eye. He bends down and picks it up, noticing it's a woman's hanky. The fragrance emitting from it causes him to raise it to his nose. "This is what I smelled a minute ago," he utters, then pulls it away from his face and flattens it out trying to determine the initials at one corner. It's nearly impossible to read in the dark, but the letters are a good size and block in nature. "SH, hmmmm, SH . . . I wonder whose this is."

The fleeing women reach the bank of the creek and are moving along at a good pace until Selma stops and catches June's hand.

"Someone's coming," she murmurs, at the same time pulling her friend down over the creek bank. "Lie down, and don't move," she orders, and flattens herself to the ground.

Fewer than ten seconds pass when the group led by John passes not more than three feet from their heads. They can feel the wind off the passing feet.

"That was too close," Selma says after they move away. "Wasn't that John leading those black people. They must be going to meet Robert."

"I've always known that John has been aiding runaway slaves. He's been doing it for years, but we've never talked about it," June realizes the truth.

"Yes, I know, the same is true for us. He's never brought it up, and Lord knows I'll never mention it. He's probably out here somewhere as well," Mrs. Housler adds.

"Let's keep moving," June insists. "I won't feel safe until we get home."

Since they're already down the bank next to the creek, they wade the water, climb up the other side, and head for the Anderson home.

They're now out in the open in a rolling meadow. There is nowhere to hide, nothing to crouch behind, or shadows to give them cover. They pick up their pace, and walk silently side by side. Nerves are settling down after they've walked a few hundred yards, when June says.

"I think we're going to make it. It's not far now."

"I don't know, June, I just saw something drop down over that rise ahead of us. We'd better get out of here."

"What was it?" June is frantic again.

"I'm not sure, but I believe it was more than one person. It's probably Charles with another group of runaways. We need to move, and move fast. Where shall we go? There's nowhere to hide here," Selma surmises excitedly.

June's mind races as she looks at their options, "The only place I can think of is our guesthouse. If we can get there, we can wait an hour, and then go home. What do you think?"

"I think we have no other choice. We have to move now. Run, I'll follow you!"

Chapter Ten

In the front upstairs bedroom of the Andersons' guesthouse, Randall is busy trying to open a wooden box he found sitting in the corner. He's moved the lamp from the dresser and has it setting on the floor, close to his work. He doesn't notice that his dog Queenie has left the bedroom, and disappeared into the darkness of the hallway.

"This box is locked up real good," he says out loud. "Maybe I can pry the hinges loose. But if I do that, then they'll know it. The bottom . . . if I turn it over, I can knock the bottom up inside, and no one will be able to see it when I'm done. I need something to hit it with."

He's struggling at the task when Queenie bounds into the room, prancing and whining. She bounces up and down, back and forth, her toenails clattering, wanting his attention.

"Quiet, Queenie, you'll wake the dead," his voice echoes in the darkness. "What's wrong?"

The dog prances to the doorway and back, whining.

"Someone down there? Someone's coming I'll bet!"

He picks up the lamp and snuffs the flame with a quick puff of his breath. The room goes dark as if the flame consumed the light as it died. Queenie stops her antics and sits down against his leg.

"Good girl," he says. "Let's be real quiet for a minute and see what's going on."

He creeps through the blackness to the window. It's a bit lighter outside, but he sees nothing out of the ordinary. However, he knows not to ignore the dog's warning.

"Come on," he whispers. "Let's go downstairs and be sure no one's out there."

Together, they feel their way through the dark hallway to the stairs, then follow the banister to the first floor.

"I know I saw a light up there in that window on the second floor." Selma, a bit short of breath from running, swears to June as they approach the guesthouse.

"I don't see a thing," she replies.

"It went out, but I know I saw it. What're we going to do now? Will this nightmare never end? It's been one thing right after another. We're going to get caught and have some explaining to do." Selma's voice is subdued, but her inflection let's June know she's strongly apprehensive and weary.

"Pull yourself together. We're not going to get caught," she declares.

"Now, let's use our heads. We can't go back home right now. John and Charles are meandering around with I don't know how many sets of eyes and ears. We stand a better chance of hiding in the house and waiting for daylight if we have to. I didn't see a light in there, and there isn't a sign of one now. You must have imagined it. No wonder either, with all that's happened to you today. Can you see my reasoning here? I think we stand a better chance of not being seen if we go into the house and stay there, at least for a while." John's wife is adamant.

"What if somebody's in there? What if I'm right about the light and somebody's in there? What then?" Honest fear shows through the leery woman's voice.

"Well, if someone is in there, they probably won't want to meet us any more than we want to meet them. If we go just inside the front door, we can get out if we see or hear anything at all."

"No. I have a feeling that someone's waiting on us just inside the door."

"Okay then, you wait on the front porch, and I'll go in the back door to let you in. That way you'll know it's safe. How's that?"

"I don't think we should split up. What if something happens to you?"

"Listen to me." Mrs. Anderson's tone suggests she might as well do as she's told. "Nothing is going to happen to me. There's no one in there. You wait on the front porch, I'll circle around and go through the back door. It'll take me a little longer, so don't get in a panic. Now let's go."

June starts trotting toward the back of the house. Selma stands still for a few seconds, then reluctantly heads for the front porch.

Randall peers through the downstairs windows from inside the house. He moves from one window to the next, attempting to prove to himself that there's no one out there.

So far, so good. He's detected no movement at all. He's about to brush off Queenie's warning, when he hears the boards creak outside the front door. Frozen in his position in the center of the room, he thinks he hears footsteps moving toward the door. He has to find out who it is for sure. He moves to a window on his left of the door, his heart thumps in his throat. Queenie stays close to his leg making no noise except that of her toenails on the floor and the opening and closing her mouth when she pants. He puts his face against the glass pane to be in a position to see through.

"Uh! Oh! It's Miss Selma. What's she doing here? Is she with my parents out here looking for me? I can't let her catch me; I better slip out the back door and go on home. Come on, Queenie, let's get out of here right now," he whispers so softly he can barely hear himself.

He makes his way through the dark shadows past the stairway, then to the doorway into the kitchen. The sound of the knob turning on the back door causes him to freeze in his tracks again. Someone's coming through the back door into the kitchen!

"I'm trapped!" The two words scream through his mind. "I have to hide!"

It takes only a few seconds to sense and eliminate his options.

"If I go upstairs, there's no way out. I'll be trapped up there. There's no good place to hide down here. The only place is the cellar, if I can make it before they catch me." He turns and runs for the trap door, Queenie right behind him.

"It has to be here!" He frantically searches on his hands and knees, trying to find the ring used to pull the door up from the floor.

Whoever it is, is in the kitchen and headed his way.

"It must be under this rug!" Time's running out, footsteps are headed his way.

"Here it is!" He pulls the trap door open at the same time he slides the small rug across the floor with a fling, then grabs Queenie by the loose skin on the back of her neck, and with some difficulty throws her down through the opening. He follows instantly and closes the door down over his head. He's amazed that except for the thud when she lands on the cellar floor, the dog makes no sound at all. And if not for the rug folding over on itself as he threw it, there's no trace of them being there. His heart feels like it's going to jump out of his chest, pounding, pumping. He tries to regulate his breathing to keep from being discovered. His dog accepts everything very well as long as she can keep herself brushed up against his leg.

It's easy for him to hear the sounds from upstairs. Footsteps cross the room to the front door, then the door opens, and another person enters. They walk together to the center of the room.

"See, there's no one here. We'd better not light a lamp. A light can be seen for miles on a night like this. Let's make ourselves comfortable and sit in the dark. We can talk without fear of being overheard or interrupted. We'll wait an hour, then go to my house. I want you to spend the night there with us."

"I know that voice, it's Mrs. Anderson. They must have everybody out looking for me. I'm in big trouble again. I swear Lord, if I can get out of this, I'll never do anything wrong again." Randall's words to himself are not at all consoling.

He sits on the third step down of the ladder, his head almost touching the joists of the upstairs floor. Queenie sits on the floor at the bottom, looking up at him with her ears raised, as if expecting an order.

"Thank you, June, I don't want to be alone," Selma responds.

"Good, then it's settled. Let's sit here on the sofa and rest a bit. That run over here has all but worn me out. How about you?" Her friend's idle conversation isn't what Selma wants to hear.

"Charles hates me, you know," she begins. "He hates me because I'm black. We haven't been man and wife since before the evening John caught you and me together. All this time, I thought he was still upset over that. But, tonight he as much as told me, it's because I'm black. I don't know what to do. I can't change my color to please him.

"At the same time, I'm tortured with loneliness. I never see anyone, except Jacob and Alberta Mae. They're wonderful people and I love them, but I need my husband and a few friends. And I think mostly, I feel useless. No one needs me for anything. My life is counting for nothing."

Randall is hearing everything. He knows the words, but isn't able to feel the emotion in their meanings. Carefully, he steps down the ladder to the floor. The air in the cellar is musty and damp, aiding the cool of the night to settle into a person's bones. The window allows a small amount of light during the day. At night, however, it seems to be part of the wall. He's unable to determine where anything is setting, forcing him to sit on the floor next to the ladder. He knows if he starts feeling around, he will, more than likely, knock something over. If he lit a lantern the light would surely show through the window and give him away. Out of choices, he sits, listens, and waits.

"If I had children of my own," Selma continues, "I'd be busy with them. Oh, how I would love that, a child of my own. Charles has been against it from the start of our lives together. Now I fully understand why. He doesn't want a half-breed.

"Do you see what I mean, June." Selma's meaning was a statement, not a question requiring an answer.

"Charles will be better off without me. He can start over, maybe with a younger woman, and have a child or two. As long as I'm around, both of us are destined to be miserable. If I don't do away with myself, he probably will in time."

"Now you hush that kind of talk. You're going to do no such thing, and Charles would never think of hurting you that way," June orders in a strong firm feminine voice.

"A lot of people need and depend on you. I know you're not able to see it right now, but the world wouldn't be the same without you—" She barely gets the last words off her tongue, when—

Queenie lets out two loud barks, waits a few seconds, and follows with two more.

"There's a dog around here, really close," June exclaims and jumps to her feet. "Someone's here, or real close by. You check out front, I'll check the back!"

Selma dashes to the front window, while June runs through the kitchen. She's still looking through the kitchen window when Selma appears behind her.

"There's a lot of people standing out front. I can't tell for sure, but I think it's either John or Charles, and a dozen or so Negroes. I heard him say he's sending one of them around here to see if it's clear, they're coming inside. They've caught us." Her subdued voice is tense and shrill.

"Not yet, they haven't," June insists defiantly. "There's a cellar under the living room. Get moving, you're coming with me."

Randall is standing at the foot of the ladder, listening to the running footsteps and low voices, not able to make out what's happening upstairs. He's looking straight up when the trap door flies open, allowing a gush of air into the cellar.

Although he can't see them, he knows the two women are coming down the ladder. With no time to do otherwise, he grabs his dog by a front leg and pulls her with him across the damp dirt floor to a place he believes is a corner of the room. He crouches down with Queenie in front of him and waits in the dark.

Immediately, a person starts descending the ladder. The rustle of a dress and petticoat, along with a wisp of perfume sent throughout the cellar by the air movement from the open door, lets him know it's one of the women. As soon as he hears her feet hit the dirt floor, the second person starts down. This time the trap door is closed. It's pitch dark, but he visualizes the second person stepping off the ladder. They both stand there, motionless, breathing heavily, waiting to see if they've been noticed.

The tension is broken by the sound of the front door opening, then swinging back to bump against the wall. The noise echoes through the cellar, stirring fear in the guts of the three souls hiding there. Heavy footsteps stop as the door closes, then proceed across the room into the kitchen. The back door opens, and a lot of people enter.

There's no movement, barely any breathing, in the cellar.

"Go into the room over there. There's a chest in the corner with some blankets in it. Drape them over the windows, then we can get some light going," A voice resonates, filling the house.

Selma, June, and Randall all recognize the colonel.

Footsteps move to the living room. After a bit of scoffing around, all hear: "We can't find a chest in here. Where is it?"

"There used to be, someone must have moved it. Go upstairs and get the blankets off the beds. Might as well cover the windows up there while you're at it. See if you can find a lamp or two," Charles reacts to the adversity.

Fast footsteps resound from everywhere it seems. A few minutes pass as blankets are put over all the windows of the house.

"They're all covered, colonel, sir." A voice not heard before relates. "We found all these lamps, too."

"Let me have one of them," Mr. Housler instructs.

Thirty seconds pass.

"There, now we can see. There's some matches over there by the stove. Get the rest of the lamps going.

"You, women, there's supplies in that cupboard. We can't chance a fire, but we'll make do. There should be bread, cheese, some fruit, and maybe some raw vegetables. Get everybody fed. The rest of our group will be here before we know it. Go on now, get busy, there's a lot to be done. You'll all stay here until tomorrow, then we'll all move on."

At this point, Selma is convinced they will never survive the night.

"They're not leaving until tomorrow," she says with no more volume than that of her breath escaping. "I told you we shouldn't come in here. I told you this would happen. What are we going to do now? I want out of here. This place gives me the creeps."

"Be quiet and let me think," June's whispered voice is terse and irritated. "Let's sit down right here and let me think."

"This floor is nothing but mud. I'll ruin this dress if I sit down."

"You heard me, Selma, sit down and be quiet, and I mean it!" The pressure is being felt by Mrs. Anderson; she doesn't need the aggravation.

They both stoop down, and then, sit on the floor.

"There has to be another way out of here," she puzzles. "If we wait until daylight, we'll be able to see. I'm sure we'll find it then."

"And that's supposed to make me feel better?" Selma challenges. "You were sure we'd be safe if we came in here in the first place."

In a flash, Selma's on her feet, climbing the ladder. June jumps up, grabs her by the waist, and pulls her to a stop just before she pushes the trap door open.

"What in the world are you doing now?" she asks angrily, "You'll give us away."

Selma is obviously overwhelmed and afraid. She's shaking all over and trying to get loose from June's ever tightening grip.

"Settle yourself down. What's the matter?"

"There's something down here with us," the quivering woman complains as she squirms to get loose. "It just licked me, I felt it's hot breath on my arm."

With that, she gives another lurch toward the trap door and freedom.

Randall jerks when Selma makes her move to the ladder. Not until then did he realize that Queenie has slipped away in the dark.

He almost blurts out, "It's only Queenie." But he just can't do it. Not yet. He knows it's only a matter of a few minutes before they discover him, and this would be a good a time to speak up. But he just can't do it.

Before June can respond, she sucks in a deep breath that shatters the silence of the cellar, and unintentionally tightens her grip on Selma with the force of fear.

"You're hurting me, let me go! I'm getting out of here!" Selma isn't whispering anymore.

"Stop it! Calm yourself. You're right about something being down here. It just brushed by my leg! It's big, too! I can't see anything! I have no idea what it is, but it's big, I can tell you that!"

"What'll we do?" The voice of the woman on the ladder tells the other two cellar dwellers, she's ready to scream.

Young Mr. Stoker knows he can't wait any longer, but instead of saying, "It's me, Randall, and Queenie," he strikes his remaining match. It bursts into light, immediately illuminating the room enough for all to see each other and Queenie.

The women are so surprised, his first vision of them is their eyes, as big as saucers, straining to see at the sudden flood of light. Their eyes, along with their gaping mouths, give their faces a gaunt look normally reserved for the dead.

With just enough time for their eyes to focus, they say in unison, "Who's there? Randall, is that you?"

He's already standing and moving closer to the women. They aren't sure what's happening and don't move a muscle. The match stem is getting shorter and shorter.

"I'm sorry Queenie scared you," he says. "She won't hurt you, she just wants attention, that's all."

"What are you doing here?" Selma asks sternly with a shaky voice, forgetting to whisper.

"I just came over here to see what I could find out about Sheree. I know she's not in that box in the ground. How come you're here?" he asks innocently, since he knows now they aren't after him.

"It's a long story. Is there another way out of here, do you know?" June doesn't want to explain.

"Yes, ma'am, there is. Who's that upstairs? Sounds like an awful lot of people. Are they all looking for me?" He asks, as the match sears his fingers forcing him to drop it. Darkness folds in on them again.

"Darn, that was my last match. I saw a lantern hanging on the ceiling in back of the ladder, the other time I was here. If I had another match, I could fire it up . . . if you want me to," he adds.

"Can you get us out of here?" June insists, ignoring his words.

"There's a tunnel behind that shelf." He points as if the women can see him.

"But I'm not going in there again. There's something living in there. I heard it before, and it walked right over my hand when I was in there."

"I'm not going to crawl through any tunnel," Selma draws the line. "I've had my fill of excitement for one day. I say we give up and hope for the best."

"The both of you can stay here if you want to, I'm not. If I can find my way through that tunnel, I'm going. I have some matches. You can come with me, or not, it's up to you." These words don't surprise Selma. She knows her friend and expects no less.

"Perhaps I'll reconsider," she says. "If we can have some light to see by, and if he leads us, I'll go."

"We have to take the chance and light the lantern. We need to see to uncover the tunnel, and for sure we'll need it once we get in there. Do you all agree?"

Two yeses.

June strikes a match, locates the lantern, raises the wick, a touch of the flame, and the cellar is dimly illuminated. The shadows of all three run across the floor, bend and go up the wall. Queenie is walking, tail wagging, around and between them.

"Is it behind that shelf there?" she points.

"Yes, we can slide it out from the wall on this end," he replies as he walks to the shelf and puts his hand on it.

"June, you steady it while we slide it away from the wall," Selma directs.

Together they move the shelf to expose the door. Randall drops to his knees and pulls it toward him. It scrapes the floor, but opens silently. June bends at the waist, holds the lantern just inside the entrance, and peers into the hole in the wall.

"It's quite small isn't it?" she comments as Queenie walks to the opening and sniffs the floor. "How did you know this was here?"

"No time for that now," Selma interjects. "It's a long story. We need to get moving while we can. Who's going first?"

"Not me," the boy is quick to inform all. "I'm telling you there's something in there."

"I'll go first, but just remember, I'll be the first one out on the other end too," June's voice is challenging, but goes unanswered.

"You follow me, Randall, since you know the way, and Selma, you and the dog after him. Don't forget to shut the door after you get in there with us. Ready? Here we go," June drops to her knees and begins crawling into the tunnel, her right arm in the air with the lantern in her hand.

The Stoker lad follows as soon as there's enough room, as does Queenie, and then Selma, who squeezes around to close the door behind her.

The tunnel door no sooner closes than a knock resounds from the back door of the house. Everyone upstairs freezes in place.

"Blow out the lights," the colonel whispers loudly.

"Colonel . . . it's me, John," his voice is heard through the door.

With the lights out, Charles opens the door. John, Robert, and the twelve men and women walk into the kitchen without speaking.

"What's going on? Why do you have the windows covered here and have a light in the cellar?"

"Close the door and put that blanket back up, and I'll tell you. Fire up the lights everybody." His voice is loud enough for those upstairs to hear but goes unheard in the tunnel.

"Well?" John pursues.

"Now, don't let this upset to you." Selma's husband says under his breath as he moves close to his two friends, "Selma and June are in the cellar."

"What?" John and Robert say at the same time.

"Keep your voices down," he cautions. "I don't know why they're here or what they are doing, but I think we surprised them, and they hid in the cellar. They've been making one awful commotion down there. If we were Indians, we'd have them both scalped by now." He chuckles. "I thought I'd wait until you got here, then decide what we should do."

"How do you know it's them?" Robert asks.

"I heard their voices plain as day. No mistake, it's them all right."

"We're a little early, I know, but we decided not to wait," John explains.

"Robert said he heard crying coming from up close to the willow when he got there. He didn't see anybody, but he smelled what he thinks is perfume on a handkerchief he found at the foot of the tree. Show it to him, son."

He hands the kerchief to the colonel. "See, the initials here in the corner, SH."

"This is Selma's," he confirms. "What in the world are those two women up to tonight? Are they keeping an eye on us do you suppose?"

"Let's get them up here and find out. We can't let that light burn down there. Someone could see it," John starts for the living room, with Charles and Robert close behind.

Mr. Anderson, the elder, takes the ring of the door in the floor with his first two fingers of his right hand, gives a tug, and pulls it up without a sound. He lays it all the way back on its hinges on the floor, and peers down into the dark cellar.

"Come on up, ladies, we know you're down there."

No response.

"No sense in hiding anymore. You might as well come on up, you can't go anywhere," Colonel Housler gives it a try.

No sound of any activity from the gloom below.

"Are you going to make me come down there and get you?" June's husband shows some irritation in his voice.

There is no response.

"Hand me a lamp. I'm going down."

John carefully sets the lamp on the edge of the opening, turns his back, and puts his left foot through the hole in the floor. After locating the top step of the ladder, he lowers himself down. After taking a moment to get his balance, he picks up the lamp in his left hand, and carefully descends into the cellar. Robert and the colonel watch the shadows change on the floor as he walks around the confines with the lantern held high.

"They're not here now," he says loudly. "The shelf is pulled away from the wall again. I put it back in place the other day when I was here. They must be in the tunnel."

"Tunnel, what tunnel?" This isn't the first surprise for Robert tonight, and he thinks, probably, not the last.

The movement is not easy for June crawling in such a confined space using only her one hand, supporting the lantern with the other. The floor is a little wet and the walls damp.

The light exposes roots on the walls and ceiling that Randall couldn't see when he was here before. Some hang down several inches, causing constantly changing strange shadows from the lantern's light. The sounds, which are muffled by the uneven walls and ceiling, are those of hands and knees on the dirt floor, the movement of clothes, some heavy breathing, and the occasional "Oooohhhhhh" from Selma, when she puts her hand down into a small pool of slime. They are all discovering the large amount of fumes given off by an oil burning lamp.

"Ssshhhhh!" June commands. Everybody freezes.

"Did you hear that? Listen!"

The fading pitter patter of moving feet is heard by all.

"That's it!" Randall excitedly announces. "I told you, there's something in here."

"What is it? Did you see it?" Selma asks.

"No, I didn't have a light, and I wasn't for staying around to find out anyhow. Noise doesn't carry in here, so, whatever it is, it's not all that far away." It's apparent from his tone, he has no interest in any attempt to confront the unknown in this tunnel.

The leader of the group speaks up with determination. "Well, it was running from us, so I don't think it'll be any bother. Let's keep going."

Selma's first thoughts are as one might think.

"I'm so glad I'm way back here. I've got June, Randall, and Queenie, ahead of me to fight whatever it is. This is strange, but I feel alive in an odd sort of way. I haven't felt this alive in years."

She takes notice that Queenie has her nose up sniffing the air.

While there's plenty of room to crawl through the tunnel, it's still easy to bump the sides with your shoulders, or your head on the ceiling. They crumble a little when the occasional collision occurs, causing the dirt to fall to the floor or down onto their heads and backs. Some of it finds its way down their necks, under their clothing, and bounces around on their skin. The sound of the crumbling dirt gives them a feeling of insecurity. If the tunnel roof collapses, nobody will attempt to dig them out. No one knows they're there.

June stops briefly to change hands with the lantern.

"How did I let my life bring me to this? I can't believe I'm crawling through a tunnel. When I get out of here, I'm going to take control of my life. This is ridiculous." She moves forward with more determination than ever.

Randall is blindly following June. Stopping when she stops, moving when she moves. What else can he do? His thoughts, however, are not on this trip through this tunnel. He's more concerned about his life when he gets out of here.

"I'm sure going to be in a lot of trouble. There won't be any explaining, Miss Selma and Miss Anderson will see to that. I bet I get a big whipping for this. I don't know which is worse, being in here, or getting out there."

June stops. "We have another tunnel going off here. Which way do we go?"

"To your left, ma'am. The right leads to the well, and there's no way to get out of there. I don't know where the left one comes out because I didn't go that way, but turn to your left anyhow," the boy behind her recommends.

She turns left and the others follow. As soon as Selma passes the opening on her right, a thought passes through her mind. I wonder where that thing we heard went? If it went in there, toward the well, then it'll be behind me. I can't even see behind me. I don't like this. Maybe I can get Queenie behind me. I'm going to try."

Try as she does, there isn't enough room for her to get past the dog. Queenie is too big and heavy for Selma to force her to do anything. More so, since, she doesn't understand what the woman behind her is trying to do.

Randall thinks Queenie is bothering Mrs. Housler, so he tries to keep the dog closer to him.

"I give up," Selma says out loud, "I'm stuck where I am. That thing will just have to kill me and drag me off somewhere."

While her mind is occupied elsewhere, she forgets the difficulty of crawling with her knees fighting the long dress she wears.

"I may not have much of a life, but I'm not going to be left in here to die. I'm getting out of here if it's the last thing I do."

Three or four minutes pass in silence as they continue, plodding on their hands and knees, making their way through the dank hole in the ground.

June stops.

"Eyes are glaring at me from the lights reflection!" she says with a lot of concern.

Selma and Randall both bob and weave to see around their leader.

Queenie is immediately excited, jumping, yelping, trying to get past Randall. Finally, she gets her front feet on his back and walks on him as he collapses to the floor. June is the next blocking the collie's way, but not for long. Gaining momentum, she hits the woman with a force causing her to fall flat. The lantern flies out of her hand, lands upside down, allowing oil to flood from its canister, which douses the light.

The dog stomps right over her and slips into the unknown. It's so dark, you can't see your finger if you poke it in your eye.

The collie runs for some distance, then stops. The trio hears a low growling, and a medium pitched howling, that sounds like a human baby, then a noisy, fierce fight.

They remain still and listen.

Lots of growling with clenched teeth, yelps of pain, and the sound of ripping flesh, fill the tunnel. The weight of the animals' bodies are easily heard as they slam into the walls and scuffle on the floor. After a few minutes, silence. Several more minutes pass, then it starts all over again, with more fury than the first time. A loud painful sounding yelp ends the battle. Then silence seems to go on forever.

June is still lying on the floor in the same position, Randall is up on his hands and knees, straining to see through the darkness, and Selma is sitting, curled up in a ball, with her arms around her bent legs, her head lying on her knees.

No one moves.

The sound of feet on the dirt floor starts off faint, almost unheard, and begin to get closer—louder. Not running, but walking, staggering.

June can think of only one thing! The lantern! Light! Fire! She knows she has to get the lantern lit fast! First she has to find it. She pats the floor, rubbing her hands around in circles, hoping to touch it!

The steps are getting closer! Louder!

None of the three is sure if it's Queenie, or the thing! They have nothing to fight it with! They can't run! All they can do is wait!

"I have it!" she yells. "If I can get it lit!" She frantically searches her pants pockets for the matches! The other two hear the sound of a match being struck on the metal of the lantern, then a welcome explosion of light. And a lot of light it is, because the spilled oil on the outside of the lantern ignites. She raises the chimney to get to the wick, down goes the glass, then the fire on the sides dwindles and fades.

She positions herself to face the onslaught of whatever it is, holding the lantern as high as possible. She can see glowing eyes just a few seconds before the bloody face of Queenie appears. She's hobbling on three legs, holding her left front paw up off the floor. Other than that, she appears to be okay.

"Good girl, good job, Queenie. You showed him. You're a hero, you saved us."

The injured dog lies down on the floor in front of June and begins licking her injured paw. The relieved woman holds the lantern close and looks at the bloody places on the dogs head and face.

"I don't see anything too serious. Just several small cuts. She's got blood all in her mouth though. Maybe she bit her tongue," she reports.

"Or maybe it belongs to that thing, whatever it was," Randall offers.

"We should get moving." The woman in front informs the other two. "Most of the oil drained out of this lantern, and I don't know how much longer it'll last. So, let's go."

The rest of the trip through the tunnel is uneventful. They never see a sign of the animal Queenie fought, just some clumps of fur and blood at the battlefield. There were several smaller holes in the wall beyond the bloody scene, the mystery animal probably drug itself away through one of them.

After what seems like a lifetime, they arrive at the end of the tunnel. A ladder leans against the front wall. A wooden floor shows itself eight or nine feet above.

"I wonder where we are, and what's going to be up there when I open that door?" June's feelings are understood and felt by Selma and Randall. Queenie is lying on the floor licking her injured paw.

"Well, here goes." Mrs. Anderson rises, and starts up the ladder.

The lantern, she has set on the floor, goes out. No one says a word.

She feels her way up until her outstretched arm lets her hand touch the door.

"I'm opening it now. Wish me luck," she whispers.

One more step up and she's able to push the door open. It makes a scratchy, rusty, sound, and lies back on the floor with a solid thud. One more step up, then her next one will put her head and shoulders above the opening.

Just as she is ready to make the final push with her leg, two sets of hands grab under her arms and pull her straight up and out. She screams loud and long, and starts swinging her arms wildly, kicking her legs in the air.

"Quiet, Mama, it's us," Robert assures her. "Daddy and the colonel are right here."

"Dammit, you almost scared me to death. Do you know that!" she yells as she attempts to compose herself.

The men release her to stand unassisted.

"Sorry, honey, we didn't think," John apologizes.

"Come on up, Selma, the colonel is here with us."

The next one on the ladder to show himself is Randall.

"Randall?" the colonel questions. "I didn't know you were with them."

"Queenie's here, too, sir. She's hurt. She had a fight with some animal down there. She saved us." His words are spoken respectively and timidly.

"Well, come on up out of there, we'll get her. Selma, can you get her started up the ladder, I think I can pick her up with one hand and pull her out."

She gets the dog to the ladder, and lifts her front paws up as high as she can.

"I'll hold your legs." Mr. Housler says as John lies on the floor and begins to reach down through the hole. "Here, Robert, give me a hand."

John lets his body slide down until he's able to get a good handful of the skin on the back of the dog's neck with his right hand.

"When I give the word, you two pull me up. Ready. Pull."

He pulls hard on the dog as he comes up and is able to get his left arm under the dog's front legs. This allows him to turn her over on her back to slide her up the ladder and over the edge of the floor.

As soon as he releases her, she's on her feet shaking herself violently.

Next to appear with her head above the floor is Selma. The colonel and Robert lift her out as they did June.

"Where are we?" she asks.

"You're in the barn. What are the three of you doing here, and what in the world possessed you to crawl through the tunnel?" Two questions the women wish they didn't have to answer.

June looks at Selma, and Selma at June, stalling for an answer. It would be obvious except it's dark in the barn, so no one sees.

"How did you know we were in the tunnel?" June asks, hoping to dodge John's questions.

The colonel speaks up, letting the women off the hook for the moment.

"You were making so much noise, it was impossible to ignore the fact that you were in the cellar. What are you doing out here tonight, Randall? Do your folks know you're here?"

"No, sir, they don't." His reply is no surprise to anyone. He conveniently skips the first question.

"What's going on with you people?" Robert demands. "Are all of you afraid to answer a question? It's as if you're strangers to each other. Aren't we all close friends? Are there more secrets I don't know about?"

Silence. Although none of the adults like Robert's blunt, tactless, onslaught, they all realize he's absolutely correct. The four of them each have reasons and agendas of their own.

Young Mr. Stoker speaks first.

"I'm going on home. Come on, Queenie." He holds his breath and walks toward the barn door. Fear is with him as he moves. He expects a voice will stop him and trouble begin. Out through the door and into the night air, he's on his way.

The atmosphere hasn't changed in the barn. It's as if the first one to say anything will be pounced upon by the others. Finally, John speaks.

"Robert, why don't you escort your mother and Mrs. Housler back to our house. The colonel and I need to get our group settled for the night. We'll be along shortly."

"Good idea, Daddy, I'll be glad to."

June and Selma have nothing to add, so they move toward the barn door.

"I'll see you at the house later then," Robert comments as he follows the women.

They walk, with Robert fifteen steps behind, past the guesthouse, through the small front yard, to the wagon road leading to the Andersons' home.

Chapter Eleven

"Here it is, Thursday night already. I've been here for three days now. There's no time to do anything except for what they tell me. Eagle sat beside me today at dinner. I know I shouldn't trust anybody, but he's really nice. I think I like him. He said someone would come to my room late at night Saturday, eleven o'clock or later, to take me to a secret meeting. They will come to my door and knock twice, then once. He told me the people at the meeting will answer all my questions about this place, and that I shouldn't be afraid, he'll be there too. I asked him what will happen if we get caught. He said not to worry, we won't. The building monitors go to bed at ten thirty every night.

"He told me it's important, and to be ready to go when they get here. No shoes, though, just stocking feet. He said not to say anything about it to anybody. Not to worry. He's the first person to talk to me since I arrived here, except for the instructors, and Sparrow, when he brought me to my first room.

"Our instructor said we'll begin studying languages, world geography, world history, world culture, physics, geometry, self-containment, and self-confidence. I've never heard of the last two. Of course, we'll still be working on our sports and such. I don't know when we'll have time to do it all.

"I wonder what would happen to me if I'm not able to keep up with the others. Hey, that might be my way out of here. If I have a terrible time learning, maybe they won't want me any more and let me go. We'll see.

"I'd better get to sleep. Morning comes early around here."

She wiggles under her blanket and closes her eyes.

June and Selma walk along the wagon road toward the Andersons' home. Robert is trailing them by eight or ten steps.

"I think we did a good job of taking control of things back there in the barn, don't you?" June asks Selma.

"Oh my, yes, I expected the worst. I suppose it will all catch up to us later this evening. But you know, I believe I was looking for a good fight. I think I wanted one," Selma acknowledges.

"It's all about control, my girl, control and leverage," Robert hears his mother's sassy voice.

"These men think they have it all over us, but if you think about it you'll realize that at the end, we always get things our way. That was proven again back there a few minutes ago. If we had dropped to our knees begging for forgiveness, they would have had the control. We didn't and they didn't."

"Are you telling me that we aren't going to answer to them at all for getting caught out together tonight?" Mrs. Housler asks.

"It's either that or put up with the paddling and frowning they'll put us through later. Frankly, I think it's time for us to stand our ground." His mama's words slam into Robert's ears.

"Have they forgotten I'm back here?" he thinks. "I can hear every word they say. What are they up to now? Are they just playing with me, or are they serious? Is this how women are when they're alone together? And what are they doing out together tonight?"

Selma comments break Robert's thoughts. "I believe I'll go home instead of staying the night with you."

"Now, Selma," her friend begins.

"Hear me out before you get all worked up," she cuts her off. "I believe I rediscovered myself back there in that tunnel. The thing missing everywhere in my life is spice. There is never much new, always the same things day after day after day. I've felt alive tonight for the first time in years. I vowed to myself back there, if I survived that tunnel, I would change. I'm going to look for the life I want. I'm going to stir things up and see what floats. I'm going to be a different woman."

"What about all that talk a while ago? I can't let you go off by yourself. What if that mood comes back over you again? I'll feel better if I know for sure that you're okay. I can't let you hurt yourself," June pleads. "Besides, you're not going home by yourself in the dark. And remember too, John and the colonel will be along shortly."

"I'm over that mood for good. I know now if I'm going to have any sort of life, I must arrange it myself. I want some time alone to think about that before Charles and I speak again. He can come on home from your house. I'll be ready for him when he gets there." She seems to have it all figured out. Her voice and manner are sure, smooth, and confident. This woman June hasn't seen since long before for that night they were caught together.

"Robert can accompany me home after we drop you off. You don't mind, do you Robert? You can bring me up to date with all that's happened to you over the years," Selma continues with a hint of coyness in her manner and voice.

Both women look to Robert for an answer.

His mind churns as he weighs and considers his options. A sense of pressure is upon him that has a new feel about it. Any other time he would simply agree, but now it's different, his daddy and the colonel are involved. If he goes with Mrs. Housler, is he choosing the side of the women? In fact, shouldn't he speak up to let both of these women know he's a man, and should be considered that way? He's not a little boy any more, a boy to be directed around at the whim of an adult female. His father and the colonel are expecting their wives to be together at the Anderson home. It's his decision, and once made, he'll stick by it.

"Yes, ma'am, I guess I could do that. If it's okay with Mama," he quietly replies.

"Did I just say that? My goose is really cooked now. Say no, Mama, make her stay here tonight," he prays.

Selma holds her tongue and looks at June.

Mother Anderson has picked up the 'scent of the hunt' in her friend's proposal.

"Surely she wouldn't act improperly toward Robert, a boy, barely a man. She's up to something." Thoughts flash through June's mind.

"What's going on in that mind of yours? You're acting as if you have something up your sleeve. What's going on?" she blurts.

"Why Honey, there's nothing, I'm just a little giddy, happy to have found a way to a fresh start to go on with the rest of my life." Selma sees how June is fishing for a devilish motive. "You can see that, can't you?"

"Frankly, I don't know what to think. It seems unlikely that a cure for your ailments could be so easily found. But on the other hand, I suppose you should do whatever you believe is best. I must insist, however, that you get word to me in the morning as to how you feel about it all. If I don't hear before noon, I'll be on your doorstep. Agreed?" June's voice, while sympathetic, is stern.

Young Mr. Anderson is scheming, trying to be ready with an answer for the two men back at the guesthouse. They are bound to ask him why he allowed this to happen.

"I'll just say Mrs. Housler was going home alone if I didn't go with her, so I thought I'd better." Perfect, it's the truth, and his mama will swear to it.

June stands at the edge of the front yard of her home and watches the two disappear into the darkness. She turns and walks toward the house, around to the back, onto the porch, and through the back door, her mind preoccupied.

"Ms. Anderson! Look at you! Where you been? I thought you was upstairs in your bed," Belle's loud voice of surprise startles her. She jumps and pulls back.

"Belle, I . . ."

"You're mud all over. Are you hurt? Who done this to you?" Belle is excitedly concerned.

"I'm sorry, can I tell you about it later? I want to get cleaned up before John and the colonel get here. They'll be along in a few minutes. Right now I need to get upstairs." June brushes past her housekeeper to bounce up the stairs to her bedroom.

They walk toward Der Bote in silence for a few minutes. There's no road directly between the farms, so, the surface of the ground is uneven with rocks, stones, and clumps of grass, making the footing a little doubtful. Selma, on Robert's right, pushes her hand between his upper arm and side.

"You don't mind if I steady myself with your arm, do you?"

He doesn't answer, just keeps walking. He has to admit to himself, it does feel good to have a woman on his arm.

"I imagine you have had any number of girlfriends at school, being away and all. Am I right?" she assumingly asks.

"Not really, Mrs. Housler," he replies nervously.

"Please, call me Selma."

"Yes, ma'am."

"I don't understand why some bright young woman hasn't chased you all over the school up there—a fine, handsome man like you," her words are tuned in a teasing manner.

"There're not all that many females around the school," his words are a little stiff. "I didn't have the time anyhow."

"Oh I see. Have you been to bed with a woman?" his mother's best friend's soft words go through his ears, down his throat, and land hard in his guts.

His voice quivers as he makes an attempt to answer, "Mrs. Housler, I don't think we should be talk—"

"My name is Selma, Robert," her steamy sexy voice cuts him off as it reaches his ears.

She stops walking, turning him toward her by keeping a firm grip on his arm. She steps forward, closing the gap between them. They are inches apart.

The young man's heart is going to leap up his throat into his mouth. He's unable to see the detail of her face, but his eyes lock on the shine of her wet lips as they move when she speaks, coming closer and closer.

"Don't you think it's time?" she whispers.

Her arms casually slide up and around his neck. He feels his reflexes weakening, making it impossible to resist. The pressure on the back of his neck from her weight pulls his shoulders and head down. She carefully, deliberately, raises up on her toes to meet his advance. Through the faint light he notices her eyes are closed, her inviting lips parted. The space between them closes—this is going to happen. It can't be stopped now. He doesn't want it to.

Instinctively aware of the softness of her body, he pulls her close. She feels small in his arms. So willing. So wonderful. Lost in the lust of the moment, he wants more. Their lips touch, barely pressing. He realizes she wants this to happen as much if not more than he does, and senses her need for him growing stronger. Never has he allowed himself to feel this way, go this far. Vaguely aware he is releasing his most guarded, private emotions, he sets himself free. Hunger for this woman consumes him.

Selma feels Robert's lips touch hers so, so . . . gently.

"Ohhooo," a low soothing voice of pleasure escapes into his ears. It feels so good to be in a man's arms. It's been in the back of her mind too long. Sensing his passion, she lets herself relax completely to their first kiss. She feels safe and secure in his arms when he effortlessly, and ever so carefully, lifts her off the ground. She allows the feeling of giving herself to him to move through her body. More, she wants more.

A little turn of her head to the side allows their noses to pass, enabling their kiss to further their craving for each other. A glowing hotbed of ecstasy pulls them closer and more deeply together.

He lowers her to the ground, and slides his left arm from under her back to the back of her neck. She pulls herself tighter to him. That's all he needs, their mouths glued together, her complete willingness. He starts caressing her body. It makes no difference that he can feel very little through the dress, petticoat, and underwear. Just knowing where his hands are sends his lust to the breaking point. Unable to hold it back, he lets his body stiffen while a deep guttural groan of pleasure escapes through his lips into Selma's mouth with slow gush of his breath.

She immediately realizes he's dumping his emotion, and kisses him harder, running her hands through his hair and around his face, until the waves of uncontrollable fiery desire subside.

Gradually, he moves his mouth from hers and rises up on his left arm.

"I'm so sorry, Selma, I'm ashamed of myself. I never thought it would be like this. I'm sorry," he whispers apologetically.

"It's okay. It's hard for you to tell, but I did the same thing," she breathes, soothing his ego.

"I can do it again," he eagerly suggests.

"No, honey, I'm afraid I let this get way out of hand. I should have never seduced you, my best friend's son. I must be out of my mind, although, I don't regret it. You are really something," she says, again for his peace of mind.

"Come on, take me home. Your mama will start wondering where you are."

They stand up, straighten their clothes, and begin walking. Robert tries to catch her hand to hold, but she starts fumbling with her bag to find a hanky. He decides not to make advances right now.

"Did you get the feeling back there, that someone was watching us?" she asks.

John and the colonel are busy making sure the group of escaping slaves is getting fed and dressed in some clean decent clothing. The large locked trunk, located in the upstairs bedroom, is full of various pieces of clothing in an assortment of sizes. The men and women are busy talking, and laughing, as they munch on the odd assortment of food, selecting the garments they need.

Since they've been on the move for what seems like forever, there has been little time to wash or mend clothing, or to take care of themselves. The only way to avoid the slave hunters is to keep moving day and night, stopping only to eat a meager meal, and rest a few minutes. They feel safe inside the house. The food is simple, but it's plentiful, and they can rest an entire night. Tomorrow morning will again bring the worry of being caught as they travel. The thought of a few more weeks of tense movement, and then a life of free men and women, keeps them going.

"Now listen up," the colonel speaks loudly, standing in the living room. "Gather around me here.

"We both would like to stay with you tonight and get to know you a little," he says motioning to John and himself. "But we have found it better if we go on our way just as if you aren't here. We don't want to know your names. We can't tell something we don't know, nor can you.

"Upstairs in the attic is a box full of arm bands. Before you leave here tomorrow, each one of you is to put one on your right arm. Everybody around here knows the colors to be those of local folks. So, it will be unlikely that anyone will question your movement. You'll leave tomorrow in small groups of two or three at a time. So, after we leave here tonight, choose up your traveling partners for the next part of your trip, and make sure your arm bands match.

"We'll be back tomorrow, shortly after daylight. We'll give you more instructions, and get started. In the meantime, keep the windows covered until you go to bed. Then take the blankets off the windows and use them to keep warm. You need to post a sentry to keep a watch for anyone moving around outside. Split it up in shifts, so everyone can get some rest. And don't go outside for any reason. Any questions?

"All right then, we'll see you first thing in the morning."

Selma and Robert have said nothing to each other during the rest of the trip to her home. His thoughts are on the events of the last few minutes, while hers are mind searching, trying to understand why she has acted this way.

His thinking soon turns toward how to further this relationship.

Her's runs to her relationship with her husband.

"We're almost there. No sense you going all the way. I can go on my own from here," she says, keeping her distance.

"I don't mind, Mrs. Housler," he reaches, catches her hand in his, and steps toward her. "A swallow of water would be real nice right now."

She's startled by his movement, but has expected some sort of further advance. Her words come void of tact and are sternly terse.

"Stop it! Nothing more is going to happen between you and me. I was out of my mind to lead you on like I did, but it stops now. I can't get involved with you, nor you me. Think about your mother and father!" she exclaims rather loudly and jerks her hand from his. "Now get out of here and go on home."

Robert stands dumbfounded. He didn't expect this. What was all that about back there? He can feel blood rush to his face in embarrassment.

Her words are mean and leave no doubt about their intent. He lets his empty hand fall to his side, and hangs his head as he turns to leave. After a few steps he turns to look back at her. Unable to see the features of her face, or the form of her body through the darkness, his memory of her in his arms is vividly fresh. The touch of her, the smell of her, her whole being is part of his mind, to be recalled as he desires.

"I respect you Mrs. Housler, but this isn't over. I know you feel the same way I do. You'll think better of this in the morning. Good night." He fades away into the night, as do the sound of his footsteps.

She watches to be sure he's gone. Satisfied, she turns toward the house.

"If only you knew the truth, young man, if only you knew."

As she enters the house through the back door, Randall and Queenie slink past in the shadows, allowing a wide spread between themselves and the house.

June is setting the last needed cup on the kitchen table, when John and the colonel appear through the back door.

"I brewed a pot of coffee. Are you interested?" she inquires. "I told Belle to go on to bed."

"Sounds good," her husband says.

She finishes filling two of the three cups and continues.

"I had Robert walk Selma on home. She's worn out. She said she'll be up waiting for you colonel."

"Well, I'm in no hurry to get home. It'll probably be mighty chilly in that house for a couple of days. We had a little spat earlier this evening. I don't suppose she mentioned it, did she?" he fishes.

"You can be sure she did." June's words come too easily through her lips. "It's none of my business, I know, but I must say, you really hurt Selma with your nasty words and insinuations. I fear for her being. I wanted her to stay with me for the night, but she wouldn't hear of it. She said she was all right when she left here, but I wouldn't count on it. She had a strange way about her. I don't know what she might do to herself. I think you should go home now, and waste no time about it. I know I'll certainly feel better if you do."

"It's worse than I thought then. Exactly what did she say?"

"I'd rather she tell you herself. I don't want to put words in her mouth. Would you like to borrow a horse? The quicker you leave the sooner you'll be home."

"I'd better go," he says as he turns to leave through the back door. Two more steps will put him on the porch. But before he can put his hand on the door, it swings open with a creak, and Robert walks into the kitchen, almost bumping against him.

His mother immediately senses something has happened. His hair is a mess of entanglement all over his head, and she notices lipstick on his cheek as well as the corner of his mouth.

She must act quickly. These two men must not see what she sees. She puts her hand on the colonel's back and encourages him through the door as he says, "Good evening to you all."

"Selma is home safe, isn't that right, Robert?" June's voice follows him out the door.

"Yes, ma'am," he automatically agrees.

In one fluid motion, she takes her son by the arm, turns him away from his daddy, and grabs a wet rag from the dish pan.

"Let me wipe that dirty, sweaty face of yours. I hope you feel better than you look," her goal is to remove the lipstick before John sees it.

"Aw, Mama, quit fussing over me. I can take care of myself," he says as he squirms and tries his best to avoid her onslaught. She accomplishes her mission.

"June, leave the boy alone," John speaks up. "Can't you see he's not in the mood for that right now?"

"All right, all right, I will. Would you like a cup of coffee, honey?" She waves her hands in surrender.

"No, I think I'm going to clean up a little and go to bed. It's been an interesting day." He feels his motives are apparent to his mother, so, he wants to get away before the questions start flying.

"I'll settle this right now," she thinks.

"Your father would like that, wouldn't you, John? Then you can start on me. Well, that's not going to happen tonight. You and I can talk tomorrow, after we sleep on it. Go on to bed, I want to talk to my son for a few minutes. I'll be up in a little while," June states and demands, testing her control of the situation.

John shakes his head in dismay.

"Damn!" he says, and gets up from his chair. He looks at them both, then proceeds to follow her instructions.

The kitchen is silent for the next few minutes as Robert sits down at the table and June pours coffee into the third cup, then puts it in front of him. She sets the pot back on the stove and sits on a chair next to him.

"Okay, now, and I want the truth. What did that woman do to you out there tonight?"

Queenie sits outside Randall's bedroom window and watches as he struggles to slide through head first into the room. He puts his hands on the wooden floor and wiggles his body from side to side, slithering, inching through the opening. At last, he's inside.

He creeps across the floor to the edge of his bed. When he pulls his shirt up over his head, a hand grabs his arm and pulls him out of the bedroom into the kitchen. With the shirt dangling from his left arm, his eyes focus on his mama and papa. There's no time to think; this is happening too fast.

"Where've you been, boy?" Alberta Mae demands.

There's not a hint of pleasantness in her voice. Her expression is a scowl. He glances at his daddy. The frown on his forehead, squinted eyes, and clenched thin lips let's him know big trouble is at hand.

"Answer your mama, boy. Where you been?" Jacob isn't fooling.

"I went over to the guesthouse to see if I could find out about Sheree," he confesses. He had to say something, and there was no time to think about it.

"How come you're all covered with mud, like you was the other day?" his mama pries.

"I was in the bedroom of the guesthouse looking around when Miss. Selma and Miss. Anderson showed up. I couldn't get out, so Queenie and I hid in the cellar. Then it was just a little bit when they was chased down in the cellar with me by a whole lot of people. Then the three of us crawled out of the cellar through the tunnel. Mr. Anderson and Mr. Colonel was right there to catch us as we was coming up into the barn. Mr. Robert was there with them, too."

"What did the colonel and Mr. Anderson have to say about all that?" Jacob continues his interrogation.

"Not much, I guess. I got out of there as quick as I could. I didn't wait around."

"Is that all there is to it? Nobody wondered what you was doing there?" Jacob's wife senses more trouble in the wind.

"No, ma'am, they didn't. But I did stop and wet my kerchief in the water trough at Mr. Anderson's house. Queenie had a fight with something in the tunnel and got cut up a little bit. I cleaned the blood off her fur. She's okay, though."

"Queenie had a fight with what in the tunnel?" Jacob's interest is piqued. "Was anyone hurt?"

"Naw! Queenie kicked its butt. She's a hero. I don't know what it was. We never got a look at it, probably a polecat, or a coon, or something. It's mighty dark in that tunnel when your light goes out."

"The only thing is, while I was wetting my kerchief, the three of them, Miss. Anderson, Miss. Selma, and Mr. Robert, showed up. I had to hide behind the trough until they left. Then Queenie and I are walking along and come up on Miss. Selma and Mr. Robert, standing, hugging, and kissing each other. They lay down on the ground and Mr. Robert got on top of her. Then they got up and came on home. I had to wait before I could get by them and I heard Miss. Selma tell him in plain certain words to go home and leave her alone." Randall is glad he has told it all. Now he awaits the punishment he knows he deserves.

Jacob and Alberta Mae can't believe their ears. The fact is, any news is rare to their ears, and it is normally of an uneventful nature. This involves people who are important in their lives. They look at each other in wonderment.

Selma has been busy cleaning up, changing into her gown, and getting ready for bed. When she hears Charles come into the house, she walks to the head of the stairs at the same time he stops at the bottom.

"Come on up here, Charles. I need to talk with you."

Obediently, silently, he climbs the stairs, and follows her into the bedroom.

"Close the door," she instructs.

The room is lit by a single lamp giving off enough light to move about, but not sufficient to see much detail. Still, he can see her face.

There's a glow about her, almost an aura. The reflections of the lamp's light dance in her dark eyes. He sees her lips move and hears.

"Undress."

"What's going on he—" he starts to say.

"Take your clothes off and come over here," she orders. "I've been waiting for you."

She watches her husband as he, a little reluctantly, begins to remove his clothes, first his coat, then his vest. He lays them carefully over the back of a straight chair. He turns toward her and stares for a few seconds, then unbuttons his shirt and slides it off, pulls off his boots and pants, leaving just his long underwear and socks.

"All of it," she orders.

He unbuttons this remaining garment, removes it and his socks, and places them on top of his pants, again turning toward her.

"Come here," she instructs as she reaches down, with both hands, pulls her gown up over her head, and casually tosses it aside.

She has reasoned that what she did earlier this evening wasn't wrong. It was with the wrong man. Still craving and needing what was not finished with Robert, she's going to get it from her husband. She's determined that Charles will remember this night.

June and Robert sit at the kitchen table locked in the situation.

"Mama, I've told you, I'm not going to talk about it. I'm not saying anything happened, but if something did, it's none of your business. I told you and Daddy already, I'm going to have a life, and there are some things you don't need to know." He toys with her.

"Well, you're too old and too big for me to beat it out of you, but I know she at least kissed you, or you her. Please tell me, honey. If you don't, I'll think only the worst about her. I swear, whatever you tell me, I'll tell no one," she begs.

"Nice try, but I know no matter what I do or don't say, you'll confront Mrs. Housler with it anyhow," he correctly points out.

"Are you saying, if I want to know I should talk to Selma?" June continues, not wanting this conversation to end.

Robert rises to his feet, bends over and kisses his mother on the cheek and says, "No, I'm not. I'm going to bed."

June watches as he leaves the room and thinks to herself.

"At times he reminds me of a little boy, but at other times, he has the wisdom of a much older man. I must learn to respect that in him, I suppose. Now I have two of them on my hands. That doesn't change a thing, though, I'll find out, one way or another."

Chapter Twelve

"John, it's time to get up," June cozies to her husband. When he doesn't stir, she rolls over on her side and shakes him gently.

"Wake up, it's time to get up. It's a little after five." She sits up on the bed, turns to allow her feet to drop to the floor, and grabs her robe. She stands up to put her arms through the sleeves, then turns to see if he's moving.

"Don't lie there and go back to sleep. What time are you meeting the colonel?"

"He'll be here about six," he sleepily yawns.

"You'd better get a move on then. I'm going down to help Belle with breakfast."

"Yes, ma'am, general." His response is to let her know he hasn't forgotten last night, although you would think it falls on deft ears since she ignores him, and leaves the room.

At the same time, at Der Bote.

"Selma, honey, why don't you just laze around today. Stay in bed for a while. I'll have some breakfast brought up to you later on." The colonel is up, preparing for his day. There's a cheery melody within his words.

She rolls over off her stomach to look at her husband through the dim light of a lamp.

"Come over here," she calmly, snugly, begs.

"No time for that right now. I need to be at the Andersons' before six."

"Well, I'm glad I'm on your mind that way, but all I want is a big hug. Come over here." This time her tone is more insistent.

He sits down on the edge of the bed. They embrace with their faces side by side. She whispers in his ear.

"Last night was wonderful. I love you. Do you hate me for acting like a harlot."

"My darling wife, you must know I love you too. I've misplaced how loving and warm you are, and you'll never know how much I've missed you. I believe you did exactly the right thing last night. It was so arousing, it's given me an idea. Let's pretend last night was a rehearsal for tonight, only this time, it'll be your turn to undress for me." His words flow into her ears as warm nectar. He carefully pulls away and stands up to get dressed.

"Get yourself home early then, and we'll make an evening of it," she says with the most lustful tone of solicitation she can muster.

It's eight AM before Selma enters the kitchen to see Alberta Mae preparing a breakfast tray. "Is that for me?" she asks feeling a little wicked about staying in bed for a good part of the day.

"It sure is, Miss Selma. I was just about to bring it up to you. Do you want me to put it here on the table? It's real nice out on the verandah this morning."

"Good idea," Mrs. Housler answers, "Let's take it out on the verandah. Find something for yourself and come sit with me, we can talk for a while." There's no mistaking the twinkle in her voice.

This is music to her cook and housekeeper's ears. Maybe she can find out what all went on last night.

"Yeesss, ma'am, you go ahead and get settled. I'll bring breakfast right along."

After they begin eating, and express the pleasantries of the beautiful spring day, Selma rinses her mouth with a gulp of coffee, and begins to relate.

"I'm sorry I stormed out of here the way I did last evening. I had to get away by myself. You recall, of course, I went to meet with June?"

Alberta Mae, having cake in her mouth, responds with a tacit yes.

"Well, it's a long story, so I'll try to shorten it as best I can. You must promise not to breathe a word of it elsewhere. Agreed?"

"You got my word," she assures back, anxious for the facts to come.

Selma recounts the entire evening, from her first words with June, through the close call with Robert at the willow, and then John with the runaway slaves. She explains her run with June to the guesthouse, and being forced into hiding in the cellar when the colonel arrived. The explanation of the tunnel keeps them both on the edge of their seats, concerned at times, and laughing on occasion. Their exit from the tunnel at the barn concluded her tale. Conveniently, she's left out any mention of Randall and Queenie.

"So, June, Robert, and I left. We dropped her off at home, and he walked with me the rest of the way here," she finishes. "What an evening it was."

Mrs. Stoker waits for a mention of Randall. It's obvious Selma doesn't want to cause trouble, but it can't be left this way. She must know that Randall saw Robert and her together. She must have an explanation ready for her husband, should he hear about it.

"I know it's not my place, ma'am, but I have to tell you that you left one part out of your story," she says with a good bit of humility.

Selma's surprise is evident. "What?"

"I mean Randall. You left out the part about Randall and the dog."

Mrs. Housler's mouth drops open, but Alberta Mae continues before she can say anything.

"He told Jacob and me last night. We caught him sneaking back through his bedroom window. I wasn't going to say anything, but you got to know what he saw."

"What?" Selma's volume shows her embarrassment and concern.

"He saw you messing around with Mr. Robert."

"He saw what?" Now, the colonel's wife's voice is excitedly loud and shocked.

"He says he saw you and Mr. Robert kissing and rolling around on the ground."

"Oh my God! Oh my God! I'm so shocked, I—I don't know what to say!"

At this point, she's exposed and frantically searches her mind for a way out.

The tension breaks when Sachel appears through the open doors from the house.

"Excuse me Miss. Selma, Mrs. Anderson and her son Robert are here to see you."

Frantic at this news, she splutters, "Tell them I'm not at home!"

"I'm sorry, ma'am, but they already seen you two sitting out here."

An earlier meeting is in progress on the Anderson farm.

John and the colonel are in the living room at the guesthouse just finishing up their instructions to the runaways for their trip today.

"Besides the colonel and me, there will be seven other wagons show up here over the next four or five hours. That gives us a total of nine. You've all split up in groups of two or three, so four wagons will take two of you, and the other five will take three.

"The folks driving these wagons are well known around here, so they shouldn't be questioned by anybody, especially while you're wearing those arm bands. My daddy told me a long time ago, if you want to hide something really well, figure out a way to put it out in plain sight, and no one will ever see it. That's what we're doing here. If someone does stop to talk to your driver, just keep still. He'll handle it."

John looks at the colonel and nods, giving him a chance to speak.

"We'll cover forty miles today on this part of your trip. You'll get an hour to eat and rest at dinner time, then you'll be moving again. About halfway through your trip today, you'll change wagons. Fresh drivers and horses will take you on. They'll fill you in on all the things you need to know while you're with them. If all goes well, you'll all be at your final destinations in two or three weeks. You'll have your freedom.

"All right now, John will leave with the first group of three in a few minutes. Get your things together and be ready. You'll move as soon as the wagons get here. You'll not be hiding, you'll be riding as passengers. My wagon will be the last to go. Don't worry, put your trust in your driver. He'll tell you what to do in case of trouble.

"Ready, John?" Colonel Housler winds it up.

An affirmative nod is given.

Mr. Anderson and three of the runaways leave through the back door. The passengers each carry a pillow case containing their meager belongings. Outside they see a buckboard type of wagon, with straw and hay piled here and there on the rear section. A matched team of sorrels stand in the harnesses, calmly waiting.

"Put your bags up here behind the seat. We'll cover them with some straw. For a while, I want all of you in the back of the wagon. Later on you can take turns up here with me. All set? Here we go." He slaps the reins out over the horses' backs, gives a left hand gesture of "see ya" to the colonel, and the wagon jerks into motion.

Charles watches as the wagon disappears around the corner of the house before he returns inside. Although he's been involved with moving runaways for years, it never gets any easier. They change the way they move them and take as few chances as possible, but the danger is always there.

"I know why I do it," he thinks to himself, "I wonder what John's real reason could be. He's likely to be governor of this state in a few years. Why does he take such a chance?"

The pressure is building on the verandah at Der Bote.

Alberta Mae's eyes are as big as silver dollars.

"What you going to do, Miss. Selma?"

"Stall them! Stall them for a few minutes."

"Sachel, you bring them out here and get them seated. Tell them I just went to freshen up, and I'll be right back."

"Alberta Mae, you get them whatever they want," Selma fires instructions like a general on a battlefield.

As Sachel leaves the verandah, she jumps over the banister, off the backside edge, and runs wildly around to the back of the house. As she lands on the back porch, she stops to catch her breath and think.

"What do they want? June told me last night if I didn't let her know how I'm doing, she'd be over here to check on me. But I would have to believe that Charles gave her a report on me when he went to their place earlier. Why is Robert with her, why isn't he with his father? He wouldn't tell her about last night, would he? I'll never have the answers unless I go in there and face up to them. I'll let them do the talking. Whatever's said, I have to remain collected, and be able to think. Stay calm. Okay, here I go."

"Good morning, June," she bubbles as she steps out of the house onto the verandah, "Did you come all the way over here just to check on me this morning?"

She turns her head toward Robert.

"And a good morning to you, sir. I thought you would be with the colonel and your daddy today."

"Good morning," he all but sings, and squirms a little in his chair.

"Checking on you is partly the reason we're here," June answers. "I have some other puzzling news to discuss with you, too."

Selma sits down at the table with them, as Alberta Mae fusses with a tray of cookies and coffee, lingering, listening.

"Can you leave us alone, Alberta Mae?" June's request stings Selma's ears.

As soon as her housekeeper leaves the verandah, she asks curtly.

"What in the world is on your mind to cause you to treat her that way? You know she's not used to that. She's part of our family."

"Well, if you want her to hear what I have to say, call her back, but, if you think her being here is going to stop me, think again." June bluntly implies.

"Go ahead . . . say whatever it is you need to, I'm listening," Selma stiffly comments, feeling a little combative after hearing the tone of June's abrasive voice.

"I want to know what the two of you were up to last night. Robert looked like he had been to a bordello when he came home. His face was covered with your lipstick, his clothes and hair were a mess. But mostly, it was the look on his face. I want to know what happened." She finishes with a glare aimed into Selma's eyes.

Mrs. Housler feels a sick dread come over her body. She suddenly aches in the pit of her stomach. Her eyes drop away from June's, as if she's looking down at her coffee cup.

What to say? How can she explain the absolute worse thing one woman can do to another? The silence is deafening.

"I told Mama last night that it's none of her business, Mrs. Housler. But she just won't let it be. She wants to make something out of nothing." Robert's words put the air back in Selma's lungs.

With a renewed sense of control, she continues with the young man's message.

"Then, I'll tell her Robert."

"I gave your son a big hug and a kiss on the cheek after he brought me home. I was welcoming him home from school, and thanking him for walking with me. I believe we all looked a fright after all that went on last night. I had to wash up and change clothes before Charles came home. I know I saw Randall's dog jump up on Robert a couple of times, too. You're getting yourself all worked up over nothing. Believe me, I know I'm a lonely person, but I would never do anything to hurt you like that. I know you know that." The words roll off Selma's lips as if she's reading from a script.

The wind leaves June's sails as she listens to her friend. It makes sense, she supposes. There's nothing out of the ordinary. Robert could have smeared the lipstick from his cheek to the corner of his mouth while wiping sweat. And Selma's right, everybody was a mess last night.

She sits, contemplating, and feeling foolish. She can believe this explanation if she wants to. It's plausible. She looks back and forth at Robert and Selma, pausing to study their faces for a few seconds each time.

"It appears I was very, very, wrong," she suggests. "I don't know how to apologize to you. To think I let this get under my skin. Well, I won't blame you if you never speak to me again, I am truly sorry. I don't understand, though, why you just didn't tell me this last night Robert. It certainly would have saved me a lot of embarrassment."

"I was having a little fun with you at first, then it made me feel good when you thought a woman was after me. You wanted to protect me, so I let you do it. I can see now that was a cruel thing to do, and for that I'm, also, deeply sorry."

June listens to his words and pretends to believe everything he says. She turns to look at her just newly reunited old friend.

"How can I ever begin to make this up to you?" June asks with heartfelt emotion.

Feeling victorious and righteous, Selma retorts with a wink of her eye.

"I'll think of a way, dear. Don't you worry about that."

"Now that we have that settled, I'll leave you ladies to yourselves and see if I can find Randall. If you'll excuse me, I'll ask Alberta Mae of his whereabouts."

The women both nod as he rises from his chair. When he starts through the door into the house, Alberta Mae appears. Unknown to any of them, she was standing within earshot of their conversation and heard the whole thing.

"He's probably still out back at home, Mr. Robert. You want me to get him?"

"Nah, that's okay, I'll find him. Thanks." Robert smiles, and hears the start of an apology being constructed by his mama to Alberta Mae as he leaves.

When he steps off the back porch, he sees Randall sitting on a straight chair, next to the porch, in the front yard of his home. Queenie is next to him with her head on his lap, being stroked and petted. A boy and his dog, not an uncommon picture, but this morning it gives a special feeling of tranquillity.

He examines his feelings as he walks toward the young boy. "I can have a good life here, doing things I want to do. Helping Daddy, learning to run the farm, helping with the runaways, it can't get better than this. And let's not forget that a woman likes me. This has worked out better than I could ever have imagined. I must find Sheree, though. I'll not be able to rest until I know she's back here safe with us."

"Morning, Randall. Hi, Queenie." His words are warm and sunny as he reaches to scratch the dog's head.

"Morning, Mr. Robert," he replies, acting rather shy.

"Hey, have you forgotten me, your good friend? My friends at school all call me Bob. Mama won't hear of it, but I wish you would."

The young boy is unable to conceal a big smile. "Yes, Mr. Bob."

"No, no, just plain Bob" Robert smiles and holds out his hand.

Randall reaches out, accepts his friend Bob's hand, and gives it a shake.

"Do people ever call you Randy?" he asks.

"Only Sheree, she's the only one."

"Can I call you Randy then?" He sits down on the edge of the porch.

The you boy's face lights up like sunshine, his eyes sparkle. He nods his head yes.

"Well Randy, you and I need to get our heads together and see what we can do about getting Sheree back. You know she isn't buried there at the graveyard, don't you?"

Bob continues after getting a "yes" nod to his question, "I need to know everything you know about it, and I'll make sure you know everything I know about it. Deal?"

"Okay." Again, the boy's face is one big smile. It's good to have a friend.

Their conversation goes back and forth, first Randy explaining in detail all that's happened. Then Bob adding to it with anything he knows. An hour passes before the back door screen opens and June steps out onto the porch.

"Come on, son. We need to get back home."

"Okay, I'll be right there."

"Now remember, we're going to get Sheree back. It could take some time, but we won't give up. You'll stay in touch with me and me you, right?"

"That's right Bob. If you need me, I'll be here," Randy responds. Now he's confident something will be done to help Sheree.

June and Robert climb aboard the surrey and head toward home, waving goodbye to Selma and Alberta Mae.

A few minutes pass as they're both lost in thought. Only the sound of the wagon wheels moving over the ground, and the horse's hooves clopping, can be heard above the birds calling to each other.

"You know I don't believe a word of it," she prods and looks at her son.

"Don't give me that 'what' look, you know what I mean, Robert. I was wrong when I placed all of the fault with Selma. You're as bad as she is. You're not as innocent as I thought. Keep in mind, young man, I'm watching you. And that's all I'm going to say about it."

He grins at his mother and simply says, "Good."

Time moves on at the Company's compound near Atlanta.

"Saturday night is finally here. Will they come and get me to go to the secret meeting? I'm not too sure about why I'm going, but they tell me it's important for me to be there. No one has said a word about it since this past Thursday." Lilly runs her plans for this evening through her mind.

Knock, knock, knock.

"They're here. I wonder who's on the other side of that door? I'll open it slowly. It's an older girl. I've never seen her before. She has a finger up to her lips.

"I'm following her down the hallway in my stocking feet. She opens a door, pulls me through and starts running up a set of stairs, taking two steps at a time. I'm right on her heels out into a hallway. We run almost the entire length of it, through another door, and up another flight of steps. We stop on a small landing at the top and she puts her finger to her lips again, then taps softly on the door in front of us with her knuckles."

Knock, knock, knock.

"The door opens, and we step out onto the roof of the building.

"I'm following her to what appears to be a tent of some sort. The moonlight helps, but mostly I'm letting her guide me around all sorts of round things coming up through the roof, all over the place. We're at the tent and entering through an opening being held back by an older boy. I don't know him either.

"We're inside, she's lighting a lamp."

"I can see a little better now. This tent is made of blankets being held up by wooden poles, which are being held in place by people. It could collapse and disappear in a few seconds, and I'm sure that's the whole idea. There's just the one lamp burning, so it isn't very bright in here. It's hard to make out all of the faces, or for that matter, to see how many people are here."

"Is everybody here?" A clear but low feminine voice is heard.

"Are we all here?" An unanswered question. "Our time is short, so, we'll get right to it. You new people are here to learn what's in store for you here at La Nesra. Understand, no one will harm you as long as you do what you're told, and when you're supposed to do it. Believe though, these people deal with those opposing their wishes very swiftly, and very harshly. Do not get caught breaking the rules. If you get caught for being here tonight, you're on your own. No one will help you. Learn to take care of yourself. Let others take care of themselves. Do not allow yourself to be taken in by an older, more mature person. Some people here will use you to their benefit, if you let them. Understand they will sacrifice you to better themselves. Our strength is in our numbers and our bond to each other. If this group asks you to perform a task, you need to decide if it's worth the risk to you. If it isn't, don't do it.

"We know what you're hearing makes little sense at the moment. You'll relate to this meeting more and more the longer you're here. Over time you'll determine who in our group you can trust, and whom you can't. But I can tell you, without question, the people here tonight can be trusted. Of course, the five of you, being new, are unknown to us. We'll learn to trust you, or not, very quickly.

"Within a few weeks, you'll be given the name of your group leader. Until then, until we get to know you better, should you need to talk with us, drink your water straight down at your supper meal, and turn the glass upside down on the table. Someone will contact you. Once you're given the name of your group leader, you can contact him or her directly.

"I'm sure the faculty and guards are aware of our group. As long as we pose no threat to them, it's unlikely they'll put forth much effort to expose us. Our purpose is to take care of our problems and situations ourselves, not to break their rules. Before you leave here, you'll receive a list of those rules, and their punishments for breaking them. You'd normally receive this information from them in about six months. Check the punishments carefully, some of them are inhumane. Break the rule, get caught at it, you get the punishment. There are no exceptions, no excuses. No one from our group can help you, nor will we try. It would only bring grief down on us all."

"All right then," a male voice announces, "it's my turn. We realize you have many questions about why you were chosen to be here, and what to expect in the future. I'll tell you. This part of the Company is like an advanced school used to train people to fill positions all over the world. These positions are many in number and include these as examples: artists, musicians, cooks, scientists topographers, bookkeepers, carpenters, veterinarians, mathematicians, economists, lawyers, blacksmiths, farmers, linguists; the list goes on and on.

"It sounds almost normal for an advanced education, doesn't it? The truth is, all of these positions, and others I've not mentioned, make up a work force separate and apart from the world you know. Every one of these people will become an extremely educated spy, killer, or information slave. They look like everyone else, but have greatly advanced skills, and a total commitment, which are used to further the needs of the Company. They mix with the rest of humanity and have a normal life, with the exception that they are called upon constantly to do a 'job'.

"You say to yourself. I won't do that, they can't make me. I say to you, yes, they can, and they will. Their methods are subtle, but effective. After a few years here, you'll agree with them and devote yourself to their causes, whatever they are.

"As long as you obey their rules, they'll slather you with kindness, affection, and material things. They'll boost your ego and self-confidence to the point you'll believe you're capable of anything. Money is plentiful, and merely a tool to them. You'll have anything you need or want, except your freedom. And when they ask, you'll inform on your friends. You'll hurt people, even murder them. You'll have no allegiance to your country, or your families. The Company will be your country and your family.

"Every few years, a group of special people arrive and begin their training. The five of you are the new group. Each with the mind of a genius, and matched with a talent far from ordinary for a normal human being. They have definite plans for you, bet on it. They've had plans for you since the day they found you, probably when you were born. They brought you all here from all over the world. Your families are very well off financially today because of you. It's no accident that you're here. It's been planned for years. No one is coming to get you, there is no escape.

"You can resist if you like. A few have tried not to learn, thinking the Company would let them go free. Some have tried to escape and return to their homes. Well, they've all disappeared during the night, never to be seen again. I can't say for sure what happened to them, but I can imagine. Should you manage to escape and by some chance reach your home, you'll realize that no one will associate themselves with you. The Company has told them they'll be held responsible if they take you back. Being held responsible means to be gruesomely murdered. Read the rules and punishment pages you'll receive in a few minutes. I think you'll agree with me. Those who have tried to leave, have not gone free. They're probably still with us, buried on these grounds somewhere, or cremated in the large kiln here in the cellar.

"This group's advice to each of you is, be the best you can at whatever you do for the Company. Enjoy every minute, anytime you can. You'll have a life that will make a difference somewhere. What difference? Where? Who's to say.

"This meeting is adjourned. You'll be taken back to your rooms now.

"God bless us all."

Chapter Thirteen

Five Years Later

"John, it's 1860. It's imperative we start your bid for governor. There's a lot of support for you right now. If we wait any longer, I'm not sure it will be there. The winds of war are blowing, and if an outbreak should occur, it could give our competition a vehicle to stir fear into the hearts of the voting public. We're all aware that people hesitate to change an incumbent during the time of war," Mr. Howard Clevenger says, his muscular hands rest on the large mahogany table as he stands at the end, and addresses the eight men seated. Mr. Clevenger is a wealthy, well liked, politically-connected, plantation owner with a desire to see a change in the governorship of the state.

Cigar smoke floats like clouds in the still air of the library of the Clevenger home. The wooden sliding doors are closed, which signals everyone in the household not to disturb those inside. It's getting late in the afternoon and the restlessness of those present is beginning to show. They've been at it since just after dinner without a break, except when a fresh pot of coffee was brought into the room.

The men are getting anxious for their business to be completed, so that they can get refreshed and dressed in their finest garb. They'll all attend the grand ball being hosted by the Clevenger family, here on their estate, slated to begin two hours hence this evening.

A number of participants have arrived as early as three days ago due to the distance they have traveled, and have been guests of the house. These eight men, and their wives, are among them. The men have spent most of the last two days together here in the library.

Others, from nearby, with invitations to attend the grand ball have been arriving throughout the day today. The house is teeming with activity. The servants must attend to every detail. Everything is expected to be perfect.

People are sitting in rocking chairs on the huge front porch watching carriages stop at the front gate to allow those inside to disembark. The carriage then proceeds to the rear of the house where their luggage is removed and delivered to an assigned guest room. Children are running, chasing each other, playing tag, yelling, and having a good time. Three mongrel dogs chase after them barking and yapping as they play.

"I agree with Howard, John. If we fail to make our move soon, the likelihood of another opportunity such as this looks slim. I believe we should make the announcement this evening. The vast majority of our resources, both power and money, will be a captive audience. It's time to change the politics of this state.

"Should a war break out while the current regime is in control, most certainly, this state will line up with the Confederate South. We must not allow that to happen. Our sources indicate that the majority of voters in this state support the views of the Union North. We can place our man at the head of this state, but we must do it now," Congressman Adrian Berkshire asserts, as he taps his cigar on the edge of a large ashtray in front of him. Sounds of agreement and encouragement resound from around the table.

As Howard sits down, giving up the floor, John Anderson rises to his feet with a serious look on his face.

"Gentlemen, I know it would appear to you that I'm dragging my feet and delaying our bid for the highest office of this state. Be assured, that's not my purpose. You all should know by now . . . I'm ready.

"I agree with most everything I've heard here this afternoon, and I believe that our platform will be readily accepted by the voting public. I'm convinced we can win this race. However, two points remain to be agreed upon.

"Number one, we need a strong man to be my running mate. A man who will support our platform with all of his energy. A man we can all trust, and with pride call our lieutenant governor. That man is Martin Schoener.

"And number two, we need to label our party affiliation.

"I don't identify with any major party today, you all know that. I'm of the opinion, however, that the Republican Party will be a political survivor for years to come. While the name is somewhat new, less than four years in the making, the fundamentals of its structure will insure a strong backing and eventually cause it to be one of the most powerful political movements in this country.

"The platform of the Republican Party puts less fiscal power at the Federal level, while stressing more power and responsibility for the states. The Republican Party believes in a strong Union of our states, as well as a strong defense program to thwart the efforts of those who would like to see our country divided into separate kingdoms.

"Further, I would like to add, a statesman from Illinois has declared his intentions to campaign for the presidency of our Union. He will, for reasons I am not able to address, in all likelihood, work from the position of the Union party platform. Be assured, however, his beliefs and his history are those of the Republican Party. With his stand on a single Federal government for our part of North America, and his unwavering policy to emancipate the slaves, I believe he will be the next president of the United States.

"I will run for the governor's office of this state on our platform with the Republican Party's point of view.

"When we can agree on these two issues, we can make our announcement.

"What do you say, Marty, are you in agreement? Are you ready?" John is confident of his nomination of Marty as lieutenant governor because he's lobbied for over a year to get the support he needs to do it.

He sits down as Howard gets back on his feet.

"Well, you heard it, gentlemen. Are there any other comments or questions to be heard?" He pauses to look around the room at each man.

"No?" He pauses again.

"You are each a vital part of our campaign committee. Your vote will be taken seriously. Cast it carefully, and if we are unanimous with our support of John and Marty, we'll make the announcement this evening.

"Are we ready for a vote?" Silence.

"Those voting for the nomination of John Anderson for governor, and Martin Schoener for lieutenant governor, raise your hand.

"It looks like we're ready, we're unanimous."

In the intervening time, on the farm next to the Andersons' place.

Bob and Randy are sitting on the back porch step of the main house at Der Bote. It's an overcast day, predicting rain with almost certainty. You can get the smell of it in the air, though there's no breeze at all.

The rattling of pans and dishes is heard from the kitchen behind them as Alberta Mae prepares supper. A fragrance of fresh baked bread seeps from the kitchen out through the back door screen and is occasionally noticed by the two friends, apparently just passing time, talking with each other.

Bob, at twenty-two years of age, has made an impact within his family and the Stokers. He's taken it upon himself to provide the Stoker children with an education; they, along with Charlotte, study with the Andersons' tutor, Mr. Knoble. It's been a total success.

Randy is a ravenous student. He's progressed far beyond the hopes of his parents. Bob beams with pride as his protege continues to amaze those around him. The twins can read, write, as well as work with numbers, and time is on their side. They'll be well educated by time they reach Randy's age. The two older sisters have no interest in getting an education. All they want is to get married and have babies. Through Bob's insistence, they are learning to read and write.

Young Mr. Anderson hasn't forgotten that evening with Selma. She still teases him on occasion, but has allowed nothing further to happen. She's ever present in the back of his mind, and he gladly accepts any attention she allows him, hoping things will change someday. Deep in a private place of her mind, Selma has a very special feeling for her best friend's son. She's never known such a young man. His pleasant tenacity and affection warms her soul. But she gets her release with her husband these days, which enables her to control the relationship.

Bob has a lady friend he's been seeing more and more frequently. Elizabeth Sanders is the daughter of Cole and Caroline Sanders, lifelong friends of the Anderson family. She and Bob occasionally meet at her father's farm.

They're not officially a couple, but Elizabeth is smitten with him. She's five years younger at seventeen, although she looks every bit his age. Robert hasn't yet looked at her the way she wants, but she's not about to give up. She knows this is the man she wants for life.

Bob hasn't forgotten his quest to locate Sheree either. He's made contacts within one hundred miles in all directions, looking for a trace, or clue, to her whereabouts. It's difficult, since he's not able to openly discuss Sheree with just anybody. Almost everyone believes she's dead and buried. He has to use caution so as not to draw unwanted attention.

"I've heard that a train station worker saw a young girl, in a trunk, being put on a private railroad car about the time Sheree was taken. Word is the train was headed for Atlanta," Bob informs his friend.

"Atlanta, Georgia?" Randy asks.

"That's what I hear. It's the first piece of information I've been able to come up with these last five years. I'm not sure how good it is, but I think we have to check it out," he continues.

"How are we going to do that?" Randy's curiosity is peaking.

"Well, I made up this story and told Mama and Daddy I want to go to Atlanta for a month or so. You know, take some time off for myself. They think it's a good idea because they're going to be busy with his running for governor, and want me to run things at the farm when I get back. So, I'm planning to leave within the week."

His words are music to Randy's ears. At last, at long last, something is going to be done to find his lost friend Sheree. A big grin consumes his face.

"Now, here's the best part. Are you ready? Do you want to come with me?" Bob springs a surprise.

"Me? Me, go with you to Atlanta, Georgia?" The seventeen-year-old boy's voice gets loud and excited. He jumps from his seat on the step and dances around.

"I sure do want to go."

Then reality starts settling in.

"My folks won't let me go. And besides, I don't have money for the expenses." The excitement turns to a blue feeling and his voice fades.

"I've thought about that too, Randy. We can't tell them the real reason we're going, just like I didn't tell my folks, but if you can get me invited for supper tonight, we'll ask them together, and see if we can work it out. One thing's for sure, we won't know until we try, and I want you to come with me." Bob has Randy lined up, now all he has to do is convince Jacob and Alberta Mae.

Mama Stoker feels a deep sense of gratitude toward Bob for taking her children under his wing and providing for their education, so it's easy to get him invited to supper this evening.

"Of course he'll stay for supper. I'll have it no other way. You tell him that, honey. I'll have it no other way," Alberta Mae responds to her Son's inquiry, not slowing down her process of setting the supper table for the Housler's.

"Tell him supper will be ready in about an hour or so, and to wash up before he comes to the table."

"Thanks, I'll tell him," Randy says, stopping her as she passes by to put his face alongside hers and giving a hug. He knows she likes it when he hugs her and he wants her to know he loves her. If it happens to help with her decision about his trip, well, let's be honest, that's really why he did it.

The entire family is present at the Stokers' supper table. The seating is a little more crowded with Bob joining them. Jacob has just finished thanking the Lord for the food on the table and asking for His blessing on all present. Quiet settles in as plates are being loaded with food from the bowls and platters.

Jacob breaks the silence as if he's been told to do it in this manner.

"Mr. Robert, what's on your mind that's caused you to have supper with us the evening? You know we welcome you here anytime, but this happened on the spur of the minute, and is the first time since you've been back."

"Am I that easy to see through, Jacob, or do you have a God-given gift that none of us here knows about?" Robert's answer eliminates any uneasy feelings, and brings chuckles around the table.

"I always feel like one of the family here in your home. So, if it's all the same to you, it'll make me happy if you all call me Bob."

As if previously rehearsed, to the person, the family all speak in unison.

"Okay, Bob."

Laughter rings throughout the Stoker home.

When silence again takes over the kitchen, everyone is eating and relaxed, then Bob speaks again.

"Now you can't let Belle know I said this Alberta Mae, but you're the best cook in the county. This is a delicious meal."

"Boy, I don't yet know what it is you want, but I can see you'll do or say about anything to get it," she says laughing with pride.

With that the whole table erupts in laughter again.

"Man-o-live, I can see I might as well say what I want to, so here goes."

"I want to take Randy to Atlanta with me for a month or so." Without waiting for a response, he continues.

"I'm taking some time off before Daddy starts his bid for governor. He and Mama are going to be really busy then, and they're expecting me to run our farm. Anyhow, I'd like to take Randy with me. I'll handle his expenses, and take good care of him."

Jacob and Alberta Mae look at each other and then at Randall.

"Son, are you sure you want to go to Atlanta? You know black folks aren't treated the same way there they are here. They won't let you eat or sleep in the same room with white people. You can't even stay on the sidewalk if a white person is coming at you. You won't be able to stay with Bob, unless he is willing to stay with the black folks there. Besides that, it's dangerous. There's only white man's law in Georgia. None for a black man. I've been told stories of a negra being killed just for looking at a white woman. With all this talk about a war, no black person, man or woman, is safe that far south."

"I'll protect him," Bob speaks up.

"How are you going to protect him?" Jacob insists. "You'll be called a negra lover and suffer for it yourself. And besides that, if the two of you get caught up in trouble, it won't help your daddy win his election."

"We'll be careful about our movements around Atlanta. We'll not be out after dark, and we'll stay in the background, so as not to be noticed," Bob argues.

A moment of silence follows.

Bob continues, "I can see that you have Randy's, as well as my well being in mind with your concerns, but I think it'll be a great opportunity for him to see the world as it is out there, away from here. He'll learn a lot from it. I've been away on my own for nearly ten years. I have some savvy when it comes to survival in a large city, and Atlanta is one large city. No one knows we're coming, and no one will notice we're there. We'll be back before you know it. If he's to further your family's name and position in this white man's world, he has to know what he's dealing with, and how to work with it. This is a good place to start. Let him come with me. Please?"

Bob hit the nail smack on the head with his last comment. Jacob and Alberta Mae look at each other, then Randy, and finally at Bob. When Mama Stoker speaks, everybody at the table knows what she says is the law.

"I see what you mean, and what you say is true, I can't argue that. He can go."

Randy jumps up from his chair, runs around the table kissing his parents, all the time shouting thank you, thank you, thank you. She takes control when she says.

"Set yourself down, honey, I'm not done talking yet."

Randy finds his chair as his mother continues.

"You can go with these rules. In the first place, Randall, you got to listen to Bob when he tells you something. You got to do what he says. He knows a whole lot more about it than you do, so you got to do what he says. Do you hear me?"

A repeated nod and a "yes, I hear you" satisfies her on rule number one.

"If trouble starts around you, you get away from it as quick as you can, and you take Bob with you. You don't try to be a hero or be somebody who's trying to change the world and the way it is. You turn tail and run, even if you're not part of the trouble. They can't hang the two of you if they can't get their hands on you."

"It'll never come to that," Bob interjects. "We won't let it come to that."

"I hear what you're saying." She speaks with understanding. "But I know how young boys are. I had five brothers growing up, and I know how boys get things in their heads and won't let go. They were sold off when they turned eighteen. My youngest put up such a fight not wanting to leave his family, they couldn't drag him off, so they shot him dead on the spot. Right there in front of us all. Nothing was done about it. We just buried him the next day."

Bob wants to tell her how sorry he is that she had to go through such a horrific occurrence, he wants to promise her nothing like that is going to happen to Randy, but the truth is, she knows no one can guarantee such a promise. At this point, she's already said Randy can go. Any further comment from him won't help and will likely hinder.

"Just two more things then I'll be done.

"We've got some money saved up and we've been looking for a way to help Randy with it. We'll give you seventy dollars, Bob, for his ticket, board, and eats. You dole it out as you see fit. He's had no money his whole life, so he needs to learn how to use it.

And the last thing is, you both be back here by the end of six weeks. You see to it. That's our rules."

"Agreed." Bob readily accepts her wishes and looks at his friend.

"I agree, Mama, and don't you worry, I'll take good care of Bob," he replies seriously.

The entire family laughs at the same time again, leaving Randy with a look of 'what's so funny' on his face.

All the while the Stokers are talking around their supper table, the Housler's are involved with their own discussion, while eating their evening meal.

"You know, Charles, these last five years have been the best of our married life. I'm happy knowing you truly love me and always have. I'm at a loss to understand all those empty years. I suppose I never will." Selma relates as an invitation for her husband to speak.

"I've known for the last five years that you would eventually ask for the truth. But I'm still undecided whether you can hear it and feel the same about me afterward. That's always been my dilemma. I love you and I don't want to lose you." He could have said anything to stall her off, but, his words only add a draft to the smoldering ashes of their relationship of years ago.

"I will always love you, darling, and I'll be here for you forever. I don't know how to say it any other way to make you believe me. I can only assure you that it's the truth. I honestly feel that whatever your deep heavy secret carries with it will only bring us closer together, not come between us. So, please tell me. Tell me, so I can understand and share the burden of it with you."

With no comment, he gets up from his chair and walks into the kitchen to be gone for a few seconds to reappear with a coffeepot in his hand. He stops at Selma's side to top off her cup, then moves to his chair around the corner of the table to her left. Instead of sitting down, he drags it back to Selma's side. Then he reaches with his free hand to secure his cup and saucer and places it on the table in front of his chair, and fills his cup with coffee before sitting down.

Then, with little or no expression on his face, he turns toward her and puts the palm of his right hand on the left side of her face in a soft caring manner. She responds by turning her head slightly to nestle his hand. He then slowly, gently, slides his fingers down under her chin and lifts just enough guide her head to face him.

He sits still, looking, taking in her face. A full minute passes.

She can see water welling in his eyes.

He leans forward, softly places a tender kiss on her lips, pulls away, turns to face the table, and takes a sip of his coffee.

She's so taken with all that's just happened, she almost breaks into tears wanting to tell him to say nothing. Wanting to console him in her arms and forgive him for everything—anything. She wants to tell him again she loves him and how much this last five years have meant to her, but she doesn't. Instead, she takes a deep soblike breath and says nothing.

"You must swear," he begins, "you can say nothing about this to anyone. And I mean June Anderson as well as anyone else."

"I swear to you, Charles," she whispers, and places her hand on his arm.

He takes a deep, deep, breath and lets it out slowly through his nose and rounded lips, as if blowing.

"I'm not who you think I am."

Looking in on those at the Clevenger estate, we find final preparations are being completed for the gala to begin.

John walks into the room he and June have occupied for the last few days, in the home of one of their closest friends, the Clevenger's. He sees her sitting at the vanity brushing her hair. She looks in the mirror to see her husband and turns to greet him.

"I'm glad you're finally here. You need to hurry and get all spruced up. You've just over an hour before we're expected downstairs at the welcoming line. Did the meeting end the way you wanted? Am I going to have sex with our next governor later tonight?" Her words are dancing in the air as he closes the door.

"That silver tongue of yours will get you in deeper than you care to one day. I'm not sure if Adrian thinks of you that way. Perhaps he does, but you'll have to ask him. I hear he's frisky in bed," he answers without hesitation.

"Adrian . . . you don't mean Adrian Berkshire do you? Adrian Berkshire couldn't govern a popcorn stand. There isn't a chance that committee would choose him over you, not a chance." She comes up off her chair to put her arms around her husband's neck.

"Now, you tell me the truth, or I just might find out if what you say is true about him, although I doubt that it is. He has to be at least seventy years old." She kisses her man, then pulls away at half an arm's length, and waits for his answer.

"Unanimously, not one opposing vote. I was successful in getting everything I wanted. Marty and Rachell will be here in a few minutes for a drink to start our celebration. You'd better put something over your underwear, or Marty's going to find out everything he's ever wondered about you.

"I can hardly believe it. It's really happening. The announcement will be made this evening shortly after supper. We're on our way, after all these years." Mr. Anderson's mind is spinning, jumping from one thought to another.

He stops talking to look into his wife's eyes, pulls her close to his chest, lifts her off the floor, and spins around and around, finally falling onto the bed. He raises up on his elbow to look down at her face.

"Do we have time for sex before they get here?"

Giggling, she wriggles out from under him and is desperately looking for a robe when a knock sounds through their door.

"They're here. God, I can't find my robe. Don't you open that door until I'm ready."

He lunges off the bed, headed for the door, chuckling as he goes.

"John, you heard me, it's not funny. I'll never speak to you again if you open that door."

A second knock resounds.

With her robe on and tied, she glances at the mirror to check her hair and says, "Okay, I'm ready."

He opens the door to see Marty, holding a bottle of champagne, and Rachell, holding four glasses. Without hesitation they barge into the room. He closes the door behind them.

"Before it leaves my mind, John, there's a fellow looking for you. Says he needs to speak to you personally, wouldn't give me his name. I told him you wouldn't be down for an hour or so. He said he'd wait." Marty is ready to dismiss this information and get started with the celebration.

"What did he look like? Have you seen him before?" John inquires.

"No, I've never seen him before. He's a tall slender fellow with a full heavy black beard. He's dressed smartly and well mannered. I have no idea who he is, or where he came from. Don't worry about him. If he really needs to talk to you, he'll find you later. He probably has a pocket full of hundred dollar bills to contribute to our campaign, and wants to give it directly to you."

"You're right." John blurts. "He can hunt me down later. Let's make a toast."

Rachell passes out the glasses filled with champagne. Four glasses are held up forehead high.

"To a successful campaign and the demise of our competition," John shouts.

The glasses clink as they meet in midair. In another moment they're empty.

Other toasts are made until the last of the champagne is consumed. It's put both couples in a great relaxed mood, ready for the fancy ball.

"We really must break this up for now," June observes. "We need to get dressed and present ourselves to our supporters downstairs."

"The same with us," Rachell joins in. "We'll see you in a bit."

An hour later.

"Come on, John, hurry up, we're late. You know they won't start letting the guests into the ballroom until the entire welcoming line is there. We're holding up the whole evening." June's nervousness is beginning to work on her.

"They'll wait, honey. I'm just about ready. This darn tie."

"Come here, let me fix it." Her voice is a little cranky. "There . . . now put your coat on, let's go." They leave their room and walk through the hallway, noticing the absence of people.

They stop at the head the staircase to allow Marty and Rachell, who just started down the open stairway, to complete their formal entrance.

Couples have gathered in the spacious entryway at the bottom to watch the most powerful men in the state and their wives descend the stairs. Everyone there is dressed in their best fancy clothes.

The women are wearing their new, never before seen, one of a kind, evening gowns. Mostly, even their husbands have not seen them in their fabulous dresses. Smiles and good humor abound everywhere.

All eyes normally fall upon the wife and her gown, as she descends the stairs with her beau. Oooohs and aaaahs are heard, along with occasional clapping, indicating the crowd's appreciation of their appearance.

June is unable to see the front of the gown Rachell's wearing, but from her vantage point, it's stunning. It's made from a silver material having a soft shimmering shine to it. She has her hair up on top in a beehive sort of style, with three long curls hanging down each side and the back. The dress must button in the front, since no buttons are to be seen down the back.

"She's probably hanging out of that dress in the front," Mrs. Anderson thinks as she nervously waits. "She has huge breasts. She hasn't been able to hide them in that dress, you can bet on it.

"What if she gets a better reception than I do? I'll be so embarrassed. She has always had a way of being flashy, without looking trashy. And she has a considerable amount of God-given beauty. She'll probably win the award for the most beautiful gown tonight as well. I should have worn that bright red gown. I feel homely. I'll probably stumble down the stairs."

June is so caught up in her negative thoughts she's not aware it's their turn to proceed. John moves to the first step, almost dragging her behind him.

"Keep up with me," he directs without moving his lips.

The air becomes still, and the noise of chatter and clapping fades when Marty and Rachell pass the waiting greeters.

June is about to collapse from the look on the faces she sees below. People are just standing and looking up at them. No one is acknowledging their descent. A feeling storms over her, she and John will be the first couple ever to go all the way down with no reaction at all.

They reach the fifth step from the top of the staircase and she is about to fill John's ear with how she feels, but a hearty wolf whistle and a loud round of applause begins. Another few steps and the applause explodes even louder.

With her confidence back, a broad smile spreads across her face.

That encourages individual comments to be heard above the cooing of the crowd.

Beautiful! Gorgeous! Splendid! Breathtaking!

"You're the belle of the ball," her husband utters through his teeth without breaking his smile.

"They like me. They really like me," she tells herself. "I still have what it takes. This is going to be a great evening."

To June, it seems like she's stood for hours welcoming guests. She and John are introduced to each and every couple as they enter the ballroom. Her face feels like it will crack from the constant smile.

"I need a good stiff drink," she thinks. "Oh, if I could get off my feet for five minutes. How many more people will fit into this ballroom anyway?"

Suddenly there are no more people to greet. The front of the greeting line is following the last couple through the doors. John is at her side and whispers in her ear.

"My feet are killing me. Let's get something to drink."

"What happens now?" she breathes in his ear.

"We'll have a drink or two and chat until supper's ready. Then we'll all be seated for the meal. Afterward, the men will drift outside for a cigar, coffee, and brandy, while the women clean the tables and wash the dishes."

"Very funny," she snaps back with a hesitant smile, clinging tightly to his arm.

"Actually," he continues. "After we eat, the servants will clear away the tables and set up smaller ones around the edge of the room. The orchestra will get set up and begin playing for the dance. That'll go on until someone decides it is time to select the best gown of the evening. After that the band will play as long as it's needed, but people will start drifting away."

"Who decides which is the best gown?" June's reason for asking is obvious to her husband.

"Let me put it this way, my beautiful wife. Don't offend any of your gentlemen callers this evening. Each man at the table is handed a ballot while eating his meal. He must write the name of the woman wearing the gown of his choice on the ballot. Then our hostess will count the ballots when she feels all the men have made their decisions and placed their votes in a box provided."

"I had no idea—" she starts but is interrupted when he continues.

"So, you see, the women will be very gracious this evening. They take this event quite seriously. At least, as long as they think there's a chance they might be chosen for the award. Believe me, the men will circulate and become acquainted with as many ladies as they can. I expect you'll be a very popular girl."

"The women don't have a say then?"

"That's right, it's considered that the women would all vote for themselves anyway, so, it would be pointless," he replies.

"You mean some of these husbands will cast their ballot for someone other than their wives?"

He really doesn't want to answer this question. It'll lead to other questions later in the evening. He stalls, thinking, but before he's able to reflect, she continues.

"Are you saying, I'm being put out here on my own tonight. You're not going to be with me?"

He's not quite sure how to take the intent in her voice. Is she concerned about being left alone to deal with all these men, or, is she looking forward to the attention?

"Just relax and enjoy yourself. You look like an angel. With that beautiful face and wonderful smile, you'll melt the heart of every man here. There's no doubt in my mind that you'll win the award," he boasts. "The fact that you're the wife of the next governor of this state might help a little too."

"Oh John, you know just the right things to say," she coos.

Just about to banter again, he feels a tap on his arm. As he turns he sees a slender, rather tall, full bearded man. He's dressed in a black suit and appears to be in a serious mood.

"This is the man Marty said was looking for me," he thinks.

"May I have a few words with you in private, Mr. Anderson. It's very important." He speaks with confidence and no emotion.

"This is not a good time, sir. Can't it wait until tomorrow? What's this about? Who are you?" John barrages him with questions.

"I'm just a messenger sent to transport you immediately to a meeting of utmost importance. Please come with me. I have a carriage waiting."

Mr. Anderson takes him by the arm and pulls him from the ballroom into the hallway.

"Do you expect me to leave this house alone with you? I don't know you. Unless you have better information to offer, I'm afraid I'll have to ask you to leave."

"Mr. Anderson, I can only tell you that it's a matter of national importance. I have two gentlemen in the carriage outside that cannot be seen here, now. Please come outside and sit in the carriage with them." The mystery man calmly counters.

John ponders as he walks away a few steps and back to face the man in black.

"I'll tell you what I'll do. Have your driver take the carriage and the two men into the barn east of this house and wait for me. The driver is to walk outside and close the doors."

"Now, hold on a minute." He walks back to his wife who is watching him and the stranger.

"Find Marty and send him to me . . . quickly, honey."

"What's going on? What's the matter?" Her eyes show excitement and concern.

"Just do as I ask, quickly now." He answers and turns back to the imposing figure standing in the hallway.

By the time he reaches the visitor, Marty arrives, almost running.

"What's the trouble?" He blurts out twenty or so feet away.

"I'm not sure. This gentleman wants me to go with him to a carriage outside to meet with two men. He won't say who they are, just that it's a matter of great importance. I've explained I won't do that, but I will meet with them in the barn if the carriage is put there and left by him and the driver. I need you to watch my back."

"I don't think this is a good idea. Let me go and invite them inside. We can meet in the library. There's no good reason to take the risk."

The stranger addresses Marty. "Sir, there is no harm intended to anyone here, and certainly, no harm is expected by the men in the carriage. I have explained that these two men cannot be seen here. The matter to be discussed is of national importance. I'll have our driver drop the two men inside the barn, then return here with the carriage.

"You can stand outside the closed barn doors to be sure no one interrupts their meeting. Will that be satisfactory?"

John and Marty look at each other for a few seconds. John nods his head in agreement, then Marty nods in support of his wishes.

"Let's do it," John orders, and turns toward a side door with Marty on his heels.

The man in black leaves though the front door with no further comment.

Darkness has moved in unnoticed by the large group inside the house. The outdoor air is crisp and smells of wood smoke from the fires in the kitchens. Mr. Anderson and Mr. Schoener move swiftly toward the barn some one hundred yards away.

"Let's get in there and get a lantern lit," John proposes. "I'll stand back in the shadows until I see what's going on. If you stand by the door, you can keep an eye and ear out for trouble. Do you have your pea shooter with you?"

"Yeah, do you want it?"

"No, but keep it handy."

The carriage arrives just as they step up to the open barn doors. John continues on inside, while Marty stops to face, and block, the team of horses. He smells their musty breath, and feels the heat from their bodies, when they stop directly in front of him.

The slender stranger they met inside climbs down from beside the driver, then turns to see a lantern burning farther back in the barn. After stepping aside, Marty motions the driver to proceed. The carriage moves with a jerk as the horses take up the slack in the rigging. Once it's completely inside, a 'whoa' is heard.

John watches from his position in the shadows as the team clomps toward him. The dim light of the lantern is all but obscured by their size and bulk. They stop not three feet from his position, stomp their feet and snort.

From outside, Marty hears the carriage door open, the springs squeak a couple of times under the weight of the men getting out, and the door slams shut.

Mr. Anderson hears the driver click his tongue three times, and order the team "back, back." The carriage jerks again and backs out of the barn. As soon as the team clears the open doors, they close, sealing him inside with the two nameless men.

It's difficult for him to determine their identity as they, too, are standing back away from the lanterns light. He's sure they're unable to see him for the same reason.

"Who are you, and what do you want of me?" His voice is firm and uninviting.

Meanwhile, back at the Housler farm, Der Bote.

The colonel raises his head and turns toward Selma, his arms still on the table, his coffee cup in his right hand as it sets on a saucer.

"I'm not who you think I am." She's not sure of the meaning of what her husband just told her, and doesn't know what to say. Motionless, she looks at him.

"My birth name is Hans Briermiester. I'm originally from Boston, Massachusetts. Almost everything you understand about my past is a fabrication, a lie. I was forced to move to this part of the country due to threats made upon the lives of my family. I thought I could run and hide from them, but they soon found me. They murdered my wife. They tied my son and me to chairs and made us watch as they used a knife to cut her over and over again. She begged them to kill her—and finally they did. They cut her throat and forced us to watch her bleed to death. They took my boy with them. I've seen him once a year for a few minutes since then." He turns back to face his cup and bows his head.

Selma is dumbstruck.

"Why?" It's the only word she could get to come out of her mouth. She is immediately so sick at her stomach she has to fight to keep from vomiting. Emotions overcome her. She can only sit and wait for him to continue.

"When I was a very young man, twelve years old, I did whatever I could to earn a little bit of money to help feed our family. My mother and father came from Germany, so, they didn't speak the language here. He was a skilled potter, but could find little work, forcing him do odd jobs, as he could get them, to get by. My mother, and my sisters, bless their souls, took in sewing, mended garments, and scrubbed floors at an inn near our home. I'm the youngest of five children, the only boy, the only one born in this country. Times were hard."

She sits as if she's frozen in her position, listening intently, not moving an eyelid.

"I, by chance, became acquainted with a group of men who used me to run errands. They paid me cash each time I did something for them. I brought home more money than my father most of the time. The errands turned to transporting goods. I didn't know it, but the goods were stolen. When I discovered the truth, they trained me how to pilfer and gave me more money than I'd ever seen. I only stole from people who could afford it, and only took what they told me. This went on for several years, until I turned seventeen.

"One fateful day, the owner of a store caught two other men and me thieving part of his supply of fur coats. We all fought and scuffled around, but as it wound up, I took a knife away from one of them, and somehow—I don't know how—I stabbed him with it. I stabbed him in the chest. We ran. Later I was told he died; I killed him."

"My God!" The words came out of her mouth before she could stop them.

"I've done some terrible things, Selma; terrible, horrid, things."

The colonel picks up his coffee cup and with two large gulps, empties it down, sets it on the table, then leaves the room.

She sits in dismay.

When he returns, he's carrying a bottle of whiskey and two glasses. He puts a glass in front of his wife and keeps one for himself.

"I think you need this as much as I do." He pours whiskey into her glass as he speaks, then turns the bottle to the rim of his and fills it completely. He sits down, picks it up, takes a mouthful, and swallows with a grimace.

She doesn't move except for her eyes watching.

He can't be certain she's seen him pour the whiskey in her glass. "Are you all right? Do you want me to continue?" His head leans down sideways to look at her face.

She blinks her eyes as if she's just awakened from a bad dream and sucks in a deep breath, then empties her glass with three swallows, and sets it on the table with a bang.

"Is this all true, or are you making this up just to shock me? If you have, you can stop now, I've heard enough," she says, still struggling to get her breath from the sting of the whiskey.

The colonel can't take his eyes off her. He's never seen her look so completely lost, so spent, drained. He wants to take her into his arms and tell her it's all a lie and that he'll make it up to her if it takes the rest of his life. But he can't, it's all true.

He thinks and sips at his whiskey. Perhaps it would be better if he leaves out many of the details for now and deals with her questions later.

"No, honey, I can't stop now. You must know it all to understand."

"I know, you're right, Charles, we have to get it out in the open. Fill me up," she says, and brushes his hand with the bottom of her empty glass.

He continues. "Well, time passed, and I kept working for them. I couldn't get away, they held me by threatening to turn me over to the police for the murder. During this time I met my wife, and after a while we had a child, our son. Then, these men used them against me. I knew they would hurt my family if I failed to do whatever they asked.

"Eventually they told me I had to murder another person. I couldn't do it, so I let the intended victim know about it. He thanked me over and over. He said he'd leave Boston and never come back. That way, I could say I'd killed him and no one would know the difference. I was very naive at that age, so when he asked me I gave him the names of the men wanting him killed. Needless to say, he went directly to the authorities who in turn went after the men. Knowing it wouldn't be long until the law, or the friends of the men they arrested, would be at our door, my wife, my son, and I decided to leave Boston. We were packing when three of the friends showed up, killed my wife, and took our son. I left immediately, and after moving several times fearing they had located me, I settled here. I thought I was free of them about the same time I met you. I believed I'd never be able to have a love relationship again, but I fell totally in love with you.

"Not long after you and I married, two of them showed up in town and pulled me aside. They had teamed up with a large organization, one that has eyes and ears everywhere. They told me, in no uncertain terms, to do as they asked, or they would kill my son, and you. I knew I couldn't go through that again. So, for these past many years, I have been living two lives; our life together and another to appease them."

Selma has hung on every word she's heard. The shock has left her to pity her husband, to hate him, to love him, to doubt him, and to realize she can never believe another thing he says or does, in that order. "Is that it? Is that all of it?" Her voice is testy and sharp as her words are delivered with a whimper.

Charles nods affirmative.

"I don't know what to say. Hell, I don't know what to think, what to believe. I need some time away from you. You, you stay out of my way until I have the time to understand all of this. Move into town for a while, or something, but get away from me. I'm going to bed. Don't be here in the morning. Do you understand?"

She runs upstairs to her bedroom, jumps onto the bed landing on her stomach, and bursts into tears. Thoughts race through her mind, flashing from hating him for the deception, to reliving the last five years of a warm loving relationship. It's all mixed up, too much to think about.

Two hours pass.

Unable to lie in bed any longer, she goes downstairs, out through the front door, and sits on the edge of the porch, with her feet on the top step. The colonel is nowhere to be seen. Lost in her thoughts, she's not aware of a person walking toward her from the side of the house in the darkness. When the figure is not but five feet from her, she's startled to hear, "Good evening, Selma, it looks like it'll rain for sure, doesn't it."

Trying to get her heart out of he throat, she stands up to recognize Robert.

"Oh, it's you, Robert. What are you doing here?" she speaks softly.

"Well, I just finished supper with the Stokers, and Randy and I are—" She mutes him by placing her finger against his lips.

Two steps forward puts her close enough to put her arms around his neck and pull him to her chest. Her actions and silence are not understood by the young man, but he doesn't object one bit.

"What's the matter? Is something wrong?"

"Everything's wrong. My whole life is wrong. It couldn't be worse. Why does life have to be so hard, so uncertain?" she exclaims, starting to sob again.

"What can I do?" he whispers, and puts his arms around her and hugs gently, his face in her hair.

"Just hold me. I need you to hold me."

They stand together, she sobbing, he wondering what to do next. Finally the tears subside, and a need creeps over the couple locked in each other's arms. She pulls away.

"What do you want me—" he tries to speak, but again she puts her finger to his lips and takes his hand.

She moves toward the steps stretching their arms out between them. When she notices that he's not taking her lead, a look back over her shoulder tells him to follow. Up the steps, across the porch, through the door, they disappear into the darkness of the house.

Back at the barn on the Clevenger estate.

"Mr. Anderson, I must apologize for the manner in which we have arranged this meeting. I have, just today, received information which makes this intrusion necessary. My name is Sam Porter. I'm here with my most trusted friend Gail Hamilton."

John is surprised with the names he hears. These men are associated in the highest echelon of politics today. "Gentlemen, how can I help you?" His humbleness is becoming to the visiting men.

Everyone steps from the shadows to meet at the lantern.

"May we call you John?" Sam Porter asks.

"Please call me Sam, and this is Gail."

John nods. "I'd like that, please do."

"Well, John . . . firstly, let me explain that officially we're not here this evening; this meeting has never taken place. Secondly, I don't think we're taking any risk with you, but I must I ask you not to repeat a word of our conversation to anyone. If you'll hold your questions as I speak, I'll gladly answer any you have when I am finished."

John shakes his head affirmatively.

"I'd like to make you aware that we directly represent the man whom we believe will be the next president of this Union. Just let me say, decisions have been made, and the outcome of the election has been determined. Due to the grave certainty of a civil war, it has been decided he can be the only choice possible. The war will be a bloody, and hard fought, North against the South, state against state, brother against brother. It could last six months or six years. It will be written in history as one being fought to determine the freedoms of mankind, namely the slaves. The Union will proclaim the slaves should be freed as guaranteed by our constitution, while the South, with as much determination, will support the institution of slavery as it exists here today. It will be a just and noble cause, which will be fought gallantly by both sides. This war will require the population to choose a side, pulling every mother, father, son, and daughter together, or apart.

"There are those among us, however, who know and believe that this war is meant to be a harbinger of the future of this great land. This battle will serve a much different purpose than determining the freedom of the slaves. It will determine whether this vast country of ours will be kept as a Union, or be split into sections to be governed by rich, powerful, tyrants. Self-appointed, they would each control as much of this land as their wit and brawn would allow. It's feared that, eventually, they would attack each other, bringing larger and larger sections of this country under the control of fewer and fewer men—dictators. It's possible that this entire young democracy of ours could shift from a land of freedom to that of a prison under the rule of a warlord."

John stands amazed at what he's hearing, and wondering what it has to do with him.

"I can see by the look on your face, I've caught you by surprise with my candid observations. Depending upon your ambitions, I'll see that you are made privy to information which will more than support my statements. This is a real existing threat with a voracious appetite. Knowing and believing these facts, our future leader has agreed to accept the presidency, and will defend our Union from all comers. The longest and hardest fought battles are going to be waged under the cover of pretense. They'll not go down in history written with a decided victor, nor will heroes be acclaimed. Our president, for instance, will be remembered for the civil war and slavery, win or lose, not for thwarting the efforts of these aforementioned tyrants."

Mr. Porter continues. "These people must be stopped. They must be defeated soundly, and left with nothing to resurrect their cause. There will be no second chances. This covert war must be engaged now, we must be the clear victor, and as difficult as it will likely be, take no prisoners."

John is having difficulty staying quiet. He understands Sam's excitement concerning his motives, but what's his part in this, perhaps outlandish, story.

"I'd best cut to the chase as I can see you're about to lose patience. Please bear with me a few more minutes," Sam explains. "But first, Gail, get that flask. You and John have a little nip while I get this said."

Gail, holding two small glasses, reaches inside his coat vest pocket to produce a silver flask. He fills one, hands it to John, fills the other, and slips the flask back into it's place, then takes a sip as he watches Mr. Anderson do the same.

"John, we know about you. For instance, we know you've been moving slaves for the last fifteen plus years. We know about your daughter's accident, and the empty grave beside her grandfather. We are aware she's in the hands of the organization I've spoken about, and we know of the rest of her brothers and sisters, and where they're living their lives. I'll tell you one thing you probably don't realize. All five of your quintuplets are alive. The organization has two of your daughters."

"What?!" John exclaims.

"As you can now understand, we know who you are, a man of integrity. A man who has made several difficult choices, and has placed his personal needs and wants aside to enable himself to continue his purpose in a political life, to help the people of this state. Your effectiveness is easily measured by your success. Now, I believe you have this evening accepted the opportunity to run for the office of governor. You have been able to influence the necessary people with political clout, and money, to get you elected."

"Frankly, whether you continue with your bid for the governor's office, or not, makes no difference to us. We need you, your connections with the people in your circle, your experience with working covertly, and not the least, your connections with the organization that has your two daughters. We want you to join with us secretly. We want your skills with us as we begin our war on this unseen enemy of the Union."

"I'll accept your questions," Mr. Porter says, and stands silent.

"Whooee!" Air escapes through John's lips. "I don't know where to begin."

There is silence in the barn as he paces a few steps, side to side, thinking.

"I'm closely involved with many faces," he explains. "I'm not sure at this moment if I have the gull, or the objectivity this job will require. I mean, what about the man standing outside that door. His list of questions for me is growing as we speak. I'm not sure it would be a good idea for me to run for governor and take this on at the same time. Could I do justice to both? Who can I take on as an ally? It could take weeks, or months, to determine where to place my trust. By this time, all those people in that house are expecting me to be the next governor of this state. What do I say to them?"

"We can't answer those questions for you." Gail Hamilton speaks. "But I can tell you that your country needs you, and needs you badly. It won't be easy, but we know you're up to it. We wouldn't be here otherwise."

Sam adds. "Your choice of comrades is extremely crucial to your effectiveness. I'm, therefore, heartened by your concern. Trust your instincts. They'll not fail you."

"You want me to be a spy, is that right?" John's eyes bounce from one man to the other.

Chapter Fourteen

The home of Charles and Selma Housler.

Selma leads Robert through the house then pauses to look up the flight of stairs. He stands behind her, holding tight to her hand. She lets out a puff of breath as though her mind is made up and begins to climb.

He balances the weight of his body with his left foot on the bottom step, when a feeling of something cold, like the steel of a knife blade, hits between his shoulder blades.

"Robert! Stop right there!"

There is no mistaking this demand is meant to be obeyed. The even tempered words have never been spoken with more controlled, icy, fury.

He stops with a jerk, pulling his hand free of Selma, and turns to see the silhouette of a man in the doorway of the kitchen. The waving, flickering, lamplight behind him causes an eerie picture in the hallway.

"Go home, Robert! You've no further business here!"

Robert believes the voice is that of Charles Housler, but he can't be sure.

"Should he stay and defend Selma against this intruder? Or, should he leave her to deal with the situation on her own?" His thoughts bring him to realize he shouldn't be in this house under these circumstances in the first place.

"I've asked you to leave, Robert, I'll not ask you again! My wife and I will work this out between us! Your interference is not needed! Now go!"

Selma, standing five steps up on the stairway, says. "Go Robert, I don't need more trouble than I already have. It's okay, I'm all right. I'm in no danger. Please go."

He looks at her, then turns and leaves the house.

"I'm not going to ask what your intentions were with that young man. I believe I know, and it won't help to hear it from you. The truth is, I understand. I didn't stop him because I'm upset with what you were about to do. I stopped him because I know in my soul you would regret it, and that regret would play a big part in your decision of whether to stay with me or not. I certainly don't blame you for needing someone. Hell, call him back if you think it'll help you handle the pain I've caused. But I would rather see if we can get a through this mess called our lives on our own." The colonel turns back into the kitchen.

She sits on the step and hangs her head; her clasped hands lie in her lap. Distress ebbs from her being out into the darkness, while a lonely dreariness tries to settle into her soul. Silence lays heavy on her shoulders.

Robert secures his horse from the barn, and is on his way home. His horse moves at a walk. He rides unaware, lost in his thoughts of a few minutes ago.

"I've never felt more respect for Mr. Housler than I have right now." He thinks. "I've done him an injustice. I don't know what's going on between them, but I owe him an apology. He probably knows how I feel about her, and even with that he's never said a word in anger to me. He doesn't deserve this, at least not from me." At this moment, he climbs a step up the ladder of maturity. "It's over. I have to get her out of my mind, find someone my own age, move on with my life, and leave her to figure things out her own. I'll only complicate her problems. I'll love her forever, and it won't be easy, but I'll do it."

At the barn on the Clevenger estate.

"We want you to be a great deal more than a spy, John. We want you to head up a group of men who will gather facts and theories. We want you to take command of our covert operations in this battle," Sam continues.

"But I know nothing about this cause. I have no military training. Certainly, there's a man out there somewhere better qualified for this than I am."

"There is no such person. A war such as this has never been fought on this soil. We don't need the blood and guts of an army general. We need an ambassador, a man who can win minor political skirmishes and know their importance in furthering our cause. We need an organizer, a man with energy, with wealth of his own. Most importantly, we need a man of unquestionable character, who will act on his own, reporting only to the highest power in this land," Mr. Porter explains.

"Report only to you then?" John asks.

"Oh no, not to me. But to someone you know you can trust," Sam answers.

"How will this endeavor be funded?" Another good question.

"A fund of five million dollars has been established as a starting point. The money isn't government funds, it's from men who know of and believe the dangers facing us in the near future. These men are committed to fund this operation regardless of the costs."

"Are you saying that I'll report only to God, and that I alone will put together a plan—a scheme—to defeat the Company?" His question is poised with emotion.

"You want me to take on the responsibility of saving our country single handedly. Mr. Porter, I think you need to reconsider your proposal. No one man on this earth should be placed in such a position. How do you know I won't be the biggest tyrant of the bunch? Why couldn't I turn out to be your biggest enemy during this civil war, work against you, and do it with your money?"

"Thank you, Mr. Anderson," Sam points out. "I couldn't have said it better myself. That's exactly the reason you are the man. Alone? Oh no, you won't be alone. There are at least fifty strong, bright, able men, who are aware of this meeting, awaiting your decision. They are all sworn to counsel and support your lead."

John's mind is churning, looking for answers. "Out of all these men you mentioned, how many of them have turned down this proposal before you decided to offer it to me?"

"I believe you are asking whether you are our first choice." Sam understands.

"We've been working for over a year to locate and convince the right man for this undertaking. We made a list of seventy-eight possible candidates. From there, we eliminated seventy-five of them on our first pass. We then put the remaining three names up for a vote by the thirty-three deciding members. The vote was unanimous in your favor."

"Well, I need time to think about this. How in the world can I hide it from the people closest to me? My wife? My family?" John poses.

"That will be just the first of many such problems you'll need to address. But there's no time to waste," Mr. Hamilton interjects. "We need a decision before we leave this barn. Sam and I need to carry your response with us. It's imperative we begin this operation without further delay. If it were me, dealing with the state's problems while putting these plans together would be something I'd avoid. I wouldn't run for governor. This is far too important. And John, let me say one last thing to you. There will be no glory for you in this. You'll never be mentioned in political circles or recorded in history for what you do. You'll do it because you know it must be done. This battle could extend well beyond the end of the civil war. The first strategy must be to stifle their efforts to support the Southern states, and by doing so, quite possibly allow the Union to win the war. Beyond that, your battle will continue until you've put them out of business."

"Suppose, just suppose, I agree here and now. What's the next step, the timing?"

"The perfect solution would be for you to disappear from the memory of your family and most of your friends, which would give you a free hand to start immediately. Since that isn't practical, I would think not more than a week, less if possible. As to your other question, you will be contacted by a group of our mutual friends. You'll know what to do from there," Mr. Porter concludes.

"Am I to be voted out of this position the first time someone doesn't agree with my thinking? Or, perhaps, be spied upon with reports of my efforts filtering back to you or someone else?" John asks good questions.

"The job is yours until you decide you've won the battle, or until someone blows your brains out during your sleep. It makes sense that your efforts cannot become a political issue. You and your organization will operate on your own. The United States government will have nothing to do with it. In fact, the government will deny your existence and offer no support whatsoever. Oh, I imagine you'll be spied upon. It will be impossible to be effective and not draw some attention. You handle that yourself." Gail Hamilton's reply carries all the truth intended.

"What will happen if I uncover a spy in your administration. Would it make sense for me to expose him or her to you?" Mr. Anderson forges ahead looking for information.

"You shouldn't give us his or her name. You should expose them for what they are. Then the government can deal with them. Remember though, don't expose yourself in the process," Sam warns.

"Any other questions?" A pause.

"No, it looks like I'll learn as I go."

“One thing you haven’t asked that I probably would if it were me,” Gail suggests. “Aren’t you curious about what the job pays, you know, what’s in it for you?”

John looks at them both and says as he sticks out his hand in agreement. “A man shouldn’t take on a job like this for money. The reward for something like this has to come from the success of his efforts. That’s the only way to sleep at night. Besides, I’ll get any money I need from that five-million-dollar war chest.”

A chuckle can be heard among them as three hands come together.

“Your decision has helped me more than you can realize. Thank you. Gail and I will pass your words along. You should hear something from the group shortly. Get yourself situated around to arrive in Richmond no later than Thursday of next week. Be prepared to be away from home for some time.” Gail’s remarks are exciting to hear.

Things are quiet at the Housler farm.

There’s not been a sound in the household for some time. There’s no sign of Sachel or Alberta Mae, who usually are seen moving from room to room completing chores. They heard part of what was said and decided to stay out of the way.

Selma starts to move by standing up on the step, holding on to the rail. She turns as though to ascend the stairs, but stops, turns, and steps down to the hallway floor. Pausing again with her hand on the large round knob of the bottom post, she braces herself with a deep breath and walks briskly into the kitchen.

Her husband has pulled a chair away from the table and placed it by the back screen door, hoping to catch a little cool breeze. He’s sitting there, looking out into the darkness.

“Charles . . . you did the right thing with Robert. Understand, no matter how it looked, I wouldn’t have allowed him to touch me, not that way. But don’t blame him, he’s just a fine young man learning his way around in his world. He has feelings for me, you know, and I used him to get back at you, to hurt you, like you’ve hurt me.” She confesses.

“Yes, I know that, honey. I’ve known since the day after he walked you home more than five years ago. You needed someone then, and again now. He happened to be there. Don’t fret about it, I’ll apologize to him. And you’re right, he’s a fine young man, with a young man’s wants and needs,” the colonel assures.

“About you and me,” he moves on, “these last five years loving you and being together have been the happiest days of my life. There’s been no lies about that. All those feelings, all those precious special moments together, all real, all true. I know they’ve meant the same to you, too. Let’s not throw it all away. I’m truly the man you have been with this last five years. All those years before, I was living two lives, but no more.” His words are spoken with conviction and emotion.

“I need to tell you that I’m not certain I can keep the promises I made before I knew the truth about you.” Selma purposely doesn’t answer the unasked question in his words. “I’ve always wondered Charles, why me? Why would you, looking like you do, having the means to pick any woman you want, why would you pick me? I was, and am, a nobody.

All I brought to this marriage was me. Then for you to treat me the way you did for so long, well, I need some time to sort this whole thing out."

"Please, honey, sit down for a few minutes. I want to explain and try to give you the answers you're looking for." He pauses to see if she's staying or leaving the kitchen.

She pulls a chair away from the table and sits some ten feet away.

"Go ahead, but I think you'll only make a bad thing worse."

The colonel believes he can, perhaps, sway his wife's thinking. Now that the initial shock is past, his explanation will be heard with a different attitude. He must be careful not to upset her again. She shouldn't receive any new information. Any discussion of his unlawful activities has to be avoided. If this conversation isn't handled properly, he'll lose her forever.

"I'm not going to sit here and tell you I know the weight of your heart, and the suffering I've caused you over our lifetime together. I know I've forced you to doubt me, and yourself, as well. You should in no way blame yourself for this mess. The fault is totally mine." He forges ahead. "Do you remember the first time we laid eyes on each other? I stopped to water my horse and was talking to Carl, the owner of the farm where you and your family lived. He and I had been acquainted for some time, so I stopped by whenever I was close to his place. I was gazing around listening to him speak when my eyes froze on you standing there barefoot in the vegetable garden, bent over with a hoe in your hands. I'll never forget that image of you. I felt my insides stir when I realized you were looking back at me. Do you remember, honey?"

"Yes, I remember. How could I ever forget?" Her reply is tempered with a warm knowing tone.

"Carl couldn't help seeing our attraction for each other. I had helped him with some financial problems and some work around his place a while before that, so he asked me if I was interested in you. I told him I'd never seen a more beautiful enticing woman. He said he'd send you with me. At first, I didn't realize what he was saying, then it hit me. I must have looked bewildered because he said you belonged to him, and he'd give you to me in payment for helping him. I told him I couldn't do that, and that ended the conversation. The thing was, I couldn't get you out of my mind. I kept going back to his farm, making up all sorts of excuses to be there, just to see you from a distance. Finally, one day he says to me, 'I think you'd better take me up on my offer. Her name is Selma. I hear she likes you too.' I told him the feelings I had for you wasn't for that of a servant. I told him I was in love with you, and at that, he handed me your freedom papers. He had them all made up, signed and sealed. You were a free woman. Remember, honey?"

"Yes, I remember you walking toward me with those papers in your hand. I was so nervous I thought I was going to wet my pants. I didn't know what the papers were all about, but I thought you were the most handsome, gentle, settled man in the world. You handed me the papers and told me I was a free woman. I could do anything I wanted. At first I didn't realize what all that meant. The only thing I knew for sure right then was I was totally in love with you, and everything about you. All you had to do was ask, and I would have went with you anywhere. But you didn't ask me to do anything, although I knew you wanted me.

You said you'd be back in two weeks, two whole weeks later, to talk to me and my family. You took my hand and kissed the back of it. Lord, I never had such feelings as I had that day. Then you left me standing there with the bucket in my arm, chickens picking at the corn I was tossing on the ground, and my family standing here and there with their mouths wide open. Oh yes, I remember, and just look at what's happened to us." Selma shows excitement when recalling those early days, and sadness when her awareness of the present returns.

They take a long look at each other. Moving his chair closer to face her, he takes her hand and kisses the back of it, as he did back then. Still holding on, he says, "Selma, will you marry me, again? You are more beautiful today then you were the day we met. I can't live without you. Will you forgive me my past sins, and together with me, make a new better life for the both of us? I swear to you, we'll be partners sharing everything, and I'll never do anything again to make you mistrust me. I'll live my life making you happy."

"You're asking me to put your previous marriage, your son, and your criminal past behind me, when I just learned of it a few hours ago. I'm not sure I want to do that. I don't know if I'll ever be able to do that." Selma's words are the spoken truth. He senses he's losing her.

He raises her hand, kisses it again, then places it carefully on her lap. He tightens his hold just a little before relaxing to remove his hand from hers. As he pulls away, she grabs and grasps his hand with a firm grip.

"God, oh God, help me, I love this man. My brain tells me I should run, but my heart makes me stay." She looks upward and prays.

He watches his wife's eyes as she lowers her head to look directly into his. He feels a calmness come over her, he sees a glow around her face.

"Thank you, thank you, my darling, you'll not regret this," he gratefully mutters.

"I'll pray every day for us, Charles. I want us to be together, but I need something to hold on to. You have to promise me that you'll break away from these people who have their hold on you. We'll fight them together if we must. And another thing, I'm your wife, and I want to be looked at and treated that way. You have to include me in your entire life, as your wife. Now, I don't know how long it will take me to accept everything you've told me, you'll have to be patient while I sort through it. And you'll answer my questions openly and honestly. If there's anything else I should know, tell me now. This is your chance. If you start adding things after today, I'll have no choice, I'll leave," she finishes.

"Wait. One more thing, I want a baby . . . our baby."

The Howard Clevenger mansion is in full swing with the gala building to a new high. Those inside have taken no notice of the meeting in the barn one hundred yards away.

The carriage is pulling away carrying a driver, a tall stranger dressed in black, and the two men who were never there. John Anderson and Marty Schoener stand watching it disappear into the night.

"What went on in there?" Marty asks, his curiosity peaking.

"Help me close these doors and I'll tell you." John's voice reveals the hush-hush nature of the meeting.

Once the doors are closed sealing them inside the barn, the mask of secrecy complete, John begins, “You’ll not believe this . . . I just agreed to accept a position as the head of a yet to be named organization. The purpose of this organization is to save this country of ours from itself. As of this moment, you and I are the only two people that know this organization exists, and right now, I’m the only member. This organization has all the funds it will ever require. It will operate covertly to influence the outcome of the upcoming war, as well as protect this land against a mighty enemy for a time unknown.

“Have I piqued your interest, Marty?”

“What in the world are you yammering about, John? Who were those men?” His friend is a little agitated.

“I’m not able to disclose that at the moment, but if your interested, you can be my number one man. What do you say? Will you help me?”

Marty stands there in the light of the lantern staring at his friend.

“Are you serious?” he finally says. “Help you with what? Hell, I don’t have a notion of what you’re talking about.”

“I’ll give you as much detail as I have, but it has to be later. Right now, we need to decide on a way to get me out of this race for governor. I won’t be able to do both jobs. We need a good convincing story, something everybody can believe. Any ideas?”

John’s message is not only vague, but now he has his friend pacing, throwing his hands into the air.

“Do you hear yourself?” Marty’s voice can be heard half way to the house.

“Are you insane. You’ve worked the better part of fifteen years to get this nomination, and now you want to throw it away. And, oh yes, you want to back out on the evening of your nomination. You can’t be serious.”

“I’m as serious as a knife in the chest. Trust me. Help me get past this evening, and I’ll explain it all to you later tonight. I’m not going to run for the governor’s office. This new position is too important, the timing is critical. You can tell me to go to hell later, just help me get through this evening, all right?”

Marty paces back and forth, back and forth, thinking. A full minute passes before he stops in front of his friend.

“If you drop out of the bid for governor, I won’t have a job anyway, so what do I have to lose? I’m in. What do you want me to do?”

“Bless you, my friend, I’ll thank you properly later.

“Our problem is to get me out of the governor’s race without causing a lot of commotion. Howard won’t make the announcement if I’m not there to accept the nomination. Perhaps the best thing would be for me to just leave, and let you deal with the wolves in there. Unless you have a better idea?”

“No, no, John, that’ll burn too many bridges. We don’t know who we might need with our new commitment. You should go back in there and make an announcement to one and all. Explain that you have an emergency—one of a personal nature—and must leave immediately. I’ll pull June and Rachell aside and prepare them. I’ll tell Howard not to make the announcement, and that we’ll be back in touch with a complete explanation.

Then, I'll have a couple of porters pack our trunks and load them on a carriage. We'll go as far as town and find an inn. We can talk, and go from there. How's that?" Marty smartly asks.

"Beautiful, just beautiful. I particularly like the part where you do all the work and I politely beg off. I'm glad you're with me. Let's get a move on."

Forty-five minutes later, the Andersons and the Schoeners are inside a carriage on their way to town. The two women know nothing except there is an emergency of some sort. They're both a little testy about leaving the ball in such a hurry.

"What's the big emergency?" Rachell starts.

"Yes, why did you drag us out of there so quickly?" June piles on.

"We'll talk about it later. Marty and I need to have some time privately before anything is said. Relax, there's no emergency. Everything's fine," John announces firmly.

June snorts a short breath and sasses. "You mean, you pulled us away from our first formal ball for no good reason. Rachell and I were having the time of our lives. I've never seen so many finely dressed, handsome, rich men, all together in one place, all wanting our attention. We'll never be invited to another one, not after the way we left there. This had better be good."

The men say nothing.

"I suppose we can always tear up these gowns and use the material for horse blankets or something. You men know we can never wear these gowns again, don't you?"

The men remain silent.

The women settle back into the leather seats seething when their husbands won't argue with them. After a while with the lack of conversation, and the swaying of the coach, they fall asleep. The rest of the trip to town is quiet.

The carriage driver stops at the first inn he comes to along the deserted main street of town. He jumps down from his seat and opens the door. John moves out first, as the wives stir. Marty is right behind him.

"Put our luggage on the walkway, driver. Here, take this for your trouble." John orders, and hands the man two dollars. "Don't tell anybody where we are."

"Yessir," the driver confirms. "I ain't seen you. I don't know nothing."

John rents the last three unoccupied rooms in the inn. Luck would have it they're all in a row on the second floor. He assigns a room to each of the women and asks them to a get a good night's sleep while he and Marty meet in the third room. He tells them their husbands could be up most of the night. They're a bit on the grouchy side, but they're tired and still a little liquored up, so, they agree to turn in for the night.

Mr. Schoener asks the night desk clerk to have a pot of coffee and something to eat brought up to their meeting room. John smiles at his friend's efficiency and notices a gnawing in his own stomach. They enter their room, remove their jackets, pull off their fancy ballroom shoes, and get comfortable: this is going to be a long night.

Mrs. Anderson's husband thanks his friend for all he's done this evening, and for the patience he's exercised through it all. He, also, explains his meeting with the two men in the barn, and cautions him to forget their names. Keeping to the facts of that meeting is a problem for him, since his mind is filled with thoughts of how to get started and the urgency of it all. Finally, he stops speaking when the coffee and cold fried chicken arrive. Cornbread, with a bowl of butter, and a canning jar of preserves are also set on the only table in the room. He pays the delivery man and tips him generously. Both men begin serving themselves and within a few minutes, with their mouths full, their meeting continues.

Marty swallows some cornbread, takes a sip of the hot coffee and says, "This tastes good, I didn't know how hungry I was. I'm still with you, so I guess I'm as crazy as you are, or maybe worse. The question is, what do we do first? Where do we start?"

"You know, oddly enough, the Lord created heaven and earth in six days, then rested on the seventh. Think about it, that's exactly the time we have to put our plan together. We're in mighty good company, and with His help, we'll think our way through this huge undertaking. As for today, this first meeting, I believe we should decide who can be included with our trust, namely, how about our wives? Can we, or should we, take the chance and tell them what we're doing? And we both have sons who could be of a great help to us, if we decide they can be a part of it. We should consider our friends, all our friends, and determine who can best help us with a list of all that needs to be done. We'll have to place our trust with any number of people. The size of this undertaking demands we take the risk. Lastly, there's only so much we can do until we have the meeting next Thursday. We'll see a few of our volunteers then, and believe me, I'm very anxious to meet them." John lays out his thoughts.

"I believe you're right on target with what you say, so I'll put my foot in it, right up to my ankle. Let's inform our wives and two oldest sons. This job will take every minute of our time, so they have to know. We don't need to tell them every little detail, just enough to let them know what we're doing. Agreed?"

John ponders for a few seconds. "Agreed, we'll tell June and Rachell at breakfast."

"Okay, that's a start, now I want to ask you about . . ." The meeting goes on.

Time moves on at the Housler's farm.

The colonel and Selma have held on to each other most of this evening, reliving their past, looking for ways to find each other again. First sipping wine, then brandy, they finally make their way to their bedroom to make up properly.

It is past one AM, Charles is lying on top of the blanket on his side facing his wife. Selma is lying on her back with the blanket pulled across her waist, her knees and legs exposed. He's happy and content knowing she's not leaving. But he's troubled, feeling she expects his past to go away with the snap of a finger. His mind isn't in the bedroom with them.

"She doesn't want to hear any more about it, unless she asks. I'm not permitted to introduce anything new, and that's one of my problems. There's so much she doesn't know, things she must understand. Breaking away from the organization won't be that easy. They'll defame me, and come after her. They'll almost certainly murder my son.

"We'll not be able to stay here on the farm. The organization will stir up the people around here, they won't let us stay. They'll run us off—if they don't bury us here. I have to tell her so she'll understand the dangers and consequences. Should I wait? If I tell her now it'll break the mood of this evening, and probably ruin everything. How do I tell her, I've been spying on all of our friends and acquaintances, or about the runaways, and how none of them ever get to where they'll be free? What will she do when she finds out I'm working for the Confederate South?

"If a war starts, I'll wear the uniform of the Confederate army. She doesn't know about all the information I've passed along to the Southern leaders concerning the Northern army and their commanders. What does she think will happen when her best friend's husband, John Anderson, learns of my betrayal of his trust. When he learns I've put his future in jeopardy, will he do his best to destroy me? Will June believe her when she tries to explain that she knew nothing of it until now? The Andersons, as well as this whole community, will know where our loyalties lay." He tells himself to relax. "Nothing will happen until I make my intentions known, and I won't do that until she understands the dangers and problems threatening us."

The meeting at the hotel continues with John and Marty hard at it, working out the 'first approach' details of their new undertaking.

John is saying, "One man I am confident we can trust is Colonel Charles Housler. I've known him for years. He's always kept his commitments, and he knows how to keep a secret. Would you agree with me?"

"I've only known him through you, but you obviously have seen him in action and trust him. Therefore, so do I."

"I'll speak to him as soon as possible when I arrive back at the farm. I'm sure he'll be of great assistance to us," John says confidently.

Chapter Fifteen

Sally and Lilly are sitting, talking at La Nesra, the Company's compound near Atlanta.

"It's hard for me to believe I've been here for over five years, Sally. I can barely remember my mother's face. I yearn to see them all. I think if I could just get some news from them, find out if they're well, things like that."

"It's against the rules for you to have any contact at all with your family. You might as well get it out of your mind," Sally explains, again, to her close friend.

"I know I can talk to you without getting into trouble. We've become good friends over the last few years. I'm not planning anything, I mean, you know I'll not try to leave here. This is my home now."

"I know, Lilly, but you only keep hurting yourself by hanging on to those memories."

"What's it like out there? Has the world changed? Is it still there?"

"It's still there, honey. I'd like nothing better than to explain everything you want to know, but if I did and you said something you're not supposed to know, or if you made a little slip, you'd be punished. Then an investigation would take place, which would put me in a terrible position. It would ruin our friendship. I wouldn't be permitted to spend time with you." She reminds the fifteen-year-old girl.

"You're really in a mood today, Lilly. Tell me, what's really on your mind?" Her direct approach almost always works with her friend.

"It's been over a month since I last saw you, that's too long. They're still doing these terrible things to me, and I don't have anybody to talk with about it. It's a lonely place where they make me go. Sometimes I'm there for days, or a week at a time, by myself."

"I'm here now, tell me, what are they doing to you?" Sally has an idea of Lilly's complaints, but wants to hear it from her.

The young girl is more savvy than Sally realizes. She says to herself. "I must be careful about what I say. I can trust nobody here, not even Sally. I'm not the only one here that she's friends with. I know because two other students told me about her. They say she pretends to be our friend, when she's really gathering information about us to give to the people who keep us here. I can't tell her everything, but I need to keep her believing we're good friends. I might be able to use her to get out of here. So, I need to talk with her as if I trust her completely. Here goes."

"They put those needles in my arm and put me to sleep, but I don't really go to sleep. I can still hear everything that's going on around me. They talk to me, tell me things I have to repeat back to them when they wake me up. Once they put me to sleep for two weeks, I know because that's what they told me. Have you ever been all alone by yourself for that long? Not being able to move even your toe? It seems like an eternity. I have to occupy my mind or go crazy. So, I try to remember things—anything—like my family, my other life. It's hard to do. Then, they carry me around. They put me here and there, only to move me again. They don't know how rough they treat me. I've had bruises all over my body. See, like these here on my leg. When they wake me up I'm really sore and stiff. My life here isn't much fun. They make me do all sorts of stretches and things to limber up, and that hurts, too. Then they feed me. They make me eat, and eat, and eat, and drink, and drink, and drink. All this time, they keep asking questions."

"I know, it's their job. They're working with you to find out how to keep you strong and healthy while you're asleep. Your body doesn't age when you're asleep, but it does take a certain amount of nourishment to keep you alive. Not much, but something. They put needles in your blood vessels and give you food through them. I understand they're close to being able to keep you alive indefinitely while you're in that state. That means you could live forever." Sally seems excited about the possibilities.

"Some life, though, huh?"

The older woman sees that her charge needs a bit of cheering up so she begins her ritual of positive attitude, and the meaning of life. She no sooner gets started than Lilly cuts her off.

"I'm really exhausted today. Can we do this next time you're here?"

"Sure, honey, I don't see why not. I'll leave so you can rest." She rises from her chair and departs in a bit of a huff.

"I usually like the time she's here, but not today. I'm glad she's gone.

"Little does she know, but I can see, as well as hear, when they put me to sleep. They don't know it, but they're teaching me to put my feelings aside and use my mind to control my emotions and actions. So, when they put me to sleep, I get my mind off of what they are doing to me and use it to make my plan. I'll leave here one day. I'll find my family again. I've made several good friends who are students here, too. I slip out of my room and meet with them. We have a special place on the roof where we go whenever we can, at eleven o'clock at night. Sometimes there are as many as eight or nine of us there, all at one time. My favorite person is Eagle. He's easy to talk with, almost like Randy. He wants to be more than just my friend, but I won't do it. I tell him this is not a good place for that, but he keeps trying. Maybe someday, I will. I won't allow myself to get to like him too much. I don't want to feel responsible for him if something should happen.

"All the while they're studying me like I'm in a specimen in a jar, I'm working with my mind to see if I can make something happen. I swear, when they put me to sleep, I can see and hear a lot better than when I'm awake. My mind is clearer too. I feel like my brain has a lot more energy and strength. If I concentrate really hard it feels like I can almost sit myself up. I don't think I move, though, because if I did, they'd see me and say something. There's always someone in the room with me. I just have this feeling, I think that maybe I can get up and move around even when I'm asleep. I've tried to do it when I'm awake lying on my bed, but I don't seem to be able to concentrate hard enough. I'm just waiting for a time when they put me to sleep and leave me alone in the room. I'll find out then.

"I have a condition in my brain, a chemical difference than that of most other people. I was born with it. They tell me they put more of a certain chemical in my blood and cause me to go to sleep. Then when they want me to wake up, they put in another chemical to cancel out some of what they put in before. This is another thing I'm working on with my brain. I think it might be possible for me to cause myself to go to sleep that way. The problem is, I don't know if I can wake myself up. If I can learn to wake myself up without them, I can do it when they leave me alone in a room at the laboratory. There's no bars on the windows there, nor locks on the doors from what I can tell. This could be my way out of here. We'll see."

At the Anderson farm, John has just explained to Robert about the new organization he's founding and has asked his son to assist with these new responsibilities as well as running the farm. Robert grasps the concept without hesitation.

"Just let me know what you want me to do, and I'll do it. Will Randy and I still be able to go to Atlanta like we've planned?" he asks.

"I think you should go, son. I have a lot to do over the next few weeks, so we probably wouldn't see each other anyway. Don't be gone more than six weeks, though. You'll need to pay some attention to matters here at the farm, as well as help me. One of the duties I'll ask you to perform will be the security of our farm, the colonel's Der Bote, and that of Cole Sanders's place."

"Great. I'll be here when you need me. We're leaving day after tomorrow." Robert rejoices.

The atmosphere around Der Bote has been calm over the last few days. The colonel and Selma look at each other from a distance and speak only a few words, then only if absolutely necessary. They need to gain an understanding of their new relationship, knowing it will take time. It's different in their bedroom at night, however. The thoughts of their problems seem to leave them when they enter the room. They don't analyze what could be seen as odd behavior. The involuntary feelings come from somewhere inside them when they lie on the bed gently kissing and caressing until they make love, then fall asleep in each other's arms.

Dawn comes early at the Anderson farm. John awakens to realize his left arm is lying flat under his wife's neck. She's lying on her back still sleeping. Carefully, he bends his elbow while sliding his arm around her left shoulder, picks up slightly, and rolls her toward him.

She stirs.

He continues to roll her over until he feels her breasts against his bare chest.

"I'm one lucky man to have such a woman for a wife," he thinks as he looks at her beautiful face and pulls her closer. He lightly slides his free hand down her side over her hip and onto her thigh while placing a tender kiss on her lips.

June awakens with surprise. Without thinking, she throws her husband aside and jumps up, out of his grasp. When she realizes where she is, what was happening, and what she's done, she's a little embarrassed.

"Is this all you men ever think of, John? Can't a person even sleep without fear of being handled?"

As the words come out of her mouth, she wishes she could swallow them back. Wanting to find a way to start over, she takes a few seconds to get her thoughts together, too long for her husband.

"You're right. A man should only want to hold his wife when it fits her schedule and her mood." The words are spoken with severity. He's out of bed, on his feet, and looking for his clothes.

"John, I . . ." she tries to say.

"Forget it," he clamors.

"But, John, I didn't . . . ," she tries again.

"I said to forget it, I know I will." His remarks are sent with apparent contempt. He grabs his clothes and boots, and leaves the room, speaking over his shoulder.

"I'll see you at breakfast. You'll recall, we're due at the Housler's for dinner at eleven."

Charles Housler is busy in his tack room waxing a saddle when he notices Robert walking toward the house. He steps outside, so as to be seen, and speaks as quietly as he can and still let the young man hear him.

"Good morning, Robert. I see you're up early. Had your breakfast yet?"

"Oh, hi, Mr. Housler. I didn't see you there. Yeah, I was up early and ate a couple of hours ago. I came over to talk with you, if you have a few minutes."

The colonel is a bit impressed by how this young man is approaching him after what happened a few evenings ago.

"Certainly, fact is, I want to talk to you too." He puts on an intentional smile to expose his friendliness.

"Let's go into the kitchen and get some coffee."

"If it's all the same to you, sir, I'd just as soon not go in there right now, you understand." Robert is choosing his playing field.

Again, the colonel is impressed.

"Sure, son, I understand. What's on your mind?" Spoken as if he doesn't know.

"Well, sir," Robert begins, "about the other night, I acted in a very improper way toward your wife. I admit to you, Mr. Housler, I'm fond of her, but I assure you, I'll not again find myself in a similar situation. You were absolutely right by ordering me to leave. I had no right or good reason to be there. I swear to you, it will never happen again. Will you please accept my apology? I won't feel right about myself until you do."

The colonel looks at this brave young man. He knows what must be happening in his mind at the moment. Many a man, young or old, would never find the courage to do what he's doing. They would just stay away, hoping things would air out over time.

Selma's husband speaks.

"How can I accept your apology when you've done nothing wrong? What I saw the other night was you trying to console my distraught wife. Something I wasn't able to do at the time. I've known about your feelings for Selma for a long time. It makes me feel proud that my wife is desired by a man such as you. I know you'd never act on your feelings, you respect family and friends."

He continues. "I'll ask a favor of you, though."

"Yes, sir, anything I can do."

"I'd like you to take Selma aside and tell her you and I have no problems with each other. It'll mean a lot to her, and me. But don't mention I asked you to do it."

"If you really want me to, I'll do that," Robert says, at the same time thinking it will give him a chance to talk to her in this way one last time.

"Yes, thank you. I appreciate it," the colonel finishes.

"Oh, by the way, your folks are visiting us for dinner today. Your daddy said it's urgently important that they meet with Selma and me. Do you have any idea what it's all about? Is it about his bid for the governor's seat?" Charles shows his concern.

"I believe I'm aware, Mr. Housler, but I know he wants to explain it all to you. Now, if you don't mind, I'm going to see if I can find Randy. If Alberta Mae will let him, I'd like to leave for Atlanta tomorrow, a day earlier than we planned. Daddy wants us to get back as soon as we can, so, maybe we can get back sooner if we leave tomorrow."

"That's fine. Don't forget about Selma now," the colonel reminds.

"That's where I'm headed right now," he answers and turns toward the house.

When he enters the kitchen, Alberta Mae and Selma are sitting together at the table with their breakfasts. Alberta Mae starts to get up when Selma says.

"Robert, hi. I didn't expect to see you here this morning. I noticed you and Charles talking out by the barn."

"Please don't get up, Alberta Mae, finish your breakfast. Mrs. Housler, can I speak with you alone somewhere?" He quickly interjects.

Alberta Mae sits back down, rolls her eyes, and turns her head, when Selma says.

"Let's go into the parlor. No one will bother us there."

"What's on your mind?" She's quick to ask as soon as they're alone.

"Well, I want to tell you that your husband and I have talked and there's no problem between us, no problem at all."

"That's good to hear," she snaps back. "Is that all?"

"No, it isn't. I don't know what's going on between you and the colonel, and it's none of my business, but I figured something out that I need to explain to you."

Her posture straightens and stiffens, he has her attention.

"I have loved you for the last five years, and always will in my own way. But I know it's not right, and I need to find a relationship that can lead somewhere. I don't blame you, you never encouraged me, except for that first night when I walked you home."

She interrupts. "You don't have to do this Robert, I know already."

"Oh, but I do, Selma, I have to do it for me. Now hush and let me finish."

"From now on, I'm your loyal friend, and that's all. I'll never approach you that way again, and if you come to me, I'll pretend I don't know what you're doing, and laugh it off. But if you ever need anything—anything—I'll be there if you ask. Okay?"

"That's fine," Selma responds, feeling somewhat let down, not quite realizing why.

"Now," the young man has more to say, "whatever your problems are with the colonel, I'm strongly suggesting that you work them out. He's a good man. If you love him, and I think you do, go out there to him right now and make things right. Life is so short, why not enjoy the parts you can. I've learned that few things in life are completely good or completely bad. There are no perfect people on this earth, only those with goodness or badness in their hearts. He has a good, giving heart. You might never find that in a man again for the rest of your life."

She looks at this twenty-two-year-old man standing in front of her and feels the wisdom of his words. It all seems so simple. Nothing is all wrong, just as nothing is all right. If the bad outweighs the good in something, it will stay way that until enough good is done to shift the weight back the other way. These last five years with the colonel have been good. One could say, very good. What will the next five years bring? No one knows, but if given the proper chance and encouragement, good can win out. We can change everything, anything, together. This is all Selma needs to push her to the conclusion she's wanted to reach all along.

"Oh, Robert, thank you, thank you," she says as she throws her arms around his neck and gives him a big hug. He's still bewildered when she lets go and runs out the back door looking for her man.

"Boy, you sure got some way with womenfolk." He hears Alberta Mae say from the kitchen.

"Come in here and hug me too. I want to thank you for cheering things up around here." He steps into the kitchen, puts his arms around Randy's mother and says, "Is it okay with you if we leave for Atlanta tomorrow instead of the day after?"

"And you know just the right time to ask your questions, too." She answers cheerily. "You know I'm not going to say no now. If you leave a day early, that means you'll be back a day sooner, right?"

Colonel Housler is busy polishing the saddle when Selma steps into the tack room. The smell of sweaty, tanned, leather fills her nostrils. The polish and rag drop as if a sixth sense tells him she's there. He turns as she runs the last few steps throwing herself at him.

"I've come to my senses." She exclaims. "I need you to be my husband, all day and all night, forever."

"What in the world's come over you, girl?" he asks excitedly.

"It was Robert, Charles. He said some things to me that made perfect sense. He has a clear understanding of life beyond his years, but I don't think he knows it."

"I know, honey. He doesn't know it, but he's destined for big things in life. John and June must be immensely proud of him. Speaking of John and June, they're due here in a couple of hours. I'm not sure about their purpose. It could be they want to tell us about their trip and his nomination for governor, but for some reason, I have the feeling it's more than that. I also feel it's important for us to let them know about our dilemma. If we're to keep their trust and friendship, we must."

Selma replies, "Yes, I know, but it would be a shame to ruin their news by hanging out our dirty laundry as soon as they get here. Let's allow them to talk through their news, and we'll show our support for them. Then when it all settles down, we can tell them everything. You can pick the proper time. How's that?"

"That's a good idea. That's the way we'll handle it," he agrees.

They spend the time before the Andersons arrive discussing their problems, and getting to know the dangers of pulling away from the organization. They feel the power of working together grow as they speak. They'll disarm the threats made by these evil, vicious, people.

John and June arrive later then planned, causing the dinner to be held for some time. They sit down at the table as soon as the initial greetings are exchanged. Alberta Mae starts serving the food immediately. No excuse is offered for the Andersons' tardiness, and none is requested by the Houslers.

"Okay, you two. How was your trip? I can't wait to hear about the grand ball. Now, tell us everything. Leave nothing out." Selma starts the ball rolling, her cheery kindness is warming to her friends.

John speaks first. "There's plenty of time for that later. Right now, I have something of great importance to discuss with the both of you. I'll ask you to have Alberta Mae and Sachel leave the house and close the doors." He sees his friends' surprise. "Please accommodate my request, my reasons will be perfectly clear in a few minutes."

When the last of the dishes containing their dinner are placed on the table, Charles kindly asks his cook and butler to leave the house.

"Let's start eating, I'll fill you in as we enjoy this wonderful meal." John directs as if he's the host of this dinner party.

The room is quiet, except for the rattle of silverware against china, and the movement of clothing as the food is passed around. As the last serving bowl is placed on the table, John clears his throat and begins speaking.

"I'm not going to run for the governor's office. At the last minute I was given information which has changed my goal in life. Hear me out, then I'll try to answer any questions you have." He goes on to explain, without exposing the two men at the barn.

Charles and Selma sit agape. June eats slowly, gently laying her fork on her plate between bites and sipping water from the crystal glass in front of her.

"And there you have it," Mr. Anderson concludes.

"I'm here to recruit you onto my team. I know of no better people than the two of you to help turn the tide of this threat to our country. You are the salt of this earth, and have proven your loyalty, again and again, to the ideals of this Union. Can we count on the both of you? You'll be doing a great service for your country."

They look at each other, both with the same thoughts. "How can we possibly tell these people that for as long as we've know them, we've been spying for the other side?"

The colonel must say something, anything. He needs time to think. “Well, err . . . what did you have in mind for us to do?”

“I’m not sure at the moment. It’s going to take at least sixty days for me to get organized and set a strategy. Marty and I are attending a meeting to learn more next week. I hope you can join us.” John is trying to show patience.

“Are the women invited to the meeting?” Selma tries to give her husband a little breathing room.

“I think not.” June volunteers. “From what I understand, there’s going to be quite a number of men there, and the meetings could go on for a week or so. I’d rather not go, unless it’s deemed necessary. Besides, with Robert away, I need to be here.”

“When are you leaving?” The colonel looks at his friend.

“I’d hoped to leave Thursday morning.” John senses a stall.

“Listen, if you feel this request is an imposition, or beyond the point of being reasonable, then by all means, tell me now. I won’t think any less of you. I’ll respect your honesty. I’d rather know now than find out later that you want to withdraw.”

“It isn’t that.” Selma offers.

“She’s right, John, we’d jump at the chance, but there are circumstances involved that you don’t know. If you did, you wouldn’t be asking.” Charles Housler believes he has put the stopper in the bottle.

“Okay, what’s going on. This isn’t like you at all. What’s so wrong that you can’t tell us? This is us sitting here with you.” June charges head first.

The colonel and Selma look across the table at their friends, then turn their heads allowing their eyes to meet. The questions are in both their minds. Should we tell them, or not? What will their reaction be if we do? The tension builds in the room. Finally, Charles turns his head to face the Andersons and says, “This pains me more than you can imagine . . .”

At La Nesra.

Four of the Company’s doctors have given Lilly an injection to put her into a comatose state once again. They wait for it to work, then they will proceed.

“Here I go again. I can feel my muscles moving away from my control. It starts with my extremities and moves in toward the center part of my body. It’s almost like turning the fire down on a lantern. It starts to shrink, farther, and farther, until it’s just a flicker, it sputters, then it’s gone. There’s nothing left but a tiny glow on the hot tip of the wick. When it cools, the life once there, is no more.

“I can hear them talking, and can see them if they move into my line of vision. I’ve learned to see clearly in all directions in front of me. Wait, what are they saying?” Lilly has decided to learn as much as she can each time they induce her to sleep.

“Her color looks excellent. Everything is connected properly. Ah, yes, this is a good beginning,” a doctor affirms.

“Lilly, I know you can hear me. We’re going to leave you alone for the next twenty-four hours. We want to determine how your system will react when you have no stimulus around you. Someone will check to see how you're doing every few hours, but other than that, you'll be left alone. Don't be frightened, you'll be fine. We're leaving the room now." A different doctor explains.

"With the way this table is setting, I'm unable to see the door. I hear people walking . . . there, the door is shut. I wonder, though, are they all gone. Let's just wait an hour or so to see if anyone stayed in here with me, somewhere I can't see them. I've learned to start a count in my head and keep it going while I think about other things. My count is close to one second apart, so I know sixty is one minute, and three hundred and sixty is one hour.

"Wait, someone just came into the room. They're turning the gas light way down low, almost off. It's almost dark in here. There goes the door shut again. I'll start my count over."

An hour later.

"It's been at least an hour since I've heard or seen anything. I must be alone. This is the opportunity I've been waiting for. I'm going to try to get up and move around. Okay, here goes. I need to center all my energy to my mind. Close out everything else.

"It's getting black. Concentrate. Pull my feelings and senses together in my mind. It's black. I feel like I'm falling, drifting. What is this place? It's black, and empty.

"Uh-oh, something's pulling at me, pulling me back where I was. No! I don't want to go back! Concentrate, harder, keep it going. There are things in here with me. I can't see them, I can feel them, but I'm not afraid. I'm still falling downward. Keep trying.

"Uh-oh, I'm moving sideways now, faster and faster. There's no wind or anything, yet I know I'm moving sideways. Something has a grip on my arms and is pulling me faster and faster. It looks like daylight up ahead, I can see a glow of light. The farther I go the brighter the light. It's getting really bright now. I can't stand it, I have to shut my eyes, but my eyes won't shut. This really hurts bad.

"Uuuuuuuhhhhhhhhhh! I've stopped. That felt like someone dropped me from about three feet off the floor, flat onto my back. But it didn't hurt at all. My lungs are filling with air fast. I'm taking a really deep breath. That feels so good. Where am I?

"It's still dark. Wait a minute, I'm still in the laboratory. Hey, I can turn my head and look around. I did it, I can move around. I can wake myself up!

"Wow! I did it! Let's see if I can get up off this table. Not too fast, don't want to fall. Well, that was easy enough. I'll try to walk across the floor to the door. Everything seems to work all right, I'm not a bit wobbly or weak. I'd better go back and sit on the table, just in case someone comes in. I'll figure out what to do next.

"Oh my God. Oh . . . my . . . God. That's me, still lying on the table. But I'm over here. How can that be? How can I be here, and there, at the same time?"

People are waiting for an explanation at the Housler farm. Selma interrupts her husband as he begins to speak.

"Wait, Charles, are you positive you know what you're doing?"

"What do you think I am about to do, honey? Have you learned to read my mind?" he says coyly.

"You're right, I don't know, but shouldn't we talk about this before you go off on your own deciding what's best for us?" she counters.

"Let me ask you then, shall we explain our situation to our friends, or shall we take advantage of their kindness and say nothing? If we agree, there's no reason for a delay. And if you'll recall, you said not two hours ago that I should pick the time to explain our problem. Do you remember?" He recalls.

"Totally, my darling, I agree with you totally. It will be good to get some peace of mind," Selma concedes.

"The two of you have got me to be a nervous wreck sitting here listening. What, in the world, has happened? What have you been doing that we don't know about?" June is unable to hold back her anxiety and excitement.

"Tell them, Charles, leave nothing out. I'll not say another word until you've finished," Selma urges.

"Would you take a bet on that, John?" Colonel Housler asks, smiling and chuckling.

"Not on your life, colonel. I know her better than that."

Feeling somewhat settled now that the decision has been made, Charles takes a moment to ponder the starting place of his explanation. Seriousness envelops the room again as he opens the doorway to his past.

"When I was a young lad, probably twelve years old or so . . ."

Back in the laboratory, Lilly has just discovered she's out of her body.

Her heart pounds as she paces back and forth from the door to the table where her body lies, apparently lifeless. Back and forth, back and forth. What to do?

"I must settle myself and think. I'm out of my body. Instead of waking up, I somehow came out of my body. How do I get back in? If they come in here to check on me, how do I—wait,—I'm still there on the table. They won't suspect anything for twenty-two hours yet. I've plenty of time to figure this all out. I wonder, am I a ghost, I can touch my arm and feel it, I can feel my hair. There's a mirror over there. Let's take a look. Nope, I can't see myself. Can I pick things up, or better yet, can I open the door? I can feel the knob in my hand. Wonderful, maybe I can travel through things. I'll put my hand through the door. No, that didn't work. This is strange if I can't see myself in the mirror, that means I'm not physically here. So, if I'm not here, why can't I put my hand through the door?

"What would happen if I walked out into the hallway, would they see me? Will I cast a shadow? I can turn the gas light up and see. No, no shadow, so, the light must go right through me. They probably can't see me then. I'll go out there and take a walk. Maybe I can walk right out of here for good, but that will leave my body behind, and that's doesn't seem like a good idea.

"I'll walk down the hallway to see if anyone can see me. If they do, I'll pretend I'm walking in my sleep. Here I go.

"I've passed five people now and not a one of them has given any notice of me. They can't see me, that's for sure.

"I need to get some keys to the outside doors and gates of this place, and this is a good time to do it. Where can I find some? Who would have keys to everything?

"Someone in the workshop, that's it. They go everywhere to work on things. I'll have to go outside to get there, though. But then, what's the difference? Outside, inside, it makes no difference: they can't see me.

"That was easy. None of the doors are locked. I've not been in this building before, but this is the place, the sign says so. I need to locate where they keep the keys. There's voices coming from that room over there. I'll peek inside.

"Those two men in there appear to be resting and eating their dinner. Talk about luck, there's a big ring of keys lying on that old desk over there. I'll walk right over there and pick them up and get out of here. No one will know. Here I go. Careful, don't make any noise. I've just about got them. Aha, I have them, now to get out of—

"What's happening? I don't feel right. Something's pulling on me hard. I'm sliding across the floor on both feet, backward. The keys are slipping out of my hand."

One of the two men yells. "What was that . . . ? How did my keys fall off that desk."

"I'm moving faster and faster backward. Out of the workshop, zooming across the ground, and into the main building. I seem to be retracing my steps, backward. Up a flight of steps, down a long hallway, around two corners, and into the room where I'm still lying on the table. Without hesitation, I'm airborne and hurled back into my body with an unheard thud. Then I hear."

"She's back. We have her back. Wake her up, quickly now." The doctors comment.

"There's that familiar warm burning sensation again. It's starting in my lower body and working its way down my legs and up through my chest and arms. It's almost to my head. It feels like a thousand hornets in my brain. I'm awake."

"How do you feel, Lilly? You gave us a little scare. When we checked on you, we noticed your body temperature had dropped to seventy-four degrees. We gave you the injection to awaken you, but it didn't seem to work. We were unable to locate a heartbeat or your respiration. Finally we held a mirror up to your mouth to detect signs of a breath, and that's when the medicine did its job. We're so glad to have you back with us."

"I think I'm all right. I'm curious though, what is my body temperature, normally, when I'm asleep?"

"We've recorded it as low as eighty-six, but that was for short periods of time, such as fifteen minutes or so. Normally it should keep steady at about ninety-two degrees. An interesting development now is that your temperature was still dropping when you woke up. It's almost back to normal now," the senior doctor mentions

"What would cause that?" She feels more comfortable that they don't know all that was going on, that she was out of her body.

"We don't know yet, but we will. Why don't you go back to your room and get some rest. There's nothing more to do here today."

"That's fine, I do feel tired. Can I go now?"

"Just one more thing, did you wake up and move around in the halls a little while before we woke you up?"

"No, of course not, how could I do that?"

"I don't know that yet, either, but at least a half dozen people reported they saw you walking the halls."

At the Housler home, Charles Housler concludes the explanation of his work as a spy for the South, and of his criminal past. "And that's the whole ugly mess."

John and June sit amazed at what they've just heard. A dropped pin would rattle in the silence of this moment.

"Say something," Selma demands.

John stares at the colonel, while rubbing his chin on both sides with his thumb and forefinger, lost in thought.

June picks up her glass of water and takes a long dry sip.

"John, I understand what a shock this must be for you. I ask only that if you have to reveal us to the authorities, give us a few days to get our affairs in order. I promise, we won't run. I'm through running." The colonel isn't begging, just asking for some time.

June speaks first. "Selma, you poor dear. I don't know what to say. we love you and Charles. John, isn't there something we can do? There must be something."

"I think," Mr. Anderson's sober voice is heard, "there's only one right thing to do. A man has to live with his conscience; the colonel his, and me with mine." A pause as he lets his mind work a little farther along the problem.

"Under the circumstances, the only solution is for the two of you to jump on our wagon and let us help with your problem, while you help with ours. It seems to be a perfect match if you think about it. First though, let me say this. There might be a lot of things you could have said today to convince me of where your loyalties lay, but your honesty about your past, when you could have kept quiet and joined our organization as a spy for the South—well, it confirms my thinking to the limit. I know I can trust you. I'll bet my life on it. With that said, think about this. You two keep your ties with this other organization. I won't be surprised to discover it's the same as the one I'm sworn to defeat. Keep up with everything you're supposed to do. Hell, we'll even feed bogus information to them, through you. That'll take the pressure off for the time being. If they get wind of what we're doing, we'll pull your tail in amongst us and circle our wagons. They won't touch you or yours.

"I'm not sure exactly how or what you can do to help put these people down, but I've a feeling you can play a mighty important role in our attempts down the road. What do you say? Are you with me on this?"

Before they can answer, June exclaims.

"John Adams Anderson, I love you. I love you. You're the man I married."

Selma's eyes are welling up when the colonel says. "John, my true friend, I will support you to my death. Selma and I will forever be in your debt. I'm at your service. I'll be at your side whenever, wherever, you need me. Selma and I truly thank you both."

As the men put their heads together, the women get up from the table and move out onto the verandah. They sit down on the white chairs overlooking the rolling green hills of Der Bote, and Selma says.

“Did you and John have a fight this morning before you got here? The reason I ask is that you are always so punctual, never late for anything.”

“The truth is, we had a little tiff before we got out of bed this morning. I was half asleep and overreacted to his advances. I felt really bad about it, but then he said a few things and that peeved me. Believe me when I say, our morning coffee cooled quickly at our breakfast table.”

“Jim hitched the buggy up inside the barn, so, when I was ready to go, I walked out there to meet John. One thing led to another, and well, you’ve heard of a roll in the hay have you?” She winks feeling she took advantage of the opportunity.

“What is it about a man and his barn?” June says to her friend’s wonderment.

Chapter Sixteen

The word of Lilly moving through the hallways while her life body was in the laboratory has caused a commotion, prompting her friends to corner her at their secret meeting place on the roof. There are six people, three boys and three girls, at the meeting commencing at eleven fifteen PM.

"Tell us," insists Rose, the girl with the ability to change her appearance. "Did you really leave your body and walk around the hallway?" She continues tauntingly.

"Take it easy, Rose. Let her tell us in her own way. It makes no sense, though, how could she do that?" Falcon's logical mind finds it disturbing, although he's not sure why.

"Falcon's right, Rose, we don't know anything about it. If she did it, it's her business. If she wants to tell us, she will. If not, well, it's up to her, and we'll not insist on anything." Eagle speaks up, protecting his friend.

They all look at Lilly, who is beginning to think they can't see her, otherwise, why would they be talking about her this way.

"Well, the doctors say people saw me running around in the halls of the building, but I've no memory of doing it. All I know is, they put me to sleep with their chemicals, and when they woke me up that's what they told me. He said six people saw me, but I have no idea who they are. Do any of you?"

No response.

"Were you over at the library building yesterday, Lilly?" Lester, a younger boy fairly new to the group, asks.

"No. Why?"

"Well, I was on an errand for Mr. Vaughn, and I saw you there. When I tried to talk to you, you acted like you didn't know me and walked away. I know it was you, I'd swear to it, only, your hair was a little different. I mean, it looked shorter than yours."

"I haven't been in that building for at least a week, and I'll swear to that."

"This is a strange thing for even the Company to do. What are they up to now?" Rose puzzles.

"We don't have enough information to come to a conclusion. We need more facts." Falcon determines.

"We should do some investigating to see what we can find out, and meet back here in two days. Keep it among the six of us. Bring no one else in. Agreed?" Eagle suggests.

"Agreed." All join in.

"Good. We should focus on locating a girl that looks like Lilly. Everyone's talking about it right now, so our questions shouldn't raise any suspicions."

"Now, all of you clear out of here. I want to talk to Lilly alone for a minute."

As the last of the four leave into the darkness, Eagle says.

"I don't believe for a minute that there's nothing to this. It doesn't sound like you, something else is going on in that pretty head of yours?"

"You're my friend, and you don't believe me? What do you want me to say?"

"All I mean is, I hope you and I are building a relationship, a trust between us. I like you a lot, and I think you feel the same way about me. Shouldn't we be able to be honest with each other? Besides, you know I'm able to understand things about people's thoughts and feelings, and I know you're holding something back. I just don't know what it is yet."

"I like you a lot too, but I'm not able to completely trust anybody, and I think you could resort to just about anything to get me into bed, and I know I'm not ready for that. Another thing we both know is that your need to know everything about everybody consumes you at times. Would you sacrifice me for information? I'm not sure about that. And while we're on the subject, if our relationship is meant to be, it will withstand the time it needs to build and blossom. Be patient, try to understand me, my situation, my needs, and be there for me. We'll prove ourselves to each other a little each day. In the meantime, be my loyal friend, and if you want me the way you say you do, slow down, quit asking. When the time is right, we'll both know it. Oh, one other thing. How can you be so sure you can trust me?" Lilly unloads on the young man.

"You said it before, I make it my business to know. Sometimes I wish I didn't have this ability to almost read minds. I don't know how I do it, it just happens, so it's almost impossible to turn off. People pull away from me when they realize what I can do. They don't trust me. I sense their fear of exposing their thoughts to me. But it doesn't work that way. I don't hear their thoughts in my head. I just get an understanding of their thinking. It's difficult to explain." Eagle tries to encourage Lilly to trust him by explaining why it appears he's always prying and probing.

"Our relationship is moving so slowly it's driving me crazy. And that's because we spend very little time alone. Shouldn't we try to be together more?" he asks.

"I'm not sure I can do that right now, I need to think about it. You know and I know, if we get caught together, like now, they'll make sure we're kept apart . . . probably forever. They won't allow the type of relationship you want to grow. I should go now."

"Yes, I know. I'll see you in two days, right?" Eagle's eagerness is apparent, her words haven't deterred him at all.

Robert and Randall arrived in Atlanta just before noon today. Since they didn't want to attract attention, they hired a carriage and driver to look for a place to stay on the near edge of the city.

They've located a small, but clean, three-room cottage, and have it rented for four of the six weeks they plan to be here. They have a living room, a bedroom, and a sparsely equipped kitchen arrangement. Best of all, they don't have the worry of a black man and a white man staying together. Their privacy is afforded by the main house which completely blocks the view of the cottage from the street. They can come and go without being noticed anytime, day or night, a perfect situation.

"What are we going to do first?" Randy's voice is raised with anticipation.

"Well, I think we should do some sight seeing. We'll get the lay of the land and determine if we can locate the whereabouts of the Company. It could be just that simple. We can ask around a little too. Not so much as to raise suspicion, though." Bob replies, at the same time unpacking his belongings and placing them in the dresser drawers.

"I expect it'll take a week of poking around to come up with anything. We might have to split up to double our efforts. I mean, you can go places and ask questions where I can't, and the same is true for me." He continues.

"I'm glad we ate earlier. I don't know about you, but I'm tired. Let's get some rest, then we can talk about it over breakfast in the morning. How's that suit you?"

"Yeah, I'm tired too," Randy responds.

As he lies in the double bed, alongside his friend, Randy thinks about all the new things he's seen over the last few days. The train ride was more than he could imagine. The meals and their accommodations were excellent. And to be in Atlanta, with buildings as many as five floors up are everywhere. What a sight. And the people, people are everywhere, coming and going. The noise, Bob says, goes on all night.

"These people must never sleep," he thinks. "Tomorrow we'll start looking for Sheree, I can't wait. I know we'll find out where she is. I just know it." He drifts off to sleep with his girlfriend on his mind.

Back at the Company, Lilly has slipped through the dark hallways, into her room without being noticed.

"It's after midnight already. I'm glad I'm safe back in my room. As soon as I get ready, I'm going to bed and try to make myself go to sleep the way they do it.

"I wonder, who's the girl Lester saw? Does she really look that much like me? Why was it I couldn't see myself in the mirror, but the people saw me in the hallway? What happened to pull me back to my body lying on the table? I'll get answers to these questions, and others, if I can do that again. I'll figure out how to leave my body and get back, before I try to escape. A few more days won't make any difference.

"Okay, I'm in bed lying on my back. Let's make sure I do it right. Close my eyes and concentrate, concentrate on putting everything out of my mind, emptying my brain. Bring in the darkness, welcome it. Think negative. Think black. Stare straight with my eyes closed until I see circles of light, then the circles should start moving around.

"Look straight ahead. Concentrate. I'm doing it. I'm doing it. I'm falling, sailing downward like a leaf from an oak tree. Gently falling. I'm not alone anymore. There are things all around me now. I can't see them, but I can feel them, almost touching me. It's totally black. I'm sailing downward. I don't want to stop, I don't care if I ever stop. It feels so good, so wonderful.

"Something just passed me so close I can feel it pulling my arms straight out over my head, slowing my fall. I'm turning and starting to move head, first with my arms straight out over my head. Something's pulling me, faster, faster, faster. There's a warm spot in my belly. The sensations of my arms and legs are all being slowly sucked into the warm spot. All of my feelings are moving toward the warm spot.

"Light, I see a small amount of light ahead. I'm moving faster and faster toward it. It's getting really bright now. Uh, oh, it's too bright! I can't look at it, but I can't look away! I can't breathe, need to catch my breath!

"Aaahhh, that's better. That was scary. I'm not being pulled along any more, I've stopped. I wonder, can I move? I can.

"I can sit up, and there I am, still lying there. I look like I'm asleep. I did it. I don't know how I'll ever get back in there, or wake myself up, but here I am, outside my body, looking at me lying there in bed.

"It just occurred to me: suppose I'm asleep and dreaming. Maybe the other girl Lester saw was in the hallway. Perhaps, I was asleep and dreaming there on the table the whole time. It could be that's all this is, a dream. It seemed awfully real to me, though. I was outside and went to the maintenance office. I had the keys in my hand.

"If this is a dream right now, it's certainly realistic. Let's see how far it'll go, how long it'll last. I should make the best of this opportunity regardless.

"The first thing I need to do is turn up the gas light a little. I can pick things up with my hands just fine. As I recall, I couldn't put my hand through the door, so, I must not be a ghost. Let's check if I can see myself in the mirror. This is strange. How can other people see me, and me not cast a reflection in the mirror? Maybe the mirror is broken somehow. Although, I can see the reflections of things here in the room. If I take it over there to the light, I'll pick it up by the frame and carry it over there.

"My God! My thumb just went through the glass of the mirror when I tried to pick it up. My heart is really pounding now. Oh my! Oh my!

"I wonder, if I toss something soft at it, if it goes through the glass, then it isn't me, it's the glass. I'll try one of my stockings.

"It bounced off. It didn't go through, not even a little bit.

"I'll try holding a pencil by it's tip and touching it.

"It goes through just like there's no glass there. Let's see if the pencil sticks out the back side when I put it through the front. Nope, there's nothing showing through. Where does it go? Should I put my hand in to see what's there? Will I be able to get it back out, or will something grab me and pull me in? If I put just my finger through, I could pull it out real fast if anything happens. I'll try that. Careful now, be ready to pull out fast, just another inch to go. I'm barely touching the glass with my finger. A little bit of pressure makes it dent in, and when I pull away the dent disappears. Little circles spread out from where I touched it, like the ripples in a still pond. I'll push a little harder. It's denting again, just a little harder. Oh, my finger went through and the dent sprung back out, so my whole finger is in there. If I pull it out, will I still have a finger? Yipes! Something's rubbing against my finger, maybe licking it. Pull it out!

"I'm afraid to look. Is it still there? I'll put my other hand over my eyes and peek through the crack of my fingers to see. Here goes, open my eyes, it's there, my finger's still there. Thank you, God. Wheeeeoooo, that was scary. I should try to put my whole arm through, but I can't. Not right now anyway, it's too scary.

"Hey, I wonder if my other me will cast a reflection in this mirror. If I can pick it up by the frame, and hold it over my face. Careful now, I don't want to drop this heavy thing. I'll just set it on my chest and lean it over. I'll bend down a little, so I can see.

"Uh. Oh. Something's happening. Something's pulling at me, I'm moving, can't stop. Up toward the ceiling and down toward my body on the bed."

"Darn! Darn! I hit the bed hard. I feel like I'm spreading out, like I've been a small ball, and now I'm spreading out through my body, spreading through my arms, legs, my neck and head. That buzzing, it sounds like a thousand hornets. Louder. Louder. That was a bright flash of light."

"I feel my lungs sucking in a lot of air, fast. The sound of my voice groaning startles me wide alert in an instant. I'm lying here in my bed, wide awake, shaking all over. Has this all been a dream? My clock shows it's almost one thirty. Have I been asleep and just scared myself enough to wake up? But then, how did this mirror get in bed with me?"

Daylight begins to brighten the city of Atlanta almost an hour before the sun peeks up from the horizon. The bright ball sends its rays to lick the dew from the grass and warm the backs of two young men as they walk toward town.

Bob and Randy appear to almost step on their own shadows, which are cast long and flat in front of them. Their feet are never quite able to hit the ground before the dark images leap from beneath the soles of their boots. Men on horseback, carriages, and various wagons, pass them by, all headed toward the downtown Atlanta. The road of red clay emits a small amount of dust from the animal's hoofs and wheels of the slow moving procession. An occasional friendly, 'morning', is sent their way to be answered in like kind.

"Let's eat at the first place we find. Then we'll split up and meet back there at noon?" Bob's statement is in the form of a question.

"That's a good idea," Randy readily says back. "Just what are we going to ask people? And how do we say it without them wanting to know why?"

"If they ask, I guess we should say we have business there. Something like, oh I don't know . . . something like, how about we have a delivery coming in on a couple of wagons, and need to know where to take it. It can be grain, like horse feed, or something. Use your imagination."

"Are we going to call this place the Company, or something else?" A good question from Bob's younger friend.

"That's a very good point my friend. It could be a school, a college, or a hospital, for all I know. We might have to change our approach from day to day until we locate it. Watch how people react when you mention the Company name. It might give us a lead as to whether we're on the right track."

"Let's eat here, this looks like a decent place, My Mama's Home Cooking. Keep in mind now, we'll meet back here at noon. If trouble finds you, get back to the cottage any way you can. If you don't show up here by twelve-thirty, I'll leave and go there. You do the same if I don't show up. Got it?"

"It's a good plan. Should you give me some money in case I need it for something?"

"Oh yes, I'm glad you asked. It completely slipped my mind. Here, take this five dollars. I'll remind you not to show it around. That's a sure fire way of getting robbed." The more experienced of the two cautions. "And here, these are your papers proving who you are. Don't let these get out of your sight either."

"Thanks, I'll be careful."

It's almost eleven o'clock before Randy realizes how much time has passed. He's already seen a great deal of the downtown area, and has talked to a few men, the idea of approaching more white people makes him uncomfortable. So, he's decided he should approach only black people. A random selection has produced no indication of the location of the Company.

"I'll try two more people, then I'll head back to meet Bob," he says to himself.

"Pardon me, sir, can you tell me where I can find a place called the Company?"

"And who are you to ask that kind of question?" The black man dressed in a driver's garb wants to know. He's standing, holding the reins and stroking the forehead of a horse, which is harnessed to a black surrey.

"I come ahead of a wagonload of grain for them, sir. Can you tell me?" Randy's reply is conveyed with certainty and clarity.

"You got any money, boy?" The driver asserts, putting him on the defensive.

"No, sir, I've never got any money." He wonders if this is the way things are in the big city. Everything costs money, nothing's free.

Before anything else can be said, a man emerges from a bank directly across the board sidewalk from the side of the surrey. He's dressed in black with a tall round-brimmed hat. The driver notices him and speaks.

"Excuse me, Mr. Vaughn, sir."

"What is it?" The man is irritated by the driver's impudence.

"This boy here is asking about the Company, sir. He wants to know how to get there. He says there's a load of grain coming and he needs to know where to take it."

The man in black happens to be Mr. Vaughn, the headmaster of training at the Company.

"Come here, boy." His instructions are stiff with sarcasm.

Randy walks around the driver, steps upon the sidewalk.

"Now, tell me boy, and be quick about it. What business do you have with the Company?"

"It's a load of grain, sir." He replies and bows his head. He knows not to look the white man in the eye.

"I know they grow all their own grain. They don't buy grain from anybody. Now who are you, and why are you nosing around?" Mr. Vaughn snaps back.

The young man is surprised by the man's manner, and doesn't reply as quickly as expected.

"Speak up, boy, I haven't got all day! I asked you your name, and why you want to find the location of the Company!"

"I'm sorry I bothered you, sir," he answers and turns to walk away with his head still bowed. He knows any further explanation will cause more questions, and he doesn't want that to happen. He also feels that these men know the location of the Company, and might lead him there.

"Hold on! Come back here! Don't walk away from me until I'm through with you, boy!"

Jacob's seventeen-year-old son can feel the tension building. This is real trouble brewing, just like his mama said. Should he stop and go back, or run like blazes? If he runs and they come after him, he'd better make sure he doesn't get caught. The thought of his clubfoot slowing him down is a strong consideration. The thing is, can he outrun the driver? On the other hand, if he turns back to face the man, he'll likely be questioned until he tells the truth, and that will cause more problems. There's only one choice.

Run! Run like the wind!

Down the street of hard red clay he streaks, past a general store, up onto the sidewalk, and through the swinging doors of a saloon. There are a dozen or so men standing at the bar, and sitting at small round tables inside. Without hesitation he speeds past them, around the end of the bar and through a doorway, looking for the back door. Luck is with him, he grabs the doorknob and in a second he's out behind the building.

Turning to his left, he sees what appears to be a barn with one of the two large doors ajar by a foot or two. He makes a beeline toward the opening, thinking he can find a place to hide inside.

When he enters, he's gulping air trying to catch his breath. A quick look back through the opening to see if anyone has followed him shows the surrey driver just now coming out of the rear door of the saloon with three of the men from inside the bar behind him.

"I don't see him," the driver pants. "The only place he could be is over there in the blacksmith's barn."

The four men start walking toward the partly open door. Randy is watching and starts to panic. "Hide in here, or run out the front. If I go out the front, people will see me and tell them where I went. They don't know for sure that I came in here. I'd best hide in here somewhere. But where? Not much time to make up my mind."

He turns away from the door and moves forward to find a hiding place. He takes two steps before he plows smack into the chest of a big man standing not three feet away.

"Where you going, son?" the man calmly asks. "Is somebody after you."

"They're right behind me!" he gasps.

"Come here . . . get in this barrel. I'll cover you up with this saddle blanket." This bulk of a man instructs.

"There's water in there." Randy counters.

"Not enough to drown you, get in there quick!" the big man demands.

The water is cold as he puts his feet in and lowers himself down into the dark murky liquid. The barrel is about half full, but with the size of teenager's body, it rises up near his chin. The man throws the blanket over the top, shutting out any trace of light. It's dark, cold, and wet, in this old wooden barrel. The smell of horse sweat from the blanket makes it difficult to breathe.

The barn door screeches as it swings farther open.

"Smitty, you see a young black boy run through here?"

"Naw, sir, I ain't seen nobody come through here." Smitty replies. He wants to ask why they're after the boy, but knows he can't show any interest.

"You're sure now, are you?" Two of the men walk past the smitty toward the front of the barn, looking here and there, wherever they think a boy could hide. One man climbs the ladder to the haymow, while the driver keeps an eye on the blacksmith.

"Oh, yessir, I been right here. I'd have seen him if he did."

The two men return from the front of the barn at same time the one in the haymow climbs down the ladder.

"Nothing." They all report.

"He must've ran off in some other direction then. Looks like we lost him," says Mr. Vaughn's driver.

"What's in this barrel here?"

Randy's heart leaps when he hears the words.

"It's just water, sir."

"Is it fit to drink?" One of the men from the bar asks at the same time he slips his hand under the blanket and wets his fingers, two inches from the boy's head.

"I wouldn't, sir, it's been sitting there like that for a while. I only use it to temper my work with. I can't remember how many shoes I've stuck in there to cool them off. I keep it covered to keep small animals out of it. You know how rats and the like want to get on the side of a barrel for a drink and fall in. Then they can't get out and they drown in there. The first thing you know, they're stinking up the place."

The man pushes the blanket back a little, scoops up a double handful of the cool liquid and splashes it in his face. Then pulls his kerchief from around his neck to start drying off.

"Let's get back inside. We'll never find him now, he's long gone." Nothing further is said. After a few seconds of silence, the boy in the barrel hears the door squeak shut.

Suddenly the blanket flies off the top of the barrel. His heart is pounding in his throat, and his body reacts from the cold water, causing a chill to go down his back.

"You can come out of there now, son, they're gone." Smitty's voice is good to hear. "I expect you're safe for now."

He climbs out of the barrel sloshing water over the sides as he comes. He dries off with an old towel, while answering Smitty's questions as to why he was running.

"I never heard of the Company, but I can sure take you right to the place where Mr. Vaughn lives and works. It's called La Nesra. It's a big place, with high walls all around it. No one knows much about what goes on in there. What business you got with them anyway?" Smitty finally asks.

Randy is so grateful for this man's help with hiding him from the men on his tail, he decides to place some trust and tells him everything.

"So, this Bob is probably waiting for you now, over at Mama's Cooking?" the owner of the blacksmith shop asks.

"That's right, and I need to get back there as quick as I can. If not, he'll be wondering about me, and I don't know what he might do," young Mr. Stoker explains.

"I don't think you should leave out of here just now. They're probably going to watch for you for a while. I tell you what, I'll send my son to tell your friend where you are, and bring him back here. How's that sound to you?"

"I don't want to get you into trouble on my account, you've done enough already." He offers the smitty a chance to change his mind.

"I'm glad to do it. If we don't look after our own kind, then no one else will. You just stay right there for a minute. I'll get Luke on his way, and see if I can find you something dry to put on. Luke's about your size, so I can probably get something." Smitty moves toward the front of the shop.

The driver of the surrey is explaining to Mr. Vaughn that they lost sight of the boy they were chasing. "So, we got no idea where he got off to." He finishes.

"I expect that blacksmith has hid him somewhere." Mr. Vaughn declares. "No point in causing any more of a commotion, though. I believe I know who that boy is. Get me back to La Nesra. I've got some thinking to do."

The surrey is pulling away from the sidewalk as Luke, the blacksmith's son, walks past, headed for My Mama's Home Cooking.

It's almost two o'clock in the afternoon at La Nesra, when Sally walks into the office of Mr. Vaughn. "I'm told you need to see me," she says as she approaches his desk.

"Yes, Sally, sit down. There's a little job I need you to do. Earlier today, I encountered a young slave boy in front of the bank. He was asking questions about the Company. When he walked toward me, I noticed he has a clubfoot. I'm all but sure he's the boyfriend left behind by Sheree Anderson, otherwise known to us as Lilly. If that's the case, he's probably not by himself, not here in Atlanta. I want you to check around and see what you can learn. If what I suspect is true, this could be the perfect opportunity to put Amber in place. I understand she's ready for assignment. Do you agree?"

"I agree, and she's anxiously biding her time, waiting for the opportunity to prove herself. What do you have in mind?"

Upstairs in the same building, Lilly lies on her bed resting. The instructors and doctors have given her the rest of the day off to relax and prepare for tests scheduled tomorrow.

"No one will check on me for about three hours, they want me to rest. As long as I show up for supper at five o'clock, my time is my own."

Lilly has decided that everything happening to her is strangely true. She's able to live outside her body, and now knows how to get back. It has to do with the mirror being put in front of her face. Although she casts no reflection while outside, she's able to move about as if she's still in her body. Since the pencil went through the mirror when she held it, and the stocking bounced off when she threw it at the glass, it must mean anything she wears or holds can be taken through the mirror with her. She knows, while not ready to admit it to herself, she'll have to explore the mirror from both sides of the glass.

"I shouldn't be wasting this time I have alone. I should go outside of my body and explore. The problem is, if they see me, they might try to lock me up after putting me back in my body, thinking they can keep me there. I could still get out of my body, but if the door's locked, I wouldn't be able to get through it. The only other thing I can do is explore behind the mirror. Do I want to do that right now? I don't know if I'm ready for any more of that. For one thing, I don't know if my mirror is big enough for all of me to fit through. It's a heck of a lot smaller than me. What if I get stuck? If all of me is on the other side of the glass, will I be able to get all of me back? What will happen if I'm on the other side of the glass and someone holds a mirror up to my face on this side? I should think about this for a while and not do something I'll regret.

"Hey, I know what I'll do. I'll get out of my body and go to the meeting tomorrow night. I'll find out if I look the same to other people, or if I'm some sort of a ghost or spirit or something. I wonder, if someone touches me, will their hand go right through me, or will they feel me, like they do now. There's a lot I don't know about all of this. I have to keep trying in order to learn all I can. That means I shouldn't waste this free time.

"I'm going out of my body and see what more I can find out about this mirror. I'll check the time on my watch and write it down before I leave my body. That way I can look when I come out, and compare it with what I wrote to see if it's the same. If it is, then I can be sure to get back in time to go to supper. "Okay, lie down, and concentrate. Wow, that was easier than before. My watch is the same as I wrote down, except for the time it took to get here. That's good.

"I'm scared to death to do it, but I know I have to. I'll just start by putting my hand through the mirror. If that works, then I'll put my whole arm through, and just keep going like that until I'm all on the other side. If it gets too spooky, I'll just pull back.

"Should I hold my breath, or what? There's no way to know for sure. I don't know if I'll be able to breathe in there. I'll make sure my head is the last part of me to go through. Wait, I know, I'll keep a grip on the frame on this side with one of my hands. That way I can pull myself back through if I have to. Okay, here I go."

Luke found Robert at My Mama's Home Cooking, and has brought him to the barn. Randy and Smitty have described everything that's happened.

"It's hard to believe, all this, and our first day here." Robert exclaims at their progress. "This is good work, but be more careful. How would I ever explain to Alberta Mae that your body's coming home on the next train from Atlanta?"

"It's the truth, Smitty saved my life. I would never have thought about hiding in the water barrel. And I thank you, so much, sir!" Randy sticks out his hand to shake.

"What do we do now?" he continues.

"Well, if Smitty will rent us a wagon, and tells us how to get there, I think we should find this La Nesra place, and take a look."

"I've got a buggy and a horse you can use all the while you're here, but I can't charge you for it. Not now that I know about why you're here and all," Smitty volunteers.

"No, that won't work. We have to pay you. We don't want any of our doings being traced back and placed at your feet. You have to live and work here, we don't. So, charge us your regular price, we'll gladly pay it. You shouldn't be seen with us any more than is necessary." Robert reminds everyone of the dangers involved.

"I see your point. You're a good honest man. I'll be here if you need me, though, do you hear me?" Smitty replies.

"Count me in on that too," Luke speaks up.

It doesn't take long for the twosome to arrive at the edge of the tall wall at the front entrance to La Nesra. They know they've found the right place since the name is clearly chiseled into the marble slab attached to the brick pillar next to the front gate.

"This place is a fortress. Look at how high the walls are, and take a look at the size of the steel bars and frame of the gate. I doubt we could ever get over those walls or slip through that gate. What do you think?" Bob asks.

"Let's follow the road around and see if we can find a spot that's not so well protected. Something like a rear entrance," Randy agrees.

They move along, following the towering walls. At last the wall bends at ninety degrees and continues back away from the road. A smaller stone wall, one which can be easily stormed and conquered by them, continues further along.

They stop, dismount the buggy, and in a few seconds are standing on top of the smaller wall looking out at acres and acres of farmland. Several groups of cattle can be seen off in the distance. A few buildings, probably barns and coops, dot the landscape. They can see the tall wall bending again farther back in the fields. Apparently the tall wall seals off the living area, while this smaller one acts as a fence to keep out law-abiding intruders.

"Any sense of us going on around?" Randy's question has already been answered in Mr. Anderson's mind.

"No, it would be a waste of time. It goes all the way around. There's not going to be an easy way to get in there, and that's a fact. Let's go back to My Mama's and get some food. My stomach is telling me I missed dinner today."

"Mine too. Let's go."

Inside the walls of La Nesra, not two hundred yards from the front gate, Lilly is still trying to get courage enough together to see what's on the other side of the glass in the mirror.

"I'll do it this time. I'll do it this time. I will do it this time. I will. I will."

"Here goes, I'm pushing with my fingers. Aahhh, my hand is through. I'll wiggle it around a little. Nothing? I'll push my arm through now, all the way up to my shoulder. I'll stretch out my arm to see if I can feel anything. Nothing? How will the rest of me ever fit through the frame of this mirror? It's hardly a foot square.

"What will happen if I get stuck half way through? What if the mirror falls over and lands on its face? I could be trapped in there forever? I'm getting my arm out of there right now. That didn't hurt anything, it's still the same. I know, I'll lay the mirror on the floor. That way I can put my feet through first, then if I need to get out fast, it'll be like climbing out of a hole.

"Okay, now, sit on the floor and dangle my feet down through the mirror. That's easy. Bend my legs and let my feet slide farther down. This is working better, I feel like I can get out if I need to. Now, if I slide my bottom across the floor toward the mirror, my thighs will slide through, if I don't get stuck. This is really easy. It's like my thighs and hips got smaller and slipped right through.

"Hold on to the sides of the frame, and lower more of me down. Careful, don't let my hands slip off. I'm clear up to my shoulders, this is very strange. Nothing bad is happening that I can tell. I still feel fine.

"Now I have to know what it looks like in there, I can't turn back now.

"I'll lower my shoulders down through, but I still have a good grip on the frame.

"I'm up to my neck. My head is next. Here goes.

"I still have my hands locked onto the edge of the mirror's frame on the outside, but I'm inside.

"There isn't any floor in here, but I can stand on my feet. It feels solid, like it will hold me. I can see myself and I look all right. My arms are stretched up to a lighted square, and my hands are through it on the other side. One at a time now, I'll let go with one hand and pull it in here with me. If I can put it back through, maybe I'll let go with the other one too. Not so fast girl, how do I know if the lighted square will still be there if all of me is in here?

"I can't believe it's me doing this, but I have to know. I can put my hand in and out, in and out, in and out, easy. Here comes my other hand through, and, and . . .

"Whhoooeeee! The light is still there, I can put my hand back through. Dear Lord, this is hard on a person's nerves.

"What now? Don't move too much. Be deliberate about everything I do.

"Look around. It's like seeing, but there's nothing to see, nothing to look at, except myself. I wonder, hmmm. Can I see back through the mirror, or will I get my own reflection from this side? Let's see. This is really something. I can see my whole room perfectly. It's like a picture that moves around in front of the mirror as I move my eyes. It's like the mirror is an extension of my eyes. This is fun. I can see my clock setting on the dresser where I left it. I still have plenty of time to explore. I like this, it's really fun.

"If I move around some, will I lose sight of my mirror's light? I'll back away a little and see. Will you look at this, there's a shiny silver thread coming with me from my mirror. It's not attached to me, it's just following me. When I walk toward the mirror it gets shorter, when I back away it gets longer. It appears it will stay with me if I move around and be there to lead me back. I'll turn my back toward it and walk away. It's staying right with me. Well, I never, this is great. I believe I can look around all I want and just follow this thread back whenever I want to.

"Now that I look closer, I notice some other lighted areas like mine. They're all sorts of shapes and sizes, little ones and great big ones. What will happen if I try to look through one of them? Let's see. Here's one about the size of mine.

"Peek a boo, I see you. Ha ha ha. This is fun.

"Oh goodness, I can see through it the same way I can see though mine. It's the hallway outside my room. There's my door. It's got my room number, forty-one, on it.

"Let's try another one, wait. Yep, my thread is still with me.

"That big one over there, it's the same. I'm looking at the room where we all eat our meals. I can see the tables and chairs. People are setting dishes and glasses in place for our supper."

"Peek-a-boo, I see you," she waves her hand hello. "Ha ha, this is fun."

"One thing though, there's no noise in here at all. It's too quiet. I'm going to yell and see what happens. Here goes.

"I'm yelling as loud as I can, but no noise is coming out. This place is starting to give me the creepies. There's no noise for my ears. I feel like I want to put my fingers in my ears to block out the noise that isn't' there. That doesn't make any sense, I put my finger in my ear and now I hear voices. It's as if I'm in a crowd of people and they're all talking at the same time in different languages. When I take my finger out of my ear it stops, back in, I can hear it again. This is getting to be too much to comprehend. I'd better get back to my room and figure this out before I go any farther. I'll just follow my shiny little thread."

The ride back to the stable to park their rig with Smitty gives Bob and Randy some time to rest and think. Both men are examining the possibilities of breaching that tall wall.

After giving the traces to Luke, they walk the rest of the way to the restaurant. The aroma coming from the kitchen increases their hunger. The dining room isn't fancy, and not all that clean. The wooden floors are black with age. Worn wooden tables, no tablecloths, and chairs, make up the only furniture. Two cooks can be easily seen in the kitchen, busy filling food orders as they are brought to them The room is about a third full of customers, allowing plenty of room to sit down.

"What's your pleasure, boys?" The voice of a stout masculine-featured woman drowns out others in the room from her perch on a stool near the kitchen. They haven't sat down yet, but they're glad to shout their order back.

"We'll have two of your biggest steaks with a pile of fried potatoes and onions, along with a loaf of your fresh bread, and lots of butter." Bob responds with at least the same volume.

"What you drinking with that?"

"Two big glasses of cold milk, and a pot of coffee." Randy yells.

"Coming up." Is heard by all throughout the room.

No sooner have the men sat down at their table than the door swings open, causing all in the room to look. In walks a redheaded female dressed in her best. She's the best looking woman these customers have seen on this end of town for some time. It takes a few minutes for the conversation to start again as patrons turn back to their food. The woman swaggers deliberately to a table as near to Bob and Randy as possible, and sits down to face them. They are unable to keep from grinning at each other acknowledging the very noticeable woman, who seems to have taken an immediate interest in them.

"Afternoon, ma'am," Bob speaks to be polite and to break the tension.

The redhead, sitting straight in her chair, gives a tacit nod and mouths a voiceless hello, never taking her eyes off him. Another couple of minutes is all he can stand of her constant stare.

"I'm sorry, ma'am, can I help you with something? I don't know why you're staring at me so." He gets right to the point.

Randy is squirming in his seat. He's heard about women like this, but never expected to be confronted by one.

"What a beautiful woman," he thinks, unable to keep from smiling at her. "I can sure see how a man could get all caught up in a woman like her. I'm glad it's not me she's after. I'm going to bump his leg and give him a nod to go ahead."

Just as he bumps Bob's leg with his, he hears her say. "It's what I can do for you that matters. May I join you and your friend?"

Randy is so excited he can hardly believe he hears himself say. "I wish you would, ma'am."

Bob looks at his friend with big eyes wondering where that urge came from. He's usually timid around women he doesn't know. There's nothing left to be said, the redhead is on her way to their table.

"Thank you, I appreciate your invitation," she says through her smile as she sits down and looks at each of them carefully.

"Have you placed your order yet?" Again, she looks at each of them.

"Yes, we have." Bob replies with a bit of nervousness in his voice.

"Good, don't worry about me. I'm not here to eat. I'm here on business." The beautiful busty female informs them with a sly little grin.

These farm boys can't believe how fast things are moving with this conversation. It's like a whirlwind. They have nothing to say, just waiting to see what happens next. They glance at each other and back at her.

What a day this has turned out to be. They don't realize it, but the room suddenly goes silent. The only noises are those coming from the kitchen. Apparently, the woman was speaking loud enough for others to hear. Her next words are going to be heard by everyone in the room, and most of them think they know what they'll be.

Suddenly, as if the wind has changed, she jerks her head and says, "Oh my, my, what do you all think I am doing here. Oh no, it's not that. You all think I'm a prostitute, am I right?" There's not a sound in the dining room. "Well, let me assure you, I'm not. Now get back to your own business."

What a disappointment for Randy. He still expects the conversation to continue down that path when she leans toward them both and whispers.

"I work at La Nesra. I hear you want to get in there unnoticed. Is that right, am I talking to the right two men?"

Bob says. "And who, may I ask, are you?"

"My name's Sally. As I said I work there. I've been known to help people when they have a need to get behind those walls. It's like a fortress you know. And just so there's no misunderstanding, I get paid for what I do for people like you."

"How do you know about us?" young Mr. Anderson continues.

"Word gets around this town quickly. Well, do you want my help or not?" She avoids an answer that will satisfy him.

"That's not good enough. How am I to know you won't be leading us into some sort of trap. You'll have to do better than that." Randy is glad to hear his associate demand more information.

"I pay people for information. The darkies around here have eyes that see all that goes on. They bring it to me, and if I'm interested, I pay them. Your friend here was overheard talking to a Mr. Vaughn earlier today. He was also seen running away. When you put those two things together, what's a girl supposed to think?" She curtly informs them both.

"Now, what's it gong to be. I can help you, or I can tell a person at La Nesra where you are? See, I get paid either way. They won't give up until they find you, you know." She looks directly into Randy's eyes. "I've seen it happen before."

"Supposing we go along with you, how will it work. Give me the details of what I'm paying for." The older of the two pursues.

"I'll tell you where to be and at what time. I'll let you inside, take you where you want to go, and stay with you until you finish whatever you want to do. Then, I'll lead you back outside again, and from there you're on your own." She lays it out in front of them.

"My interests are locating a girl you have inside La Nesra. And we're interested in more than just talking to her, she'll be leaving with us."

"That's your business, none of mine. I'll get you in and get you out."

"It looks as if we have no other choice. But listen to me, if this is a plan to trap us out where no one will ever know what happened, I'll make it my business to be close enough to you to snap your neck before they get to me. Remember that."

Randy hears Bob's words with amazement. He has more respect than ever for him.

"It'll cost you fifty dollars. I'll take it now, and be careful not to let anyone see."

Randy is surprised at how brazen and tough this beautiful female can be.

"Half now, and the other half when we're on the outside with the person we're here to get," Bob insists.

"Okay, that's fine," she says, takes the money from Bob's hand under the table, and stands up. "It will take a few days for me to get everything ready. What's the name of the person you want me to find?"

"Her name is Sheree Anderson. That's spelled S-h-e-r-e-e."

"I'll find her and bring you a picture when I see you again. Be here, at this time, three days from now, and be ready to go that same night."

The intimidating redhead is gone as quickly as she came.

They look at each other as their food is being placed in front of them.

"What have we done? What in the world have we done to ourselves as well as Sheree." Randy says under his breath to Bob.

Chapter Seventeen

"It's been three days since I first entered through the mirror into that place of a different sense of being. I've been back there every day exploring farther and farther away from my room. Last night was the meeting with our group of, somewhat, trusted friends. I left my real self in my room and met them as my out-of-body me.

"No one noticed the difference. They treated me the same as always. Even Eagle didn't know I was not myself, and that was the true test. Now I'm sure no one will.

"Nothing much new was learned about the girl in the other building. A scant few of the people questioned admitted they had seen her, but knew nothing about her. It was agreed that everyone would keep an eye and ear open for information, and discuss it at our next meeting.

"Eagle tried to get me to stay after the meeting, but I said it wasn't possible right then. I said I would let him know when we could, and that we could determine where to meet then."

"When everybody stood up to leave, Falcon brushed close against me. A little unusual for him I thought, but his purpose was to secretly push a note into my hand. He said nothing, didn't even look at me, and left. I rushed back to my room to resume myself in my physical body, and immediately unfolded the note. It read: 'Something is going on that I don't think I should mention in front of the others. I've heard bits and pieces of conversations, which, if you line them up with a logical sequence, could mean two men are coming here tomorrow night to get you. I don't know who they are or when they'll be here, and I'm not exactly sure it's true. I thought you should know.' There was no signature.

"I burned it, then spent most of the night trying to decipher the meaning of it all. In all likelihood, Lester is mistaken about the look alike girl in the other building. Falcon's understanding of the information in his note apparently comes from pieces of several, or who knows how many, different conversations. Chances are none of it is true, or it could be that someone's trying to locate me and is coming for me tonight. If they are, two things need to be done. Number one, since Falcon has heard of their coming, the security people here must know of it too. They'll probably set a trap to catch them. Number two, I should be ready to go with them. Since they won't know how to find me, I need to find them before they get caught. We can all leave right then. Gosh, I hope it's my family coming after me."

Daylight comes with its usual serenity, its light spreading across Atlanta maintaining a constant speed, reaching for La Nesra.

Lilly awakens and begins her day as usual, a physical workout with her group, a quick bath, and breakfast. She manages to get the last bite off her plate at the same time she's summoned to the laboratory. It can mean only one thing, more tests.

"I hope they do whatever it is they're going to do and give me the afternoon off. I need the time to lay out a plan."

She hurries through the building to the laboratory. She will know in a couple of minutes. The doctor greets and addresses her as she enters the room.

"Lilly, we're going to put you to sleep for the next twenty-four hours to conclude a few tests regarding your ability to accept nourishment. We've noticed you're starting to look fatigued and lack your normal energy. The rest, along with our injections of food mixtures, will do you good. Lie down on the table and get comfortable. The door will be locked when we leave you alone so you won't be bothered. Okay, we'll get started."

She obeys, but her mind is busy elsewhere.

"They're doing this to foil any plan someone might have to get me out of here, I just know it. They don't want me to be in my room, and no one will think to look for me here. I can't escape if they can't find me, and worse yet, I need to warn them that they're walking into a trap. What can I do? I know, I'll get out of my body and find them. But if they lock me in here, I won't be able to get out. If I had a way out, I could find them as soon as they come into the yard. I could warn them, and bring them back here to get my body. But how? How can I get out of here if the door is locked? Falcon would say to look at it logically. That's it, as soon as they leave me alone, I know exactly what I'll do. I'll get some rest for now, I didn't get much sleep last night, and this is going be a long day."

Bob and Randy have spent the last two days close to their rented cottage. Randy is forbidden to go anywhere, except to relieve himself, and to eat at My Mama's Home Cooking. They both fear he'll be seen and reported to Mr. Vaughn of the Company. There's no good reason to take a chance when they're so near to finding Sheree. As they eat their breakfast they again ponder the possibilities of the redheaded woman's plan.

"We both know this is probably a trap. The company doesn't want us poking around asking questions with them not knowing what we're up to. They probably figure the best way to handle us is to get us out of the way. What better way than to catch us inside their walls. Then, they can do anything they want and there'll be damn little we can do about it." Bob's words are received as the whole truth of it all.

"But what different can we do? I don't know how else we'll ever get in there," Randy points out.

"I'm not totally convinced that Sheree's even in there. Just because we've found the Company, doesn't mean she's there." Bob wants his partner to counter his statements.

"It's the only thing we've got right now, Bob. We have to check it out and be sure she's not there. That Sally woman is supposed to bring us a picture of her. If she has a picture, she must be in there. Right?"

"Oh, I know you're right, but I want to be sure we've thought about everything. We can't do Sheree any good if we're both dead. That's all," Mr. Anderson worries.

“Maybe we should ask Smitty and his son to go with us? Maybe they can bring some of their friends.” Young Randall keeps pursuing.

“I think our best chance of getting in and out of there is just the two of us. If we take a crowd, we have to worry about them too,” Robert negates.

“What if one of us held on to Sally outside while the other one went in to get Sheree? That way we could trade her if we get caught?” Randy’s not going to give up. He’s going after his friend, one way or another.

“Let’s say we do something like that. We still need something to convince them we mean business. Something like a gun, only bigger.”

“Like nitroglycerin!” the younger of the two exclaims.

“What do we know about nitroglycerin, Randy? It’s mighty touchy, I can tell you that. Besides, I doubt if we could put our hands on any if we wanted to.” The older of the two dismisses the idea.

“Well then, maybe we could use gunpowder to make some kind of a bomb we could throw at them. We could stick a fuse in it so it would explode after we throw it. We could fill up a bean can and seal off the top with a piece of fuse sticking out. Then, if they come after us, we can put fire to the fuse and throw it.”

“That’s it. We’ll tie Sally’s arm to mine so she can’t get away. We’ll show her the explosives and let her know we’ll use them if trouble starts. Even if the bombs don’t work, they won’t know it, and we’ll bluff our way out of there. That way, Sally will know I can carry out my threat of killing her. If it’s a trap, they’ll see we can cause some serious damage before they get to us.” Bob knows this isn’t a good solution, but it’s probably the best they’ll be able to do.

“Where are we going to get gunpowder?” A good question from Randy.

“I’ll talk to Smitty this morning. Maybe he can tell us where we can find some.” Bob suggests a place to start.

In the meantime, an invitation-only meeting is about to begin.

John Anderson and Marty Schoener stand facing each other, leaning with one elbow resting on the oak mantle of the fireplace in the library of the plush Monticello Inn on the outskirts of Baltimore. They’re expecting fifteen or more people to arrive shortly. This is their first exposure to the men who have joined together to form the organization which is to be used to expose and eliminate a formidable unnamed foe. They have no idea who their guests might be.

“You know, here we stand awaiting the appearance of some unknown group of people, to establish a yet to be named spy organization, which is meant to combat a foe with the magnitude of a giant, the name and whereabouts of which has yet to be determined. It sounds a bit ridiculous, I must say.” Marty is making conversation to lessen the tension.

“We’ll give them one hour, if no one shows, we’ll pack up and get on with our liv—” John stops short when people start entering the room.

Over the next three or four minutes, eight men and two women appear through the doorway and find seats in the room. No one speaks.

He's relieved to see his good friend Howard Clevenger in the mix. The last man through the doors slides them closed and sits down. No one has taken a seat at the table, where twelve chairs are set. There, now, are no other empty seats in the room.

John and Marty take their elbows off the mantle and turn to face the people scattered around the room, neither is sure what to do next. No one, it seems, is going to speak. They all sit calmly, looking at the two men standing.

After collecting his thoughts, John explains.

"My name is John Anderson. I'm probably unknown to all of you, except for Howard. I've been asked, and have accepted the responsibility of creating an organization to counter the efforts of a large spy agency within our national borders. The man here with me is Martin Schoener. He has agreed to act as my good right arm."

The room remains silent.

"It's my understanding that you have agreed to my appointment prior to my knowledge of it, and have committed to support my efforts." He baits his audience.

Silence.

Both John and Marty, are wondering where this meeting is headed. John turns left and paces three steps, turns back and paces to the spot he just left. Then turns to his right and says, "Who in this room will support me? I'll need a verbal and physical affirmation." With that he sits down at the head of the empty table.

Marty moves to the opposite end and sits, leaving five empty chairs on each side.

One by one the rest of the group exchange their seats for one at the table.

When all are present, Marty interjects. "This is half of what the man expects. We'll go around the table starting here at my left. Let's hear your mind."

"You're first," he declares, his face sober, a frown between his eyes, as he puts his pointing finger against the man's chest and taps twice.

"I believe you've just answered our first question about the two of you completely," the man says.

"You'll both do, without a doubt. Do we all agree?" He asks the rest of the table.

A resounding affirmative response is heard along with bobbing heads.

Howard Clevenger rises to his feet in front of his chair.

"It's good to see you, John, you too, Marty. I'll not apologize for our façade a few minutes ago. These men and women needed to see a little of what I know you two are made of. I was involved with your selection to lead this soon-to-be organization. I wasn't at liberty to say anything before you accepted, however. You had to make up your own mind. I couldn't take the chance of influencing your decision. The ten of us here will serve as your initial staff. Our talents vary greatly, so together we should be able to handle most of what you'll require. I'll personally vouch for the integrity and trustworthiness of each and every person at this table. You'll soon learn of our eagerness to cooperate and work with your plans. All here understand that you are the commander of this force, and if for any reason, you feel any of us are not what's needed, it's your duty to dismiss us from this group." Howard concludes as he sits down.

"One other thing John, have you decided to run for governor, or will you pass on the nomination this time around?"

"Regretfully, I believe this new task at hand will require my total attention, Howard, so, I'll depend upon you to remove me as a candidate. Let's speak privately later today, if that's agreeable."

A nod from Howard affirms his wishes.

The group's leader stands and continues, as he starts casually moving around the table. "I must believe that this position I have accepted is not desired by any of you. If it were, I wouldn't be here. So, I'm not going to thank you for the opportunity, but rather I'll inform you that your involvement will be as though you have this job. No one man on this earth can possibly take on a task of such enormity. I'll lead you, I'll organize our efforts, and I'll make the tough decisions. But I'll require all of you to be up to your necks with the execution of our planned efforts. If any of you believe you are unable to make this type of commitment to me and your country, leave now, for we don't have the time to baby sit a person of your caliber. We'll all have more respect for each other if you leave, rather than have you stay and become a weight around all our necks. Anyone?" He waits to see who might change their minds.

The room is quiet except for the sounds of bodies being adjusted in their seats.

"Our creed will be defined and put in writing. A copy will be served upon each of you as soon as possible. Keep in mind, I'll ask for your commitment to each and every mandate, including our protection of each other. Should it be determined that one of us is living outside our creed, such as, cohabiting with the enemy, justice will be swift and final. There will be no exceptions. Is that clear?" He knows a control statement must be made today, and leave no room for misunderstanding his intentions. "Also, any of you belonging to a fraternity group such as the Freeman Organization, or a sect of it, will be expected to continue with them as usual."

"That includes you, Mr. Anderson, does it not? I'm Henry Furman." The voice comes from an elderly man sitting between the two women.

"It does." John answers without hesitation

"Is this the entire group, Howard? Are there more to come?" Marty inquires.

"We're all here. There are others who will fight our battles with us, but are unable to totally commit themselves as are we."

"Let's relax, ladies and gentlemen. If the ladies don't mind, I think I'll remove my coat and get a cup of coffee before we continue." John says, hoping to relieve the stress in the room.

A good move on his part, people rise from their chairs to get coffee and light their pipes and cigars. The ladies remove their shoes when they reseat themselves. The older of the two produces a cigarette sized cigar and fires it up. A few of the men remove their suit coats and hang them on the backs of their chairs. A few minutes pass as John confers with Marty and Howard. The voices settle, and activity subsides when he walks to the head of the table and lays several papers down in front of him.

"I think it'll be a good idea to agree upon and understand the scope of our operations. We must all start with the same access to knowledge, and realize our boundaries. We will quickly find the need to protect ourselves, and a short time later discover we must protect the rest of the world as well. We must be aware of the current and future political parties' agendas, and support them whenever we can, never veering from our ultimate goal. There's going to be a war between our States. It will not be our business or responsibility to align ourselves to fight. But we will use the cloak of the war to further our own purposes whenever we can." John stops to sip his coffee, and glances at the papers on the table.

"First things first." He observes, as he continues. "Number one, who are we? Do we need a name for our organization? If so, what shall we call ourselves? Consider our field agents, the people we assign to carry out missions. We'll need a method of identifying with them, and a way of conversing that is not known to our enemies. Number two, I spoke about our creed, the rules we live by. The rules we will adhere to while running our organization. We need to identify our creed and reduce them to paper. Number three, what is our total purpose? Once answered, this should be split up in three pieces: our immediate, intermediate, and long term goals. Number four, how shall we enlist those people we'll need to attain our goals? We'll need a method of training our people to be put in the field, and a code name designation for each operation we have working. And number five, we need a staff to accumulate and disperse large amounts of information. We'll, also, need a school to train our entire force. It should be separate from the training program for our field people, for obvious security reasons."

"Marty will pair you up in groups to work on these needs. He can explain in more detail, if you like. I'm going to adjourn our meeting until three o'clock this afternoon. By then I'll want to hear your responses to your areas of concern. In the meantime, I'll be available to meet with you as you deem necessary. Until three o'clock then."

The day moves along for the team in Atlanta.

It's going for two o'clock in the afternoon before Bob returns to the cottage where Randy has been waiting since breakfast. He's carrying a two gallon wooden barrel, a handful of candles, a small coil of blasting fuse, and a burlap bag that rattles as if it's full of glass bottles.

"I was beginning to wonder where you were." Randy relates from his seat on a straight chair under a tree behind the cottage. "What all do you have there?"

Bob doesn't respond until he gets closer to his friend. He sets the burlap bag on the ground, then with both hands, carefully, sets the keg down beside it. He lays the fuse and candles on top, and looks up. "I have everything we need. I asked Smitty about the gunpowder, and explained what we were planning. He knew right away everything we needed, and how to put it together. He took me to the back door of a gun shop and asked a friend of his to fix us up with all of this."

"It looks like you've got enough there to blow up all of Atlanta."

"Yeh, I know, but I wasn't sure how much we'll need, and I wanted there to be enough. We probably won't use it all. But wait, I'm not finished, there's more. Listen to this. I'll bet Smitty has done something like this before. He's arranging a way to get us out of Atlanta after we get Sheree. I bought three horses from him, and he's going to have them waiting for us about a half an hour north of here, all loaded up with the supplies we'll need for our trip back home. Like he says, we can't go to the depot and wait for a train, they'd catch us for sure. We have to make our way back home on horseback. It's our best chance of not getting caught."

"Man-o-man," Randy exclaims. "I never even thought about all that yet. I'm sure glad he's on our side."

"There's more," Bob continues. "Luke is going to be waiting for us when we come out of La Nesra with Sheree. He'll be about a quarter of a mile northeast of the Company's compound with a fast team and carriage. If we can make it to there without getting caught, he'll take us right to Smitty and the horses."

"Now, this is a plan." Young Mr. Stoker voices with excitement. "You're right Bob, these guys have done this before, and God bless them for it. I feel really good about this whole thing now. We're going to get Sheree back, after all these years."

"I believe you're right, my friend, but we still have work to do. There's ten empty pint whiskey bottles in that bag. We have to dry them out and fill them with gunpowder. Then we'll cut a piece of fuse for each one, and stick it down in the powder, leaving a few inches stick out. After that, we'll seal them up by melting these candles and pouring the wax on top. Once the wax sets up, we can carry them in our pockets or anywhere. If we need to use them later tonight, we can light the fuses and throw them, just like you said. That should keep those people at the Company at a distance. What do you think?"

"Like I said, now we have a plan. But how are we going to light the fuses?" Randy asks knowing he'll be so nervous he'll never to able to strike a match, let alone light a fuse.

"Cigars, my man, cigars." Bob boasts proudly at the same time he pulls two from his shirt pocket. "Before we go in, we'll light these up and keep them lit all the while we're in there. All we have to do is touch the fuse to the fire on these stogies and away she goes. The truth is, I wish I could take some credit for all of this, but Smitty's the one who put it all together. Something to remember though," he cautions, "When these bottles explode, glass is going to spray out in all directions, at us, as well as at them."

"That means we should get behind something first, if we can." Randy's reasoning is right on target.

"Let's get busy, we don't want to miss our meeting with Sally." Bob moves toward the burlap bag as he speaks. "We'll each take two of these with us, and we'll leave the rest of them with Smitty and Luke. They can divide them up and put them with the carriage and the horses."

Inside the Company's compound a few miles away.

"That was a lengthy nap. I must have slept for at least three hours. I see they've left me alone, and turned the lamp down. That's a good sign that they won't be back for a while. Getting out of my body is easier every time I do it. Here I am, looking at myself, there on the table. I'll never get used to this. It's unbelievable.

"Since I can go through the mirror in my room and move around in that other place, maybe, just maybe, I can go back out through one of those other white places. I mean, if I can see the hallway through those white holes, maybe I can climb through one. I'll go through a mirror here, and if I can, I'll get into my room by going through my mirror there. From there I can get out and do what I want. They won't lock the door to my room, not with me locked up here in the laboratory.

"Okay, I need a mirror. Don't tell me there isn't a mirror in here somewhere. I don't see any. Damn the luck, there has to be a mirror in here somewhere. Don't panic, search, look in every drawer, behind every door, everywhere."

A few minutes pass.

"I've looked everywhere, there's none in here. I'll turn the gas light up so I can see a little better. I'll pull these cabinets away from the wall. There might be something behind one of them. Well, look here . . . it's a good size piece of a broken mirror. It must have fallen off the wall and broke and they missed this piece when they cleaned it up. I'll just move it over here on the floor. Oooppps. My fingers go right through it. I can't pick it up. There's no frame for me to grip. Let's see if I can slide it sideways toward me by pressing on the edge of it. Okay, that works. I'll slide it out from behind here so I can press my fingers on the edges of either side. I should be able to pick it up that way.

"A little more, ah there, now if I can pick it up. Careful now, don't want to drop it. Gently place it on the floor. There, I'm all set. Here goes, I'm sliding through, I'm in. Now to find my room, that silver thread doesn't follow me any more. I don't know why, but it doesn't. I believe my room is that way. Distance doesn't seem to mean much in here. It's almost seems that if I think of where I want to go, I go there.

"This feels right. This must be it. I'll peek through. It's my room all right. I should be able to climb through this white square hole and be in there. Here goes. Amazing, I'm in my room.

"The first thing to do is to get rid of this white shirt, then I'll see about getting out of here and up on the roof. I think that's the best place for me to be when they come. I'll be able to see them enter through any of the gates from up there, then I can run down and tell them before they get caught. I'll have to get my body back before I can leave here with them, though. I'll explain it to them, they'll understand. They'll be able to figure out a way to get the laboratory door open.

"Oh, I'm so excited. Another few hours and I'll be out of here and on my way home. I can hardly wait. I want my life back. I want to hug my whole family, and friends, especially Randy. I wonder who's coming to get me. Probably Daddy and one of his friends. I'll get to the roof and stay out of sight until dark. They won't be here before then. I hope there's a moon tonight so I can see through the shadows."

The meeting at Baltimore is about to resume again.

Mr. Anderson calls his meeting to order at exactly three o'clock. The lack of empty seats at the table tells him all are present.

"I would like this to be an open forum. Your voices and opinions are needed and appreciated," he begins.

"Marty, I'm going to ask that you and Howard host this part of our meeting. I'd like to observe and take notes." He sits down as Marty gets to his feet.

"A couple of things before we get to the meat and potatoes of things." He sets the stage for his part of the meeting, and starts by explaining to John.

"We've split our group into five committees of two people each. Since Howard knows these folks, he's met with them and determined the best committee for each of the five areas you discussed earlier. I've acted as an overseer and advisor with each committee, so I'm going to introduce each committee in the order you asked your questions, and let each one lay out their thinking as to how their goals can be accomplished. Anybody have a problem with that?"

No objections are heard.

"Committee number one, you're first with the name of our organization, names for our field agents, and a method of communicating with them secretly."

The older man sitting between the two women rises as Marty sits down.

"I'm Henry Furman. This young lady next to me, Mrs. Caleb Ross, and I would like to report as follows: What's in a name? We feel it should easily identify our group and be remembered after hearing it the first time. We suggest the name Sentries of National Security. That can be shortened to S.O.N.S. or SONS. We can then be aptly referred to as the Sons of our Homeland. Are there any other suggestions?" he asks and listens for responses.

The table is unanimous, voicing their acceptance of the name Sons.

"Then the Sons we are. Good," John affirms.

"In regards to the names of our field agents, the two of us agree. For the purpose of protecting their identity, there should be no definite reasoning when naming them. When an operation begins, the head of the operation should be responsible for naming it. Further, that name should be known only to those with a definite need."

"I want to know every name, every person, every detail of all operations planned, or working, on a current basis. No exceptions. Any operation must have my approval before it begins. Is that clear?" Their leader wants to be involved.

"Absolutely, Mr. Anderson," Henry assures. "We understand your need to know."

"I agree with your thinking, Henry, and please . . . call me John."

"Thank you, John. Now, as to a method to communicate secretly with our field agents, Mrs. Ross and I feel that no one method should be used. We should have a dozen or more contrived codes, which change frequently to keep our foes busy trying to decipher our messaging. We'll staff the people we need to accomplish this area with the help of committee number five."

John nods affirmatively.

The rest of the meeting consists of the same proceedings, until all of the five committees have their plans approved by John and Marty. It's a beginning. Everything has a starting place. The Sons must grow rapidly, yet carefully, with the proper people. John feels good about the group he's met today. They're all true patriots, with power, connections, and money.

As the meeting breaks up for the day, he stands at the doorway shaking hands, thanking each person for their participation and loyalty to their country. A second meeting is planned two days from today to get into more detail with the committees.

Randy and Bob are now recognized as regular customers at My Mama's Home Cooking on the outskirts of Atlanta. They are twenty minutes early for their planned meeting with the fiery, aggressive, redheaded, Sally. They have coffee in front of them as they sit at a table away from the windows, waiting.

"She's supposed to bring us a picture of Sheree, right?" Randy addresses his friend.

"That's what she said. It's been so long, I don't know if we'll recognize her without it. She's all grown up now, just like you are. I believe she's sixteen, since her birthday is already past this year."

"I'll bet she's one beautiful woman." His partner's remark seems a little strange to Robert. He had forgotten that school kept him away much of the time his sister was growing up, but he remembers now that they were close.

"You can bet on it. You've seen Charlotte. She's gorgeous, and she's always looked a lot like Sheree," Bob replies.

"I hadn't thought of it until just now, but if the picture Sally shows us doesn't look anything like Charlotte, we might have to change our thinking about going in there."

"Yeah, I guess you're right. I never thought of that either. I sure hope it looks like her. It will, I know it will." Sheree's best friend hangs on to hope.

"Here she comes. Right on time," Bob whispers.

The statuesque, flashy, redhead arrives like a breath of fresh air. Her clothes are bright with color and the scent of perfume drifts in the air around her.

She walks directly to them and sits down at the table, her back to the street.

She fumbles in her bag and produces a tin type photograph of a young girl.

"Here's a picture of your Sheree, boys," she declares, "just like I promised."

Bob takes the tin type from her and positions it so he and Randy can view it at the same time.

"It's her! It's her for sure!" Randy's voice is loud with excitement.

"Ssshhhhh! Young man! You don't need to tell all of Atlanta about it," Sally warns.

"How old is this picture?" Bob asks.

"Not more than a year, I'd say. I swiped it out of her file in the office. You can't have it, I have to put it back before they know it's gone." She wants it understood.

"Are you still of a mind to get her out of there?"

"We are." Randy delivers the answer with certainty.

"All right then, this is what I want you to do."

"You be at the northeast corner of the big wall at sundown. I'll open the small steel door there as soon as I can after the last rays of daylight are gone. I'll lead you to the girl, and once you've got her, I'll lead you back out to the door. Then you're on your own."

"I hope this whole thing is as simple as you make it sound, Sally. We'll be there when you open the door, but I'm warning you again, if this is some sort of a trap, you won't live to see us caught. Do you understand? I mean every word I say." Bob tries to put fear into the mind of the redhead.

"Stop worrying. I do this three or four times a year for different people. Just do as I say and everything will be fine." Sally exudes confidence.

"Is there any cover close to the door?" Randy asks.

"Not much," she answers. "They won't let anything grow close to the wall. The closest trees are about fifty yards away. I'd stay there until dark, then move up to the wall if I were you. I won't leave you out there very long. I can't make any money that way. And while we're talking about that, make sure you have the rest of my money with you."

"That's not a problem. We'll see you shortly after sundown." Bob confirms.

"I'll be there to let the two of you in, and that's a fact." She's on her feet and out the door as quickly as she came, leaving nothing but the lingering hint of her perfume.

The clock moves at a snails pace for three people in Atlanta this afternoon, causing them to think, rethink, and think again, about the possibilities of a catastrophe waiting to happen inside the walls of the Company's compound.

Time for action arrives when Luke pulls a closed carriage to a stop in front of the cottage. He's there to pick up Bob, Randy, their personal things, and their equipment for their trip to the wall.

Each will carry two of the glass bottles loaded with gunpowder. Each has a cigar, with matches to light it, and Bob has a length of rope.

As planned, Luke will keep three of the bottles in the carriage. The other three will be dropped off with their personal effects to Smitty as they pass the blacksmith shop on their way to the Company. He'll take them and their horses to the meeting place.

They're on their way.

Luke pulls the reins toward himself, and pushes the brake lever with his foot to stop his horses.

"Whoa!" He commands the team. The carriage rolls to a stop.

"This is about as close as I dare take you. That clump of trees over there must be the ones she's talking about." He points as he explains to his two passengers They can hear him, but can't see him from inside the carriage.

"Look around, do you see anybody?" Bob's voice is just loud enough for Luke to hear. "Can we get out now?"

A few seconds pass.

"It's all clear. Come on out," their driver says.

"I see what you mean. That clump of trees is about the only thing around here, they must be the ones," Randy confirms.

"There's not much cover between here and there." Bob notices.

"You're right about that," Luke agrees. "They could probably see you from the top of that wall. But from what I can tell, there's no better place."

"We'll just have to take the chance. You'd better get going. No sense in giving them this rig to spot if they're looking. I don't know how long it'll take us to get back to you, but you're going to wait on us about a quarter of a mile over that way there, right?" Mr. Anderson asks, looking for reassurance as he points.

"I'm not leaving without the both of you; I'll be there, count on it."

Randy feels the plan coming together as Luke speaks.

Meanwhile . . . up on the roof inside La Nesra.

"Well, I'm here, and I can see most of the yard of the compound. This water-retaining wall is plenty tall enough for me to hide behind and peek over. It's starting to get dark, it won't be long now. As soon as I see them, I'll run downstairs and warn them. Then we'll go to the laboratory, get my body, and get out of here.

"Uh oh, something's going on. The guards are moving around everywhere. They're hiding behind things! It looks like they're setting up a trap. This is not good at all! They're getting ready for Daddy to sneak into the yard, then they'll pounce on him.

"What should I do? Oh, Lord, what can I do? I can't get down there to warn them, there are too many guards. They'll see me for sure. I have to settle down and think. If I yell, I don't know if Daddy could hear me from here. It might draw attention to me and cause a commotion down there, though. He might hear it and know it's a trap.

"But then, the first thing the guards will do is go to the laboratory to see how I got out of there. They'll make sure I never get a chance like this again. That's no good. There has to be another way. Think! Think!

"I wonder . . . If I throw a mirror from here to the ground, I can go through the mirror in my room and come out down there. If it's dark enough, maybe they won't see me. It will be a whole lot easier to warn him if I'm down there. It's worth a try.

"I've got to get another mirror and throw it down there, so I might as well bring the one from my room up here while I'm at it. I can go through it from up here and save time. I've got to get moving, I need to be down there in time to warn them."

Minutes are ticking away at the clump of trees just outside the wall.

"Just a few more minutes, and we can move up to the door. How are you feeling? Are you scared?" The older of the two young men asks nervously.

"I'm shaking all over right now, but I think I'll be okay as soon as we get started. This waiting is killing me."

"Yes, me too. If everything goes right, this will all be over in ten or fifteen minutes." Bob's statement is for his own benefit, but it spurs Randy's belief anyway.

"Everything's going to work out, you'll see. I've got a good feeling about it all." His words are music to Bob's ears.

"Are you ready?"

An affirmative nod from Randy.

"Let's go." The loud whisper leaves Bob's lips, and they're on their way.

Running is a chore for Randy, especially when he has to crouch down with his legs bent, leaning forward at the waist. To him, it seems like a mile to the wall from the trees.

Bob reaches the wall expecting his cohort to be a little behind him, but when he turns he sees him getting up off the ground about twenty yards away. But he's on his way again and comes rushing in gasping for air.

Panting, Bob whispers rather loudly.

"Stand with your back flat up against the wall. They won't be able to see you as easily. What happened to you?"

"Aw! I got my feet tangled up and fell flat on my face."

"Are you hurt?"

"No, I'm okay, but I broke one of my bottles. The glass cut my leg a little bit."

Bob looks down at his friend's leg. He can see a growing wet spot of red on his pants. "How bad is it?"

"I'm not sure, my pocket's full of glass and gunpowder."

Concerned about the amount of blood he sees, Randy puts his hand down into his pocket and begins to remove one piece of glass, and one handful of gunpowder at a time. He's quickly able to determine that a sliver has cut through the material of his pants pocket and embedded itself into his leg. It's a small oddly shaped piece that's holding the gash open, allowing it to bleed profusely, which makes it slippery, difficult to grip with his fingers without getting cut again.

"Here, try this." Bob tosses a kerchief.

With it wrapped around his hand and fingers, he's able to remove the sliver with ease. It doesn't hurt when he pulls it out, even though it was buried at an angle, and punched more than an inch into his leg.

For right now, the best thing he can do is put pressure on the wound. He wraps the kerchief around his thigh, and ties a knot on top of the bleeding cut. There . . . with any luck, that should stop the bleeding.

"Are you going to be able to come with me?" Bob is obviously questioning the wisdom of Randy proceeding any farther.

"Light your cigar," Is his way of saying, I'm going with you.

They wait in silence.

All of this while, Lilly is frantically trying to find a mirror to toss down onto the ground from the roof.

"Darn, any other time I'd be falling over mirrors. Now I can't find a single one. Time's running out. The only thing left to do is go through the mirror in my room and try to find another mirror close to a downstairs doorway. Maybe I can slip past the guards. It's my only chance. I've got to try."

Back at the wall, the plan moves forward.

The not often used, steel door creeks and squeals as it swings open. How can anyone not hear it? The rescuers are hugging the wall about ten feet from the entryway.

Sally leans through the opening to look outside.

"I see you there, boys. Come on, let's get going, we don't have all night."

"Are you going to be able to do this, Randy."

He knows Bob is concerned about him keeping up with the pace. He expects his foot to slow him down, but now this leg?

"You lead the way, I'll be right behind you." He assures his friend.

"Give me your arm, Sally," Bob demands as he reaches for her.

"Why?" she asks, startled by his move.

"This is why." He puts her arm next to his and hurriedly wraps the length of rope he brought around both his wrist and hers. "Tie this tight."

Randy does as he is told.

"Now, I can be sure you're close to me, so, if anything happens we don't expect, the sound of your neck breaking will be the first thing they hear. Can you see this bottle in my pocket? It's filled with explosives. If trouble starts, I'll light the fuse with this cigar and, *boom*, all hell will break loose. Do you get my point?"

Sally neither speaks nor acknowledges him in any way.

"Lead the way," he says, and the three of them cautiously enter the compound.

Following her from shadow to shadow, creeping their way across the courtyard, the two men are unaware of the many sets of eyes following their every move.

From a darkened room, Mr. Vaughn watches through an open window. A sinister grin gives him the appearance of a madman.

"Just as I planned . . . just as I planned," he muses and chuckles with satisfaction.

Lilly is frantic.

She has entered the other side of the mirror and is desperately trying to move about to locate a white opening that will let her out into the yard to warn her liberators.

"I'm too worked up to think straight. Slow down Lilly, slow down. Get your mind on the problem at hand. I need to find an opening that will let me out in the yard. Think it again, and again. Okay, now I'm moving along, feeling like I'm headed to the right place. Keep thinking. Keep trying."

At the same time, not far from her, the boys continue to follow their redheaded leader through a series of shadows until finally, she stops at the base of a flight of six stone steps leading up into a building.

"She's in here. Ssshhhh. Quiet now, a whisper will echo through these halls," she cautions with a breath of volume.

The man with the bleeding leg is bringing up the rear of their group, constantly looking backward, expecting to be captured at any second.

Up the steps and into the building they go. The injured leg is starting to give pain to its owner, and blood is moving down his thigh again. He tries to apply pressure with his hand as they climb the steps, still it trickles down his lower leg into his boot.

Sally and Bob are getting farther and farther ahead of him. Maybe if he took a few seconds to tighten the kerchief, it would stop the bleeding.

"Bob," he whispers, trying to let him know he's stopping.

His call goes unheard by the other two as they have moved out of earshot ahead. They keep going, unaware he's not with them. As he's tightening the kerchief tighter around his thigh, Randy gets an insecure feeling that someone is watching him from behind. He looks over his shoulder to see a four-foot-tall mirror with etchings all around the edges, hanging on the wall in a massive frame. He's about to continue the chase and follow the other two, when he notices movement in the hallway. As his comrades pass by doorways, shadows of people creep out just enough to watch them from behind.

"They didn't see me stop, so they don't know I'm here. I'd better keep it that way for now. They'll be coming back this way with Sheree. So, if there's trouble to be had, I might be a big surprise for these shadowy characters. I'll wait right here.

"I should get this bottle of powder ready, just in case, but I can't puff on this cigar. They'll see the glow of the fire here in the dark." He's talking to himself so he won't feel so alone. Although his back is almost against the wall, he senses something's moving behind him.

Lilly continues to search for the right opening. At last, she sees a hallway through a large white hole. This is it, the floor below my room. Darn, who's this? A guard or somebody just stepped in front of the white hole. I can't get through with them standing there. "Move, darn you, move!"

Nothing is slowing the progress of the redhead and Robert.

Sally pulls him along with their wrists bound to each other, up a flight of stairs and down another hallway to room number forty-one. Finally she stops and says, "This is it. This is her room."

"Open the door and go in," he urges.

She opens the door to expose a dimly lit, small but efficiently furnished room. Lying peacefully asleep on the bed is a young woman, snuggled in blankets.

"Close the door and turn up the lamp," he orders. "I want to see her face."

Sally stretches her arm out to reach the door, and pushes it shut. Stretching their arms still farther she reaches the lamp with her other hand, and gives the valve a quick turn. The room brightens as the flame leaps up.

Bob looks down into the face of the girl and realizes it is Sheree. It takes his breath away to see her after so long a time. Gently, his hand covers her mouth, and he whispers.

"Sheree . . . wake up. I'm your brother, Bob."

The girl jerks violently trying to get free of his grip. Her screams are muffled by his hand.

"It's okay, Sheree. You're safe. I'm your brother. I've come to take you home."

Her eyes are darting wildly first his face, then to Sally's, then back to him.

"Hush now, listen to me. I'm your brother, Bob. Randy is right behind me. We've come to take you home. We don't have much time. We need you to get dressed so we can get out of here. I'll take my hand away from your mouth if you promise not to scream. Okay?" The girl nods her head yes.

Back in the hallway, the tension is building.

Lilly continues to wait for the person in front of the white square to move. She peers around this shadow of a person to see out.

"Why is this guard just standing here? Move, I tell you, move! Of course he can't hear me, I can't hear me unless I put my finger in my ear."

Things can't happen fast enough in room forty-one.

The young girl has settled down to where Bob and Sally believe she's ready to make the trip back to the steel door and the world outside.

Through the hallway, and down the stairs they move, quickly, and quietly. One more hallway and they'll be out of the building.

"I wonder what's happened to Randy?" Bob worries to himself.

Meanwhile, Lilly is about out of her mind, trying to get out through the white square.

"Hey, this guard just looked right at me. He's no guard, it's . . . it's Randy! My Lord, it's Randy! He looks just the same, only older. I'd know him anywhere. I'll just reach through and tap his shoulder. I have to be careful, I don't want to scare him to death. Here goes . . ."

On the other side of the mirror, at the same time, Randy is becoming more and more aware of something behind him. He's about ready to run down the hallway to find Bob, when he sees Sally at the bottom of the stairway, followed by two other figures; they're moving toward him fast.

"Sheree?" He utters and takes three steps toward them.

Lilly's arm is through the mirror, she's just inches away from tapping her boyfriend of years ago on the shoulder. Then she hears her name, and he moves away, out of her reach unless she moves farther out of the mirror.

Bob and the two women are moving like the wind, their steps make no sound as they rush toward Randy.

Thinking they're unable to see him, he moves out more toward them, giving Lilly a full view of the hallway.

Instinct and fear of getting caught take over, and she pulls her arm back into the mirror. She can plainly see the three people moving toward the mirror she's standing behind.

"It's my brother, Robert. He's here with Randy. That's Sally, and that's—ME?

"Something's really wrong here. Did they go to the laboratory and somehow wake me up. But then, why am I still here?"

An eerie feeling comes over young Mr. Stoker as he moves away from the wall, making him stop and turn to check his back. He sees nothing but the large mirror mounted on the wall.

"I don't care if the world hears me, I'm going to scream at them," Lilly exclaims silently.

"You've got the wrong girl! She's not me! Here I am! She's not me!"

"They can't hear me. I'll go through the mirror, then they'll know. I'll tell them." She can see how fast everything is happening, time is running out.

She is about to make her move when footsteps of people running at the other end of the hallway prompts the fleeing foursome to move speedily past the mirror, out through the doorway, and down the stone steps into the courtyard.

She's barely able to stop moving completely through the mirror into the hallway when five or six guards run toward her and turn through the outside doorway, chasing the escaping liberators. She can't go out there now. There's no point. Her brother, Randy, and her impostor, are gone, being led by her friend Sally.

"I'll get back up on the roof and see what's going on from there."

Once outside, the foursome heads directly for the steel door. Randy's having a lot of trouble keeping up. His clubfoot makes it hard enough, but now his injured leg feels like it's ready to fall off, and he's getting weak from the loss of blood.

"I don't think I'm going to make it!" he yells. "Go on without me. Save Sheree."

Lilly is standing on the roof witnessing the whole thing, emotions are riding high. Her brother is taking an impostor with him, and now Randy is collapsing in the courtyard and will surely be caught. She can't help herself.

"Get up and run, Randy! Run! Don't let them catch you! Please don't let them catch you!" She's too far away for him to hear with enough clarity to realize it's her, yelling.

Bob hears his friend and knows he won't leave him behind. With a jerk he frees his arm from Sally's, and pushes her with the girl, through the doorway.

As he moves toward Randy, who is now sitting on the ground leaning over trying to light the fuse of his remaining whiskey bottle, Bob pulls a bottle from his jacket pocket and touches the fuse to the tip of his cigar.

Psssszzzzzzz . . .

The fuse comes to life, sputtering, spitting sparks and smoke. There's no time with such a short length of fuse, so he throws it almost immediately.

He reaches the injured Randy at the same time the bottle explodes sending fire and shock waves, along with shards of glass, in all directions. Without hesitation, he scoops his friend up in his arms as if he is picking up a feather, and runs like a deer back to and out through the metal door. He hears the thundering of horses hooves hammering the ground getting closer and closer. Everyone is expecting the worst, when around the corner of the wall comes a closed carriage with a strong team at a full run. The driver is none other than Luke.

"Whoa, horses! Whoa . . . !" he yells standing up in the drivers well, leaning back on the reins, pulling to a stop.

"Get in, and let's get out of here," he yells.

"Here's your money, Sally. Thanks for your help."

Bob hands her the money while hanging on to Randy with one arm, follows Sheree to the coach, and lifts his friend inside behind her. He steps up on the entry step and yells to Luke, "Whip 'em up. Let's get out of here."

The carriage jerks rigorously and jumps forward. Once moving, Luke turns the team back in the direction he came from, toward where his father is waiting with fresh horses for the threesome.

Once inside the coach and knowing all are safely aboard, Bob yells up at the driver, "What are you doing here? We're supposed to meet you."

"I know," Luke yells back. "But I had a strong feeling that you needed me, so I had to come for you. Lucky I did, huh?"

"I'll say," Bob bounces back. "Randy was starting to get a little heavy."

Once the carriage disappears around the corner of the tall wall, Sally turns around and walks back through the steel door. Mr. Vaughn is standing just inside to meet her.

"How did I do? Do you think they believe they've saved their Sheree?" she asks.

"Oh, I do, I truly do. You've done an amazing job, Sally. We now have our agent placed in a perfect position. If she's as good at her job as I think she can be, we'll be listening in on the Anderson business for years to come. It's taken years of planning and preparation. And we've been lucky catching this opportunity. But now I can say, it's all been worth it.

"What did you think of that chase we gave them?" he asks amused.

"I thought for a minute there you might catch Randy. Did anyone get hurt from that blast?"

"I don't think so, but I'm sure we have a scorched spot where it hit."

Meanwhile . . . up on the roof.

Lilly sits with her knees pulled up to her chest, her arms around them.

"It was their plan all along to put that girl in my place. My family will think it's me. Only the Lord knows what will happen now. I will get out of here, somehow, and get to my family to tell them about this impostor. I swear, I will."

"I might as well get back to my life body. I'll go to my room and go through my mirror there."

The emotionally exhausted young girl runs down the stairs and hallways back to her room. There she slides through the mirror and emerges from the broken mirror lying on the floor of the laboratory.

"I'm at the laboratory, but where am I. My life body is not here, the table's gone, and the door is open. What's going on here? Did Bob and Randy really wake me up somehow and get me to go with them? Was that really me?"

Chapter Eighteen

Luke has the team whipped up at a run, still slapping the reins across their backs, putting as much distance between La Nesra and his passengers as possible. The closed carriage bounces up at least a foot in the front, at the same time it rocks down in the back, swaying from side to side, leaning to the left, then to the right. It's a wild ride for the three people inside, lifting them off their seats to careen off each other's bodies. The noise of the horses' hooves, the banging of the carriage body against the resisting springs, and the wind rushing around the open windows, make it almost impossible to hear anything said between the passengers. Randy reaches out across the space between the facing seats to take his liberated friend's hand.

"It's really good to see you, Sheree!" he yells. "I was beginning to think this day would never come!"

"I can't tell you how glad I am to see both of you!" she shouts back as she gently squeezes his hand and reaches for Robert's with her other one, all the time trying to keep her seat. "You finally found me, and have freed me from those people. I'll never be able to thank you enough!"

"You look just like I thought you would!" Her brother clamors above the noise. "You're an exact image of your sister, Charlotte, except for your hair!"

"I can't wait to see everyone! I hope they haven't all forgotten me! I've missed all of you so much!" she responds loudly, again gently squeezing Randy's hand.

"Well, Daddy's away right now for a few weeks, but Mama and the rest will all be glad to see you! They don't know we came to find you, so they aren't expecting us to bring you home. It'll be a total surprise for them!" Robert bellows.

"I don't know how you did it, but I prayed every day you'd come for me! Are you okay, Randy? Your leg looks like it's still bleeding! Does it hurt a lot?" she yells.

"It's almost stopped now! It doesn't hurt all that much, it's just that I'm feeling kind of weak. I might need a doctor."

"That's because you've lost all that blood!" Robert exclaims. "Once we get to the horses, we can find a spot to settle down for the night, and get a good look at that cut. If we get caught now there's no telling when we might get you to a doctor!"

The injured young man pulls his hand away, and slides back in the seat to lean against the side of the carriage. Conversation stops allowing the noise of the tossing carriage to take control inside the coach.

Mr. Vaughn, Sally, and the director of security are meeting at La Nesra, discussing their successes this evening.

"A week ago, I had no idea how we were going to instate Amber in place of Sheree with the Anderson family. Imagine what we've accomplished here this evening? All these years of carefully training Amber, the constant weeks and months of indoctrination, it's all been worth it." He congratulates himself over what he sees as an almost impossible task being thought out and brought to a perfect conclusion through his genius. A seldom seen smile creeps across his face.

"The two of you have accomplished what some have said to be impossible. Without you, this wouldn't have happened. You're to be commended for your services, and I'll see to it. Now, however, let's go over the details of this operation to be sure we haven't missed something. Sally, did you give Amber the name of her contact?"

"Oh yes, on several occasions."

"Who is it then?"

"Messenger," she replies.

"How will she find Messenger?" He knows the answers but wants to hear it all again.

"All she has to do is pay attention, and the name will appear. She merely must recognize it when she sees it. This agent will be expecting her. With them looking for each other, their meeting is a certainty." Sally confirms.

Mr. Vaughn continues. "Will the Anderson family accept Amber as their own, believing she's their daughter Sheree? Has she been trained well enough that they won't be suspicious? Is she mature enough to continue the charade without detection?"

"I can answer all three of your concerns with six words. Yes, they will, and she is. You see, the Andersons all believe Amber died at birth. She is truly one of their own. She was removed from them, and has never known them to be her family. Her loyalties are to us. She's been fed information over the span of her life to the point of knowing herself to be Sheree Anderson. She knows no other life, no other purpose, and her appearance proves her to be their absent daughter. They'll accept her with open arms, covet her, and protect her. There has never been a more perfect person for such an endeavor. Her character as Sheree Anderson will become a reality as soon as she settles into their lives. She'll believe she is Sheree, but will have our interests at heart. Any information we haven't provided her, they'll accept as a slip of the memory. Since she's been absent for so long, they won't expect her to be perfect. They'll accept her as she is." Sally's words are a cradlesong to Mr. Vaughn's ears.

"I'm unable to express how satisfying it is to hear your words, Sally. Thank you." He squirms in his chair with excitement. Turning his attention to the director of security, who has been sitting quietly listening to the conversation, he says.

"Did anyone see you when you took Amber to Lilly's room?"

"We were very careful and had her covered with a long coat, so, if anyone saw her, they wouldn't know who she was. She was all dressed for bed facilitating us to get her to her room and get out fast. We closed the door and posted a sentry across the hallway to be sure no one would check on her," the director matter-of-factly states.

"Tell me what you think. Did we make it seem real enough for those two young men not to be suspicious? Did we do enough? Should we have done more?"

"I think we would have caught them if we had pursued them any harder. They have to believe it was all real. We didn't expect the young slave to get hurt, so we had to hold back to allow the other young man time to rescue him.

"That explosion was a surprise, but because we were holding back, we received just two powder burns and a few scratches from flying glass, that's all. It could have been a lot worse. I think we acted the way they thought we would."

"Should we have chased them after they boarded the coach?" Their leader hangs on to every word he hears.

"No . . . they'll figure we know where they're headed, and that we can find them anytime we like. And again, I believe there was a good chance we would have caught them if we had given a proper pursuit. No, I'm sure, we did the right thing."

"Now . . . tell me how you handled Lilly while they were inside here with us." Mr. Vaughn is exploring, picking at everything.

"We put her to sleep in the laboratory in the middle part of this morning, just as we planned. Then, about three this afternoon, we moved her and put her in the pantry area. Then, just before they came, we moved her again to the armory. As you know, there are no windows, and the whole building is encased with steel. We didn't want to take any chances that someone would tip them off as to her whereabouts. She's still there," the director responds. "We're the only three who know her location. I moved her there myself."

"Let's leave her there for now." Mr. Vaughn directs. "We'll meet again tomorrow morning to determine if anything comes to mind we might have overlooked. If there's nothing further right now, I'll see the both of you in the morning."

Lilly is sitting with her legs crossed, elbows resting on her knees, on the floor of the laboratory, next to where the table holding her body had been. The piece of broken mirror is still lying on the floor beside her. Tears are streaming down her cheeks.

"I don't know what to do. They must have found a way to wake my body up and took her with them, not knowing I'm not in there. Is that even possible? Maybe it is. I'm too upset to think straight, not able to concentrate and piece things together. I feel like I need to find my life body, only I don't know where to start. I never thought it would come to this, but I need some help. I have to trust someone, take the chance. But who?

"Eagle would love for me to come to him, and I know he'll do anything I ask, but I just don't trust him. The only other person I know well enough is Falcon. He told me about the people coming to get me. He tried to help me then, maybe he'll help me again. He has a totally logical mind too, and that's what I need. If I give him all the facts I have, he can put it all together and sort it out, logically. Okay, now that's decided, and I know where his room is, I can sneak down the hallway from here, or I can go through the mirrors, that is, if he has a mirror in his room. If I go down the hallway someone might see me, so, I'd better go through the mirrors.

"Here goes, wow, it gets easier all the time.

"Think Falcon's room . . . Falcon's room.

"I'm moving, I'm going.

"I'm here . . . I think. Look through the white block.

"It's him all right. He's sitting at his desk with his back toward me. I don't want to scare him out of his wits. I'll put my head through the mirror first and say something. When he turns to see me I'll pull back, and then sort of creep up on him."

"Falcon, it's Lilly, don't be afraid of me. Come and stand in front of your mirror and watch for me."

"Boy, I just got my head back in time. I don't think he saw me. Here he comes looking at the mirror."

"Is that you, Lilly? I heard you but I can't see you. Where are you?" he puzzles.

"Here goes my hand through the mirror . . . not too fast now."

"Lord, oh Lord, what's going on here!" His voice shows excitement.

"I'd better get on with this before he does something I don't want him to. I'll put my head through next, sort of slowly, and then not stop until I'm all the way through."

"Oh my God, I must be asleep, I have to be dreaming. This can't be happening. It can't be real." He feels like he should run, but his legs are as heavy tree stumps, and his feet must be nailed to the floor.

"I'm real, Falcon. It truly is me. Here I'll touch you and then you can touch me."

He pulls away, but not before she touches him on his face with a soft brush of her hand.

"Now you touch me, anywhere. You'll see it's me. Here, touch my arm."

Falcon hesitates; he tries, but he doesn't seem to be able to move his arms.

Lilly reaches, takes his hand, and rubs it up and down her arm.

"I know it's terribly strange and seems impossible, but it's true. It's me, and I just came out of that mirror. I can see you need a minute to catch your breath, so, I'm going to tell you some things, and then I'm going to ask you for your help. Come over here, sit on the bed with me. Come on, I won't bite you. Okay, now listen carefully, I have a lot to tell you. Are you listening? This whole thing started almost six years ago . . ."

Smitty's waiting in a gully behind and below a small growth of trees, some four miles northeast of La Nesra, a place known well by his son.

Luke masterfully guides the carriage over the edge of the gully and down into the dry creek bed. He stands on the brake and pulls reins to stop. The carriage abruptly comes to a standstill, continuing to rock and weave several times before settling down.

"What a ride!" he calls down to his daddy. "I've got 'em all, and they're still alive!"

"Glory be! I'm surely thankful for that. I was starting to get worried. Did you have some trouble?" Smitty's tone and demeanor shows his concern.

"Randy's cut his leg real bad. We need to get it looked at as quick as we can. He's been bleeding a lot," Luke explains as he jumps down from the driver's box.

The team stomps from hoof to hoof, panting hard, snorting and blowing, trying to clear the mucus from their nostrils. Their sides, chests, and rumps are covered with white foam. The odor of horse sweat can be tasted, and their body heat can be felt from three feet away in the cool evening air.

"Let's get him out here and get a look at it. Maybe there's something we can do right now," Smitty orders.

Bob helps the hurt boy through the doorway of the carriage and gently lowers him into the waiting hands of Smitty and Luke. Then, he and the young woman follow to watch as they place him on the ground, leaning him against the bank of the dry waterway.

"I see what you mean. Looks like half of this boy's blood has run down his leg," Luke's father observes. "Get these pants off and let me see what's happened under there."

Randy's boots have to be removed before his pants can be taken off. He doesn't scream, but he moans with his mouth shut as they do what needs to be done.

"Grab that lantern off that first horse there, and get me one of those canteens while you're at it. Let me wash this off so I can see." The blacksmith is still giving orders.

A lit lantern and a canteen of water are brought to him.

"This is a good clean cut, no dirt or anything in it I can see. How'd you do this?"

"I fell when I was running and broke one of those whiskey bottles I had in my pocket. A piece of it went in my leg. I got it all out though." He grimaces.

"It's still seeping blood. If you move around much, it's likely to open up and start bleeding all over again, and I don't think you can stand too much more of that. We got to fix it right here and now, before you go on any farther," Smitty decides.

Everyone knows the risk of staying in one place too long, but there's no other choice. His leg has to be stabilized, or he could bleed to death.

"What you going to do?" young Stoker questions, his eyes growing larger in the light from the lantern.

"We have to seal up the wound with a hot knife." The older man is quick to reply.

"It's called cauterization," Bob explains. "Usually, a hot iron is held against the skin and sears the wound shut. I've seen it done, it works."

"But we don't have time to build a fire, and the lamp fire isn't hot enough, not to mention we can't get caught here." Smitty insists, pondering. "Luke, get me one of those whisky bottles of gunpowder. I'm going to need a handful."

"Now, listen to me, boy, I'm going to dry the blood off your leg first, then I'm going to spread the powder all over and around the edges of that cut. We have to move fast so it doesn't soak up with blood. As soon as I get it on there, Bob's going to touch a match to it, then it's going to flare up and get real hot, and that's what we need. It should do the job, but it's going to hurt like hell for a little bit."

"What other choice do I have? Do it quick." Randy knows this must be done.

"Let's lay him down so he doesn't have to watch this whole thing. Sheree, sit there on the ground, put his head on your lap, and hold your hand over his eyes," Bob orders.

"Gladly," the young girl replies.

Randy doesn't mind having his head on Sheree's lap. In fact, he's thinking this all might be worth it. His thoughts turn to the days of their close friendship, especially the day he kissed her. He's about to mention it to her when it feels like—someone has cut off his leg! His whole body stiffens with reaction to the pain of the burning gunpowder. Sheree tightens her hold, keeping him still on her lap.

"Yeeeeoooowwww!" he screams.

The surge of pain lasts for about ten seconds, then settles down to a feeling of a hot branding iron pressing against his leg.

"If I can get this smoke to clear, I'll get a look and see how we did." Randy hears Smitty say.

"Look here, Bob, what do you think? It looks good to me."

The smell of burnt flesh, mixed with the smoke from the gunpowder, is thick in the air as he bends down to get a close look.

"That looks good. You did a fine job. All we need to do now is keep it good and clean, it'll heal on it's own. Unless we have a problem, we'll have Doc Shaw look at it when we get home." The boy's best friend reports the good news for Randy's ears.

"Well, I know and understand that you want to be out of this state as soon as you can, but bouncing around on the saddle of a horse won't do him any good. He needs to rest, get some grub and water." Smitty is concerned Randy's condition will worsen.

"Friends of ours live about three miles east of here. We can take him in the carriage that far, and let him rest the night in a nice warm bed. We can get a couple of decent meals in him, then you can leave tomorrow morning. He'll be in a whole lot better shape to travel, and we'll be sure his leg will hold up for the trip. What do you say, boys? It's your decision." The smitty looks at Bob.

"Absolutely." Bob is quick to agree, feeling the responsibility for the safety of his sister, and Randy, lighten a little.

"I don't know how you do it, but you seem to be connected everywhere. I believe you can do just about anything you have a mind to do." He continues, "Do you know everybody in the State of Georgia?"

"It's not that so much. Let's just say I work for a different railroad than the kind you rode in here on. Our railroad is made of people, whose business it is to move people on the run. Enough said?"

Bob drops his head down and slightly to the left with a nod of understanding.

"Let's move," Luke urges.

Lilly is just finishing her explanation to Falcon, who hasn't said a word other than 'My God' several times since she starting talking.

"So, that's the whole story. I really need your to help. I don't know if my body is here or with Robert and Randy. If it's here, then they're taking an impostor with them."

"Aren't you going to say something?" A pause. "Anything?"

"I don't know what to say," he begins.

"You know how I am. I need to understand the facts and the reasons behind them. You've got to give me a little time to digest all of this. It's absurdly strange, you know. I mean, the last part as how you can put yourself to sleep and rise up out of your body. I wouldn't believe any of it if I hadn't seen it with my own eyes. And then, there's this business of you traveling through mirrors. Wow!"

He starts pacing the floor while Lilly sits on the edge of his bed, her head and eyes following him back and forth. There's silence in the room for five minutes or more, during which Falcon is thinking. She's relieved, at last, to see him stop in front of her and say.

"The first thing we do is find your body. It'll take the two of us a long time to search this whole place, and we already know it's not where it would normally be. I feel strange calling your body 'it,'" he says.

"Then call my body Sheree, and call me Lilly. How's that?"

"Yes, that'll work a lot better. You need to stay out of sight until we can determine what's going on, and where they've taken Sheree. I'll get our group together, and we'll search this whole place in a day's time. I won't tell them about you. I'll tell them we're looking for Sheree, only I'll call her Lilly." He shakes his head with wonder. "We'll find Sheree, then we'll decide what we're going to do about your impostor."

"I've not noticed Falcon before just now. He has really nice deep blue eyes, and is not a bit bad looking. I like the way his lips move when he speaks, it sort of . . . stirs one's blood. And his voice, it seems to soothe me, it gives me a secure feeling. I imagine he has a good body under those clothes. It's amazing, I've never noticed him this way before."

"Where can you stay so no one will see you?" he asks.

"I don't know, I suppose the best place would be on the other side of the mirror."

"How will I find you, if I need you for something?"

"I'll stay close to this mirror. If you need me, stand in front of it, and I'll come through to you. If you find Sheree, you can bring me to her by holding a mirror in front of her face. Don't ask how it works, but it does, and I'll be drawn back into my body."

"Do you sleep and eat when you're in there?" he says curiously.

"I don't know. I've not spent that much time in there up to now. Good question."

"I'll try to get something for you to eat from the kitchen in the morning, and put it here in my dresser drawer. If you need it, you'll know it's there. Okay?" he offers.

"That will be wonderful of you. I appreciate your concern."

"Is there furniture and things like that in there? I mean where will you sleep or even sit down?"

"I've not seen a thing, except for the white shapes, which all seem to be the backsides of mirrors. They're all over the place. Until you just mentioned it, I never thought about it . . . there's nothing in there. At least, nothing as we know it."

"Maybe it would be best if you spent the night here with me then. We have a lot to do tomorrow so we can use the rest. We can share the bed; I mean, you sleep under the blankets, and I'll sleep on top of them." he suggests.

"Well, I don't know . . ."

"Don't worry, I would never do anything that could make you think badly of me. I like you too much to do that. You'll be safe here."

"Did he just say he likes me?" His words linger in her mind.

"That will be fine as long as I can keep my clothes on."

"Oh, I think you definitely should, just in case you have to jump through the mirror for one reason or another. I'll keep mine on, too."

She lies back on the bed and rolls over to occupy the half close to the wall. Falcon turns the light down to a dim glow, and lies down beside her.

It's been quiet for ten minutes. Her thoughts keep coming back to him.

"He's so nice to me, and caring. Most of the boys around here, including Eagle, have one thing on their mind all the time, but not him. I wonder what his real name is. Does he have a family who misses him and wants him back? He must be as lonely for them and his home as I am mine. I've never seen him with a girl, I'm not sure if he has a close friend at all. He's so unassuming, doesn't ask for anything, doesn't expect anything from anybody.

"He said he likes me, but he didn't say in what way. Does he like me as a friend, or does he like me as a girlfriend? Hmmmmm? I'd sure like to know the answer to that question. Stop it, you silly girl. There's no time for this sort of thing right now. Keep your mind on the problems at hand. But what if he does see me in the lovelike way?

"I know I like him—more and more—the longer I'm around him. I should give him a little signal that I like him too. I know, I'll roll over on my side and lay my head on his shoulder. Not get all over him, just lay my head on his shoulder. No . . . I'd better not.

"I shouldn't, but this urge is getting stronger. I think I will. Here goes.

"There. Mmmmmm, this feels really good. Is he asleep? Does he even know I'm here? Oh, oh, wait, he's moving his arm. He's putting it around me and pulling me over to his chest. Oh wow, he's holding me and softly caressing my arm.

"My breasts are pushing against him, it's making me feel like I want to be a part of him. I could stay here forever and never move. I've never had these kinds of feelings."

On the other side of the bed.

"I can't believe she wants to be close to me. I swear, I won't move another muscle all night, if she just doesn't pull away. She's probably in a desperate mood right now, and when it changes, she won't even remember this, or me. She's never shown the slightest interest in me until now. I wonder if she can hear my heart pounding; her ear is right on my chest. I'm getting a strong craving to turn on my side toward her and put both my arms around her, but I'd better not. She'll just pull away, and besides, I promised her I wouldn't. But what if she wants me to? Will she think I'm not interested in her if I don't?

"One thing's for sure, the way I'm feeling right now, if she doesn't pull away real soon, I'll have to. I want to kiss her, and I don't mean a peck on her cheek. What's the matter with you? Think about what you're doing. This is not her real body lying here beside you, it's not the real her. You're going to turn her against you before she has a chance to get to know you. Fight these urges and be satisfied that she wants to be this close to you tonight."

Back on the other side of the bed.

"I know he's awake. What's going on in his mind right now? He probably thinks I'm some sort of harlot by the way I've forced myself on him. I don't care, I want to snuggle against him. If that's all I get from this tonight, then I'll have to live with that. But right now, I'm going to snuggle against him."

"She's moving. Wait, she's nestling closer, she just put her leg across me. She's sliding her arm across my chest, hugging me. Is this really happening to me? I don't know what to do or where this is going, but I'll remember it for the rest of my life. I can't hold back any longer." The young man is stifled with overwhelming new feelings.

"I hope I've not gone too far with my eagerness. I don't want to scare him off. Something's about to happen, he's moving, rolling over to face me. His arms are both around me, he's pulling me close to him, and he's sliding down in the bed. His lips are just three inches from mine." Her heart is pounding. What will happen next?

"The closer I pull her to me, the tighter she hugs me. I can't stop now, I'm going to kiss her and see what happens."

"Kiss me, Falcon. Kiss me now, or I'm going to kiss you."

"I'm sorry, but if I don't kiss you, I'm going to go out of my mind." Falcon breathes heavily.

"I can feel all of the air going out of me as I melt into his arms. His soft lips are on mine and I'm kissing him back."

Their kiss is tender at first, then their bodies won't let them do anything but consume each other.

"She's kissing me back. Thank you, Lord, she's kissing me back hard. I need her closer to me. I want her to be a part of me. Her lips are so soft, taste so good, and her face is so beautiful. I want to swallow her in one big gulp."

He doesn't know why, but he starts caressing her lips with his tongue. She parts hers just enough for him to enter her mouth. They're squirming, trying to get closer.

"His tongue is getting farther and farther into my mouth. My breath is so heavy moving through my nose against his face, it doesn't seem to leave before I'm sucking it back . . . mmmmmmmmmmmmmmm."

"What's happening to her? It's like all her resistance is gone. Is she okay? This is going too far too fast, I have to stop.

"I want her, and that's for sure, but now is not the right time. She should be herself, in her own body, when we go any farther than this. I might never get the chance again, but now is not the right time."

"I'm sorry, Lilly, I can't go any farther than this right now. Please understand, I want to, but I just can't." He pulls away and sits up on the bed to look down at her.

"Did I do something wrong? I did, didn't I? You probably hate me for it too."

"No, no, you didn't. Everything about you is wonderful, and a lot more than I deserve. It's just, well, I want things to be back to normal when we go where this is leading. I want all of you, not just the part of you from behind the mirror. Do you see what I mean? I need to know all of you wants all of me. I don't want you to regret later what we do here now," he says, and makes himself get up off the bed.

"You're the sweetest, most understanding man I've ever met, and I'm glad you feel that way. But let me get this straight; you like me, right?"

"Lilly, I think I fell in love the first day I saw you, and I would have said something a long time ago, but I thought you and Eagle were together. I mean, I thought you liked each other, and well, maybe you do, and maybe I'm making a fool of myself." He turns to face her squarely, and waits for a response.

"To be honest with you, I'm not sure I know what love really is. I know I've discovered feelings for you that I didn't realize I had, and I know I don't have these feelings for Eagle. I feel really good about what just happened here between us, and I want it to happen again. I won't say I love you, but it could be I do. So please, don't pull away thinking I don't care for you, because I do. I like you more than a lot, so come here and I'll prove it to you. Kiss me again. I won't seduce you . . . not until you're ready."

The carriage comes to a noisy stop in front of a house which is not much more than a large two-story shack. Luke wastes no time, and jumps down to assist Randy's exit to the ground. Sheree steadies him from behind as they lower him down.

Bob and Smitty have followed on horseback, leading the extra two horses.

The front door of the unpainted structure opens to expose an elderly black man, dressed in a pair of tattered bib overalls. No shoes, no socks, and no shirt. A lamplight behind him causes a moving shadow to fall over the single step, and off on to the ground.

"Who's that out there?" he yells with concern.

"It's me and Luke, Mr. Sorrels. I brought some people with me, and we need your help." Smitty answers with the same volume.

"Is that you, Smitty?"

"Yeah, it's me all right. Sorry if we scared you. Can we come in?"

"You sure can, you know you're always welcome here. Come on now, get yourselves in here. I don't see none to good in the dark these days. Come on in here and let me get a look at you all."

Luke ties the team to the hitching post, while Robert secures the reins of the saddled horses to the rear of the carriage. One by one they enter the house, with Randy leaning on Sheree for support.

"Where's Miss. Sorrels?" Smitty asks.

"She went to bed early this evening, said she was tuckered out. But I hear her stirring, she'll be down here in a minute. What you fellas doing out this time of night. Looks like one of you must have caught a ball or something?"

Smitty explains as Mrs. Sorrels climbs down a ladder from the second floor, and greets everyone with a big broad smile before she starts poking up a fire in the cookstove.

The coffeepot, which is always on the stove, is sending steam through the pouring spout by the time the story of the escape is described to the elderly couple.

"Sounds to me like you fellas need a place to stay tonight. You staying too, are you, Smitty?" Mrs. Sorrels asks.

"No, no, but Randy needs to rest for while. He's lost a lot of blood," he explains.

"I'll bet the whole gaggle of you could eat something too," she continues. "And, young man, I want you to start drinking water. You can't make new blood without a lot of water. So, get to it," she orders, pointing to a large water bucket, with a dipper hanging alongside, setting on a table in the corner of the room.

"Sheree, you come here and help me get things together so we can eat. And Smitty, you and Bob take them saddle horses around to the barn for the night, and give them some grain. And you, old man, set yourself down there at the table and stay out of the way."

Everybody laughs at the way she's taken over and shouts orders.

"We all better do as she says, or she might get to be a little bossy." Mr. Sorrels chuckles.

An hour later all are seated around an oval-shaped table, the top of which is worn paint bare. There are just three chairs, so an old wooden crate, a two-foot-tall piece of tree stump, and two ash buckets turned upside down, give them all a place to sit. The conversation has been mostly catching up on the news between good friends that haven't been together for a while. The food is plain, but tasty, and plenty of it.

Bob casually looks around the table at this mixture of people. Smitty and Luke are absolutely comfortable here. Mrs. Sorrels has practically adopted Sheree, who seems like she's known these people forever. By the looks of him, Randy's leg must be kicking up a lot. Still, though, he's a part of everything that's going on.

Mr. Sorrels is glad to have the company. He probably doesn't get the opportunity to visit too often. Finally, he takes a good look at Randy, and says, "It's time we settled this young man down for the night. Mother, make a place down here for the three of us. Then you and the young woman can sleep upstairs."

"Are you and Luke sure about leaving? There's room in the barn for your team, you know," he addresses Smitty.

"We have a business to open up first thing in the morning, so we have to go. But thank you for the hospitality anyway," Luke responds.

A thought crosses Bob's mind.

"Is it going to be safe for you back at your livery? I mean, what if someone got a good look at you, or your rig, and knows who you are. It could mean real trouble."

"Aww, don't concern yourself with us, we'll be just fine. After all these years, I reckon most people around here expect things like this from us. Besides, I don't want to leave this rig setting out here overnight. It would be a dead give away for anybody looking for you." Smitty speaks with wisdom.

"We can't thank you and Luke enough for all you've done. If you ever need for anything, just get word to us, and we'll come running. We never could have pulled this off by ourselves." Bob's tone shows his sincerity.

Smitty and Luke leave with the team and carriage, pulling one saddled horse behind them. The women retire to the upstairs, while the men make themselves comfortable on the wooden floor of the kitchen, using the comforters and blankets supplied by Mrs. Sorrels. Quiet settles over the Sorrels' humble home.

It's morning at La Nesra.

Falcon awakes with a jump and sucks in a deep breath. He glances at the clock setting on his dresser.

"It's six thirty already." He thinks at the same time realizing Lilly is asleep and snuggled against him, half lying on the bed and half on him. He looks down at her with amazement.

"If she still likes me this morning, I . . . she will, she has to." He kisses her hair. "I love you Lilly, I think I always will," he whispers softly, knowing she's asleep.

"I heard every word you said, Falcon. I know I have a smile on my face, but you can't see it. I want to jump up and smother you with kisses, but for now, I want you to think I'm still asleep. So, I'll just lie here and enjoy myself, pretending. I'll think this really hard. 'I love you, too.' If you heard me, kiss me on the head again."

Falcon knows he must awaken her so they can start their day. What better way is there to start than by kissing her on the head?

"My God, did he hear me? He just kissed me on the head."

"Time to rise and shine, young lady," he feels her stir a bit.

"What time is it? Oh, I see what you mean. You need to get moving, or you'll miss breakfast. I'll just lie here and watch you change your clothes."

"Not today, you won't. I'm wearing these same ones. I'll be out of here in a jiffy. What are you going to do while I'm gone?"

"A little bit of exploring, I think, behind the mirror that is. I'll see if I can get a clue as to where Sheree might be."

"Good idea. I'll see you shortly after dinner. Say one, one thirty or so." With that he's out the door and on his way.

Bob let's Randy sleep a little longer while he slips out of the house into the barn to feed and saddle the horses. He's just pulling the last cinch snug, when he's aware of movement behind him. Startled, he turns ready to fight.

"Oh, it's you, Sheree." He lets out a breath of relief. "I didn't know you were there. What are you doing up already?"

"I'm helping Mrs. Sorrels with breakfast. She's putting it on the table now, so let's get in there while it's still hot." She all but sings.

"Just finishing up. Wait a minute, sis, and I'll walk in with you."

"I haven't heard anything like that in a long time, brother." She gleefully shares. There's no doubt in her mind now, she's going to be a part of the Anderson family.

Bob puts his arm around her shoulder, and together, they walk briskly to the house.

"How's Randy this morning?" he asks.

"A lot better. The rest helped him a lot, and the cut is starting to scab over. Mr. Sorrels put some salve on it and wrapped it with a bandage. He says that way it won't stick and tear the skin off when it's looked at again. Mrs. Sorrels is going to try to get the blood out of Randy's pants and keep them for him so he can pick them up the next time he's through here." She advises.

During breakfast the discussion is mostly about the trip back to the Anderson home. It's determined that the best way to get there will be to use the horses to get to Chattanooga. There they can sell them along with the gear, and board the train. The travel time will be cut by two-thirds. Once they get close to their destination, they'll jump from the moving train before it gets to the station. That is, if Randy's leg will hold up. From there they'll walk the rest of the way home.

"I think we'll stop off at the Sanders' place and leave you there, Sheree, until Randy and I can be sure there's no one from the Company at our place. They could easily telegraph ahead and have somebody waiting to ambush us. You remember them, don't you?" Bob suggests.

An affirmative nod from Sheree.

"You won't recognize Beth, err . . . a, I mean Elizabeth, she's all grown up now," he continues.

"And she's sweet on Bob, too," Randy proudly announces.

Laughter erupts around the table, as Bob's face glows with embarrassment.

"We should get moving if we're going to be in Chattanooga by tomorrow afternoon." Young Mr. Anderson averts further comment by changing the subject.

"I'll help clean up these breakfast dishes before we leave." Sheree volunteers.

"We'll have none of that this morning," Mrs. Sorrels insists. "He's right, now get yourselves out of here. And be real careful, I sure would like it if you came back by again when you're down this way."

Good-byes are said while the horses are brought around from the barn. Once mounted, the three wave, thank their hosts for their hospitality, and they're on their way.

At La Nesra, Lilly sits on the edge of the bed pondering her day.

"Here I am, alone. I won't see Falcon for at least five hours. I miss him already. I'll just have to make the best of it, that's all. I'll do what I said and explore around on the other side of the mirror. No sense putting it off, here I go.

"Nothing's different, it always looks the same. Just space, but the space isn't distance, or at least not like distance I know. These white places must all be mirrors, like doorways to the other side. I don't see another soul. I can talk but nothing comes out. If I put my finger in my ear, I can hear myself speak. I can also hear all sorts of other voices and noise. I wonder? If I put my hands over my eyes, will I be able to see things. Here goes. Oh my, it's scary. I couldn't keep my hands over my eyes. There's people or things everywhere. I'll try again, this time I'll keep my eyes covered.

"It's unbelievable. There are people all over the place in here. They seem to have heads and arms of a sort, but their bodies tend to fade away the farther down toward their feet they go. Oddly, it feels normal.

"Some of them are looking at me, with their wide open eyes. They just seem to float around, without moving anything, floating everywhere. There's no floor to support them, or me for that matter; and they move in all sorts of directions, some of them higher up than others. It's like they're flying, without wings, almost.

"Wait a minute . . . a girl is stopping to look at me. She's not trying to touch me or anything. Her eyes have hollow circles around them, sort of like a black eye. There she goes—not far—here she comes again and she's bringing several with her. They're floating right here, looking at me. Their eyes don't move up or down or from side to side, they just stare straight ahead. They're circling around me now, and moving up and down. I can make them go away by taking my hands from my eyes, but are they gone, or are they still there and I can't see them? They don't seem to want to hurt me, and I'm not afraid of them any more.

“The girl is pointing to her mouth, she must want something to eat. She’s shaking her head no. Then she must want me to say something. She’s nodding her head yes. How can I speak to you? She’s pointing to her head, and grimacing her face. You want me to think it? She’s nodding yes. Well, of course, she’s been reading my mind all along.

“Okay, now I’m getting somewhere.

“You can read my thoughts, but how can I hear you?

“She’s pointing to her head and grimacing again.

“I should concentrate, is that right? She nods yes. I don’t need to put my finger in my ear? She shakes her head no. I’m listening . . . I’m listening . . . listening.”

Can you hear me? Can you hear me? Refer to me as Zola. Can you hear me?

“I hear you. I can actually hear you, Zola. My name is Lilly. Where is this place? Who are you? I mean, what are you? I mean, oh, I don’t know what I mean.”

Hello, Lilly. I have read your brain pattern and that is how I can communicate with you in your mind. I am speaking in a fashion familiar to you. I will try to explain a few of your concerns. You will answer one of my queries, after I respond to one of yours. I will begin.

You have found your way into the corridor of life. I am one of the many sentries with the mission to serve and protect all within this corridor. This is the place where souls are reserved until called upon to be born or reborn into another dimension, probably from where you come.

My question. How did you get here? Did you expire, or are you passing through?

“No, I didn’t die, but I seem to be able to leave my body and move around without it. I accidentally discovered that I can climb through a mirror and get into here. I plan to go back there and get back into my body, when I can, and live there. So, I suppose, I’m just passing through. Are you all dead people? Exactly where is this place?”

We are not dead, not as you know the word. A flesh and blood body dies an decays away, but a soul lives on forever. Upon death, a soul transports here to prepare to be introduced into a new body. This corridor of life is located in a minus nine dimension atmosphere. Perhaps, I should explain more clearly. I sense you are not understanding. You understand that you come from a three dimension place. One dimension is width, one is height, and another is depth. The corridor of life has twelve less dimensions than yours. Removing the three you are familiar with will reduce your ability to see, hear, and sense, to zero. Beyond that now, continue to remove nine others to reach our atmosphere. Several of them are time, distance, and levity.

There are other different life supporting places, such as this. The most advanced occupying many fewer dimensions than yours, and those with more than yours. Your race on earth usually is able to comprehend none other then their own. The senses of your beings in your world do not detect them, but they are there. We all co-exist together. Do you grasp what I am relating to you?

“I understand everything you’ve said, and I believe you, but it’ll take a while for me to accept it.”

I am sure that is true. What is your purpose here?

"Well, right now, I've lost my life body somewhere, and I'm trying to find it. I'm sort of exploring to see what this place is all about. I've found that I can go back and forth through mirrors, and move from one place to another that way. And now, I know where this place is and how to communicate with you. It's a long, long, story. Simply put, right now, I'm looking for my life body."

Yes, I know. I have learned from your mind while you were thinking. I am now aware of everything that has happened to you. If you open up your mind with your thoughts, I can understand your brain waves.

Is your purpose here to use this information to help or hinder your dimension? If you plan to help your mankind, perhaps I can assist you. If you plan to harm your mankind I must sever our communication now.

"To be totally honest, I don't have any plans of doing either one. I'm just trying to help me. I'm a prisoner of where my life body is being kept. My family is probably in great danger from an impostor, who happens to look like me. I must tell them of the threat to their lives. To do that, I need to find a way to get free long enough get back to my home. If I must, I'll come back here after I alert them, but it's imperative that I warn them of the danger."

I can see you mean no harm to anyone by being here. Let me determine if I can assist you. I am feeling flashing images of a male of your kind. What importance do you place on this being?

"You must mean Falcon?"

I now understand . . . you opened your mind to me. Trust this person. He will fight to protect you. Let your mind float with your thoughts. Think about your fears and reasons for being a prisoner. I will try to determine a solution for your needs.

"I'll try. Let's see where shall I start?"

I have a response for you. The logic of your situation would lead to this conclusion. First you must locate your human body. You must then locate a place where your body will be safe from exposure to any and all of your mankind, except Falcon, and place it there. He will guard it for you. You will then leave your body and enter here. I will assist you to step through a mirror into the bedroom you occupied at your home. As soon as you have finished with your mission, you will reverse your travel, return to this place and enter your body. The travel time should be expected to total no more than four seconds of your measure. The risk cannot be determined without a complete knowledge of all variables.

"That sounds like a very good plan. I wouldn't be gone but a few hours, maybe a day, at the most. I feel a whole lot better. I can probably go there, do everything I need to do, and be back before Robert, Randy, and the impostor get there. This is good, really good. Thank you. Thank you a lot.

"Can you help me find my body? And how will I find you when I come back to go to my home?"

Beings here do not answer to a name. Think the name Zola, and turn. I will be aware of the name while others will not. I will come to you. Responding to your next question, you should be able to concentrate your mind powers and find your body. It should pull you to it. I believe you have tried with no results. That indicates your body is located behind a barrier. Look for it to be where it is fortified densely or heavily guarded. You must believe it is where it can be easily accessed by those who placed it there. I am unable to supply any additional information.

"It looks like our talk is over, she's leaving. Darn, I have a lot of questions to ask her too. I don't know why I didn't think of this plan. I'm better than this. I need to get my mind off my emotions and on track with my problems, except my emotions when it comes to Falcon, that is. I've been here quite a while, so I'd better get back and wait for him."

"Oh, he's here already I see. I don't want to startle him, so I'll say hello before I go all the way into the room. Hello, I'm back. Here I come."

"I don't think I'll ever get used to you coming through that mirror, Lilly. It's truly astounding," he says. "Where have you been, have you had a productive day?"

"You won't believe this. I have a plan, a very good plan. Let me tell you about it."

"Wait, I have some good news, I think. I've tried to talk privately with everyone in our group today. They're all looking for Sheree. Eagle is upset that you're missing, but anyway, Lester saw one of the security people pushing a laboratory table into the armory late yesterday afternoon." Falcon excitedly discloses.

"Well, I'll be, the armory's wall and ceiling are made of steel, aren't they?"

"I think so, why?'

"That explains why I can't find my life body like I usually can. She's right."

"Who's she? Who's right?" His curiosity is peaking.

"I have some news for you too. After you left, this morning, I went through the mirror to explore and see what I could find out about that place in there. Well, wouldn't you know I . . ."

Eagle is heavily concerned that Lilly is missing, and has made excuses to be away from his duties for the afternoon.

"Where could she be?" he thinks. "I want to find her before anyone else does. She'll be very thankful to whoever rescues her. It'll help our relationship tremendously. The others will check in all of the obvious places. Where would no one think to look?

"It's possible she's escaped, or maybe tried to escape and was caught. That would mean the cellar; solitary is down there. They wouldn't put her there unless she did something to deserve that treatment, and I know she would tell me if she had a plan to escape. I doubt she's down there. What about the barns or the equipment house? No, there are no locks on any of those doors. That only leaves the armory. But why? Why would they need to lock her in the armory? There's more going on here than Falcon's telling us, so I'll not mention my thinking to anybody.

"I'll need some keys if I'm going to get in there, it's sealed up like a tomb, and rightly so. There's enough explosives in there to make a big hole in the ground out of Atlanta. I worked in there for a while, about four years ago. What do I recall about the way it's laid out? It seems to me there's an air vent that's covered with some heavy screening on the north side. But it's above where a man can reach. If I can get up there and take the screen off, I can probably slide through and get in."

"I have to find out if she's in there. I'll go during supper, that way fewer people are milling about," Eagle concludes.

Falcon is speaking to Lilly.

"I can see that your friend in there wants to help you. She's absolutely correct with her logic. Given the known facts, it's the one way you can be gone, do all you need to do, and get back before they actually miss you. We have two immediate problems, however. Assuming Sheree is in the armory, how do we get her out, and secondly, where shall we put her afterward?" he points out.

"Just a minute, who says we have to remove Sheree from the armory. If she comes up missing from there, that's probably the last place they will expect her to be. Think about it, we break in and leave evidence of it. We take Sheree and place her in an ammunition crate, or something, and stack it with all the rest. They'll never know. They'll believe she's left the armory and is somewhere else in the compound," Lilly suggests.

"I like your thinking, but wouldn't it be better if we didn't alarm them by indicating the security of the armory has been breached. Follow this." Falcon's logical mind is gearing up. "What if Sheree isn't there? Let's get me inside the armory without raising suspicion. If Sheree isn't there, no one will be any the wiser. If she is, I'll stand guard over her until you get back from your mission. I'll be prepared to hide should they come to check on her. That way, if they move her to another location, I'll follow and watch where they put her. It's entirely possible they won't come to the armory at all."

"I like that, now, how do we get in there? I might be able to get the keys." Lilly proceeds, "If Zola can help me to get to the maintenance building without being seen, I believe I can snitch the keys we need to get in through the door. There's rarely ever a guard there. You'll have to be careful not to be seen, though."

"I think we can make this happen. It all makes perfect sense." Falcon is excited with the prospects of this evening.

"Get in there with Zola, and get those keys."

With a quick shake of her head, Lilly moves toward the mirror.

"I'm in, now . . . spin around and think her name. Zola, Zola."

Yes, Lilly, I am here. Are you called Lilly, or Sheree?

"The truth is, Zola, my real name is Sheree, but the place I am living changed it so no one could find me."

The truth is all that is accepted, Sheree. Why are you here?

"Can you help me locate the maintenance building at La Nesra, and find a mirror I can go through to get in there? I need to borrow some keys without them knowing it. I'll return them, so I won't be stealing them."

For what purpose?

"I need to get Falcon inside the armory so he can guard my body while I go home to warn my family at our farm, like you suggested."

Yes, I can. Open your mouth and breathe me inside.

"What? You want me to do what?"

I will help you. Do as I ask. Open your mouth and breathe me inside, now.

"Oh boy, I did, and she is."

Close your eyes . . .

Open your eyes, and breathe me out.

"We haven't moved, have we?"

Look through the medium.

"You mean the white spot, right? Well, I'll be. Will you wait here for me to take me back, Zola?

You will find me as you found me before.

"Thank you. I'll be back in a jiffy."

Lilly peeks through the white opening into the maintenance building.

"Okay, there's nobody there, so, here I go.

"Darn this mirror is hanging on the wall above a wash basin full of grimy water. I'll try not to spill it. It isn't easy climbing down from a hole in the wall headfirst.

"Look out! I'm slipping! I'm going to fall."

Splash!

"Uuuuhhhhh!

"That didn't hurt one bit, but I knocked over the basin and made enough racket to be heard a mile away. And now, there's water all over the place. I'll hide for a minute to see if anyone comes to see what happened. Lucky for me there's no one in here. They must be out somewhere working on a job.

"No one's coming, so I'll get the keys and be on my way. The last time I was here they were lying on a desk. Let's see, in there, I believe. No keys here, look around. Look in the drawers, in the wooden baskets on the desks. Check to see if they're hanging on a wall. Maybe they're in the keyhole in the door. Is there a work jacket or something like that lying around here?

"They must have all the keys with them, there's none here anywhere. What now? Darn, I have to wait for them to come back, what other choice do I have?

"I need to hide. I'd go back through the mirror, but I'll probably fall down the wall again when I try to return. So, I need to hide in here somewhere. I'll get under that desk there in the corner, that's where the keys were lying the last time I was here. Maybe they'll toss them there when they come in."

Time passes.

Eagle watches his clock and waits for supper to start being served. He has already made his excuses, and is not expected at his normal seat in the eating area. His plan is to get a ladder and a pry bar from the maintenance building to enable him to reach and loosen the screen on the airway at the armory.

"This is working out just grand. There's no one out here right now. I'll slip into the shop and grab everything I need," he mutters to himself as he crosses the courtyard.

Lilly patiently awaits the maintenance crew's return.

"Someone's coming. They're here, finally.

"There's only one of them. I wonder if he has his keys? I can only see him from his knees down. If I lean out a little, maybe I can see the . . . oh no . . . it's Eagle.

"What's he doing here? I can't show myself, he thinks I'm missing.

"He's taking a ladder and a tool. Whoooeeee! He's gone. I can breathe again.

"Hurry up folks, I've been here a long time. Falcon's probably wondering where I am. I wonder if Eagle is still lingering around here somewhere. I think I'll take a peek out the front door and see. Just a few more steps.

"Uh-oh! Voices and footsteps! It's them, the maintenance men, they're back and ready to come through the door. Hide! No time to get back under the desk! Hurry! They're coming in here! They're going to see me! I'll pull this small cabinet away from the wall and duck down behind it! Darn, I can't get all of me back here! My leg, my foot, they'll see my foot sticking out! No time, I have to stop moving! They're here and coming toward me!"

"What the hell happened here? Look at this mess, there's water everywhere, and the pan is lying there on the floor. Somebody's been in here fooling around again, getting into things that's none of their business. One day, I'll catch the bastards while they're at it, and there'll be hell to pay." A man's deep gruff voice echoes through the room.

"There's three of them. One of them will see my foot for sure. I have to do something, and I mean right now."

"This old greasy rag here on the floor. I'll tie it around my head to cover my face, then I'll jump out and scare them. If I run around them, maybe I can spot the keys, grab them and make a run for the mirror. It's risky, but I have no other choice. I'll use the element of surprise to my advantage. Here goes. Look for the keys. Too late!"

"Hey, somebody's foot is sticking out from behind that cabinet over there. Someone's hiding back there."

"Hey, you, come out of there."

With no other choice, Lilly jumps up and runs hard right at the man closest to her. There's no keys on him that she can see.

"This guy is quick!" the man yells. "Get him before he gets away!"

She passes the first man, and heads for the second one standing off to the left and closer to the mirror.

"What the hell . . . ?" he screams, still startled at her appearance.

She moves straight at him.

The third man turns to see a figure moving fast through the room, jumping over trash containers, and spare parts lying on the floor.

"Get him!" the first man yells. "He must be the one who made this mess! Don't let him get away!"

"Let them yell. I'm a lot faster than they are. They think I'm a boy."

She sees no keys showing on the second man either, and swishes past him before he can react to block her path.

The third man is standing almost in front of the mirror, right next to the wash basin which is lying upside down on the floor.

"I missed him, Pete, get him!" the second man shouts, as he dives for her and slams to the floor on his side.

Since there's no time to do anything else, she decides run straight at the third man, push off the wash basin with her foot, jump to the top of the wash stand, and dive head first through the mirror. The first two men are right behind her.

"They're faster than I thought, I need a burst of speed!" she urges herself.

The third man is moving to unintentionally block more of the front of the mirror, hindering her approach. He's reaching out his arms.

"I'm moving at full speed! I'll run right over him!

"His hand! He has his keys in his hand!" She is surprising herself with her ability to focus on something other than evading these men.

Her foot is on the wash basin. She pushes hard. Up she goes, toward the top of the wash stand. The maintenance man's arm is reaching for her waist.

"I have to grab the keys from his hand as I go by. Got them!" She glows with her success, and plows hard into his arm as he tries to get his other one around her. Her speed makes him slide off down to the calf of her leg. She shoves off the top of the wash stand with her left foot, and tries to kick him loose with the right one.

"That broke me loose." She senses and stretches her arms and hands out in front of herself to dive through the mirror.

"Darn, they've got my foot. They're pulling me back out of the mirror."

"Think! Think fast!"

"Zola! Zola! Help me! Help me fast! They're pulling me back, I can't stop them!"

Breathe me in, Sheree.

She feels a thud as her body moves instantly through the mirror, causing the men on the other side to slam into it and the wall.

Breathe me out.

"I'm suddenly very calm, not even breathing hard. I have the keys I need, see?" She tries to display her success.

Zola says nothing and turns away.

"That was too close. Thank you very, very much, Zola."

The three maintenance men stand looking at the mirror, then each other, and back at the mirror again. "What just happened here. Did you two see what I just saw?" the boss says breathlessly. "Did that guy just jump through that mirror, or am I seeing things?"

The other two men agree verbally as well as by their actions.

"We can't tell anybody about this. They'll lock us up as being crazy."

Falcon is concerned for Lilly. "Where in the world have you been all this time? I've been worried, and look at you, you're all wet and filthy."

"It's another long story. I left the maintenance room a mess, but I have the keys. Here, take them."

"There's a half a dozen keys on this ring. Which one fits the lock on the armory door?" he questions.

"I don't know. You'll have to try them and see."

"What if the armory key isn't on here? Hmmmmm? You can't answer that either, can you?" He grins when he realizes this is the best she's able to provide.

Eagle has successfully removed the screening from the air vent and is climbing down crates and barrels to the floor inside the armory.

"It's really dark in here. Light a match and find a candle or a lantern. Aaaahhh, that's a lot better."

"Lilly, are you in here? It's Eagle," he speaks loudly.

No response.

He walks carefully through the maze of wooden boxes, crates, and barrels containing powder, bullets, and guns, while holding the lantern high, searching.

"What's that there?" The closer he gets, the more it looks like a table with a body lying on it.

"Will you look at this? It's her. It's Lilly. Looks like she's asleep."

He puts his hand on her shoulder and shakes gently, expecting her to open her eyes.

She lies motionless.

"She must be under one of those sleeps they make her do. If that's the case, nothing I do is going to wake her up. What do I do now? I can't ask her what she wants to do, and I won't get any credit for finding her. What would I do with her if I took her out of here? I'd better just tell the rest where she is and let them figure it out."

"Look at her there, sleeping. She's a beautiful girl. I wish we were closer than we are. I've dreamed of having relations with you for a long time, Lilly. Will we ever, I wonder?" he says out loud.

"Come to think of it, who would know if we did it right now. You don't mind do you?" he says more boldly.

He gazes at the young woman, pulls the blanket off her body and drops it to the dirt floor at the foot of the table, while holding the lantern high in his left hand. Then he moves a large box closer and sets it on top to light the scene. Carefully, using both hands, the slow process of loosening the buttons of her blouse begins. Excitement builds within him.

After laying the open blouse to the sides, he puts his fingers under the lower edge of her undergarment and lifts it up and over her breasts.

"I've wished for this moment for a long time, Lilly. I'm sorry you're not here with me. And I know this is wrong, but I can't stop now." He speaks to her, hoping an explanation will ease his conscience.

After fumbling with the buttons of her trousers, he takes the cuffs and pulls them down over her legs and feet, then stands looking at her almost nude body in the dim wavering light.

"In a moment, you'll be mine." The lustful voice breaks the silence while he removes her blouse and bra.

He feels the cool flesh of her hips against his fingers as he slips them under the sides of her underpants and pulls them slowly toward him.

He's starts to remove his own, when his ears pick up the sound of someone coming through the door. A sick feeling envelops him with the thought of being caught like this. With no time to extinguish the lantern, he slips away from the nude Sheree to hide in the blackness of the shadows among the crates.

"Who's this coming in here? If they catch me in here, with her like this, they'll probably shoot me." The words scream through his head as he crouches down.

His wait is but a few seconds, someone is coming.

"Sheree, my dear girl, are you in here? I've come to get you."

"It's Falcon. He must have figured this out the way I did." Eagle is a bit relieved that it's him rather than an official of the compound, but not for long.

"He won't have any problem finding her with the lantern still burning. And when he sees her, the way she is, lying there on the table, he'll tell everyone. I need to get out of here without him seeing me. But how?"

"Oh my God, Sheree, who's done this to you?" Falcon's words fill the building.

He didn't expect to find her this way. His first thought is to cover her up with the blanket he sees lying on the dirt floor.

Acting quickly, Eagle moves around in the darkness and picks up the steel pry bar he brought to loosen the air vent screen.

Her close friend is busy spreading the blanket over Sheree, when Eagle silently sneaks up from behind and swings a sharp blow of the pry bar to his head.

Falcon sinks to the floor.

"I'm sorry I had to do that, but you'd do the same thing if it was you in this spot.

"I might as well finish what I started, Falcon. Maybe they'll blame you for it."

Eagle grins as he steps over the unconscious Falcon, and jerks the blanket off Sheree's nude body.

Chapter Nineteen

Falcon's eyelids flutter as he tries to regain consciousness after being struck from behind by Eagle. His head spins, and throbs with every beat of his heart. Seconds pass in slow motion while he struggles to collect the strength to move, to focus his eyes. The sounds he hears make no sense.

Uhh . . . ! Uhhh . . . ! Uhhhh . . . ! Uhhhhhh . . . !

It takes every bit of energy he can muster to force his head up from the dirt floor. His vision starts to clear the closer he gets to a sitting position. The whole room moves with wavy outlines of shadows. His attention is drawn toward the light of a lantern, to fall upon the back of a man who appears to be naked from the waist down. As suddenly as the light of his life extinguished a few minutes ago, the fire of survival ignites within him, he realizes where he is, and the reality of what's happening.

With a mighty push he's on his feet, staggering left and right, backward and forward. He reaches for the edge of a wooden crate to balance himself when he sees Eagle, standing at the foot of the table holding Sheree. His body is lying on her, her legs dangling in midair on either side of his hips.

"Get off her, you cowardly bastard!" he orders sternly, with a guttural monotone voice, just loud enough for his assailant to hear him.

Eagle, startled, straightens up on his feet instantly, and turns to face him.

"You're too late, laddy, I'm finished with her. I was just catching my breath. You can take your turn now." He smirks, and pulls up his pants as he brags to the injured young man about his accomplishment.

"I said to get away from her."

"Or you'll do what? It looks to me like you're in no shape to give orders to anybody."

"You're going to pay for this Eagle, you'll pay for this dearly. I'm going to see to it." The longer Falcon is on his feet the steadier he gets, his strength slowly coming back.

"If you think you can report me to the people here, you might as well forget it. I'm one of them, you know. I've been working with them all along, passing information as they need it. I'll tell them you did this. Who do you think they'll believe, you or me? Besides, if she was awake, she'd tell you she's been teasing me, leading me on, for a long time now. This was bound to happen. It was just a matter of when. Why do you care about her anyway? She's nothing to you . . . she's nothing to anybody. Get over here and have your way with her. No one needs to know about it, in fact, she'll never know who did it unless we tell her." Eagle attempts to build a case by getting his accuser involved.

“Sheree . . . ,” Falcon starts and catches himself just before he reveals that Sheree can hear when she’s in this sleep. That would mean Eagle would probably try to silence her permanently. He begins again.

“I’ll know . . . I’ll always know, you filthy piece of hog droppings; and she will too, as soon as I tell her.” Falcon purposely stalls, allowing time to recuperate further. “People don’t want to be associated with the likes of you. They’ll throw you to the wolves, and you know it. You’re finished, you’ll be lucky to get out of here with your life,” he counters Eagle’s assertions.

“There’s just one little thing you’ve forgotten, you fool. You’re the only one who knows what happened here, and you’re not leaving here alive.” Eagle’s words are delivered as cold as the look on his face. He starts moving toward Falcon like a bull with his head down.

With no time to react differently, the weakened Falcon moves to the left to avoid the head on rush. Still a bit off balance, he’s knocked to the ground by the raging man’s flailing right arm. The momentum of his rush causes Eagle to miss his target, and slam to the dirt floor with a thud.

Falcon rolls when he hits the floor, lands on his knees, and turns to face his opponent. He knows his chances of winning this fight are slim. With barely enough strength to muster one more defensive move, that leaves him with no offense at all. The pain in his head is making it difficult to see clearly or concentrate.

Eagle is up to his feet immediately and turns to once again rush headfirst toward his intended victim. From five feet away, he dives intending to flatten Falcon to the floor. Knowing there is no time to dodge his aggressor a second time, the man on his knees attempts to brace for the inevitable collision by extending his right hand to meet the dirt floor. It’s then he feels what appears to be a steel bar. Just closing his grip puts it in his hand.

Without hesitation, believing it’s his last chance, his hand comes up with the pry bar moving across his body to the left. The heavy weight of the steel, along with the force he’s able to put behind it, hits his aggressor’s left forearm and pushes it across him to the right, which allows the bar to strike Eagle on the left side of his neck. Instinct moves Falcon to his right to keep the weight of his opponent’s body from smashing down on him.

Disoriented from the unexpected blow to his neck, Eagle is unable to guide his forward motion and can’t protect himself as he plunges into a stack of two crates. His head slams into the bottom one, pushing it out from beneath the one on top, allowing it to crash down on his body. Stunned, he writhes aimlessly, attempting to free himself.

Falcon, now lying flat on his stomach, expects Eagle to be on top of him at any second, and isn’t aware the pry bar is still clutched tightly in his hand. Energy exhausted, he must rest a few seconds.

Fifteen seconds pass.

Eagle rolls the crate off his back and staggers to his feet. Falcon raises his head to see his foe in the shadows, towering, moving over him with a smaller crate raised over his head. In a few seconds, he’ll be ready to slam it down and snuff the life of the only person able to expose the truth.

With barely enough might to get out of the path of the threat, Falcon rolls toward Eagle instead of away. As he moves, he swings the steel bar hoping to bash his enemy in the chest, causing him to lose his balance with the crate, and force him to let it fall harmlessly to the floor. But Eagle has already started the crate moving down toward the spot where Falcon is lying, and has added the muscle of his body behind it, keeping his grip to guide it all the way down. That puts him in a moving arch over the rolling Falcon, who brings the steel bar up, pointing it at the oncoming man's chest.

Falcon sees the crate moving down toward him, it scrapes his knuckles as it narrowly passes the steel bar and brushes his shoulder before crashing to the floor behind him.

Eagle moans, "Uuuuhhhhhh"

Falcon feels his limp body and arms fall against him.

Caught between the crate, the steel pry bar, which has dug itself into the floor barely missing his back, and an unconscious Eagle, the pinned man struggles to slide out from beneath his confinements. A warm liquid is creeping its way down his chest and back, giving him immediate concern. The darkness of his cell makes it impossible to determine what it is, or from whom, or what, it might be leaking. His heart pumps harder.

"This has to be blood, and by the amount of it, one of us is badly injured. I don't think it's me, but I'd better get loose before he's able to make another move." Falcon says to himself under his breath.

Wriggling back and forth, up and down, side to side, he's able to worm himself free, disturbing nothing at the scene.

He struggles to his hands and knees, then puts his hand on the crate that narrowly missed him to help push himself to a standing position. Eagle's head is lying on top of the crate, facing him, not a foot away. His eyes are open with a fixed stare, and his mouth gapes breathlessly.

The winner of the fight bends down to look into the space that just confined him. Although the light isn't good, he's able to determine that the flat slanted end of the steel bar has caught Eagle in the center of his chest, just below his rib cage. When the other end of it jammed into the dirt floor as he moved downward with the crate, he was impaled by his own weight. The pry bar was thrust up into his chest. Blood oozes down the steel bar, soaking the dirt floor.

"I suppose this is justice, you miserable devil, but I would rather Sheree see you accept your punishment. Maybe knowing you'll never be able to do anything like this again will be good enough for her. I hope so." Falcon's comments fall on deaf ears as he turns to Sheree to lift her by her shoulders and pull her up so her legs are again on the table.

"I can't leave you like this Sheree, they shouldn't see you like this."

After gently putting her underwear over her bare breasts, adjusting her blouse so it can be buttoned, and moving her arms to her sides, he picks up her pants and underwear from the floor to slip them on over her legs and hips covering her nakedness. Then he picks the blanket up from the floor, covers all but her shoulders and head, and smoothes out any wrinkles he sees.

"There, that's a whole lot better. Now if someone comes in here, they'll never suspect anything has happened to you," he thinks as he stands looking at his abused friend.

"I should have taken better care of you," he speaks out loud, stumbling with the words. "I should not have allowed this to happen. I should have been more careful when I came in here. There's no words to say how sorry I am that I was unable stop him. You don't deserve this. You've been through so much in your life already, now this. Please believe I did the best I could; it just wasn't good enough. I'm not sure how I'll ever tell you, but you have to know. I'll be here for you, and I guess that's about all I can do." He brushes water from his eyes, and leans down to kiss her on the cheek.

"I know I said I would hide Sheree if I found her, but with all this, I think I'd better try to get you back into your body." He speaks as if Lilly is listening.

Cautiously, he rises to an upright position, at the same time putting his left hand to the back of his head trying to determine the extent of his injury. The pain isn't getting any better, but his vision has improved. He looks at his blood covered hand and says, "Get a grip on yourself, Falcon, you've got a big mess to clean up in a short amount of time. Where do I begin? Logic tells me I need some help, but the only person I can trust is Lilly. With everything that's happened here, will she be able to keep her wits, or will she break down and be more of a problem than help? Who am I kidding, I have no other choice, I need her help.

"How will I get to her? With this blood all over my clothes, I don't dare try to make it to my room. Someone is bound to see me and ask questions. There are no other clothes here for me to change. Sheree's are too small and Eagle's are soaked in blood worse than mine. What to do?

"I remember Lilly saying if I ever needed her back in her body, to hold a mirror up to her face. Well that's a thought, but I don't have a mirror. Where can I get one? I'm sure they've not stored mirrors in with these explosives on purpose, but, there's a chance they might have stored a trunk containing someone's personal belongings. These crates all look so much alike, but a trunk should be easy to find." He thinks as he turns around scanning the area illuminated by the lantern.

"I'll have a quick look around. You never know, I might get lucky." He grabs the lantern and reaches up to hold it as high as possible and begins his search, holding the back of his head with his other hand.

Meandering through the pathways between the crates and barrels soon makes him realize there is no orderly system being used to store these munitions. It's as if they're placed on the dirt floor where space permits with no consideration for the age, type, or frequency of use. A few appear to have been hurriedly ripped open, allowing some of the exposed contents to fall to the floor. Lead shot, sidearms, long rifles, cannon shot, along with wooden barrels spilling black powder, are scattered on the floor partially blocking the passageways.

"What's this? Smaller wooden boxes. Something's printed on the sides and top. Let's get the lantern over here for a look. D-y-n-a-m-i-t-e," he spells out.

"Whoa! I've heard about this, but I've not seen it before. From what I understand it's dangerously unstable. I'll keep clear of this, and that's a fact."

He continues his search for a trunk.

"A spark or a lit match in the wrong place would cause this whole building to go up like a candle. The sooner we get out of here, the better off we'll both be."

"Will you look at this, it looks like a pile of old, discarded, military uniforms. Most of this is good for nothing but rags. They're full of dust and have a strong musky smell to them." He mutters while sorting through the assortment of shirts, pants, pantaloons, coats, and underwear.

After a few minutes, he has selected, and dressed himself in a faded yellow shirt, or perhaps it's white and yellowed with age. The sleeves balloon at the cuffs, while the front is pleated with ruffles in a vertical pattern. And a pair of light gray pantaloons, which fit skin tight, with the legs reaching to the midcalf. Instead of a hem, the pants have a dark green band sewed around the bottom of each leg.

"This is the best I'm able to do. They're not exactly stylish, but at least there's no blood on them. I'll stuff my clothes back under the bottom of all these old things. Nobody will find them there. I need to get out of here without delay. If they find Sheree here with Eagle's body, they'll look for answers. But if they find me here with them, I'll hang for sure. If I can get outside, lock the door, and get a few feet away before anyone notices me, I have a chance. I'll be back later, Sheree.

"Okay, I'm outside. It's getting dark, that's good. Get the key in the hole, Falcon, stop shaking. There, it's locked. Now turn and walk casually toward my building. So far, so good."

"Hey, you! Falcon!"

"Damn! Someone has seen me. How do I explain this getup for starters?"

"Hey Falcon, it's me, Lester. What are you doing in the armory this time of the day, and how did you get those keys?" The young man announces loudly as he runs to his friend's side.

"Thank God, it's you Lester. You just took twenty years off my life by yelling at me that way. What are you doing out here this time of the day? And keep your voice down." Falcon tries to turn the tables.

"Looking for you. Everybody's looking for you." Lester's voice changes to a whisper.

"Why?" Falcon breathes with a sense of urgency and surprise.

"You're missing, I mean, when you didn't come to supper, they checked to see if you had given a reason you wouldn't be there. When they didn't find anything, they sent security to your room; then right after supper, they alerted everybody to look for you. They must think you're trying to escape." Lester is about to burst with eagerness.

"Now, why were you in the armory? I saw you come out and lock the door. And why are you wearing those pitiful clothes?"

"There's no time to explain it all right now. Help me get to my room without being stopped by security, or anybody else, for that matter. I'll tell you later."

As the two young men move toward the doorway of Falcon's building, trying to hurry without raising suspicion, Mr. Vaughn appears as if he's been waiting for them on the stone porch. He watches, and waits for them to climb the several steps.

"Damn, the luck." Falcon's words can be heard by Lester, but not Mr. Vaughn.

"Well, well, Falcon . . . I see you've found him, Lester. Good work." He finally says when they approach not more than an arm's length away.

There's no smile on his face, but his forehead wrinkles as he raises his eyebrows, looks out over the top of his glasses, and gives an approving nod.

"Yes, sir, I did. He was just coming out of the armory. He has keys to lock the door and all. I've not yet discovered what he's doing there in this outfit of yesteryear. All he wants is to get to his room," Lester gleefully volunteers.

The trapped man is stunned by the way Lester has turned on him. His mind is moving rapidly trying to determine his next move. The Company man continues before he can say anything.

"I don't know how, but I expect he's missed his friend, Lilly, and somehow determined she's in the armory. Am I correct young man? Was she there?"

Falcon picks up on his lead.

"I don't know, sir. I didn't get inside. I was fumbling with the keys, trying to find the right one, when Lester yelled at me."

"He says you were coming out of the armory when he saw you, and you were locking the door. Are you saying Lester is wrong with what he saw." Mr. Vaughn is playing a game.

"He's mistaken, but you're correct when you say I was looking for Lilly. I've looked everywhere for her and she's nowhere to be found. Everybody has looked for her and discovered nothing."

"Why the urgency? Perhaps she's ill and being treated at the medical office."

"Well, sir, rumor has it she was taken last night. Two men supposedly came in and abducted her." Falcon is amazed at himself, the way he is able to play the game. If he can turn Mr. Vaughn's attention away from the armory, perhaps he won't be so sternly reprimanded.

"And she isn't at the medical office. We checked."

"I see." Mr. Vaughn seems to accept the explanation.

"I won't ask about the way you're dressed, but, explain to me those keys with which you have somehow been entrusted."

"Think fast, and be convincing." Falcon tells himself in a flash.

"I'm afraid you've got me there, Mr. Vaughn. I went to the maintenance building, looking for Lilly. The place was a big mess, things were upset everywhere. No one was there, so I looked around and found them lying on the floor. I thought maybe I could use them to check inside some of the locked buildings. I didn't get much of a chance, though. The armory was the first place I went." He holds out his hand offering the ring of keys.

"You shouldn't be snooping into things that don't concern you. You know better than that." He sternly scolds the young man.

"I don't know if what you're telling me is the truth or not. So, go on to your room and resume your normal activities. I'll think about all this, and if necessary, deal with you later.

"Now go on, get to your room. You too Lester." Mr. Vaughn orders strictly.

Lester and Falcon split up and head for their rooms on a run.

Lilly is sitting on the bed, her legs crossed, impatiently waiting for Falcon to return. She jumps up as he enters the room.

"Look at you. What have you got on? Whose clothes are those? Where have you been all this time? What happened to your head? There's blood in your hair. Good Lord, I've been thinking all sorts of things." She accuses, asks all her questions, and lets him know she cares about him in one breath.

"This has been the worst day of my life. I was banged on the head from behind. It'll be okay, it's not bleeding any more," he pants.

"I didn't know what to do. If something happened to you, I'd never forgive myself. Don't ever do this again, okay?" Again, she explains her frustration.

"Ssshhuuushhh, Lilly, stop rambling and sit down here on the bed with me. I have something to tell you, but get a grip on yourself, you're in for a shock."

Her eyes get big with fear and wonderment. She feels uneasy, tense. Falcon's never acted this way with her before. This must be bad, bad, news.

He takes her hand, and gently kisses it as they sit on the edge of the bed. This day gets harder as it drags along.

She takes a deep breath and lets it out, preparing herself.

"Tell me," she compels.

"I found Sheree in the armory," he begins solemnly.

"Is she all right? What's wrong?" Lilly interrupts.

"Let me say what I have to say. Keep quiet."

"I found Sheree in the armory. There was a lantern burning so I was able to see her lying on a table . . . naked."

"Oh my God!" she starts.

Falcon puts his finger to her lips. "Keep quiet or I'll never get this out."

Her face is aghast as she sits stiff, her mouth agape, not breathing.

"I found a blanket on the floor and was trying to cover her up, when something hit me on the head. I don't know how long it was, but the next thing I saw was a man having intercourse with her."

"Oh Lord, no! My God, no!" Lilly screams in tears. "I've always been afraid something like this would happen. I always knew it would—sooner or later."

He takes her in his arms and consoles her as best he can. A few minutes pass as she settles down.

"Who did it? Who was it?" She demands coldly and pushes away from his arms.

"Promise me you won't try to leave this room and I'll tell you. There's nothing you can do about it now. Promise?" He calmly responds reaching to pull her to him again.

Feeling dirty, needing a bath, she allows herself to be pulled to his chest. She doesn't know why, but she feels safe.

"Promise," she whispers.

"Eagle, it was Eagle."

Lilly jumps up from his arms onto her feet.

"I'll kill that son-of-a-bitch!" she exclaims. "I'll make him wish he had never been born!"

Concerned that she'll bolt out the door, he jumps up, wraps his arms around her, lifts her off the floor, and throws her on the bed, with him on top. She struggles to get loose, but his weight and strength convince her to relax and give up the fight.

"You won't be able to kill him. He's already dead," he says in a low voice directly into her ear.

"What do you mean, he's already dead? How did he die?" Lilly's mind spins wildly, zeroing in on the obvious. "You did it, didn't you? You killed him, but how?"

"I came to my senses just as he finished with her. I didn't know until then who had hit me. It took me a few minutes to realize what was going on, and get my faculties together. When I told him I was going to report him, he said he was going to kill me. I really didn't have any choice, I had to fight him. We scuffled around for a few minutes until finally he dove at me and landed on the end of a pry bar."

"Oh, you poor thing." Lilly puts her hand up to his face.

"It stuck him all the way up in his chest." His eyes fill with tears. "He let out his breath with a groan and died lying on top of me. His blood drained all over my chest and back before I could get out from under him." Unable to control his emotions any longer, Falcon begins to sob.

"So, that's the reason for the clothes," she thinks, as her arms find their way to hold him.

Feeling more in control, she questions.

"Where is he now? Where's Sheree? Is she still lying there naked? Is she still locked in there, with him dead, and her lying there naked?" She conjures the scene.

Falcon collects himself and sits up on the bed, allowing her to move about.

"I found Sheree's clothes and dressed her before I left. But he's still there, lying there just as he died."

"I'm so sorry you had to go through all that, and you did it for me."

"I couldn't stop him. When I woke up it was too late." His tears well up again, but before he can wipe them with his hand, she is in his arms, lovingly kissing his eyes.

"It's not your fault, you dear wonderful man. You've done more than anyone should ask of another human being. You're amazing. With all that went on, you took the time to dress Sheree. You took the time to protect me, the only way you could. I couldn't before, but I can say it now. I love you, Falcon. I love everything about you." She hugs him tightly with many thoughts running through her head.

"Can he love me now that he knows someone else has had relations with me? It's the only time it's ever happened, and he must know I wouldn't have allowed it if I could have stopped it. Seeing me naked that way, has it turned his mind away from me?"

She has tears in her eyes as she speaks. "Please don't blame me for what's happened. It's not my fault either, and I need you to help me get through all this."

Falcon carefully pushes her away far enough to see her tormented face.

"I love you too, you breath of heaven, I adore you. I'll always love you, no matter how hard you try to get me not to sometimes. The truth is, I'm glad it was me who killed him instead of you. This way you don't have to live with the memory of it, and it helps me to know that I did all I could."

Their lips meet, and for a moment they're separated from the distressed life being forced upon them. They soar together, their love for each other carrying them higher and higher. Slowly, though all too soon, their passion ebbs, and the weight of their reality is once again upon them.

"There's a bit more." Falcon looks into her eyes and says without expression.

"What more?" she asks, wanting it all to end.

"Vaughn caught Lester and me coming into the building."

Lilly's eyes reflect the expectation of doom.

"Nothing happened. He let us go explaining he would think about my story of finding the keys lying on the floor in the maintenance building, and never actually being in the armory. I told him Lester saw me as I was trying to unlock the armory door to get in looking for Sheree."

"Do you think he believed you?" she asks.

"For the moment, I think. The problem is, as I see it, he'll believe me until he finds Eagle's dead body. Then all bets are off."

"Then, we can't let him find Eagle's body," Lilly states very matter-of-factly.

"He took the keys from me, honey." Using the 'honey' word makes him feel good inside.

"How did Eagle get in?"

"Good question. The door was locked when I got there, and Eagle was inside already. There must be another way in. There has to be." He continues, "We need to do something with his body, but right now, I need to lie down for a couple of hours. I still have this horrible headache, and I feel like I have no energy at all."

"You probably need something to drink and a little bit to eat. Here, let me clean up that bloody spot on your head," she says as she approaches him with a wet towel.

"Some water sounds good to me right now," he says.

"I'll get you some, just sit still."

Falcon gulps the water she brings, and patiently sits as she carefully washes the blood and dirt from his head wound.

"There you are, that's a lot better. You lie down and rest, and I'll make my way to the medical office to get something to bandage this cut in your scalp. Then, I'll slip outside to the armory to take a look for another way in there."

"Lilly, I don't wan—"

"You hush. I'm not going to try to go in there by myself. I'll let you rest for a couple of hours, then I'll wake you up, and we can go together. Okay?"

He feels so weary right now, he'll agree to almost anything.

"I suppose so." He lies back and is asleep when his head hits the pillow.

"I'm sorry, sweetness, I pray you're all right, but I can't wait around for two or three hours. Things need to be done without delay, and I'm just the person to do them. I'll be back as soon as I can," she whispers into his ear.

She moves swiftly through the halls, out the entry doorway, and down the few steps to the courtyard, without being noticed. Her first stop will be the maintenance building to pick up a few things. Preparedness and simplicity are the best plan.

"Just as I'd hoped, there's no one here. It looks like nobody has cleaned up the mess I made yet either. Let's see, I need a shovel, a hammer, some nails, some rope, and a knife. And oh yes, I want that mirror I jumped through earlier when those three men were chasing me.

"That didn't take long, I have it all but a knife. There's no knife or blade of any sort here I can find. I'll take this small saw instead. Will you look at this? A burlap bag, just what I need to carry these things. The shovel won't fit, but that's okay.

"The trick will be to get out of here and inside the armory without getting caught. I'd better get a move on, I have a feeling in my bones, uh, oh, someone's coming."

She swiftly moves outside and hides behind the corner of the building. The footsteps get closer. She waits.

"Where would a person on guard duty get the notion that he could leave his post when his relief doesn't show up. You're as close to being a total idiot as any man I have ever known. You know, I could have you shot for this?" the director of security verbally pummels a young guard, as they turn the corner of the building at a fast pace.

"Did you see something move over there?" The subject is changed quickly when the director catches a glimpse of movement out of the corner of his eye.

"No, sir, I didn't." the guard replies. "And sir, I didn't abandon my post. I was on my way back when you met me. I went to look for Whitey. He's more than an hour and a half late."

"That's no excuse for leaving your post unattended. You're to stay at your post until you're properly relieved. Is that clear? Do you understand?."

"Yes, sir, I do, but what if he never shows up?"

"You know as well as I do, each and every one of our guard posts are physically checked by the captain of the guard every three hours, religiously. You should report to him and let him handle any problems. Do we understand each other? Anything further?" The security boss has lost his patience, and has apparently forgotten the movement he detected earlier.

There is no response.

"Then you stay here and guard your post until Whitey or the captain of the guard relieves you."

"I'd better move on before that security guy comes this way for a look. I can't let the things in this bag rattle around either, he'll hear it for sure. Lucky for me, there's not much of a moon tonight. I'll take the long way around to the armory. That'll put me farther away from the guards."

She moves stealthily from shadow to shadow, keeping anything she can between her and the guarded areas. At last, she's just fifty feet from the armory building.

"I don't remember any windows at all, or a door, other than the main one. There has to be another way in, though. I'll take it one side at a time and give them a good look over. I'll start on the side toward the big outside wall, away from the guards' line of sight." Her plan is set.

She runs bent over toward the wall, with the burlap bag held in her left hand. It bounces in the air, while the shovel, grasped at the end of the handle by her other hand, drags the ground on her right. After reaching her darkly shadowed destination, it doesn't take long to determine that there is no way to enter the armory from there.

"I'll peek around the corner to see if anyone's watching the back wall. Easy does it. There's a ladder leaning up against the armory wall. This feels like a trap. I'd better have another look. Peek around, carefully now. Well I never . . . there's a big square of screen just above the ladder. This must be the way Eagle got in. I'd like it better if it was facing toward the big outside wall like this one here. The chance of being seen would be a whole lot less. I guess you play the cards you're dealt. And I know I'm going in there, so let's get up that ladder. Take a good look around first. I don't see anything. Here goes."

She runs straight for the base of the ladder some thirty feet away. Once there, she leans the shovel against the armory wall and immediately starts climbing toward the screen. The heavy burlap bag requires the total use of her left hand to move it up. It swings back and forth under the ladder as she climbs, pulling her off balance. The higher she gets the more vulnerable she feels.

"Someone's watching me, I can't shake this creepy feeling running up and down my back. If they jump out of the shadows, I'll fall from up here for sure."

She's as far up as she can go. If she lets go of the ladder with her right hand she can reach the screen, but she won't be able to hold on to anything with the bag in her other hand. That thought is scary, she's not that far off the ground, but it looks like it's a long way down. She notices the screen is held in place by setting on partially driven nails at either end on the bottom. It can be lifted, turned sideways, and slid through the opening it covers.

"Just do it. Look out, I almost lost my balance, but I've got my right hand on the screen. It looks like screen, but it's actually a heavier metal. It must be four feet by three feet. It rattled a little bit when I grabbed for it. Eagle probably was planning on coming back out this way so he left it loose.

"What do I do with it if I pull it open? It feels heavy, so if I try to hang on when it starts moving, it'll pull me to the ground with it. This is not good."

The bag is getting heavier, pulling at her left arm, and her grip needs to be adjusted. Thinking she'll change hands for a few minutes, she swings it under the ladder, let's go of the screen with her right hand, and wraps her right arm under, to meet her left hand and the bag.

Instead of swinging under as planned, the burlap bag hits the left side of the ladder, causing it to start sliding to the right. Since the only thing keeping her on the ladder is her weight leaning against it, her first instinct is to reach up with her empty right hand for the wall. But instead of hitting the wall, her hand strikes the screen with a smack. It rattles, dislodges itself from the two nails, and starts falling straight down. It hits the top of the ladder, slips between it and the building wall, creating a sled. At the same time, the radical movement of the ladder causes its feet to start sliding away from the armory wall.

Although she tries to slow the fall by scraping the fingers of her right hand down the wall, it's to no avail. The ladder moves out from under her, and follows the screen down. Lilly, burlap bag, screen, and ladder, all hit the ground with a violent crash.

Her head bounces off the screen and the wall as she lands on top of, and facing, the ladder. Her left arm, under it, still clutches the burlap bag full of tools.

From inside the bag, the handle of the hammer pushes up between the rungs to strike her ribs on the left side, causing her to let out a yelp. A bit dazed, she feels pain coming from various parts of her body. Her head, chest, right hand fingers, ribs, and left arm, all send signals of distress.

"Can I move? I need to get my left arm free."

"Damn! Someone must have heard me! They're running this way!

"There's no use trying to get away, they'll be here before I can get to my feet! I think my left arm is broken and probably my ribs. I've really loused things up now. I hope they just shoot me and get it over with!

"Damn! I should have waited for Falcon like he wanted."

She struggles to free her arm by rolling off the left side of the ladder, as two men come running. She expects to be grabbed and pulled to her feet any second.

"Lilly, are you all right?" The words are angelic music to her ears.

"Oh, Falcon, it's you. Thank god."

"And me too," Lester chimes.

"There's no time to talk, get the ladder back up to that opening. Lilly, you have to get up the ladder and into the armory, right now. Lester, you follow her, then I'll throw this bag up. You toss it inside to her, then I'll hand the shovel up. I'll bring this piece of steel screen up with me, and get inside with the two of you. Then we'll pull the ladder up and inside with us. If we're fast enough, they won't find anything when they get here. Now move!" Falcon calmly fires instructions in a loud whisper.

"What was that? It sounded like something fell, and then some woman screamed!" A guard shouts to his brothers in arms.

"Where did it come from?" The three frantically working people hear the guards yelling. "Over by the armory!"

Lilly, the bag of tools, and the shovel are inside.

"Go around the other way to block an escape!" another guard shouts. "We'll go this way."

The screen is moving through the opening; the two items left outside are Falcon and the ladder, a few more seconds is all they need.

The two groups of guards converge at the back of the building from either side.

"See anything?" one pants.

"Not a thing." Answers are heard.

Peering out through the opening in the armory wall some eight feet above them, Lilly, Falcon, and Lester, calm their breath as they hold on to the three feet of the ladder they were able to pull inside. If the guards look up, they'll see the rest of it extending out over their heads from the opening in the wall above them.

"Should we try to slide this in, with them down there?" Lester whispers to the other two.

"We'd better not move it at all." Falcon responds, forming his words with his breath instead of his voice. "If they hear any sound, they might look up. Just sit still and wait."

Inside the armory, several wooden crates were already stacked high near the opening, allowing the three desperate young adults to move through the window easily. Other crates are stair stepped down to the dirt floor. It appears they have been stacked this way for this very purpose.

The guards chat with each other for a few minutes walking about in various directions, speculating about the noise, and the absence of a cause. When nothing is discovered, they meander off, one at a time, in various directions.

"That was too close for me!" Lester says in a low voice.

"Me, too," Falcon concurs. "Let's get this ladder in here while we can."

"What about the screen?" Lilly suggests. "Should we put it back in place?"

"Naw, this isn't going to take us that long. We'll put it back when we leave," Falcon answers.

"The lantern is still lit," he continues, and starts moving down the arrangement of crates to the floor. He waits for his associates as they climb down after him.

"Which way?" Lester urges as they group together amongst the crates, boxes, and barrels.

"Over here." Falcon moves toward the light of the lantern.

They follow close as he leads them through the maze created by the random placement of the stores in the building. Shortly, they emerge into the open space, where the lantern is seen setting on a crate.

"There's nothing here!" Lilly exclaims. "Where's Sheree!"

"She was right there—lying on a table, right there—and Eagle was over here." Falcon grabs the bail of the lantern and takes it with him as he moves to show where Eagle was lying dead.

"It's gone, it's all gone. There's not even any blood on the floor over here," he says with amazement.

In unison, the three of them conclude this is a trap, and they walked right into it. Nobody moves, expecting to be captured.

When nothing happens, Lester is the first to speak. "Should we look around to see if they just moved things? Maybe, it's all still in here somewhere."

"I think we should get out of here while we still can. We need some time to sort this whole thing out," Falcon snaps back.

"What about me? What do I do now?" Lilly's voice drops off into the silence of the dim light, and shadows.

Chapter Twenty

Today is the third day since Lilly, Falcon, and Lester made their way into the armory to find Sheree's and Eagle's bodies missing. They replaced the screen over the air vent window, and returned the tools to their proper location as best they could, It was considered a good idea to keep Falcon and Lester away from each other for a few days to see what the Company planned to do in a way of their punishment, if anything. Nothing has changed. Eagle's body has not turned up, Sheree is nowhere to be found, and no one is talking about it. Her injuries healed themselves within an hour of her fall from the ladder, amazing those who knew.

Falcon just walked past Lester in the hallway, slipped a note into his hand, and kept on moving. Lester, surprised, without thinking, raises his hand to look at the paper.

"Meeting, my room, one thirty, today." He looks up, but Falcon is gone.

"What are they up to now?" He wonders.

The train carrying Bob, Randy, and Amber, posing as Sheree, moves along at five miles an hour around a long gentle curve just outside of town. That puts them some twelve miles, as the crow files, from the Anderson homestead. As planned, they're standing on the platform at the rear of the last car, awaiting Robert's signal to jump to the passing ground.

"Get ready." He instructs. "Throw your bag off first, then jump right after it. You first Randy, then you Sheree. I'll be the last off. Got it? Jump when I say, go. Get set . . . !

"Go!" One at a time they jump to hit the ground and roll.

Bob brushes dust from his shirt and pants as he gets up, then looks back along the tracks to see if his traveling companions are okay. Randy is up and walking toward Sheree. She's sitting on the ground, her legs stretched out flat in front, adjusting her bonnet. Randy reaches her first, and offers his hand to help her up, which she accepts. Everyone is okay. No injuries from the jump.

"The Sander's place is a good two hour's walk from here," Bob comments. "Let's get started. Maybe Elizabeth will feed us when we get there."

Each carrying their belongings, they turn away from the tracks and start walking three abreast across the once plowed and productive tobacco field. A gentle breeze picks up the dust from the heels of their boots, blowing it in a drifting fashion, to allow it to settle again a few inches away. Only remnants of last year's crop that have not yet rotted away appear here and there.

It's a beautiful warm day, a good day to be getting back home.

The Andersons' home has been abuzz since five o'clock this morning with the expected activities required to attend to the needs of last night's house guests.

It's John's first night home since he met with the money and power people in Baltimore. He brought Marty and Rachell Schoener with him, while Colonel Charles Housler, with his wife Selma, arrived from their farm to join them for a late supper. No business or politics was discussed last night. The evening was meant for relaxing, and to allow the six of them to begin further bonding of their relationships. It was, after all, the first meeting of Rachell and Selma. The Schoeners' plan to spend the next week at the Andersons' home, and are expecting their three children to join them here the day after tomorrow.

These six people are the core of the new organization, the Sentries of National Security, abbreviated, the Sons. The Houslers, June, and Rachell, are not yet aware of the name, or any particulars regarding their new venture. Everyone is eager to be part of the conference to take place in a few minutes. The finishing touches are just being handled by the household help, then the doors of the den will be closed before the meeting commences.

Instead of sitting around the wooden table, as might be expected, the overstuffed chairs and sofa seem more inviting as the couples find their way to a seat in the room. Two chairs are moved from their place against the wall, and positioned to bring everyone closer, facing each other in an oblong circle. A low, long, table holding the coffee and tea service occupies the center. Johnnie cakes, cookies, jellies, and butter are there for the taking, since none of the six were hungry for breakfast earlier this morning.

The women are dressed in casual clothing, with their hair down and loose, there are no corsets, or other confining garments. The men are dressed with their suits and vests, but the accompanying ties, coats, and cuff links, have been left in their rooms. The cuffs of their sleeves are rolled twice up their arms.

"Let's get started, folks," John begins. "I think the best way to start is for me to briefly touch on all that's happened these past few days. That should put us all on the same page before we get into anything new. Now remember, this is an open forum. It's expected that you'll interrupt to ask questions or make your mind known. There are no secrets in this room, nor is any area to be protected. Our ladies have joined us today to allow them to have an understanding of what their men are doing, and to get a feeling of the importance of our endeavor."

With a look of a homeless threesome, Bob, Randy, and Sheree's impersonator hoof it into the front yard of the Sanders' home. Elizabeth and her mama are working at the side and toward the rear of the house, hanging clothes on a line,

"Beth!" Robert calls.

She turns to notice him and drops a pair of her father's wet pants in the dusty dirt to run wildly, throwing her arms around his neck as she jumps to his chest.

"You're home!" she shouts. "I missed you so much. I'm glad you're home."

Party because she's in his arms and he's glad to see her, but mostly because he tries to keep his balance, Robert turns around and around with Beth clinging to his neck.

"I missed you, too. It's good to be home and see how beautiful you are." Words come out though parched lips without thought, at the same time he's consuming the eagerness, attention, and fragrance of this young woman, who seems to adore him.

"Hi, Mrs. Sanders!" He lets go with one arm and waves.

"You remember these two, don't you?" he asks Beth as he sets her feet on the ground.

"Sure, I do. Hi, Randy, it's good to see you back." She lets go of Robert to give him a one arm hug.

"And I know you weren't expecting her, but this is my sister . . ." Beth cuts her man off.

"And you're Sheree, right?"

"I sure am," Amber answers, nodding her head yes.

"My, how you've grown, and how beautiful you are. I wouldn't know you if not for your sister Charlotte. You look exactly alike. We weren't expecting you to come home with Robert and Randy, so you make it all that much better. I've been praying to keep you safe and to bring you home, Sheree. He's answered my prayers. Everyone has missed you so much."

"I can see why Robert is sweet on you. You've become a grown-up woman, and everything, since I've been gone. I always thought you were the prettiest girl around here, but you're more lovely than I remember." Sheree piles on the compliments with a shovel.

"Robert, you'd best put a rope around this one. Don't let her get away."

All four laugh at her candidness.

Mrs. Sanders has made her way to the group from the clothes line.

"You've brought us a surprise, Robert?" Her statement is a question.

"How in the world did you find her?"

"Luck was on our side, Mrs. Sanders. It's a long story and I'd like to tell you, but right now, I sure could use a long drink of water."

"Where's my mind? Come on in, you three, I'll bet you're hungry, too." She observes.

"Yes, ma'am." All three chime as they move with her toward the house. Robert and Beth, their arms around each other's waist, bring up the rear.

After swilling down a large glass of water, the three travelers sit around the kitchen table watching Mrs. Sanders and Beth prepare a feast of eggs, ham, and fried potatoes. The meal is served with fresh, made-this-morning biscuits and gravy. Coffee and milk washes it all down. Mmmmmmmmm. Fit for a king.

All the while they're eating, the story of locating, planning, and liberating Sheree is explained. Mrs. Sanders makes Randy drop his drawers, so she can see his injured leg. The chatter is filled with laughter and happiness.

"And that brings me to ask a favor of you and Mr. Sanders." Robert addresses Beth's mother as he finishes the tale and his meal.

"We'll help you if we can, honey," she replies. "What is it?"

"I'd appreciate it if I could leave Sheree here with you for a day or so, until I know it's safe and no one's waiting to pounce on her when I take her home."

"We'd love that, wouldn't we, Mama?" Beth immediately assures.

"You can stay as long as you like, child. You're welcome here." Caroline gladly supports her daughter.

"Thank you very much," Sheree begins. "You're all so nice to me, It's been a long time since I've been around friends and family. I hardly know how to act. I won't be any trouble, and I can help out with anything you need done."

Cole Sanders is coming out of the barn from putting his horse in out of the sun, just getting back from his trip to town this morning. Robert and Randy are coming out of the house, leaving to make their way home. The women are right behind them, chatting and giggling.

"Hey, Robert!" He announces his presence. "I didn't know you were back from Atlanta."

"Yes, sir, we just got here about an hour ago. Randy and I are on our way home now."

"Who's that with you there on the porch? Sheree . . . ! Sheree Anderson, is that you?"

"It's me all right, Mr. Sanders, I'm back home." Sheree's look-a-like makes an assumption that pays off.

"How in the world—? How did you . . . ? Does your mama and daddy know you're here?" Cole's surprise is obvious as he stutters. "You're all grown up, girl. Look at you. You must be, what, fifteen or sixteen now?"

"I'll be sixteen on my birthday," she proudly relates.

"Well, you sure are a sight for these old eyes. Your folks are going to be shocked when they see you. What a fine young lady you've grown into."

"Robert has asked us to look after her for a few days, Cole. Until we're all sure there's nobody chasing them that would take her back. I told him we wouldn't have it any other way," his wife volunteers.

"We'll be glad to help in any way we can," he continues. "So, you boys are on your way home now, you say? You wouldn't stay for a few more minutes and tell me about how you found Sheree and got back here, would you? While we're talking, we can saddle up a couple of horses to get you home. What do you think?"

"We can't refuse an offer like that, now can we Randy?" Robert answers as a tired Mr. Stoker nods in agreement.

"That's just fine, boys, Caroline, would you bring me a cool drink of water out here to the barn? I sure would appreciate it, honey."

"While I'm thinking about it," Cole has more to say, "if Randy here takes both horses home with him, I'll be over there later this afternoon, and I can bring them back with me then."

"It's no trouble for us to bring them back, Mr. Sanders," Randy assures.

"No, no, that's okay. I've got business with the colonel, so, I've got to be over there today anyway. I might as well bring them back with me." Cole affirms as they walk into the barn.

Back at La Nesra.

Lester knocks on the door at Falcon's room. It is exactly one thirty.

"Hurry up!" goes through his mind. He's not wanting to be seen standing in the hallway.

Falcon opens the door, reaches out to take Lester by the arm, pulls him in, then shuts, and locks it behind him. Lilly is sitting on the bed.

"What's going on?" He's quick to ask.

"Lilly and I have been talking over our situation, and there's a few things we don't understand that need to be cleared up," he begins.

"Okay, such as?" The young man feels he is suddenly on trial.

"Whose side are you on? First, you turn me in to Vaughn, then, the next thing I know, you come running to my side to help us out by the armory." Falcon is blunt.

"I'm on the side of right. I believe the way these people are treating Lilly is wrong. As for Mr. Vaughn, he had already seen us, so the only choice we had was to give him what he probably already suspected anyway. And by the way, that was a good bit of fast thinking on your part. I know you want to trust me. It's risky, but all I can do is prove myself as we go along," Lester responds.

"Another thing is, aren't you the least bit curious about everything you've seen and heard? You've not asked a single question. It doesn't add up." Lilly fires another question.

"I figure you'll tell me sooner or later; and if I start asking a lot of questions, you probably will think I'm some sort of spy for the Company, and I'm not," he assures.

"What's in this for you?" Another blunt question from Falcon.

"Well, I want to get out of here as bad as anyone, and I think the two of you will be able to do it. I want to go with you." His responses all seem to make good sense.

"What do you want to do?" Falcon looks at Lilly. "Do we accept him as one of us, or do we kill him."

"I don't want to kill anyone else today. Let's believe him; we can kill him later if it comes to that. Let's shake on it." Lilly smiles back, and extends her right arm.

Falcon and Lester move toward her and place their hands on hers. Their hands are still touching, when they hear the lock on the door turn, and watch it slowly open.

The doors are shut on the den at the Anderson farm.

The meeting has been going on for some time now. Everybody has been brought up to date, so most questions and misunderstandings have been explained. John and the colonel have carefully informed the Schoeners of their previous involvements, and spelled out their loyalty to the Sons. They have been at it for several hours, except for two short breaks to freshen up, so it's decided to put things on hold and move around for a while. As they rise from their seats, they hear Belle yelling, coming down the hallway.

"Ms. Anderson, come quick! Mr. Robert's home! He and Randall are out front right now getting off their horses."

The Andersons hurry to the front door and out onto the porch. The Houslers and Schoeners are a few steps behind. June is the first off the porch to greet her son with a big hug and a kiss on the cheek. John is right behind her, putting his arms around the both of them. Selma has Randall wrapped in her arms, as he tries to squirm away. The colonel and the Schoeners are left standing on the porch.

Robert notices Marty as someone he should know, but is unable to bring him to mind. He pulls away from the hug, expecting an introduction.

"Robert, you remember Marty Schoener. You met him a while back out by the pond." John refreshes his son's memory. "And his lovely wife, Rachell."

"I do now, Daddy. Nice to see you again, Mr. Schoener," he says, walks to the edge of the porch, and sticks out his hand to Marty.

"It's a pleasure to meet you, ma'am." He tips his hat to Rachell.

A hand is on Robert's shoulder giving a gentle signal, 'turn around.' As he turns, Selma slides her arms around him, puts her left cheek against his left cheek, her body against his, and kisses him up near his ear.

"I'm glad you're home," she whispers before relaxing her grip to push away, and say quite happily for all to hear, "Welcome home, you dear boy."

Not knowing what to make of it, he gets a different feeling in his guts. He feels embarrassed, not for himself, but for her.

"We got Sheree, Ms. Anderson! We brought Sheree home with us!" Randy can't wait any longer to tell it all.

At first, because she's caught up with Robert's arrival, the news doesn't register with June. She has a dazed look about her face, then it hits hard.

"Is it true? Is it really true?" she screams, jumping up and down. "Where is she?"

"Yes, Mama, it's true!" Robert confirms excitedly. "We left her at the Sanders' place until we could check things out here, They weren't happy with us in Atlanta when we broke her out, so they could be on our tail. Have you seen anybody?"

"No, not a soul. Nothing out of the ordinary at all. How in the world did you find her?" John is quick to answer and ask.

Before he can answer, June insists she be taken to her daughter immediately, and it is instantly known it will be no other way. She's going.

John turns to his guests, shrugs his shoulders and puts the palms of his hands in the air, "It looks like I'll need to postpone things for a while. The truth is, I want to see my daughter, too."

"Hell, why don't we all go?" Marty suggests.

The idea is accepted unanimously by actions instead of words. Everyone gleefully clamors while hurriedly going inside the house to collect clothing and articles needed for the trip.

"Belle, ask Jim to get the big carriage ready with a team. We'll all fit in there together," John directs.

"I think I'll go on with Randy to see him home, then I'll come on over. These two horses belong to Mr. Sanders, and I'd like to get them back to him. Then, I'll ride back here with you." Robert informs his father.

"That's fine, son; remember though, and I don't care if it's two o'clock in the morning, I want a brick by brick layout of what all you and Randy have been through bringing your sister home."

"I'd better get ready now though, I think your mother will leave me here if I don't." He grins and turns to go into the house.

At La Nesra, Lilly, Falcon, and Lester stand agape as the door swings open revealing Mr. Vaughn, and Sally, standing side by side. Behind them is the director of security and two guards. They stand in silence.

"Lester, if I find out you've had a hand in this, you'll regret it." Falcon grits his teeth and says under his breath.

Sally is the first to speak.

"We wondered how long it would take for the three of you to get back together. We've been watching you all along, and I must say, together you're really creative. But to no avail I'm afraid. It's time for us to get everything out in the open. Any effort to leave this room will be a waste of your energy, and futile. You might as well relax and accept your destiny."

Mr. Vaughn's expression is darkly grim. "I'm going to explain a few things to each of you. Just to let you know where you stand."

"First of all you, Lilly. You with your out-of-body antics, the mirrors and such. You're not the first we've had here with these abilities, and you won't be the last. We've allowed you to explore at will, in fact, we've encouraged you. All the time, however, we've also known we can pull you back inside your body simply by getting a reflection of your face in a mirror. I know you're aware of that, too. Now, think about it. If we want to imprison you inside your body, all we need to do is fix a mirror in front of your face, and put you to sleep. You won't be able to leave your body as long as it's there. We also know you can hear when you're asleep, and we are almost certain you can see, to a degree at least.

"Creating an unbearable prison for you is an option we hope we never need to use, But, keep in mind, my dear, I'll put you there if necessary. I'll put you there and store you away where no one will ever look for you, let alone find you. Do you like the idea of being with yourself, alone, day after day, week after week, year after year, forever?

"I'll make you a two-part promise. The first, as long as you become a part of this organization, work with us, and stay loyal to our cause—without attempting to leave, physically or spiritually—you'll have no problem with me. The second part, if I discover you've tried, or are trying to, physically escape La Nesra after today—or if you leave your body spiritually without my knowledge and permission—I'll put you in that prison. There will be no discussion about it, I'll put you there and remove your name from our records. It will be as if you never existed. Do you understand?" Mr. Vaughn looks Lilly in the eyes as he makes his threats.

"I heard what you said," she responds, biting her lip to hold her tongue, seething inside.

"We found Eagle dead at your feet in the armory, Lilly," the director of security informs the group. "There's a hole in his chest you can put your hand into, yet there was nothing at hand that could have made such a wound, Therefore, we considered that your out-of-body self killed him."

"I didn't kill him," Lilly coldly interrupts. "I've not been in the armory."

"Uh, uh, uh, we know that isn't true, but let the director continue," Mr. Vaughn taunts.

"It didn't take long to put things together, Falcon. We found your clothes where you hid them under a pile of old discarded uniforms. They're covered with blood. A little more searching gave us a pry bar, just the right size to cause the hole in Eagle's chest. We found blood on it, too. Now, when you couple all this to the fact you were seen coming out of the armory with keys in your hand, dressed in an old-fashioned uniform, and later, the three of you made your way into the armory through the air vent at the back, led us to just one possible conclusion. You killed Eagle, Falcon, not Lilly."

"What do you think the punishment should be for killing a fellow student?" Mr. Vaughn gloats as he speaks. "We can have you shot or put in the dungeon to rot."

"You're a bright young man." Sally picks up the conversation. "Wouldn't it be a waste to snuff the life of a young man with his whole future in front of him? It doesn't have to be that way We're at La Nesra, there's another choice. We can pretend it never happened."

"What's the catch?" Falcon poses.

Mr. Vaughn puts the pointing finger of his right hand up to keep Sally from responding.

"The catch, as you put it, sir, is simple. If you are caught, or suspected of plotting against your friends, here at La Nesra, if you attempt to escape, or if you, in any way, indicate you do not support our cause, your sentence will be handed down swiftly."

The director of security speaks, "Do you understand?"

"For how long?" Falcon asks.

"Forever! You young squirt, forever," Mr. Vaughn smirks.

"We saved you for last, Lester, and for good reason." The director points as he speaks. "Except for helping these two get inside the armory, I don't know what part you played in this whole thing. The problem I have with you is you'll do about anything to escape from here. We know you've tried to build support with others here, but have failed to come up with a plan. If we can't trust you, what good are you to us?"

Mr. Vaughn interjects, his finger in the air again.

"From this day on, it will be your responsibility to keep these two on track. You are to monitor their activities and report back to us anything they do or say against La Nesra. Take this responsibility very seriously, Lester. For if they are caught breaking the rules we just gave them, and you haven't kept us informed, we're going to hold you responsible."

"You mean I have to spy on them?" the intended informer relates in a distasteful manner.

“Call it what you will, as long as you report to us,” the director answers.

“I think we’re through here. This meeting is over.” Sally insists.

Lilly feels uneasy inside. These people don’t realize all that’s happened. They don’t know why Eagle is dead, how he died, or why Falcon had to do it. It’s not his fault. They have to know.

“Let Lester go, he’s not a part of this,” she urges. “There’s more to be said that doesn’t concern him, something more I need to tell you.”

“No, Lilly, don’t do it. It won’t change anything. It’ll just complicate things more,” Falcon interjects.

“Go, Lester! Go to your room,” Sally demands.

As he leaves, the director closes the door, keeping himself in the room, leaving the guards in the hall.

“Now, what don’t we know, Lilly,” Mr. Vaughn puzzles.

“Please, don’t. If you’re doing this for me, don’t. It’ll make no difference to them. Please,” Falcon begs.

“Go ahead. Get it off your chest,” Sally encourages.

“I’m sorry, Falcon, I have to tell them,” she begins.

“In the first place, neither Falcon or I have been trying to escape La Nesra. I was out of my body, and when I tried to get back, Sheree was gone. We call my physical body Sheree in order to cause less confusion. I was a nervous wreck, not knowing what to do, so I asked Falcon to help me. That was the first he knew about my ability to leave my life body. We looked everywhere with no success. Then we realized the only place my life body could be was in the armory. I got the keys and gave them to him to go there to look. When he got there, he found Sheree lying nude on a table. Then Eagle hit him on the head from behind. When he came to his senses, he saw Eagle having intercourse with her. A fight started, and after a scuffle, Eagle fell on the pry bar. Falcon was just protecting her, and that’s all. He wouldn’t have killed Eagle on purpose. It was an accident.”

“Is this true, Falcon?” Mr. Vaughn asks with an unexpected bit of understanding in his voice.

Before he can reply, Sally interrupts with a question for Lilly.

“Are you saying Eagle raped you, when you were outside of your body?”

“That’s right, Sally,” Falcon affirms, “that cowardly bastard raped Sheree while she was in one of those sleeps.”

“I’ve not been able to get back to my body since then, and it’s about to set me crazy,” Lilly adds. “That’s why we went to the armory later, and crawled through the air vent—looking for Sheree—whom we all know now, wasn’t there.”

“Perhaps we’ve been a bit hasty with our conclusions.” The older Company man is beginning to act like a human being, which is noticeable to everyone. “I’ll have your life body taken to your room, Lilly. We’ll let things settle down for a few months, and if we’ve had no further problems with the two of you, I’ll see that these incidents are erased from your records. I’m not at all happy with the way Eagle acted. Knowing this leads me to believe he would have met an early demise by someone's hands, if not yours. Let's see if we can get back to normal tomorrow." He concludes.

Bob and Randy arrive at Der Bote, dismount, and are entering the kitchen of the Stoker household.

"Hi, Mama," Randall says calmly and quietly, so as not to startle Alberta Mae.

She turns to see her son and Bob.

"Oh my Lordy, Randall, you're home." She shuffles her feet across the kitchen floor to put her arms around him. "I wasn't expecting you back for another two weeks or so. Hi, Bob, it's good to see you brought my boy back, all in one piece too. How come you're back early?"

"We got our business done sooner than we thought, and so, here we are," Randall replies.

"It seems to me that I was told you were going to Atlanta to see the sights and have some fun. What's this business you're talking about? What business did the two of you have in Atlanta?" She senses there's more to be told.

"I know that's what we said," Bob explains. "We didn't want you to worry about us, so that's the way we left it. The whole truth is, we went to see if we could find Sheree. We didn't know if we could or not, so we thought why worry you for no reason."

She stands, her feet firmly planted, hands on her hips, with the 'you lied to me' look on her face.

"Don't get all upset." Randall tries to smother the flames building inside his mother. "We found her."

"You, the two of you, found Sheree Anderson . . . in Atlanta?" she asks in disbelief.

"And we brought her home with us," he assures.

"We sure did, Alberta Mae. We got lucky, had some help, and when all was done, we brought her home." Mr. Anderson supports her son.

"I can't believe it. And you two did it on your own, and you're still alive. Don't say anything else, I'm going to get Jacob. He's going to want to know all the details just like me. No sense telling it all twice."

"If it's all the same to you, I'm going to head on over to the Sanders' place. We left Sheree there, so my whole family is on their way there now. Randy can do a fine job explaining it all." Bob excuses himself, mounts his horse, and with the reins of the second horse in his hand. When he turns to leave he catches sight of Alberta Mae trotting toward the barn to find Jacob. He hears her yell to the rest of the family as she goes.

"Randall's home and he's got a whale of a story to tell us. Come on inside while I get your daddy."

Robert arrives at the Sanders' farm to see two matched grays, hitched to their big carriage, setting on the shade side of the house. He rides his horse at a walk leading the extra horse with an empty saddle to the barn, stops, dismounts, and takes them inside.

One at a time, he puts a horse into a stall, removes its saddle, blanket, and bridle, and closes the stall door behind them. "I'd better not feed you since I don't know when you were last, but I imagine you could use a drink of water." The words come out loud as he grabs a water bucket and dumps the contents into a trough serving both stalls.

"It's really warming up this afternoon, I could use a swallow of something myself." He thinks as he walks across the barnyard toward the house.

"Ahh, there's a tin cup and a bucket by the well." He thinks to himself, blowing out a breath and wiping the back of his hand across his brow. Just as he empties a second cup into his mouth, and spits the last swallow out into the yard, Beth's voice is heard.

"I saw you come in. You look all hot and worn, you poor thing. Come on in here out of the sun, your whole family's here. Did you see Daddy? He's on his way over to Der Bote."

"Hi, honey, no, I didn't catch sight of him, but we could have passed each other, him on one side of a hill and me on the other. I guess he left before Mr. Housler showed up here. He said he was going to Der Bote to see him today sometime. How long has he been gone?"

"Not all that long, I guess, He'll be along in an hour or so, I'm sure. Come on in, and I'll get you a tall glass of lemonade."

The sun has been going down for the last half hour when the Andersons decide it's time to take their entire party home. They drift out of the house into the yard, stretching and yawning.

Mrs. Sanders and Sheree stand on the porch bidding all a good evening, while Beth and Robert sit in the carriage alone. They slipped out of the house a few minutes ahead of the others to have a quiet moment together.

"I know it's only a few days, but it's been long enough for me to yearn for you to be home again, I never realized I could miss a person like I've missed you," she says, with a velvety gentle voice, at the same time snuggling her face against his neck and chest.

"I've thought about you a lot, too," he replies softly.

"Darn," she says. "They're coming already, I didn't get to say half of all that's on my mind. Come over tomorrow, can you?"

"Yeh, sure I can, I can't be sure what time though."

"That's okay, I'll be here all day. You promise?"

"I'll be here, I promise."

The others climb aboard the carriage while Robert walks Beth around the corner of the house, back to the porch where Mrs. Sanders and Sheree wait to wave goodbye to their guests. It was decided during the evening that Sheree would spend two days at the Sanders farm. Then she would move home to be with her family.

"Good night, Mrs. Sanders, Thanks for your hospitality, and for taking Sheree in the way you have." Robert expresses from his heart.

"Think nothing of it. We're glad to do it," she acknowledges.

"I wonder, though, Robert, I'm getting a bit worried about Cole. He should have been back a couple of hours ago, and it'll be dark before long. I know it's a lot to ask, but could you wait around for a spell, I've got a feeling there's trouble brewing. It sure would be a comfort to have you around until he gets home."

"Oh, it's no trouble at all, ma'am. I know what you mean, just let me tell my family to go on without me." He assures her.

"Mother, you're scaring me!" Beth exclaims, but is really asking, what do you think is wrong?

Robert returns to find all three women on the porch with their arms around each other, facing the setting sun.

"Would you like me to get a horse and go out for a look around before it gets too dark to see anything?" he asks.

"Would you do that for me, honey? It would sure make me feel better." The older woman confesses.

"I'll go with you," Beth states, looking at her mother. "Is that okay with you?"

"It's all right with me. Sheree will keep me company, but it's up to your young man." Caroline lets him know he's in charge.

"I don't see why not," he responds. "Two sets of eyes are better than one. Come on, let's get saddled up."

The ride home in the carriage is mostly a quiet one. Everybody arose early this morning, so, the busy hours of a long day have taken their toll. Catching a nap is next to impossible because of the constant bouncing and noise of the rig. The few comments to be heard are about Sheree, her appearance, and her version of the escape.

It's a beautiful evening. The sun is about down, but the temperature hangs warm at eighty degrees. The moon is full and the sky free of clouds, displaying millions of stars in the heavens. The clopping sound of the horses hooves compete with the night critters and insects. A lonesome whippoorwill calling to its mate, barn owls far off in the distance, and the 'croak' of bullfrogs, as they answer each other, create an early evening symphony. The soft breeze, that has made the day more bearable, calms as the sun drops over the horizon.

Lights from the Andersons' house extend through the windows out into the yard, casting shadows in all directions. The carriage jerks to a stop, and Jim appears out of the darkness to grip the halters of the team, John knows he'll take good care of them before he retires for the day. Once the carriage is empty, Jim leads the horses toward the barn.

"Well folks, make yourselves at home, I'm sure there's coffee and something to eat there in the kitchen, if you've a mind. And whatever you might want to drink in the way of something to help you sleep is there in the den. But as for me, I'm going to bed, I bid you all a good night." John announces and starts up the stairs.

"I'll be right up, dear, Don't go to sleep," June tells her husband, not thinking how it sounds.

Everyone laughs causing her to retrace her words and laugh with them.

"Can I do anything at all to make anyone more comfortable?" she asks as a good host should.

"No, thanks, June, I think we're all pretty much tuckered out too. I'm sure we'll follow you in a few minutes." Marty answers for the group.

"All right then, remember, there's food in the kitchen, and there's always a pot of coffee on the stove. I'll see you all in the morning. Good night." She turns to follow her husband up the stairs.

Good nights are heard from the remaining four.

June steps into their bedroom to see John disrobing, getting ready to climb into bed.

"Whew, it's warm in here. Push the curtain back to let some air in," she instructs her husband.

John obediently responds to her wishes.

After closing the door, she crosses the floor to sit on a chair in front of their dresser, allowing her reflection, and his, to be seen in the mirror.

"She's not my daughter." She expresses unexpectedly, with the tone of a stern judge stating a fact.

"What?" he replies, puzzled, partly because he's not sure he heard correctly.

"That girl, over at the Sanders' place, is not Sheree. I don't know who she is, but she's not my Sheree."

Robert and Beth are nearing the main house of Der Bote having seen no sign of Cole or his horse. The house is dark, except at the back porch where light from the kitchen glows through the screen. As they stop and dismount, Alberta Mae appears through the doorway.

"Land sakes, what are you two doing out here this time of night? Is something wrong?"

"We're not sure. Mr. Sanders headed over this way more than five hours ago, and he's never made it back home. Has he been here today?" Robert's voice is serious.

"No, sir, Bob, he's not been here today. I've been in and out of this house all day, and I've not seen hide nor hair of him. Let me ask Sachel just to be sure. I'll be back in a minute or two." She disappears into the house.

Robert and Beth stand silent, holding their horses reins, awaiting her return.

She comes out pushing the screen door ahead of her with a platter holding two glasses of cold milk and several pieces of corn bread.

"Sachel's not seen him either. I guessed you might be feeling hungry and thirsty so I brought you a little something," she explains.

"Thank you, this looks real good." Beth shows her appreciation by taking a glass in her free hand.

Robert takes a piece of corn bread with his free hand and the milk with the hand still holding the reins.

"Albert Mae makes the best corn bread in the county, Beth. You'd better get a piece." he brags.

"My daddy said he had business here today with Colonel Housler. It's not like him to just wander off. Something must be wrong." The inflection of Beth's voice lets Robert know she's ready to resume the search.

"We'd better get going, Thanks a lot."

"If he shows up here, I'll tell him you're out looking for him and to get himself home." Randall's mom calls after them as they ride off.

There's no definite trail to follow between Der Bote and the Sanders' farm. Most people would take the easiest, shortest, ride, but Cole apparently hasn't done that; and it adds to the puzzle. The moon makes it bright enough to see anything not hidden in the shadows. Just to be sure, the two riders take the time to zigzag back and forth, looking under trees, in the hollows of the rolling hills—anywhere they think he might be lying injured, maybe unable to move. No luck.

There's no sign of his horse or of him at the house when they approach. Mrs. Sanders and Sheree are sitting on the porch step, looking out into the darkness. They stand up as the horses get nearer.

"Did you find him?" Caroline's voice is heavy with concern, knowing the answer.

"No., nothing; we went all the way to Der Bote and back, and we didn't see a sign of him." Beth's discouragement is relayed by her actions and the tone of her voice.

"I don't see much sense in searching any more until first light. We have no idea where to look. I'll get the horses fed and put them up for the night. Then, I'll fix a place and bed down in the barn. I'll know if he shows up that way, and if he doesn't, I'll be up early to get a fresh start." At this point, Robert doesn't know what else to do.

"I'll make up the daybed, there's room in the house for you. No sense you sleeping in the barn," Mrs. Sanders volunteers.

"If it's just the same to you, I'd rather stay in the barn. I don't know, I guess I need to be out here just in case he comes home," Robert politely insists.

"All right then, but don't leave here without your breakfast, you hear me? I won't sleep with Cole not here, so I'll be up early." Robert knows none of the three of them will get much sleep, and that she needs something to do. "We'll get Lou and the rest of the hands to help out in the morning."

"Yes, ma'am." He turns, with both horses in tow, headed for the barn.

John is fully awake now that June has flatly stated "that girl at the Sanders' place is not my daughter."

"You're going to have to explain yourself. Why would you say that?"

"A mother knows her children. The way she smiles, the way she uses her eyes, and gestures with her head. Things like that. It's not her. She's not Sheree."

"She looks like Sheree to me. God, she's the image of her sister, Charlotte. If you changed the color of her hair and her skin tone, you couldn't tell them apart."

"Maybe you couldn't, but I could. That young woman isn't Sheree."

"I'm going to have to think about this, honey. Robert and Randall went after her, they found her, freed her from the Company, and brought her home. Are you saying they took the wrong girl? If that's the case, why wouldn't she say so?"

"I don't know, at least not yet. I need to think more about it. Promise me this, will you? Look into it. Let's not just accept her as ours and never know for sure. I tell you I've never been more sure of anything in my life. She's not Sheree."

Robert puts the horses in their stalls, gives them a small feeding of oats, and a fork of hay. He throws the saddle blankets over a pile of straw as the base for his bed. Beth brought a blanket and pillow. After taking the feed bags off the horses, it seems to be a good idea to hang the burning lantern on a nail above the open doors of the barn. Then he strips his clothes down to his underwear, lies down on the saddle blankets, and spreads the comforter from the house out over himself. He's glad Beth remembered a pillow.

The day has been long with its stressful moments, so, it feels good just to get his weight off his bones, to lie down. His mind rehashes the activities of the day. The horses seem restless, as if they know Cole isn't home. Could they miss him tending to them? Probably.

It seems like hours have passed without sleep. His body jerks at the loud snort of a horse clearing its nose.

"I wonder if it's getting light yet?" He turns over to sit up, attempting a look out through the open barn door. It's startling to see a horse standing inside, facing him. The flickering of the lantern flame keeps the shadows moving on the walls and floor. After rubbing his eyes for a few seconds, another look proves the horse is indeed there.

His first thought is, 'how did you get out of your stall?' But then, as his mind's eye clears, he notices the horse is still saddled, the reins are dragging the ground.

"What the—?" Adrenaline shoots through his body. The comforter flies aside, he's on his feet in a heart beat. It's then he's aware of something hanging from the stirrup. Barefoot, clothed in just his underwear, he moves silently, swiftly, to the horse's side. It's a leg, all twisted and attached to the body of a man lying on the dirt floor face down, his arms stretched straight up over his head. The leg and foot are pointing in the opposite direction of where they should.

Nothing moves except the horses head and ears as he approaches. He bends down, one knee on the floor, to pull up on the man's nearest shoulder, wanting a look at his face. Anyone can see that this poor body has left the saddle to get caught in the stirrup, and has been dragged for miles. His clothes are shredded and torn, exposing his legs, arms, and back, where bruises, scrapes, cuts, and blood, make it difficult to see skin. There's blood all over the back of his head, some of it dried and matted with dirt and debris in his gray hair. His free leg lies under the horse.

"Oh God. It's Cole," he whispers. The fear of knowing the worst makes him hesitate before putting his fingers against his longtime neighbor's neck.

"There's a heartbeat. Faint, but it's there. Thank the Lord."

The horses hear him declare, "I should free his leg before anything else, I sure don't want this horse to walk off with him. I don't need to worry about hurting him, he's out cold. Uuggghhh! I don't like doing this. There, he's free. Be careful, Bob, lay his leg down easy." Talking out loud helps somehow.

"Now, we'll just put you in a stall so you're out of the way." He explains to the horse while shoving him saddle, bridle, and all. He closes the stall door, slips his clothes on, and runs to the house.

Mrs. Sanders is sitting in the dimly lit kitchen, her rocker facing the open door to the porch. Having never been to bed, her open eyes stare out at nothing. Her head snaps to attention to see Cole coming through the door. But it isn't Cole, it's Robert. He speaks.

"He's home, in the barn. He's hurt real bad, but he's alive. We need to get Doc out here right away."

Sheree and Beth are coming down the stairs to hear the news. "What can we do?"

"Run down to Lou's shack, and tell him to get to town and bring Doc Shaw right away." Mrs. Sanders takes charge and will handle it from here. "Get some water from the well and bring it to the barn! Hurry! Show me, Robert."

Mrs. Sanders arrives at the barn to see her husband lying face down on the dirt floor. Her first move is to check his pulse at his wrist. Satisfied, she carefully moves over him to determine the extent of his injuries. "How did he get here?" she asks.

"His horse dragged him home, with his foot still caught in the stirrup. See there, it's all twisted the wrong way." Robert cringes as he explains. "It looks to me like he's left the saddle for one reason or another, and got his foot tangled up. Whatever it was must have spooked his horse and caused him to run."

"We'd better not move him too much until Doc says we can," Cole's wife cautions. "I'll put a cool compress on his head as soon as Sheree gets here with the water. That shouldn't hurt anything."

At that moment, Sheree arrives with water splashing over the sides of a bucket.

"Lou's on his way. He said to tell you that he'll get Doc back here as quick as he can." Elizabeth rushes into the barn explaining. With no other way to console her, she puts her arm around Caroline's shoulders and looks down at her father.

Caroline Sanders has a stout build, carrying her one hundred forty pounds on a five-foot-three frame, but is trim and firm. She's never been a raving beauty, but her soft friendly brown eyes and easy broad warm smile make her beautiful in her own way.

Cole and she were childhood sweethearts and married when she turned fourteen, him eighteen. Elizabeth is their only child, as her birth was difficult and left her mother unable to bear another. Caroline's almost white, gray hair is worn wrapped in a bun up on the back of her head. It's long when she lets it down, but only Cole can attest to it. He's been the only one to see her that way for the last twenty years. Their love for each other has grown into an understanding. Unable to remember the last time she's heard or said those three words makes no difference, the love is still there and they both know it.

Robert looks at his pocket watch in the light of the lantern, one forty-five.

"It shouldn't take more than two hours, two and a half at the most, for Doc to get here," he announces.

"Hold on, honey, you're home and we're getting you some help. Just hold on," she says quietly to her husband as she kneels, resting on her heels, beside him.

Time moves at a snail's pace. Two thirty, ten past three, three forty-five, fifteen past four.

"They should be here any minute," Robert stresses, pacing back and forth just outside the barn door.

Sheree made a pot of coffee for them and the soon-to-arrive Dr. Shaw.

Four thirty comes and goes, ten minutes to five, five thirty.

The worried young Anderson man has the urge to announce he's going to town after the doc himself, with the words ready to come out of his mouth—then.

"Horses on the run, faint, but coming this way!" he yells.

Cheers come from the front porch of the house where the help, every man, woman and child of them, have gathered to pray and wait for the doctor to come.

Elizabeth and Sheree appear from the barn with their heads tilted up toward the sky. "Thank you, God, they're here."

Mrs. Sanders hasn't moved a muscle since Lou left, except for putting cool water on Cole's head. The rinsing of the white dish cloth has turned the water in the bucket a dark clear red.

Doc arrives, jumps from his horse, medicine bag in hand, and walks briskly into the barn, paying attention to no one.

"I'm awful sorry, Caroline. There was a ruckus in town just as Lou woke me up. I had to take a bullet out of a man's chest before I could leave. Why don't you move over here, out of the way, and let me see what's going on here. Robert, bring that lantern closer," Doc orders. "I need to see what has to be done first. There's scissors in my bag there. Cut his clothes off. By the looks of them that won't take long."

Caroline is the first to begin cutting, Beth and Sheree are right there with her.

Doc starts with his leg, the one turned the wrong way. "Don't move him much until I stabilize this leg; I don't want to put a sliver of bone through an artery. Robert, see if you can find me a couple of pieces of wood, something two or three feet long, and maybe a couple of inches wide. And have someone bring me ten or twelve strips of cloth about three inches wide and three feet long." Doc knows he needs to splint this mangled limb, and he'll need all of the sterile bandages in his bag for Cole's other injuries.

Doc has Sheree get another bucket of clean water, and begins to wash the blood and dirt off Cole's bare back. "This is going to take a while Caroline. Why don't you let these young ladies here take you back to the house, I'm here now, I'll take care of him. So far, I'm not seeing anything worse than his leg. I've got to turn him over yet, but I'm betting I'll find things the same as his back. Now, go ahead, and I'll make sure you know of any changes. He's a tough old coot, I believe he's going to make it."

Caroline slowly gets to her feet and with the two young women at her elbows, they move from the barn toward the house.

Robert returns with the requested boards just after the women leave.

"Get Lou in here to help us," Doc commands.

Lou is standing just outside the barn doors and hears he's needed inside.

"Take a hold of his foot, Robert, and pull with a steady pressure; firm, but not too hard. First thing we're going to do is turn him over, so watch for bones trying to push through the skin on his leg. Lou, you turn Cole over this way on his back, and I'll work his other leg as he goes."

"I don't think I can lift and turn him over at the same time," Lou says.

"It'll probably take two or three moves to get it done, but you can do it." Doc assures. "How about you, Robert?"

"I don't move his leg, am I right?"

"That's right, we'll turn him to face the right way, You just hold the leg still, and let us know if you see any bones trying to poke through," Doc repeats patiently.

"I'm all set. Let's do it," Lou announces.

"All right, now remember, I have to move his other leg under his bad one as you turn him. Easy does it."

"Ready? Now."

"Uuuuhhh!" Lou strains from lifting Cole.

"That's good, now, again."

"Uuuuhhhhh!"

"One more time will do it. How you doing, Robert?"

"Looks good, Doc."

"Okay, Lou, now."

"Uuuhh!"

"That'll do. Hold that leg steady; I need to look him over before we set it."

"He's going to need a few stitches to close some of these cuts, but I don't see anything all that serious. It's hard to tell about his head wounds. No way to know how hard he hit."

It takes another hour and a half for Doc to clean, stitch, and bandage Cole's wounds. Setting his leg is the toughest part. It takes the three of them, pulling, and pushing to align the broken bones. His twisted hip popped back into place in the process.

Elizabeth moves between the house and barn to report the progress to her mother.

Daylight has replaced the darkness as a new day begins.

"That's about all I can do for now. We can move him without too much worry. We just need to be careful not to drop him. Have a bed made downstairs, and bring a couple of clothes props; we'll make a litter with this comforter here, and get him inside," Doc directs Beth on her last trip.

While Robert and Lou move Cole to the house, Doc explains to Caroline that the broken bones, cuts, and bruises will heal in time. He was glad Cole was unconscious when they worked on his hip and leg, but now it's the thing that concerns him most.

"There's no way of telling what, if anything, is wrong inside his head. We need to give it some time. The next forty-eight hours will let us know. If he wakes up enough to swallow, give him plenty of water, all he'll drink. If he wants to eat, that's okay, too. He's going to be in a lot of hurt, so here's a bottle of pain killer. It'll make him want to sleep though, and I'd rather he didn't for a few hours. So, watch how much you give him. No more than a tablespoon every six hours. A little more often if he complains a lot, no more than three days though."

"Is it morphine, Doc?" Sheree asks.

"It's almost the same thing. You know, I thought you were Charlotte Anderson when I first saw you, but I can see now, you're not."

“I’m Sheree Anderson, Doc Do you remember me?”

“Remember you? Lordy girl, how could I ever forget you? I buried you a little over five years ago.”

Mrs. Sanders interrupts, “Is there anything else we should know?”

“That’s about it. Like I say, I believe he’s going to be okay. I’ll be back out here tomorrow to check on him, but right now I need to get back to town. Office hours, you know, and I need to check on last nights patient. People will be looking for me.”

“What do I owe you? Whatever it is it won’t be nearly enough for all you’ve done.” Caroline ponders, wanting to settle up.

“I don’t have any idea, Caroline. Right now, you just take care of Cole, and we’ll work something out later on.”

Handshakes, hugs, and thanks are given all around. Doc mounts up and leaves for town.

The Andersons are up, getting ready for the day ahead. He knows his wife would like nothing better than to convince him someone is posing as Sheree. A piece of information he’s kept from his wife to protect her, keeps coming to the front of his mind. The night of the ball, in the barn, an ambassador of the next president of the Union told him his daughter—the one supposedly born dead—is actually alive and well, living at the Company. Perhaps June’s right with her suspicion. But why? What would the Company have to gain? To his knowledge, the Company, as yet, has no idea that he’s in the process of building an organization to counter the Union’s enemies. They probably believe he has a chance of being the next Governor, but that’s not a sure thing. If they have placed her as a spy, what must they have in mind for her to do?

“What’s in store for you today?” June inquires as they finish dressing.

“The boys and I are having a meeting that should last until dinner. By the middle of the afternoon we should have some free time on our hands. Why?”

“I was thinking, do you want us gals at your meeting? If not, maybe we’ll go into town for a while. I think we would all enjoy that.”

“Go ahead, just keep your eyes open. We wouldn’t want you all caught in a crossfire of some war mongering rebels and yanks.” John is relieved that the women won’t join the men in the meeting, but is a little edgy about them going alone.

“Why not have Jim and Josh drive you in?” he continues.

“Great idea,” she replies. “That’s what we’ll do. We can have a good time, just us girls.”

While the entire household is around the dining-room table enjoying breakfast, Robert arrives from the Sanders’ farm. All conversation from that point on is about Cole, his accident, and his current condition. As anyone would expect, consensus of the group follows that his horse threw him, and that he was dragged. Robert informs the Anderson family of Sheree’s request to stay and help out at the Sanders’ place, at least until they know the outcome of Cole’s injuries. He excuses himself to lie down for a few hours.

The five women: June, Selma, Rachell, Charlotte, and one of Josh's daughters about Charlotte's age, along with Jim and Josh, leave in the large carriage for town. It's about nine o'clock and already the temperature is nearing eighty degrees. It's going to be a hot, beautiful sunlit day.

The men file into the den to start their meeting. The large oval table seems agreeable to them today, so they gather at one end, remove their coats, hang them on the backs of their chairs, and sit down. Belle brings a coffee service and sets it near them on the table. She closes the doors as she leaves.

"Word from Washington has it that the war is unavoidable. Five states are already drafting documents to cede from the Union. Others are certain to follow. Our organization must be in place and effective within a year. Otherwise, the business of the war will engulf our efforts, and dilute our efforts. Marty and I have a plan, which, we believe, will make it happen. It's all here in these pages." John hands the colonel and Marty each a binder, three fourths of an inch thick. "I'd like to go over it to get your input before we declare it the framework for the Sons."

The afternoon, and the next two days pass without big problems Cole Sanders has regained consciousness, but is having difficulty recalling the details of his accident. It's as if his memory has been erased back to two days before. Doc says this happens sometimes with head injuries. It could take six days or six months to clear up.

Sheree is coming home today for the first time in over five years.

The Schoener's children arrived to become a handful for Belle and June. The Houslers are commuting from Der Bote, as necessary.

Robert is getting closer by the day to Beth.

June has been trying to catch John alone since breakfast. Finally, she sees him leave the house through the back door by himself. She has to run to catch up.

"Can I talk to you?" she asks, as she comes to his side.

"Sure, what about?" He keeps walking toward the barn.

"Sheree, what else." She stops and puts her hand on his arm, causing him to turn toward her.

"She'll be here shortly, and I'm not sure how to handle things. I need to feel that you believe me about her, or at least you haven't closed your mind to it," she frankly states.

"I don't disbelieve you, honey. I'd just like to have some proof of my own before starting anything. I'm checking a few things out, but I need some time."

"How much time?"

"Sixty days, maybe?"

"That's two months. I'm supposed to live with a stranger for a daughter, under this roof for two months, and keep quiet about it? You know me better than that, I'll never be able to do it."

"What's happened to the woman I married? Is she still in there with you? She would look at this as a game, her against the stranger. Who's smarter, slyer? Who can put on the best façade?" he challenges.

"You mean, if she's here to spy on us, why can't I make her believe we've accepted her as Sheree; only to spy on her?" June's eyebrows raise, her nose thins a bit, and a little smile forms on her lips.

"Exactly, just for sixty days," he confirms.

"I'll do it, as long as you believe me." She needs assurances.

"I think we'll have more than enough proof by then." He gives his wife a hug, then turns toward the barn.

"I love you, John Anderson." Reaches his ears as he walks away, causing him to raise his right hand in acknowledgment.

Three days pass.

Rachell Schoener and the children are leaving tomorrow, and none too soon for June and Belle. Cole Sanders's memory is almost completely returned. He's requested Colonel Housler to come to see him, claiming unfinished business.

Marty is helping John and several of the farmhands move some hay up into the loft of the barn. He looks out across the barnyard to the horizon. "Rider coming, John."

"Who is it?"

"Can't say for sure, but the way he's dressed it looks like the colonel."

They both drop their hay hooks and walk out toward the end of the corral, which is attached to that side of the barn.

"It's the colonel, all right," Mr. Anderson determines as the rider gets closer.

"John! Marty!" the colonel greets his friends with a smile as he dismounts.

"What brings you out our way?" John asks.

"You've heard Cole Sanders is on the mend and has his memory back, I suppose?" the colonel inquires. Then, without waiting for an answer, he continues. "He's asked me over to handle some unfinished business, and I thought you both might like the opportunity to stop by and see him too, unless you've already been over there since his accident. We can ride over to his place together."

They look at each other. Since it seems to be John's call, Marty says, "It'll get us away from this work, and you've not seen him since his accident."

The three men make their way to the Sanders' farm and sit talking with Cole about his ordeal. Caroline is as happy as she can be, tending to her husband, making everything just so for his friends.

After thirty minutes, Cole says.

"Honey, will you quit fussing over me, and get that telegram for the colonel? I was in town the morning before my accident, and was at the telegraph office to pick up my mail. This telegram was there for you and Virgil asked me to drop it off. I told him I'd be glad to do it, and I would have, if I hadn't had this damned accident. Anyway, here it is now."

Colonel Housler has no idea what the telegram is about as he accepts it from Caroline. Without thinking, and from curiosity, he opens it immediately.

"You've got me." He explains, "It just says, 'You have company coming,' that's it. It's signed, 'Barker.' I have no idea what this is about. Someone must have mixed something up somewhere." He tucks the paper into his breast pocket.

Another half hour passes with friendly conversation.

"We're tiring you Cole," John says. "We'd better let you get some rest. Besides, it's time we're getting home."

The three men leave and are just out of sight of the house.

"What was that all about, Colonel?" John wonders about the telegram.

"It said just what I read, 'You have company coming, signed Barker.' It probably means another agent has been assigned to this area, and I should be on the lookout for him. I've not seen nor heard anything though."

"Charles, I'm getting the feeling that the organization keeping you in check is the same one we've been charged to deal with, the Company. It's too much of a coincidence. I think I know who the agent is, but I'd rather not say right now. I want to see how the contact is managed. That is to say, how you are eventually contacted. You'll understand completely shortly."

Six weeks pass in a blur.

Lilly is in the medical building, at La Nesra, complaining about an illness.

"I don't know, doctor. I'm not able to keep a thing in my stomach in the mornings, even crackers come up. It usually passes, though, and after a couple of hours, I can eat okay; if I watch what it is."

"Let me examine you. How long has this been going on?" the doctor asks,

"About a week now," she replies.

"How's your monthly visitor?" he asks.

"I'm a little late, I guess."

"You're pregnant, young lady," he blurts out indignantly. "I'll have to report this. Who's the father of this child?"

At the Anderson farm, Sheree has made herself completely at home. Everyone has accepted her back; everything seems to be falling into place.

"It's time I make a move to find my contact." She thinks, lying in bed, before going to sleep. "Sally and the director of security told me to look for messenger. They told me they would let my contact know I'm coming." Peaceful sleep comes easily for the young woman.

It's morning before she knows it; time to start another glorious day.

"What a wonderful place this is to live," she says to herself. "The people here are so nice, so unassuming, so honest with their feelings for one another. A person could get used to a life like this and never want to leave." She finishes dressing and bounces down the stairs to greet everyone for breakfast.

John is away for a few days, so she expects to see June, Robert, and Charlotte at the table in the kitchen, with Belle busy cooking, Robert is missing.

"Morning, all," she chimes. "Where's Robert?"

"He left earlier to pick up Randy at Der Bote. They're going fishing," Charlotte replies smartly.

"Oh, I see." Sheree sits at the table, thinking.

"Der Bote . . . Der Bote; that's German for 'the messenger.' It couldn't be, could it? Could it be that simple? If it is, which one is it: the colonel, or his wife, Selma? I'd better be sure before I expose myself, and that's a fact."

June sits across the table looking at her impostor daughter.

"You little hussy. What's going on in that mind of yours? I've got the proof I need now. Pooch, your horse, wants nothing to do with you. He'd rather be with me—and that's saying something. Your dog, Peaches, growls every time you get close to her. I kept thinking, there must be a way to prove it to John, and finally it just came to me. Sheree fell off a wagon and hit her head on the edge of the steel wheel when she was five years old. There was an inch and a half cut under her hair. Doc had to sew it up, and it left a scar. I checked when you were asleep, you little devil. It's not there. Just wait until John gets home, this will all be over."

Chapter Twenty-One

At La Nesra, Lilly is meeting with Mr. Vaughn in his office.

"I don't want you to worry about a thing, my dear. Your being pregnant is not the end of the world. We've had pregnancies here many times over the years; we've yet to lose a mother or baby."

"But I don't want to be pregnant." Lilly addresses the much older man. "I'm too young, and the baby won't have a father. Don't you understand? I was raped; I don't want his baby. Can't we get rid of it somehow?" Her voice quivers.

"To abort the child would cause a good deal of danger to you. Besides, it's been determined, after much consideration, that we want this child." Lilly cuts him off.

"Then I'll get ri—"

"You'll do no such thing. You'll probably murder yourself in the process." He is hotly adamant. "I'm going to explain to you now how we are going to handle this, and you can take this as a warning. If you give me, or anyone else, the idea that you plan to harm yourself or your baby, I'll put you in chains for the duration of your pregnancy. Now, listen to me, you'll see—it won't be all that bad for you. You'll have everything you need or want. We'll pamper you and your child to extremes. As we speak, work has begun on a small cottage to house you and your baby. It's back away from this building, and will be completed by the time you'll want your privacy. It'll have a nursery, a midwife or maid's quarters, and all the necessities of home."

Lilly interrupts.

"Oh, I see, you're planning to stick me away—somewhere out of everyone's sight—and slip my food under the door so no one will have to look at me."

"Settle down. We're planning nothing of the kind. Just sit still for a few minutes and let me explain." Mr. Vaughn is doing his best to control his impatience. "You will be permitted to have any one female live there with you, for as long as you like. She can keep you company, and you'll have someone other than your maid to help out."

"I can pick anyone I want?"

"Yes, that's correct. Anyone except one of our staff, of course."

"What if I choose Falcon?"

"I believe I said any female, now, didn't I?"

"Will I ever see Falcon again?" she asks, wide eyed.

"Of course, you will, let me continue. Your circle of friends will have no restrictions whatsoever. But because of your need to rest, there will be a curfew. Other than that, you can associate with whomever you choose, and that includes Falcon."

"Is Eagle really dead?" An unexpected question.

"Yes, Lilly, he's no longer with us. Now, will you settle down and let me tell you a few things? I don't want to be here all day. I have other matters that need my attention."

"I'll try." Her exasperated remark makes her squirm in her seat.

"Good. I'm going to take a chance with you. I'm going to explain some of the real reasons you're here, and the reason we replaced you with Amber."

Lilly's eyes turn to immediately focus on the face of the man speaking.

"Oh, I see I have your attention now. Do you think we aren't aware that you know about the switch. I'm convinced you have totally underestimated our abilities to know everything that goes on here. Be quiet for a few minutes, I'll open your mind, and let you know who you have been dealing with these last six years."

"The Company is a world-wide organization with people and ties to just about everything. It's been around for centuries, so it's had a lot of time to build and infiltrate every nook and cranny of our society. Training facilities are set up and operating all over the world, educating, and producing people. People with the proper training, ready when they're needed, are strategically placed in various positions, enabling our organization to have eyes and ears everywhere. Our purpose here, at La Nesra, with you, and the others, is to train agents. The difference among here and the other facilities is, they train people to do regular jobs, while we train people with special talents. We get the cream of the crop. Our people—you—will be used to accomplish special, unexpected assignments that could change the future of this world. You'll learn as we go along that our Company is farther advanced in technology, such as the sciences, mathematics, life zones, and hyper travel, beyond anything you understand. Our sole purpose is to bring all the countries of the world together, all working for the same goal, the same end. Each nation will have the same level, or standard of living, and the same opportunities as any other country on earth. Peace will reign since every living soul will have everything they want or need."

Lilly interrupts, again. "It sounds to me like a world full of slaves with someone telling them what they need and what they'll have. I suppose they'll all dress alike, too?" Her attitude is one of defiance. "I mean, look at us here, we all dress alike, boys and girls."

"Well, as oppressive as it seems to you right now, consider that you won't be one of them. The people chosen to be trained here are destined for much larger responsibilities. For which, the rewards are enormous."

"I imagine there's a person who's getting filthy rich from everyone's efforts. Some tyrant?" She counters looking for a fight.

"See, this is why you're here. You understand completely, but it's not one person, it's the Company. The Company, of which, you are a part."

"But why?"

"It would take days to go into the detail you're looking for. You'll learn as you go along," he summarizes. The actions of his hands reveal there is more coming, and he wants to move on.

"We've trained Amber for years to be you. She doesn't possess the powers you have, but having her take your place will put you in a position here to become more than you can imagine."

Lilly straightens up in her chair.

"You were brought here some six years ago to begin your training. Your family didn't want to let you go, and you didn't want to come. We have believed that as long as they pine for you, there will be a chance they will come looking, and they have. Lilly, Amber is a perfect duplicate of you. They will never suspect anything. She'll live the rest of her life as you. Your family will accept her as their own, and your continued existence here with us will be unknown to them."

She feels agitated, boxed in. "What about her, won't Amber get tired of being me? What if I get out of here and tell them what you've done?"

"Think about it. She's there, she's Sheree. If you try to discredit her, you'll be the one on trial, not her. As for her getting tired of being you, she is you. That's all she knows. She isn't acting out a part, she's you. How does one get tired of being themselves? Besides, we have, also, trained her to do a job while she's you?"

"To spy on my family and friends, right?" Lilly curtly interjects.

"That, and to keep an eye on a few other agents we have working in that area. Frankly, though, the job we gave her is to give her a purpose more than anything else. We don't expect much in the way of reports from her."

"It sounds like you've thought of everything," she calmly concedes.

"I doubt it, but we'll deal with it when something shows up," he says, feeling self-assured. "Now, let's talk about you and your impressive powers."

"We, of course, are aware of your ability to leave your body and move about as an apparition, having mass and volume. Because of the mass and volume, you are unable to pass through solid objects as you would imagine a spirit might do. You've discovered you can pass through the face of a mirror, and move around in a world on the other side. Am I correct so far?" He looks into her eyes and waits for an answer.

"So far." Is her hesitant response.

"Do you understand anything at all about your ability to do this? Would you like to know more about it?" Her mind races as she hears his words.

"Yes, I mean, no. What I mean to say is, I don't understand much about it at all and, yes, I want to know everything."

"We'll start at the beginning, then," he offers.

She adjusts her position in her chair, getting ready to listen intently.

"You were born with a nerve property in your brain which allows you to sleep in an almost deathlike manner. A chemical put into your veins can induce the sleep, while another can wake you up. Your body contains these chemicals within itself, but, it takes a trauma or a shock of some sort for it to be induced into your system. Now, you've learned to produce them at will, and have the ability to control when you sleep and when you awaken, all by yourself." When he stops to take a breath, she interrupts.

"Oh, I see, but what abou—?"

He shows the flat of his right hand to quiet her in mid-sentence.

"While you appear to be near death, your soul is in a state of leaving or staying inside your body. You've discovered the way to float free and away from your physical self. Now, look at it this way, positive and negative. Positive is your physical body, while negative is your out-of-body persona, one with mass, volume, and intellect. To explain further, a photograph is produced by first creating a negative, then through a chemical process, a positive or likeness is installed on tin or paper to produce a picture. So, to get a picture of a bowl of fruit, you open a hole in a closed camera allowing the reflecting light of the scene to fall upon a piece of light sensitive material, called a plate or film, creating a negative. After processing, the negative becomes positive again, only in a different form, it's a picture, not a bowl of fruit. Does this make sense to you?"

"I think so, but I have to tell you, I don't much care about all the reasons I can do these things. I want to know what else there is I can do. I want to know what that other place is all about. How long can I stay out of my body? Who are those people in there?"

"Aren't you the least bit interested in why and how this works for you?" he asks.

"Like you say, later on maybe, but not now. There's time to learn all that. Tell me about the place inside the mirror?" she replies.

He settles back into his chair while letting out a long breath through his slightly parted lips.

"I guess I'll never understand the need of youth to move along so quickly. It seems to be all about what's next instead of using time to notice anything taking place now. But that said, I suppose there's nothing wrong with jumping ahead for a while.

"Have you met Zola?" he asks, surprising Lilly that he knows of her.

"You've met her?" She says, her eyes brighten at the news.

"Not personally, but I have a good amount of information about her, and others of that kind. What do you know about her?" He encourages the young girl to trust him.

"I know she's very kind and helpful. I feel like I can trust her. It's strange, I mean, how she looks with no legs, yet she moves around so fast. I think things and she knows all about me. I hear her inside my head, not through my ears." Lilly begins to let down her guard.

Mr. Vaughn leans over his desk toward her and becomes very serious. A frown forms on his forehead and his eyes narrow. He says.

"Be very careful when you're in their world. It can be a very dangerous place to be for those with little understanding of it."

"What do you mean? I've not seen anything dangerous in there."

"Zola is an angel. There are countless other angels, much like her, whose task it is to keep peace in that world. These angels don't have emotions as you might expect. With no feelings for the souls in there, they have the ability to exterminate any unwanted being with no remorse whatsoever. They know their jobs and do them efficiently. Should you give any one of them the slightest reason to doubt you. Well, you won't be coming back to this world."

"Wow! If that happened to me, what would happen to my life body here? Has it ever happened to anyone you know?" She's totally drawn into the conversation.

"Yes, I've known one or two. A body left here without its spiritual form doesn't have a life. It's like being left in a coma."

"What happens to them, I mean, what if their spirit is lost forever . . . in there?"

"The body stays alive as long as it's attended to with its physical needs, food, water, air, and elimination. If left unattended, it will eventually die."

"What happens to the spirit if the body dies? Does it die too?"

"The complete answer to that will take some time to explain. Simply put, if the spirit is in the body when death occurs, it leaves and travels to the hall of spirits. If the spirit is not in the body, then it will roam, not belonging anywhere, until it finds its body. Then it can enter its dead human body, and thus be transferred to the hall of spirits. A spirit is unable to live in a normal way here if its body is not alive. The way they have to live is gruesome"

"Are there any, right now—alive bodies, I mean—waiting on their spirit to come back?"

"Oh my, yes, not here at La Nesra, but there are many, several hundred perhaps, being kept alive, waiting. A mirror is fixed in front of their faces, just in case their spirit is being held captive somewhere. If the spirit breaks free, it will be pulled back to its body."

"Have some of them came back?" She's intrigued with the excitement of it all. "I'll bet if they do, they'll never go back in there again."

"You're right there. They would be noticed almost instantly if they were to go back, so, they're not permitted to enter there again, although, some of them want to go for their own reasons. Another threat thrives there as well, Lilly. Not every soul that moves from here to there is as pure and good as you. Some have been around for scores of years, moving in and out as they work their devious plans against mankind. They've learned to avoid the angels' wrath with façades of purity, all the while using that world, with its advantages, against their foes. To become their target means there is no safety there, or here. They are relentless with the chase, never to be satisfied until their prey is eliminated."

"How can I tell who they are?"

"At first, you won't be able to, but the more you work there, the more obvious it becomes."

"He seems to have all the answers, but how?" She thinks as she listens.

"How do you know all of this?" Her insides quiver awaiting his response.

"If you think about it Lilly, it's obvious."

Life goes on at the Anderson farm.

June rises to her tip toes to give her husband a welcome-home kiss as he enters the house through the front door. A big squeeze, another kiss, and they relax, pulling away just enough to see each other's faces.

"I've missed you," she says with a smile. "It's good to have you home."

"Me too, honey, this traveling and being gone almost all the time is hard. Some days I wonder if it's all going to be worth it. I can do something else, you know," he says with a bit of despair.

"Now, John Anderson, that's not the man I married. We'll get through this. In a few months, maybe a year, you'll have people in place and won't need to be at the helm every minute. I never thought I'd have an opportunity to say this to you, but, you're country needs you. Can you take us all with you when you go back?"

"I've thought about that, but I probably wouldn't see you all that much, most of my time is spent in meetings, or over a pile of papers at my desk."

"A few hours a week is better than nothing at all. I say, we'll all go with you, expecting to stay ten days or so. Let's see how it works out. Perhaps we should think about getting a place there, and sort of move back and forth."

"Let's plan on that. When I leave, you're all coming with me. I feel better already." His broad smile lets June know he is pleased with her.

"Where are the children?" he continues

"I believe the girls are upstairs working on Charlotte's hair. Those two have become really close over these past few weeks. You know, if we don't send that girl pretending to be our daughter packing, I'll have to get her some clothes. She's been wearing Charlotte's up to now. She didn't bring much with her." Two birds with one stone; she cannot believe she's been able to get to this topic so soon.

"Yeah, I know," he begins. "I stopped in town long enough to ask Doc to join us here at the house tomorrow morning for a meeting about that very thing. And on the way home, I went by Cole Sanders' place to see how he's doing, and invited them too."

"If Robert's around, I'd like him to ride over to the Houslers and do the same with them. I want to be sure we make the right move with Sheree."

"Good." She supports her husband's thinking, especially if it gets the impostor from under her feet. "He's around here somewhere with Elizabeth. It seems like they're together from dawn to dark any more. You never see one without the other. I'll ask Belle to round him up. Now, let's get you some coffee and something to hold you until supper."

"That's the best offer I've had for some time," he says gladly.

"Then you're going to really like my offer for later tonight," she whispers coyly, smiling into his eyes.

They walk toward the kitchen, their arms around each other's waist.

Upstairs in Charlotte's bedroom, Sheree is working on her sister's hair.

"Will you hold still and quit being silly. You won't like it when I pull your hair with this brush," Sheree warns.

Charlotte's hair is considerably darker, as is her skin, than her sister's. Their builds, facial appearances, and ages would lead you to believe they're twins, which, in fact, they are and then some.

"Daddy's home, I hear him downstairs. Mama's always happy when he gets home," she observes.

"Why's he gone so much? Where does he work? What does he do that keeps him away so much?" Sheree's questions seem to fit the occasion to Charlotte.

"I think the government, over at Maryland. I don't know what he actually does, though." Charlotte turns on her chair to look at her sister when she hears.

"Do you think he still likes me? I feel like Mama doesn't, not all that much anyway." Sheree puts as much feeling into the words as they will hold. "I don't know, sometimes I think she doesn't believe I'm your real sister."

Charlotte wastes no time responding. "Well, the reason for that is, you and I both know you're not, she probably knows it, too."

"Do you think I'm not your sister?" Sheree feels her heart sink. She thought she was secure with her identity.

"Oh really now, I've known since the day you got back. Don't worry, I won't tell. You're a nice person, even if you're not my sister. And I'm having so much fun since you came here I'm not going to mess it up."

"Why do you think I'm not your sister?"

"It's everything. You don't talk like her, you don't act like her, but mostly, I think it's the way you treat me—and Randall. Sheree didn't know it, but I knew about her and Randall. She would never miss a chance to spend time with him. You act like you don't even know him, and it hurts him. She would never do that. And me—Mama had to make my real sister play with me. She never wanted much to do with me. Now we're together most of the time. I know you're not her."

"I've been gone a long time. A person changes when they're gone away from their family. You don't know what all I've been through. It would change anybody."

"Well, I know this: Pooch never liked me the same way he liked my sister, and that goes for Peaches, too. Now, Pooch would rather be with me than you; and Peaches runs and growls when you go toward her. Animals don't forget, they remember people."

Sheree is reeling from the onslaught. To admit she isn't her sister is impossible, she knows that. How to counter Charlotte? That's what she has to do, and quickly. To wait or say nothing will only add credibility to her thinking.

Charlotte speaks again.

"Like I said, I don't care if you're my sister or not. I like you and that's good enough for me. I get lonely around here. And besides, I've never had a best friend."

"Thank you for that. You know, where I've been, I've not had a best friend either. I don't know how right now, but I'll prove to you that I am your sister, Sheree. So, let's keep your opinions between us. There's no sense in upsetting everybody for no good reason." She can breathe now. Thank goodness Charlotte continued to speak her mind. Sheree's training tells her to change the subject, indicating a lack of importance of their conversation.

"Mama says she's going to buy me some new clothes. You know anything I get you can wear, if you want to."

"I'll be glad to get mine back," Charlotte truthfully answers, then smiles and says, "But since you offered, I'll take you up on it."

"Sheree! Charlotte! Can you come down here for a few minutes? Your Daddy's home," June yells up the stairs.

Without responding, the girls drop what they're doing and bounce down the stairs, looking for their father.

He's sitting at the table in the kitchen with a cup of coffee, and a slab of Belle's sugar cream pie. He gets up as they enter to give them each a hug.

"Have you two been minding your mother while I was away?" he jokingly asks.

"We're not babies, you know." Charlotte replies with a smart attitude.

"Oooppps. My mistake." Her father admits with a big smile.

"How long will you be home?" Sheree asks quietly, not able to use the word *Daddy* just yet.

"A few days I expect." He replies with the same quiet manner.

"Your mother and I were just talking about the two of you. How would you like to go into town with Belle tomorrow, to do some shopping? We're going to be tied up most of the morning and Belle says she'd like to pick up several things. I'm sure you can find something for yourselves. And I know your mother will work that out for you." He wants to be sure Sheree is nowhere close to the upcoming meeting.

Meanwhile, back at La Nesra.

"It's obvious." Mr. Vaughn has just replied to Lilly's question of how do you know about life on the other side of the mirror.

"I don't know what you mean. What's obvious?" she asks.

"Well, you're looking at a being whom lost his physical body many years ago," he replies curtly.

"You mean you're—?" she starts, only to be cut off.

"I am. I most certainly am." He assures as he looks away from her gaze.

"But how?" She continues.

"I was an agent, and moved from the old country through the corridor of souls to get into position for a mission here in this country. When I returned, my body wasn't there. I was told my physical body was either misplaced by my caretakers, or stolen and hidden by some demented soul. I searched for the better part of ten years to no avail. I was able to carry out many assignments during those years. As with any, the possibility of making enemies is part of the job. I made several, and they chased me all over the world. I imagine they came across my body and did something with it. The Company sacrificed a decoy on my behalf, which threw them off my trail. Then they placed me here about forty years ago. I've not been bothered by them since. But I'm not able to go through the corridor of souls, or do anything to bring notice to myself, or my whereabouts. I'm not a prisoner, but I'm stuck right here, probably forever." He turns his head away in despair.

Feeling a bit of empathy Lilly asks softly, "Why are you telling me all of this?"

"The truth is, I've given a you lot of thought you, and decided just recently to move along with your training. Your first assignment will be to locate my life body. Until your baby is born, I'll teach you everything I know. Then as soon as you feel you're able to leave your child, we'll get started. How does that sound to you?"

"You mean I'll be able to leave here? Who'll take care of the baby?" She's quick to reply.

"Your maid will take care of your baby as if it's her own. And yes, you'll leave here. You'll be my eyes and ears, traveling to whatever place necessary to find my body. You do understand that your life body will be kept here, of course. You'll travel through the corridor of souls and communicate with me on a daily basis."

"Is this some sort of test?" She poses a good question.

"One of several you'll be asked to pass before you'll be permitted to physically venture beyond these walls. We must be certain of your loyalties." His answer seems to be an honest one.

"Am I correct in thinking your body must still be alive? Didn't you just say a spiritual life when your life body has died is a gruesome one? You acted like you dreaded the thought of that. Is your life body dead or alive?"

"Another good question. It must be alive and being tended to, otherwise, I wouldn't be able to lead the life I have today. To explain more fully, if the spirit stays on the other side of the mirror, it requires no nourishment. Just as all the souls there require no nourishment. If the spirit exists on this side of the mirror and their body is deceased, it must feed itself. Since there is no practical way to digest normal food when in that state, the only way to be nourished is with fresh blood."

"Like a vampire?" She feels creepy when the words come out.

"Exactly." He confirms. "In addition, it should make sense that at times, a soul belonging on the other side of the mirror, ventures to this side. While it requires no food on the other side, it does on this side. Hence, another vampire type of spirit."

"Wow!" Lilly exclaims.

"Are you able to see yourself in a mirror when you are out of your body?" he asks the young pregnant woman.

"I see what you mean." She confirms with an eerie tone. "So, I imagine you're concerned that something will happen to your life body causing you to either drink fresh blood here, or die; or go over there where they'll probably murder you. Right?"

"There's my dilemma. It's been a long time, and I live in fear every day. Not that I know it for a fact, but I understand that the craving for fresh blood becomes obsessive to the point of killing living things to get warm fresh blood."

"Even people, I'm sure." She drops her eyes away from his now gaunt face. "Then vampires do exist, just not the way we read about them. Do they fly, and do they have to stay out of the sun?" She continues

"I've never heard of one flying, but perhaps some of them can. The reason they stay out of the sun is it depletes a waterlike substance from their skin, and after a period of time, it makes them sort of transparent, like a ghost. They must feed again before they look normal. The blood they drink is visible until it's consumed into their bodies. It isn't a pleasant sight. Otherwise, they can move about as freely as they want, anytime of the day or night."

"Do they have long hollow teeth they use to suck up blood."

"I hope I never find out. I hope, to God, I never find out." He winces.

"Back to Amber, Mr. Vaughn. Am I to understand that she means no harm to my family?"

"That's absolutely correct. She's there only as an informant."

Lilly feels better hearing that. She can relax and come up with a new plan if there's no immediate threat to her family.

"Besides," she says to herself, "given time, they'll know she isn't me."

It's nine thirty in the morning at the Anderson farm.

Charlotte, Sheree, and Belle are boarding the large carriage—along with two of the hand's teenage-girl children—and Jim and Josh, headed for town. The men occupy the driver's box, while the women have seated themselves in the two plush bench seats closest to the front, leaving an empty seat behind them. Jim, with the reins in his hands, turns to look back over his shoulder, checking to see that all are seated. A push of his foot releases the brake, then a ripple of the reins out over the team and a soft 'giddup' starts the carriage moving. Hands wave goodbye from the carriage.

The group here at the farm for the meeting consists of John, Doc, the colonel and Selma, Cole and Caroline Sanders, their daughter Elizabeth, Robert, and Randall.

Belle was up early this morning, preparing for the meeting. All there is left to do is for June and Selma to serve dinner when needed. Coffee and iced cinnamon rolls are already in the living room, where their meeting will be held. The Andersons felt the seating would be more comfortable and informal. Curious faces file into the living room, randomly finding seats, and settle down. John remains standing, for the moment, enabling him to attract everyone's attention.

"Feel free to get up and move around when you've the mind. Here's coffee and some sweets to tide us over until dinner. Help yourselves." A few do exactly that.

"I'd like you to speak up when you have something to say. You've all had a part, one way or another, with the subject of our meeting, namely, the homecoming of our Sheree. June and I feel, uaahh . . . that is to say . . . June and I believe that the young lady, Robert and Randall so courageously brought home, is not our daughter Sheree."

The room becomes a din of involuntary comments.

He continues, "We think an impostor has been put in our midst by the very people who took Sheree over five years ago."

"But John, how could that be?" The colonel's voice rises above the rumblings of the others in the room. "She looks just like her sister Charlotte. She knows everybody and acts like she's been here all her life."

"Yes, I know, but I have information that I have hesitated to pass on to you because I saw no need, until now. I believe the reason she looks like her sister is that they are sisters, but she's not Sheree. I have it from good authority that our first daughter didn't actually die when she was born. She was revived and kept by the Company."

"Oh my God!" June's voice rings throughout the room. "Why didn't you tell me?"

"I saw no sense in getting you all upset at the time, and until this young woman arrived here with Robert and Randall, I couldn't be sure of the information."

"Ohhh, this changes everything," she continues. "I was ready to do all sorts of things to get her out of here, but now . . . She is my daughter.

"Now I don't know how I feel." Her hands fall to her lap as she hangs her head.

"Now hold on, John, we don't know for sure she's not Sheree. How can we be sure? Does anybody else here think she's not Sheree?" Caroline Sanders speaks up.

Randall speaks.

"Maybe it's not my place to say, but she don't seem the same to me. I mean, I know it's been a long time, and a person can change, but Sheree and me were friends before. It just don't seem like we are now. She don't want anything to do with me, not even talk. And Queenie don't like her, and she liked Sheree a lot."

Doc speaks up. "I seem to remember fixing a cut on Sheree's head years ago. It should have left some sort of scar. That might be one way to make certain."

"June says she has already checked, Doc, and the scar isn't there. Isn't that right, honey?" John speaks for his wife.

She raises her head, her face solemn and grim.

"Yes, that's right. The scar isn't there." She lowers her head again.

"Can I do something for you, June?" Selma is concerned for her friend. "Perhaps you should lie down for a few minutes."

"No, what I need is a good stiff drink. John, fix me a snifter of brandy. I know it's early but will anyone else join me."

Selma is the first to volunteer her support. "I won't let you drink alone. Get me one, too." Then, to everyone's surprise, Caroline Sanders adds her order to the rest.

The meeting takes a little break as Mr. Anderson pours brandies and hands them out to the ladies. "Anyone else like a little something with their coffee?" he asks with a smile. "I believe I'll sweeten mine up a bit with bourbon."

The men, except for Robert and Randall, take him up on the offer. After setting the bourbon bottle on the coffee table, John looks around to see that everybody is comfortable and begins again.

"I believe there is little doubt that the young woman with us is not our daughter Sheree. That means Sheree is still with the Company—somewhere. In my mind, it also means the Company has had this plan for a long time. The question is, why? What good will it do them to have a spy in our midst?"

"Maybe I can cast a little light on that," the colonel speaks up. "She could be here to check on me, or for that matter, to replace me. Although I've not said a word to them about my relationship with you and our cause, they have their ways of knowing things."

"What are you two talking about?" Cole Sanders interjects. "Is there something I should know about?"

The meeting has taken a turn that John expected, but it's too early on to get into that right now. "Cole, I don't mean to put you off, but if you don't mind, I'd like to stay on the subject of Sheree. We'll answer all your questions and fill you in on everything before you leave here today. That I promise you."

Cole nods his head in agreement.

"I'm not certain how we'll ever know for sure why she's here unless we keep up the charade. On the other hand, can we ever be comfortable knowing there's a spy in our homes. And that's the reason for this meeting. I feel we all have a share in this and the decision should be made by us all. Should we keep going the way we are now, or, would it be best to confront our spy, listen to what she has to say, then deal with her?"

"What do you mean, deal with her?" June is quick to ask.

"I'm not sure. That would be decided by all of us, too."

"You're not planning to hurt her, are you?" Elizabeth poses, with a defensive tone in her voice. "She's no more than an older child."

"I'm not planning anything. But keep in mind, this older child has been placed in our lives to do something, or to cause something to happen. You don't have to be a grown person to pull the trigger of a gun, or light a fuse to a keg of powder." the colonel exclaims loudly.

"I'm thinking we should lock her up until she tells us everything we want to know." Cole knows no one will support him, but it's one solution.

"People, people," June gets to her feet as she speaks. "Before you get a rope and turn into a mob, remember this child, in all likelihood, is my daughter, my flesh and blood, and I won't stand for any harm coming to her."

Doc rises to his feet and raises his hands to calm the clamor.

"Sit back down June. We all know none of us here are going to do any harm to this young woman. Now, let's look at this logically. I believe John's right when he says this plan of theirs has been laid out for years. They wouldn't spend all that time and effort for just one big bang. They want her here for the long haul. They've put her here for a longtime purpose, a purpose she probably doesn't even know about. Whatever it is, we'll never know unless we play along and keep our eyes and ears open."

"I agree with Doc," Robert opens up for the first time after sitting quietly listening. "The whole parcel of us can surely out think and out maneuver one little girl. Let's give her a long leash, give her room to show us what she's up to."

"I now think that's best too." The colonel changes his mind. "It might be possible to pass information through her, back to the Company. I mean, if we want to know who she's working for and how they'll react to information coming from her, let's feed something to her that will bring a result we can see."

"That sounds like a plan, Colonel. What do you have in mind?" John agrees.

"Nothing specific, but perhaps something to pull them out and cause an action of some sort. Once we see them react, we might be able to use her to get inside them."

The women, including June, readily agree, since they want no harm to come to the girl.

"Cole, speak your mind, if you've got something to say," Doc urges.

"When you put it that way, it looks like the best thing to do," he agrees.

"Let's hear from Randall and see if we can make it unanimous," John says, as all eyes fall on the young man.

He takes a deep breath before speaking, not use to being the center of attention in a grown up situation. "I can see where you all are right with your thinking. I just wish we hadn't brought all this to you by bringing the wrong Sheree home. It all makes sense now.

Bob and I, we both thought it was too easy. Everything seemed to lead us to bringing her home. I'll bet our real Sheree is in that place La Nesra somewhere. I just know it."

"June, are you going to be able to keep up with all of this?" Her husband knows this will never work without her involvement.

"I have to. It should be easier since I know she is, at least, one of our own. Calling her Sheree hasn't been a problem at all, since we don't know her by her real name. Can we leave it this way? Let's plan another meeting in about six months. If she gets settled in here with us her loyalties to the Company might dwindle, maybe she can belong to this family as she should," she finishes.

"That's a good idea," Elizabeth adds. "She was so sweet to us all when Daddy had his accident. She was right there to help in any way she could. She didn't have to do that; there's goodness in that girl. It won't be difficult for me to be around her, I like her."

"Yes, thank you, Elizabeth." Caroline Sanders supports her daughter. "We need to remind ourselves that this child's life has, more than likely, been that of a motherless, fatherless orphan. She doesn't know what it's like to have family, people who truly love her. I believe we should do our level best to bring her to our way of thinking."

"Well, she's done a good job so far. You two are swooning over her, knowing she's here to spy on us. And the rest of us feel pretty much the same way." Selma's thoughts are delivered in a joking manner. "I haven't been around her all that much, but she appears to be a normal girl for her age. I think we're on the right track, but, let's not let our guard down too quickly. I wonder if we should meet again in about ninety days. Six months seem quite a ways off."

John picks up the conversation. "We all agree to keep up the facade, so, let's take it a day, a week at a time, and meet again when we think we need to."

"That's fine John, but there's one more thing." Doc has a point to make.

"How do we go about explaining Sheree to the folks around here. Remember now, we buried her over five years ago. There's a marker in your family graveyard with her name on it to prove it."

It's a beautiful day at Atlanta.

Lilly and Falcon are strolling across the courtyard, hand in hand, headed for Mr. Vaughn's office.

"I'm glad you don't mind my keeping the baby," Lilly comments.

"It's the right thing to do. I'm really glad you made the decision." Falcon assures.

"Well, like I said earlier, I'm going to carry it, and I'm going to give birth to it, but from there, don't expect a whole lot from me. I don't want Eagle's child." She continues, "Mr. Vaughn has an assignment for me as soon as I'm able after the baby comes. That's why I want you with me this morning. I'm going to tell him I need your help to see if he'll let you come with me."

"I doubt that he will, Lilly. If you have to travel through the corridor of souls, I won't be able to go with you."

"I know, but he has his personal reasons for putting me on this assignment. So I think, maybe, he'll do it because I want him to."

"What's in that pretty head of yours now? Can you tell me what the assignment is?"

"I'd better not. It would be better if he told you. It could take quite a while to accomplish though, I can tell you that. But we'd be together, away from here." She turns on her best, cute, I have a plan, smile.

"You are up to something, and I love you for it. Hey, I'll do it. Why not? I must have a charmed life after the way I lived through our last experience together."

"He's expecting us, so let's get in there and give it our best. Remember, though, if he doesn't agree to it today, we still have at least seven months to change his mind." She opens Mr. Vaughn's door as she finishes speaking.

"Good morning Lilly . . . Falcon." He looks up from a stack of papers lying on his desk, and points to the chairs where he wants them to sit.

"Morning, Mr. Vaughn," Falcon says with respect.

Lilly does not respond.

"What's on your mind now? I know you must want something; people normally don't make an effort to see me." He rests back in his chair looking straight into her eyes, glancing back and forth.

"I'll get right to the point," she begins. "Yesterday while we were talking, you said if I wanted or needed anything, I should ask for it, right?"

"That's what I said."

"I would like to have Falcon assigned with me when I go to work for you, after the baby is born."

"Why?" An expected question.

"It'll be my first time on my own, and I'd feel better, safer, more at ease, if he's with me. Also, I probably shouldn't communicate directly with you. I know you don't want you-know-who to find you. Another thing is, if I get myself into trouble, there'll be someone to help me, or at least keep you informed."

The older Company man doesn't appear to be the least bit agitated with her proposal.

"If I am going to send someone with you, why would I choose a person who has no more experience than you. Wouldn't I be more likely to send an experienced agent?"

"Because Falcon and I are good together. Our mutual abilities to calculate, plan, and reason make us a formidable force."

"Ahh, yes, I've seen that in action," he agrees, showing his teeth with a seldom seen smile for the second time in Lilly's memory.

"So, we can do it then?" She pushes for a positive response.

"Have you told him about the assignment?" His words make Falcon feel like he's a piece of the furniture, or not in the room.

"No, sir, not one word. It's your place to do that." She feels in control of this meeting.

"Well, I have to say, I can see the merit of your suggestion. Hmmm . . ."

After two full minutes of silence, he shifts quickly, heavily, in his chair to look at Falcon nose to nose.

"Are you in agreement with all this?"

"Yes," the startled Falcon blurts out.

"You'll start right now, then. It's your job to make sure Lilly is protected, twenty-four hours a day, seven days a week. Understand? You're her bodyguard."

Lilly squirms a little in her seat and smiles inside at his choice of words.

"By starting now, you might get an idea of the amount of work it is to keep up with another person. I'll start filling you in tomorrow. Be here right after our noon meal."

"Now, get out of here, I've work to do." His attitude is almost playful.

The meeting at the Anderson home has been brought to a stop with Doc's remark ending with, "there's a marker in your family graveyard with her name on it . . ."

Everyone's mouth drops open as he pulls his pipe and tobacco pouch from his coat pocket, puts the bowl inside the pouch and packs tobacco with his first finger. Silence prevails as they watch him put the pouch away, place the stem of the pipe between his teeth on the left side of his mouth, and fumble for a match.

"Here, I'll get you a match, Doc." Selma jumps to her feet headed for the kitchen.

"I've been pondering on what kind of a story we can come up with about Sheree being back home from the dead, without depending on our impostor," he continues.

"The way I see it, she'll have to help us pull it off."

Selma is back with several matches and hands them to Doc as she says, "Maybe we could say Sheree is the daughter of June's long lost sister, or something like that?"

"I believe the point is we can't introduce her at all as Sheree, as my sister's daughter, or anything else, unless she's agreeable to go along with it. Doc's right, we have to confront her with everything, or board her up in the barn." John's wife nails it down.

"If we're going to tell her we know she isn't Sheree, then we should introduce her as who she really is. No cover up—no more lies," Cole offers.

"What if she refuses to work with us?" A good question from Robert.

"I suppose we should plan for that possibility, but I think, under the circumstances, she won't want us to expose her to her superiors. It'll mean she's failed at her assignment, and whomever it is she's working for won't like that one bit," John states as a fact.

"Then, who will tell her? All of us? And what would we say. How much will we tell her?" Caroline adds her voice.

The colonel offers his thoughts. "There's no sense in telling her we're all part of anything. Let her figure it out for herself. You can bet once we tell her we know she's an impostor, she's going to think this meeting is all about her. As for who tells her, I offer John and June. I think she'd expect to hear it from the two of you."

"Yeah, you're right about that," John affirms as the rest nod their heads and speak all at once in agreement.

"Just don't ask me to do it. I'll help, but you have to do it." June wants the room of people to understand her position.

"We'll do it tomorrow morning, if that's agreeable?" John states and asks.

When there is no further conversation about the matter, he moves on, deliberately.

"That's settled then. Thank you, one and all, for your wisdom and input. Now, ladies, perhaps you'll excuse us if we move to the den. I need about an hour with the lot of these fine gentlemen."

"Does that include Randy and me?" Robert inquires. "I think it would be a good idea, unless it's something personal."

John looks at the other three men, then back at Robert.

"Absolutely." Is his only comment.

The men rise from their seats and move toward the den with their spiked coffee in hand. Doc picks up a cinnamon roll as he passes the tray setting on the coffee table. Once all are inside the room, John closes the door. He waits until all are seated around the large table, and the noise has settled down, then gets Robert's attention with a wave of his hand. He points to the humidor of cigars on the desk, then motions with his finger to pass it around, and begins.

"Just to clear the air a little. Doc and I had a conversation yesterday about our impostor. It seemed to the both of us that it was important to get all of the issues out in the open. That is, to discuss all of the perils and obstacles involved, amongst us, before a decision was made to confront her with it. To that end, it was decided to take the long way around, as we did, believing we would eventually all come to the same conclusion. I think now everyone has a good understanding as to why there's only one way to go with her. We're doing the right thing."

He pauses a few seconds, deliberately giving all in the room a chance to respond.

No takers? He moves on.

"Doc, I'm not taking anything for granted here, but I figure you'll support me, or you'll take what you hear here to your grave. So, I'm just going to move on. If you decide you want no part of it, just get up and leave."

Doc nods affirmatively.

"Cole, I accepted a tremendous responsibility several weeks ago. I've opted out of the race for the Governor's position. Should I have won that election, it would be impossible to handle that responsibility and that of the new challenge ahead." He smiles at the possibilities. "I need all the help I can get with this new endeavor, and would like to have you on board with us. The thing is, this job is sensitive in it's nature, and the only thing I can tell you right now is that it's of national importance, and very urgent. Would you be interested in helping us out? Will your health allow you to do it.?"

"Well," he replies, "Doc tells me that my injuries are all healed and what I have now is what I'll deal with the rest of my life. I'll walk with a cane, and you know good and well, that doesn't lend itself to farm work. I still can't remember how my horse threw me, I don't know if I ever will. Other than that, I'm in pretty damn good shape for my age, and I need something to do. Something to live for rather than sit around and watch other people do all the work. I've got too much spare time on my hands. A man doesn't have to pay too much attention to understand you're working on something that must be of dire importance. You're never home anymore, and Robert seems to have taken over the running of your place. June and the Houslers don't have the time to stop by and visit. To be honest, I was beginning to feel—well—sort of left out. Hell, you all know me. I go back a long way with your families, before you were born, most of you. With me, you get what you see. If you want me, I'm in. Does that satisfy your question?"

"I'm glad to hear you say it, Cole. Welcome aboard."

John turns his head to the other side of the table to look at Randall.

"Randall, are you sure you want to throw in with the rest of us? You know, of course, if you join with us and we let you in on what's going on, there's no leaving, you're in for good. The only way out is a pine box." John stops to hear his answer.

Other than Randall, the rest of the room laughs out loud at John's approach to a serious question.

The young man's eyes stretch big and round as his forehead wrinkles up in the middle.

"Yessir, if Bob says it's okay, then it's okay with me, too." An honest answer. Nothing else is needed.

"Great, and welcome aboard to you, too."

"Now listen, because I'm going to fill you in with some surprising facts and interesting information. This will make you fully understand the importance of our meeting a few minutes ago. I am, with the help of all of you and others to come . . ."

Back at La Nesra, Lilly and Falcon left Mr. Vaughn's office and have located a bench in the courtyard, away from curious ears. The morning sun is warm and comforting as they sit for a moment in silence, reflecting on the meaning of their just adjourned meeting. Falcon speaks first.

"Can you tell me now? What's this all about?"

"I think he expects us to talk about it now. That's probably why he didn't go any further with it today, he wants us to discuss it first," she answers. "My assignment is all about him. He, apparently, has the ability to move through the mirror the same as me, by leaving his body. Just as my body was taken from me, someone has hidden his somewhere over forty years ago, and he hasn't been able to find it. To make matters worse, he's done some things that have turned the wrong people against him, they want to capture or kill him. He knows a lot more about the place on the other side of the mirror than I do. He says he can't go back there. If he does, his enemies will kill him."

"So, what does he want you to do?" Falcon urges.

"He wants me to find his life body. I think he's just tired of it all, and wants to get back into his body, even if it means dying to do it."

"Man-oh-man, where do you start with something like this? I mean, his life body could be anywhere in the world." Falcon begins to sense the enormity of the problem.

"I hope he can give us a place to start. Otherwise, I don't see how else we could have a chance," Lilly explains. "The truth is, I don't care if we ever find his body. If you and I can get out of here, on our own, what do we care? This could be our chance to get away from here and be together."

"I knew you had something up your sleeve." His face spreads into a broad smile. "Tell me more."

"Okay, I will, but this part is sort of hard and a little bit scary for me." She sits for a few seconds, obviously, preparing herself for the unknown.

"Here goes," she says puffing short breaths. "I love you. I love you more than anything. I don't care about any of this." She refers to La Nesra and the Company. "I only want to be with you."

Falcon makes a move as though he is about to speak. She shakes her head no, and raises her hand from her lap to place it on his arm.

"Let me finish this," she whispers. "I'm not sure how you feel about me, but all I want from life right now is you. I've thought about you, and I've thought about us. I care more for you every day I live. I want to be with you for the rest of my life. I've even thought about my family, and I don't think I'll ever be able to go back there to live with them. I'd like my parents to hold me and hug me again, but, the older I get, the more I think they gave me away for money, and that brings tears to my eyes. I don't think I'll ever be able to forgive them for that. I'll miss them, and my brother and sister, and I'll miss my friend Randall, but I'll just have to live with that. It's an awful thing to think, let alone say, but I just want to be away from it all. I want some peace. I can't remember going to bed at night feeling safe, except for the night I stayed with you. I don't like the idea of feeling sorry for myself, and I know all of this will pass in time. It's just—where will I wind up in life? Will I eventually turn out to be another Mr. Vaughn?"

"Lilly—" Falcon tries to interrupt.

"Let me finish what I need to say!" she demands.

"This life I live has been forced upon me. I've had no hand in it. This is not what I want to do with my life. I curse the day I was born with this affliction. I want to be a normal person. I want to have your babies. I want us to be together—be a family, doing normal life things. I want a dog for our children to play with, I want to cook your meals, and darn your socks. I don't care where we live as long as we're together. I don't care what you do for a living, as long as I'm with you. Do you see why I don't want this baby? I can't nurture this child. It will remind me of everything I want to forget. I'll never have any peace. I don't know, some days I feel like I can have some sort of life in spite of all that's been going on. Then other days, I feel like I'll start screaming my brains out until they come to drag me away, and lock me up."

She stops for a few seconds to look into Falcon's eyes and admire his handsome face. "Do you really love me—for me I mean, for what and who I am? Do you want any of the same things I want? Can you see us together, for the rest of our lives? If you don't, please, don't say you do, then let me discover later that you don't. Give me the truth now, and I promise I won't hate you for it; I'll love you for it. If that makes any sense?" She places her hand back on her lap, closes her eyes, lowers her head, and braces herself for his response.

"You want the truth, huh? I'm not sure you can handle the truth, but if you want it, I'll give it to you."

She doesn't expect his answer to start like this. Deep down, she believes he loves her too. She can't help raising her head to look at him. Her face tells him he's right. She's almost in tears and he hasn't started yet. He knows, though, she has to hear what he has to say first in order to understand his response to her question.

"You've made this all about you," he soberly, quietly explains. "You've not once asked me about how I feel about this place, about my life. You don't even know where I was born, or how I happen to be here. Your interests, to my knowledge, are centered around you. I believe you mean it when you say you love me, because I believe that's the way you feel right now. You're downtrodden, overburdened, and just plain lonely. Once your situation—your life—changes, what then? Where will I fit in when you get your zest for life back? The honest truth is, neither of us has ever been in love before, at least not the forever kind of love. How can you or I say 'I know I love you and I will forever', and know it to be true. We can't, or I know I can't, and I won't mislead you."

As he speaks, Lilly hears his words, but is understanding them differently then they are said. She hears. "I'm lonely too, but I don't want to take the chance of getting hurt, so I probably should pull back away from our relationship, push her away. Besides, my logical mind tells me we should know each other a whole lot better before we make any commitments."

"Shut! Up!" she says firmly, each word forming a sentence.

"What?" He's surprised.

"Do you love me or not? Yes or no!"

"Oh God, yes!" Three words, eight letters that light the fuse of passion between them.

"Then take me somewhere and prove it to me. I'm here in person now, and I want you more than you can ever know," she coos, her tear-filled eyes shining with tenderness.

"There's a place in the main barn, in the back of the hay loft. No one will look for us there." Eagerness is written all over him.

As they move toward the barn, arms around each other's waist, she says in a teasing way. "You seem to know a lot about taking a girl to a secret place to have your way with her, don't you?"

"Only you, I've been thinking for a long time about you and a place we could go to be together. Now come on, move it, we're wasting time."

Six o'clock comes early this morning at the Anderson farm. June rolls over in bed to nudge John awake.

"It's time to get up, honey."

"Yeah, okay, I'm up," he responds, under his breath.

John rises to his feet from the bed, walks over to the wash stand and pours water from the pitcher into the bowl. He fills his cupped hands and bends down to splash his face, hair, and the back of his neck. While he dries himself with a towel, he hears his wife's words.

"We have to tell her today, don't we?"

He knows she's spent most of the night, lying awake, dreading the task ahead.

"Yes, that's right. I told you, don't worry about it. I'll take care of it, you don't have to be there unless you want to."

"I do have to be there. She'll need her mother."

Breakfast passes without incident, although Robert keeps looking at his sister. It's as if he's trying to be sure she's an impostor. No one seems to notice but June. The conversation centers mostly around the girls' trip to town, and the purchases they made.

As soon as all are finished eating and leaving the table, John whispers to Sheree. Then they walk together toward the den. Robert sees what's happening and quickly occupies Charlotte by taking her through the kitchen and out the back door.

June, not wanting the den doors to be closed before she gets there, grabs a cup of coffee and runs up to the doorway, stops, then walks inside. He motions for Sheree to take a seat. June sits next to her, while John takes up a position on the opposite side of the table.

"We know you're not our daughter Sheree," he begins, feeling it is best to get the shock behind them.

She says nothing, but turns an ashen gray as the blood leaves her face.

"We've known for some time now. We mean you no harm, you can be sure of that, but it's time to get at the truth. Will you admit to us that you're not our daughter?"

Silence.

June speaks up. "We believe you probably are our real-life daughter, but not Sheree."

John gives his wife a look that can only be interpreted one way. "Will you let me handle this?"

"I don't know what to say." The shocked young woman looks back and forth at them as she speaks, trying to appear unaffected by the news.

"You can start by telling us the truth. You're not our daughter, Sheree, are you?" John makes it look as though he's losing his patience.

She looks into each of their faces for a few seconds, then down at the table.

"No, I'm not."

"Who are you, then?" his next question follows quickly.

"My name is Amber."

"What a beautiful name," June interjects, then realizes she should keep quiet.

"Why are you here pretending to be Sheree?"

"I'm on assignment from the Company; I'm here to connect with an agent."

"Why? What are your orders? What's the agents name?" John stays hot after her.

"I'm supposed to settle in with your family and friends, and wait for instructions from them. I don't know the agent's name. They said I would know when I saw it."

"How long have you been at the Company?"

"As long as I can remember, all my life, I guess"

"Are you sure you're not here to cause us problems?'

"Like I said, I'm supposed to locate and meet up with an agent in this area, and make you think I'm your daughter. From there, I don't know. They didn't tell me anything else. When they find out you know who I am, they'll punish me somehow."

"Well, your secret's out. How long did you think you could fool all of us?"

"I never really thought about it, I suppose. I never believed you wouldn't accept me as your daughter. All I've heard, all my life, as far back as I can remember, are things about you and your lives, and things about Sheree. I feel like I am her. I think, given time, I could really become her."

June wants to be a part of this conversation in the worst of ways. She squirms in her seat, wrings her hands, and tosses her head, as she listens.

"What do you think we should do with you Amber?" John wants to hear where her loyalties lie, if possible.

"Don't tell the Company. Just don't tell them." The Andersons can see a bit of fear on her face.

"It'll be impossible to pass you off as Sheree around here. It can't be done. So, whatever we do, we have to call you by a different name. Your real name would be the best."

"Call me Amber, then, but the only thing is, if the Company checks up on me and finds out you're calling me Amber, they'll know."

June is unable to hold back any longer.

"Let's call you Cheryl. That way if a question comes up, you can always say Sheree is another name for Cheryl."

"Cheryl . . . well I'll be damned. Good thinking, June. That's perfect." John congratulates his wife.

The young girl beams at the possibility. "Cheryl, with a C, right? From now on, just refer to me as Cheryl."

"Okay, that's settled. Now, we'll pass you off as the daughter of a sister of June's. In other words, our niece." John puts the plan together.

"Why are you doing this?" Cheryl asks boldly.

"Would you rather we just turned you over to them?" June now challenges.

"I don't understand. I'm here to spy on you, and now you're treating me as if you want me to be a part of your family?"

"Would that be so bad?" John's question is meant to infer the plan is exactly that. She should be a part of the family.

"Oh no, I'd like to be a part of this family. I love it here. You've all treated me so kindly. This is a good place to be, but how can you be so sure I still won't spy on you and let the Company know what I find out. They'll expect something from me from time to time, I'm sure."

"Cheryl, we think you are, and I mean truly are, our daughter. We think you were taken from us as an infant, taken by the Company to be raised, and sent back to us as you are now. I think Charlotte and Sheree actually are your sisters." June savors every word coming from her mouth.

"If only that were true." Her eyes tear up allowing a bead of water to run down her cheek. "Would I be one of a set of triplets? We all look so much alike."

"It'll be true as long as we want it to be," June continues. "We won't be able to spread it around though. Remember, you're my sister's daughter. And yes, you are the first of three girls I gave birth to that day. You're the oldest."

"I have two sisters, then? Will Charlotte know the truth? She already knows I'm not Sheree. She told me so."

Mama and Papa Anderson look at each other and shake their heads in unison.

"Oh yes, we must tell her the truth, after all, she's your sister," June sings out.

"I have sisters—I can't believe it—I have two sisters."

"Let's get real serious for a moment ladies. This is no game we're playing here. The price for making a mistake could be deadly."

"I need to hear from you Cheryl, that you will pass on to the Company only the information we give you; that your loyalties are with this family, and the causes of this family. Do you agree?" John needs her confirmation.

"I swear to you . . . Uncle John, I'll be like a daughter to you and Aunt June." She grins at the play on her words.

"You'll never have to question my loyalties. I've always dreamed of having a family, but I never really expected to get one. I'll never do anything to hurt anyone, I swear it."

Chapter Twenty-Two

The Union party's candidate from the state of Illinois has just been elected to the office of president of these United States. Democrat voters voiced their distaste for their party by splitting their votes among the three democratic candidates, giving none of them a chance to overcome the united Union organization. Had all of the democratic votes been cast for one person, the Union party would have lost the election. Needless to say, there is a tremendous amount of temper between the political parties, as well as among themselves. A shaky start at best for a new president-elect. People closest to him are advising to keep a low profile for a while to allow hot heads time to cool down.

The Southern states, for the most part, do not support the new president. To show his intentions, the governor of South Carolina has made public before the election, that if a Union candidate wins the election, his state will secede from the Union. It is expected that other Southern states will soon follow their lead, probably setting the stage for the beginning of a civil war. It's widely known that the new president will not support slavery, although during his campaign he has voiced a willingness to listen to all sides in order to arrive at a peaceful resolution.

It is clearly understood that he is a staunch supporter of the Northern Union, and that a separation of the existing states will not be tolerated. He has made known that Union forces will be used to ensure a one-nation configuration. He has further indicated that the Union will wage a war, if necessary.

Violence caused by raiders, both for and against slave ownership, haunts the upper Southern states. These bands, at times, are made up of a hundred or more men, men that enjoy the killing, pillaging, and devastating beyond the need of their cause. No one, or anything, is safe during a siege. Their objective appears to be to kill every living thing in sight, steal what they fancy, and burn the rest.

Union soldiers have little effectiveness trying to stop the attacks since the raiders base their success on randomly selected targets, hitting hard with a fury, and running afterward. It is not uncommon for these groups to plunder, then move fifty miles in a day to wreak havoc on their next defenseless victims. The sight of a band of these self-appointed liberators, or liberty defenders, drives a stake of terror through the hearts of every innocent man, woman, and child in their path.

At Der Bote, the farm and home of the colonel and Selma Housler.

Robert has urgently requested his father, Colonel Housler, Cole Sanders, Marty Schoener, Doc, and Randall to an early morning meeting, out of the earshot of Cheryl.

John and Marty have traveled from Baltimore to arrive at 5 AM. Doc and Cole arrived about twenty minutes earlier. The two travelers need to freshen up before getting down to business, allowing time for the others to prepare to eat.

A sound of a coffeepot perking, along with the sizzle of bacon and eggs frying in a large iron skillet, fill the kitchen, emitting an aroma that floats through the house. Plates, coffee mugs, water glasses, and silverware adorn the dining room table.

"You can get yourselves started on this; I got plenty more coming up in a few minutes." Alberta Mae assures as she sets out platters of food, then returns to the kitchen. She quickly appears again with a pitcher of milk, and a pot of coffee, to set them on the table before the men can get seated.

"Eat up, gentlemen," the colonel invites. "John and Marty can catch up when they get ready."

The platters are being passed around when the two arrive to find an empty seat. Once the plates are filled and the platters are back on the table, John speaks up.

"I hope this is important." His tone sends a message of concern to his son. "What's this all about?"

All heads turn toward Robert, as the men lay their forks on their plates.

"Daddy, you put me in charge of the security of these farms when you left. I'm worried that we're going to get some trouble—and I mean big trouble—from these raiders I keep hearing about. The word I get is they're not leaving a single thing standing. They're burning the buildings and the crops, murdering farm animals and anybody else who gets in their way."

"They're nowhere close to here, yet," Marty interrupts.

Robert counters immediately. "They could be here within the next week or so. It looks like they're moving this way, and they're covering a lot of territory in a day's time. I think we should have some sort of plan before they get here. Right now, we have no way of protecting ourselves, and I don't want to wait until they come through town, killing and burning, headed this way. We need some time to get ready." His voice shows concerned excitement as he uses his hands and arms to support his words.

Silence at the table.

"Why do you think they'd come through town first?" Doc asks.

"That's what I'd do if it were me. I'd catch the town asleep, early, just like now. I'd take the town before coming after these farms. I'd figure I'd get more resistance from the town's people, than from our farms."

"He's right about that," the colonel agrees. "He's got a good point here."

Randall's eyes are wide with anticipation. This isn't a story in a book about being threatened. This is real life.

Marty speaks, "There's no one here at this table who wants anything to happen to these farms or anyone on them. John, after hearing his concerns, we can't just leave for Baltimore, and not make arrangements for this possibility. He's right. We might have a little more time than we think with winter coming on, but now's the time to get ready with a plan, whether it's ever used or not."

John feels as though he's being harshly judged for no reason. He hasn't said a word to indicate he feels any differently than any of them, but he did start off with a gruff attitude toward his son. He casts his eyes around the room, letting them settle on the startled look of Randall's face.

"Randall," he starts, "you might as well jump on this wagon, too. Say your piece."

"I guess I feel just like the rest of you, but what can a handful of us do about an army of these raiders coming through here. They'll run over us like we was a babe in a bunting. We don't even have a good place to hide. We sure don't have guns enough to make any kind of stand. And besides that, nobody here has shot a gun enough to get more than one shot off before they get their ramrod shoved down their throat by one of those murdering bastards." This speech from Randall stops them all in their tracks.

"I think he has just put it all in perspective," John says with a leery smile, and puffs out a short breath at the reality he's heard.

"Son, I owe you an apology," John addresses Robert. "No castle could ask for a better sentry. I am sorry for the way I started out here this morning."

Quiet settles in as a few moments of thought passes over the men. The silence is interrupted when Alberta Mae appears with more food and another pot of coffee.

"You all better eat before this gets cold. I ain't heating anything up again." She leaves as quickly as she came. Smiles and chuckles from the group at her demeanor relieves the tension in the room.

"What do we do about it?" John inquires as he looks at each man, one at a time.

Doc begins. "We don't want to create a panic whatever we do. So, let's not overplay our hand. I suppose just about everybody around here has already heard as much as we know, and that being said, they'll probably welcome any plan we come up with. The merchants and businessmen in town have a lot to lose if the worst should happen. I'm just not sure who, or how many, are willing to pick up a gun, that's all."

The elder Mr. Anderson adds, "We should get the Mayor to call a meeting of the town leaders. That might get us a feel for what they're willing to do. We need a man to head this up. If you all agree, I'll recommend Robert."

"I don't know, Daddy, will they take me seriously?" his son expresses honest concerns. "I'm probably still just a kid in their eyes."

"Well, if it's okay with the rest of you, I'll take care of getting Robert started with the townspeople. They all know me and they'll listen to what I say," Doc volunteers.

"Any objections?" John asks the group.

No takers.

"That's a start then. Keep us all informed, son. Now, what about our farms, how can we help protect ourselves?"

Meanwhile, at the Anderson farm.

Cheryl has been unable to sleep well for the last month. Since the day of the discovery of her true identity, she's been the perfect niece, trying her best to become a part of the Anderson family. It seems to get easier as each day goes by. Everyone trusts her more and more, and treats her like she's one of them. There's been no mention of her loyalties, or who she is, since that day. Everything appears to be working as expected, but . . .

"I've been lying here most of the night, awake. The easier it is to fit in, the more I think about why I'm here in the first place. I can't get it out of my mind. I don't want to hurt anyone in this family, but on the other hand, I'm here on a mission. True, I'm not sure what that mission is just yet, but I feel like I should find out who my contact is and see what develops. If my contact doesn't hear from me soon, he, or she, might tell the Company. And that would mean, they might come looking for me to see what's going on. I'll be in big trouble then. I'd better do something. I think I'll find a reason to go to Der Bote by myself over the next few days. Maybe I can find out who my contact is. It must be either Selma, or the colonel."

At 10:30 AM in Atlanta, Lilly is standing in the doorway of her small, new home at La Nesra, watching Falcon approach.

"You've been gone quite a while," she announces as he gets nearer.

"Yeah, I had to wait about forty-five minutes to see him. He was tied up doing something or other," he answers.

"How'd it go?" Her need to know is obvious with her tone.

He reaches the doorway as she steps aside enough to allow him to brush past her, then she follows him into the living room.

Falcon throws himself down into an overstuffed chair and looks up at her.

"We have a little problem." He frowns.

"What? What's wrong?" Her aggravation with the direction he is headed shows.

"Do you remember back when we first talked to him about our being together after the baby?"

"Yes, I do. Why?" A tense 'come on, let's get on with it' is in her voice.

"Well, we thought we could get out of here together, and get away from the Company. Then you and I could have some sort of normal life together. Remember?"

"Yeah, so?"

"Today he tells me that when he said I would be your bodyguard, to protect you, he meant just that. We understood I could go with you, but he meant I would guard your life body here at La Nesra—while you're out going through the mirrors, or wherever, to locate his life body. I'll be the only person, other than him, to know where your real body lies while you're gone. My job will be to take care of you here."

A flash of anger goes through Lilly's body. Being six months pregnant has changed her attitude toward everything. She doesn't like the way she looks, the way she feels, or her role in this whole thing. She has the tendency to fly off the handle with a mean temper.

"Damn! Damn! Damn! Why the hell does everything have to go wrong! Just once, just one time, I'd like to see something go right around here. I'm so sick of this, sometimes I think I won't be able to breathe if things keep closing in on me. This baby is the curse of my life, and I didn't want it in the first place. Now look at me, I'm stuck, I have no other choice now. I just wish this was all over. I don't care any more what happens, I just want this baby out of me." Her ranting can be heard for quite a distance.

Ten seconds pass before she continues in a much quieter, calmer, voice.

"I know one thing. Once I get rid of this one, there's never going to be another one. I'm never going through this again. And now, to top everything off, all of these plans we've made mean nothing. Vaughn and his crew win again." Her emotions shift from anger to hopelessness as tears begin rolling down her cheeks.

This isn't the first time Falcon has heard this outburst. He's found it's better to let her rave until she's finished before saying anything. Once, he tried to console her—to settle her down—but instead, she verbally attacked him, saying mean things he knew she didn't mean; but they hurt anyway. He waits until she's finished with her tirade, then quietly says.

"I love you, you know. You've never been more beautiful to me than you are right now. I want you more now then ever. I wish that baby was mine, and do you know why? It's because you wouldn't say these things if it was ours. You'd love it the same gentle way you love and care about me. I don't know much about all you're going through, but I think part of you doesn't want to get attached. You know this baby will be taken away from you as soon as it's born, and because you were taken away from your family against your will, you think you're doing the same thing to your child that your parents did to you. Think about it."

"I have thought about it. I think about it all the time. I can't get it off my mind, and it drives me crazy. I know I shouldn't want it, because it Eagle's, but something keeps making me want to love it. Maybe you're right, maybe I should just relax and let my feelings take me wherever." Lilly's tears subside, but her eyes are full of water as she looks at Falcon.

"This baby is yours, too. That's a fact that will never change. Not today, not tomorrow, never." He informs with love and support. "Listen to me. If you want to leave the baby here, and the two of us leave together, that's okay with me, but to tell the truth, I'd rather we take it with us. We can raise it together, like it's ours. I'll love this baby because it's part of you. I'll be its daddy, and no one needs to know any different."

"Do you really think we can?" Her face perks up with hope, her eyes blurred with tears. "We'll have to start all over. A baby is a big responsibility. Our whole plan will have to be changed," she continues eagerly.

Falcon reaches his left hand toward her, which she gladly accepts. He pulls her to his lap and puts his arms around her. She feels so good to him. A little tickle starts in his stomach then goes all the way around him. He puts his right hand on her baby and caresses gently, she puts her head against his. The smell of her hair lures him to raise his left hand to touch her face. The feeling from his stomach spreads up to his head and down to this knees. It's overwhelming.

"I love you with all my heart, Lilly. Will you marry me?"

She doesn't respond immediately, but that's because she's can't believe she heard what he said. Suddenly, she sits up on his lap to look into his face.

"What did you say? Say it again!" she urges.

"I said, I love you with all my heart, will you marry me?"

"Oh my God, you're serious. You want to marry me? You want to marry me, me—looking like this?"

"If they'll let us," he assures. "And if they won't let us, we'll marry ourselves."

She sits on his lap, staring at him, not moving.

"You're insane." She finally reacts. "You are out of your mind, you darling, wonderful man. You've lost your senses."

"Is that a yes, or no?"

"You really do love me, don't you? I mean, you love me the way I am, you don't want to change me, you want me the way I am?"

"I adore you. Why can't you believe anyone can feel that way about you? You're all I want, or will ever want in a woman. If you marry me, I'll prove it to you every day for the rest of your life."

"What a day this has started out to be. Wow! I'm getting married, and we're having a baby." Joy spreads over Lilly's face as she sinks back down into his arms, and places a gentle, loving, sensual kiss on his lips.

He pulls away catching his breath.

"I'm taking this as a yes."

The meeting at Der Bote regarding a plan to protect the farms has changed to a meeting about the progress of the Sons organization. John has been explaining a more clearly defined purpose.

"So, you see, there's no doubt that our main target is the Company. We now have well over one hundred pairs of eyes and ears gathering information and passing it on to us. It won't be long until we're a force to be reckoned with. We know already that the Company is playing a big hand in stirring up this pending war. They're not concerned with the politics or slavery. They want this entire nation under one control—theirs. They want one person, one of theirs, to rule this whole continent. Their ultimate goal is to, one day, rule the entire world. They won't have men fighting with guns and knives, but you can bet they'll be somewhere behind the planning of the battles to be fought.

"Our job is to thwart the efforts of the Company, and to overcome them anywhere, and in any way we can. We'll use our eyes and ears to gather all sorts of information about them and the Confederacy. That will be passed covertly through our people to the proper officials of the Union. They'll use it as they see fit. We'll not show ourselves to our enemy while in their midst, nor will we face them openly on a battlefield. Our war will be fought under the cloak of freedom, with a purpose of shutting down their efforts in any way we can, not allowing them to take over our blessed land. Our plan is coming together, gentlemen. We'll be able to start making a difference in just a few short months.

"Is there anything else? If not, let's break this up. I don't know about the rest of you, but I'm beginning to feel the lack of sleep." He finishes.

"I believe we're all done here." Robert's words end the meeting. "Mr. Sanders, can I see you privately for a minute before we leave?"

"You bet, let's step outside."

The two men step through the kitchen out on to the back porch.

"What's on your mind, son?" Cole asks.

"Well, sir, as you know, Beth and I have been seeing each other for some time now, and, err . . . aaahh, well . . . well, I want to ask her to . . . aaahh . . . marry me. Er, aaahh—that is to say, aaahhh—if she'll have me, and, err, if you approve." Robert stutters through his nervousness.

"I was wondering when this subject would come up," Cole calmly replies with little emotion. "All she ever talks about is you anymore. As I say, I've been expecting this day for some time now. Do you truly love her? Are you sure?" His tone is serious.

"I do, sir. I love her with all my heart. I swear to you, I'll take care of her and make you and Mrs. Sanders glad you gave us your blessing."

"I'll need to talk it over with Caroline before I can give you an answer. We've always done things together, you know." Cole's honesty is exactly what the young man expects, and he knows that's what his future father-in-law wants from him.

"Beth doesn't know it, but I've already asked her mother, sir." Robert waits for the blast of a quarrelsome response since he asked her first.

"Is that so?" Cole states his question. "I see you've got things well in hand, my boy. That being the case, I'd be proud to have you in the family." Cole presents a broad warm grim and sticks his hand out to his future son-in-law.

"The truth is," he continues, "Caroline mentioned your conversation, so I'm real glad you told me about it. You're the kind of man my daughter needs. Smart, honest, and hard working. When are you going to ask her?"

"Right away—today." Robert cheerfully relates.

"Do your parents know yet?"

"No, not yet. I plan to tell them after I talk to Beth. I know they'll be real happy about it, they both love her a lot."

"If you want to ride back to the house with Marty and me, shake a leg, son. We want to get a couple of hours sleep before it gets too late in the day." Robert hears his father call from the kitchen.

"You go ahead, Daddy, I'm going with Mr. Sanders back to his place to see Beth. I'll catch up with you later."

"That's fine. See you soon, Cole, we're leaving." John's words cause Cole to turn back into the kitchen, leaving Robert standing on the porch.

Before the screen door can shut, Randall pushes it again, and walks out announcing. "What you got going on with Mr. Sanders that's so secret?"

Robert can't hide a broad teeth baring smile.

"Don't say anything around where Daddy can hear you, but I'm going to ask Beth to marry me? I don't want to say anything to my family until I ask her and I know for sure she wants to?"

"Oh no, you're going to do what?" Randall chides in jest. "What can I say to talk you out of this?" He's unable to keep up the charade for more than a few seconds when he sees Robert's smile fading in disbelief. He takes two steps toward his friend to put his arms around him in a big hug. “It’s about time. You two practically live together now. If there was ever a couple meant for each other, it’s you and Beth. When are you going to ask her? Better do it quick, while you’ve got the nerve.”

“I’m going back with Mr. Sanders to their place right now, I’ll ask her today. He’s already said it’s okay with him.”

“I’m really happy for you, and I can tell she wants to marry you. It’s written all over her face every time she looks at you.”

“Thanks for the support, I sure hope you right.”

“You ready? Let’s get moving.” Cole pushes the screen door open and appears from the kitchen.

Meanwhile, back at La Nesra.

“What? You want to do what?”

“We want to get married.” Falcon repeats to Mr. Vaughn.

“Why? You’re together most of the time now.”

“We want to be together as man and wife,” Falcon continues.

“Live together as a couple,” Lilly adds.

“You mean, give your baby a father; that’s it, isn’t it? What’s going on here? You know, you might as well tell me the truth.” His expression changes from a blank to one of a ‘I’m-way-ahead-of-you’ stare over the top of his glasses. His abrupt candid response leaves the pair speechless for the moment.

“Listen to me. It makes no difference whether you’re married or single, when you give birth, your baby belongs to the Company, period. If you think you’ll get married and the three of you will somehow leave here, you might as well put it out of your mind.”

“It isn’t that, Mr. Vaughn. I just want my baby to have a father, and not be a bastard from the start of its life,” Lilly speaks up.

“And I want to give it my name,” Falcon enforces.

“I hear what you say, but I don’t see the point of it. The baby will have a name—one supplied by the Company. On the other hand, I suppose, if I don’t agree to it, you’ll put on a ritual of your own, and pretend to be married anyhow. This is a new one. I don’t recall any of our students wanting to get married to each other. Ahhhhmm.” He settles back in his chair behind the desk and begins to rub his chin with his left hand.

“A simple ceremony, correct?”

Falcon and Lilly look at each other, then respond in unison.

“Correct.”

“Let me sleep on it tonight. I’ll let you know tomorrow, sometime after dinner.” Mr. Vaughn dismisses them, as if they’re no longer in the room, by turning his attention to the paperwork on his desk. Once they’ve left, he looks up and allows his face to sport a small, knowing grin.

The couple is quiet until they’re outside in the courtyard.

“What do you make of that?” she asks.

"I don't know; he's up to something though. You can put your money on it," he responds. "I think he'll probably let us get married, but he's also probably going to shackle us to here, so we can't leave with or without our baby."

"He'll have to let me go one way or the other if he wants me to look for his life body" Lilly offers. "He's most likely thinking he'll keep you here just as he already planned. That way I'll have an even bigger reason to work my assignment and come back for you."

"If that's true, then nothing's really changed. We'll be no worse off than we are now, and be married." Falcon determines and speaks with a feeling of victory in his voice. "We'll know for sure tomorrow."

Cole and Robert dismount their horses at the hitching rail in front of the Sanders home, as Caroline and Beth emerge from the house to greet them.

"You're back sooner than I expected," Caroline comments.

"Yeah, well, we got an early start. You got something on the stove for dinner? I feel like I want to eat a little early today," he answers.

Robert makes a beeline to Beth's side.

As her parents disappear into the house, he takes Beth's hand and, without an explanation, leads her off the porch toward the barn. Once inside, he gestures to her to sit on a bale of hay. Obliging without hesitation, she watches him get down on his knees in front of her. The look on his face causes her eyes to open wider, supporting the sober, questioning look on her face.

He reaches to take her hands in his and raises his face to allow their eyes to meet. A few seconds pass as he takes in the vision of her.

"I love you more than anything in this world," he says softly. "I need you so much. I think about you the first thing every morning, and I see your face the last thing every night. I can't wait to be with you every day."

Beth watches the words being formed on his lips before she hears them through her ears. She feels a familiar emotion starting in the pit of her stomach. One that comes over her every time she gets near Robert. This time it's different, stronger than ever before, and it's flooding out all over. Her face is getting warm—hot—in anticipation as he continues.

"I don't have much to offer you, but I promise, I'll work hard to give you the life you deserve, and I'll always be here for you, with you. I want to raise our children with you."

Beth's eyes are welled with tears of joy as she looks at her handsome young man gazing into her eyes with such a commitment. She's barely able to keep her seat desiring to hold and caress him.

"I want to spend my life and grow old with you. Will you do me the honor of being my wife? Will you marry me?"

A chill goes down her back when she hears those words, "will you marry me."

It takes only a second for her to give him his answer. She leaps off the bale of hay, knocks him over backward, and lands on top of him when he hits the ground.

"Yes! Yes! Yes! I'll marry you. I feel the same way too. I'll be proud to be your wife," she yells, smothering him with rapid kisses around his face and forehead, settling on his lips, where she lingers. His arms come up around her to pull her firmly against his chest. They lie there, locked in their embrace of joyous emotion.

Caroline and Cole turn around and come back out onto the front porch when they see Robert leading their daughter to the barn. They stand there waiting, and finally hear her shout her acceptance. They turn to give each other a gentle hug, then turn again, with their arms around each other's waist, to gaze at the open barn doors.

"Our little girl has become a woman," Cole comments with a tear in his eye and a quiver in his lip.

"She has, honey. And she has your brains and sentimental ways with people too. She'll be just fine," Caroline compliments, and squeezes his hand.

"And she's got your good looks, along with your way of saying something to make everything okay, no matter what." Cole looks at a tear flowing over his wife's lips. "You're right, they'll be just fine. I'm sure glad you married me, Caroline. What would have happened to me if you hadn't?"

"I've wondered that, too."

It gets to be supper time before the betrothed couple finds their way to the Anderson home. It was hard for them to leave the Sanders' warm, heartfelt joy for their engagement.

"Hi, you two, I was wondering if you'd be here for supper," June remarks as they enter through the back door. "It's almost ready. So, get washed up. It'll be on the table in a few minutes."

The couple looks at each other and grins.

June catches the look and stops in her tracks.

"Okay, what's going on?"

Beth puts her finger up to her lips for a second, then whispers.

"We're engaged, we're getting married."

"You're getting married!" June's voice can be heard all the way out to the barn.

John, Charlotte, and Cheryl come bounding down the stairs, through the hallway, and into the kitchen.

"You're getting married?" Charlotte and Cheryl ask at once.

"They sure are!" Belle chimes out with a belly laugh.

"When did this all happen?" John asks with amazement.

"Just this afternoon," Robert answers.

"When? I mean, when are you getting married?" Robert's proud mother blurts.

"I want to be a June bride, if that's okay with you?" Beth addresses her new mother-in-law-to-be.

"I'd like that. I'd like that a lot," she confirms.

"Do your folks know? Wait, don't answer that. That's what that whole thing with you and Cole was about earlier today, wasn't it?" John puts it all together.

"Well, congratulations!" he continues loudly. "This is a happy occasion. Belle, break out some champagne for us all. Let's celebrate the upcoming marriage of our son to the daughter of one of our best friends. I couldn't be happier. I wish Cole and Caroline were here right now."

"Beth, I hope you know how we all feel about you," June speaks with emotion in her voice, almost breaking into tears. "You're already one of the family. We all love you so very much. Hearing this news is like melting it all together, making our family even more united. My prayers have been answered."

With that, June, Beth, Charlotte, Cheryl, and Belle all gang together to hug each other and cry, while John and Robert exchange handshakes and manly hugs.

Beneath her joy of experiencing a moment like none other in her life, Cheryl's mind is trying to put it all together in a way to satisfy her feelings. She's torn between having a family, and her sworn allegiances to the Company. "I can't do anything to hurt these people. They're all so happy and committed to each other. They aren't out to hurt anybody. They love and trust each other. They know if they're threatened by someone or something outside the family, the family—no matter what—will be there for them. I want that, I need that. But if I don't do something, the Company will probably come after me and hurt me, maybe even kill me. Then they'll send someone else in here to do what they sent me here to do anyway. It could be better for me to do some things, not hurt anyone, just enough to keep them at bay, enough to give me some time to figure this all out. I'd better go over to Der Bote tomorrow."

Cheryl is up and out of the house early enough to be at Der Bote around nine. Luckily, and probably because of the news last night, no one asks questions when she announces she's going to Der Bote this morning. So far, so good.

Instead of going to the front door when she arrives, she spins the reins of her horse, Pooch, around the hitching rail, then walks around to the back of the house and onto the porch. She puts her face close to the screen to peer into the kitchen. There's no one to be seen. The screen door is unlocked, and opens with a creak and scratch as she enters.

"Hello! Anyone home?" she calls out.

The house is silent.

She moves into the hallway, stopping at the foot of the stairs.

"Anybody here?"

The house remains quiet.

"I wonder where everyone is?" She says to herself. "I should probably wait on the front porch for a while. But on the other hand, this might be the perfect time to see if I can find anything to tip me off about my contact. Let me think, where should I look first. His desk . . . the colonel's desk might give me a clue."

She slips into the den to find a large wooden desk setting crossways in a corner with a chair, a flag on a standard, and a floor lamp, behind it. She begins to look through a stack of papers lying in a pile on the corner. Nothing there.

"I'll check the drawers," she says under her breath.

"This one's locked. I wonder what all's in there?"

She opens the middle drawer above the seating area and discovers a letter opener.

"This might work. If I can pry down on the drawer, the catch might clear enough for me to get it open."

A loud snap!

"Damn, it broke. I'd better take it with me. They might not miss it if it isn't here, for sure they'll wonder how it broke if I leave it. I'll slip it into my pocket. I'll run into the kitchen and get a knife or something."

As she is about to enter the kitchen, the screen door squeaks and scratches outward. Almost falling from trying to stop her forward motion, she barely has enough time to pull back into the hallway when she hears footsteps enter the kitchen, coming toward her. Her choices are limited and a decision must be made. Stay where she is and explain why she's there, or hide somewhere and slip out of the house a bit later. Her self-preservation instincts take over and command her to hide.

Upstairs! Run!

Up the stairs she goes, taking three steps at a time, down the short hallway through a partially open door. She closes the door almost shut, leaving enough room to see out. Wait! Control her breathing! Stop panting! Quiet!

After a few minutes of watching through the opening in the door, seeing no one coming up the stairs, she decides to look around the room. It's almost dark with the drapes pulled. There's barely enough light to see the furniture, a chair with clothes lying over it next to the bed. The bed—someone's in the bed! Her heart pounds so loud she grabs her chest with a thump and freezes in her position.

There's no sound or movement from the bed.

"I wonder who it is? If I can get a little closer, maybe I can see."

She creeps carefully, making sure the floor doesn't creak under her weight, to the side of the bed closest to the persons face. She bends down to get a look.

"Charles! Are you going to sleep the day away?" the loud voice of Selma coming up the stairs resounds through the entire house. She's coming down the hallway.

"Did you hear me dear man?" Her voice is louder than before.

The person in the bed begins to stir.

"Hide! Where?"

Selma enters and walks directly to the curtains to pull them apart allowing the daylight to the flood the room.

"Come on, Charles. You'll not want to go to bed tonight if you sleep all day. Get up, it's a wonderful day."

"You're right," he mumbles. "Come here and help me up."

"Why? Can't you get yourself up this morning?" She thinks she knows why.

"Just come here and help me up," he says quietly.

"Oh, all right, but remember, there are people up and about in the house." She moves to the side of the bed knowing he's going to grab her and pull her down with him.

He does just that, and pulls her to him to begin kissing her neck and face.

"Uuummmm, you taste good," he coos.

"So that's it. Now I know what's on your mind. Let me up, I'll close the door, get out of these clothes, and be right back. Now don't lose your place, or you'll have to start all over again."

Charles loosens his hold, allowing her to get up and move away from the bed.

She closes the door, then turns toward the bed to stop dead in her tracks.

"Do you have another woman in here with you?"

"Yeah . . . she's under the bed," he banters.

"I smell perfume that isn't like any of mine."

"You're serious, aren't you?"

"Well there is, or has been, someone in here wearing perfume unlike any I own, or have ever worn. Believe me, I know the scent of my own perfume."

Alberta Mae's voice comes up the stairway.

"Miss Selma, there's a horse tied out in front of the house. I think it's the one Ms. Charlotte rides. You know, I think they call him Pooch. But I don't see her anywhere down here. I just came from our house, and she's not there either."

Selma looks at Charles, and Charles her.

"Charlotte, if you're in here, you might as well come out. We'll find you anyway," she commands.

Charles is trying frantically to get his pants on over his long johns by balancing on one foot. Bent over, he's tugging them over his other leg.

"This is humiliating," Cheryl thinks. "I'm certainly not much of a spy. I'm failing miserably. I might as well get this over with, they're going to find me anyway."

"It's me, Cheryl," she explains as she slides on her back from beneath the bed.

The couple, agape as they stand motionless, watch her get to her feet.

The colonel's eyes expand. "Honest, Selma, I didn't know she was there. I was joshing."

"What are you doing in our bedroom—under our bed?" Selma asks grimly, ignoring her husband. "How did you get up here in the first place?"

"I know this looks pretty bad, but let me explain!" Cheryl's face is as red as a hot poker.

Charles manages to get his pants on, but is still without a shirt, and stands scratching his mussed hair with his left hand, obviously still a bit bewildered by what's happening.

"Yes, explain, please. I can't wait to hear this!" Mrs. Housler exclaims in an accusing manner.

By this time, Alberta Mae is standing in the doorway.

"Oh my . . . my, my," she wonders out loud.

"Well, first, I called from the back porch into the house and no one answered. So, I came into the kitchen and called and called again. Then I heard a noise, like someone was upstairs. So, I went to the bottom of the steps and yelled up here. And then, when I didn't get a response, I came up here looking for somebody—anybody. I didn't find anybody, so I was on my way back down when I heard someone coming through the back screen door. And well, I got scared of being seen coming down the stairs, so I ran in here. I got under the bed when you came down the hallway. I know I shouldn't have came in your house with no one here. I'm really sorry." She's been taught to tell the truth as much as possible, then fabricate a story as required.

"Did you hear her come in here, Charles?" Selma asserts.

"No, I didn't hear her at all. You woke me up."

"What's that thing sticking out of your pocket, honey?" Alberta Mae inquires.

"Oh, no!" The letter opener, she sees the broken letter opener. The young woman almost swallows her tongue at the thought of getting caught with such a piece of evidence. "Ignore her, don't acknowledge a thing she's said. Maybe, they'll let it pass."

"I'm really sorry I've caused such a problem. I didn't mean any harm. I just came over to visit with everyone for a little while, that's all. Please forgive me." The begging starts.

"A similar thing happened to me when I was a child." Charles indicates his understanding of the situation. "I was afraid I'd be blamed for something I didn't do, so I made things worse by hiding, and then got caught. I can see how this happened."

"That's right Mr. Housler. That's the reason I hid. I was afraid I'd be blamed for something, somehow, so I went and hid. I haven't done anything, and I didn't come here to do anything, except to visit for a while. I'll understand if you want me to go and not come back," Cheryl continues.

"Yes, well, I guess I can see how that could be the case. Let's go downstairs and give Charles a chance to get dressed. We can sort this all out down in the kitchen over a cup of coffee," Selma directs.

"I've got to get rid of this letter opener," Cheryl realizes. "If Alberta Mae asks again, I'll have no choice but to explain what I'm doing with it. But if I don't have it, she'll think she was mistaken and didn't see it."

As Alberta Mae and Selma turn to leave the bedroom, She slides the letter opener out of her pocked and lets it fall, almost silently, to the rug on the floor. Then gives the two pieces a nudge with her toe to push it back under the bed.

The three women descend the stairs and enter the kitchen. Alberta Mae reaches for the coffeepot as they sit down. Selma speaks first, after sipping of her coffee.

"Now, tell us Cheryl, why are you here? You and I both know you didn't come here just to visit," she asks, bluntly to the point.

"Can I speak with you privately, Mrs. Housler," Cheryl asks.

"Anything you have to say to me you can say in front of Alberta Mae."

"Anything?"

'That's right"

The colonel has wasted no time getting dressed and coming down stairs. As he walks into the kitchen, Alberta Mae jumps up from her seat to her feet.

"Eggs and bacon okay with you this morning, sir?" she inquires.

"That's fine, but some coffee first," he responds as he sits down.

"I'm glad you're here, Mr. Housler, because the real reason I'm here concerns the both of you." She decides to get it over with and just ask if either of them is her contact.

"I have an idea that you already know I was sent here to spy on everybody. When I left the Company to come here they told me to make contact with another agent in the area. They told me I would know my contact when I came across him or her. They said to look for the messenger. So, I know that Der Bote is German for 'the messenger.' I guessed that means one of you is my contact." She points at Selma first, then the colonel.

"You think one or both of us are spying on the people around here?" Selma acts astonished at the accusation. "I take it then, you're trying to make a connection with your fellow spies. Is that right?"

"That's right. But not for the reason you're probably thinking."

"And what are we supposed to be thinking?" Mrs. Housler's tone shows her temper is being tested.

"First, I need to know if one of you is my contact. Are you?" Cheryl insists on an answer.

"I'm tired of the cat and mouse game you're playing. Tell us why you're here and what you want from us. If you're not able to do that, I'm taking you home to John and June and let you explain your presence here to them. Now, the next words out of your mouth will tell me what I need to do." The colonel lays the two pieces of the broken letter opener on the table as he speaks.

Selma grins and squirms on her seat when she hears her husbands words. Alberta Mae is busy fixing the colonel's breakfast, pretending she's not hearing a thing.

"No, don't do that." Cheryl weakens at the suggestion. "I couldn't stand to cause them any more grief than I already have. Please don't do that."

"Then you'd better start talking, and this time the truth!" Selma pounds her righteously.

"I came over here to see if I could find out which one of you is my contact without you knowing it. I'm afraid if I don't let the Company know how I'm doing, they might send someone to check on me. I thought if one of you is part of the Company, too, then maybe you could help me—somehow. I was looking for something to tell me which one of you it is when I broke the letter opener trying to get your desk drawer open. I never did see or find anything. That's when you came in and I ran upstairs, and that's all there is, that's the truth. Please believe me, I'll never do anything to hurt you or anybody here. But if the Company comes and does some things, you'll all think I caused it and blame me for it. I was trying to protect us all. Can you see that? Do you understand what I mean? What else can I do?"

"It seems to me that someone has to start trusting somebody if this whole thing is ever going to be settled," Alberta Mae speaks up unexpectedly. "Right now, nobody can trust nobody."

"You've made a good point. We have to start somewhere if we're ever going to be able to relax around each other again." Selma's temper has gone back into hiding. "Personally, I'd like to be able to get to know who you are, and someday be your trusted friend. With that in mind, and with Charles's agreement, we'll take a chance and accept your explanation. I can sense the worry in your thinking. Just one thing though, if you hurt my dear friend June in any way, you'll answer to me. And answer to me you will."

"I'll go along with this because I think it's the right thing to do. But I caution you, Cheryl, you don't know my wife like I do. Listen to what she says and heed her every word. She means it. Don't become a target of her scorn." The colonel supports his wife.

"I'd like to take this a step further, however. If, after you leave here, you have second thoughts about our understanding, leave this area of the country under the cover of darkness, without a word to anyone. Just vanish, and never come back. That would be the best way to end your charade for all concerned. Agreed?"

"Oh, yes, sir, but I'm not going anywhere. I want, so badly, to be able to trust, to be trusted, to have a family, and close friends, like you all here. Be sure of this, if there is a fight to be fought, I'll be at your side. I swear it."

Chapter Twenty-Three

The date is late March,1861.

The seceding states of the South have selected a president of the newly established Confederate States of America. Montgomery, Alabama, will be their capital city.

The newly elected Union party candidate was inaugurated to the office of president of the United States on March fourth. The nation's capital was, and is, Washington DC.

The threat of war lies over the land like a heavy hand with a grip that can be denied by no one. Southern states have begun to withdraw from the Union as their Confederacy takes shape. It's expected that a total of eleven states will join their effort. To say, however, that an overwhelming majority of the Southern population supports the ideals of the Confederacy would be a stretch of the truth. Since the feeling of the need for free slave labor lessens the farther north you travel, the Union states are strongly supported by the public, both philosophically and financially.

The Union states along the northern border of the Confederacy are a boiling pot of slave owners, abolitionists, peace seekers, and those interested only in their own gains regardless of who wins the war. Loosely noted, those States are Missouri, Kentucky, Ohio, Pennsylvania, Maryland, and Delaware.

Husband against wife, brother against brother, sister against sister, father against son, family against family, clan against clan, the war will be fought to free the slaves; but many will fight each other to settle old personal grievances, and do it righteously, at least in their minds.

The number of bandits and outlaws are on the rise. It's easy to place the blame for the problems of these times upon the war. Law enforcers are outnumbered to the point that many localities have taken the attitude of "there's not much we can do"; the Federals will deal with it when the war starts.

John Anderson is spending more and more time away from home, working day and night, building his organization. The more people he brings into the Sons as agents, the more people it takes to support their efforts. It's growing faster than he ever dreamed. He's amazed to see how many are willing to devote their lives to their country. He hasn't seen his farm for over three weeks now, so he feels the need to get home more every day.

In Atlanta, Georgia, at La Nesra, Lilly has given birth to her child, a girl. The only name associated with her at this point is 'baby.' The parents were married with a small legal ceremony on the third day of December, eighteen hundred sixty. They live together in the small house built especially for Lilly during her pregnancy. Their plans for escaping the grip of the Company are decided, but they are biding their time, waiting for the new mother to fully regain her strength before putting them into action.

Robert and Beth are busy planning their June wedding. His mother June and Caroline are working together to make it an event to be remembered. Robert is also busy with the Anderson farm operation, and his self-felt responsibilities to keep the farms closest to theirs protected.

Randall hasn't given up on the idea of rescuing Sheree from the Company, but with Bob tied up with his commitments, he can find little or no support. He spends a good deal of time educating himself by reading anything and everything he can get his hands on.

It's been noticed that he and Charlotte are together more often than ever these days. They've been seen sitting for long periods of time, talking, and at times poking at each other laughingly. They are a topic of discussion within the families, but nothing has been mentioned to the youngsters.

June, along with Charlotte and Cheryl, is in town today, and is standing in the general store. Jim and Josh came with the ladies to provide some security.

"Cheryl, you'd better get a move on if you're going to be on time for your appointment at Miss Eliza's for your fitting. You know she doesn't like for a person to be late," June says to her "niece."

"I'm going. Are you coming with me Charlotte? You can see how beautiful my new dress is going to be. It's destined to be my favorite," Cheryl answers cheerily.

"Do I have to go, Mama? I'd rather stay here with you. I don't care about her old dress." Charlotte whines like a small child. You would think she's envious, but she knows she can have any, or as many dresses as she wants. All she has to do is ask.

"I suppose not. You can go by yourself, honey, but be sure to be back at the carriage in about an hour." June handles the small problem as she looks through her bag for the list of supplies she needs for the farm.

"Okay, I'll see you later." Cheryl holds her hand up, wiggles her fingers goodbye at Charlotte, and out the door she goes.

It is a bit chilly today for the thin shawl she has around her shoulders, but Cheryl likes to be noticed. She likes heads to turn when she passes by people on the street. For that reason she lets the shawl hang down between her arms and sides, keeping her front side open to be viewed. A small pleasant smile is on her lips, and she walks with a bit of a spring and swing in her step. Her gaze is straight ahead but watchful of everyone she passes to view their reaction.

Just another two blocks, then a left turn will put her at the entrance of Miss Eliza's shop. She steps down off the wooden sidewalk to cross an alleyway. Some ten steps on the moist ground will take her to the next stretch of board sidewalk.

She's ready to take her second step when she feels the grip of someone's hand on her upper left arm. She's pulled off balance and falls sideways toward the alley. When she turns her body to the left to catch herself with her right hand, another hand grips her upper right arm, and she's forced back through the alley to the rear of the buildings. It happens so quickly, she doesn't think to scream or fight back. A right turn at the back of the building puts them behind cover. She takes a breath to yell, but before she can utter a sound, a hand covers her mouth, and an arm slides around her waist to get a firm grip.

"Hush! We don't want to hurt you! There's an old friend of yours here who wants to talk to you. If I take my hand away, will you promise not to make a fuss?"

After a few seconds, realizing she has no chance of getting away as long as he has her in his grasp, she nods yes, and her abductor gradually loosens his hold.

She moves away and turns to confront her foes. A good hard swift kick and she'll run down the alley toward the main street and safety. "One . . . , two . . . , th—"

Before she can get moving, a voice comes from behind her. A familiar voice, one she had hoped she would not hear for a long time.

"Amber, it's Sally. Remember me?" Sally comes from behind and turns to face her as she passes. "I haven't seen you for some time. You look good. Someone's taking care of you, that's obvious."

Cheryl ignores the small talk. "What do you want? Why are you here?"

"Our friends at the Company say they haven't heard a thing from you since you left. They want to know what you're doing, so they sent me to find out, that's all. I'm sorry we had to approach you the way we did, but the opportunity presented itself and, well now you're here and we can talk," she relates.

Cheryl has no response. She's dreaded this day since the day she arrived at the Andersons home.

"Have you been able to settle in with the Anderson family?"

"You could say that."

"Do they believe you're their daughter, Sheree?"

"Not exactly" Cheryl needs time to think, time to make a plan. "Listen, I'm late for an appointment. Let me meet you somewhere tomorrow afternoon. I'll tell you everything you want to know then."

"No, that will not be acceptable, I need information now. If you'll stop fencing with me for a few minutes and answer my questions, you can go."

"Well, I don't know what you want me to say," she states indignantly.

"Oh I see. Okay, we'll play your game. I want answers to a few little questions, such as: Who do they think you are? And why haven't you communicated with your contact? We know the Houslers have moved slaves through here over the years, are they still at it? What's John Anderson doing with his time since he pulled out of the governor's race? You know, things like that." Sally shows her contempt for Cheryl's attitude.

"I've not been able to locate my contact. I thought it was the Houslers, but now I don't think they are." Cheryl skips the first question intentionally.

"They're not your contact, I can tell you that. Why did you think they were?"

"I was told to look for the messenger. Their farm is named Der Bote, which is German for 'the messenger,' that's why. If they're not, then who is it?" Her attitude is showing again.

"Under these circumstances, I'll not tell you that right now." The redheaded woman finds it easy to take an attitude herself and replies curtly. "Take her to the barn. We shouldn't stay out in the open like this any longer."

"Where in the world is that girl? I asked her to be back here in no more than an hour. It doesn't take that long to put on a dress for a fitting." June's getting impatient.

"I heard you tell her, Mama. Want me to go see what's holding her up at Miss Eliza's?" Charlotte volunteers.

"Please," she responds insistently.

Charlotte's gone no more than six or seven minutes, when she returns to the carriage on the run. "She's not there. Miss Eliza says she hasn't seen her today."

"This is not like her at all. This town's not big enough for her to lose herself in it, something's wrong. Something must have happened to her." Mrs. Anderson gets more upset as she speaks. "Let's get over to Doc's and see if he can help us find her."

"Jim, you and Josh go back to the farm and get Robert. Tell him what's going on, and that we need him here as quickly as possible. Tell him to bring all the help he can. Hurry Jim, I think we have a big problem," she gives orders, feeling vulnerable.

The carriage turns around in the middle of the street to head the other direction. A crack of the whip above the horses backs gets them running. They're out of sight in a few seconds.

Doc has explained that the only thing he can do is ask the town deputy to form a search party, so, he goes with the women to the deputy's office. The law enforcement officer is naturally curious about their reasons. Once they're related, he says there's no need for a search party, he'll handle it himself without bothering the townsfolk. June is upset to say the least.

"You expect me to sit here and wait while you—by yourself—hunt this town over for my niece. That'll take too long. Someone could take her miles from here before you get started," she yells at the lawman.

"Time's passing while you're screaming, ma'am. I'll get started as soon as you settle down," he defiantly advises.

The carriage, with Jim and Josh aboard, arrives at the farm with a flurry of commotion. They take turns yelling for Robert and the hands as they roll up to the front of the house. Belle, who is sweeping the front porch is the first to react. She drops her broom and runs to meet them.

"What on earth is wrong?" she yells. "Where's my girls? What's happened to my girls?"

Robert is the next to appear out through the screen door to leap over the porch steps. The hands come running in at the same time.

"Ms. Cheryl is missing! We can't find her in town! Ms. Anderson said we should come and get you, and get back there as quick as we can!" Jim's out of breath as though he ran all the way from town. "She says to bring as much help as we can!"

"Change these horses out, and get the buckboard hitched up. Then saddle four horses. I want outriders with these wagons. All you hands climb aboard as soon as they're ready."

"Count me in, Bob." Randy volunteers from his position on the porch. "I'm going, too."

"I was counting on that Randy, thanks. Belle, you and Randy get as many handguns and holsters as you can. We'll need close to fifteen if my count's right, and grab the ammunition we'll need. Get me Daddy's double barrel scattergun, too. Everybody hurry now, I want to be out of here in fifteen minutes!" he shouts orders.

June has been pacing the floor since the deputy left to start his search. Back and forth, back and forth.

"June, will you sit down somewhere?" Doc begs insistently. "You're going to wear a hole through that wood floor, and you're about to drive me crazy."

"I can't help it, Doc I can feel Cheryl slipping away from me. It brings back those old memories of Sheree, the day they took her. But what can I do? I've been ordered to stay here, out of the way. Well, I'm about ready to kill something, and I guess it shows." June explodes at Doc's suggestion.

"To hell with the deputy, Mama. Let's you and me go down the street asking some questions ourselves?" Charlotte's statement comes out as a question. "What's he going to do? Put us in jail? He doesn't have a jail."

"Let's go!" They head for the door as Doc lowers and shakes his head from side to side.

June is on the sidewalk and waits for her daughter to close the door to Doc's office. All at once, the carriage, the buckboard, and four outriders storm into town, coming to an abrupt stop in the middle of the street in front of them.

Robert is the first to jump down from his saddle to trot toward his mother and sister. The rest of his help climb down and walk the same direction, grouping together as they go.

The deputy hears and sees their arrival and jogs up the dirt street to see who's invading his town. He first sees a familiar face, then the scattergun.

"Robert," he muses as he nears the group, his left eye squints as the left side of his mouth bends up slightly.

"Cliff," he replies coldly.

"You here on a mission?" the town peace keeper asks without changing expressions.

"If you mean, am I here to find my kin, I am, and I've brought my own help. Do you have a problem with that?" Young Mr. Anderson turns to face the deputy, and switches the scattergun to his right hand.

The men from the farm start to separate when they see him take the stance.

"Whoa! Whoa, now!" the deputy shouts. "Don't start throwing lead. No one's going to get all shot up over a missing girl. Hell, this job don't pay that kind of money."

"That missing girl, as you call her, is my cousin, Cliff. Now, what's it going to be, are you going to help us, or do I need to deal with you first. Whichever, I start in thirty seconds."

"What do you want me to do? Just tell me and I'll do it," Cliff settles himself.

"My men and I will do what needs to be done. You'd better hope I don't find out this is all due to your bungling ways, deputy. You just stay where I can see you, and tell these townspeople what we're doing as we go. Got it?"

"I will, just tell your men to relax a little."

Robert ignores his request.

"Jim, take two men and stake out that far end of town. We'll start on the other end and come toward you. We'll wait until you're in place before we start. Be on the lookout, there's no telling what we might flush out of here."

Jim motions and the three men mount up and take off at a gallop to the edge of town. Once there, a wave of their hands starts the search.

"He's just like his father," June says loud enough for Charlotte to hear.

"Daddy would be proud of him today, too, Mama. I guess he already knows it though. That's why he left him in charge while he's away."

After twenty minutes of searching, they've found no sign of Cheryl. Robert, Jim, and several hands walk up to the barn behind the smitty shop.

"Two of you go around to the back, Jim and I will go through the front," he announces.

Guns in hand, hammers back, the two men enter the barn looking side to side, up and down, expecting something—anything. Jim speaks first.

"Look over here. This looks like Miss Cheryl's shawl."

The back doors swing open and two hands enter. That gives Robert the opportunity to look where Jim's pointing.

"It's hers all right," Robert confirms. "Get everybody in here. We have to search this whole barn."

It takes the men ten minutes to look everywhere. Under piles of hay and straw, behind and inside crates and boxes here and there, the haymow, and beneath a pile of feed sacks. No luck. They're glad nothing turned up because it most likely would have been a lifeless body.

"Okay, let's keep going and clear the rest of town," Robert instructs. At this point he doubts he'll find his cousin, here in town anyway. Twenty minutes later, he's walking up to his mother. His men, scattered down the street, follow him.

"She's not here. We've looked everywhere."

"What now? What can I do? I need to do something," June begs.

"You can get some supplies together for four men for two or three days. Randy, Jim, Josh, and I are taking the horses to see if we can pick up some tracks."

"We'll have them back here in a few minutes. Come Charlotte, you can help?" The two women head for the general store.

Twenty minutes later, the supplies are packed, tied to the horses, and the men are getting ready to leave. Robert gets a hug from his mother.

"Be very careful, son. I'll die if something happens to you."

"I will, don't worry," he says to soothe her. He mounts his horse and notices Randy's empty saddle. As he looks around, Jim points him out.

Randy and Charlotte are standing together, back away from the group, her hands on either side of his neck, with his on either side of her waist, looking at each other's face.

"Let's go, laddy," he calls out.

Two heads turn to look, then back for a quick peck on the lips, and Randy is in the saddle, ready to go. Robert can't hide a broad grin. Knowing Randy as he does, a pairing of him and his sister suits him just fine. The four men wave as they turn their horses and gallop away.

As soon as the horses are out of sight, June turns to her daughter. "Let's get over to the telegraph office, we should send word to your father. If we don't, he'll be upset when he finds it out, and you know we don't want that along with everything else."

June studies for a few minutes over the blank paper pad determining just what message she'll wire to her husband. "There's no sense getting him all stirred up, he can't do anything from Maryland. There's no good way except to tell him outright." She decides to herself. Her hand moves the pencil across the paper, then she lays it on the pad and pushes it toward Virgil.

"John. Cheryl has been abducted. Robert is out tracking those responsible. I will keep you informed. We are all safe. Do not worry. June."

"Is that it?" he asks, after reading the message out loud.

June nods.

"Mmmm. Let's see here," he ponders "that'll be forty cents."

"I'll get it out right away" he says, as he turns and sits at a table holding the telegraph key.

"Let's get back to the farm. There's nothing more we can do here." June concludes and moves through the door with Charlotte at her elbow, headed for the carriage.

June's messenger stands on the front porch at Der Bote awaiting a response to the note she wrote on the way from town. Mr. Housler is reading.

"Selma! Come here please! We have a message from June!" he calls throughout the house.

Selma is surprised to see the colonel standing with a piece of paper in his hand, and the door open with a black man standing, waiting.

"What sort of message?" she asks urgently.

The colonel doesn't speak, just hands her the paper.

"Selma, please do me the favor of coming to our farm as quickly as possible. Cheryl has been abducted. Robert, and Randy are out trying to catch up to those responsible. Charlotte and I are left here alone, and I need your company and support. Please come, if you can. Signed, June"

She raises her eyes from the paper.

"He's waiting for an answer," the colonel calmly, quietly explains.

"I hope you don't mind, Charles, but I have to go, you know that."

"You take this message to Mrs. Anderson. Selma will be there immediately." Charles instructs the messenger.

"Thank you, Charles. Alberta Mae, are you in the kitchen!" she calls out.

"Yes, ma'am. Is there trouble?" Their cook and housekeeper enters the hallway.

"Yes, I'm afraid so. Randy and Robert are out chasing after some people who have taken Cheryl away from the Andersons. She wants me to keep her company at her place until they return. I should take a few clothes with me, enough to last three or four days, I would think."

"Yes, ma'am, I'll help you pack."

"Have Jacob hitch the blacks up to the surrey," the colonel instructs Jacob's wife. "I'll take my wife to the Andersons, and return as soon as I know everyone's settled and safe. I shouldn't be gone all that long."

John Anderson is standing behind his desk at his office in Baltimore stuffing his case with papers. Marty Schoener is sitting across from him watching.

Arrangements have been made for the Son's chief to run his horses all the way to his farm. He'll exchange them at intervals for fresh mounts allowing him to continue nonstop except for food and drink. He figures he can be there late tomorrow night, or early the next morning.

"I'm sorry, Marty, I know this isn't the best time to leave you here on your own. But June wouldn't send a message like this unless she thinks I should be there. I don't know what all has happened, but you can bet our little innocent niece has a hand in it somewhere. Just when you think you can trust people, well, you know what I mean. As I said, I should be back in no more than a week or ten days. You won't have to explain to anyone, but if you should need a reason for my absence, just say I'm away conducting meetings with prospective agents. That always works."

"Go, John, and don't worry about it. I'll handle things here. This place isn't going to fold up in ten days. I just hope June's problems are something that can be handled. If you need any help once you get there, just get a message to me. If necessary, I'll bring the cavalry."

"Thanks, Marty, I appreciate it. Anything else we should discuss before I leave?"

"Yes, there is one more thing, and I know we've talked about it before. But it's becoming a real problem, and getting bigger every day."

"Are you back on the 'right to kill' warpath again? Darn it, I've told you any number of times, I don't have the power to authorize our people to kill without being held responsible for it. If they kill, they're going to be judged for it, and if necessary, pay the consequences. That's all there is to it."

"I hear every word you say, but try to put yourself in the position we've asked some of these people to assume. The Company has given each and every one of their top agents a license to kill. When our people face one of these devils, we don't stand a chance. You can't ask a person to take on a gun fight with their hands tied. It won't be long before these brave souls will be murdered, or resort to resigning to protect themselves. We need to act now. Just let me take the top twenty most exposed people. Let me give them something . . . ?"

"Like what?" John inquires with exasperation.

"I don't know—say, you can shoot back, as long as they shoot first—anything. You know, I guess I should have asked this question directly some time ago," Marty continues.

"Who has the authority to give us the go ahead?"

"That's just the point. No one, no one with any political authority who knows about us will talk about it. I can't take it to the mainstream judiciary branch, they don't know we exist."

"I seem to remember you telling me, you're the head cheese here. The buck stops with you. You should make the decision." Marty pushes hard.

"Maybe I already have." John suggests. "I'm hesitant to give anyone the right to kill someone else. What will I be saying with a gesture like that?"

"You know, if the president came in here right now and pinned a general title on you, you wouldn't hesitate to send soldiers out to kill or be killed. Tell me, what's the difference here?"

"I suppose, the fact that the president gave me the responsibility to do exactly that. Oh, I see what you're saying," John's expression changes as he pauses. "I see what you mean. It appears he's already done that, hasn't he?"

Marty lets a big grin spread across his face.

"You sly old fox, you led me right down that path. You've been up nights thinking about this haven't you." John smiles at his friend.

"All right, you've got it. But pass out this license carefully, because I'm authorizing you, and only you, to do it. Put my name on the top of the list, and get with me as soon as I get back to let me know those you've selected. You might consider the mission, as well as the person, when you're deciding."

"Bravo. We'll start kicking some ass and making a difference now!" Marty is elated with the new possibilities.

The plan of the search party is to disperse outward about a hundred yards apart, starting a half a mile outside of town. Then together, they'll make circles around the town, expanding outward on each turn, looking for tracks that will give them a clue as to the direction of the abductors. The odds are probably not in their favor, but it's their only sensible option. Ten minutes into their second turn, and out of the sight of each other because of the rolling hills, the monotony of their search is interrupted by the sound of two shots. Everybody in the party knows to converge on the man doing the shooting. He's found something. Jim fired the shots. He's down on one knee looking at the ground when the three riders arrive within a few seconds of each other. All dismount, walk, and bend down to look down at his find.

"See here. Hoof prints headed that way." He points the direction. "I didn't think much of them at first, until I saw one is carrying double. It could be them. Three horses carrying four people."

"It's probably them. Those tracks are fresh too, not more than a few hours old," Josh observes.

"It has to be them," Randy confirms.

"Then, let's go!" Robert commits easily, since there's nothing else to go on.

Tracking takes time when the trail is good. This ground the fleeing abductors are following is hard and rocky, making it difficult to see the signs. They know what they are doing, slowing their trackers down. Several times, the four men giving chase have lost the tracks and have had to ride in outward spiraling circles to locate them again.

"It's going to be dark in a few minutes, Bob. Let's find a place to settle in for the night? The light's getting bad, and if we're not careful we'll wander off the trail so far we'll never be able to pick it up again. We can start again at first light," Randy suggests.

"If it's okay with the three you, I'd like to keep moving for a while. I've got this feeling if we don't catch up with them tonight, we'll never see Cheryl again. Mama gave me this compass back in town, and I've been watching the general direction of these tracks. No matter how they drift off, side to side, they always come back to north-northeast. I think we should give it another couple of hours, and if we don't have something definite working by then, yeah, we'll stop. We can unwrap some of these sandwiches Charlotte made and eat in the saddle. What do you say?"

"He's never led me wrong before." Randy supports his friend. "And as long as he feeds me, I'm ready."

"Let's go." Josh seconds Randy's intended motion.

"We better get our jackets on before we set out. It's going to get chilly when that sun goes down." Good advice from Jim.

On they trudge, their horses walking single file behind Robert. He stops every half hour to adjust their direction by using the compass. After a couple of hours, the only noises made by the group are those of the horses' hooves, constant, rhythmic, clopping; and those of night creatures moving about in the bushes and weeds as the riders pass.

Their leader stops, thinking he'll give up for the night to let his men and animals get some rest. The three come to his side thinking he's checking the compass again.

"Over there," Jim comments quietly. "Is that the flicker of a campfire?"

"Where?"

"Over there." He points.

They all look, straining their eyes to be the first to agree with him.

"I don't see anything," Bob relates after thirty seconds of searching the darkness.

"Me neither," Josh agrees.

"I must be seeing things, but I swear I saw something. I probably wouldn't have seen it at all if we hadn't stopped. It was just for a second, and then no more. These old eyes must be playing tricks on me." He's ready to dismiss his belief and move on.

"How far off did it seem to be?" Randy inquires.

"Oh, I don't rightly know, maybe a quarter of a mile."

"It's the only hint of a sign we've had all day." Bob points out. "Let's give it a half hour in that direction. If we don't come up with something by then, we'll settle in for the night. Agreed?"

"That's good." Is heard from Josh. They fall into a single file when they start moving again.

They've traveled some seven hundred yards, when Bob stops again. This time he motions the other three to his side. "Look there." He points to his front and out to the right. "That's a campfire, for sure. We'd better leave our horses here, so we don't roust them out when we move up. Tie them to these bushes. We don't want them running off if they hear some gunfire. All set? Follow close to me. No talking."

The men move smoothly, quietly, weaving past shrubs and briar patches. Bob drops to a squatting position and waits for the others to catch up.

"Randy, you and Jim split off here and go around to the other side. We'll wait until we see you come up, then Josh and I will go in. You lay back and cover us. Don't make a move until we do, but after that, do what you think needs done. Got it?" He doesn't wait for a response. "Let's go."

Bob and Josh move like cats, slinking, sneaking closer to the campfire. Side by side, they sink to one knee, then his leader leans to whisper in Josh's ear.

"There's two bedrolls, over there." He points. "See that shack over there?" He points again to a small building some fifty feet away from the campfire. "That's probably where they're holding Cheryl. We know there's three of them from their tracks. There's two out here, so one must be in the shack with her. When we see Randy and Jim, we'll go in and try to take control without any gunfire, but be ready for anything."

"Yessir," Josh breathes a whisper.

"They're here, let's do it." The pair walks quietly into the clearing, guns in hand, hammers cocked. Bob takes the first bedroll by putting the muzzle of his scattergun against the neck just under the chin, of the sleeping man.

"What the hell!" He reacts loudly at the touch of the cold steel.

The other bedroll jerks and the blanket flies off to expose the second man startled by the yell, moving to a sitting position, gun in hand. He starts to turn to confront the problem, when the barrel of Josh's handgun presses against the back of his neck.

"Drop the gun, and don't make another move!"

With their attention focused at the action by the campfire, Bob and Josh barely hear the squeaking of the hinges on the door of the shack as it opens.

Bzzzzzzzz, bzzzzzzzz, bzzzzzzzz, the noise of angry hornets passing over their heads is heard just before the sound of gunfire!

Josh dives for the ground and starts rolling back away from the fire. Bob jumps in the opposite direction, turns the barrel of his shotgun toward the sound of the incoming bullets, and squeezes the trigger. He hears the left barrel erupt, and feels the jerk of the firearm in his hand, as he slams to the ground. At the same time he looks to see a silhouette outlined by a light at the door, from inside the shack. The right barrel sounds off.

The silhouette jumps to the side, and their two captives waste no time getting to their feet to disappear into the darkness.

His shots are answered immediately.

The hissing of bullets goes over the heads of the two men temporarily pinned to the ground close to the fire.

Gunfire blares, and fire flashing from gun muzzles is seen coming from the bushes where Randy and Jim lie flat on the ground.

Gun smoke floats heavy above the ground making it difficult to see through the moving shadows cast by the campfire. The light in the shack is just a glow in the fog, the smell in the air is unmistakable.

Robert feels uncomfortable, being between the shooters and the campfire. His movements might be easily seen.

A single shot breaks the silence.

The light in the shack goes out with the sound of shattering glass.

No one moves, no one shoots, seconds pass.

"We don't want to have to kill you, and by now you should realize we can. We have you outmaneuvered, outgunned, and outnumbered. All we want is the time to get out of here without you on our tail." One of the abductors yells.

"What about the girl?" Bob replies.

"She's in the shack! You can get her after we're gone!

"We're leaving one man here to watch until the rest of us are gone! If you move before you hear our horses leave, he'll shoot the girl before you can get to her. You understand?"

"We understand!" Randy yells back.

Almost immediately, the doorway of the shack starts to brighten again, with a flickering, fluttering, light.

"The shack's on fire!" Robert shouts.

"You wait until we're gone!" a voice orders.

The light gets brighter and brighter as the fire grows in intensity. The seconds pass like hours. They all know the old dried out wood of the shanty will burn like kindling. It's more than Robert can stand.

"To hell with you! Shoot if you have to, I'm getting her out of there!" he blares as he gets to his feet and heads for the shack.

No gunfire.

"Come on boys, let's get her!" Randy yells.

Being the first to arrive at the open doorway, it takes Bob just a second to realize the heat is too much to go in that way.

"Go around back, see if we can get her out there. Hurry!"

The four turn the corner at the back of the shack to see a small window, starting about five feet off the ground. The glass is missing, thick smoke is pouring steadily out and up.

"Boost me up there!" he orders.

"Let me go! You're too big!" Randy counters.

No one argues.

Bob cups his hands, Randy puts his right foot in the step, then feels himself being lifted. As soon as he's off the ground, another set of hands are under his left foot, and a pair on his back keeps him steady. Up, up, he goes. He's all but thrown up and through the small opening.

"Thud!" He lands on the hard dirt floor of the shack. The heat is more than he expects, and the roar of the flames is frightening. Looking quickly, he sees Cheryl tied to a wooden chair, gagged, and slumped over.

"Throw me a knife!" he yells to those outside. "She's tied up with rope to a chair. I can't get her out this way."

Immediately, a hunting knife falls to the floor within his reach. He grabs the chair, pulls it and Cheryl toward the rear of the shack four feet farther away from the flames, then with one swipe of the blade, cuts the ropes. He forces the gag out of her mouth, and lets it rest on her chin and neck. He picks her up from the chair, turns and lifts her up toward the small window, but he's not able to push her high enough to get her through. He rests her back on the edge of the windowsill, then moves his hands to get better leverage.

"I'm going to give it all I've got, so be ready to catch her. I've got to throw her out! There's no time!" he yells. A big deep breath of smoke filled air and, "Uuumpphhh!"

Cheryl moves up and out through the opening, clearing the sill with her feet, to sail three feet beyond into the waiting arms outside. Fear and adrenaline are the muscle behind his super strength.

Jim is the first to return to the window to help Randy, who, as yet, is nowhere to be seen. Inside, the heat is unbearable, it's getting impossible to breathe! Time is running out! Randy backs as close to the blaze as he can without catching fire himself, takes a step and a half and leaps for the windowsill. His head, shoulders, and arms go through the hole, but with nothing to push his feet against, he hangs in midair. Jim grasps his arms and pulls as he yells for help. Josh is there in a heartbeat, but pull as they do, they're unable to move him up wall. Their leverage is all wrong.

"Can you run out through the door!" Bob yells.

"It's too hot!" he answers, almost in a panic. "If I don't get out of here, my clothes are going to catch fire!"

"Sit down on the floor and see if you can use both feet to loosen the boards at the bottom. We'll pull them away, and you can slide under!" Bob screams with urgency.

Bam! Bam! Bam! Bam! Randy's attempts can be heard outside.

Jim and Josh are on their hands and knees with their fingers under the bottom edge of the boards pulling, trying to get them loose. The flames are licking out through the small window, and up over the shed roof. The smoke is thick, the roar of the fire sounds like a waterfall. The kicking stops.

"Randy, don't you give up now, dammit! Kick these boards loose now! You hear me?" Jim yells as he thinks the worst. Fear shoots through the hearts and souls of all three men.

Bam! Bam! Bam! The kicking resumes.

The rusty nails holding two of the boards screech and move just enough to let Josh get the tips of his fingers under and behind them. A mighty pull and they give away, bending at first, then a second, higher up, row of nails let go, enabling the men on the outside to make an opening large enough for the endangered young man to start squirming through on his side, head first. Jim holds the boards up out of the way, and Josh grabs his shirt. Then with another mighty lunge backward, he scrapes Randy through, free of his fiery prison.

"Yeeoowww!" Josh screams. "His clothes are so hot they burned my hands! He's on fire!"

"Roll him over and over on the ground, get him back away from the fire! Then get those burning clothes off fast!" Bob yells while in the process of picking Cheryl up in his arms to move her away from the heat.

After getting Randy out of his burning clothes, they all turn to look back at the fire, now fully engulfing the small shed.

"How's Cheryl, is she alive?" Randy asks.

"She's breathing, so I guess that's good, but she's unconscious. I don't know if the smoke and heat got to her, or if maybe they gave her something to keep her quiet. I don't see any burns anywhere, but it's hard to tell in this light. Her clothes don't seem to be burned," Bob replies.

"What about you?" he continues. "That was just too close. Are you burned anywhere?"

"I have some spots that are giving me some pain, but I think all and all, I'm okay. The only thing is, I don't have any extra clothes. I might be able to wear my underwear when they cool down, but the rest of them fell to pieces when we took them off. My boots are all right, though."

"It's cool out here tonight, so you're going to need something," Jim points out.

"Oh, I almost forgot. I took my jacket off before the shooting started. It's lying over there."

"Why?" Bob wonders.

"Well, it's almost new, and I didn't want to ruin it with stuff—you know—stuff like bullet holes and blood, so I took it off," Randy replies seriously.

Everybody chuckles, which seems to lessen the stress of the moment.

"Mama sent a change of clothes with me. They might be a little big on you, but they'll do for a day or two. They're in my bedroll on my horse, and there's some salve we can use on your burns in my saddle bags, too," Bob relates.

"Jim, will you and Josh go get the horses and bring them over here with us. I'm uneasy thinking our fleeing abductors might come across them. I never did hear their horses leave. And besides, we can't have Randy standing around here in his birthday suit when Cheryl wakes up."

Jim and Josh giggle, along with Randy, just thinking about that, then leave to get the horses.

"You're face looks mighty red, Randy. I can't tell for sure in this light, but I think your eyebrows are gone."

Bob's comment prompts the young man to carefully touch his forehead, feeling for eyebrows.

"Oooohhhh!" A noise comes from Cheryl, who is lying flat on her back on the ground. She rolls her head a little to the right and moans again, "Ooooohhhhh!"

"She's coming around," Bob says, and moves to bend down beside her. "Can you hear me, Cheryl? It's Robert."

Randy moves quickly to find his underwear and jacket.

She opens her eyes slightly. "I'm so tired," she whispers

"Are you all right?"

"I just need to sleep." She closes her eyes and is gone again.

"I think she's going to be okay. They probably gave her something."

"That's good news." Randy is sitting on the ground, back away from the light of the burning shack, carefully pulling his underwear on over his tender skin.

They both get to their feet when they hear Jim and Josh coming with the horses.

"What a relief, I was worried they wouldn't be there," Bob confesses.

The salve applied to Randy's burns brings welcome relief from the pain. And although they don't exactly fit, he greatly appreciates the loan of a pair of pants and shirt.

While Jim and Randy unsaddle the horses and give them a few oats with their feed bags, Josh puts a coffeepot on the campfire. Jim rigs a string line between two trees, close in to them, and ties the horses halters to it.

Bob tries to get Cheryl to take a sip of water with no success. He picks her up and lays her on a blanket, wraps it back over her, then places another one on top of that. A folded saddle blanket serves as her pillow.

After a fresh cup of coffee, and splitting a can of fruit, the three men lay out their bedrolls and prepare to retire.

"I've been thinking about all that shooting tonight. Those shots were coming fast and furious, faster than one person can do," Randy suggests as he lies down and tugs at his blanket.

"Yeah, I know, we'll take a look when it gets light. Maybe we can get a clue," Bob proposes. "Right now, let's try to get a few hours sleep."

"Do we need a guard?" Jim asks. "I'll take the first watch."

"No, I don't think they'll be back tonight," Bob decides. "Let's all get some rest, we've got a long day tomorrow."

In a few minutes, all is quiet around the campfire. Snores and deep breathing can be heard from the exhausted, unauthorized posse. It's been a long day. Robert lies awake, his ears attentive to the sounds around him. He's glad his friend Randy is able to sleep through the pain of the burns he received. The crackling of the fires and a faraway barn owl keep him company. There'll be no sleep for him tonight.

Several miles farther to the north-northeast, three horses stand, saddled, tethered together around a tree, just back from the edge of a dry wash. Their riders sit side by side down in the wash, leaning against the bank, wrapped in their blankets, trying to get warm for the rest of the night. Maybe, if they're lucky, they'll get a few hours of sleep.

"Do you suppose they got her out before the fire got to her? Don't you think those sleeping powders you gave her put her in more danger than necessary?" Sally asks, actually concerned for Cheryl's safety.

"Who knows? Who cares? We win either way," Benny, a Company man and cohort of Sally's, says smartly as he moves to cover himself more completely with his blanket.

"It would be a shame, you know, a young girl like that," she continues.

"I think her plan was a stroke of genius. Think about it. She told us everything she knew, but needed a way to be trusted more by her kin. By tying her to that chair, and burning the shack, they'll really believe she's one of them now. They won't understand how we could do that to one of our own. They'll believe every word she says, that is, if she lives through the fire. If she doesn't, well, then, what have we lost? Just a young girl with questionable loyalties, and besides, it was all her idea in the first place."

"Yes, I know you're right, I just have to handle it in my head, I guess. We need to get to a telegraph office as soon as possible in the morning. The right people need to know what we learned today."

"You people from La Nesra never cease to amaze me," Benny continues. "It's easy to pass out orders across your desks, but it's a little different when you come out here with us—the animals—as I've heard us called. We're the people who carry out those orders. If you think you can have a conscience and still do your job out here. Well, you can't, and if you're out here very long with us, you'll learn that. How will you feel when you find out the girl survived the fire and has turned against us? The word will come down from the Company to kill off a few of her family. How do you suppose you'll feel about that?"

"Oh, shut up, Benny. Not everybody's like you, you know. Just because you love this sort of thing doesn't mean I have to." Sally curtly finishes, throws her blanket up and out, then pulls it back tight around her, then turns to face the other way.

"You know, I could go for a woman like you. You're sassy and not bad looking either. Old Nate here, he won't say anything, will you, Nate?" Benny breathes with a suggestive inference in his voice. "Come on over here and let me get you warm."

She throws her blanket off, jumps to her feet, takes two steps to be in front of the man, then places the muzzle of her revolver on his lips. Slowly, so he can see clearly and hear the clicks, she pulls the hammer back with her thumb.

Benny's eyes are wild with surprise!

Nate jumps up, not knowing what's happening.

"Stay where you are, Nate, unless you want some of this, too."

"Open your big mouth, asshole!" she orders.

Slowly, his lips part and the end of the barrel slides into his mouth. The brassy oily taste of the cold metal makes him want to gag.

"Listen, and listen good. I'm not the little prissy miss you mistake me for. If you or your partner here, either one, try to lay a hand on me, I'll kill you both. I'll carve you up in little pieces, feed you to the wild dogs, and laugh while I'm doing it. And remember this, as long as we're working together, don't let me catch you looking at me in a way I take for disrespect, or I'll shoot off one of your ears, wash it clean, and wear it around my neck on a string. Do we all understand each other?" She pulls the gun barrel from his mouth.

He hangs his head, no comment. She prods his nose with the gun.

"Yes, ma'am."

"Nate?"

"Yes, ma'am."

It's morning at the Anderson farm, where June and Selma sip their second cup of coffee while they talk at the kitchen table.

"You don't know how much I appreciate your being here with me." June expresses by putting her hand on Selma's.

Selma looks at her dear friend's face and smiles a little smile, keeping her lips together. "I'll be here as long as you need me, honey. There's no rush for me to be anywhere else. You and I will have plenty of time, at long last, to enjoy each other's company. Is there anything I can do around here, I mean, like help out with whatever Jim and Josh would do?"

"Not a thing. Belle has everything well in hand. I had no idea she even knew what all those two do every day. Well, I can tell you, not only does she know, she was barking orders to our hands when I came down this morning. I truly believe the woman can run this place all by herself." June smiles and tee hees through her nose. "I'm just amazed."

"I hope Charles made it home okay last night. It was close to midnight when he left. I begged him to stay, but he claimed he told Alberta Mae and Jacob he'd be back, and he didn't want to worry them," June relates her intent.

"Yes, I know he can be a little stubborn at times. If she doesn't find him there this morning, I'm sure she'll send someone looking for him."

"When do you expect to hear from John?" Selma changes the subject.

"Before noon, I would think. That is, if Virgil can find somebody to bring a message out this far. If we don't hear something by the middle of the afternoon, we'll go into town. I really don't expect him to drop everything and rush home." She continues, "There's no need for that, I suppose. But if I hadn't told him and something happened, well, I had to tell him."

"I hear what you say, but if I know John, he'll be here before Robert gets back." Selma's words are encouraging.

"I hope you're right. I just feel so selfish when I want him here. His work is so important to this country, and I want him here. I hope you're right though." The ease she feels with her longtime friend, urges June to explain further.

"I don't like to talk too much about feeling things that might happen in the future. I mean, like having a dream or just a sense of something that's going to happen. But for some reason, I feel a big fire, I sense people burning in that fire. It's a terrible thing to think, let alone say out loud," she confesses.

"Who's in the fire, or where is the fire?" Selma's immediate questions are meant to arouse her friend to tell more.

"I believe a man and a woman, maybe two men and a woman. As to where . . . somewhere close."

Selma now knows the real reason June wants her man home. She believes the worst is about to happen. Someone, or some people close by, is going to die in a fire.

"What starts the fire? Is it lightning from a storm? A broken lantern? What?" Selma knows if it was she who felt this way, she'd want to talk about it.

Meanwhile, at the camp of the four rescuers, and Cheryl, they are beginning to stir. Robert, who fell asleep in spite of his efforts to stay awake, is roused by the sound of wood breaking as Jim attempts to rekindle the smoldering fire. He jumps up, spins around, takes in, and calculates the situation this morning. His actions startle the man by the fire.

"Whoa, settle down!" Jim says in a monotone voice. "Everything's all right. We're all okay."

Robert realizes where he is, and for the next fifteen seconds he stands there, looking around at the bedrolls on the ground as if he's missing something. Then he shivers all over and moves toward the fire that Jim has coaxed back to life.

"We get the coffee going and we'll get the rest of them up," Jim remarks.

"Yeah, good idea," Bob confirms. "Little chilly this morning."

"A little different than last night, huh? That shack's nothing but a pile of ashes this morning. We're all mighty lucky to be here this morning. It's a great morning." The farmhand smiles at the happy ending.

Fifteen minutes later.

The fire is hot and the coffee is almost ready. The warmth feels good in the nippy March morning air.

"I'll stir them up," Bob says getting to his feet.

One by one, he jostles Randy and Josh awake with his hand. Cheryl hasn't moved from the position she was lying in last night. He reaches to touch her forehead. Her eyes open with a jerk. One deep breath and her screams can be heard for miles around as she wraps herself into a sobbing ball.

"She's alive, and that's a fact," he exclaims, falling back to catch himself with his hands. He picks her up, holds her to his chest, and whispers. "Sssshhhhh, everything's all right. Hush now, everything's okay. They're gone, we've got you. You're safe with us now."

Slowly, but steadily, she settles down, relaxing in his arms, against his chest.

The other men stand around watching.

"That's a girl, you're doing fine. Would you like some coffee?" he asks.

She sits up on his lap, looks at him, then turns her head to take in the rest of the group. Short quivering snuffs of air in through her nose, along with the jerking of her stomach, result from her sobbing. A slow, long, forlorn, pucker deforms her face, then she smashes her head into Robert's chest again.

"I'm so sorry, I'm so sorry, I didn't want to—I tried my best not to. I hate myself. I couldn't help it, they made me."

"It's okay, honey. We know, it's not your fault," he consoles her.

"You don't understand, I told them everything. I told them anything they wanted to know." She pushes away to give him a teary, sorrowful, look. "I'm so sorry, I wish I could take it all back. I would if I could."

"Don't you worry about it, we can get into all of that later. Right now, you're okay, and that's the important thing. What did they do to you? Are you hurt?"

"They twisted my arms and legs and threatened to hang me by my neck. And they probably would have if they hadn't seen the bunch of you coming from way off," she sniffles and whimpers.

"So, we took off running again until we made it to here. They took me into an old shed, and said they'd lie in wait to kill all of you from ambush if I didn't answer their questions. When I still didn't answer, they said they'd go back to the farm and murder everyone there, but not until they killed me by setting the shed on fire, with me in it. I couldn't take it any more. I was so tired and scared of what they'd do, I—I just told them. I answered all their questions. Then they gave me some water, and that's all I remember until now."

"You don't remember the fire?" Randy asks.

"What fire?"

"We'll explain all that later," Bob answers, understanding she was sedated.

"Can you stand and walk?"

"I think so, but I feel sort of silly in my head. Kind of dizzy."

"Let's try."

Cheryl gets to her feet with the help of her older brother. He lets go.

"Walk to Randy."

One step, two steps, she weaves, wobbles, and falls to the side.

Josh is there to catch her and break her fall.

"Let's get some food into you and see if you can stay on a horse. We'll stop in town on the way back and let Doc get a look at you before we head home."

"Jim, as soon as you have some breakfast, go on ahead of us back to the farm. Tell Mama we found her, and she's safe. You can tell her we'll be home as soon as we can, and not to worry, we're all okay.

"Without us to slow you down, you can probably be there by the middle of the afternoon. We shouldn't be all that far behind, unless Doc finds something wrong. If that's the case, I'll stay in town with her, while Randy and Josh come on home."

"What are we going to do about those three who took her?" Randy wonders.

"Let them go, for now. We'll quiz her when she feels better. Maybe she knows them," he answers as if she isn't there to hear him.

The horses are saddled, packed, and ready to go. It's decided that since Randy weighs less than anyone else, he and Cheryl should ride the strongest horse. Because of her weak condition, she'll ride in the saddle, and Randy will ride behind her with his feet in the stirrups.

Jim walks into the group with his hands cupped, holding some metal pieces.

"Look at this. I went looking to see what I could find out about all that shooting last night, and look at this." He holds out his cupped hands.

Bob is the first to speak.

“Those are shell casings. The bullet, powder, and the primer are all packed in there together, and they’re fired from a new kind of gun. I’ve seen pictures before, but this is the first I’ve seen firsthand. I didn’t know they were available.”

Cheryl speaks.

“It’s the Company, Bob. They have all the latest weapons. I’ve trained with them myself. Those are small ones, to fit a handgun, but they have them for rifles too. I’ve not seen it, but I was told about a gun that’s hauled around like a cannon on wheels. Only, instead of one barrel to shoot one ball, it has ten or twelve rifle barrels in a circle, with a crank on the side, like a rope crank on a well. The bullets it uses are tied onto a belt somehow, and it feeds through so when the crank’s turned, one bullet after another is fed to the barrels and they shoot faster than anyone can imagine. I heard it being fired once. It was scary.”

“I read about that too,” Randy joins in. “If I remember right, it’s called a Gatling gun. It said it can shoot three times for every tick of the clock. Now that’s fast.”

“Man-o-man, what’s this world coming to?” Jim says, amazed.

“Put those in your pocket. We might need some proof of this later on.” Bob gestures.

“Let’s get mounted up. Jim you go on ahead, like we decided. We’ll be along, but remember, we’re going to stop in town to see Doc before coming home.”

Jim is on his horse and slips out of sight before the rest of the group kick their horses to a walk. They’re homeward bound with their purpose fulfilled, a good feeling.

The day wears on.

It’s about two thirty in the afternoon when Jim rides at a gallop to the back porch of the Anderson home. His horse, all lathered up, is slobbering and snorting. He jumps to the ground as Belle comes through the kitchen door, pushing the screen out of her way.

“Where’s everybody?” she yells before he can get a word out.

“They’re all okay. Is Miss. Anderson around? We found Miss Cheryl and got her back. I promised to tell her as soon as I got back.”

“She’s not here right now, she went to town with Miss Selma and one of the hands to see if there’s a message from Mr. Anderson.”

“I have to go tell her!” Jim turns to climb back in the saddle.

“Now, listen here, that horse is all tuckered out. They’ll be back here in an hour or so, I expect. You just settle down a little, and wait right here for them. Come on in the kitchen and I’ll get you something to drink. Are you hungry?”

Jim follows as Belle leads the way.

“The truth is, they’re all going to come through town so they can have Mr. Doc see if Miss Cheryl’s okay. So, maybe, Miss Anderson will see them there anyhow?”

“Now see there, that’s even more reason for you to stay here.”

Meanwhile, in town, the open carriage is parked in front of the telegraph office. Selma and the driver are waiting for June to pick up a message from John, if there is one.

"Nothing, June," Virgil explains. "Do you suppose he's just coming home so he's not going to answer? If you want to go on home, I'll make sure you get it right away if it does come in."

"Oh, I don't know, maybe we'll wait around for an hour or so. After that, I wouldn't expect one today."

"Whatever you think's best."

She turns and walks out onto the sidewalk.

"Nothing yet. I'd like to wait for a while, maybe something will come in. Let's walk over to the restaurant and get a piece of cake. I'll show you where we found Cheryl's shawl on the way," she explains to Selma.

Back at the Anderson farm.

Belle insists that Jim has a piece of pie and coffee while she fixes him eggs, bacon, and biscuits. It isn't difficult to convince him, he hasn't eaten anything since breakfast almost seven hours ago.

She sits and encourages him to give her every detail of the chase and recovery of Cheryl. He's wiping up a little bit of egg yolk from his plate with his last bite of biscuit when.

"Help! Oh God! Help! Help!" Screams come from the backyard, getting closer.

"That sounds like Alberta Mae!" Belle shouts and runs out onto the back porch with Jim on her heels.

Chapter Twenty-Four

Belle and Jim rush from the kitchen of the Anderson home out onto the back porch, when they hear what sounds like Alberta Mae, running, calling for help. They see her coming across the yard, arms flailing, dress and apron flopping up and down, trying to scream between gasps for air.

"Help! Oh, help us please! They're coming! They're coming!"

They run toward her; she frantically toward them. She stumbles into their arms allowing them to gently lower her to a sitting position on the ground.

"What's wrong? Who's coming?" Belle yells excitedly, looking into the terror-stricken face of her friend.

Alberta Mae, totally exhausted, pants and gasps trying to get words out.

"No time! Got to get help! Oh God!"

Jim sits on the ground to pull her back against his chest, trying to get her to relax and settle down. Belle kneels and sits back on her heels in front of them. She takes the woman's hands and looks caringly into her eyes.

Jim speaks calmly, slowly, "Now, take a minute to get your breath and tell us."

"Take your time, honey, we'll help you, you know we will," Belle soothes.

After several seconds of panting and wheezing, she begins to get her senses back. Belle wipes tears and nose drippings from the stricken woman's face with the end of her apron. "All right now, tell us real slow."

"The raiders! They're coming! They're coming, and they're coming fast!" she blurts with a short breath between each burst of words.

"Are they at your place right now?" Jim reacts.

Alberta Mae, settling down more and more, pulls herself together. She sits up quickly and turns to face both of her friends.

"We had a rider come in, riding hard, from the next farm over from us. He told us all that the raiders is killing and burning everything on their place, and they're headed this way. He was working a field when he saw them, and there wasn't any use for him to try to help, he said. There's maybe thirty or more of them. He figured he'd best let us know. They're coming right behind him, he said! I wanted to stay and gather up my kids and things before we all come over here, but the colonel told me to get over here and tell you right away. I told him that Bob said if this happened we was all to come over here. He said Jacob and him would get everybody over here as quick as they could. So, I just did what he said and ran over here as fast as I could."

"Do you want me to go over there and help?" Jim asks, looking at the two women.

"Dear Lord!" Belle frets. "Why is this happening when all our menfolk are gone? I don't know what to do!"

Then as if resolution is born within her soul from above, she gets to her feet. Knowing she has the responsibility whether she wants it or not, a calm takes over.

"Just do what you know is right," she says to herself out loud.

"No Jim, I think you'd better stay here and help us get ready. The colonel and Jacob can handle that over there. They know to bring everybody here, so we should get things ready for them."

"I'm going back, then," Albert Mae explains. "I've got to know my man and kids are safe."

"You can't go back there now. You barely made it here in the first place." Jim tries to discourage her.

"I'll take that horse." She points to the still froth covered, exhausted, animal Jim rode in on. "I'm going, and I'm going on that horse! You'll have to fight me to stop me!" She yells, gets up, and strides toward the horse.

Jim is right behind her, so Belle thinks he'll do his best to keep her here. Instead, he helps by lifting her up into the saddle. She's on her way back to Der Bote.

"I couldn't help myself, Belle. That's where I'd want to be if I was her."

She nods her head "me too."

"How many hands do we have here right now?" she demands.

"At least eight, I think, maybe ten. I've been gone, so I don't know where they all are," Jim shoots back.

"Send one to town to tell Miss Anderson, and send one to Mr. Sanders place too. Bring the rest of whoever's here to the kitchen as fast as you can."

Jim throws his hand up signaling "I understand" and runs toward the barn.

She walks swiftly back into the house. Gathering up the guns is easy since she just put them away when the hands came back from town after looking for Cheryl. She piles everything, guns, ammunition, and knives, on the kitchen table planning to hand it out to the hands as they come in. A horse leaves at run, a few minutes pass; a second horse leaves. The sound of a slap of reins against the horse's hindquarters, and a couple of 'yahs' fade as the rider gets up to speed.

"There's only going to be eight or nine of us until Mr. Housler gets here with however many he brings. If Mr. Sanders gets here in time, we might have as many as twenty or thirty of us ready to fight. That'll give them something to reckon with. And if some help can get here from town with Miss Anderson, those raiders will get a big surprise," she says out loud with no one to hear. "We'll put them that ain't big enough to fight down in the root cellar. They'll be all right there. Then we'll get these shutters closed here on the house, and we'll lock up the barn. We'll put a gun through every hole that's big enough, and them that ain't shooting, can load. I'm sure glad Mr. Robert told us all how to go about this."

Jim comes running into the kitchen swinging the screen back making it slam against the house.

"The riders are on their way to town and Mr. Sanders' place. It looks like there's only eight fighting men, counting me, left here right now. I sent them to get all their families and bring them here. What now?"

"Start closing the shutters, and when the hands start showing up, put the children in the root cellar, then get the barn closed up. If the wives can shoot, we'll give them a gun, if they can't shoot, then they can load. Mr. Housler and Mr. Sanders should be coming in before long, so split them and their people between here and the barn. Make sure there's shooting supplies here and there." Belle gives orders like a general preparing to defend her fort.

Jim turns and is gone in a flash.

Time passes. Belle has the armament laid out, and ready. The shutters being closed cause the house to get dim inside, eerie with streaks of sunlight coming through the cracks.

The sound of people talking, trotting with things jostling gets closer to the back porch. The screen door opens, and the hands with their wives and children come filing into the kitchen. Belle gives directions to these familiar faces. They follow the instructions without question. Soon, all are accounted for, and the children are in the cellar under the house.

"Is the barn closed up, Jim," Belle inquires.

"Yep." The only response required.

"Well, when Mr. Housler gets here with his bunch, we'll see if he wants to put all his with guns in there. If not, the rest can come in here with us. Then when Mr. Sanders shows up, we can put them where we need them. Okay?"

"That's what we'll do Belle," Jim agrees.

"Hand out these guns to them that know how to use them. See if you can put a loader with every shooter. Make sure to give the long guns to the good shots. They can hit what they aim at farther out."

Jim moves to the table to start passing out guns, and pairing up shooters with loaders.

"We going to have enough to go around?" Belle worries.

"Looks like more than enough to me," he assures. "We'll probably need them all when the rest get here."

In the back of her mind, Belle knows there's a stash of powder and fuses in the barn. She knows Mr. Housler can put it to good use too, and that's one reason for positioning him there. Another is for him to pull attention to the barn, away from the house. The idea is to get the raiders in a cross fire situation. These are all Robert's instructions.

Robert has given each farm in the area two plans. First, and most importantly, one to save their lives by getting to a safe place if they're caught by surprise, alone. Secondly, one that provides a strategy if their farm becomes a fort to be defended by everyone close by. The towns people, also, have a plan to protect themselves, and have agreed to support the farms with manpower and guns. Each plan of action is determined by where the assault begins, and the direction it is headed. Homes that had no shutters in the past, do now. Gun slots are built into them, allowing those inside to rain bullets on the intruders. Each house to be defended has a large supply of ammunition, rifles, handguns, and powder. If the residents are forced to leave ahead of an attack, the orders are to take all the armaments they can carry and destroy the rest.

Because of it's proximity to the other farms, the Andersons' barn has been fortified, as well as the house. Robert has seen to it that every farm house, and every building to be defended, is properly outfitted.

"That's about all we can do for now," Belle tells everybody who's listening. "All we can to now is wait."

And wait. At first everybody in the house is perched, cocked like a hammer on a gun, ready for all hell to break loose.

And wait. A few shooters have set their guns down and leaned them up against the wall. Still their eyes survey the outside through the cracks in the shutters.

And wait. Jim has opened the back door, and is standing a few feet beyond the back porch looking in the direction of the Housler farm.

"That's smoke, all right! Looks like things are burning over there!"

And wait. Now, Jim and several of the hands are standing midway between the house and the barn, looking at the black clouds rising from behind the horizon. Der Bote is burning.

"Where are they?" Belle frets. "Lord knows they should be here by now."

"And where's the Sanders family? They're not here either."

Jim turns to look in the direction of the Sanders' place. "There's smoke over there too!" he yells and points.

"You get yourselves back in this house!" Belle orders. "There's no telling what's going on out there! You all get in here where it's safe!"

And they wait. Almost two hours have passed. No people from anywhere have showed up.

Someone from the front of the house yells.

"There's horses coming . . . lots of them! I can't see them, but I can hear them!"

Everyone who has a peep hole to look through strains to see the oncoming onslaught of riders. Closer! Louder! The first shot is expected to be heard any second.

"Get ready!" Jim yells.

It sounds like the horses are coming up the front steps before they rumble to a stop.

"You in there! This is Cliff, the deputy from town! Are you in there?"

"It's the towns folk, they're here!" a voice yells from the front hallway of the house. "There must be twenty or more of them."

"You all stay in here and be ready if any shooting starts!" Jim yells as he and Belle leave through the back door to cautiously approach the bunch gathering at the front of the house. They don't want to walk into a trap.

As they turn the front corner of the house to present themselves, a carriage clears the crowd, and pulls to a stop with the horses facing the house. Out jumps Selma, Charlotte, and June.

"Oh, thank the Lord, you're all right?" June shouts as she rushes to hug Belle, and then Jim, with Selma right behind her.

"Where's my husband and our people?" Selma asks, fearing the worst, not wanting to hear the answer.

"I don't know, Miss Selma. Alberta Mae came here to warn us, but we couldn't stop her from going back. Nobody else has come over here from your place," Belle replies.

"And nobody from Mr. Sanders place is here yet, either," Jim adds. "We sent a rider after them just after Alberta Mae made it over here, and he's not back yet."

"There's a lot of smoke in both directions, look there—and there." The deputy points as the women turn to see.

"I've got to get these men back to town as fast as I can. If those raiders attacked Der Bote, the Sanders' place, and not here, they probably did it to pull us out of town. That could mean they're going to hit there next, before we can get back."

"Aren't you going to leave a few men with us so we can check the damage at Der Bote and the Sanders' farm?" June asks insistently.

"I'm likely to need every man I've got. Besides, the raiders are gone by now. There's nothing this posse can do over there."

"What's the matter with you, deputy? There are families at both of these places that need our help, and you can't spare five men?" Selma is concerned and angry. "If you pull out of here without leaving some help, well . . . I hope you know what you're doing. If it works out that a few of your men could have made the difference of people living or dying, you'll answer to my husband, and you know it."

"Can't spare a man!" he yells, and turns his horse back toward town. The rest follow leaving the four women, and Jim, standing, watching.

Selma hangs her head, and with four nervous steps turns completely around.

"I have to go, June. I can't stay here, not knowing. I have to go."

"I know," she replies. "I'm going with you."

"Belle, you stay inside and keep it boarded up. Charlotte, you stay here and help Belle. Jim, you get three more guns, and come with us."

With nothing further said, the two women climb into the carriage where the driver still waits. Jim is soon at their side with enough guns for the four of them.

"Let's go!" are his words as he falls into the seat.

"I see you're back," June expresses to Jim as the driver snaps the horses and pulls the reins to back up and turn.

"Did you find Cheryl? And where's the rest?"

"Yes, ma'am, we did. Mr. Robert sent me ahead to tell everybody. They took Miss Cheryl to town to see Mr. Doc, so he could check her over to be sure she's okay. Nobody got hurt real bad, but Miss Cheryl and Randall was in a fire and . . ."

“Whoa. Start from the beginning and tell us the whole story.” June has heard what she needs to hear now she wants the details.

Back in town.

It’s just after five thirty in the afternoon when Robert, Randy, Cheryl, and Josh, stop in front of Doc’s office. Randy’s the first to the ground from behind Cheryl to help her off the saddle. She’s still a little wobbly, but stronger for the most part. They help her up the steps to the sidewalk, then Bob takes her arm to lead her into the office.

“I see you found her, although she does look a little beat up,” Doc notices.

“Yeah. She’s still dizzy and the like, Doc. Can you look her over and see if there’s anything wrong? I think they might have given her something to make her sleep, but I’m not sure about that. I’ll just wait, if that’s okay with you,” Bob relates.

“You haven’t heard, have you?” Doc cocks his head and mashes his lips together as he finishes speaking.

“What?”

“Well, a rider from your place came running into town and said there’s trouble at Der Bote. He said it’s the raiders. Your mother, Charlotte, and Selma were here in town, so they and maybe twenty men left here about an hour ago, headed out there.”

Bob’s expression changes to one of urgency.

“You’ll be all right here until we get back.” He addresses Cheryl by looking at her. “Don’t let her go anywhere, Doc. I’ll be back in a couple of hours.”

Cheryl, who has sat down on the edge of the examination table, jumps to her feet and exclaims, “You’re not going anywhere without me, buster! They’re my family too!”

Bob looks at Doc with a “what do we do now” look.

“Let me give her a quick once over, it’ll take about ten minutes. You can wait that long.”

“Yes, I suppose so. I’ll tell the boys what you told me while I’m waiting.”

“Don’t try to slip off without me, Robert Anderson. I’m going home with you, or by myself.” He hears her shout at his back when he turns to go outside.

Meanwhile, between the Anderson farm and Der Bote.

The carriage carrying June and Selma bounces along violently, moving at a fast pace, heading for the burning Der Bote. Conversation has waned since the end of Jim’s explanation of Cheryl’s rescue. No one questions the details. Fear and gloom of the unexpected forms over the four men and women. Nothing is said between them, but each knows the others are praying for the safety of their innocent families and friends. Eyes watch the black billowing smoke which becomes more of a reality with each turn of the wagon wheels.

“Oooohhhhh!” is heard from Selma as they crest the last knoll now being able to see Der Bote. Everything’s on fire. The house, the main barn, the Stokers’ home, the tack shed, the equipment barn, anything that will burn is engulfed in flames. The black smoke from the entire area seems to rise in individual stacks, then form together when it gets caught up in the wind, to become one long dark cloud. The black cloud blocks the sun and casts a shadow on the ground.

"Stop!" June commands. "Let's not ride into a gunfight, we have to use our heads!"

"Charles!" Selma screams, and jumps down from the stopping carriage to fall and roll over sideways twice.

June is at her side before she can get to her feet.

"Wait, Selma. Let Jim and me," she says firmly. "Give us just five minutes, please, honey, it's for the best."

"Damn those dirty rotten bastards!" Selma screams, sobbing wildly. "Why did they do this to us? What did we ever do to them?" She falls to her knees, clutches her hands together and raises them above her head.

"Dear Lord, please help me. Please let me find Charles and the rest of our family here alive. These people are my whole life. Please spare them and take me. I can't go on without them. Please Lord, take me. These people are innocent of any crime against anybody. They're all hard working people, with only good in their minds for one another. Oh, please, help me find my husband alive, then take me."

She lowers her arms down to let her hands fall into her lap as she sits back on her heels. Then, in one motion, she turns away from June and puts her arms out and down so she's on her hands and knees, to start gagging and vomiting.

June moves to put her arms around her waist and her cheek on the back of her head. There's nothing to say, just hold her.

"My whole life is going up in smoke. I hurt so bad inside," she says quietly and sits back on her heels to face her friend. June uses her hanky to dry her tears and clean her face.

"It's gone. They're all gone. What will I ever do without them? Charles, Alberta Mae, Jacob, the girls, and the twins, all gone. Even the hands, all those innocent children—gone."

"We don't know that for sure yet, honey. I'm going to try to get closer to see what's what. Will you stay here while I do that?" June motions for the driver to come to stay with Selma while she and Jim look for survivors.

They walk the three hundred yards cautiously, but briskly, guns ready, toward the fire and smoke. There is no gunfire, no sign of life at all, nothing. The closer they get, the more they are taken in by the devastation, the needless destruction of life and property.

The heat is incredible, too hot to get close enough to see anything in or about the buildings. Bangs and pows sound through the roaring and crackling flames when sealed bottles, jars, and cans explode. A few more degrees and they would not be able to stand the heat to search the grounds between the fires.

Flames roar out of the upstairs windows of the main house, shooting ten feet into the air. The downstairs is an inferno. The walls have burned through in many places, signaling the eventual collapse of the entire structure. Nothing could live in there.

Dead cattle lie in the feeding pen close to the barn. The smell of burning hair and baking flesh is repugnant. Two horses, apparently shot where they stood saddled and waiting, lie dead side by side, their reins still wrapped around the hitching rail. Queenie, and two other dogs, the hogs, ducks, chickens, all lying dead, scattered everywhere as if they were chased, then finally shot. The barn has already started caving in on itself, adding fuel to the raging blaze.

Jim and June go their separate ways trying to look everywhere they can, then meet at the center of it all.

"I don't see any sign of life, do you?" she says, wiping tears caused by the thick smoke from her face.

"Nothing! It's too hot, I can't get close enough to see anything!" he almost yells.

"Where else can we look? Where would they be if they're alive?" she asks earnestly. "There's nothing we can do here. We won't be able to get near these fires until morning."

"The smokehouse, someone might be in the smokehouse."

"Where is it?" she asks.

"Over here, I think," he says over his shoulder, moving away.

The smokehouse, which is fifty yards from the fires, facing away, is tunneled into the side of a rise in the ground. It's larger than most of its kind, being fifteen feet deep by ten feet wide at the floor. Then it goes up about eight feet to a hollowed dome at the ceiling. There, a chimney has been hollowed and shored up through several feet of soil to stick up two feet above the ground on top, then protected with a rain hat. The entire interior is lined with adobe bricks. The door, which measures four feet wide by six feet tall, hung on a steel frame with steel hinges, is made of thick hardwood, and opens outward. To keep animals from getting at the meat being smoked, a wooden bar lies across two ell-shaped steel holders, which are bolted to the frame.

They approach from behind the rise to walk down and around to the door. The wooden bar is laid in place, securing the door from the outside.

"Not much chance of anyone being in there," Jim observes.

"Open it," June blurts.

He lifts the bar from its cradled position and tosses it aside, then grabs the handle and pulls the creaking door open with his right hand, his gun cocked and ready in his left.

At first glance there's nothing, no one. But it's dark, so he takes a step inside.

A whimper!

"Miss June, somebody's in here. I just heard a little whimper."

She's quickly at the door trying to peer around him into the darkness.

"Who's in here?" he says with authority.

"Just us, you're not going to hurt us, are you?" A crying voice comes from the rear of the bricked blackness.

Realizing it's a child's voice, June coaxes, "Come on out, honey. Those bad people are gone. We're from the Anderson farm. Don't be afraid, we're here to help you. Come on, come on out."

The sound of running footsteps cause them to turn to see Selma and the driver coming, which pulls their attention away from the voice in the smokehouse.

"I can't wait back there, I have to know!" Selma loudly explains as she nears.

June notices that she has calmed herself, and for the moment, at least, is acting level headed.

"We haven't found a thing so far. The fire's too hot to get near. I doubt we'll be able to do much until morning. I'm so sorry, I don't know what to say." She can only imagine what her friend feels.

"Hi, Sadie. You don't know how happy I am to see you. Is anyone else in there with you?" Selma says, as she ignores everyone and passes them by to bend down just inside the smokehouse doorway.

They turn to see an eight-year-old child standing in front of Selma.

"Yes, ma'am."

"How many?" June asks instantly.

"Tell them to come out," Selma speaks softly to the young girl, taking her hand, ignoring her friend's question.

"Come on out here, it's okay. Miss Selma's here," Sadie calls into the darkness.

One by one, timidly, children begin coming into the light from the back of the smokehouse. Two more girls, and four boys, aged between three and seven. They all appear to be unharmed, the youngest rubbing her eyes from the bright light.

"How did you get in there?" Jim wonders.

"Mr. Jacob made us go in there, and he told us not to come out until he came back after us."

"Where are the rest of the people? Did you see where they went, or have any idea where they might be?" June feels she has to ask, although she does not expect to learn anything.

"No, ma'am," the oldest speaks as most of the rest shake their heads no.

"We heard a lot of yelling and shooting for a while, then it all got quiet, until now," the seven-year-old volunteers.

"Were the bad people here before Jacob put you in there?" Selma pulls the two youngest to her for a hug.

"We didn't see anybody else. Just everybody was running around and yelling."

"Let's think about this for a minute," June suggests. "There's no sign of a fight here anywhere. Wouldn't there be a body, if not ours, then one of theirs, around here somewhere? There's no guns lying around, no hats, it's like there was no battle at all."

"Well, I know Charles," Selma pipes in. "He wouldn't give all this up without a fight. He'd go down fighting."

"That goes for Jacob, too," Jim adds.

Selma's hopes start to rise, the more she says, the faster she talks. "So, if they didn't stand and fight it out, they must have had a good reason. Maybe they didn't have time to get ready, maybe they ran instead. Maybe Charles felt it was better to run and hide, to save more lives. I remember him telling Alberta Mae and Jacob, 'Don't get yourself killed trying to protect these material things. Save yourself if these raiders come. Your life is far more important than all these belongings.' Jacob took the time to hide these small children because they would slow them down if they're running."

"Say they did run and hide . . . Charles wouldn't lead those killers to any other farm around here. If he ran, it would be in a different direction than our place, or the Sanders'," June surmises.

The colonel's wife gets to her feet, her face lighting up with hope, takes a deep breath and exclaims. "Then that means they must be somewhere that way." She points her finger, waving her arm from side to side, and starts to move in that direction.

"Wait!" Mrs. Anderson orders. "Let's get the carriage. We might need a way to carry someone if they're injured when we find them, and we can load these children in there with us. We'll start crisscrossing, back and forth, all over out there. If they're there, we'll find them."

"I'll bring it over here." The driver reacts as he speaks.

Meanwhile, back in town at the doctor's office.

Robert has been calmly pacing back and forth on the sidewalk, waiting for Doc to check Cheryl for injuries. He said it would take ten minutes, it's been twenty. The office door opens and Doc appears from inside.

"I don't like the looks of her. She's having real problems focusing her eyes. She can't follow my finger at all. I know she's going to have a fit, but she should stay here, somewhere close for a couple of days, so I can keep an eye on her."

"Then she's staying, Doc. I don't care what she says," Robert asserts.

"Well, you come on in here and tell her then." Doc motions as he speaks.

Cheryl is dressed and putting on her shoes as they enter the office.

"I heard, but I'm not staying here. I'll be worried out of my mind. I'll stay out of the way, I won't be any trouble."

"Then you heard Doc say you can't even focus your eyes, didn't you?"

An affirmative nod.

"If there's a fight going on at the farm, we'll have our hands full, and I won't have time to worry about you. You're staying right here, and I mean it. I'll be back to check on you later. You understand?" Her brother lays down the law.

"Doc, can you do me a favor and get her settled over at the hotel? Tell them I'll be in to square up later on."

"Yeah, sure, I'll do that," Doc replies.

"And see that she get something to eat."

Doc smashes his lips together, looks over the top of his glasses, and nods yes.

Robert addresses Randy and Josh as he leaves the office, "Let's go."

They mount their horses, and ride at a gallop out of town.

"Come on, young lady, we'll go over to the hotel and get you checked in," Doc tells Cheryl.

"I won't stay there. I'll leave as soon as you're gone," She sasses.

"Look, I don't care what you do, it's not like I know you all that well. But I'm a doctor, and I know about injuries. If you start off on your own, more than likely, we'll find you tomorrow, somewhere between here and the farm, lying on the ground on your back, with buzzards sitting on your chest, pecking at your eyes. There'll be enough of you left to bury, but nobody will be able to tell exactly who you are. Ever seen how fast buzzards can clean meat off a bone? Why, I've heard many a story about buzzards starting to peck at people before they're even dead. But then . . . you know best. Makes no difference to me at all."

Back at Der Bote.

The carriage is loaded down with four adults and seven children, but the horses manage to keep it moving. Each adult has a child on their lap. The others are crowded in whatever space they can find.

The idea that Charles Housler would not lead an attack to an adjoining farm narrows the search area down by at least half, maybe two thirds. The carriage is moving at diagonal swipes of a hundred and fifty yards each, back and forth across the area where the searchers hope to find a clue to the survivors of the attack on Der Bote. The position of the sun tells those on board they have less than two hours before it's too dark to see.

"How far do you suppose they could get on foot?" Selma wonders.

"It's hard to say," June answers. "If they were being chased, they'd be running. If they weren't, they'd probably be walking fast. Even if they had horses there probably wasn't enough for everybody, so they wouldn't go off and leave anyone. I think they would go only as far as they absolutely had to. They wouldn't leave this area. So, if I'm right about all of that, then I'd say no more than two miles, probably less than that."

"You continue to absolutely amaze me," Selma praises and places her hand on her friend's arm."

She places her hand on Selma's and gives it a little squeeze.

The search continues.

"Someone's sitting on the ground up there." The driver points, and pulls the reins to head the horses in that direction.

All faces are stressed trying to see to make an identification.

"That looks like Albert Mae," Jim yells from his seat next to the driver. "It is, it's Alberta Mae."

The carriage continues at its same pace and pulls to a stop about twenty feet away.

Everybody jumps to the ground and soon surround the lone black woman, sitting on the ground, with her man, Jacob, lying on his back, with his head on her lap.

Selma sits down beside her, realizing Jacob isn't moving.

"Is he?" she whispers.

Alberta Mae doesn't move or change her expression.

"He's gone, Miss Selma. He's in a better place now. My man's gone to heaven."

Not a sound can be heard from all those gathered around the two women.

"Are you hurt?" She puts her hand on the stunned woman's shoulder.

"Yes, ma'am. I think my leg's broke. I can't move it. It hurts too bad. We would have got away, if not for that. Jacob, he . . . was trying to help me, when one of those hellions rode up, and just shot him. I thought he was going to shoot me too, but he thought better of it, spit at me, and rode off." She lowers her head to look lovingly at her husband's lifeless face. "He just rode up here and shot him in the back."

June fights back her tears to say. "Are there any others of ours out here?"

Alberta Mae raises her head to speak. "Yes, ma'am, they're scattered all over out here. I don't know who's still alive, but we was all well away from the house before the raiders got there. I see you found the babies, that's good. Jacob put them there thinking it would be safer than to bring them out here. Looks like he was right."

She looks down at his face again. "You was right, honey. You can stop worrying about those children now. They're all okay."

"Do you have any idea where Charles might be?" Selma asks cautiously.

"He was here with me and my whole family until I broke my leg, then Jacob made him go on with our kids. I never thought I'd see the day when Jacob told the colonel what to do, and then to have the colonel up and do it. But he did, and the colonel took our four kids off over that way."

"How long ago?" the colonel's wife continues.

"I can't rightly say. I've sort of lost track of time, sitting here with Jacob."

"It's going to be dark before too long. If we're going to look for him and the children yet tonight, we'd better get moving," June advises.

"Will you be all right if June and I go looking for Charles and the kids?" Selma poses.

"Don't worry about me. As long as I sit still, I'll be fine."

"We're not going to leave you sitting here. You need to get your leg looked at, and get out of this night weather," June asserts. "Jim, find some sticks or boards and make a splint for her leg. Get her and Jacob in the carriage, then take them and the children back to our farm. Selma and I are going to search as long as we can see. Don't bother sending anyone back to look for us tonight, it'll be dark before long. We'll be all right together."

"Yes, ma'am."

At the Anderson farm, Robert, Randy, and Josh are just arriving.

All is quiet as the trio let their horses trot up to the front yard of the Anderson home. The men's eyes are scouring every possible hiding place for a sign of a threat.

Nothing.

The shutters are closed tight over the windows and there's no light inside the house. Shadows from the barn and house are lying long on the ground, as the sun sets.

"Mama, it's Robert, are you in there?" he yells from the saddle of his horse.

"Glory be, it's Mr. Robert."

The men hear Belle's voice and climb down from their mounts.

Before they can tie the reins to the rail, Belle and several hands appear from around the corner of the house.

"It's so good to see you, honey," she says and gives each of them a big hug.

"Where's Mama? I stopped at Doc's office in town and he said she came back here, that there was a threat of a raiding party." Robert's concerned, he doesn't see his mother.

"They was here, and so was a bunch of men from town. But the men went back to town, and Miss June and Miss Selma went with Jim and a hand over to Der Bote. It looked like it was on fire from here. There was an awful lot of black smoke over there."

"Where's their people, why aren't they here?"

"I don't know, Alberta Mae came running over here to tell us the raiders was coming, and we couldn't stop her from going back. We thought they would all come back over here, but we haven't seen anybody. There was no keeping Miss Selma from going over there, so they all went. They took the buggy. There was a lot of smoke coming from over there. We saw some coming from Mr. and Mrs. Sanders' farm too. So, we was expecting them to come over here, but no one has showed up as yet. We've just been locked up tight, waiting for something to happen."

Robert listens and studies for a moment.

"Randy, if you want to go on over and check on your family, go, but don't take any chances. If it doesn't look right, come back here. While you're doing that, I'll go over to the Sanders' place. Josh, you're welcome to come with either of us, or you can stay here. It's your call."

"If Belle can pack me up a couple of her biscuits and some water, I'll go with Randy," he replies.

Robert nods his head with understanding and mounts his horse.

Belle is back out of the house, in a few minutes, with a bundle of biscuits and two canteens of water. "You two be careful going over there. If there's trouble, get yourselves back here," she issues orders.

During the ride to the Sanders' farm, Robert's mind is occupied with questions. "We didn't see a sign of a posse on our way home from town. Why not? Is it just a coincidence that the responsible men from our farm are gone when the raiders show up? Why did they hit Der Bote and the Sanders' farm, and not ours? Why didn't the people from both places follow our plan and go to our farm? Why didn't the posse go to the burning farms to see if they could help? At least one of them?

"I can't keep beating my horse this way. She's been on the move since early this morning." As he pats her on the neck, he says out loud, "Good girl. Good girl. You've sure done your share today. Once we get back home, I'll see that you get extra grain, and the day off tomorrow."

Electing not to run his tired horse, he moves along steadily at a walk. Antsy, he moves around on the saddle more than usual, making his mount a little nervous. She tosses her head from side to side, twisting her neck, and puffing air through her nostrils.

"All right, all right, I hear you. I'll sit still. We'll get there when we get there."

Twenty minutes pass.

Smoke has formed a large long cloud which is drifting away from Robert's approach to the Sanders' homestead. The closer he gets, the blacker and thicker it becomes. His hopes of this being an isolated blaze, such as an accidental barn fire, begin to disappear. Finally, he can see the house and barn.

"Whoa! I'd better leave you here. I don't want you getting spooked by the fire and smoke." He jumps down from the saddle.

Turning his head from side to side, he surveys the burning remnants of the home and buildings. The blazes have engulfed the house and barn, having destroyed the second floors of both. Three walls of the barn are still standing but leaning in toward the fire. It won't be long before they collapse. When the second floor of the house crashed down, the front side of it must have fallen first, because it pulled the whole front wall in on top of itself. When the fire leaped up the slanted dry wood, it burned through, causing the back wall to fall to the outside with the floor on top of it. There is nothing left to save. All of the outbuildings are not much more than ashes. His body jerks as the reality of what has happened here slams home. This is real, the Sanders' home is gone.

"Where are they? I hate to look, I'm afraid of what I'll find." He directs his attention to locating clues as to where they might be. "No sense in trying to see if they were caught in the fires. They're too hot right now. It'll be morning before anyone can get near them. I'll walk around and see what I can find."

"Elizabeth! Can you hear me? Mr. Sanders, Mrs. Sanders!" he yells at the top of his lungs.

No response.

"Aaawwww, damn! They killed all of their livestock. It looks like they shot them right there in the holding pen. Poor things, I hope they didn't suffer. By my count there's four horses, and twelve, thirteen, fourteen head of beef and cows. I wonder how many more were caught in the barn with the fire? Where is everybody? I don't see a sign of a soul anywhere. What a damn shame. What kind of a person would do this? Why?

"There's a small orchard out in back of the house. Maybe they made it into there and hid." He thinks and turns toward the house, walks around to the back, giving the hot crackling fire plenty of room.

The edge of the orchard begins some fifty yards behind the house. As he nears the first row of trees, he sees two of the Sanders' hands, lying on their backs, eyes and mouths open—dead.

He fills his hand with his gun. There's no time right now to check on them. He needs to keep an eye out for lingering trouble. The raiders might have left someone here to pick off anyone who comes to help the Sanders family.

Two rows deep into the orchard, he comes across Cole Sanders sitting on the ground, his legs stretched out in front, his arms pulled behind him, back around the trunk of an apple tree, and tied. Five obvious bullet holes have left him lifeless.

He stoops down to close Cole's eyes with the fingers of his left hand. It's then he sees Caroline lying on her stomach, under a tree, not fifteen feet away, with a pitchfork thrust deep into her back, the handle sticking straight up.

Four quick steps puts him at her side, kneeling down, to see if she's still alive.

"Mrs. Sanders, can you hear me? It's Robert."

She opens her eyes trying to see him, but her strength has drained with her blood.

"Closer," she says with a raspy whisper and a short pant of breath.

He bends down close to her face.

"They took her and all our young womenfolk." Her voice evidences the pain she is suffering. "They said they'll sell them off in New Orleans. These devils was sent here to do this by someone in town." She takes a few short breaths. "I heard them talking, they're going to hit Der Bote too." She closes her eyes and gasps several times, then continues. "Thank God you're here. Did they kill Cole?"

"Yes, I'm afraid he's gone. But you're alive, and we need to get you some help."

"It's too late, I can't go on without Cole anyway. But you've got to find Elizabeth. Promise me you'll find her." Her speech comes out in short bursts as she musters all her remaining strength to raise her head to look into his face with unfocused eyes. One last attempt to get a breath and she falls back to the ground. A fixed stare proves life has left her body.

"I will. I swear to you, Mrs. Sanders, I will. If it takes the rest of my life, I will."

Unable to hold back any longer, he bends down to put his head against hers and sobs. The more he cries, the more old memories of times past flood over him. Times when he held the hurt and grief back, not letting his emotions take over. Times when he had to be a man. There's no one here to witness anything, he can let it all out.

Meanwhile, back at Der Bote.

Randy and Josh have just arrived to witness the roaring fires. They stay in their saddles silently surveying what's left of the lives of the families who lived here.

Randy senses the terror his mama, papa, brothers, and sisters must have endured. He didn't expect to find anybody here, but he hoped he would meet up with Miss June and Miss Selma, somewhere along the way, with news about his family.

"I don't know what to say," Josh is the first to speak. "I've never seen nothing like this in all my born days."

"There's no one here, Josh. If they were caught up in the fire, we won't know until we can sort through the ashes, and that won't be until tomorrow afternoon, probably."

"Yeh, you're right, Randy. I sure hope everybody is okay."

"I know, me too. We might as well get back to the Andersons' place. Nothing more we can do here," Randy concludes as he pulls his reins to turn his horse around.

They're just leaving the yard of Der Bote when Josh stops his horse and points off to his right.

"Look there, that's a carriage full of people headed over this way!"

"You're right. That's Jim up front with the driver, and that looks like Mama and Daddy in the second seat. And there's a lot of children with them." Randy's spirit rises quickly.

They dismount, allowing the carriage to come to them. As it gets nearer, Randy can see his father is lying against his mother, bouncing uncontrollably. The look on her face tells him his daddy is dead, or dying.

"Stay in the carriage children. We're not here for long." Alberta Mae's voice is heard as the carriage pulls to a stop.

Randy treads to his mother's side, and places his hands on top of the carriage wall.

"Is he . . . ?" he asks solemnly.

His mama's face puckers as tears flow from her eyes down her cheeks. Unable to speak she nods yes.

He hangs his head, and kicks the sole of his boot on the ground. Taking a deep breath when he straightens up, he moves his hands from the carriage, and turns to look away.

"Come here, son. Come to your mama," she begs and reaches her arms out to his back.

He turns to accept her embrace.

"Let it out, honey. It's no good to keep it bottled up."

"Aw, Mama, I never told Daddy how much I loved him," he cries. "Now he's gone. I never got the chance to make him proud of me, and now he's gone."

"He knew, son. He knew you loved him, and if you'd heard him talk about you when you wasn't around, you'd know he's always been proud of you. Just the other day, he was telling me how he wanted you to be a lawyer, or a schoolteacher. He said he knew you are plenty smart enough, and you could do it. All he ever really wanted for you, his oldest son, was for you to be better off than him. Just live your life from here on out, that'll make him proud. He'll know, he'll know for sure."

"It hurts, Mama."

"I know, Randall, I hurt, too. But we'll all get through this and go on. That's the way of things. None of us are here to serve each other for long. We're all here to serve the Lord, and Jesus wants your daddy with him now. He's in a far better place with our Lord," she speaks through her heartache and suffering.

After a few minutes, Randy notices her splinted leg.

"You're hurt?" he questions.

"I think my leg is broke. We put these sticks on here to kind of hold it on place until we can get it set.

"Look at you, you look like you've been too close to a fire. Your hair looks singed all over," she comments.

"And that's the truth of it," he answers. "But I'm fine now."

"Where are you headed now?" Josh asks.

"Our place. We figured we could make Alberta Mae comfortable there while we get Mr. Doc from town," Jim replies.

"Are you in pain?" Randy is concerned.

"I'll be all right. All I need is to get off this bouncy wagon. Things will settle down then."

"Then let's get her there. We can talk things out after we get her settled down." He moves to mount his sorrel.

Less than a mile away from the spot where they found Alberta Mae, June and Selma walk side by side searching for survivors of the Der Bote disaster. Their hopes are high of finding the colonel and the Stokers' other four children. So far there's been no clue as to their whereabouts, or any of Der Botes hands.

"It's going to be dark in less than an hour. If you want to go back, I'll understand, but I'd rather keep looking." Selma gives her best friend a chance to call it off for the night.

"I think not!" she answers loudly, with certainty. "We'll keep looking until we find them, dark or not. I can't go home knowing they're out here somewhere, maybe injured and needing help. If you need to rest a while we will, but then we'll keep on going."

"No, I'm fine," Selma assures. "This handgun is getting heavy though."

"I know, mine, too, but I feel better knowing I have it."

"Should we start yelling their names?" June wonders. "I don't think firing a shot will do any good. It could scare them to move farther away from us, and it might attract attention from the wrong people."

"I believe those raiders are long gone. Let's try yelling their names," Selma concludes.

"Charles! Charles Housler, can you hear me!" she yells as loud as she can.

"Charles, it's us, Selma and June! If you can hear me, give us a sign!" she yells again.

A gunshot reports through the silence.

It's too far away to be startling to the two women, but they stop, look at each other, and smile.

"If that's you, Charles, fire one more shot," Selma screams with delight.

A few seconds pass.

A second round explodes from a distance off to their left.

"Stay put, we're coming!" June is quick to shout. "That came from over there, that direction." She points.

For the next few minutes, the women move swiftly across a meadow, toward a group of trees covering three or four acres. Once they're close enough, Selma lets out another yell.

"Where are you, Charles!"

A faint female voice can be heard from the far edge of the small forest, off to their left.

"Here! We're over here!"

The two turn and run side by side, knowing they've found at least some of their missing souls alive. Another two hundred feet, and—

Hell breaks loose!

Bursting out of the woods into the meadow behind them come four mounted riders, shouting and shooting. Bullets whiz all around the two moving women.

"Run for the woods!" June orders.

They are almost there when she hears Selma grunt.

"Uuummpphh!"

She sees her spill, head over heels, and spin twice before landing on her stomach with her head pointing toward the oncoming assault. Without thinking, she jumps to the ground on her stomach, facing the attackers!

Now, a much smaller target, she raises up on her elbows, both hands on the grip of her gun, pulls the hammer back with her right thumb, takes aim, and—

Pow!

The closest rider leaves his saddle and bounces over his horse's back to the ground.

Again, she pulls the hammer back, takes aim—

Pow!

The gun jumps in her hand, and the closest charging horse drops to it's knees, causing it's rider to slide off the left side, to land on his back. His mortally wounded mount then collapses, falling to its left to land and trap the man's lower body under its side, his torso between the horses front and hind legs.

It takes her a few seconds to get control of the gun again, which puts the last two intruders almost on top of her. The gun explodes again and she rolls to her right, away from Selma, thinking an incoming horse is going to trample her. Instead, it rears up over her head, throwing its passenger backward, before falling on its side with its head twisted upward from the exiting rider pulling on the reins. It lands not more than two yards from her. With no time to get ready to shoot again, she looks up at the remaining horse and rider. His broad-brimmed hat casts a shadow over his face, making it difficult to determine his looks. His attempts to control his animal is making it difficult for him to get into a position to shoot. Even so, she can see the gun in his right hand coming around, moving to point toward her, he'll get the next shot off before she can.

"Go ahead, you bastard. I'll see you in hell." She closes her eyes and screams.

Pow!

The expected impact of the incoming bullet from his gun doesn't happen.

She opens her eyes to see the rider rolling off his horse.

"What the—?"

Selma, now on her feet, staggers from behind the horse, holding a smoking gun.

"Selma! You did that? Thank God, I thought you were dead!" June can't believe her eyes.

"I think I am," she replies, her voice failing at the end. She sinks slowly to a kneeling position. The gun leaves her hand to hit the ground with a thud, then she falls hard on her face into the grass and weeds.

June scrambles to her feet thinking the battle's over, and starts to move toward her, when she hears movement from behind. Turning she sees the third rider getting to his feet not fifteen feet away.

He's picking up the gun he lost when his horse threw him. She cocks the hammer and raises her weapon with both hands in one motion, points it at him, and says coldly.

"Leave the gun where it is and run as hard and fast as you can. Killing you will be easy for me right now."

The man, on his feet, bent over, with his hand on the gun, freezes in his position.

"Don't think too long! I need to tend to my friend, and you're keeping me from it! Make a move with that gun, or run! I'll count to three! Listen hard to two! You won't hear three!" she shouts grimly.

"One!"

The man reacts by turning upward to face her, bringing the gun with him, yelling.

"What the hell!"

Pow!

The gun jumps in her hand.

The bullet strikes him in the center of his chest, killing him instantly. His momentum and determination cause him to squeeze the trigger and fire wildly as he falls backward to the ground with a thump.

She sees movement from another of the riders, the one trapped under his horse.

Calmly, she walks toward him to kick his handgun out of his reach, then looks down into his face. He's not more than a boy, younger than her son Robert. So young and innocent to be here doing this. Her attitude softens.

"Do you want me to shoot you, or leave you here like this." Her voice is monotone, without emotion.

"Don't kill me! Please, please, don't shoot me!" he begs.

She looks down at him knowing he will never get out from under the weight of his horse on his own, then turns away, leaving him there to die.

With her gun in hand, hanging limply at her side, she moves to Selma, lying still, where she fell. She kneels down, takes a grip on her shoulder with her left hand, and rolls her over. A bright red spot on her forehead above her right eye, back toward her ear, is oozing blood. There's a puddle on the ground where she was lying, and now, since June has rolled her over, the blood is making its way back into her hair, but she's alive.

Realizing the bleeding must be stopped, June immediately thinks. "I need something to bandage her with something to put pressure on the wound."

Before she can lay Selma down, the rattling of brush and footsteps coming from the woods gets her attention. Footsteps, moving toward her.

"I have just one shot left!" Goes through her mind as she raises her handgun to point it in the direction of the onslaught.

"I'll use it, then I'll grab Selma's gun, she still has four left."

A daze starts to come over her, almost like her strength is draining through a hole in her body. Her actions become mechanical as she waits for the worst. The stress of fighting off the onslaught and killing two people give her a deep down feeling that she cannot deal with another assault like the one before.

"Will anyone truly know what's happened here today?" goes through her mind.

"They'll be coming out of the woods any second now! Get ready!" she tells herself, still kneeling at Selma's side.

"Fire one shot, then get Selma's gun!" Her head is spinning, she's having trouble focusing her eyes.

"There they are! Fire one shot, then get Selma's gun!"

"Miss June! Miss June!" she hears her name from far away.

"It's us, Miss June, Randall's sisters! Don't shoot!"

She shakes her head violently from side to side batting her eyelashes, trying to see more clearly. The two women reach her and take her in their arms, causing her to begin to cry.

"Thank God, you're all right," she says, hugging the two girls.

"We saw everything from over there, Miss June. You were wonderful, fighting off those cowards like that," the oldest explains.

"Selma . . . she needs help," June urges. "She bleeding from a head wound. We need to stop it with a bandage or something."

The younger girl strips a piece of material from her petticoat while the older one moves to lift the wounded woman to a sitting position. The bandage is applied snugly, and the bleeding slows.

"She'll be okay now," the younger woman assures.

June is settling down and getting her faculties back. "Is Charles with you? Where are the boys?" she snaps urgently.

"Mr. Housler is there in the woods. He got shot in the back. The bullet went clean through him. He's lost a lot of blood and is awful weak, but he's alive and awake. The boys went on over to the next farm to get some help. We stayed here to tend to him."

"What about your hands? Where are they?"

"We don't know . . . Everybody went in different directions."

"Those men you just shot was after us. They saw us run into these woods. They started searching down at that end and was coming this way. If you hadn't showed up when you did, I don't know what we would have done."

"How long have the boys been gone?" June asks.

"Two hours by now. They should be back any time."

"Have you seen Mama and Papa?" the oldest girl asks.

June looks around surveying the situation, ignoring the question, then speaks.

"See if you can round up those two horses. We'll get some long branches and wrap their bedroll blankets around them to make a couple of stretchers. We'll tie those to the saddles and let the horses pull Charles and Selma behind them. I don't think we should stay here any longer than we have to, so I'll leave a note on that dead horse over there for the boys. That way they'll know we're headed back to our farm, and that they should do the same. I'll tell them to bring that bastard trapped under his horse with them, too, so we can turn him over to the law to be hanged for these senseless killings."

Back at the Sanders' farm.

Robert's emotions subside to his thinking as he begins to rationalize the situation at hand. "Elizabeth is alive, I have to find her." His mind speaks to him. "I need to find her before they do Lord knows what to her. But, what about these bodies lying all around here? I need help to bury them, but if I go to get help and leave them here after dark, the wild dogs and wolves will tear into them, and the vultures will probably be after them if I don't get back before daylight. I have to take them with me. My horse won't be able to carry all that weight, even if I'm able to load them all on her. I can probably put two on her, she can handle that. But what about the other—wait, I know, I'll use my rope and drag the two hands behind. I'll put Mr. and Mrs. Sanders on my horse, then I'll walk, leading her, dragging the two hands behind us.

“That’ll work. Then when I get them back to our farm, I can go looking for Elizabeth and let our hands take care of the burials.”

At the Anderson farm.

Darkness has set in before the carriage with Alberta Mae, the body of Jacob, the driver, and the children of the hands arrive. Randall, Jim, and Josh let the reins of their horses fall to the ground as they dismount.

After making sure of whom the arriving people are, Belle and a few of the Andersons’ hands appear from inside the house to lend a hand.

Two riders are sent to town to get Doc.

Jacob is hoisted to the shoulders of three men and solemnly taken into the house to be laid out in the parlor. The horses are unsaddled and the team unharnessed, then led into the barn to be watered and fed. The carriage is left where it stopped. Afterward, every living soul is taken into the house, which is again locked up to make a defense if needed.

Belle has been busy feeding and caring for all the needs of the refugees. Time has passed quickly when Randall enters the kitchen to announce.

“Someone’s coming!”

Every light in the house is extinguished. Eyes peer through any hole or crack available, attempting to determine friend or foe.

“I count three, walking, leading two horses pulling something,” Jim advises from his position at a window in the den.

“Are you still up in there?” June’s voice is a welcome sound to all inside.

“Light them lights, Miss June is back!” Belle orders loudly, making her way to, and out through, the kitchen door to the back porch.

June speaks when she sees Belle coming with Charlotte right behind her.

“We’ve got some injuries here. Charles is hurt very badly. He’s been shot in the back and has lost a lot of blood. He needs a doctor as soon as possible. And Selma, well, I just don’t know. She’s got a head wound from where a bullet grazed her. It doesn’t look all that bad, but she won’t wake up.”

“The doctor should be here any time now, Miss June. We sent for him some time ago for Alberta Mae’s leg. What about you, honey, are you hurt? And what about you girls?” Belle replies.

“We’re okay,” the oldest girl answers. “But you should take a look at Miss June, she’s been through an awful lot.”

By this time others have appeared from the house, and have started loosening the ties holding the stretchers to the horses.

“I’m okay, don’t bother with me,” June remarks. “Get them in the house and make them comfortable.”

“I’ll take care of her, Belle,” Charlotte relates as she appears at her mother’s side to put her arm around her.

“You’re side’s all wet,” she observes and pulls her hand back to look at it. “It’s dark like blood. Have you been shot, too? Let’s get you into the light.”

The stretchers, with Charles and Selma, are carried into the house, followed by June with Charlotte's help, then the girls, and Belle.

"Have you told the girls about their daddy?" Charlotte whispers to her mother.

"No, I thought it was best not to until we got safely here."

A quick inspection leads Belle to the conclusion that June has been hit by a bullet. It ripped its way through her dress and undergarments to make a quarter of an inch deep gouge, three inches long, at a downward angle, back to front, along her side. From the amount on her dress, it didn't bleed all that much.

"Wheeee! You are one lucky girl. Another two inches and you'd be on one of those stretchers yourself, and you didn't even know it, did you?" Belle comments with amazement.

"I don't know when it happened, but I can see that it did. I never felt a thing."

"Better get out of those clothes so I can clean that up and put a dressing on it," Belle strongly suggests.

"Don't fuss over me!" she snaps. "Doc can look at it after he tends to Selma and Charles, and sets Alberta Mae's leg. I'm all right, except maybe for—

"Charlotte, march yourself into the den and bring me a bottle of brandy. I suddenly need a stiff drink. And offer something to anyone else who wants it," June exclaims.

She moves to follow her mother's instructions, and motions to the Stoker girls to come with her.

"Your mama needs to talk to you," she says quietly as they leave the kitchen.

"My baby girl is becoming a woman," June thinks proudly to herself as she watches her daughter softly handle a horrible situation.

The Anderson homestead has had its ups and downs over the years, housing those coping with the problems and joys of life. Its residents have always bounced back bringing renewed energy and hope with them. Tonight, however, it feels grim in its joints.

June sits at the kitchen table with a bottle of brandy in front of her, sipping at the rim of a snifter. Sobbing and wailing, along with continual prayers, can be heard from other rooms of the house.

Charlotte is sitting across from her mother, her elbows and forearms lying on the table, her hands clasped, gazing admiringly.

"May I have a drink from your bottle?"

June's attention turns to her daughter.

"Are you sure?" she asks.

Charlotte's yes nod prompts June to slide her glass across the table.

"Try it. If you like it, get yourself a glass. Don't gulp it now, it's sort of warm."

The glass is raised to her nose, and the young woman takes a whiff as she has watched her parents do. Then she lifts the bottom edge of the rim to her lips.

June watches intently as the dark liquid moves up the edge, across her lips and teeth, into her daughter's mouth.

"Not too much, easy does it," the older of the two Anderson women, thinks.

Charlotte lowers the glass to the table, and slides it toward her mother while sloshing the liquid about her mouth. Then squeezing her jaws tightly against her teeth, and her mouth shaped in a small smile, she swallows with an exaggerated gulp.

Without changing her expression, she gets up, and leaves June to think whatever she wants, only to reappear with a glass matching that of her mother's. She picks up the bottle by the neck, pours two fingers of the brandy, then sits down, never letting go of the snifter. She slides the bottle toward her mother, and shows a teethy smile.

"Not bad. Not bad at all," she coos, then takes on a serious look.

"I love you more every day, Mama. You amaze me the way you take on life. The way you get involved. The things you do without letting consequences get in your way. I want to be just like you. I want the softness you make people feel with your words, and I want your temper—and ire—that make people listen and respect you for who you are. And most of all, I want to have babies, and be the mother you are to me."

With that she raises her glass in salute, and downs another swallow.

June sits agape, in awe; words fail her.

A voice from the front of the house exclaims.

"Doc's here. They all just pulled up out front."

June doesn't move, she looks across the table at her daughter.

"You know, honey, that's the nicest thing you've ever said, or ever could say to me. I had no idea you feel that way about me."

"There's a lot you don't know about me. I want you to know me, but there never seems to be enough time. There's always something else needing your attention. After all that's gone on around here today, I've been frantic, worrying something would happen to you, and I would never get the chance to tell you how I feel. I know this is a lousy time, but I've learned today that this might be all we have."

June reaches out to place her hand on Charlotte's, both of which are lying on the table surrounding her glass. She looks intently, serenely, into her daughter's eyes and says softly.

"Oh, oh my, I'm so, so sorry. I love you so much. I've never stopped to consider how you must feel about . . . well, that's changing right now. You're old enough to understand. Let's set our glasses and this bottle on top of the cupboard for later. You know, I want to be in there with Doc. He's going to need some help, so come on, let's go—we'll get back to this, I promise, because there are some things you should hear, too."

Charlotte nods her head with an exaggerated yes and rises from the table, glass and bottle in hand, headed for the cupboard. Once both glasses and the bottle are placed safely out of the way, mother and daughter scurry from the kitchen to the front of the house.

Doc is down on one knee bending over Charles, who is still on the stretcher, lying on the floor. He listens to his patient's heart and chest sounds, then cuts away his shirt with scissors to get a look at his wound. He gets down close to look at the edges of the ghastly irregular hole in Charles's upper right chest. Motioning to June, he says, "Help me raise him up so I can see his back."

Charlotte is right there to help, making sure she's not in Doc's way as he cuts down through the collar of Charles blood soaked shirt, then rips it with his hands all the way down to the waistband of the wounded man's pants.

"Looks like the bullet went in the back and came out the front clean. I don't know how, but I think it missed his lungs, they sound clear of anything. The bleeding has stopped, at least on the outside. I don't dare try to probe around or move him too much. He might start bleeding again, and he sure as hell doesn't need that," Doc surmises out loud. "The best we can do for the time being is clean him up and get some bandages over these holes. You girls can do that while I look at Selma and Alberta Mae. Don't move him any more than you have to. If he starts to get any worse, we might have to get some blood into him. Here Charlotte, take my stethoscope and listen to his heart and lungs. Count how many breaths he takes and how many times his heart beats in a minute. Check him every ten minutes and let me know if they change any, any at all. Got it?"

"Yessir, I can do that, Dr. Shaw."

Doc glances at her thinking "How long has it been since I've heard my last name?"

"Okay, that's fine. Now, let's check on Selma." He rises to move across the room to where she is lying on her back on a couch. June follows.

He lifts her legs to slide them toward the back of the couch to make room to sit on the edge. Then he carefully takes her chin in his hand, and turns her face to his right, exposing the bloody wound on the side of her head.

"The Almighty has been with these two people today. Another half inch and she wouldn't be with us right now. Fetch my bag from over there, June. Let's see if we can wake her up. This doesn't look all that bad." He's relieved at what he sees.

"Hand me that bottle of ammonia and a piece of that bandage there," he urges as she sets his bag on the floor beside him. He wets the bandage with a little of the ammonia and waves it slowly under Selma's nose. Nothing at first, but then she starts to toss her head and fuss.

"She's coming out of it," he announces.

She opens her eyes, bats her eyelashes a few times, then startled, tries to jump up.

He's right there to hold her down.

"Hold on there, girl! You're safe. Stay still for a minute or two. We don't want you passing out again."

She rolls her eyes around trying to focus, trying to understand where she is.

June stoops down at her side.

"It's me, honey, it's June. You're here at my home. You're all right. You're going to be just fine."

"Charles?" Selma raises her voice. "Where's Charles?"

"We found him. He's wounded, but he's here with us. He's alive," June relates as she takes her hand.

"Can I see him?"

"In a few minutes," Doc replies. "Give yourself a chance to recover a bit. You took a bad blow to the side of your head, and you've been unconscious for quite a while, so you just lie there, I'll let you know when you can get up. I'll bet you have one whale of a headache right now," he continues.

"Yes, you're right about that," she replies.

"Well, the only thing I have that will help will also make you sleepy, and I don't want you to sleep for a while. Can you put up with it?"

"I will. Can I have something to drink?"

"I don't see why not. Tell June what you want. I need to check on Alberta Mae," Doc says as he rises from the couch. "Charlotte, here's another job you can help me with. Take some of that alcohol out of my bag and clean the blood and grime off her wound. Then put a clean dressing on it and tie it off around her head."

"Okay," she agrees.

June has just returned to Selma's side with a hot cup of coffee, when she hears Jim in the hallway calling her name.

"Where's Miss June? Mr. Robert is coming up out front, leading his horse. Looks like he's got bodies tied to his saddle."

"I'll be right back. You stay here on this couch, you hear me, Selma?"

June hurries to the hallway and follows Jim outside to see Robert standing, looking down at the ground, with his horse behind him. The moon is bright and the sky cloudless, making it possible to see.

"What on earth?" she says quietly, then trots toward her son.

"Oh no, what's happened?" She takes him in her arms with a gentle hug.

He stands there with his arms down at his sides, holding the horses reins.

"They're all dead," he says calmly, without emotion.

"Who's dead?" she reacts.

"The Sanders family and all their hands. Those murdering bastards killed them, all their stock, and set everything on fire."

"Elizabeth?"

"I'm not sure. I found Mrs. Sanders just before she died. She told me they took Beth and the other women to sell to someone in New Orleans. But I don't know that for a fact. I couldn't leave these bodies back there overnight, so I brought them with me. I had to drag two of them behind my horse. I couldn't figure another way to do it."

"Jim, get some help and take these bodies to the barn where they'll be safe," June orders. "Come into the house, you look exhausted." She pulls on his arm to get him moving. "Are you okay? Are you hurt?"

"No, I'm not hurt or anything. No one was there when I got there. Mrs. Sanders was taking her last breath when I found her. Everybody else was already gone. They shot Mr. Sanders five times, and stuck a hay fork in her back. I brought the bodies of two hands with me, I didn't see any others. I don't know if they were caught in the fires, or maybe they ran off and hid somewhere. I don't know."

"I know it's a terrible thing to see and go through. There's no way to reason why anyone would act this way toward another human being. The people who had a hand in this today are deranged somehow. There's just one way to deal with them, and that's kind for kind," his mother sympathizes.

"Mrs. Sanders said something that I don't know what to make of. She said the men who did this are from town. She said she heard them talking amongst themselves. They said they were going to hit Der Bote, too. Why would anyone from town be a part of anything like this?"

"I don't know, maybe we can all put our heads together and sort it out. First, though, you need to get something in your stomach and rest. Except for the hands, we have the whole Housler farm family inside here. Alberta Mae has a broken leg. I hate to give you more bad news, but Jacob was killed. The colonel has been wounded badly, and Selma was nicked on the head with a bullet."

"Isn't that Doc's buggy?" he asks.

"Yes, he's inside," she replies.

Charlotte meets them in the hallway as they enter the house.

"Dr. Shaw needs you, Mama. He's ready to straighten Alberta Mae's leg.

"You come with me, brother. You look like you can use a good stiff drink and some food, in that order," she continues.

"Oh, there you are, I've been looking for you," Doc addresses June as she enters the room where Alberta Mae sits in an overstuffed chair, her leg propped up on a footstool.

"Just when were you planning to tell me you took a bullet yourself today?" His tone is one of aggravation.

"It's nothing, Doc, I'd rather we give our attention to those that need it right away, I'm fine. This little scratch can wait," she answers matter-of-factly.

"I'm the doctor here, and I'll be the judge of what can wait and what can't," he scolds her. "Now, bring yourself over here next to this light so I can see your little scratch."

Feeling like a small child, she minds his words.

"You can either take your dress off or let me cut it away a bit." Doc offers a choice.

"Snip away," is the reply.

After using the scissors for a few seconds, he is able to pull her garments away from the wound to make an assessment.

"Well I'll be—no bullet made this wound. I don't know how you did this, but you've run a good size stick into your side, clear up to a fork, and it's broken off and stuck under your skin. Do you mean to tell me that you don't remember doing this? This had to downright hurt when it happened."

Her mind flashes back over the day. The only time it could have happened is when she threw herself to the ground as the four riders, with guns blazing, came pounding down on Selma and her.

"What do we do now?" she poses, ignoring his question.

"Well, now we have to get it out of you, that's what we do."

"I'm sorry, Alberta Mae, but you're going to have to wait a little longer," he explains.

"I'm okay, this leg has settled down a lot since I got here," she concedes.

He continues, "Randall, see if you can find Charlotte and bring her in here."

Randall leaves the room.

"There's no way of knowing how deep down inside your body that stick has gone, June. I don't know if it's punctured anything in there or not. So, to be on the safe side, I think we should treat this as a serious operation, and put you under with some ether. That way, if I do have to open you up to sew some holes shut, you won't feel a thing."

Charlotte appears just as her mother responds to Doc's suggestion.

"You're not putting me to sleep, Dr. Cedrick Shaw. If this stick has to come out, I'm going to be awake to see it happen." Her remarks are delivered with a defiant, demeanor.

Charlotte, obviously, already aware of the problem, blurts in agreement without thinking. "You tell him, Mama."

"You women, you think you know it all. Just remember, I warned you. If that's the way you want it, so be it."

"Charlotte, clean off the kitchen table, and get some water boiling. We'll do this out there. And make sure there's light for me to see what I'm doing. While she's getting ready, June, let's you and me set this leg. You get up there and sit your bottom down on Alberta Mae's lap to stop her from sliding off on to the floor when I pull on her leg. Randall, find me three or four flat boards about two inches wide, by at least a foot long, but not more than a foot and a half, and not less than a half inch thick. Make it quick now. While he's doing that, Charlotte, tear me up a sheet or something, in strips three inches wide and about four feet long. I'll need them to tie off the splint we'll make with the boards. Make at least eight of them. Scoot!"

"I'm going to take this bracing off your leg now. I'll be as careful as I can, but it's going to hurt unless you want me to put you asleep."

"You just go right ahead and do what you have to do, Mr. Doc. I'm ready for it," she contends.

"You hold her leg as still as you can, June. Here we go."

The boards and bandages are at his side before Doc gets the field splint off her leg.

"Randall, you get up there behind June and hold your Mama back when I pull. She's going to want to come straight up out of that chair."

"Yessir." Randall lays his chest across his mother and wraps his arms over the wings and back of the chair.

Doc ties two of the bandages around his patient's ankle, and passes an end each to Charlotte and Jim.

"Now, I'm going to pull and line up her bones. I want you two to just keep a steady even outward pressure going until I get the splint tied off. Can you do that?"

Responses are affirmative.

Doc takes Alberta Mae's leg, just above the ankle, in both hands and pulls with all his might. Charlotte and Jim keep their lines taught.

Alberta Mae howls in distress.

The doctor runs his hands carefully up and down her leg, his fingers checking from side to side, front to back, down her shin bone.

"Once more!" he signals to all.

This time he gives her leg a jerk and hears Alberta Mae say "Oh my, what a relief."

Charlotte and Jim maintain their outward stretch of her leg.

Again, Doc's fingers do their job.

"That's good. Hold it right there until I get this splint set and tight, and we'll be finished."

Three minutes pass as the boards are placed along each side of her leg and strapped on with the bandages. Finally, he stops and signals Charlotte and Jim to relax their grip.

"That should heal up so that you'll never know it was broken," he advises his patient.

"You two can let her up now," he speaks to June and Randall.

"It all fell right into place, it was a clean break. It's going to swell and get awful sore for a couple of weeks, but I'd say if you don't put any weight on it for a month, everything should be okay," he instructs.

"Thank you, Mr. Doc. It feels a whole lot better already. I surely thank you," she says gratefully. "I'll do exactly as you say."

"All right, it's time for you, Miss June. Charlotte, bring my bag and that bottle of alcohol to the kitchen. I'm going to want you to pour a little of it over my hands after I wash them." He moves to the kitchen following his next patient.

Charlotte appears with the bag and alcohol.

"My tools are wrapped up in a white cloth in there," he says, pointing to the bag. "Drop them into that pot of boiling water for a few minutes. Then pour the water off except for enough to keep them covered."

"Okay, I'm ready, pour some of that alcohol over my hands, and start handing me my tools as I ask for them. Use one of those clean bandages to pick them up with."

He moves to the kitchen table where June is lying on her back.

"On your side." His way of telling June to turn over.

"Dampen a towel with cool water and give it to your mother. She might want it to wipe her face, or maybe put between her teeth. Okay, we're all set. Here we go, I won't hurt you any more than I just have to. Hand me my scalpel. It's that one with the knife blade on the end of it."

She picks it out of the water and hands it to him immediately. "I know what a scalpel is," she informs him.

June winces as Doc makes a small incision enabling him to get a pair of forceps under the stick buried beneath her skin.

"Hold on," he says quietly. "Forceps," he commands.

No sooner did the words leave his mouth than the handles hit his hand. Charlotte is a step ahead of him.

He carefully pushes the open jaws under her skin and closes them around the exposed piece of wood. Very gently at first, he tugs with a little twist. When it doesn't budge, he puts the fingers of his left hand on either side of the wound and pushes in at the same time he pulls the forceps toward him.

June twists and lets out a guttural, muffled squeal.

This time the stick moves and slides out about an inch. He sees the end of the side of the fork he feared was deep inside her. He is relieved to see it is far less serious than it might have been. Blood starts running down her side and back. He holds his hand out. Charlotte slaps a clean bandage in it without being prompted. He places it over the wound and presses firmly.

"Well now, good news, it looks like it's not as bad as I thought it was. Get another grip, June, a bit more and we'll have it."

Still holding the bandage in place, he repositions his fingers to either side of the stick, and turns the forceps to pull straight out, sliding it from under her skin. One smooth pull and out it comes, bringing a fresh supply of blood with it. He holds the stick, which appears to be at least three inches long, over June's side to show her.

"That's an ugly looking thing to have stuck in your side," she says. "Are you finished?"

"Almost. We'll get this bleeding settled down, then we'll look for any splinters. I don't think we'll have to stitch it up, so we'll just clean it real good, put on a bit of salve, and bandage it up. The point of this stick that went straight into your side turned out to be no more than an inch long, and by the amount and the color of the blood I've seen, I'd say there's been no bleeding inside there at all."

"Looks like you were right all along, just a scratch," he kids.

She chuckles, feeling relieved.

"Charlotte, come here and hold this compress while I clean up a little," Doc instructs his help.

"I'll be happy to, Doc, but first, I need to check on Mr. Housler, Mrs. Housler, and Alberta Mae. I'll be right back," Charlotte replies and leaves the room.

"You've raised yourself a dandy there," he comments.

"I know," she replies quietly. "I'm a bit late in finding that out, too."

Although several observers were in the kitchen when the procedures began, all left during the operation. Doc and June wait, she still lying on her side on the kitchen table.

Suddenly, Robert appears through the door out of his mother's sight, with the first finger of his right hand pressed upward over his lips, signaling Doc to be quiet.

Following him is a man who gently lays his hand on June's shoulder and whispers.

"Hey, it's me."

June turns slowly to see.

"John!"

Chapter Twenty-Five

The time is two hours before dawn the morning after the raids.

Tap. Tap. Tap. Silence, not a thought of sound.

Tap. Tap. Tap. Tap.

Cheryl stirs from her sound sleep in her bed at the hotel in town.

Tap. Tap. Tap.

"Someone's at the door," she thinks, her mind still fuzzy. She pushes herself to throw the blankets aside and swing her feet to the floor.

Tap. Tap. Tap.

"I'm coming. Just a minute," she says, loud enough to be heard through the door, then grabs a robe and threads her arms through the sleeves as she approaches the source of the tapping. A twist of the key, and a half turn of the door knob, allows her to pull the door inward just a crack.

"Who is it? What do you want?" she asks using her firm serious voice.

"Sally. It's Sally, Amber. I must speak with you."

Sally's voice causes Cheryl to slam the door, and turn the key. Blood courses through her body putting her senses on edge.

"Get out of here! I have nothing to say to you!" Her voice shows her surprise.

"It's not what you think, Amber, let me in. I need to talk to you."

"Who do you have with you?"

"No one, I'm alone."

"You're supposed to be long gone. Why are you still here?"

"I can't explain through this door, everyone will hear me. Let me in."

"Wait until I get some clothes on."

Sally sees the light of a just lit lamp appear under the door. A few minutes pass, then she hears the key turn in the lock, and watches the door swing back slowly.

"Call me, Cheryl. Everybody knows me by that name."

"Fine, Cheryl it is," Sally agrees.

As soon as her visitor clears the doorway, she closes the door, and locks it.

"I don't want any surprises, I'm sure you can understand that," she relates to the woman who recently kidnapped and tore her away from her family. Why are you here?"

"I'm here to arrange an alliance with you."

"I'm listening," Cheryl encourages.

"Well, whether you believe me or not, I would not have left you there tied to a chair with that shack on fire. That was totally unnecessary, and way too dangerous. You might have been burned alive."

"You're forgetting, it was my idea. And why aren't you on your way to Atlanta?" Cheryl cuts her off.

"Will you quit fencing with me and let me say what I'm here to tell you?" Sally appears to be losing her patience.

"I'm not going to Atlanta. I've decided I'm on the wrong side here. You've known me too long to think that I believe your heart and soul is anywhere but here with these people—your family. You're not going to spy on them. Hell, you love them, one and all. After we left you there alone in that burning shack, I had to keep one eye open every minute to protect myself from those two thugs we were with. The only thing on their minds was me. I warned them severely to stay away, but they must have put their heads together, and, well, anyway, they tried to catch me by surprise and overcome me. I had no choice but to defend myself. I killed Benny outright, and I'm pretty sure I wounded Nate, but he was able to get to his horse and rode off, hanging over his saddle horn."

"What?" Cheryl says in amazement.

"I had to do it. If I hadn't, they would have done what they wanted, then murdered me. They couldn't leave me alive after that. Their lives wouldn't be worth a plug nickel," Sally says calmly, matter-of-factly.

"Nate will probably invent some story to tell them at Atlanta—but, let me finish. I was pretty shook up, so it took a while to settle down and determine what I need to do. I came into town to meet with your contact to ask him to get a message to Atlanta, and you. I had to be sure you were okay. He was naturally curious about the details of my carefully worded report, so I was relating them to him when it came over me. I'm nothing to any of these people. Just a tool, an expendable tool. If I had been raped and killed out there, the Company would step on my body to get over me, and keep right on going. I'm not doing it any more. I'm through."

"Lord, Sally . . . I never dreamed. What will you do? Where will you go? Can you just up and quit the Company anytime you want to?"

"That's what you want to do, isn't it?"

Cheryl looks at her without answering, fearing she's walking into a trap.

"I don't blame you for not trusting me, but I'm going to trust you. Then maybe we can see eye to eye."

Cheryl stays silent.

"I think I'm the cause of the raids yesterday. Your contact is an idiot. He knows not to attack your family directly, because of you, so he did the next worse thing he could think of. He took what I told him and turned it into a reason to attack your family by hurting your friends. I'm just sick about it. I'm ready to put my life, my efforts, and training into helping my fellow man rid this world of the Company, and the likes of him. I want you to help me."

"Whoa, now, let me get this straight. You think you and I can take on the Company? We're just two women, we wouldn't last a month. And by the way, who is my contact?" Cheryl's response amounts to about what Sally expects.

"He's the local deputy sheriff, Clifford Messinger."

"Clifford Messinger—I don't think I've ever seen him. I can see now why I would know him as my contact. Clifford Messinger, huh, they told me I'd know when I heard the name. What did you tell him that would make him set off the raids?" she continues.

"I told him what you told me, more or less, that's all. I told you, he's an idiot. I think he has an axe to grind with your family. If I'd known how he would react, I would have never said anything to him. His ego is all wrapped up in his title. He's just a bully with a badge. I can't take back what's already said, but I can as sure as hell do my best to thwart any future effort he turns loose on your family." Sally's temper is starting to show.

"I like what you're saying, but I still don't see how just the two of us—"

Sally cuts her off. "Are you with me then? Do you want to protect all that's yours?"

"Yes, I suppose I do," Cheryl commits.

"Great! Now listen carefully. Here's what we'll do."

The place is La Nesra, at Atlanta, Georgia. A small cottage inside the walls is occupied by Falcon, Lilly, and their baby girl. The time is daybreak, the day after the raids on Der Bote and the Sanders' farm. Lilly and Falcon are finishing their breakfast at their small table for two. The maid is caring for their baby girl.

"I still think we should name our baby," Lilly remarks.

"It's not a good idea right now," Falcon counters, leaning over the table toward his wife, keeping his voice low and soft.

"If we show too much interest in her, the Company might get suspicious and take her away before we're ready. Our walls have ears, you know that. And besides, baby is going to have a last name, too." He concludes pointing his finger toward the maid in the other room.

Lilly nods her head slightly yes.

"It's been a month, husband, I'm ready," she reminds him with a whisper.

"It's been three weeks, wife, and I just want to be sure you're up to the task."

"I'm ready to go today," she assures. "What am I supposed to do when someone knocks on our door while you're gone, and says they're here to take baby? We need to get a move on. We'd better leave while we can."

"I know, you're right," Falcon agrees, and gets lost in his thoughts.

Lilly sits, waiting with her elbows on the table, coffee cup in both hands, holding it to her mouth. This is nothing new to her, it's his way.

"Okay," he breathes. "Three days . . . we leave in three days. It'll take that much time to get our supplies together. Okay?"

"Like I say, I'm ready, now."

"What about her?" Falcon points to the other room again.

"Let me worry about her. She won't be a problem. But what if they come after baby in the meantime?" she poses.

"Try to stall them for a day or so. If that doesn't work and they take her away, we'll have to go after her when we leave. We have to take her with us, and we will have just one chance—we can't come back after her later on, you know that."

Lilly nods, "I know."

Breakfast at the Anderson farm is quite an undertaking this morning. Belle, acting as the head cook and server, has been at it since before dawn. The hands' wives and girl children, all scamper at her command. The house is full of people, all of whom are hungry, and wanting to know what they should do today.

Is it safe? Should some start with their regular chores?

Who is going to Der Bote to see what is left there?

The same is true for the Sanders' place.

The colonel made it through the night, but is still in serious condition. He's awake, though, and has had chicken broth and coffee. Selma, with the large bandage around her head, appears worse off than she feels. Alberta Mae, already growling about being unable to help, is trying to get someone, anyone, to get, or make, her a pair of crutches. June isn't moving as fast today as she was last night. The soreness and aching of her wound is giving her a constant reminder of yesterday.

A lot of conversation last night, until the wee hours of this morning has John Anderson somewhat briefed.

Robert has been pacing most of the night, trying to determine his best action to locate Elizabeth.

Alberta Mae finally agreed, allowing Jacob's body to be taken to the barn and placed with the other four. Randall is easily found either at his daddy's side, or pacing with Robert.

Doc Shaw spent the night, wanting to keep an eye on the colonel and the rest. He's checked all the wounds already, and redressed those that needed it, had his breakfast, and is getting ready to get back to town.

"I thank God for you, Doc," June says as she gives him a quick hug before he climbs aboard his buggy. "You are truly a good friend."

"I'd like to add my appreciation to that, Doc," John says in thanks, extending his hand.

"That's okay," he says. "I'm glad I was able to do what I did. I imagine I'll see you later in town, John. That right?"

"It looks that way. I need to ask a few questions?"

"Well, unless I hear different from you all here, I'll be back out here tomorrow morning to check on the colonel. I'll send the parson and undertaker out here as soon as I get into town. I'll tell them to expect to be here all day." Doc climbs into his buggy, which is hitched to his rested, freshly fed, horses. He sets his bag on the floor, picks the reins off the brake lever, snaps them over the backs of his team, and with a *click, click* of his tongue, moves away. John and June wave goodbye and turn back into the house.

"See if we can get everybody together in the living room, June. I should say a few words."

She leaves to volunteer some help with finding everybody and fulfilling her husband's request.

John has time to have Belle slap a hard fried egg and a sausage patty between one of her biscuits, and grab a cup of coffee before walking into the living room, where people are gathering. The five minutes it takes him go gulp down his food is just enough to crowd everyone into the room or just outside in the hallway. After a couple more swallows of coffee, he holds up his hands to call for quiet.

"For those of you here who might not know who I am, I'm John Anderson. I'm sure, after yesterday, you all know my family on a close personal basis. If you can't hear me just let me know and I'll try to speak up. I know, too, that some of you are here from Der Bote and the Sanders' farm. We want you to know you're welcome here. Make your plans to stay as long as you need it to be. A lot went on yesterday, and I know there's a lot of aching hearts here today grieving for your kin and friends, people you care a lot about. If there's anything—anything at all—I, my family, or our extended family, can do to help you through this terrible catastrophe, please don't hesitate to make it known. Most of these people were our close friends, too.

"Along with dealing with the grief and pain, we must also find the time and strength to go through what's left of the lives of two families, to salvage all that we can. Be assured, everyone will have a roof over their heads tonight and from now on. There will be food, places for everyone to sleep, facilities to bathe and keep clean. Things will never be the same again, but as long as we all stick together, and work together, our lives will, in time, get back to where they make some sense.

"I'm asking June and Selma to take charge and organize groups to do what needs to be attended to. They'll be asking for your help, and I can tell you that all of us will appreciate anything you're able to do.

"One of the first things will be to have a search party try to locate any missing people. So, if you know of someone who's missing, be sure to tell June and Selma. We want every soul on these three farms to be accounted for.

"Another will be a burial party, to make places for our dead. Help will be here from town later today, but graves can be dug and made ready for when they get here.

"I want Robert, Randall, Jim, and Josh to get saddled up and ready for a trip to town. Make sure you're carrying iron, I know I will. If we're not back here in time for the funerals and the like, understand that our hearts are here, if not out bodies.

"Are there any questions?"

"God bless you, and your family, Mr. Anderson," is heard from someone in the crowd.

Many of the others repeat the words in unison.

The meeting starts breaking up.

After a brief, cheek to cheek, conversation with Selma, June makes her way to John and gets his attention by griping his arm and pulling him aside.

"I don't want you to leave before I get a big hug." She smiles and turns him toward her. Once in his arms and her face next to his, she whispers.

"Don't you go into town taking on every living soul there. We all know you're angry as hell—we all are—but think before you pull that trigger. I killed two men yesterday. I never dreamed I could actually shoot anybody. And if Selma hadn't killed one, I wouldn't be here now. I'm not sure how I feel about it, but I know they would have killed us both without batting an eyelash. I keep thinking a person should feel a little remorse for taking the life of another, but I don't right now. I have a feeling of indifference for their lives. I ask myself, will the bitterness pass, will the dread of living with it ebb over time. I don't know. I see clearly now that right doesn't always win out, John. Don't get yourself killed over this. Nothing's worth that. Come back to me."

"Don't worry, honey. We're not going into town with our guns blazing. But we have to ask some tough questions. They have to know, though, we'll back our play, and the quicker they believe that, the easier we'll get the answers we're looking for. I can't let the killers of these people walk away, to just let it all fall by the wayside. Someone has to pay, and pay dearly. My job is to see to it."

"Let the deputy do it. It's his job," she counters.

"The deputy isn't going to do anything. I have a file full of information about him. He's an agent for the Company. For all I know, he's part of the reason this happened. I'll have four men with me so we can watch each other's backs. We won't be looking for trouble, but we're going to get some answers. I'm sorry you don't agree with me, but you said it yourself. You were there yesterday, you and Selma. You did what you did because you had to. That's all I'm doing."

June looks into her husband's face and pulls it to hers. She kisses him on the cheek and tells him what he wants to hear. "I love you, John Anderson, and I fear for your life. If it's war they want, then take it to them. Kill them before they kill you and my son. If we have to pay for it later, we'll sweat in hell together."

With that, she pulls away and swiftly moves toward Selma on the other side of the room.

The ride to town is solemn and quiet as each of the five men reflect on yesterday. Josh thanks the Lord with a silent prayer for allowing most of his family to be safely away from the gun play and burning. Some of the missing hands of Der Bote are longtime friends of those on the Anderson farm, so he worries about them and what will happen to their families.

Jim has no family of his own. He's always said, with all the other families around, he's never needed any more. Being the driver on the Anderson farm, he and Jacob, who was the driver on the Housler farm, had a lot in common. When there was time over the years, they enjoyed each other's company, fishing at the lake or picnicking with his family. Jim was there those many years ago, when Jacob was severely beaten by John. He's always been amazed by how Jacob was able to put that all behind him and get on with his life. He truly loved Jacob Stoker and has to work at keeping his feelings from consuming him.

Randall rocks in his saddle pondering what his family life will be like without his father. His daddy was the boss of the hands, and his mama was the boss of the house for Miss Selma and Mr. Housler. He has never worried about them or his sisters and brothers because of that. But now, everything has changed.

"Daddy's gone . . . the house and everything in it is gone . . . Mama's hurt. That'll heal up, but it'll take some time. There'll be no place for my brothers and sisters to work. What's going to happen to them? Will they be sold off separately, to work on other farms? Mr. Housler might not survive his injury. What will Miss Selma do if that happens? I'm the head of the family now, and I don't know how to be the head of a family. Daddy was always so wise about life. Mama always claimed to be the boss in our house, but we all knew Daddy had his way of letting her be that. I miss him."

Robert rides up front, his horse side by side with his father's. His thoughts are about Elizabeth. "The truth is, I don't know if I'll ever see her again. I only have this one picture of her, but I thank God I have it. I can still smell her hair, and that fresh-smelling soap she used when she took a bath. Her voice is still in my head from when she said she loved me for the first time, I hope I never forget that. I don't think I could ever love another woman the way I do her. There's not a selfish bone in her body, and she would do anything for anybody, anytime, never expecting a thank-you. Her parents were so proud of her, their only child. I wonder if she saw them being killed. God, I hope not. I don't know what I'll do if I can't find her. Where to start? New Orleans is a long way off. There's a lot of towns and cities between here and there. She could be anywhere. I miss her so much, sometimes I want to scream."

John's mind is filled with neglected responsibility and regret. "I should have been home when this happened. Maybe I could have done something, anything. It's almost like Robert was pulled away on purpose, so this could happen. If I'd been here, one of us would have been at home. I feel like I've failed the Sanders' in the worst way. I pushed them into a commitment to help me. Maybe, somehow, word got out and this is their payback. And the colonel, it could be for the same reason; but with him, it could be tied to his estranged son in some way. Whatever, I won't get any rest until I know each and every one of those murdering devils have paid for their actions. I must keep in mind though, these four men here with me all have lives of their own. They have their own reasons for being here, and those have to be satisfied as well."

"Town's coming up," they hear Robert comment.

John straightens himself in his saddle and twists around to see everyone still with him.

With the horses at a walk, the group of five pull up at the sheriff's office, dismount, and wrap their horses reins around the hitching rail.

John adjusts his gun belt up and to the right a tad, before walking around the rear of Robert's mount and up onto the wooden walk. He stops there to wait for his men to catch up. When they step up onto the walk, he turns and moves toward the office door, but before he can take three steps, the door opens, and the deputy fills the empty space.

"Morning John, Robert . . . boys. Can I help you with something?" He nods his head. His words are friendly, but the look on his face shows a lot of concern.

"I need a few words with you, Cliff, can we talk inside?" John asks with a stone-sober face.

"All of you?" The lawman adjusts his stance.

"All of us," Mr. Anderson insists.

The deputy's eyes glance at each of his visitors, and with a quick turn of his head each way, he looks up and down the street, then steps back and to the side with no comment. Once everyone is inside, the law in this town closes the door and finds his way to his chair behind a small desk. He sits down, still silent, then looks intently at John.

John speaks. "What do you know about the raids on the Houslers' and Sanders' farms yesterday?"

"All I know is one of your hands came blowing into town wanting a posse to go out to your place, claiming the raiders were headed there, and you needed help. It took a little time, but I was able get about twenty men together. Then we all went out there as fast as we could. Why're you asking? You already know all that." The deputy's demeanor is one of defiance.

"You saw both of those farms burning, why didn't you split your men and see if you could help those poor people? I understand you flat refused and brought your posse back here to town. Is that right?" The elder Anderson gets more aggressive, not liking Cliff's attitude.

"That's right, that's exactly what I did. I had to get my men back to town to protect the people and stores here. By the looks of the smoke I saw, there was no helping anybody out there. Whatever was happening was over." The deputy defends his decision.

"You were asked to leave a few men to help protect my farm if the raiders showed up there, you refused that, too," Robert's dad states.

"That's right. I needed every man I had." His tone all but dares John to accuse him of anything.

"You're the so-called law around here, Cliff. You took an oath to protect every citizen in your charge. Do you have any idea of how many people died out there yesterday? You don't give a damn do you?" Temper is beginning to show.

"Who the hell do you think you are? Coming in here with your gang to scare me into something. You weren't here, you don't know how things were out there and back here in town. People here were scared, too. Now, quit pussyfooting around, if you've got something to accuse me of, let me hear it, or take your gun carrying buddies and get out." Deputy Messinger gets to his feet and lays his hand on the butt of his gun.

John squares off and watches for the deputy's hand to move.

"You're a fool if you make a play here, Cliff, and you know it," he glares as he speaks. "You're a dead man if that gun comes out of it's holster."

The Anderson group has spread themselves in a half circle in front of the desk, hands poised above their sidearms, ready. Nobody moves. One wrong word, or insinuation of a move, will fill the air with lead and smoke. The seven seconds that pass drag on to feel like sixty.

Unexpectedly, the noise of the door being opened breaks the tension and calms the standoff. All eyes, except John's watching the deputy, move to the door.

The first to appear is one of the Stoker twins, Randall's brothers. The next through the door is a young man, whose clothes are covered with mud and dust, his hands tied behind his back. The third to enter is the second of the twin brothers.

"What the—" Cliff stutters.

"This is one of the people who attacked our farm," the first twin explains.

"And he might be the one who shot Mr. Housler, too," says the second twin.

"Who are the two of you black boys, bringing a white man in here all tied up this way—making such outlandish claims?" the lawman begins. "Now, cut him loose!" he demands.

"Nobody's cutting anybody loose." A loud deep voice precedes a large man, who bends down to come through the door. "Stay where you are boys, don't anybody move a muscle."

The man is over six foot four inches tall, wearing mostly black. His keen dark green eyes flick here and there, taking in the layout. Gray, almost white hair hangs from under his hat to lay on his shoulders. A square jaw, with heavy eyebrows, and a thick gray mustache make an opposing appearance. His hands hang at his sides, just inches from the handles of a matched set of Colts, their holsters tied down to his legs. A trained eye would notice the holster hammer loops are loose, making the guns available to a quick hand.

"Something going on here? Things feel a little on edge?"

"Who the hell are you?" Cliff reacts.

"My name is of no importance here and now, deputy. I'm just helping two friends of mine bring a proven killer to jail for justice. Am I going to find that here?"

"I know this set of twins, mister, I'm John Anderson. These young men are from the farm, Der Bote, just over from mine. It was raided yesterday. That's why we're here trying to get to the bottom of it. These four are with me. Randall there is their brother."

"I'm the law here and—!" The deputy moves his hands to make his point.

Nobody sees nor hears the move, but the stranger's hand is holding a gun pointed at the head of the towns law in less than a heartbeat.

"I told you not to move, mister, I'll not tell you again. Take your hogleg with the tips of you fingers and lay it there on the desk. I'd hate to have to kill you this morning. Move!"

The gun is laid gently on the desk.

"Turn the butt, toward me."

"Now, everybody relax. Let's sort this all out. I'll start off. Late yesterday afternoon, these two men came running on foot, all tuckered out, begging me to get my men and go back with them to fend off a band of renegades that was killing and burning everything in sight. They said their sisters and a Colonel Charles Housler, who was mortally shot, were being tracked by half a dozen of those renegades, and they feared for their lives. I rounded up a few of my men, and the lot of us took off to see if we could help. Along the edge of a woods we found three dead men and this lad here, who was trapped under one of two dead horses. I found this note from a gal named June." He holsters his sidearm and produces a note from his shirt pocket.

"It says this man should be brought here and jailed for murdering and pillaging. It didn't take much, with him trapped under his horse, for us to get the whole ugly story. He named as many of the men in the raiding party as he could. I wrote them all down here, on the back of this note."

"What else did the lying bastard say!" Cliff yells.

The young man with his hands tied behind his back makes a move toward the deputy. The twins restrain him. He starts to speak but the stranger cuts him off.

"You know what he said deputy. That's why I'm here with these two good men."

Cliff jumps for the gun lying on the desk, fumbles just a bit before getting it in his hand, then ducks down behind the desk as the hammer falls, striking the sweet spot of the load in the chamber. The sound of the explosion is deafening in the small space.

Instantly, another shot sounds off.

The prisoner is hit by the deputy's bullet, and is pushed back sideways into the strangers loaded hand, knocking his arm off to the side just as his gun comes to life. His bullet smashes harmlessly into the wall.

Clifford Messinger, his gun in his hand, falls dead to the floor.

Another gun is smoking, still pointed at the dead deputy. John looks down at his hand and realizes he fired the fatal shot. His, and the stranger's gun, went off at the same time. "Damn!" he reacts.

"Nothing else you could do, Mr. Anderson," the man in black assures. "He was bound to get killed today, one way or the other."

"Did anybody get hit?" Randall implores.

"Your prisoner caught it in his shoulder. It's not bad. He'll be able to stand trial," Robert replies, as he pulls the man back to his feet. "Doc can have him back as good as new in no time."

"This man the only law here?" the stranger inquires. "You folks might want to take your prisoner and find out anything you want to know before you turn him over. He told us the deputy here was the one who instructed them to stage these raids."

"Did he say why?" Robert asks.

"I didn't take the time to find that out. He'll tell you when you ask him the right way, if you know what I mean?" the man in black encourages.

"Who are you anyway?" Randall queries.

"If it's all the same to the lot of you, the less you know about me, the better off we'll all be down the road. I have my reasons, and if you're tied to me, well let's just say, it won't help you any. If you can handle this from here, I'll drift away and nobody needs to be the wiser."

John sticks out his hand.

"Thanks . . . for all you done for these boys, and backing our play. Just so you know, Colonel Housler is alive. We have every confidence he'll make it. The girls are fine too."

The stranger nods, turns, and says, "glad to hear it," and leaves the office. Once outside, he notices the streets are clear of people. The gunshots must have driven them inside. Wanting no further involvement, he mounts up, kicks his mount to a trot, and is gone.

With no time to waste, Robert drags the chair from the back of the deputy's desk and pushes the young prisoner down on it.

"Someone go get Doc," he orders.

Randall and the twins leave the office.

"I'm sorry you had to be a part of this," John attempts to apologize to his son.

"I'm not," he doesn't hesitate to set his father straight. "I know now that you feel as strongly about what needs to be done as I do, and I'm proud of what's happened here.

"What's your name, boy." Robert asks the young man, calling him boy when he's no older than himself.

"Ed. My name's Edward Skinner.

"Look," he continues. "I know I'm caught, so I'll tell you anything you want to know. No need to get rough."

"This list, these men—all friends of yours?" Robert asks.

"I know them, but I wouldn't call them friends. I did what I did for the money."

"You say Cliff hired you to raid these farms yesterday?" John inquires.

"That's right. We each got twenty dollars gold."

"Who's the deputy work for?" Robert pushes.

"I don't know for sure, but I've heard it's some kind of company."

"Where can we find these men on this list?" John continues

"You going to kill them?" the prisoner asks.

"That's not your concern." Young Mr. Anderson warns with a sense of justice.

"I'll tell you, or—what the hell—I'll take you to each and every one and point him out. Whatever you want. Do you think they might not hang me if I help you get the rest of them?"

"They might not, but I wouldn't count on it." Robert dishes out venom sternly.

"Do you know where they took their women prisoners?" John queries.

"I don't know anything about any prisoners. Nobody told me we were taking prisoners," the young man answers freely.

The questioning stops as Doc and the boys come through the door.

The first thing he does is bend down behind the desk and check Cliff.

"He's dead. Shot right through the heart from the side, I'd say."

"Who killed him?" Doc's question is a reaction rather than a search for the guilty party. "Don't answer that if it's anyone here," he quickly corrects himself.

"That's okay, Doc. A stranger and I fired at the same time, but I think my bullet got him," John admits. "It was determined that he ordered those raids yesterday, and he went for his gun. His bullet's in Ed's shoulder, here." John points to the prisoner. "I think he was trying to kill his accuser, but I guess we'll never know for sure now."

"Good riddance, I say. He was a no good skunk," Doc lets his opinion be known.

"Let me see how bad you're shot up," he continues and moves to Ed's side.

"Ahh . . . it's not too bad, need to get that bullet out of there, though. Help me get him over to my office, boys."

The twins volunteer to help. One on either side of the prisoner, they move toward the door. Randal, with his hand holding a pistol, stops the closest to him.

"Take this, and if he makes a wrong move—kill him."

"Now, don't anybody get trigger-happy here. Like I said, I'm caught and I know it. I'm not going to cause any trouble for anybody," Ed assures the group.

"I'll send somebody after Cliff's body," Doc concludes.

No more have they left the office, when Cheryl appears.

"I have someone I want you all to meet," she explains with the first words out of her mouth, as she moves through the door.

"This is Sally," she offers as a woman follows her inside, then positions herself at the doorway to keep watch for eavesdroppers.

Robert and Randall recognize the redheaded woman immediately.

"She's from the Company," Randall speaks first. "She's the one that helped us bring the wrong Sheree—I mean, bring Amber—I mean, Cheryl, home."

John and Robert aren't the least bit surprised, since deep down they've suspected Cheryl has maintained her alliances at the Company, but Sally's entrance is totally unexpected.

"Don't start with anything until you've heard us out," Cheryl begins. "It's not what you think. Let Sally explain."

"Who's that, there on the floor?" Sally can only see the man's legs and feet because of the desk.

"Cliff, the deputy," Randall is quick to relate.

"So, this is where the shots came from. Is he dead?" she continues.

"Dead as a wedge," Randall replies with a bit of satisfaction. John and Robert both feel a bit of humor with his statement.

"Perfect!" she exclaims. "This is working out just great."

"You're Mr. Anderson, I take it."

"I am." John doesn't get a chance to continue.

"I'm glad you're here. Cheryl and I have been up since very early this morning, working out the details of a plan I know you will want to be a part of."

"We're listening," John manages to interject, with the intent to let her know Robert and Randall are part of this, also.

"Wonderful," she adds, as she turns to look them straight in the eyes, and with a nod, acknowledges their inclusion.

"To start with, late yesterday afternoon, I made a long overdue decision to sever my loyalties to the Company. And I have Cheryl's word that she's of the same mind. I could stand here for several days explaining my reasons, but there's no time for that. Just be assured that my decision has been thoroughly thought out, and is not reversible. Cheryl's loyalties haven't been with the Company since she arrived here, but then I imagine you already know that.

"We want to join forces with you to eradicate the world of the Company, and all it amounts to. Don't be surprised that I know about your SONS organization. It's a common topic of conversation in the halls of La Nesra. We—Cheryl and I—are completely trusted by those in control at Atlanta's La Nesra. They, one and all, will consider heavily any information we pass along to them. I believe I'm in a position to take Clifford's place in their structure, which has worked well for several years. Cheryl will then report to me.

"Now, the good part, I can supply you with an insurmountable amount of information, from the layout inside La Nesra, to the names of their leaders there. I will be able to get you a list of names of agents, and their whereabouts throughout this country, and in many cases, give you the nature of their assignments. We, working together, might even be able to supply recruits for the Company from your own, loyal, people.

"I know you will have many questions that need answers, and perhaps I can address them one at a time as we go along. The important thing at this moment is to agree to a new beginning. Cheryl and I will work every day to prove ourselves to you.

"Now, the hard part. It's possible that I might have been partly responsible for the raids on your farms."

The air in the office suddenly becomes heavy, causing everyone to breathe deeper.

"Believe me, I had no idea Clifford would react the way he did. I would never knowingly be part of anything like that. I came into town to relate information to him, thinking he would report it to La Nesra."

"What information?" John interrupts.

"Things I told her," Cheryl accepts responsibility. "Things like where you were then, what Robert was doing, what the Houslers and the Sanders' were doing. Things like that. I had to tell her something—anything."

"There was nothing of any real consequence, Mr. Anderson," Sally continues. "As Cheryl says, just information to fill up a report. I'm not sure if Clifford sent it on or not. It could have been the very thing that set him off."

"I doubt that's what happened," Robert interjects. "He and I had words before that. It almost came to gunplay. I've been thinking that's what set him off."

John shakes his head with confusion, and a feeling of being uninformed.

"Will someone fill me in on what's been going on around here." His words are curtly presented.

"You bet." His son agrees in an upbeat manner, wanting to suppress his father's lurking temper. He continues with the facts of Cheryl's abduction and the efforts made to get her back. With input from Sally, Randall, and Cheryl, the entire story gets laid out.

John spreads his feet a little, crosses his arms on his chest, then raises his forearm to put his forefinger and thumb on either side of his chin. Rubbing gently, thoughtfully, he balances backward and forward, heel to toe, slightly. After a minute or two of silence, he opens his arms and takes a deep breath.

"Well, well, I can see that all of us have found a way to blame ourselves for what happened, when the truth is probably more along these lines.

"You'd have no way of knowing this, but a few years ago—back before Cliff became a deputy—he'd had more than enough to drink early one afternoon, and was raising hell at the bar. He began to shoot up the place, and started breaking the furniture by throwing people around. It just so happened that Charles Housler and Cole Sanders were in town that day and heard the commotion. They went in there, dodging bullets and Cliff's drunken tantrum, and pinned him to the floor. They detained him right there, put him in a back room, locked the door, and I heard nobody paid any attention to him for a couple of days. When he got out, he swore he'd get even.

"Another time, before that, he made some advances toward June. That's my wife, Robert's mother, Sally. I had to let him know she didn't appreciate it, and I can tell you he didn't like the way I went about it. So, he and I have tried to stay out of each others way since then.

"So, do you see what I mean. The man's dead. We'll never know what was in his mind, and we'll all deal with it in our own way, I guess.

"Sally," he changes the subject and the mood. "I'd be a fool if I didn't give your proposal a chance. I need to think it over for a day or two, so as to know how it could work within our group. But, we have family things to handle right now, and I don't think you should be any part of them. Why don't you just keep your head down for a couple of days, until I get back to you."

"That's fine, Mr. Anderson. I'll be here when you're ready," she affirms.

It's a damp and balmy in Atlanta. Soft rain has been falling off and on all day. The sky is overcast, obscuring the sun.

Falcon is involved with his duties away from their cottage, where his wife and baby girl are busy with their maid, having dinner.

"How much has she taken so far?" Lilly asks her maid, who is bottle-feeding the small child. Lilly has been forbidden to breast-feed, making the feeding process a difficult time of the day for her. She's also limited as to how long she can hold her newborn.

"About half, ma'am," she answers. "She's doing real good."

Hesitantly, her eyes flicking first at Lilly, then to the baby, back and forth, she continues. "Can I talk to you, ma'am? You won't get mad will you?"

"Of course, you can talk to me, what is it? Is something wrong?" The child's mother immediately focuses on the worried look of the face glancing back at her.

"Well, I don't mean to poke my nose into where it don't belong, but I know what you and your husband are up to."

Lilly's heart sinks. "What's that?" she reacts, hoping the maid isn't headed where she thinks she is.

"You, leaving here with your baby."

"What do you want?" Falcon's wife, caught by surprise, cuts to the chase.

"I want to go with you when you go. I can't stay here. You know I have a child, too. I have to find a way out of here. I want a better life than this for him."

"No, I didn't know you have a child. How old is he?"

“He’ll be six the end of next month.”

“Where’s his father?” Lilly tries to settle herself down.

“He’s a white man here, but I’m not allowed to talk about him. If I do, he’ll hurt me and my boy. I have to get away from here.”

“Are you threatening me? If I say no, what will you do?” A hard question that has to be asked and answered.

“Oh, no, ma’am. Don’t ever think that. I’d never do anything like that. No, ma’am, never do anything like that.”

“Well then, I—I, I don’t know what to say. I’ll need to talk to my husband.”

“I had to say something today to you, because they told me to have the baby ready, so they can pick her up tomorrow, and they told me not to tell you about it.”

“Tomorrow? When tomorrow?” The new mother feels a panic coming on.

“They didn’t say, just tomorrow.”

“Good Lord. That doesn’t give us much time, does it?”

“No, ma’am.”

“Finish feeding her, then put her down in her crib. I’m going to see if I can find her daddy. You stay here, don’t leave. I’ll be back as soon as I can.”

“Yes, ma’am.”

“And Nora.”

“Yes, ma’am?”

“You don’t know how much I appreciate your telling me.”

It takes Lilly the better part of forty-five minutes to locate Falcon, and get word to him to come home. Her excuse to pull him away from his duties is that she needs help with a personal problem, one related to the baby’s birth. As she walks home, she thinks how close to the truth her excuse actually is.

“He’s on his way,” she informs Nora as she enters the cottage.

“Is she asleep?”

“Yes, ma’am, she was asleep before I laid her down.”

They sit silently, waiting for Falcon to get home. Both their minds are churning with possible solutions to their problems, looking for an acceptable exit from La Nesra.

Falcon enters the cottage in a flurry, wondering what the emergency could be, only to see the two women sitting quietly, calmly. Before he can say anything, his wife starts explaining.

“They’re coming after her tomorrow, honey. Nora says they told her to have her ready, that they would pick her up tomorrow.”

“Oh my! We do have a problem, don’t we?” he reacts to the news.

“When tomorrow?”

“We don’t know, it could be anytime,” she answers.

“That means we have to make our move quickly,” he begins. Then the realization that Nora knows about their leaving hits him.

“How did you—?” he starts to ask her, but is cut off in midsentence.

"I want to go with you, sir" Nora nervously explains. "I want me and my boy to go with you."

Falcon turns to start pacing.

"Her boy is six years old. Understand, she's asking, not demanding. She told me if we can't take her, she'll understand," Lilly properly interjects. "We're going to have to change our plan anyway, can't we include them now? I mean, I understand how she feels about raising a child in here, in prison. Besides, she can be a big help to me with our baby," the infant's mother pleads her case.

"Yes, okay, I suppose so," he agrees. "Just hush for a few minutes and let me think. There must be more to this than just them taking our baby."

The women are joyous and jump up to hug each other, then.

"Sshhhh." Lilly puts her finger to her lips. "Let him think. That's the second best thing he does."

Falcon sits at the table to put his head in his hands.

Ten minutes pass.

Without warning, he speaks and rises to his feet.

"Logic tells me they want us to attempt an escape tonight, if we plan to leave at all. I think they suspect we're going to try, they just don't know when. They're trying to flush us out, and will be waiting when we do. Then it'll be over, and they'll have caught us.

"That's why they told Nora, believing she would pass it on to us. Vaughn's trying to break his agreement with us. If he catches us escaping, all deals are off. He'll lock me in the tombs below, then he'll take baby and force you to do whatever he wants by making threats to harm the two of us. Not bad, Vaughn, old buddy, old pal—but I can't let that happen," he concludes with a bit of slyness sliding off his tongue.

"Here's what we're going to do, ladies . . ."

Chapter Twenty-Six

The Anderson farm, in the afternoon, the day Clifford Messinger is killed.

"I'm glad you're home," June greets her husband as he enters the kitchen of their home through the back door. "How did things go in town?"

"It was a mixed bag. Cliff's dead."

"Oh no, what happened?"

"The short version is he made a play against too many guns, and lost. I killed him—that was after we discovered he was the one who ordered these raids. The cowboy you left trapped under his horse made it to town with the help of a stranger and Alberta Mae's twin boys. He was in a talkative mood, and pointed the finger at Cliff. That boy is no older than Robert, and just look at the mess he's in. His name is Edward Skinner. As it turned out, he was able to give us a list of names of the men in the raiding party. He said he'd help us find them and point them out."

"What are they going to do about you killing Cliff?" June is concerned.

"I'm not sure. Doc said he'd handle everything there, and not to worry about it. You know there's no law in town now," he explains. "If they want me, they know where to find me. I'm not hiding from anybody. The truth is, he drew first on six armed men. So, there's plenty of witnesses as to what happened. I'm not so worried about that, as I am about the blame of this incident falling on the Sons. Anyway, enough of that. What's happening here?"

June tosses the dish towel she's holding onto the table and almost collapses onto a chair. "Get yourself a cup of coffee and sit down, I've a lot to tell you. I hope you agree with what I've done."

"What have you done?" he asks, and follows her instructions.

"Well, we have just entirely too many people in this house. A few of the missing hands from Der Bote and the Sanders' farm have been drifting in today. They have nowhere else to go. So, I told Selma that she could have our guesthouse for as long as she wants it. The Stoker daughters can take care of the meals and things until Alberta Mae is able to get around again. They can all pitch in and take care of the colonel. He's improving, wants to sleep a lot, but his signs are a lot stronger. We won't try to move him for a few days, it'll take that long to get the guesthouse ready and settled anyway. I figure Jim and Josh can find places for the hands from Der Bote and the Sanders' place with our hands' families. I know it'll be hard at first, but all three of these farms need to be tended to as usual. We need to keep everybody together to make sure these shaken people get what they need. We can split up the work once we get things settled down.

"Once we've buried our dead, and oh, by the way, the undertaker and the reverend arrived a couple of hours ago. As I was saying, once we get our dead buried, we can get more organized.

"My, my, I'm really going to miss Caroline. I miss them both already. And Robert—Elizabeth has been his life lately. She's such a darling girl. He has to be worried sick. Has he said anything to you?" Not waiting for John's reply, she continues.

"I sent people to both farms to see what they could find now that the fires have had a chance to cool down. I told them to send any hands that showed up there, over here. I've got people digging graves, sorting through ashes, rounding up and feeding live stock, gathering things like dishes, pots and pans, getting food from root cellars, and I don't know what all. I think it's best to keep them busy, so this day will end with some very emotionally hard things finished and over with. And Selma, that woman is a blessing. You know, she saved my life?"

"Yes, I know, honey, you told me. And you hers," John says with understanding.

"Well, there's no way I could handle all of this by myself. She's been on the run all day long, with a half-dead husband lying in there on the floor—that poor man—and a head wound of her own. And she's coddling Alberta Mae like you'll never believe. And the Stoker daughters have taken over keeping the hands, wives, and children organized, doing odds and ends. And I'm so proud of Charlotte. If she doesn't take up nursing, or become a doctor, or something, she'll miss her calling for sure. The girl is a wonder. She just seems to be everywhere, anywhere something needs to be done. And . . ."

John stops his wife's ramblings by reaching across the corner of the table, taking her hand and pulling her to sit on his lap. He puts his arms around her and pulls her close so her face is against his.

"You've done all you can do for now," he whispers in her ear. "You've done more than anybody should be expected to do. You haven't stopped since this whole thing started. I don't think you've sat down since I've been home. It's time for you to let all these wonderful people do what you've set them off to do, and get yourself some rest. I'm so proud of you. I don't know how else to tell you how much you mean to me and all these people, other than, you are our gift from God. And I want you to know we all thank Him in our prayers for loaning you to us."

Hearing her husband's soft words brings tears to June's eyes, making John aware of them as they roll down her face to reach his neck, then continue to his chest. She doesn't whimper a sound, but her tears flow freely.

He gets up, with her in his arms and carries her from the kitchen, up the stairs to their bedroom, and lays her carefully on the bed. He reaches over and folds the quilt back over her, bends down, and kisses her gently on the lips.

"Try to get some sleep. I'm here, I'll take care of things while you rest," he murmurs.

"Promise you'll wake me in an hour?"

"I promise I'll wake you the minute anything isn't going the way you planned it."

"Now, sleep. I'll close the door so no one will bother you." He straightens up and turns for the door. She takes his hand and holds on tight.

"I love you, John Anderson," she breathes.

"Me too."

Robert and Randall have taken their horses, along with John's, to the barn to remove their saddles and give them water.

"I hope Daddy's okay with killing Cliff," Bob comments.

"Yeah, me too," Randy replies. "That sure was something. That deputy was a fool, I mean, drawing the way he did. That stranger was greased lightning with a gun, and your daddy's quick too."

"I know, and that wild bullet could have killed somebody," Bob reminds.

"I probably shouldn't say anything just now, but you know I'm going out of my mind thinking about Beth. I have to do something to start trying to find her."

"I know," Randy answers. "And I'll help you, you know that, but right now I have to be here for Mama. We have to bury daddy, and I need to know she's going to be okay if I'm not here."

"That's right, and I'll be here to help in any way I can. I'm not going anywhere either until I know everybody here is safe, and on the mend. I'm deeply sorry about Jacob's death, Randy," Bob explains as he moves to put his arms around his friend. "Your daddy was a good friend to me, and is loved by everybody he knew. We'll all miss him. I want you to remember these words, and I mean every one of them.

"In good time, we will avenge the death of your daddy and everybody that died at the hands of those murdering bastards. We have their names, and knowing that, it's just a matter of tracking them down, one at a time.

"But first things first. We'll tend to things here, then we'll see what we can do about Beth, and go from there," Bob finishes, indicating the two of them will do it without the help of anyone. Right now the both of them need to think that way.

The weather hasn't improved in Atlanta. Drizzle is soaking the area for miles around. Inside the walls of La Nesra, Falcon, Lilly, baby, and their maid Nora, are putting their plan to escape into action. After receiving word that their baby is going to be taken away from them tomorrow, they have no choice but to leave immediately.

"Since Mr. Vaughn obviously believes Nora will tell us they're coming to get baby, they will be watching more closely than ever. But I don't think they'll expect us to leave in broad daylight. We'll use this gloomy weather to our best advantage," Falcon surmises to his wife. "I don't think they'll be expecting us to take Nora with us either, especially since she has a child, so they won't be watching her as closely. That's why I sent her to bring Rose and Hawk here to visit. She can move around easier than us.

"She's going to tell Rose to wear concealing clothing, maybe something like a rain coat, and a bonnet or hat that covers her face. She'll also ask her to bring a large basket containing the supplies we'll need. Then she'll tell Hawk to wear a broad-brimmed hat and accompany Rose over here. Once they get here, we'll explain completely what we need them to do."

"I hope this works. I'm a nervous wreck," Baby's mother explains.

"Just relax. There's nothing we can do until they get here. You've packed up all the things you really need for baby. We can't take much else," Falcon observes.

"That's the other thing. We need a name for baby. We can't keep calling her baby," she offers.

Falcon thinks. "What a time to be worrying about naming baby."

"Any ideas?" he asks as patiently as he can muster.

"Yes, I have a suggestion, but you have as much say in this as I do."

"What is it?" He's a little terse.

"It's the French word for joy.—Joie. I'd like to call her Joie."

"Joie, I like that. I see your point too, she certainly is a joy." He grins and shakes his head in agreement. "Joie, it is."

"We need a last name, too," she pushes ahead. "She can't start out life without a last name."

"Good God, do we have to do this right now? Can't we wait until we're out of here and relaxing somewhere on the other side of these walls?" Falcon snaps.

"We can't do anything else until they get here, and I need to do something," she fires back.

A few seconds of silence allows tempers to settle.

"We should use your real last name, you know. We're married and that's what married couples do?" she forges ahead, again.

Through the tension of the moment, Falcon sees a glimmer of humor in his wife's insistence.

"You'll laugh at the irony." A grin follows his words.

"Why? What's your real last name?" Lilly sports a little grin as she asks.

"It's Justice."

"You're last name is Justice?" she giggles.

"Joie Justice, Joie Justice—you're not fibbing to me are you? Is your last name really Justice."

"I'm afraid so, but we don't have to use it. We can pick any name we want. We can use your last name if we want to," Falcon concedes.

"No, a child should bear his father's last name." She confirms, "Joie . . . Justice. It's a fine name. That means my last name is Justice, too."

"Lilly Justice . . . Sheree Justice—I think I like Sheree the best, don't you?" she rambles on without waiting for an answer.

"Mrs. Falcon Justice. Oh, no, no, no. Can you imagine Joie introducing you later in life? 'And this is my daddy, Falcon Justice.' I know you don't want to, but tell me your real first name. It can't be all that bad. It has to be better than Falcon."

Lilly's continual chatter is wearing thin with a usually patient husband.

"Lilly, will you please shut up. You're about to drive me batty with your babbling. We'll work this all out later," he verbally spanks her.

Surprised by his manner, she starts to retort.

"My, aren't you the grouchy one—"

Tap. Tap. Tap. Someone's knocking.

Falcon opens the door to allow Rose and Hawk entry.

"Is Nora coming?" Lilly asks calmly, urgently.

"She had to lag behind to get her son ready. She'll be here in a few minutes," Rose replies.

"Come in and sit down, please. We shouldn't make our move for at least thirty minutes. That gives us plenty of time to go over the plan," Falcon explains.

"I have fresh coffee made, anybody like a cup?" Lilly polls the new arrivals.

"That sounds good," Rose accepts, as Hawk nods yes.

"Okay, here's the plan," Falcon starts explaining.

"Rose, we will need you to change your appearance to resemble Lilly. We'll empty the basket you brought and put Joie in it."

"Baby has a name," Rose interrupts happily. "I love it, Lilly—Joie."

"It's the French spelling, it means joy," Lilly jumps in to add. She is reminded by her husband's stare, the topic is dropped.

"As I was saying, we'll empty the basket and put Joie in it. Lilly will change clothes with you. All of the supplies she can carry will be put in these bags and tied under her loose garments. Since we're dressed alike, all I'll need from you, Hawk, is your hat. I'll carry the basket when we leave. When we go, Rose, you'll follow us out, dressed in Lilly's clothes, and stand to watch us leave. From a distance, with your appearance changed, no one will know the difference. And there should be no suspicion when we leave, since they saw the two of you come in. They'll have no reason to watch where we go.

"We plan to leave La Nesra through that seldom used iron door at the far back wall. Lilly was able to sneak the key so we could make a copy. We'll go directly to the far back side of the last tool shed. Its door opens on the side toward the wall, and it's never locked. We'll go inside and wait.

"Five minutes after we leave, Rose, you'll leave, still appearing to be Lilly. Nora, carrying a bundle of the remaining supplies, disguised as a baby, will leave with you. You'll both walk casually toward the main building, past the maintenance shop.

"Now, Hawk, this is where timing is the most important. As soon as Rose and Nora are out of here, you set this cottage afire. Make sure you torch it all over the place so it goes up quickly. Then run out through the door yelling, fire . . . fire . . .

"They'll believe you're me since their attention will be drawn to the fire, and besides, as far as they know, I'm the only one that's still home.

"Okay, Rose, when you and Nora—

Tap. Tap.

"It's me, Nora." Her voice comes from the other side of the door.

"You're timing is perfect. We're just going over the plan." Falcon opens the door and starts going over the details again to bring her up to date.

"Okay, now, Rose, when you and Nora get to the maintenance shop door, stop and act like you're chatting. Once you hear Hawk yell "Fire," you, Rose, slip inside the shop, and you, Nora, continue on to your quarters to get your son.

"Once you're inside the shop, you'll move the second crate, on your left, up and off a keg of powder fitted with a two minute fuse. Light it, and get out fast. Change your appearance back to yourself as soon as you can, then go back to your quarters and stay there.

"Hawk, with all the confusion caused by the fire, and with the speed you have, you shouldn't have any problem eluding the watchful eyes of our guards. Once you're safely out of their sight, get to Nora's quarters as fast as you can. She'll meet you outside. With any luck at all, the powder will blow up the maintenance shop about this time, creating another diversion, which will allow you to physically pick up her boy, then the two of you run like hell to the shed where we're waiting.

"Once you get Nora and the boy there with us, you'll leave, and get back here so you're seen amidst all the confusion.

"We'll move to the wall, unlock the door, pass through, and lock it behind us. The fire and the explosion should keep everyone busy, long enough for us to get out of sight.

"This whole thing shouldn't take more than fifteen minutes, tops. We should be on the other side of the wall, and on our way in fifteen minutes.

"Questions?" he invites.

"Where will you go from there?" Rose asks.

"The less you know, the less you'll able to tell them if you're caught. I'm sorry, but it's for the best."

"Yes, I agree," she concludes.

"Are you sure that key will turn that old rusty lock." Hawk's concern perks up everybody's ears. "You know, this plan is no simple thing. There's a lot of things that could go wrong. What if we run into someone who realizes we're out of place doing what we're doing, just for instance?"

"I know it's risky, but from my point of view, it's the one chance we have. If we all just do our part, it will come together. To answer your question about the lock, I have no idea. I can't even be sure it's the right key. I haven't dared go near that door. If they saw me looking it over, well, enough said."

"We'd better start getting ready," Joie's mother calmly observes. "Here, Rose, are some matches. You'll need them."

"I'm glad you thought of them, I probably wouldn't have," she jokes, but the possibility of that reality hits home to everyone.

Ten minutes pass as clothes are exchanged and supplies are packed. Rose's process of changing herself to look similar to Lilly, amazes one and all. Baby Joie is carefully placed in the basket, which is comfortably padded all around with a blanket. A white pillow case is laid across the open top of the carrier, and folded over itself, leaving the child's face uncovered until it's time to leave. Then it will be adjusted to cover the entire top, hiding it's precious contents.

Falcon has given Hawk a gallon can of lamp oil to strew throughout the cottage, along with a few matches.

"One last check. Does everybody know what they're supposed to do? Do you have all your props?" Falcon engages the final countdown.

No responses. Everyone just looks at each other.

"Okay, then—let's do it."

Lilly, loaded with supplies under her garments, and Falcon, carrying baby Joie in the basket, calmly move through the door, and turn as though they are going back to Rose's and Hawk's quarters.

Lilly turns to give Rose, who is dressed to appear as Lilly, a little wave goodbye.

Once the couple has moved away, Rose turns back into the cottage and closes the door.

Five minutes pass.

Rose and Nora casually leave the cottage, apparently headed for the main building. Walking side by side, they chat, back and forth.

As soon as Hawk soaks the furniture, curtains, bedclothes, and rugs with lamp oil, he strikes a match and sets fire to a broom he found in the kitchen area. A stream of flame is left behind when he drags it across the oil soaked areas. By the time he finishes, the flames are lapping out hungrily for more fuel. It's time to go, time to abandon the sacrificial cottage.

Once outside, he turns to run backward toward the nosy sentries.

"Fire! Fire! Help! The house is on fire!" he yells, his gift of speed allowing him to move rapidly, in fact, so fast that he has to force himself to slow down to make the right impression.

Smoke is already billowing out through the open doorway, and flames can be seen inside the small home. People begin to converge to help in any way they can.

Hawk continues to move backward. People, some shouting orders, pass him by with buckets and shovels. When the corner of a storage building covers his exit, he turns and runs. The route to Nora's quarters has to be circuitous to be sure no one is following. His lightning speed propels his body making it impossible for anyone with normal abilities to give chase. After putting two buildings between him and the fire, he turns again, now moving directly to Nora's.

In the meantime, Rose and Nora have split up. Rose fumbles nervously with a match, as she stands in the maintenance building, trying to light the fuse leading to a keg of powder.

"Come on! Come on!" she whispers urgently to herself.

Pppfffftttttzzzzzzzzzzzzsssssssssss.

"It's time to get out of here! Fast!" she thinks, and out the door she runs, disregarding anything or anybody in her way.

The fuse burns! When the waiting keg of powder feels the first spark from the fizzing cord, it makes a noise and shakes the ground to be felt throughout La Nesra.

Hawk hears the explosion at the same time he catches sight of Nora and her son waiting for his arrival. Not knowing from which direction he'll come, Nora's looking the other way and doesn't see his approach until he slows down some fifty feet away.

"Where did you come from?" she says in surprise.

Hawk grins with no comment, scoops up Nora under one arm, her boy under his other, and they're off like a shot out of a cannon.

The sound of the powder going off is music to the ears of Lilly and Falcon, as they wait in the shed. It means the plan is working.

"Get ready," he orders. "They'll be here any second now."

Twenty seconds pass quickly, when fast moving feet headed toward them are heard. His speed being what it is, Hawk arrives immediately, just slightly winded, with his arms full of two wide-eyed passengers. When he stops, he stands them on their feet.

"My God, I didn't know you was going to carry me!" Nora exclaims louder than she should under the circumstances.

"You couldn't keep up with me, so, I figured faster is better," Hawk replies.

Her son is speechless. He's looking up at everybody, wondering what's going to happen next.

"Thank you, Hawk. You'll never know how much we appreciate this," Lilly speaks for all.

"Yes," Falcon confirms. "Tell Rose for us too."

Hawk nods his head. An extended hand, a quick shake, and Hawk is on his way back to the mass confusion to make an appearance.

Falcon, with the basket in hand, heads for the wall with the two women and Sherman close behind. There being no cover to hide their movement, it's best to move directly, ignoring the exposure. Once at the wall, Lilly produces a five inch long steel key. She crosses her fingers, puts it into the rusty keyhole of the door lock, and with a quick glance at Falcon and Nora, gives it a counter clockwise twist. The sound of the lock opening is easily heard. He grabs the door handle and pulls. The hinges creak and screech as he labors it open.

When you're expecting to see green fields and open land as a door opens, it comes as a total surprise to be looking at, what appears to be, a tunnel into darkness, not a way through a four foot thick, stone and brick, wall.

"What the—" Lilly says in amazement. "What do we do now?"

Nora stands, totally bewildered, gripping her son's hand, awaiting instructions.

"We can't stay out here for long," Falcon explains the obvious. "We have to go in and close the door behind us. Get a candle from our supplies and have it ready to light after we get this door closed. Keep the key in your hand Lilly, we'll need it first thing once we're in there."

"Go, get in there, before someone sees us."

Reluctantly, Nora and her son step into the darkness, behind Lilly. Falcon follows dragging the door closed behind him. The daylight entering the hole in the wall from around the partially open door is closed out as the heavy metal structure squeals and screeches to seal the opening.

"Light the candle," He orders. Momentarily, a match bursts into flame, bringing life and light to the darkness.

"Here." Nora reaches to hand the candle to Lilly, who's holding the match.

"There, we have light," Falcon's wife confirms.

"Let me have the key."

"Okay, relax a little. We're locked in here now. If no one saw us, we should be safe, for a while at least." He tries to assure the escaping women and young boy.

"What is this place?" Nora asks, peering with big open eyes into the darkness beyond the candle's light. Her son has a tight grip around her waist.

"Let's find out. Stay together, we'll follow back through here a little piece and see how far it goes." Lilly holds the candle higher than her head. "Come on, we can't stay here. It can't go very far. Maybe there's away out on the other end."

Baby Joie sleeps peacefully in the basket.

Falcon begins to take in his surroundings. "This passageway, if that's what it is, spreads out to be ten or twelve feet wide. It goes up fast, too. It must be at least as high as the walls, maybe fifteen feet. There's nothing in here. The floor is stone as are the walls and ceiling. It's dry too, not like a cave." The group travels close together for another fifty feet to arrive at another steel door.

"It ends here at this door." Nora concludes with some relief.

"Yeah, but what's on the other side?" Lilly ponders mysteriously. "Do you suppose this key will open it."

"Try it." Her husband hands her the key.

"No, it doesn't work." Her efforts are in vain.

"So, now what? Me and my boy—we're stuck here in this, whatever it is, right?" Nora grouses. "I thought we were going to get out of here. If I'd known we'd wind up in a place like this, I'd never have come."

"Oh, shut up, Nora. I don't want to hear your whining. If all you can do is moan and complain, I don't want to be with you when we get out of here. You can just fend for yourself," Lilly explodes, her voice sounds hollow bouncing off the face of the stone and bricks.

"And we will find a way out of here, so settle yourselves, ladies. Let's take stock of what we have here. I believe we're safe as long as we stay in here. Do we have a good supply of matches?" Falcon starts to reason.

"Yes, plenty," Lilly responds "Let's blow out our candle, for now. We might need the air. Huddle close together, it'll make us feel more secure."

The candle is extinguished, and the last speck of light fades. You can touch your nose and not see your finger.

Confusion and activity settle down more and more as the day following the raids progresses at the Anderson farm.

The burials will take place tomorrow morning, the undertaker and parson having done their jobs. The parson will be back to conduct the funerals. Mr. and Mrs. Sanders will be interred on their farm, along with their hands. Jacob will rest on Der Bote, overlooking the lake he enjoyed so much.

A lot of work remains, considering all the dead animals lying around. It'll take several days to make places to bury such large carcasses. And everybody knows the longer it takes the worse kind of job it will be.

June wouldn't stay in bed for more than two hours. She claims she'll sleep tonight.

The immediate families of the farms, by coincidence, have settled together in the den. Present are John, June, Robert, Charlotte, and Cheryl, from the Andersons' place. Selma, along with Alberta Mae, her two grown daughters, her twin teenage boys, and Randall make up the group from Der Bote. The colonel still occupies the stretcher he was brought in on. There's talk of moving him to make him more comfortable in the morning.

Belle is in and out of the room, tending to things as they come to her mind. Sachel, the Housler's butler, crawled up to the kitchen door an hour ago. His injuries come from a lasso tied to his legs and a saddle horn, then being dragged behind a galloping horse, and left for dead. He's banged up, but he'll live.

The atmosphere in the room is mostly quiet—calm, short of peaceful. Most of the comments heard are redundant of what has happened, with echoes of agreement and support. Nonseeing eyes stare into nothingness as their owners drift in and out of thought and remembrances.

John gets up from his seat to reach the coffeepot, with the notion of topping off his cup with fresh. He stops short when he realizes who all is here, together for the first time since Lord knows when. He studies, "Once this moment passes, will it ever happen again?"

With the exception of the hands and their families, this is what's left of the lives on three farms. The thought of fresh coffee leaves his mind. Still standing, leaning over the shining oak table, cup in hand, he speaks. Because of his movement, most eyes are already on him.

"I'm not sure what to say. I don't know if I can find the right words."

He now has everyone's attention.

"Except for a few not in attendance, you people in this room are, and have been, my whole life. I mean, you are the most important people in the world to me. I just want you to know that I plan to devote my time and resources to finding and enacting justice on each and every one of the dastardly cowards who took the lives of our loved ones, and brought this grief to our farms. It'll take time, but they'll be found and dealt with. If they resist the ways of the law, then they'll feel the terror our families feel, from the business end of a bullet, or a rope around their necks. I swear to you, I'll not rest until each of them knows the wrath of our pain."

"Can I speak freely, here and now, Daddy?" Robert interrupts.

"I don't see why not, son. We're all in this together."

"Well, I don't know who all will agree with me, but I think we should band all three of our farms together. It's going to take quite a spell to rebuild the homes and buildings that are just ashes now. If we band together, we can be more of a force against anything like this happening in the future. Shares can be figured out, so it's fair to those who own these farms. And with the production from all this land, we can control a lot bigger share of the market for our products. I know this probably sounds heartless under these circumstances. But think about it. Some of us are going to be busy doing the work you just committed to do. Who's going to replace us on these farms, and free us up to do it. Right now it takes three foremen, and three drivers, to work our farms. If we put them together it only takes one foreman, and one driver. See what I mean?" Robert finishes.

"Son, you're forgetting, there's nothing left of the Sanders' family. No one left to support such an agreement," John counters.

"I'm the closest thing to an owner there is. My future wife is the sole heir to that property, and until we know for sure, one way or the other, she's still alive, and I'll vote her shares," he testifies. "Another thing, tracking down these criminals will cost money. That money can come from these combined farms. We all stand to gain from what you do, so we should all stand behind the cost."

"Sounds like you've given this a lot of thought," John addresses his son.

"Not just now," his oldest child responds to the inferred question. "I've had it in my mind for a long time now. This just seems to be the time to do something like this, if we have a mind to. The other thing is," he starts again, "if something happens and some of us don't come back from tracking down these killers, these farms will keep right on going. Keep right on going, providing for our families—or what's left of them—for years and years."

Selma's voice is heard.

"I'll need to wait to hear from Charles, but I think it's a good idea. We've talked about it several times over the last few years, and we, as you know, have no one to will our holdings to upon our death. This would be a good chance to insure that everyone at our farm could have some security in their lives. They could—and if things go right—their children, and their heirs could for years to come."

"So, am I right with thinking that you mean to give everyone shares, that, to include the hands and all," June inquires.

"One and all, Mama. Everyone would share in the efforts and profits. I've got it all down on paper as to how to go about deciding the shares and how to go about selecting those to manage it's affairs." Robert is quick to supply information.

"That would be a way for me to pull away from my current employer," John thinks out loud.

"You mean the Sons?" June's question is more like a statement.

"Yep," John confirms. "I don't see how I can head that up and still have time to deal with these raiders. Marty's going to wonder about me and my lack of commitment. Especially after I swore to him I'd stick with it, but this is something I have to do."

"What we're talking about here sounds a lot like sharecropping. Plantation owners have been doing that for years. They assign a parcel of their land to a black family and let them work it for part of the proceeds at harvest time. One of the problems they have is that the workers run up debt buying food and the like. Things they need while they're working the land, waiting on the harvest, things that were supplied free before, when they worked as slaves. They just seem to get farther and farther into debt, and that debt is worse than working as a slave. They're still treated that way anyhow," June announces.

"You're right, that's true with sharecropping, but our land here will be ours; Mr. and Mrs. Housler's, and all the hands. Contracts between us will commit us to keep it amongst ourselves, and all share in the cost of living. You said it, food, clothing, medicine, and the like. Everybody will have the opportunity to eat and drink the same things, and have the same medical care, because it will all be paid for from the same account. After all the bills are paid, say at the end of a year, if there's money left over, it will be split up among us all, according to our shares. If there's no money left over, then no one will get anything, but there will be no debt for any one person or one group to pay, we'll share and share alike," Robert explains.

Conversation at the Anderson home continues.

Falcon, Lilly, Nora, and her son, find themselves in some sort of hallway, or tunnel, inside the wall surrounding the compound. They presently sit, locked in darkness, contemplating their next move.

"How many candles do we have?" Falcon asks.

"An even dozen," Lilly replies.

"Each one will burn for say . . . four hours. Sitting here doing nothing is going to get us nowhere, so let's try this." He suggests, "Take six of the candles and light them all. Set them around so this whole place lights up. We'll look it over good, with one thing in mind, a way out. We can give it a good two hours, and still have plenty of candle time left. That is, unless we use up too much air. If that's the case, we'll have to open the door."

"Sounds good to me," his wife concurs. "I don't know what else to do."

The candles are lit and placed to illuminate their entire area of confinement.

"What are we looking for? How will we know when we find it?" Nora asks reasonable questions.

"Anything, anything you wouldn't expect to find in a place like this," Falcon encourages. "A loose stone, something sticking out of the wall, some reason for this hallway to be here."

Their search begins. Nora's son is beginning to lose his fears and starts to move around, away from his mother. To keep him occupied, she gives him a cloth sack of beans, and shows him how to throw it, chase after it, then throw it again. Hearing the bag hit the floor is her constant reminder of his whereabouts, and that he's okay.

Falcon wonders about the wisdom of this game, since the boy's running, banging, feet make a lot of noise. Not to mention the occasional yell to let everyone know how far he threw the bean bag. There's nothing in here to deaden the noise, so it echoes in the hollow.

They've been searching for thirty minutes with no results. This soon-to-be-six-year-old boy, chasing this bean bag, along with her looking for a needle in this stone haystack, is taking its toll on Lilly's nerves. She looks to see the child throwing it up in the air, back over his head, not watching where it might land, or who it might hit. Then he immediately turns to follow, grabs it up, and does the same thing again. This time it flies through the air, barely missing his mother's head, to crash to the floor. She has her mouth open and a breath ready to tell him to watch where he's throwing that thing, but his mother beats her to it, just as he gives it another fling.

"Stop it!" she criticizes. "You're going to hit someone if you're not careful!"

Her loud, stern words startle the young boy, causing him to let go of the bag in a way to force it off to the side, making it hit the wall with a thud. To the amazement of everyone, the force of the bean bag noticeably moves a stone. Falcon reacts by never taking his eyes off the spot, and moving to it fast. Once there, he puts his hands on the stone, chest high, and carefully pushes it with more and more pressure, finally putting the weight of his body behind his efforts.

It moves. The ten-inch square of rough stone slides about four inches into the wall, enough to expose a hole in the side of the stone next to it.

"Bring me a candle," he orders.

Nora grabs one within her reach and readily hands it over.

"Looks like some sort of metal handle in here," he observes and informs the others.

The young lad stands still in his tracks—watching. Probably thinking he's done something wrong. The women stand staring, their eyes glued on Falcon's hand inside the hole.

"Looks like I could pull on it, but I don't know what might happen. What do you think?" he asks.

"What if whatever happens makes a lot of noise, or maybe even opens up a hole in the floor. We'll be goners," Lilly cautions.

"What if it makes this whole place fall in on us?" Nora supports Lilly's worry.

"We don't have that many options." Falcon reminds the wary women. "We have no way of getting that iron door open to the outside, and going back into the compound will put us at great risk of getting caught. We've came this far—get back away as far as you can. I'm going to see what happens."

Unable to move it with one hand, he sets the candle on the floor, then with both hands, jerks and pulls hard. It moves about an inch, toward him, inside the hole.

A low rumble can be heard before a vibration is felt beneath their feet.

Falcon hears the women take quick fearful breaths, and watches Nora grab her son to her side. He then thinks it best not to stand so close to a place where the floor might open up and steps away from the wall.

The whole hallway quivers when a six-feet-high-by-two-feet-wide section of the wall, starting at the floor, begins to slide back within itself. It makes a heavy scouring, grinding sound, sliding on the stone floor, slowly exposing a hidden opening to a dark hallway of the same size. He picks up the candle and holds it high so it just clears the six foot opening. Pushing the light out to arms length, he leans in and around to peer into the newly uncovered space.

"Don't go in there, Falcon!" Lilly orders strictly.

"Oh my, oh, my, my, my." Nora's words are simple but express her feelings well.

"Mama, you're hurting me." The first complete sentence the child has spoken since their escape started.

"This could be our way out, honey. We have to find out where it goes," Falcon responds to his wife's command.

"What if you go in there and all of a sudden this thing closes up again. What about us?"

"Well, I'm going in there. You can come with me or not." He's eager to make a discovery.

"If you go, Miss Lilly, I'm not staying here by myself. No, siree. Not by myself." Nora lets her feelings known.

"Each of you grab a candle, and let's get moving," their leader decides.

He guides the exploration with his wife next in line. Nora pushes her son ahead of her as they start through the narrow opening. She walks backward so nothing slips up from behind, but she can't keep up that way.

The hallway turns hard to the left, then five steps to turn hard left again. Another eight steps comes to a hard right. Their leader figures they are now walking parallel to the outer edges of the wall. A hard right turn heads them toward the center. A few more steps brings the sight of a dim light ahead. The closer they get the brighter the light, and the more silently the group moves. It's as quiet as a grave. Even the sound of moving feet and the rustle of clothing are muffled. The light grows and becomes bright enough that they no longer need their candles. A hard right turn, and they stand at the entrance of a large room, twenty feet wide by forty feet long. The ceiling appears to be about nine feet. A light from above illuminates the area with a brilliance equal to, or more than, daylight.

"Look at this," he says in amazement. "I've never seen anything like it before. We're down inside a wall. Where's all this light coming from?"

"Snuff your candles, we don't need them in here."

"What are those things over there?" Lilly points as she speaks.

"I don't like it here." Nora lets her opinion be known. Her son struggles but is unable to free himself from her grip.

"Watch what you touch, people. Be careful where you step," Falcon cautions.

Together, they creep into the room, looking in all directions as they go. They pass strange-looking boxes that flash different colors of light. Wires, or perhaps pieces of string, attach these boxes to long, sort of cigar-shaped containers. They are large enough to hold an adult man, and are molded out of some sort of shiny material. The bottom half is black, but the top half is clear and thick like a canning jar, but it's not glass. They lie flat on two-foot-high carriers that have wheels on the end of the legs. The group gets close enough to one to look through the clear material for a glimpse of what it contains. Nothing. It's empty except for some wires hooked to four cuffs, and a padded place big enough for an adult person to lie down. There is a pillow that might be made from leather, and a number of long glasslike hollow wires. Some of these have three inch needles on the ends.

Falcon taps his knuckles against the outside shell. *Tap. Tap. Tap.*

"Stop that!" Lilly snaps.

"I just wonder what this is made from?" he calmly puzzles. "And what they're used for?"

Nora's son has managed to pull away enough to peer into the next container. She follows so as not to lose her grip.

"Look, Mama," he motions with his finger just as she gets beside him, and bends to see where he's pointing. "There's a man in this one." "Eeeeooooouuuu!" she screams and jumps back away from the box.

Falcon and Lilly are at the container in an instant, looking down at a man who is lying deathly still. He's hooked and strapped to all those wires, strings, and cuffs they saw in the empty one. Dressed, except for shoes, he has no noticeable wounds or bruises. His clothing is nothing more than a robe tied closed with a sash. His somber emotionless face seems pale in the bright lights, almost gray. Long hair, overflowing its space, and fingernails that extend to the point of curling back under themselves, further a sense of eeriness.

Lilly moves on to another, and another. "There's a man in each one of these things," she informs the rest.

The two rows of these sleek-looking containers are spaced allowing her to move swiftly, glancing from side to side, to see that most of them contain a body. She stops short of the end of the rows.

"Honey, you'd better come and look at this," she calls with an uncertain tone to her voice.

Falcon steps swiftly to her side.

"Look in here—does this remind you of anyone?" she asks.

"Vaughn! If you trim off his hair and get a little color in that face, it's Mr. Vaughn," he reacts with surprise.

"To be exact, it's Mr. Vaughn's body," she states with excitement. "We've found his body."

"You mean, this is the body he was going to have you look for?" Falcon wants to be certain.

"I doubt there's another," Lilly assures.

"You don't suppose it's been here all along?" He starts pointing his finger and counting. "Thirteen . . . fourteen," he finishes.

"There's fourteen of these containers, and let's see how many have people in them." He walks swiftly past the first row, and returns close to the second row, counting.

"Eleven, counting Mr. Vaughn."

"What do you make of it?" His wife looks for answers.

"We don't have enough information yet to make any sense of it," he rightly explains.

"If this is Mr. Vaughn's body, the one he's been looking for, for years, you'd have to think not many people here at La Nesra know about this room. And if anybody does, you'd think he would."

"Can we get out of here now?" Nora complains. "It's spooky."

"You can go back outside and wait for us if you want to," Falcon advises. "But be sure you don't touch anything on the way out. We don't want to lock ourselves in here."

"We need to look this place over carefully. Maybe there's a way out somewhere in here. We might be quite a while," Lilly relates for Nora's benefit.

"I'll just stay here then—with the two of you," the maid concludes reluctantly.

"Do you recognize any of these other people?" He's looking for a clue as to who they are and why they're here, laid out like this.

"Can I let my boy loose?" Nora inquires.

"Just keep an eye on him," Lilly is quick to answer. "Joie's stirring, can you see to her. She needs to be changed, or maybe she's hungry."

"Yes, ma'am."

Falcon strikes a match and touches the flame against the wick of his candle.

"What are you doing?" his wife wonders.

"I noticed when we came in here, the flame of my candle danced all over, like there was some draft or something. I'm just checking," he replies. "The air in here seems to be pretty fresh, too. I'm betting there's a hole somewhere allowing outside air to get in. That might be our way out."

He begins walking, zigzagging in and around the containers. The candle flame leans toward him as he moves, so he knows to stop frequently to allow it to seek its own direction. Walk a few steps, stop, walk a few more . . . move in the direction the flame is leaning. Take notice if it leans the same way most of the time. He follows until it stands straight up where the walls meet at the far end of the room. He looks up as he takes his last step.

"There's a square hole in the ceiling over here, but I don't see any light up there at all. For sure there's air moving up through there, but there's no telling where it goes."

"If air is going out then there must be air coming in from somewhere," Nora reasons.

"You've got a point there," he agrees and turns, pushing the candle into the air as far as he can reach.

When he nears the first bright light coming from the ceiling, the flame lies flat, trying to find a space to stand tall again, and almost dies. When he lowers it down, it regains its posture. He raises it up again . . . this time it flutters and dies.

"Air is coming through these bright lights, somehow," he relates to his comrades. "If I can get up on this coffinlike thing here, I can probably see what they are."

"Do you think it'll hold you?" Lilly cautions.

"I'll soon find out," he answers, then lays the candle on the floor, puts his hands on top of the container, bends his knees, and jumps, pushing up with his arms, to get one foot on top. It's easy then to raise himself upright—carefully—keeping his balance. Putting a hand against the ceiling gives the support he needs to keep himself steady. It also tells Falcon he's too tall for the space; he has to bend over at the shoulders to fit.

The light is shining brightly above him, about a foot away. It's too bright to peer into. Not standing completely erect, he puts his other hand up to feel around, to see if he can tell what it is. His hand disappears into the light and keeps on going. His arm is up into the light as far as he can reach. It's a big hole, by the feel of it, big enough for a man to fit through.

Lilly and Nora watch as he moves his feet to position himself directly under the hole.

"What are you doing? Don't go up in there. You don't know what's in there or what that light might do to you," his wife sternly orders.

"Aww, stop worrying, I put my hand in there. It's okay."

He arranges his hands, one on either side of the hole in the ceiling, and cautiously straightens his body and legs to push himself up into the light.

Nora puts her hands to her cheeks. "Oh my Lord."

Lilly hangs her head moving it in a no motion.

He lets go with one hand and pulls it up inside the light, then the other. There's no movement for a few seconds, then—without warning—Falcon's body jerks straight up.

"Yeeeoooowwww!" he lets out a yell.

Lilly reacts faster than she has ever moved before. Fearing for his life, she throws her arms around his legs, and holds on!

Nora screams, scaring Sherman, who lets out a series of howls, and runs to the entrance of the room. Once into the darkness he stops to peer back in timidly, expecting the worst.

Lilly's weight pulls Falcon down from his tip toes to stand flat on the container again.

His laughter is heard by all below.

"Ha hah hah hah hah! Ha hah hah!"

He bends down to touch Lilly's head.

"I'm okay, I was just joking," he confesses.

She lets go, stands up, and takes two steps backward to look up at him in anger. "Don't you ever do anything like that again!" she screams. "I thought something had you! Don't you ever do that again! You took ten years off my life!"

"I'm sorry, honey, I was just having a little fun. I didn't mean to scare everybody like that. It was just a little joke," he apologizes.

"Don't 'honey' and 'joke' me. You damned near scared us to death. You'd better leave me alone for a while, until I settle down. Joke, hah! Some joke," she berates her husband.

He gets back to his serious side by necessity.

"There's nothing up there, just some bright, slippery coating on the walls of the hole. It reflects the light from above. I don't think we could climb up through there, it's way too slippery. It's not going to be our way out, but at least we know we have plenty of air, and light—at least until dark. With the supplies we have, we can stay here for days if we have to."

After the trio spends the next twenty minutes searching the room completely, it's determined there is no way out, except for the way they came in.

"Looks like we're stuck," Nora begins. "We might as well give ourselves up."

"Stop being so negative," Lilly snaps. "We're not giving up. We are going to find a way out of here, and that's that."

Nora's son is playing with two tops his mother brought along. He spins one, then the other, watching as they bump, eventually wobbling to a stop to lay on their sides. Lilly watches for a while then walks to Nora and extends her arms, asking for Joie. With a questioning look she hands the baby to her mother.

Joie fusses and squirms, being cuddled in Lilly's left arm. She pulls her close to her face, turns away from Nora, then rubs her nose against her baby's.

"I'm your mama, baby Joie, and we're going to get to know each other. I'll bet you're hungry, aren't you?" She moves to the opposite side of the room, sits on the floor, and leans back against the wall, her Joie in her arms.

Nora breaks out a few sandwiches and apples for supper. It'll be dark before long. Everybody munches, lost within themselves, their own thoughts for company.

Mrs. Justice is the first to break the stillness by bringing Joie back to the basket, where she carefully places her down, her hunger satisfied, sound asleep.

"I was just thinking, honey, had I brought a mirror with me, I could do something to get us all out of here," she comments. "Has anyone seen one around here anywhere?"

"No," her husband answers.

"Did you say a mirror, ma'am? How in the world can a mirror get us out of here?" Nora asks intently.

"It's along story, Nora. You wouldn't believe me if I told you." Her reply is delivered in a consoling manner.

"Well, I was thinking before we left, what could I bring along that a woman like you would need once she's out of here, and the only thing I could think of that I had, was a mirror. I've got it right here in my bag. It's not real big, but it's a mirror for sure," the maid explains, at the same time she fumbles in her belongings. "Here it is!" She proudly presents a larger-than-usual hand mirror.

"Well, I'll be. Nora, you really are something. You have no idea how much I love you right now."

Nora looks at her as if to say, "It's only a mirror."

"Okay, all right, now we're getting somewhere. It's your turn, honey, put that mind of yours to work and get us a plan." She sounds off excitedly.

He sits, amazed at these two helpless women. Then he paces, sits, paces, sits—for fifteen minutes—thinking, calculating. Lilly knows to leave him alone, while Nora doesn't know what to make of any of it. Finally.

"Okay, this is what I think we should do," he starts. "Lilly, you should go and find Mr. Vaughn. Tell him you've found his body like you promised you would. Tell him you'll take him to it, if he'll agree to let the four of us and our baby go free."

"What if he says no?" she interrupts. "He has to be more than a little upset about us burning down the cottage and blowing up his maintenance building."

"If necessary, but only if you must, tell him his body is hooked up like you see it here. And tell him unless he agrees to our terms, we'll remove these things that are keeping him alive. He knows that will mean disaster for him," Falcon conjures. "Keep in mind, from what he's told us, he'll do about anything, if it means he gets back to his body.

"On the other hand, you could try to find the key to the outside door. Maybe that would be the smart thing to do, but say we get the key and escape. They'll be on our tail starting today and for the rest of our lives. Mr. Vaughn can be trusted to keep his word, so once we get it, he won't try to find us after we're out of here. We won't have to live on the run.

"One other thing I think we must consider is who these people are, and why they're being kept here like this. I have this deep down feeling there's something sinister going on—there's more to this than you and I can ever imagine. I'm all but convinced that Mr. Vaughn is tired and worn out from his years of service to the Company. All those years, pining to be back in his body, his body that has been kept from him by the same people he's been loyal to for so long. It's a strong possibility that he'll want his freedom, too. That being the case, he could help us turn against the Company. He can supply us with facts and information, enabling us to inflict some serious damage to their plans and organization."

"Falcon, you don't really think—" He cuts his wife off.

"Nothing's for sure, but, the Company has held his body hostage for years and years, making him do their bidding. The old worm could turn, and I think there's better than an even chance he will. You and I both know there isn't any lasting good going to come from anything the Company has a hand in. I'll even go a step farther and say, we can take a whole lot more from here if Mr. Vaughn leaves with us. More than these few supplies in these bags."

"You mean, like guns and things?" Lilly interjects again.

"No, no, I mean what's in his head, information enough to break the Company in half. And money . . . he can probably get his hands on more money than we can carry. We'll need it if we intend to set up an offense against them."

"Now you're talking my kind of language." Lilly agrees to the plan. She turns to address Nora.

"Nora, do you want to be a part of this, or do you want to go your own way, once we're out of here."

"I got no place to go from here. I got no family that I know of. But I'm not smart like the two of you, and I'm not a scrapper either, and I've got my child here to worry about. I probably wouldn't be a whole lot of help to you. But I sure do love your little Joie, and I could make a real good home for her, while you're both out doing whatever. And I love the two of you, too. You brought me and my boy along when you didn't have to. So, I guess, if you want me . . . ?"

"You bet we want you and Sherman, Nora," Falcon assures. "I'm glad we all feel the same way."

Lilly bends down to give Nora a big shoulder hug, then rises to address her husband.

"When do I go?"

"Right now," Falcon replies. "But remember, don't let him trap you so you can't get back here."

"Good point. If I'm not back here within an hour, place the mirror in front of my face. That'll bring me back from just about anywhere." She instructs her husband.

"What if he puts you somewhere like the armory. No—thirty minutes—you've got thirty minutes, then I pull you back."

She nods sharply, affirmative. She then places the mirror on the stone floor and wiggles the fingers of her right hand at the three of them. "You might want to cover Sherman's eyes for a few minutes," she explains to Nora, and lies down on the floor.

In less than five minutes, the two see Lilly rise from her resting place, and yet, leave herself there. Then, she carefully steps down into the mirror one foot at a time, slithers down to her arm pits, stops, waves at her husband, and disappears below the glass.

"Tell me I didn't see that. Dear Lord, tell me I didn't see that." Nora can't believe her eyes.

On the other side of the glass, Lilly gathers her thoughts and pages Zola in her mind.

"Zola. Zola. Zola."

Almost immediately a voice in her mind is present.

You called my name, Sheree?

"Yes, can you help me find a portal to locate Mr. Vaughn?" Lilly says in her mind.

Think about Mr. Vaughn, Sheree. It will allow me to determine who it is you want.

Lilly imagines a picture of Mr. Vaughn.

Close your eyes, Sheree.

Seconds pass.

You are here. Is there anything else?

"No, thank you very much."

There is no response.

She opens her eyes to look through a portal. Mr. Vaughn is washing his face and hands, right in front of her. This must be his quarters.

She looks around before entering. There are two rooms here, the bedroom being off by itself, while the kitchen, and living room are all in one. Nothing fancy about it, older furniture, worn but not dirty. Nothing here would remind you of any female's presence. It could all use a coat of paint. He has a towel up against his face when she puts her head through the mirror in front of him.

"Don't be alarmed, Mr. Vaughn. It's me, Lilly." She practically whispers.

He stops rubbing his face and stands completely still.

"It's me, Lilly, Mr. Vaughn. I'm coming through your mirror."

He drops the towel and stumbles backward at the appearance of her head coming out of his mirror. With his own experiences doing the same thing, it doesn't take him long to pull himself together.

"How long have you been back there? Why are you here?" The speed of his speech, and the tone of his voice shows he's a bit startled.

"I have just arrived. Stand back, please, I'm coming through," she requests, and climbs through the mirror above his wash stand.

He takes three steps backward to give her room, and watches her appear. "I thought you were well on your way to escaping. What are you doing here?" he asks again.

"I've found your real body. Just like I said I would."

"It's not possible. You've not had enough time for anything like that. Is this some sort of twisted joke?"

"It's no joke. I've stood as close to your flesh and blood body as I'm standing to you right now. I'm here to tell you that I'll lead you to it, if you agree to our conditions."

"What conditions?" His interests are heating up.

"Falcon, my baby Joie, my maid Nora, her son Sherman, and I are all to go free. Free and clear of La Nesra forever. I need your sworn word."

"If I swear to it, how soon can I see my body?"

"Come with me through the mirror and you can see it within a few minutes. Otherwise, it could take a little time." She puts it this way to see if he will travel through the mirror. If she has to make a quick get away, it will be good to know if he will follow.

"I can't go through the mirror, you know that. I might as well put a gun to my head as do that," he confirms her husband's thinking.

"Swear to it now, and I'll tell you where to meet me in fifteen minutes. I'll be watching, so if you whisper a word of this to anyone, I'll know it. I need to know now, because if I don't get back before long, my husband will destroy your body. I made an agreement with you to find your body. You said you'd let me go if I did that. Well, I have, so I'm not asking for anything you haven't already promised."

"But the situation has changed. Setting fire to your cottage is one thing, but four people were injured by flying debris when you blew up the maintenance building. I can't take that lightly. Other people are involved now. They'll be looking for an explanation, and eventually, the people responsible. And now, you want to take our baby, your maid, and her son with you, too. I'd say things have changed. You shouldn't expect me to keep a bargain when you have so flagrantly broken the terms," the older man concludes.

The man is correct with what he says, she can't deny that. "You've got me there, you're right, but regardless, that's the way it is now. It's all five of us, free and clear." Lilly stands her ground, ready to leap for the mirror.

He looks her straight in the eyes. "There's more to this than you're telling me, isn't there? Why would you risk coming here like this? You wouldn't unless . . . you need me, don't you? That's it, for some reason, you can't get out of here without my help. If you want me to be part of your plan, you have some explaining to do."

She tries to think fast, but nothing comes to her mind except she has to be back with Falcon before long. "There's no time for that right now. Like I said, you'll be dead if I don't get back. We can meet again later, you, Falcon, and me. But I'll not take you to your body until I have your word," she explains.

"You're not leaving here until I get some answers!" He raises his voice sternly and reaches to grab her left arm with his right hand.

His grip feels as hard as steel when she instinctively pulls to get away unsuccessfully. A feeling of panic tries to overcome her, but her training tells her to keep her wits.

"Let go!" she commands.

"I said you're not going anywhere until you tell me the whole truth!" Mr. Vaughn shoots back with excitement.

It seems to Lilly that her body is taking over from her mind. Her weight shifts to her left foot as her right foot comes up from the floor. At the same time, she turns bringing her leg up and over their arms, kicks his face with her foot, which pushes him away hard, breaking his grasp. She spins completely around to see him falling backward into the small kitchen table. It slides, under his weight, into the wall, causing him to glance off and fall onto the floor. She watches as he fights to regain his faculties. It would be a simple thing to ensue with another foot to his head, and finish the fight for good. But the adrenaline is pumping, her senses are on edge.

"No! We need him!" she tells herself.

He staggers back to his feet, wiping the back of his hand across the sting of his face, trying to focus on the incoming threat. When nothing happens, he looks for blood on his hand, then, still regaining his balance, says.

"No more. Don't hit me again. I'm no match for you. We've trained you well."

"I'm sorry, I hope I didn't hurt you, but you shouldn't have grabbed me like that." She surprises herself with words she's yet to put in her mind. She is also astonished with her accomplishment. "Wow!" she thinks, feeling quite grown up and in control. "I did that! Me! I didn't even think about it. It just happened."

"Are you ready to work something out now?" she sternly addresses the staunch Company man.

"Do you actually know where my body lies?" he replies, still recovering.

"It's the truth. There are other bodies, too. We're not sure who they are though."

"Are they just lying around, or are they in something, something that's, somehow hooked up to a support system." His eyes open wide and eagerness takes over his face at this bit of information.

"They're enclosed in containers made of a material I've never seen before," she explains.

Now he believes. How would she know unless she's seen them?

"That's all you had to say. Tell me what you want me to do."

"I'd rather take you back through the mirror with me, but I know you won't take the chance, and I don't blame you for that. I need to get Falcon and you together, so we'll meet you."

"Meet where?" he fires back.

"The equipment shed farthest back toward the rear wall. Be there in an hour. Wait inside. Come alone, and make sure no one follows you. We'll come to you as soon as we know it's safe." She lays out the plan.

"Don't worry. You've proven to me that you're serious. You'll be safe," he assures.

"I have your word that you agree to my conditions, correct?" She needs to confirm.

"I do, but you said conditions, you've only stated one," he makes a point.

"Falcon will explain another."

With the meeting finished, she leaves through the mirror as he watches her go.

Falcon, Nora, baby Joie, and Sherman wait for her return, making it no surprise when she sticks her head up through the mirror lying on the floor in the secret room.

"I'm back," she announces.

Sherman is sitting on the floor not near his mother, when he sees her head, he screams, jumps up, and runs crying to her arms. Clinging wildly to her, he turns his head to watch Lilly rise to her feet.

Falcon walks toward his wife.

"How'd it go?"

She carefully relates to her husband everything that happened at the meeting with one of the most powerful men at La Nesra.

Chapter Twenty-Seven

Mr. Vaughn is the first to arrive at the equipment shed where he will wait for Lilly and Falcon. He gazes around, looking to spot anyone whom could have followed him. Normally, he wouldn't be concerned because of his position with the Company. He could have someone's head if he caught them trailing his path. But this is different. Knowledge of this meeting must be buried in the deepest grave of secrecy.

It's been a dismal day of cloud cover and spotty rain. There's no moon to give any light, making the interior of the shed as dark as the bottom of a forty foot well. He pulls the right side of the double doors open and decides to leave it that way, then inches his way into the blackness. He takes a position just inside the door that remains closed. He's fifteen minutes early, so a wait is expected. He leans back against the door, folds his arms, and lowers his head to rest his chest.

"It's peaceful out here tonight," he thinks to himself as he closes his eyes. "There's hardly a sound of anything."

Plop. Several seconds pass. *Plop. Plop.*

"What a restful symphony. Rain dripping off a branch into a puddle out there somewhere," he says to himself and begins to realize how long it has been since he has taken time to enjoy the small uncomplicated things in life. His thoughts drift back to his life as a child. Back when he would lie in his bed at night listening to the rain hitting the tin roof of the orphanage where he stayed. Life was so simple then. Do what you were told, eat what they give you, protect what was yours, and do not be a trouble to anybody. Those were the unwritten rules.

A lonely life to be sure, nobody cared if you lived or died, or whether you stayed there or not, for that matter. To resist the desires of those who managed the affairs of the business meant a swift, severe flogging, imposed with a half-inch-thick willow switch. Meeting that switch a few times changed many an attitude over the years.

"That's how I discovered my ability to leave my body in the first place." He thinks, shifting his position against the door. "That solitude forced me to withdraw within myself to the point I stumbled into the fact that I was different from most people. The Company discovered me on the other side of the mirror, and offered me the security of a large family: schooling, training, and a reason for living. They've done right by me all these years, and now, here I am, on the verge of throwing it all away."

The sound of approaching footsteps on the wet ground draws his attention back to the present. They stop just outside the shed.

"Mr. Vaughn, are you here?" Lilly whispers.

"Yes, I'm here," he replies, and steps into the doorway opening.

"Falcon and I have talked, and what we'd like to do is put a blindfold on you. We'll take you to your life body, then we can talk," she continues.

"Yes, that will be acceptable," he agrees.

Falcon slips a folded baby blanket over the older man's eyes and ties it secure with a bandage wrapped around and around his head. Lilly offers him her arm to guide his way. The first thing she does is pivot him around in a circle several times to face him away from the shed but not toward the wall. She walks thirty-five steps, stops, and pivots him again, more steps, a pivot, and again. The last fifty feet is covered in a zigzag fashion to arrive at the open doorway into the back wall.

Falcon lags back and watches Lilly lead the eager man into the room in the wall. Then he shuts the door, lights a candle, passes it to his wife, and waits until she starts guiding him into the secret passageway, before he locks the door. He has to run to catch them before they enter the room where the Company man's life body lies in a container. Oddly, Falcon thought the light in the room would wane as the sun went down, but to his amazement, round bars around the walls two feet below the ceiling, started glowing brighter and brighter as the sun set. They give off a cool light, enough to read by.

Lilly leads the blindfolded man directly to the container containing his body.

"Are you ready?" she asks.

"I suppose I am," he responds, letting out a slow deep breath.

Falcon loosens the bandage and slips the blindfold up and over the nervous man's head. At first, he turns his head up and down, side to side, looking, taking in the scene in awe. Finally, Lilly says.

"Mr. Vaughn . . . meet Mr. Vaughn," and points to the clear covering of the container.

He steps closer to peer down at the figure. "My Lord, it's me. After all these years, it's me." He stands agape. Tears form in his eyes to roll down his face.

Falcon and Lilly move away to give him some time alone with himself.

After a few minutes, he begins examining the container. Carefully, his hands move all over it, along the top, around the ends and sides. He stoops down to look underneath. "So, this is how they do it. Apparently this container is made of some material that won't allow me to get back to my body. I don't see any way to open it. It's smooth all over," he comments.

Falcon responds, "Yes, I know. We'd better know what we're doing before we open it anyway. We don't want to destroy you now, not after all these years."

"You're right, of course," Mr. Vaughn agrees, his face beaming with joy. "But it can't happen soon enough for me."

"What do you make of all these others?" Lilly asks, taking his hand.

He follows along looking at the bodies inside. After each, he shakes his head no.

"Can you give us a clue as to what this is all about?" Falcon questions.

"Are you sure you want to know?" the older man answers, and without waiting continues. "I must confess, I wasn't sure how I felt about all of this until I stood there, looking down at myself. Then it hit me. They—the people here I work for—have known for years that my body is here. They have purposely kept it from me to keep me here, working for them. They lied to me for forty years. All this time, I was this close. They could have told me, I would have stayed anyway. I've had hopelessness handed to me every day for forty years. They did that, and are still doing it to me.

"I no longer have any allegiance to them. Why should I? They deserve only grief from me for what they've done. And by God, they're going to get it. They'll rue the day they decided to do this to me. I swear it. As God is almighty, I swear it." Mr. Vaughn's temper heats up more and more as he speaks. "I don't know what the two of you have in mind, but whatever it is, it's too good for what they deserve. If we can work at it together, I'll show you and tell you things you won't believe. We'll use their own science against them."

"I think we should all get free of this place, before we do anything else," Lilly interrupts to suggest.

"That means, we'll have to find a way to open this container," Falcon adds.

"Whoa, just a minute, hold your horses." Mr. Vaughn cools their ambition. "Firstly, do you three think you can learn to trust me. I mean completely trust me? Let me tell you a few things and offer a suggestion or two. I think in your efforts to escape, you just might have came across the tools that will influence the future of this world. It makes sense now.

"To try to put it in a nutshell, if I'm right, these people here in these containers were put here centuries and centuries ago by a civilization beyond our world, to be brought to life at a future time, to bring the riches of this world back to their world. Or, if our world doesn't measure up to their expectations, they are here to destroy Earth, and everything on it."

Lilly and Falcon stand, frozen in thought. Nora, once again, wishes she had never become part of this escape.

"These people in these containers were designated the 'death angels' when they were put here, and have been passed on to different people down through the years, to be cared for, and kept safe, you see, until their time comes. Just a very few people at a time have ever known the whereabouts of their resting places. There are those out there who would destroy them if they could find them. The Company has had the responsibility of protecting them since the very beginning."

"The origin of the Company goes way back then?" Falcon questions. "Who were these people, or maybe I should say, who are these people?"

"Well, again, for the sake of simplicity and time, the highest order of these people today are descendants of a culture from another world, the Korgots. They were left here to capture and organize the entire working force of this world. It has been, and is, their goal to control the efforts of every living thing on this earth."

"What do you mean, left here?" Lilly inquires.

"The Korgots, numbering in the thousands, came here on an exploratory venture. Once their colony was established, the vast majority left, leaving just enough here to properly further their efforts to amass and stockpile the mineral riches of our earth. Their plan is to return one day with cargo carriers, to claim and take everything, leaving a barren, depleted, used-up ball behind."

"When are they coming back?" Lilly asks, feeling a little fear creep into her body.

"I don't know. I've been told, but I don't understand. It seems that their world circles around a different sun than ours. It takes ours twelve months to circle our sun. It might take fifty years for their world to travel around their sun just one time. They're not able to travel the distance from their world to ours until they pass us at their closest point. Once they leave, they have only so much time to get here, load up, and get back. Otherwise, their world could move away, beyond their reach." Mr. Vaughn has the group captivated. "The people they left here, way back then, are to have everything ready when their cargo carriers return. It'll take time to load everything, and time, could be very limited."

"What if it isn't ready? I mean, what if the people who were left here don't get their job completed? What happens when they get here with their cargo carriers and these people here haven't been able to put everything together for them to load?" Falcon is beginning to understand the hidden purpose behind the Company's efforts.

"Try to keep this in mind, folks. I'm way, way down the ladder in the scheme of command. Some of what I'm explaining, I've been told by the Company. Some of it, I've been told by my co-workers, and some of it, I've imagined just to fill in the unexplained areas. I can only tell you what I think, so keep that in mind. The exact truth could be, and probably is, something different.

"But to answer your question, Falcon. The responsible people here will be in a whole lot of trouble. They will have had years, centuries, to get ready. The cargo carriers and passengers will have to leave at a certain time. There will be no second chances. If the people here are successful, they'll be taken back as heroes, and treated as such. If they fail—well, remember now, what I am telling you is supposition on my part—they will probably be left here and be destroyed with the rest of our earth."

"Wow!" Lilly comes to life. "It sounds to me that we lose either way. They're plan is to take everything they can, and leave us in ashes."

"That's their plan." Mr. Vaughn supports her thinking.

"So, who do you think these people in these containers are?" Falcon asks intently.

"If they are who I think they could be—let me start over. A group of a hundred or so of their most gifted and talented warriors were left behind as their ace in the hole. The concern of those leaving was that the people they left here would create their own dynasty, a dynasty that might develop a force to take over this earth, and build an offense to repel their arrival when they return. These warriors were capable of feats beyond our beliefs. It's said that as few as three could destroy our entire world before we could mount a defense. The Company's responsibility has been to guard their existence until they activate themselves just prior to the arrival of the returning cargo carriers. Any hostility toward the arriving carriers will be dealt with immediately by these warriors. Then, once everything is loaded, it will be these warriors' job to destroy our earth.

"We can't be sure, but it's thought that people here on earth whom know about the Company, and work every day against them, have been able to locate and destroy all but twenty of these warriors. These could be part of that twenty."

"Why would anybody cooperate with the Company if they're going to be burnt to a crisp anyhow?" Lilly poses a good question. "Why isn't everybody working against the Company, instead of for them?"

"There lies the crux of it all. It is said if the Company gets the job completed, and if it can be confirmed which individuals have helped get it done, then they will be taken aboard the carriers with the cargo. They will be welcomed and coddled for the rest of time. They will be saved from the ravages enacted by these warriors."

"This is beginning to sound very familiar. It almost sounds like the boundaries of heaven and hell. An evil force pitted against a good and just world of mankind," Lilly notices.

"I'm glad you sense the possibilities," Mr. Vaughn acknowledges. "When you sit down and outline the problems of the world, then lay religion beside it. Well, let's put it this way. Active participation in a religious sect is forbidden by the Company. They don't try to keep you from wondering about it, but you best not talk about it, or try to enlist anyone else with your thinking."

"You mentioned some suggestions?" Falcon recalls.

"Yes, I did. And I'll ask you all to hold your decisions until I've finished. To begin with, I want to express my thanks for your concerns about me and my long lost life body. Quite obviously, I would have never found it on my own. Whether you like it or not, you have compassion for your fellow man. Oh, I know you have your reasons for bringing me here. I imagine you feel trapped, somehow, and need my connections to get you the rest of the way out of La Nesra. You need me to set you completely free. That's why you will probably resist my first suggestion.

"You should scrap your escape plans completely. I can see that, without a doubt, as much as you want your freedom, you're compelled to fight the Company even after you're free from the bonds of these walls. Leaving here now will lessen your ability to carry out plans to disrupt the Company's activities. You need to be here, close to everything. I can be more of a help to you if you're close by. Most importantly, though, you must be aware that to do any worthwhile damage to the Company will take planning and time. If you were to muster ten thousand troops to storm the walls of La Nesra, then hang your flag of victory on a pole high over the battlefield, the effect on the Company could be similar to that of a mosquito bite on an elephant's rump. The Company must be destroyed from within by using what they do best against them. Use their purpose, their greed, to our advantage. That will take money, information, understanding, and time. Should we leave here, escape to freedom, we will have lost a great advantage forever. We must stay. We must make our plans, and we must do it together.

"I'm sure I can work it out so the three of you can stay here with very little supervision. You should be able to come and go as you deem necessary, and do it without question. I'll locate a quarters which will allow the five of you to stay together."

“I’ll keep Joie, and Nora’s Sherman can stay with us too, then?” Lilly quickly asks for guarantees.

“Absolutely. Trust me. I’ll take care of it,” Mr. Vaughn assures.

“Do we have an agreement?” he adds without hesitation.

“Who’s the boss if we do what you’re suggesting? If I leave here a free man, I’ll be my own boss. I won’t report to anybody.” Falcon’s words burn Mr. Vaughn’s ears.

He swallows hard to force his ego down his throat away from his tongue, takes a deep quiet breath and speaks calmly, as if the question means nothing to him.

“We’ll all have a say in most cases, but if I take on a task, I’ll be the boss. When you take on a task, you’re the boss. Does that satisfy your question?” he answers tersely and looks Falcon in the eye. A mistake, since he’s trying to win Falcon’s trust, and he knows it as it happens.

With no response to his question, he continues.

“Do we have an agreement, then?”

Without a negative reply, he takes it as a positive vote.

“Good. Let’s get on with it. The five of you can slip quietly into Sally’s quarters for the night. She’s away on a mission, so she won’t be back any time soon. The first thing in the morning we’ll make other arrangements and get you settled. While you’re getting set up, I’ll see what I can find out about these bodies, particularly, how to open these containers. Let’s plan to get together the day after tomorrow in my office. We can start there.”

“Now, do you trust me enough to tell me where we are?” he finishes.

“No.” Falcon immediately takes charge. “We’ll take you back to the shed the same way we brought you here. You’re better off not knowing just yet.”

The place: the Anderson farm. The time: three days after the raids.

The funerals for the victims were held yesterday. Moving from grave site to grave site made it a long day. By mid-afternoon the tears of the mourners were dried up, emotions were spent, and there was nothing left to be said. The weary group filed back to the Andersons’ home, where the women pitched in together to get a ‘make do’ meal ready for everyone. Exhausted, bedtime came early for one and all.

Belle is up at five AM rattling pots and pans, cooking, baking, and making coffee. She’s feeding the hands in the kitchen. At the same time, the wives are setting the dining room table for the rest. Alberta Mae hobbles around on a crutch made from a tree limb with the fork at the end cut off short to fit under her arm. She rests her weight on the crutch, then sort of hops with her good leg. She’s unable to carry anything to help that way, but she can supervise to make sure everything is as it should be. Belle listens from the kitchen and grins as she hears her longtime friend giving orders. He broke the mold when He made that woman, runs through her mind.

John is the first to appear in the dining room. He looks around at the table setting, and watches as the women put the finishing touches, arranging napkins, silverware, and pouring water. The place shines.

“Morning, Mr. Anderson,” she greets him.

"Good morning, Alberta Mae," he says cheerily, and walks to put his arms around her. "This looks nice, you've made me feel like everything is going to be all right here this morning. I thank you. I didn't know it, but I needed this just now."

She hugs him back, wobbling on her crutch. "I needed to hear you say it, too, honey. Now, you just set yourself down and we'll get you some coffee."

June and Selma come down together, and the rest drift in one at a time over the next fifteen minutes. Charlotte and Cheryl can be heard coming down the stairs chattering back and forth. They reach the bottom of the stairs and turn toward the hallway.

"Miss Charlotte, Miss Cheryl, there's a lady here on the front porch. Says she's been invited to breakfast." Sachel has taken over the butler duties of the house.

"Who is it?" Charlotte asks quietly.

"Didn't ask, ma'am. Want me to ask her? She says you're expecting her."

"No, that's okay. We'll bring her in," Cheryl volunteers. The two young women step to the front door and out on to the porch to see a smartly dressed woman with her back to them. She turns when she hears them arrive.

"Sally," Cheryl blurts in surprise. "I didn't expect to see you this morning."

"Hello, Cheryl," Sally greets her new cohort. "I had no idea either, until late yesterday afternoon when one of your hands brought me an invitation from Robert."

Sally turns her attention to Charlotte.

"You must be Charlotte. I'm amazed. You two look almost alike, and the both of you are an image of Lilly. Amazing."

"I'm Sally," she addresses Charlotte. "I'm a friend of your sisters. I met your daddy and your brother Robert a few days ago in town."

"Hello," Charlotte responds graciously with a small smile. "Who's Lilly?"

Cheryl immediately sees a big need for a lengthy explanation, which shouldn't be approached here on the front porch. "It's a long complicated story," she interrupts, and takes each woman's hand to pull them gently toward the door. "Let's go inside and introduce Sally to everyone. Everything can be explained over breakfast."

The men start to rise as they see Sally enter the dining room.

"Sit still, please. Don't get up for me," she suggests.

The rest settle back down to their seats, except for Robert. The three women stand just inside the doorway looking at the beautifully set table.

He moves quickly extending his hand to Sally. "Welcome to our farm," he says warmly. "Everybody, I took the liberty of inviting Sally to breakfast this morning. Since we're all going to be working together, I thought we might as well get started off on the right foot. You've met my father John, and Randy. This is my mother, June, and, that's our very dear friend, Selma Housler. I can see you've already met Charlotte."

"Good morning, everyone, I do hope my being here is appropriate. If I make you uncomfortable, it won't hurt my feelings if you'd rather I leave." She can see the surprise in their faces.

John rises to his feet, no one speaks for a few seconds.

"Nonsense. You're welcome here. Of course you'll stay. Robert's right, no better time than right now to get started. Come on over and sit down right here, beside me."

The next few minutes are a mixture of exchanging words of first meetings, welcoming remarks, and questioning glances.

Seeing everyone present at the table, the hands wives, acting on the orders of Belle and Alberta Mae, are quick to fill coffee cups, and start bringing platters of breakfast food.

The mixed conversations stop when Selma says. "My curiosity is eating me alive, Sally. Forgive me if I sound tactless, but, just who are you? I must say, I am completely impressed by your looks and dress. You're not something we usually see out here this time of the day. You are absolutely beautiful."

June and Charlotte light up inside when they hear, 'just who are you.'

Sally isn't sure whether she should start explaining, or if she should wait for one of the others. She doesn't wait long.

"Randy and I met Sally when we went to Atlanta to find Sheree. She's the one who helped us find her," Robert starts.

June squirms in her seat, but remains silent.

"She helped us get in and out of that place called La Nesra," Randy adds.

"I've known Sally a long time," Cheryl begins. "Close to ten years I'd say. She was my counselor while I was in training at La Nesra, and was a big part of the plan to put me here, with you. She's worked with the Company pretty much all her life."

Sally nods her head in agreement.

June is unable to sit quietly any longer.

"So, from what I'm hearing, you must know of my daughter, Sheree?"

Sally nods. "Yes, I know Sheree. She's known as Lilly now."

June sits straight up in her chair. Randall's heart skips a beat, and his eyes widen as he glances at Charlotte, who turns her head to catch his glimpse. John looks quickly at each member of his family, again and again.

"You've got some nerve, if I must say so!" Selma explodes. "What gall, your coming here like this after what just happened!" She gets to her feet, puts her hands on the table, and leans toward Sally.

"My husband's lying in there with a bullet hole in his back. He almost died. We just buried Cole and Caroline Sanders, Jacob Stoker, and four of our hands. At least fifteen of our hands are still nowhere to be found, and you burnt our farms to the ground. And now you're here, sitting there all primped to perfection, expecting—Lord, I don't know what. What kind of person are you?"

Sally, with her hands clasped in her lap, hangs her head.

"You bitch! I don't know what you've told these men to get them to forgive and forget, but I understand your kind of conniving, self-serving thinking. You'd better not find yourself alone with me. I'm so riled right now I could tear off one of your arms, and stuff it down your throat!"

Selma makes a move as though she's coming across the table. June grabs her around the waist at the same time John stands up in front of Sally to cut off the onslaught. The table moves causing dishes to rattle and silverware to jingle. Water and coffee splashes from the glasses and cups.

Selma slams down into her chair from June's force.

"What on earth is going on in here?" Belle exclaims, as she enters the room. "You children behave yourselves before you break something."

Selma sits in her chair, moving her head from side to side, breathing heavily through her nose, her lips pressed tightly together, seething with hate.

"If you say you'll stay there, I'll let you go," June calmly advises her best friend.

Selma turns her head to look into June's face, and glares with squinted eyes.

"Is that a yes?"

Selma sits still, but sneers at Sally, who's still looking down at her hands.

June relaxes her grip as John returns to his seat. The rest of the group resumes breathing, waiting to see what happens next.

Without giving any one else a chance to speak, Sally raises her head, leaving her hands on her lap and speaks. "I don't have the words to express my deep heartfelt sorrow for what happened here. I,—I truly do understand how you feel, and if there was a way to change it, I would. If you all agree that killing me will bring you some sort of comfort, then I'll not try to stop you. I'm not here to offer excuses. The only reason I'm here is to offer you my help in any way I can. Believe me or not, these raids were not brought on by the Company. There was not, nor has there ever been, any conversation within the Company about such an act. Cliff Messinger was the sole instigator of this hell you've been through. He organized it, and he paid for it. Your husband has a list of those individuals who actually did the murdering and burning." Her eyes move from June to finally find Selma.

"Selma, I can only say I don't blame you for the way you feel. Hate me, hell, despise me; I'd cancel it all out and bring everything back, if I could—but I can't. I can, though, do everything possible to limit anything like this ever happening again. Cliff Messinger was lying dead on the floor the day I swore to John, Robert, and Randall that I was through working for the Company. I'll devote my life, along with everything I know about the Company, to help your cause. Over time, you'll find me to be an extremely loyal person."

"Is this all true, John," Selma inquires smartly. "Do you actually think she'll turn on the Company?"

John takes a moment to collect his thoughts, then replies.

"People change, Selma. All sorts of things happen in people's lives to make them change. I don't know much more about her than you do, but if she truly wants to help us against the Company . . . well, I have to give her enough room to do it."

"I respect that, and for that reason and that reason only, I'll not interfere. But you listen to me, lady, I've got my eye on you, and the first time you give me reason, I'll cut your throat while you sleep. You understand?"

"I hear your words, I understand, but I'll ask you this . . . talk to me before you go off looking for sharp knife. Make sure you know—don't kill me later because you didn't get to do it here and now—I want to do everything I can to destroy and dismantle the Company. If you'll keep an open mind, you'll see I'm true to my word."

June changes the subject.

"Tell me about my daughter. When was the last time you saw her? Is she well? Do they treat her right?"

"I've not seen her recently, but I know her to be well. Here's a surprise though. She's married and has a child—a little girl."

Sheree's mother raises her head in disbelief. John turns to look at her. Randall feels his heart fall into his guts, and hangs his head. Charlotte stares at Sally, not wanting to look at Randall, while Cheryl sits complacent.

Robert's emotions are mixed in his unasked questions. Has she found someone she truly loves? Are they happy together? He wants to see her.

"Her husband's name is Falcon. As I said earlier, her name has been changed to Lilly. I've not heard what they named the baby," Sally continues.

"My word," Selma expresses at the news, having let her guard down for the moment.

"She has grown into a beautiful young woman, Mrs. Anderson. She's never given up on the idea of escaping and coming home."

June clouds up immediately. Water can be seen welling in her eyes.

"I want to help you get her back," Sally proposes, reaching and taking June's hand.

"Is it possible, do you think?" Robert asks.

"Oh, yes, it's very likely, especially with me working with you."

"When?" Mrs. Anderson's question is quick and to the point.

"I need to get back there to make a determination. We don't want to break her out only to have them chasing after us. We'll come up with a way to get them to release her, and her family."

June brightens at the prospect.

"Is there any further word from Ed Skinner about Elizabeth?" Robert hopes for any bit of information as to her whereabouts.

"No, I'm sorry, Robert. Folks in town have questioned him again, and again. I don't think he knows anything about her. Apparently, he wasn't with the group who took her."

"I don't know where to start," he confesses, sadly. "She could be anywhere."

"I know this isn't much, but when you don't know where to turn, try working on things you do know. Ask questions as you go. Look for hints. Carry her picture with you to show to people. Stay as busy as you can doing things that matter to you, such as, getting your sister out of La Nesra, or tracking down the rest of that raider gang," Sally wisely advises.

"She's right, son, let's be sure things are right here before we go venturing out on other business. I know it's eating you up on the inside, but going off in all directions will wind up being a waste of time," John explains and supports Sally. "If we had some sort of a lead, I'd be the first in line to go after Elizabeth, you know that. It's hard, but right now we need you right here."

"You're daddy's right, Bob," Randall advises. "We need to get the guesthouse ready for Mr. Housler and Miss Selma, and see that Mama is getting along okay with her broken leg. What if something happens and a bunch of those raiders came back to finish their job? We need to be ready."

"I'm going to town to send a wire to Marty Schoener asking him to meet me halfway between here and Baltimore. Once I get a few things worked out with him, I'll be back. That should take no more than three days. Then we can get started getting done what we know has to be finished. Use the time while I'm gone to get settled here. We'll find her, son. I know we will." John's assurances mean a lot to Robert, but he still feels he should be on a horse, headed somewhere, making an effort of some kind.

It's two o'clock in the morning when John and Marty connect with each other in a dimly lit hotel room, about halfway between the Anderson farm and Baltimore. Both men have been traveling by horseback, and look in need of rest. Unshaven, parched, dusty, and wearing the same clothes they had on since they left their origins, both are feeling hunger when their hands come together with a greeting.

"Marty, it's good to see you." John puts his left hand on Marty's right elbow as he grips his hand.

"Likewise, John." He returns the grip with a broad, hearty grin.

"News travels fast. I heard you had some real trouble at your place," John's longtime friend continues.

John shakes his head yes and explains, in detail, the circumstances back at the farm. Marty is appalled at what he hears. "I'm ready to go kick their ass. Just tell me when and where."

"There's something you can do, but it doesn't have a whole lot to do with your kicking their ass," John explains. "I need to back away from my responsibilities with the Sons for a while, maybe quite a while. For the sake of my family, and yes, I suppose my sake too, I need to settle some scores. I need to find Elizabeth."

"What are you saying?"

"I need you too take over the Sons operation, take my place. You can do it, I've seen what you can do."

"I don't know, John. These people gave this job to you, not me. I don't know if they'll stand for it."

"There's more, Marty, I need you to ferret out information for me. And I need your access to a supply of weapons and ammunition," John adds to the problem.

"Uuuuummmhhhh, knock me down. You know there's a war going to be fought shortly, right?" Marty reminds his friend. "I imagine I'll have trouble getting the supplies I need, how do you expect there will be anything left for you."

"Ship mine to me now," John explains.

"Ship them? You want me to steal them for you, free of charge, and then ship them to you. I'll say this, when you dream, you really dream. All jesting aside, my good friend, during these times, if we're caught, it could mean both our heads," Marty cautions.

"I know it's asking a lot, but if I set out without the proper backup, it'll take me twice as long. Listen, the war might not heat up for another six months yet, maybe a year. Help me. I'll be back in my chair before they know I'm gone. If they ask, tell them I'm home ill with a disease, or tell them I suffered a wound resulting from the raids. Here's a list of the supplies I need. If you can get two wagons to meet us right here, I'll have people transfer the goods to my wagons and send yours back." John keeps trying.

"My God, you want two wagonloads of weapons and ammunition? Aaaww, hell, we both know I'm going to do it. Why am I complaining? I've had a good life. Rachell will understand when her husband's sentenced to rot in prison for ten years."

"Great, thank you, Marty. How soon can you have the wagons here?"

"I might as well go all the way with this. No sense in you trying to get back here. Tell me where you want them to go. I'll just leave the wagons there and bring the horses back. That way there's less chance anybody will know they're for you. I'd advise you to move them to a secure place of your choosing as soon as you can though."

Robert steps off the front porch to walk toward his father, returning from his trip to meet Marty. John's glad to see a warm smile on his son's face.

"Welcome home, Daddy."

"Thanks, Robert, I'm glad to be back. Looks like folks are settling down and getting back to their lives. I didn't stop, but I drifted past the guesthouse on my way. I see things have moved along over there as well."

"Yep, Mr. and Mrs. Housler are over there now. Alberta Mae is able to get things done with some help. You should see her. She'd make a good army sergeant." Robert chuckles and pats his dad on the back.

"How is the colonel?"

"He's not up and about yet, but he's getting stronger every day. He's eating good now, and according to Mrs. Housler, he's complaining more and more."

John smiles at the news and nods his head knowingly.

"And Selma?" he asks.

"She's doing just fine. Her head bandage is off. It looks like she's going to have a bit of scar, but her hair will cover most of it. Funny thing, you know how heated up she got at Sally at breakfast the other day? Well, Sally's staying at the guesthouse now. I'm not saying those two are best friends, but they're getting along together. Sure surprises me." He grins as he relates.

John smiles back and shakes his head slightly.

"How's your mother?"

"Oh, she's doing all right, she says. But I catch her, when she's not looking, wiping tears from her eyes. I think she believes she didn't do enough through this whole thing. I don't know why, but she blames herself."

"Yeah, I figured as much. She feels responsible, since neither you or I was here. Then I up and leave first thing after it's over."

"I've tried to tell her to lean on me more, but you know how she is. She'll handle it herself." Robert is clearly concerned.

"Well, she needs some time, I'll talk to her, but you're right. She'll figure it out for herself. Just give her a hug when you can. You don't need to say anything, just give her a hug," John suggests, knowing it will be good for his son too.

"How about you, son? How are you holding up?"

"I'm fine. Just antsy, that's all. I feel like nothings happening. I need to do something," he confides.

"I can imagine . . ." John stops in midsentence when a thought occurs to him.

"You know I'm real proud of you, don't you? You've grown into a fine man. You have a strong will, you're wise ahead of your time, and you've got a heart big enough for five people." A pause. "We'll find her, you know. It could take some time, but we'll find Elizabeth. We won't give up until we do. You've got my word on it."

Robert looks into his daddy's face, his eyes welled with tears.

"Thanks, I didn't know it, but I needed that." He starts to walk away, but stops in thought, and turns back. "And . . . I love you too."

They each wipe tears by bowing their head, then putting a thumb and forefinger on the outer edges of their eyes, and sliding them together to their nose. Brushing the water up over their foreheads, under their hats, and running their fingers into their hair finishes the job.

"Let's get started," the elder of the two offers. "See if you can pull everybody together for a meeting right after supper this evening. I have an idea or two."

"I can do that. If you don't mind though, I'd like to do it at the guesthouse. Colonel Housler would really like to be a part of it, and we shouldn't move him all the way over here again."

"You set it up, son."

June is standing at the front door when John and Robert reach the porch.

"What are the two of you talking so seriously about?" she wonders.

"We were just noticing how much prettier you get with every day that goes by, honey" John quips.

They put their arms around each other and disappear into the house. Robert has things to do, so he's on his way to get it done.

Time marches on at La Nesra, in Atlanta.

True to his word, Mr. Vaughn secured housing for Lilly's family, her maid and son. It's a space above an old hay storage barn, which is situated away from any traffic patterns. The stairs to reach it are attached directly to the side of the building facing the perimeter wall of the compound. There's a three-foot square landing at the top, with a wooden railing all around. The door to their new home opens in, on their left.

Lilly is very skeptical at first, but once inside, she is pleasantly surprised. There are no interior walls, just one big open room. The furniture seems almost new, and it appears to have everything they'll need. There's plenty of room for Nora and Sherman. Mr. Vaughn has promised to have a few walls put up to give the two families some privacy. There are large windows on the wall straight back from the door, which allows an abundance of morning sunlight into the room. The colors in the rugs on the wooden floors stand out vividly, indicating they are fairly new, also. The kitchen area is outfitted completely. And then there's the clincher, a beautifully finished baby crib—with a matching rocker.

Lilly's words are, "I love it."

Mr. Vaughn has, somehow, snuffed out any inquiry into the fire and explosion. It's been over two days and nobody has even looked suspiciously at Falcon or Lilly.

It's late in the afternoon and time is passing slowly as the couple waits for an expected meeting with their newly determined ally.

"He should be here in a few minutes, honey. Why don't you put Joie down in her crib. Nora can watch her while we're busy," Lilly addresses her husband, who has become attached to their baby girl.

The outside stairs creak under the weight of someone coming.

"He's here," Falcon informs his wife.

Lilly is right there to open the door before a knock is heard. "We heard you coming," she explains to Mr. Vaughn, as he appears through the door.

"Yes, well . . . I could have these steps looked at if the noise bothers you."

"Oh, no, no," Falcon pipes up. "I like it. This way nobody can sneak up on us."

The Company man steps into the new home of the couple and glances around.

"Do you have everything you need?" he inquires.

"Yes, we have everything. It'll take us a few days to get settled," Lilly replies.

"Have you been able to learn anything?" she continues, as she shuts the door.

"We'll know within the hour. I've arranged a meeting with one of my superiors. He's a good man, and a trusted friend. I took a chance by taking him into my confidence several years ago to discover he has his issues with the Company, as well. To shorten the story, I approached him with our situation, not mentioning your names at first. After exchanging information, we decided we are of the same mind. Him, with his reasons and purpose, and me with mine," Mr. Vaughn discloses.

"Who is he?" Lilly interrupts.

"He would rather remain anonymous until he's had a chance to speak with the both of you. You'll understand once you hear his side of it."

"When?" is Falcon's question.

"Now," Mr. Vaughn explains. "We need to leave now to meet him."

"Nora!" Lilly calls.

"Yes, ma'am, I heard. I'll be right here. You go ahead and do what you have to."

"Let's go," Falcon urges, not asking where. He'll learn that when he gets there.

"Here, before we go, take these rings. There's one for each of you. As long as you wear these no one here will bother you no matter where you go, or what you're doing. You can come and go from La Nesra, as you wish. If someone should stop you, show them the ring, you won't have any trouble. Your maid will have the same privileges, except she'll have to be with one or the both of you," Mr. Vaughn informs them, holding out his hand.

The rings are heavy, obviously made of gold. They have a center set round emerald, flanked by a diamond on either side, giving them a striking, memorable, appearance. With a design engraved around and between the gems, it is obvious these rings are rare, and are meant to mean something to those wearing them.

"Wear them on your right hand. Put them on and don't take them off. Understand?"

As the trio descends the steps, the couple following, Mr. Vaughn explains further.

"The man you are about to meet is held in high esteem within the Company. He doesn't want to jeopardize that, expect him to be very cautious. I've given him information about both of you, so his purpose now is to determine whether to get involved with us. I believe once he decides in our favor, he can explain a lot of what we want to know, and in all probability, will help us determine and execute a plan."

Lilly places her ring on her right hand ring finger, leaving her left hand free to wear a wedding band, sometime in the near future. The weight of the ring is noticeable as she walks, her arms swinging. It's a good, sort of belonging, feeling.

"Here we are. Let me go in first to make sure he's ready," Mr. Vaughn advises the couple as they near a ground level door at the side of the main building.

Lilly raises her hand to look at her ring as they wait. Seeing his wife, Falcon does the same thing. "Kind of nice, in an ugly sort of way, huh?" he comments.

"I think it's beautiful. You're terrible. I'll bet these are worth a lot of money," she responds. "What's a woman to think. Men, you don't know beauty when you see it."

Falcon grins, expecting this sort of response.

The older man appears from inside the building, and motions with a wave of his hand to follow. Once inside, they descend a set of stairs to a narrow hallway, then move to a closed door at the end to enter a space just large enough for three chairs. A black curtain, hanging from the ceiling, meets a waist high wooden wall, separating them from the rest of the room. Once they're seated, the only sounds are the hissing of the gas lights illuminating the room and hallway.

"The door is closed. Here with me are Lilly and Falcon. I'll let you continue from here," Mr. Vaughn announces.

"Good. Very good." A firm, confident voice comes from the other side of the curtain. "Can I hear your voices, one at a time."

Mr. Vaughn motions, encouraging the couple to speak.

"I'm Lilly. I don't know what to say other than I'll try to answer your questions."

"And I'm Falcon, Lilly's husband. I must say that if it were not for Mr. Vaughn being here, I'd feel at a great disadvantage at this moment. I understand your need for secrecy, but I hope you realize our feeling of exposure."

"Absolutely," is heard, the voice of the unknown. "What motivation brings you to this point? How sure are you that this is what you truly want? Have you talked between yourselves about the good, and the bad, to come from your efforts? How far are you willing to go, and how long are you willing to devote yourselves? Talk to me, answer these questions as honestly and as truthfully as you can. Take your time."

"You, as well as us?" Falcon counters.

"You first," is the response.

Meanwhile, back at the Andersons' farm. The meeting, arranged by Robert at the guesthouse, is about to begin. Present are John, June, Charlotte, Cheryl, the colonel and Selma, Sally, Alberta Mae, Randall, the twins, the two daughters, Belle, and Sachel—and, of course, Robert. The furniture is full with the rest sitting in various positions on the floor, in a sort of semicircle. One left standing is John. He begins.

"I know it's getting late in the day for a meeting like this, but I think it's important to us all to know what's going on and where we're at with it. I just returned today, after making arrangements where I've been working, to stay here, to be here with you all, while we work our way through our problems."

A small rumbling of voices is heard supporting his intentions.

"We're all in this fix together. There's no secrets between the people in this room. You'll all know what any one of us knows, from start to finish. Agreed?"

A louder rumbling of supporting voices.

He continues.

"Within a few days, two wagons full of supplies will arrive. These supplies will help us prepare for any future raiding party bringing their hell down on us. As you'll see, they'll regret that day, should it come. Further, these supplies will help us in our endeavors to locate Elizabeth Sanders, and any missing hands, and bring them back to us."

Another, louder yet, round of voices in support of John's words.

"Each and every one of you here this evening will play a part in what needs to be done. I'm asking you to do your job assignment the best way you can. Everything, even the smallest job, is important to our success. So, when you're given something to do, do it with the thought in mind that it will better us all. Once the supplies get here, this is where we'll start."

During the rest of the meeting, the following plan is laid out, and a place to start is identified.

Colonel Charles Housler will head up the continuing efforts of the three farms. Since he's on the mend, it makes sense that he not be required to ramble around the countryside. He will be the authority, the chairman, concerning everything, and accepts the responsibility gladly. Belle and Alberta Mae will see to the two households, making sure there's food and clothing for everyone. June and Selma will coordinate information, and pass it on as required. Also, they'll keep communications flowing by encoding, or deciphering, messages as necessary. Sachel, once all of the defenses are in place, will monitor the safety of those on the farms. The Stoker twin boys and the daughters will work as runners, ferrying information to the others. The rest, John, Robert, Randall, Charlotte, Cheryl, and Sally, will constitute the offensive point of the groups efforts. Charlotte and Cheryl are part of this team due to their insistence, not because everybody thinks it is a good idea. John has made it clear that everybody is to help everyone else, wherever and whenever they can, with anything.

After all have had their say, and it seems no one has been left out, each feels satisfied with their responsibilities. Everybody plays an important part in this large, diverse, boiling pot of a family. A family tied together by grief, need, and loyalty. The six comprising the offensive arm of the group get together for few minutes to determine that their first priority will be to find and rescue Elizabeth. As a place to begin, Sally will leave immediately for Atlanta, to be followed in a few days by the others, who will trickle in one and two at a time, so as not to raise suspicion. The idea is to obtain information about Sheree, and, at the same time, ask a lot of questions about Elizabeth. If nothing develops within a few days, the group will move on to New Orleans searching for Robert's fiancee.

Everyone is excited that they are doing something, especially Robert. The wait for the supply wagons to arrive will drag. It begins.

In the meantime, at Atlanta, in a small room in the basement of La Nesra. Lilly and Falcon have been answering all of the inquiries coming from the man behind the black curtain. There's a long pause.

"I believe I'm finished. I'll answer any question you have, providing it is pertinent to matters at hand."

"Are you with us?" is Falcon's first question.

"I've not yet decided. I want to hear your questions."

Knowing they'll not discover the identity of the man not more then ten feet from them until his wishes are fulfilled, Falcon's and Lilly's questions about him would be a waste of time. Also, questions about trust are pointless. They either trust him, or try to work their plan by themselves, and since they've came this far . . . well, what do they have to lose now?

"Will you leave with us, or stay here and help us from here?" Lilly's first question seems appropriate.

"I'll remain here as long as possible. I'll provide you with information and keep you out of danger as best I can. At times, I could be in a position to offer hands on help, even physical force. I would, also, expect you to stay here as long as deemed necessary. My vision of what we must do isn't going to be accomplished in a few days. It could take months, years."

"Are you willing to tell us about the Company, I mean, what about those men in those containers we found." Falcon gets to a point they all want addressed.

"Yes, well, I'm aware of Mr. Vaughn's explanation to you. As far as it goes, it's accurate. But let's get to the real problem. The ten forms you have discovered are, apparently, part of the remaining death angels left here centuries ago to destroy our world, if necessary. It would seem an easy solution to break open their containers and mutilate them, to render them useless, thus reducing the threat to mankind by that number. However, way back then, three of them were secretly replaced with three Herculean angels. Their purpose is to counteract the uprising death angels. The three Herculean angels were intermingled among the death angels, making it impossible for those Korgots left here to determine which is which. So, in our efforts to destroy the threat to mankind by eliminating those in the containers, we could be doing just the opposite. We would take the chance of destroying the only things known that could stop the death angels onslaught. On the other hand, if proponents of the death angels were to destroy those in the containers, trying to reduce the number of Herculean angels, they would certainly eliminate some of their own, and possibly leave intact the Herculean angels."

Lilly reacts. "How do we know if the one's that have already been destroyed aren't the good guys."

"We don't. To top it off, it's written that the Company's responsibility is to be positioned, when the time comes, to eliminate the good guys before they have a chance to gain power enough to destroy the bad guys."

Lilly exclaims again. "I had no idea."

"It seems to me that we're damned either way. What happens if I take my family and leave here? Let you deal with it?" Falcon poses.

Mr. Vaughn hasn't spoken since this process started.

"We're hoping you won't do that. You're the first positive thing we've had happen for years. You've found ten of the remaining twenty, whether their good or bad, we at least now know—or rather, you know—where they are," he finishes.

"Exactly," comes the hidden voice.

"We will do all we can to entice you to stay, to help us to covertly develop information, which will enable a plan for us to thwart this dastardly effort of our forefathers."

"Honestly, whoever you are, take a good look at us. We're not much more than big kids. This sounds like a big problem to set on our shoulders. There has to be somebody with more to offer than us." Falcon expresses honest feelings.

"You've just demonstrated part of your value to us. You have a talent of seeing the evasive obviousness of a problem, the logic. You can quickly sort out the chaff from the grain, get to the basic truths, turn out the probabilities. And you're young. You'll be around for a long time. Plenty of time to hone your skills to pass them on to another to take your place. And so it goes, until it's time."

"And you, Lilly, your ability to put yourself into a deep sleep, aging so slowly. If handled properly, you could be around for several hundred years. Imagine what you'll be worth to people one hundred years from now. Especially when we perfect our information implantation system. You'll know everything that's happened while you're asleep. Take that times three, see what I mean," the voice gets excited.

"What do you mean 'information implantation system'?" Lilly asks intently.

"Stay, and you can learn about that, and hundreds of other advances, advances the common public has not yet conceived, let alone heard about. It will amaze you. It will open your eyes to the reality of mankind and our purpose here on earth."

"I'm not sure what you just said, sir, but you're asking us to sign on to something we know little about. It sounds like a lifetime job at that. Things are happening way too fast for me. Can we have a few days to talk all of this over? A week maybe?" Lilly explains and asks.

"Mr. Vaughn, what do you think?" the voice booms with a bit of aggravation.

"Give them the time. If they're forced into anything, they can change their minds once they're out of sight and do whatever they want anyway."

"All right. One week. Get with Mr. Vaughn to determine a meeting time and place."

Mr. Vaughn gets to his feet and motions with his head to move out of the room.

Once they are back at their quarters, the couple informs Nora of the situation. She doesn't want to understand it, but is glad her two friends include her and Sherman. She rolls her big eyes at hearing the facts.

"What do you think, honey?" Lilly asks her husband

"I think, if we do what they want us to, then our plans for getting away by ourselves to live a normal life are out the window. One minute I feel patriotic and want to sign on with them, but my next thought is what about you. What do you want? I want you to be happy with whatever we do. They seem to be willing to give us whatever we want if we stay, I like that. We can have some freedom, but do you want to raise Joie in this atmosphere? See, I'm all over the place with it. How do you feel about it?"

"Pretty much the same as you, I suppose. But, you know, God has put us on this earth for a reason. He's brought us together. As ridiculous as it sounds, maybe you and I are here to save the world. Maybe, whatever it is we'll do while we're here will make the difference; the difference the world needs to carry on. Should we not think so much about ourselves, and start thinking about our children and theirs. What about all those little children out there needing our help? Then you and me—can we turn our back on them?"

'When you put it that way, what else can we do?" Nora interrupts. "We got to do what we got to do."

It's been three days since the meeting at the Anderson farm. A hand has just returned from the orchard at the Sanders' place, checking to see if the supply wagons have arrived. He has reported to Robert, who is entering the kitchen through the back door.

"Get Daddy, Cheryl. Tell him the wagons are here. Whoopppttteeedeee! Now we're getting somewhere," he exclaims with glee.

John appears through the kitchen door onto the back porch.

"You say they're here?" he asks.

"Yep, just got the word."

"Well then, let's round up a couple of teams and get some help together," John resounds happily. "No sense waiting around, let's get it done."

John, Robert, Randall, Jim, Josh, and two hands arrive at the orchard out in back of what was once the Sanders' home. It's Randall's first time to see it—and the rest of the buildings—burned to the ground. The memory of seeing Der Bote burning flashes through his head.

"It's a shame, you know, it's just a damned shame. What gets into people's heads to do something like this. May they all rot in hell," he comments to the others.

No one responds.

"The wagons are back there in the orchard, about in the middle," Robert explains.

Jim, Josh, and the hands ready the harnesses and rigs, while John, Robert, and Randall walk back in the orchard to remove the branches used to camouflage the wagons. Then, one at a time, a team is taken in, hooked up, and with the help of everyone, each is pulled and pushed to the hard ground near the house. There ropes are tied from saddle horns of the saddled horses, to the wagons to help the teams manage the hills ahead. The heavy wagons leave deep ruts as the move along.

There's room enough in the Andersons' main barn to fit the wagons one behind the other with the teams still hitched. Once inside, the men anxiously remove the army tents used to cover, and protect, the supplies from the elements.

"Will you look at this. No wonder these wagons weigh a ton," Robert clamors. "These look like cannons."

"That's what they are," John is quick to explain. "See there, in those crates, those are lead balls made to come out of those cannons like scatterguns belching rain from hell. We'll build a frame and set one up at each of our homes so it will cover a path between our houses and barns. One of these balls can tear a man's arm off at two hundred yards, and we'll have twenty of them coming out of that barrel at a time. Think what that will do to a ravaging group charging down on us. Wait for just the right time and . . . *boom*. They won't know what hit them."

"There must be fifty rifles here. They sure look different though," Robert notices.

"They're breech loaders. Another surprise for those devils," John informs his son and the others.

"Ha! Look at these round iron balls with the fuses sticking out!" Randall exclaims.

"Yeah," John explains. "When that thing explodes, it sends out razor sharp, odd-shaped pieces, called shrapnel, in all directions. It's a mean weapon, not something you want to get caught close to when it goes off. The explosion is bad enough, let alone that spray of deadly missiles."

"What do you do? Light the fuse and throw it?" Randall asks, with La Nesra and the broken bottle in his front pocket, on his mind.

"That's right. The trick is to let the fuse burn down before you throw it. You don't want to give anybody time to pick it up and throw it back at you." John's words are heard and understood by all.

"There's everything we could ever need here, and plenty of it. Where in the world did you find it all?" Robert inquires.

"Don't ask, son. Let's just make sure everybody here knows what to do with it while we're gone. We'll get the colonel involved and let him know what we think, then let him do it."

"I believe anything he won't need immediately if he's attacked, should be put in the tunnel under the guesthouse. We sure don't want it to go off accidentally, from a wild shot or the like."

"Good idea," Randall agrees. The rest chime in with comments of support.

"Okay folks. The sooner we get this handled, the sooner we can get on our way to Atlanta," John encourages Robert and Randall.

Chapter Twenty-Eight

It has been a week since Lilly and Falcon met with Mr. Vaughn, and the mysterious, yet to be named, higher up of La Nesra. Nobody has bothered the couple for anything. To see if they could leave the compound, they took Joie, Nora, and Sherman out beyond the front wall earlier today to picnic under a large tree about four hundred yards away. The guard at the gate paid them little attention. They enjoyed their freedom for over two hours before returning.

Once back in their quarters, the group feels quite smug with their accomplishment.

"That was great," Lilly comments. "It felt like I was just let out of prison."

"I didn't think I would ever see past that wall in my whole life, let alone, come back in here after I got out," Nora adds.

"They didn't question us at all," Falcon joins in. "These men made their word good, I'll give them that. We'll probably hear from them before long, so, are we all in agreement? We're staying?"

"Like I said, sir, I want to be with the two of you. If you're staying, then I'm staying," Nora assures without hesitation.

"I could go either way, honey," Lilly follows. "I want you to be happy, so if you want to stay, count me in. I sort of feel like that it's what we're meant to do."

"Okay, we're staying, but I think we should know everything they do; and we should keep our eyes open. I'm not worried that our unknown person is setting a trap, what would he have to gain? He knows where we are, if he wants to hurt us, he could do it anytime, he doesn't need a trap. And he now knows the angels are here at La Nesra. It wouldn't take him too long to find them on his own. If we feel as though we're equal partners, we can work without having to be on guard against our allies."

"Yes, you're right, and since we can leave here whenever we want, they must be aware that I can go back to my family anytime. You know they've thought of that, yet they still gave us our freedom. They're sincere with what they're saying," Lilly surmises.

"We might as well show them the containers then. If their attitude toward us is the same after that, I'll believe them," Falcon concludes.

The outside steps squeak. Someone's coming.

Tap. Tap. Tap.

Nora opens the door.

"Yes, ma'am?" she asks.

"I understand Lilly and Falcon live here, are they home?"

Lilly recognizes the voice.

"Come in, Sally," she invites loudly, but not excitedly. "We're here."

"You know Falcon, don't you?" she continues as her old acquaintance appears through the door.

"Why, yes, I believe so. Hi, I'm Sally. I've been one of Lilly's counselors over the years," she addresses Falcon.

"I heard you two are married—and a baby. Where's the baby?"

Nora looks at Mrs. Justice, who responds with a nod. "I'll just get her. She's should be up now anyway." She heads for the baby crib.

"We named her Joie," Lilly smiles.

"Will you look at this. She is just beautiful," Sally exclaims and takes Joie from Nora's arms. She looks at her for a few seconds, kisses her on the nose, and hands her back. "Joie suits her. You have a lovely daughter."

"Thanks," Falcon acknowledges graciously, then gets right to the point.

"What brings you here?" He motions her to sit as he and Lilly find their seats.

"Are you in a hurry to go somewhere or something?" Sally asks candidly.

"No, we weren't going anywhere, why?" Lilly answers and asks.

"Well, I want to talk with both of you about something, but it might take me a while to get around to it, that's all." Sally is as candid as before.

She thinks to herself. "I don't know Falcon that well, and for all I know, he's very devoted to the Company. Not just that, if I say anything to Lilly about her family, if she takes that information to the Company explaining where she got it, it could seriously damage my standing here."

"Go right ahead, we're listening," Falcon replies curtly to the redheaded beauty.

"Okay." A short pause while she thinks. "Lilly, do you and your husband share the same view regarding the politics around here?"

"Yes, we do," he answers for his wife.

"Sally, my thinking hasn't changed. You've known me a long time, well enough to know that I'd get out of here if I could. You've known that for years, I've made no bones about it to anybody. Is that what you're looking for?" Lilly trumpets smartly.

She's never considered Sally a good friend, but has taken solace on her shoulder a time or two. Certainly she has no intention of revealing anything to her that might hinder the agreement she and her husband are about to confirm with Mr. Vaughn and his boss.

"I'm glad you put it that way; you've saved me a lot of stewing over my words. I'm going to take a chance on you two. I've been to your farm and have spoken with your family, and I have a lot to tell you. To begin with, they all send their love, and think about you every day." Sally starts at the beginning to explain.

John and his group arrived at Atlanta by train earlier this afternoon. After discussing it among themselves, they decided to travel together for two reasons. Firstly, tempers and hostility toward black people have increased sharply, and continue to become worse as the beginning of the war approaches. Randall will be much safer with their group. Secondly,

John can honestly pass off Robert, Charlotte, and Cheryl, as his children, all out on a holiday. They'll appear as an innocent family, here to see the sights.

Randy and Robert suggest that they split from the group when they reach Atlanta. The two of them will find lodgings out on the edge of town. Somewhere close to where they stayed the last time they were here. John and the girls will stay at the Atlanta Grand, right in the heart of downtown. This way they multiply their chances of obtaining information about Elizabeth by covering a larger area of the city. They all know to meet Sally, as planned, tomorrow afternoon at My Mama's Home Cooking.

Their mission, one and all, until then, is to ask casual questions regarding their search for Elizabeth, and keep their ears open for information about the raiders. It seems to be an impossible task, but as Sally advised earlier, work at what you know, all the while keeping an eye out for what you want to know. At least, they feel like they are trying.

Meanwhile, at La Nesra, not more than three miles away.

"My God," Lilly breathes, sitting in a state of disbelief as Sally relates the details of the raids. "Will Daddy go to jail for killing the deputy?"

"No. The local doctor there said he discussed it with certain people, and they determined to put it in the records as good riddance," she confirms.

"I'm sorry to hear about Jacob. I'll bet Randy and the rest are devastated. You say Colonel Housler is going to be okay?"

"Yes, that's right. Were you acquainted with the Sanders' daughter Elizabeth?"

"Not really. I've seen her before, but she's more Robert's age. I, well, I wasn't allowed to associate much with anybody. I understand now that Mama and Daddy didn't want people to know me because they knew they would have to explain more about my disappearance." Her voice drops off at the end letting those listening know she didn't mean to talk about that.

Sally, wanting to break her friend's mood, smiles and says cheerfully, "Elizabeth and Robert are engaged to be married."

"What? Engaged? Didn't you say she was taken prisoner by the raiders," she blurts in surprise. Without waiting for a response she continues. "Poor Robert, he has to be going out of his mind. He's a person to give his all to whatever he does, so I know he must love her with all his heart. I can't see him sitting around doing nothing, and because of that, I don't think our parents could either."

"You're absolutely right with your thinking," the visiting redhead says quietly, leaning toward the couple from her seat.

"They're here," she whispers. "Your father, Robert, Randall, and your two sisters are here in Atlanta, or they soon will be. They're supposed to arrive today."

Falcon looks at Lilly sitting with a blank look on her face, unable to muster a word. Finally he breaks the silence.

"Trying to locate Elizabeth?" he asks, never taking his eyes off his wife.

"I sure hope I can trust the two of you," Sally prepares herself to take a big chance. "Yes, they're here trying to get a clue as to her whereabouts, but their main concern right now is getting you out of here, Sheree. They're here to take you home with them." She pauses to get a reaction, but when it doesn't come, she adds, "And, I'm here to help them."

At that moment, before another thought can come over any of the three, the outside stairs squeak; someone's coming.

Nora is at the door before anyone thinks to say 'wait.' Her eyes get big with surprise when she backs away, swinging the door open, speechless. Mr. Vaughn's form blocks the light from outside as he enters. He notices immediately a "you've caught us" look on all their faces.

"What have I interrupted here?" he muses firmly, with raised eyebrows, squinted eyes, and a wrinkle on his forehead.

The atmosphere in the room becomes so thick and heavy the floor groans under its weight. Silence. A cold chill goes down Sally's back. One word from anyone in this room will bring an avalanche of trouble down on her. She could be in chains within the hour.

Nora nervously closes the door and announces, "I'll just go take care of Joie, that's all, take care of Joie, and Sherman," she yammers.

Mr. Vaughn's expression changes quickly to a grin. "I see you found your way?" he addresses Sally.

"Yes, no trouble at all," she says back, making every effort to sound calm, confident.

"Don't mean to disrupt your visit. I just want to let you know our meeting is set up for thirty minutes from now at the same place. Do you understand?" He glances at Falcon and Lilly alternately.

"Fine, we'll be there," Falcon replies.

He shakes his head in understanding, turns, and leaves, closing the door. The stairs squeak as he descends.

"Do you suppose he heard what we were talking about?" Sally is quick to ask with a worried look.

"I doubt it. He was only about halfway up here when we heard that squeak. I wouldn't worry about it," Falcon assures, as he rises to peek out the door. "He's gone."

Since Mr. Vaughn has left, and since no one turned her in, Sally is more confident and decides to cast caution to the wind. "Time's running short, so let me get on with it." She is stopped when Lilly comes out of her stupor.

"They're here, to get me? They're really here?"

Sally nods, looking into the young woman's eyes. "Yes, and I'm here to make sure it happens. I've recently made a life changing decision to place my loyalties with your family, and do whatever is necessary to stop the Company. I intend to stay on here as long as I can, but my efforts will be to, ahh, to spy on them. There I've said it. Turn me in if you must."

"Oh, if only this were true," Lilly all but cries.

Sally moves from her seat on her knees to take Joie's mother in her arms.

"It is Sheree. I swear to you, it's true. I'm going to meet them tomorrow afternoon. We need to make arrangements which I'll pass on to them. Then, it's just a matter of time, and you'll be free."

Lilly hugs their visiting messenger, and pants short cries of joy. Tears roll down her cheeks to drop from her chin into her new comradre's red hair. But then with a jerk, she lets go and pushes her away. "What about Falcon and Joie? I'm not leaving here without them. That's not going to happen. And, Nora and Sherman, we've promised them they'll be with us regardless of what we do. We can't leave them behind."

"Thank you, ma'am," is heard from farther back in their home.

"You're right, we can't, but you have to admit, it won't be easy to get just you out. It will be considerably more difficult with so many people," Sally points out.

Falcon, who has kept quiet for the most part, speaks up.

"Craps, honey, we're taking everybody else at their word, we might as well tell her. The truth is, Sally, we can all walk out of here anytime we please. We had our dinner today out under that big tree in front of the main gate. See this ring?" Falcon holds up his hand. "This is our ticket in and out of here. Mr. Vaughn give each of us one."

She takes his hand to get a good look at the ring, then holds up her own. Except for size, they're identical. She shakes her head in disbelief.

"All right, what's going on? The Company doesn't hand these out to just anybody. Have I misjudged you?" She withdraws back to her seat as she speaks.

"It's a long story," Lilly explains. "I'm believing more and more that we all want the same thing. We're all on the same side, but nobody knows it."

"She's right," Falcon picks up where she lets off. "Mr. Vaughn gave these to us because Lilly has done him a huge favor. Because of the favor, he's able to turn against the Company, just as we have. Only, he's brought another person along with him, a higher-up. Together, we plan to do as much damage to the Company as we can, for as long as we can."

"Then, you're planning on staying here?" she wonders with reservations.

"That's been our plan, but that was before she learned about her folks being here. It could be that's all changed now." He looks at his wife.

"Wait. Wait. Wait," Lilly interjects. "Don't put this all on my shoulders. Of course I want to see everyone again. It's been a long time. But I said earlier, and I meant it, I want to be with my husband and baby girl. That's what I know for sure. Beyond that it's your decision, honey. We're a family now."

Knowing his wife, this beautiful young woman, is choosing him above everything else is music to Falcon's ears. It removes any doubt of her motives, or questions of her loyalty.

"What time and where are you meeting tomorrow?" he asks Sally.

"Right after dinner at a place called My Mama's Home Cooking. It might be better, since we're all going, to meet me just before you get into town. I can lead you there. They'll be so surprised. They're not expecting you at all," she answers cheerily.

"I'm in favor of making no further commitments until we've had a chance to talk this over with your family," he speaks to his wife.

"What about this meeting in a few minutes?" she points out.

"We have to agree with them. At least for the time being."

"It's settled, then," Sally breathes a soothing sigh of relief. "Meet me at eleven in the morning, just this side of town."

"I suppose I can muster up a team and carriage with this ring?" Falcon ponders.

"I'm sure you can. Let me get out of here so you can get to your meeting. See you tomorrow. Your family is in for a big surprise," Sally feels good about herself, at least for the moment, as she bounces down the outside stairs.

"I'm glad to see you're on time," Mr. Vaughn comments as Lilly and Falcon enter the small room in the basement of the main building.

"They're here," he calls to the man hidden behind the curtain.

"Good, I'm glad. Are you enjoying your newly acquired freedom? I saw you leaving earlier today, it looked like a picnic basket you were taking with you," the man comments.

"Yes," Falcon relates. "It's nice to be able to get away for a couple of hours."

"Good. Have you made a decision?" His question is direct to the point.

"Yes, we've decided to stay. We have a need though. We need to know what you know, with absolutely no secrets between us. It's the only way I'll be able to do the job at hand. I must be certain of our position in the overall scheme of things," Falcon declares.

"I hear you, and understand your thinking. I can agree to your need to a point, but let me explain. The activity you and I are talking about is just one facet of everything I have on my hands. I'll not be able to get you involved with, nor keep you appraised of all that's going on with everything. But then, I don't think that's what your asking, is it? You're concerned with our relationship as it pertains to your efforts, correct?"

Falcon studies for a moment.

"Yes, that's right, as far as that goes. To be specific, I don't want to have to dig for information you already have at your disposal. I will expect you to volunteer anything you are aware of that pertains to my tasks at hand. In other words, I want all the facts, all the time, about anything my family and I are involved with."

Lilly feels a warm swelling of pride as she hears her husband speak.

"What else is in there?" she wonders in amazement. "And his nerve, wow."

"I can subscribe to that as long as our agreement is reciprocal," the voice counters.

"Agreed," Falcon acknowledges.

"One last thing, when do we meet face to face?"

The young man's question is unexpected by Mr. Vaughn. "That time will co—"

He is cut off by the voice behind the curtain. "Now's as good a time as any."

The curtain slides to the side to expose a man standing with his arm outstretched looking for a hand to shake.

He's over six feet four inches tall and dressed mostly in black. His green eyes are quick to take in everything. His hair, almost white, probably showing up gray out in the light, is parted in the middle to hang down the sides of his head and lays on his shoulders. Heavy eyebrows, a mustache, a strong nose, and a square jaw make him something to behold. His looks make him one imposing man.

Lilly and Falcon both think. "I've never seen him around here before. I'd remember it if I had."

"My name is Black, Tyrone Black. People call me Ty." He smiles as he waits for a hand to come toward him.

Falcon takes a big breath, rises and grabs the man's hand. Lilly stands beside her husband.

"Glad to meet you both." His voice seems stronger since they can see him.

"I believe I've met your father," he addresses the young woman.

"Really? Where?"

"It was in a deputy sheriff's office back in your hometown a couple of weeks ago. I'll let him tell you about it when you see him. Your brother, Robert, as I recall, a young black man . . . Randall, I believe was his name, and two of his brothers, were there. I imagine you're anxious to see them."

"You mean you don't mind if I see my family?" she quickly confirms.

"That's what I'd want to do if I were you. You've been away from them for a long time. We have an agreement now, and I expect you'll honor it. Beyond that, I think you should get reacquainted with them as soon as you can."

She feels like a small child, one that's been granted a big wish.

"Thank you for that," she expresses to Ty. "And, Mr. Vaughn, I want to thank you, too. This would never have happened without you, thank you."

Ty sits down on his chair on his side of the wall, and motions for the three to do likewise. He looks at Mr. Vaughn. "Now that we all know each other, let's chat for a bit. How far have you gotten with telling them about the Company?"

"Not that much. This whole thing has happened so quickly, there hasn't been time."

"I see. I'll make a few assumptions and pick my place then." He decides. "Let's talk technology. Maybe that's a new word for you, but you'll understand its meaning as we go along." His starting point piques interests.

Lilly and Falcon look at each other wondering why he doesn't ask the location of the men in the containers. That's what they would ask, first thing.

"When the Korgot transports left our earth to go back to their home, they left behind all sorts of information and machinery. The sight and use of these far-advanced abilities is what kept the human race from overrunning our intruders' smaller numbers. Things that fly through the air on their own, not like birds with wings, but round things that look like a saucer for a cup, only upside down. They fly at speeds beyond our imagination. First they're here, blink your eye, and they're gone. They left guns that shoot a light. A light so hot it melts anything it touches. Iron, steel, rock, wood, the human body, it makes no difference; the light burns right through them, like a hot knife going through a big block of butter. Things you can hold in your hand and speak back and forth to someone miles away, with no wires attached. Explosives so powerful that a piece the size of a silver dollar could level La Nesra to the ground. Machines that can see through almost anything, and never damage it. Machines, configured to all kinds of work, that crawl along the ground on pliable wheels. Round clear glass bubbles that light up to cast light fifty times as bright as a candle, yet don't melt away. Do you get the idea? Technology."

The young couple does not know how to react. From what they know as compared to what they have just heard sounds like someone's imagination running amuck.

"The look on your faces tell me you find it hard to believe. But I assure you, it's all true, and I've only just begun. It's incredible, the amount of information the Korgots left with us. If we, the humans of our world, would get along together as a big family, we could put it to use and advance our society by twenty centuries, all within a few short years. It's been obvious, however, that unless something changes, it will never happen. Greed and power, one country trying to take over another, wouldn't allow it. A single nation with this information would control the world, or destroy it trying. Well, you say, then why doesn't the Company do that? It seems that's what they're trying to do anyway. Simply put, the human species is the work force needed to accomplish the Company's goal. Even then, it can't be done without a united effort. Humanity has always had one trait shared by all. If we find something we don't understand, we fear it. What's more, if we fear it and we're unable to control it, we destroy it. In this case, if we try to destroy it, there's a strong chance we'll kill ourselves in the process."

Falcon speaks up.

"Are you saying the Company has been, and is, hiding all this new knowledge, keeping it from the human race?"

"Yes, and has been for centuries," Ty replies. "Keep in mind that the tremendous task of stockpiling this whole world's riches into one big pile can only be accomplished with manpower. The Company's objective is to enslave the entire human race with a process people will welcome, and keep on working.

"If the entire world of humanity was to rise up together, the Company would cease to exist. The strength of our masses of people would exceed the Company's ability to use the technology. After that, some people within the masses, those craving power and extreme wealth, would use the captured technology against each other, destroying the world as we know it."

"So, when the transports arrive to load up the earth's riches, they would find nothing. Not a living soul," Lilly thinks out loud. "You mentioned a minute ago, a plan the Company is working. What is it?" she continues thoughtfully.

"Remember now, you two, it's not at all as simple as I'm explaining. It would take us years to get into all the facets and aspects of what's gone on for centuries and that which is going on today. Then to explain why, well, that would take years beyond that. I'm only trying to give you a brief understanding."

"Yes, we know," Falcon assures the man in black.

"The plan has been adjusted all along to become what it is today," he starts again. "It has boiled down basically to this. The one way to get the entire human race to work together as one, without fighting amongst ourselves, is to give us the belief we are free to do whatever we want. But create an atmosphere where we can only get what we want through work. Let us work at what we want, doing what we like and enjoy. Let us surround ourselves with possessions of our choice. Allow us to mate and raise our families as we see fit. All we have to do is follow certain rules. Then give us the added belief that our reward at the end of it all, for doing a good job, is a place beyond our physical life. A place where we can spend an eternity with our loved ones, enjoying everything we can imagine. A place where grief, pain, and tribulation no longer exist. All of this and the Company takes it another step further.

"A human must be kept wanting something. We must have something new to work for, something to desire. The Company's answer to that is to release pieces of their new technology in the form of useful items. This new information is chosen carefully so as not to confuse the issue by suggesting an article before its proper time. People like us have to be willing to accept it. If it's too far advanced, we'll reject it. As I said before, if we don't understand it, we want no part of it."

"Are you saying that a lot of the new things we see these days aren't really invented by the people who claim them?" Lilly questions.

"More that you realize, but not all. Humanity is very creative. Uses of some of the technology has been applied way beyond its original purpose.

"Great care is taken to leak information to the right people situated in the right places, and doing it in a way to let them claim its origin. Give them the object with a complete explanation of what it does, then let them work backward to invent it."

Mr. Vaughn has remained quiet for some time, but interjects now.

"Does what he's saying sound familiar to you?" He addresses the young couple.

"Yes, it does," she confirms. "It sounds like the life we're living now."

"This is worrisome to me," Falcon states flatly. "If our lives are nothing but lies, if we're just puppets on somebody's strings. I mean, what's the point? What's the use?"

"Oh, don't misunderstand," Ty is quick to correct. "Your life isn't a lie. What you see and what you have are real. Your wife and child exist and are yours to hold. You have a future. You can do what you want with your lives. Your children, and their children, will do as they desire, too. That's not a lie. Your usefulness is to them, yourself, and your fellow man.

"Don't you see? The plan makes sense, and that's why it will continue to work. It's what people dream about. Add to that, the majority of the human race is made up of followers. We want to be told what to do. We grasp at something we can believe. If everyone in the world could live this life in peace with each other, with the here ever after guaranteed, what more could we ask? Why would anybody question such a life?"

"Why has it taken the Company so long?" Falcon wonders. "If this is such a great plan, what's stopping them? It's obvious they're not even close to having the whole world under their control."

"It's because of people like you, your wife, Mr. Vaughn here, and me. People like us who want more control over our own destiny. You, Falcon, impressed me a few minutes ago when you said 'I want to know what you know.' You're not willing to blindly go about your business. You want to know the whys and purpose of what you're doing. You want to know what tools are at your disposal to get your job done. You want any information you can get to help make decisions as you go. You think for yourself, with an open mind. That's what slows down the Company's plan. People like us work against the plan, in most cases unknowingly. We know what we want, and that may not be what we're told we want."

Mr. Vaughn interrupts Ty. "If we expand our knowledge to include all the countries of the world, and not just where we live, it's easy to understand how readily some nations accept the Company's teachings. Any number of countries entire population will fall easily into place, just as leaves are drawn to the ground when they are released from trees in the fall of the year. There's nowhere else to go, nothing else to turn to."

"I don't think I like what's going on here," Lilly squirms on her chair. "I'm not settled yet with what I've found out about myself. I don't understand all of that. The more I learn about all of this makes me want to run and hide. It's seems there's nothing left that's the way I thought it was. I feel confused and, I don't know, sort of like I've been left behind, alone. I don't want to hear any more about this today. I need some time to sort this out in my mind."

"I completely understand the feeling, Lilly," Ty sympathizes. "Just let me add a few words before we go. All is not lost. We've been addressing only the objectives of the Company. It isn't too late for us to make a difference. Wherever our destiny leads us, remember this. Our spirits don't die when our bodies give out. We'll live on in a place better than this life on earth, even if the earth no longer exists. The pure truth is, as yet, no one has come back from there to tell us about it. No one, and I mean no one, here on this earth, can guarantee anything to anybody else. It's all a matter of what we believe as individuals. As for me, I believe we have a life beyond this one. I don't just believe it. I know it for a fact. But I don't want the Company to have any part in it."

Lilly nods her head in agreement. "Amen," she closes.

"One last thing," Ty surmises.

"Probably, none of us asked to be introduced to this job of working for the Company. We were, most likely, forced into it through circumstance. The Company, over the years, has taught us not to ask many questions, just accept what they tell us, do their bidding, and be loyal to nothing else. Most of the people within the Company support their plan completely. I don't have numbers to back this up, but I imagine there are tens of thousands of people working for them. The only way to destroy something this size is from the inside. Turn them against themselves. Use their own tools against them. That's where we come in, and the reason you two are so important to our cause. Thank you for listening. I'm glad you're with us."

"Now, why don't you take us to those containers you found?"

They both look at Mr. Vaughn, wondering if he's told Ty about his life body.

"Ty knows about my body, I have nothing to hide from him." He anticipates their concern and explains.

"Did you bring the key?" Lilly asks her husband.

"Yeh, let's go," he answers as he stands.

"Keep in mind, folks, this is still a secret, and must be kept that way. I'm not sure if anybody else knows the death angels are here, let alone where they're located. So, let's split up and make sure we're not followed," Mr. Black cautions the group.

"Let's meet in the building where we met before, Mr. Vaughn," Lilly suggests.

They meet fifteen minutes later at the small, seldom used, equipment building as planned. The four of them then move swiftly, directly, to the door at the back wall.

Once inside, Lilly locates and lights a candle. Without speaking she leads the way through the hidden hallway to the brightly lit chamber housing the bodies.

"Will you look at this," Ty comments. "I've been through the tunnel in this wall any number of times over the years. Never suspected, or even thought about, a room such as this. How did you find it?"

"Purely by accident. How long do you suppose they've been here?" Lilly wonders.

"There's no way of knowing for sure. They could have been put here right after this place was built. That was over fifty years ago," Ty offers as he walks from container to container, peering inside each one.

"That means these were here before my body disappeared. So, someone put me here later, which means they've been back during these recent years," Mr. Vaughn exposes a possibility.

"Yes, a good point," Ty agrees. "But it doesn't necessarily mean those people are still at La Nesra, or for that matter, if they're still alive."

"Do you know how to get him out of there?" Lilly asks.

"I'm afraid not. I was just pondering our options," he answers.

Mr. Vaughn looks down at himself in the container.

"Here's the way I see it. We use me to figure out how to do it. If something happens to my body, then at least we won't have destroyed one of the good guys. I'm just happy to have found my body. I'm willing to take the chance, and if something goes wrong, well, it's my decision."

"That's very brave of you. I think it's a good decision," Ty agrees.

"Let's think about this before we go poking around," Falcon suggests as he begins to look for the logic of it all.

"Smashing this clear glass on top would be like taking a hammer to the bung on an unmarked barrel. We don't know what might start coming out of there. The air might be different from anything we know. Once we break that glass, there's no turning back. Also, there's those little wire looking things. They look like they're hooked up to his skin. They come out of the container at the bottom and go over here to hook up to this box with the flashing things. It would make sense to me that this glass top should come off without breaking. I suggest we look this thing over for a place to push or pull something. You know, just like the way we got the wall to open up to get in here," Falcon offers for consideration.

"We won't hurt anything that way. Let's do it," Lilly agrees with her husband.

They each take an area closest to them and begin looking slowly, carefully running their hands and fingers over the surface of the glass, including around the edges where it meets the container. Nothing.

Ty squats down on his heels to look up under the container, balancing himself with his hand on the top of the glass near the foot of it.

"Nothing under here," he comments and starts to rise. Unwittingly, he puts pressure on the top of the glass with his hand.

Click, click! A sound like someone has tapped the glass with a piece of metal gets everyone's attention.

When he removes the pressure of his hand the glass moves up at a slant from that end and continues to rise, bringing folding supports with it. Everybody steps back defensively to watch it smoothly level out and continue up for another three feet, then stop, held in the air by the folding supports, two on either side. The entire glass cover has moved up and away, exposing Mr. Vaughn's body.

"Will you look at that?" Lilly spurts in amazement, eyes wide.

Mr. Vaughn is the first to move back to the container to look down. "The wires, they've fallen off! They're not attached any more!" he exclaims.

"How do you feel?" Ty addresses his cohort, concerned his body might be dying.

"I feel fine . . . wonderful."

Falcon looks around from face to face gathering the feelings of his alliances. He glances at the black box.

"This box isn't flashing anymore."

Everyone's eyes move to the box when they hear his words.

"Let's not get in a hurry," he cautions. "Let's think about this. Should we take your body out of there? Are you thinking of returning to it now, or later?"

"To be perfectly honest, I'm a little unsettled with that. I never thought we'd get this far."

"It's your call, Mr. Vaughn," Ty explains.

"Could you all leave me alone here for a few minutes? I need to ponder this out for a little while, by myself."

"You bet. We'll wait out in the tunnel. Come out there when you're ready. Take your time, this is a big move." Ty spreads his arms, as he moves toward the exit, indicating to Lilly and Falcon they should leave, too.

The three wait in the entry tunnel near the door to the courtyard, milling around without speaking, mulling over all that's happened today. A single candle makes their shadows move on the floor and walls. Fifteen minutes pass.

Mr. Vaughn appears through the opening of the sliding wall to stand perfectly still in the dim light.

"Have you decided?" Ty asks.

"It's me. I did it. It's me," he says contentedly and gives a teethy smile.

"You mean, you're . . . ?" Lilly doesn't finish when he nods his head with an exaggerated yes.

"How does it feel?" Falcon asks in surprise.

"A little bit odd, I'd say, but better all the time. A little stiff, but I imagine I'll loosen up as I move around. Most of all I feel whole; I feel like I'll sleep good tonight."

"It just occurred to me," Falcon realizes. "You're container is open and empty. If anybody comes in here to check on anything, they'll see you're gone. It won't take but a few seconds for them to conclude it was you in here, after your body. They'll know you've seen everything in there. That could put you at risk."

"I'm not getting out of my body. I hope I never have to do that again." The older man stands firm.

"Not only that, we don't know how to close this sliding wall either. We need to find a way to cover our tracks," Falcon continues.

"We don't know if this wall will ever open again once we find a way to close it. We'd be better off to leave everything as it is until we can fix it all," Lilly explains.

"Yes, you're right. We're going to have to risk it until we find a few solutions to cover ourselves completely," Ty asserts. "Let's sleep on it."

"Another thought just occurred to me, I'm mortal now. If somebody stabs me in my sleep, I'll die, just like anyone else." Mr. Vaughn looks at his hands and arms.

Sunrise brings the beginning of a beautiful spring day to the Atlanta area. Falcon is up early to get breakfast, and trot over to the livery to see about a carriage for the day. His family is supposed to meet Sally at eleven this morning, just this side of Atlanta. That means they'll have to leave La Nesra no later than a little after ten to be there on time. Lilly expressed last night she doesn't want to be late for any reason.

He makes sure he flashes his ring when he asks the smithy for a rig. It turns out to be no problem at all. "Come back in a half hour and I'll have it ready for you." Those words are music to his ears. The carriage turns out to be a smaller one, just enough room for the five of them. Nora wants to change her mind about going, stating she and Sherman will only be in the way, but Falcon and Lilly will not hear of it. The words "You're coming, like it or not" are used convincingly.

Falcon and Nora's six-year-old sit up front, while she and Lilly, holding Joie, occupy the back seat, as ladies should, according to Sherman. A single horse trots along pulling the load with little effort.

Sherman has taken to Falcon and talks continuously, pointing, craning his neck, this being the first full day of his life outside the walls of La Nesra. To an onlooker, they appear to be a happy family headed to town for the day.

"There she is," Falcon announces. "Just like she said." The carriage pulls to a stop adjacent to the surrey with Sally, sitting alone, holding the reins.

"Follow me into town to the blacksmith's. You can stay there while I go on to get your family. I've thought it over and it's not a good idea for all of us to show up at the restaurant where we planned to meet. It's small, and we'd draw a lot of attention. I'll talk it over with them and decide on a better place, then I'll come and get you. It shouldn't take more than fifteen minutes. Okay?" Sally explains.

"Yeah, that makes sense. Lead on," Falcon responds.

True to her word, Sally is gone not more than ten minutes when she returns to the blacksmith's barn where the expanded Justice family waits patiently.

"Robert and Randall are staying in a little cottage not far from here. They're all going over there now. It's a perfect place to meet. Follow me," she explains cheerfully.

"Do they know we're coming?" Lilly asks, feeling a bit edgy.

"Yes, I had to tell them. They're all excited. They wanted to know if you're bringing your baby. Come on, they'll be waiting."

Five minutes later, Falcon, Lilly, and family are climbing down from the carriage in front of the same little cottage Bob and Randy rented the last time they were in Atlanta. The front door flies open when they step up onto the porch followed by happy cheers and words of gladness. Once inside, introductions are made, then it's hugs and kisses all around. Baby Joie is passed around like a hot potato, with the women all begging to be next. Sherman takes to Randy as though they knew each other in another life. He's on his lap the minute he sits down. Little by little, the commotion settles and everyone finds a seat. Some use cushions on the floor. Nora's in the kitchen bringing the coffee. Even while tussling with Sherman, Randy is unable to take his eyes off his once best friend, Sheree.

"Does she remember me?" he thinks. "I've changed a lot, I know. She might not know who I am."

He doesn't wonder too long. She gets her husband's hand and drags him behind her. "Come here you," she boldly states, her arms stretched out.

Randy dumps Sherman on the floor, and puts his arms around his friend. A long, gentle, meaningful hug ensues. Carefully, not in a big hurry, she moves away, leaving one arm around his waist, to face her husband.

"Honey, I want you to meet a very good friend, my very first boyfriend. This is Randall Stoker. I've always called him Randy.

"Randy, my husband, Falcon."

Handshakes are exchanged.

She looks into Randy's eyes and says, "We have some catching up to do. We'll make sure we have time to talk later. Okay?"

Randy nods.

Knowing a lot of information needs to be exchanged among everyone here, she leads Falcon back to his seat and sits down, glancing at her sisters Charlotte, and Amber, or is it Cheryl.

"How did you manage to get away?" John is the first to ask a question.

"Oh, Daddy, it's a long story, I want to know about Mama, and everybody back home first. I heard from Sally there was a raid. How are they?" she asks, ready to hang onto his every word.

"I wish your mother could be here with us. It would be perfect if she was here," Joie's grandfather points out.

The room gets quiet as John starts explaining the raid, the days after, including the killing of the deputy, and the sadness surrounding the deaths of so many friends. He keeps to the point and shortens the story as best he can. Eyes still well up when those who were there relive the deaths.

Lilly dries her eyes, one at a time, with the back of her right hand.

"I'm so sorry for all of you. I don't know what to say. I know how much it hurts to have loved ones taken away from you," she says without thinking.

"I'll never forgive myself for what I let happen to you, Sheree." Her daddy picks up on what she said and comments soberly. "I won't ask for your forgiveness, because I can't see how something like that can be forgiven. I'll live with it the rest of my life. All I can say is, I love you, and have always loved you. That'll never change. I just hope that one day you'll be able to look at me without thinking about what I did to you." John hangs his head as tears flood to his eyes.

"Oh, Daddy, I didn't mean it that way. I didn't think—" she starts sobbing, looking at her father, then jumps up and goes to throw her arms around him. They hold each other and cry out loud. The rest of the room is in tears watching the reunion. Falcon is crying as hard as his wife, his are tears of joy that they are together again.

"I love you too. I've never stopped loving you and Mama. My memories are how the kindest, warmest, best parents in the world took care of me when I was young. I forgive you, just love me like you did back then, make me your daughter again. That's all I want." Lilly's sobbing becomes heavier.

Charlotte and Cheryl move to Lilly's side and put their arms around her and John. A good cry follows for the next few minutes. Lilly's arms work their way around her sisters.

Robert has stayed back away to witness it all. Finally, he rises to take the few steps to close the distance between them.

"When is it going to be my turn?" he says, choking back a lump in this throat.

Lilly hears his voice and pulls away from the huddle to jump up and throw herself at him. The crying starts all over again. This time Randy joins them to put his arms around his two best friends. Then Falcon joins the group, all rejoicing the reunion.

Nora stands back away, holding Sherman in place in front her with an arm down over his shoulder, wiping tears from her eyes with her other hand.

Sally sits poised, hanky in hand, soaking up tears before they roll down her face.

After a while, when the tears have dried up, a sense of warmth takes over the small cottage, and conversation begins between and among everyone present. There are periods of laughter, and periods of seriousness. Falcon is accepted as one of the family, and is told as much. Lilly has to look around occasionally to be sure Joie is still there. Robert and Randy make a trip to My Mama's Home Cooking, and bring home enough food for everyone. Anything and everything is discussed. Lilly and Randy find a few minutes to speak privately.

"I know this must be a shock to you, Randy. Sometimes it doesn't seem real to me. With all that's going on it's almost like I'm living someone else's life. I need you to believe I thought I would never see you or any of my family again."

"Do you truly love him?" Randy tries to learn in a mature fashion.

"Yes, I do, with all my heart. But I still remember what we were to each other, and if you can, I want our friendship to be as close as it was back then."

"I want that too, Sheree. It's okay now that I know you're happy. I thought maybe you were forced into something. So, yeah, that's what I want too."

Time moves on as do the conversations. It's just a matter of time until Lilly, Sally, Charlotte, and Cheryl, come together. Lilly, knowing Cheryl is actually Amber, who was sent to spy on her family, and Cheryl, knowing Lilly is aware of it, are at odds with each other with their glances and expressions. Charlotte is speaking in an effort to bring Lilly up to date.

"So, were you aware that you have two brothers?" she asks and looks coyly at her sister.

"No, that's really news to me. Where are they? Who are they?"

"They're our duplicates. There were five of us born at the same time, the three of us and the two of them. They've been living with the Stokers all these years. I'm not sure they know who they are."

"You're talking about the twin boys, aren't you?"

"Yep, our family is a mess. Cheryl here was taken away from Mama when she was born. They told her she was stillborn, and look, here she is. Mama's swears there's no more of us, but I wonder."

Lilly sits in a stare, thinking about her mother and all she must have gone through. Cheryl's voice snaps her out of it. "I don't blame you for feeling the way you do about me, Sheree, and I can't imagine that you'll ever look at me as your sister, but, I am. I'm from the same flesh and blood as you and Charlotte. Once I met our family, I couldn't start spying on them. To be honest, I tried to force myself, but I fell in love with everybody, the farm, the neighbors—everything. I'm truly an Anderson, now and forever. I have no loyalties to the Company, none at all. I, more than anyone, know what you've been through here at the Company. Until I went home, I never knew anything else. That gives you and me a lot in common. I sense that if we can get over our suspicions and fears of each other, we can be great friends. I, for one, want to take this opportunity to try. Will you?"

Lilly looks at her sister soberly. "I don't hate you. Hell, I don't know you. Right now, I don't know what I know. Everything is coming at me from all directions, all at once. Not just here, everywhere. I haven't seen my family for a long, long time. And I'm not the Sheree they remember. I've changed, and so have they. Right now, I have more important things on my mind than making friends with you. I'm sorry, but that's the way it is. So, don't push. Things will work out the way they should, but it'll take time." Feeling she has gone too far, she cuts herself off.

"That's an honest assessment," Sally intervenes, speaking for both women. "It's a good place to start. I'll say this. I never thought I would know three beautiful women that resemble each other so much. If it weren't for your hair and skin colors, I don't know if I could tell you apart. But anyway, we're all on the same side now, and in time, we'll let go of the past. A year from now we'll not often think of these times."

Eventually, Robert and Lilly find themselves sitting together at the kitchen table.

"Do you have any idea where Elizabeth could be?" she begins, just to open the topic for conversation.

"No, not really," he responds despairingly. "We're hoping to turn something up while we're here. Since you're safe, we'll probably look around for a few days, and if nothing comes up, we'll go on down to New Orleans. They said they were going to sell her there."

"May I enter your conversation? I couldn't help but overhear what you were saying," Sally speaks from her seat at the other end of the table.

Lilly and Robert turn to look at her.

"I have a thought, that's all. You know, we have a lot of eyes and ears available to us. The Company has agents everywhere. They can do a faster and more thorough job of it. Believe me, if anybody can find Elizabeth, they can, and I can put the word out tomorrow. It could take a week or two, but we'll find her."

"You can do that?" Robert asks, afraid she's overstepping her abilities.

"She can do it, Robert," his sister confirms.

Hearing that, he lets out a yell loud enough to wake a sleeping drunk a mile away.

"Yeeeoooowwwweeeee! Ha! Ha! Haaaa!"

"I would have told you before, but I didn't know then that Sheree had her freedom. We had to get her out first," Sally explains, elated with his response.

"Good Lord, this has been a wonderful day. Thank you, Sally," he throws his arms into the air, smiles, and blows her a kiss.

"Did you hear that, Daddy? We're going to find her! We're going to find Beth!"

While all of this is going on, few realize it, but the war has unofficially started. Troops of the Confederate states have taken over several Union forts, mostly in the Southern states, with little or no resistance. A fort on the east coast is under siege and has been cut off from supplies and reinforcements for more than a week. It seems the political powers of the Union are holding back, hoping the problem will go away. They know a civil war will be costly beyond the worth of a dollar. It will take its toll on America's most valuable possession, the young men and women from both sides.

Many feel this waiting, stalling, will cost the Union a victory over the South. They feel, and are loudly vocal about it, the South should be hit hard and relentlessly. The foe should be stepped on like a bug by the powerful industrial states of the North.

The Confederate states of the South, however, have wasted no time putting a plan together. They are keenly aware of the North's ability to outproduce them with material needs to support a war. Beyond that, they understand the North can muster many more soldiers to bear arms. The vast majority of the population of this young country lives north of the line drawn across it by a stated commitment to the South.

The idea of their plan is to force the Union to spread their army thin over a large area. A strike here and there to show the South's might, and the taking of small towns will force the Union to send troops to regain the ground. Then, it will cost the North a portion of those troops to hold the position, as well as require soldiers to transport supplies to support them. Take the towns and cities, then withdraw under fire when the Union forces arrive. Keep up the pressure making it a larger and larger problem for the North. Spread them out; make them regain; make them defend; and make them supply troops along hundreds and hundreds of miles of geography.

The South also knows a war is won by securing the opposition's flag. That can only be accomplished by going after it with large, trained, properly outfitted forces, and a strategy to limit their own losses. The foe's main army must be defeated. Once that's accomplished, it's matter of marching forward, and hanging the Confederate flag as they go. Picking the proper time and place for the confrontation is crucial.

The North has been in the process of preparedness for some time. They have watched as the South overruns their forts, claiming the arms and supplies. Their carefully considered plan is to surround the Confederate South much like a large snake, cutting off any supplies expected from outside their domain. Once in place, this large snake will constrict its powerful coil, closing it tighter and tighter, crushing everything in its path. There are those in the Union military who believe this approach will take to long, cost too many lives. A strategy of marching a huge army directly to Birmingham, Alabama, to thwart the enemy at their core, their capital, makes more sense. It is expected the South will bring its biggest and best aim at the political seats of the North. Washington DC, Philadelphia, and New York City top the many on an endless growing list. It is decided, after much deliberation, to keep the capital of the Union at Washington DC, although, considering it's location, it appears to be an easier target for the South.

Those opposed to marching a mighty army to Alabama claim that approach will only scatter the enemie's forces, creating many smaller fronts to be fought, which could take years and years. They all agree that a civil war must have a clear victor. The loser must be soundly defeated, demoralized, and be glad if they must lose, that it is finished.

Factories in the North are changing their production from consumer products to those of war as quickly as possible. The Union's recruiting process is aggressive, mandating training camps to sprout up all over.

The location: the Anderson farm. Time: the afternoon of the reunion of the Anderson family at Atlanta.

June is walking from the barn, just back from town checking for word from her family in Atlanta. She stopped at the guesthouse on the way home to be sure all is well there.

The sound of horses galloping, coming closer, hits her ears. Instinctively, she yells.

"Jim! Josh! Close up the barn and get your guns. There's horses coming in on the run."

She reaches the front porch to fly up the steps, through the door, then back out on the porch, and stand holding a scattergun, awaiting trouble. Her hand goes up to shade her eyes.

"Must be fourteen or fifteen of them. They're moving around in the group, making it hard to count at this distance," she thinks.

As they near the edge of the yard, she can see they are soldiers. Soldiers dressed in gray. She's a bit relieved they're not renegades.

The group stops in front of her, back away from the porch. One man dismounts and approaches.

"Afternoon, ma'am, I'm Captain Curtis with the Confederate States of America cavalry," the neatly dressed but dusty young man says, while grabbing the brim of his hat to give it a tug.

She stands still, her finger on the trigger of the scattergun held at her waist, laying across her other arm.

"I'm the point of a garrison that'll be here in a couple of hours. My orders are to secure this house as a military quarters. We don't mean any harm to anyone here, but you'll have to leave within the hour."

June doesn't move or speak.

"Did you hear me? You're going to have to leave. Troops are on their way here."

"Look over your left shoulder, young man. Do you see that man standing there with a torch in his hand? One touch of that torch to the barrel of that cannon, and the bodies of your men will be cluttering my front yard. I haven't invited you here, so git, and don't come back!" she demands coldly, with as mean a look she can muster. June is hardened with experience. There is no fear in her and it shows.

The officer takes his hat off and wipes his brow with his bandanna.

"Don't be this way, ma'am. If you don't leave, they'll blast you out of here." He wipes the inside of his hatband as he speaks and puts it back on his head.

"That's what it's going to take. Now, get back on your horse, and lead your men out of here, or the general will have to climb over your bodies to get to me. Move!" June yells her last word.

Captain Curtis mounts up and is about to leave when he stops.

"Ma'am, I'm serious. They'll set their cannon back there out of your range and blast you until they're sure you're not going to shoot back. They don't care about you or your home. Hell, they don't care how many people they kill. They have orders too. This is war."

June waves the end of her gun at him, warning him off.

The horses leave in a thunder of hoofbeats.

"Looks like you scared them off, Miss June. Good for you," Belle announces from just inside the door, holding a rifle, ready to help if necessary.

"All I've done is buy us a couple of hours, Belle. They'll be back just like he said, and there will be a hundred or so of them then. Send one of the hands over to the guesthouse, and let them know we're coming. Then round up everybody. Let's get as much as we can loaded on our wagons. We'll get out of here before they get back. Tell whoever you send to stay there at the guesthouse, and don't let them send anybody over here. We're not going to fight. No sense in it," June issues the orders, then walks off the porch to approach Jim, who's still standing next to the cannon holding a burning torch.

"You scared him off, Jim. He didn't like the looks of you with that torch and cannon." She makes a poor attempt at humor aimed at Josh walking up.

"I'm glad we still have those two freight wagons in the barn. Load all the powder and fire arms in one of them. See if you can get this cannon in there too. We have to get out of here before he brings the whole damned army back with him, and I want to take as much as we can."

"Belle, on second thought," she yells. "I want you to take all the children over to the guesthouse. We need all the help we can get here, and we won't have to worry about them that way. I don't know what this army might do when they get here, so tell the colonel to get ready for a fight. Tell him we're bringing another cannon with us. And tell him we're bringing all our horses, too."

"Yes, ma'am, Miss June. I'll do just that. Tell whoever packs up my kitchen to bring everything they can. I got a feeling I'm going to need it. I just hope I can keep Miss. Selma from coming back over here. You know how she is," she calls over her shoulder, as she leaves to round up the children.

"Jim, Josh, should we blow the place up and burn it to the ground? That's what Robert says we're supposed to do," June invites opinions.

"No, ma'am," Josh is quick to reply. "We're taking almost everything with us. What we'll be leaving behind won't be much help to them. They'll probably kill our cattle to feed themselves, but burning the place down won't stop that."

"I think he's right, Miss June. Besides these are army people, not raiders. Maybe they won't bother much of the house, unless they just have to," Jim agrees.

"Then we won't. Let's get these wagons and anything else with wheels, loaded, and get out of here."

The next hour and thirty minutes pass without notice. June checks her watch.

"We'd better tie down what we have, Jim. We don't want to be here when they come, and it's getting close to the time," she looks at two freight wagons, two buckboards, two carriages, a surrey, and three two-wheeled carts, with horses hitched, piled high with everything imaginable, from the house and barn. Ropes are wrapped around and thrown over articles until they're secured for the trip.

"Let's roll," she commands just as Selma comes galloping in.

June climbs up to the driver's seat of the lead freight wagon.

"What are you doing here?" June shouts at her best friend.

"I just couldn't wait any longer. I was just too worried you wouldn't make it out of here in time," Selma replies, then jumps to the ground from her horse, ties his reins to the wagon, and climbs up to sit beside her friend. "What all do you have packed up here?" she asks.

"I have no idea, everybody just loaded things on their own," June responds.

"Are you driving, or am I?"

One at a time, the wagons fall into a single line and steadily move out of the yard on their way. Unknown to them, the company of soldiers moved just out of sight to wait for the rest of their garrison. Two of them lie on their stomachs just over the first rise, watching through their field glasses as the wagons leave.

"They're pulling out now, Captain," one of them calls over his shoulder.

"Good. Let me know when they're out of sight. We'll move in and take over."

Back away from the activity, a lone hunter has noticed the company of Southern soldiers, and has been watching all along. Through his glasses, he sees June send them away, and knows they stopped just over the rise. When the wagons move out, it is obvious to him, these people have been threatened to leave their home. He keeps his position to watch the wagons roll out of sight, and is not surprised when the soldiers move in. He doesn't know what they are up to, but, in his mind, this is not right.

A greeting party stands watching as the heavy wagons move slowly, but steadily, into the yard of the guesthouse.

Selma and June climb down from their seat and walk toward the colonel, who sits in a chair on the front porch awaiting their arrival. He's a whole lot better, but still requires some assistance to move around.

"Looks like you brought the whole place with you, June," he comments.

"We would've if we'd had more time," she replies with a smirk and a jerk of her head.

"Did they say why they're taking your farm?" The colonel wants to know.

"No, and I didn't ask. All he said was his boss had his orders to occupy our farm, and this is war."

"You did the right thing, coming over here. You can't fight their whole damned army."

"I know, but I'm sick inside. You know how it feels. That house and this farm has been my life for a lot of years."

"It's like John said, June. It's the people that matter, not the replaceable things."

June bends down to give him a gentle, but feeling, hug.

"Thanks for that, Charles," she says softly.

"One of the wagons is loaded with the cannon and weapons. What should we do with them?" Selma addresses her husband. "And where are we going to put all these things we brought."

"Honey, let me worry about it. I'm going to sit right here and handle everything. You and June find yourselves a place out of the way, and get settled down. See if Alberta Mae, or Belle, can bring me some coffee, and a bottle of something to sweeten it a little. Everything is going to work out. I'll see to it." The colonel's confident words of being in control, and knowing what to do, are a relief to the two women. Selma bends down to give her husband a peck on the cheek before entering the house with June right behind her.

"Jim, Josh, come over here for a minute!" they hear Charles yell behind them.

It's getting dark in Atlanta, giving a signal to those at the reunion that time has come to break up and go their separate ways for the night. Lilly and Falcon sit together on the front seat of the carriage, with Nora, holding Joie, and Sherman in the back. They've left the lights of the town behind them as they head home to La Nesra. Up to now, they've traveled silently, lost in their own thoughts.

"I miss Mama so much." Lilly's words seem loud with no noise around except for the horse and carriage movement. "I need to see her."

"You will, honey. It might be a few weeks, though. We should settle a few things here before we go anywhere," Falcon points out.

"No, I mean I need to see her now. Tonight," she insists.

"I see what you've got in your head. You want to go through the mirror don't you? Do you realize your mother has no idea about you that way. You'll probably scare her to death."

"I don't have to talk to her, or anything like that. I just need to see her. That's all."

"Well then, go, but promise me that's all you'll do. Don't go there and get involved in something. Promise you'll not go through the mirror once you get there. No matter what's going on, you come back here. Promise?"

"Promise," she swears, knowing that's all she wants to do anyway.

Once they arrive at their snug little home at La Nesra, it isn't long before Nora has Sherman and Joie resting peacefully in their beds.

Lilly gets ready and slips through the mirror, finds Zola, and is on her way to see her mother.

"Open your eyes, you are here, Sheree," Zola comments through Lilly's mind, and is gone at the same time.

Lilly moves to the white portal and peers through.

"Soldiers? Soldiers everywhere. This can't be our house. Zola's made a mistake. Wait, this looks like our home, but there's not much furniture. I need to get in there and look around. I'll be just a minute or two. I won't get involved in anything," she tells herself.

There are soldiers milling around in various stages of dress doing evening, before bedtime, things. They're lying and sitting on cots, which are set up wherever there's room.

"This is going to be hard to do. looking around without being noticed," she realizes. Getting through the mirror into the downstairs hallway is easy. Now, if she can just get a look into one of the other rooms. That's all she needs, just a peek.

She moves toward the bottom of the stairs, sort of heading for the kitchen.

"Hey! Who are you! What are you doing here!"

Some five miles on the other side of town, away from the Anderson farm, a lone hunter walks his horse through the tents of a Union army camp. Since he's alone and moving slowly, no one questions his presence. He stops in front of a large tent, one he figures is the command post. "I need to talk to the head man here," he says to a sentry standing ready to guard the entrance.

"Who are you, and what do you want him for?"

"I want to tell him about a rebel camp I saw a couple of hours ago."

The flap of the tent moves back as a Union officer steps through. The light of a lamp behind him makes it difficult for the hunter to see his face.

"I'm Major Towers," he says, standing there without a coat, his suspenders holding up his pants.

"Come on in here. See if you can find this man some coffee," he orders the sentry.

"What's this about a rebel camp you saw?" the major asks as they enter the tent and seat themselves on two straight-back folding chairs.

"I don't know if it means anything at all, Major, but I just witnessed a hundred or so rebels take over a farmhouse on the other side of town. They made the people there pack up their belongings and leave, then they moved in."

"A hundred of them, you say. That's a whole regiment. They're up to something. Anything else?" the officer asks.

"I suppose not, except there was a woman there with a lot of brass. She stood on the porch with a shotgun and run off their scouting party of fifteen men. That was sure something to see. The whole farm packed up and left right after that. I made a big circle down and away from the area, enough room so they wouldn't see me. I came into town from the South, and didn't see anything unusual going on there. They told me there that you're camped out here."

"Where is this farmhouse?"

"From here, go through town until you come to a split in the road. Then take the right fork. It's the first place you come to."

"Thanks for bringing this to me, mister. We'll see what's going on first thing in the morning. You can bed down here for the night if you like. I can offer you a hot breakfast in the morning."

"Thanks just the same, but I'll just move along. Appreciate the coffee."

Chapter Twenty-Nine

"We're supposed to wait here under this tree for them to come out. Last night, I thought I'd like to get a look at the inside, but now that I'm looking at it I'm glad we're meeting out here," John relates when his group arrives at the designated spot.

"Yeah, me, too. Those walls are very imposing," Charlotte adds.

"We might as well get down and sit in the shade. It might be a while," Robert cues.

Inside the walls at the home of Falcon and Lilly, he's pacing, wondering if something has happened to his wife. She was to be back last night. She promised not to get involved with anything going on at the farm. She should have been gone no more that two hours.

"Lilly's family is probably here by now. I can't wait any longer for her. When she shows up, send her out there. We had planned to tell them together, but it looks like I'll do it myself," he explains to Nora.

"You go ahead, I'll tell her, and don't worry, she'll be here in a little bit."

The guard opens the gate allowing Falcon through to join the group waiting on the other side of the road.

"Where's Lilly, son," John is quick to ask.

"She's not here right now, Mr. Anderson."

"Where is she?" he counters.

"It's a long story, and I wish she was here to tell you, but she isn't, so I'll have to do the best I can."

"I wish you would; we've all been wondering since last night what you have to tell us." Randy becomes outspoken.

Meanwhile, at the Anderson farm.

Lilly tried to get back through the mirror before anyone could grab her last night, but luck was not with her. A soldier caught her by the arm and dragged her kicking and flailing to his superior officer. Thinking fast, she explained that she lives here, then went on the offensive wanting to know where the rest of her family have gone. After an hour of constant questioning with no further success, the officer had her tied to a straight chair in the kitchen, and left her there under guard for the night.

Struggle as she has all night, with the bindings on her wrists tied behind the back of the chair, she's accomplished nothing except to cause burns to stain the ropes with blood. She's had plenty of time to think and listen. "They're here to capture our town. Another army is coming to set up camp on the other side, and as soon as it gets there, they'll attack from both directions. They don't expect much resistance, but they believe the Union will bring forces to take the town back in quick order. Then, both Confederate armies will retreat back here to this farm forcing the Union to commit troops to the town on a continual basis."

The only thing the soldiers will tell her about her family is 'they left.' They don't know where they went, but there was no fight to make them leave. She surmises they are probably at the guesthouse.

"Falcon is going to kill me if I don't get back home before long. I promised I wouldn't go through the mirror, but I did anyway. I want to go to the guesthouse to see if everybody is okay there, but first I have to go back to La Nesra and let him know I'm all right," she thinks as she watches the soldiers in the house move about tending to their duties.

The head man, a colonel, has just dispatched a scouting party of four men to see if the rest of the soldiers have arrived on the other side of town. He told the men to make a wide circle, to stay out of sight, and to get back as soon as they can.

"First things first," she tells herself. "I have to get loose."

"I need to go to the privy," she says to a soldier who's pouring himself a cup of coffee.

"I'll bet you do. It's been a long night. Let me find out," he says kindly and leaves the kitchen. Shortly, he returns with a smile on his face.

"It's okay, but I have to walk you there and back. He said we're to feed you when we get back, too. See, we're not so bad, are we?"

Lilly smiles back at him with no comment. He loosens her ropes so she can slide her wrists free. While he unties her feet from the legs of the chair, she rubs the stinging circles around her arms and wrists.

"Stand up and get your feet under you," he tells her. "Like I say, I have to hold on to your arm there and back. We'll go when you're ready."

She stands for a minute, pretending to get the feeling back into her legs, then moves carefully toward the hallway. The solider has a good grip on her upper right arm. Once into the hallway, she looks around to see soldiers everywhere. She thought this through during the night, and knows there's just one chance. If this doesn't work, she'll not get another.

"It looks like most of the furniture is gone, so I can't be sure there are any mirrors left anywhere, except those I can see right now. I have to get to one I can see, whether they see me go through it or not. I know the hallway mirror is here, that's where I came through. If I can see my way clear, there'll be no time to waste. I'll have to make my move, and make it fast," she thinks. "There's the mirror. There are two soldiers in the way, but I can probably knock them aside by surprise. Here goes."

She jerks forward, causing the soldier's grip on her arm to slide down to her wrist. Then she spins, throwing her left leg over her right arm, and kicks her watchman squarely in the chest with a flying foot. The unexpected force of the blow jolts him backward, allowing her to yank her wrist free. She's leaning forward, ready to dash to the mirror.

The soldier she kicked falls backward, banging into another who loses his grip on his plate of food and coffee cup, causing them to fly through the air to land with the clatter of tin bouncing onto and down the stair steps. That gets everyone's attention. With just a few steps to go, she is not up to full speed when she hits the two soldiers blocking the mirror. Aiming to separate and knock them aside, she goes between them, head down, arms at her side. If not for the surprise, they could easily stop her, but in this case, they fall off balance enough for her to slide past and leap head first at the mirror.

"Where'd she go!" she hears as her feet clear the glass to the other side.

Taking a moment to get herself composed, she watches through the mirror as the soldiers look for her, making all sorts of comments about her disappearance.

"One minute she was here and I had a hold of her arm, and the next minute she's gone! We don't know where she went!" she hears her kindly guard explain to his superior officer.

"I am here," Zola responds to Lilly's thoughts.

'It's about time you got back. You got us worried to death," Nora addresses Lilly firmly as she comes back through the mirror. "Where have you been?"

"I know, I'm sorry Nora, where's Falcon?" she responds hurriedly.

"He went out to the gate. I think your folks are out there."

Nora turns away as Lilly returns to her life body lying on their bed.

"I'll be back," she says, then takes a munch on a biscuit she snatches up from a basket on the table, as she goes out the door.

At the same time, five hundreds yards back toward town from the guesthouse, a company of Union soldiers sits mounted, idle, awaiting word from their advance patrol. It's not long before two riders approach at gallop.

"There's not much to see, Major. There's two cannons mounted in place on either side in front of the house. One's pointing this way and one the other. We didn't see any rebel soldiers at all. There's a few hands doing chores and things like that. It looks pretty quiet to us. Except for those cannons, I'd say there's nothing going on there," one of the scouts informs his commanding officer.

"That hunter last night said the first house we come to, so this must be the place. Doesn't make sense though, a man like that going out of his way to tell us about a Confederate army and all, and then them not be here," the major reiterates, adjusting his seat in the saddle.

"Could be a trap, Major," the other scout speaks up. "Maybe that hunter is one of them. Those soldiers he told us about could be hiding, waiting for us to ride into a crossfire or something."

"Yeah, well, he said there was a hundred or more of them. It's not easy to hide that many men, unless there's a woods close by. Did you see any horses or supply wagons?"

"There's no woods close at all. But there was maybe thirty horses in a corral outside the barn," the first scout replies. "But you know, around here, you should expect that.

There's a lot of stables that cater to different breeds. One thing though, there's a lot of empty wagons setting around."

"We don't have enough men with us to take on a garrison, and since we can't be sure, I'm not going to risk going in there right now. Those cannons worry me. Farmers and horse breeders don't have a need for them. I believe that hunter told the truth, whether he's one of them or not," the major thinks out loud.

"Go on back and bring the column back here, along with four cannons. We'll wait here and see what else we can figure out while you're gone. You should be back in an hour and a half," he orders.

Colonel Housler has taken his position of authority in his chair on the front porch of the guesthouse. Taking no chances, sentries are posted out about two hundred yards around the house. He has just lit his pipe when Josh comes trotting toward him.

"Our hand we sent out there just came and told me he saw two soldiers with field glasses, on horses, looking us over," he says pointing in the direction of town.

"Probably scouts," the colonel surmises. "Those devils, one farm ought to be enough. Damn! Well, tell him to go back out there and let us know if he sees anything else."

"I already did, sir," Josh confirms.

"There wouldn't be any advantage for them to swing around and come in on our other flank, so, let's move that cannon over there alongside the other one. Aim it so they'll cover a wider pattern, and load them with regular ball shot," the colonel points as he speaks. "If they start coming in, we'll warn them off with a couple of shots. Maybe that'll change their minds. Make sure every man has a gun in his hand, and get the children all in the house," he continues. "Might as well be ready."

"We're going to fight them then?" Josh needs confirmation

"We have nowhere else to go," the colonel explains. "We all know our plan, and we've practiced it over and over, so let's be sure everybody's in place when they make their move. We'll make them walk through a bloody hell to get to this house."

An hour passes.

Two of the four soldiers sent by the Confederate colonel occupying the Andersons' home to locate the rest of the Confederate troops jump down from their horses in front of the house and run inside to find their commanding officer.

"What are you doing back here so soon? You haven't had time to follow your orders," he snaps as the two men report in.

"The sergeant sent us back to tell you there's a company of Union soldiers about three miles back toward that town," one of the scouts blurts.

"What are they doing?" the officer asks.

"Nothing. Just sitting around. Looks like they're waiting, or maybe resting their horses."

"You can bet if that's just a company, there's a lot more around somewhere. Get yourselves back out there and keep an eye on them. Let me know if you see any more join up with them, or if they start moving. Stay out of sight. We don't want them to know we're here."

"Yes, sir." The two soldiers turn and leave.

"Captain!" the colonel shouts.

The captain appears at the doorway of the den.

"Sir?"

"I just learned there are Union troops three miles from here toward town. It's a small group, probably a company, but I'm betting there's more close by. Get ready to move if we have to."

Meanwhile, at La Nesra, under a large tree, across from the main gate, Falcon and Lilly's extended family have found a place to sit on the ground and listen.

He's made a decision to tell them everything. For them to grasp it all, the only place to start is at the very beginning.

In awe at times, dismayed at times, riled at times, but, except for an occasional gesture or comment in amazement, they sit silently, taking it all in.

"And so, that's where we are now," he finishes and looks around at each of them, looking for comments.

"Unbelievable!" Robert is the first to react. "So, Sheree's back at the farm."

He cuts himself short when Lilly appears through the gate, walking toward them.

After waiting for her to get close enough to hear, Falcon says, "Where have you been? I thought something happened to you."

"I'm sorry, I got tied up, and couldn't get away until now." The truth, but a lie by omission, so as not to upset her husband.

Robert continues, "So, you've been back at the farm? Is that right?"

Lilly looks at her husband.

"I told them everything?" he explains.

"Everything?" she insists.

"Everything," he confirms.

She looks around at everyone landing at last on her brother. "Yes, I needed to see Mama, so I went there last night. I don't know how to tell you all this, but the only people there are a lot of Confederate soldiers. Mama and the rest are nowhere around. I think, from what I could hear, they went over to the guesthouse when the soldiers took over our farm."

"You didn't see your mother then?" John is quick to ask.

"No, I didn't see any of our people, not Belle, not anybody. They're all gone."

"Any sign of a fight?" Robert poses.

"No, I believe, from what I could see, they must have left and took most of their belongings with them before the soldiers arrived."

"They probably need us back there," Randy joins in. "We'd better get going."

"It's too far. Whatever's going to happen will be over with before we can get there," Robert correctly informs everyone.

“It’s doesn’t sound like the Confederates mean any harm, especially since they were able to take belongings with them. Maybe this whole thing will blow over.” John looks for an easy solution to a distant problem.

“I’d feel a whole lot better about it if we knew everything is okay at the guesthouse. I mean, if they just went there to wait it out?” Charlotte points out.

Lilly raises her right arm and waves her hand a little.

“I can go there and find out.”

They all look at her and realize . . . she can.

“What are you going to do if you get there and everything is not all right? You can’t get involved there all by yourself,” Falcon worries.

“I won’t, whatever it is, I’ll come straight back here.”

“Just like you did last night?” Her husband has a good point.

“Honey, I’m sorry for that, but I came back as quickly as I could. If I hadn’t gone there, we wouldn’t know about this now. I’m okay, nothing happened to me. I’m here,” she testifies, while pulling the cuffs of her blouse down over the burns on her wrists, which are healing.

“Maybe this isn’t the time to get into this, but think about it. If we’re going to fight against the Company, I’ll have to go off on my own once in a while. I can take care of myself. All I’m going to do is go to the guesthouse, look through the mirrors, then come back here. Just like last night,” she counters.

“Let her go,” Robert urges Falcon. “If everything’s okay, then we can get on with finding Elizabeth. We won’t worry about it if we know.”

The girls join in with him, “Let her go.”

“Well, all right, but if you’re not back here in two hours . . .” He doesn’t finish, realizing it is pointless.

“Are you all going to wait here. It could be two hours, or maybe a little longer?” Lilly asks. “Just tell me now where you’ll be and I can come directly there. You can go with them, honey. I’ll tell Nora where you are before I leave.”

“That’s what we’ll do. We’re staying at the Atlanta Grand. My room number is 211. We can all wait there,” John offers. “You’re sure this will work?”

“It’ll work, Daddy, but are you sure about seeing me come back. You have to expect me to come through the glass in the mirror, and the person you see won’t be the real me.”

“Will you look the same, or will you be a ghost?” Randy inquires, his eyes bigger than usual.

The others turn their heads to look at him, then back at Lilly. A good question.

“Once I’m through the mirror, you won’t know the difference.”

“It isn’t that bad. It’s just seeing her do it the first time, that’s all,” Falcon assures.

With everybody in agreement, Lilly gives her husband a peck on the cheek, and turns to walk swiftly toward the gate, waving goodbye over her shoulder.

The Union soldier’s scouting party, waiting for reinforcements from their main camp, sees a lone soldier riding in at a run.

He jumps off his horse while it is still moving, and runs to stop in front of the major.

"There's more of them coming, sir."

"How many?" the major asks, wondering if there's enough for the job to be done.

"The word they had back at camp was about two hundred and fifty."

"I can see we're not talking about the same thing, soldier. Now, what are you talking about?"

"There's two hundred and fifty more rebs coming, sir. They got word by dispatch back at camp after we left this morning. By now they're no more than two hours out, if that."

"Did the lieutenant send anybody with you?"

"He split the troop, sir. There's a hundred and fifty behind me by about forty-five minutes. He's keeping the other half there. He said to tell you if he hasn't heard different from you within an hour, he'll take a stand just outside town and wait, or fight, as the case may be."

"I don't know what's going on here, but you can bet these troops here are meant to join up with those coming in. We've got no time to lose. Are ours bringing any artillery along with them?"

"No, sir, the lieutenant said—" the major cuts him off.

"He'll probably need them there, and, he's right. That's a good decision on his part, but it doesn't help us much."

The major grabs his left wrist with his right hand behind his back and paces four steps out, turns, and four steps back.

"Here's what we'll do."

Fifteen minutes later.

The major sits in his saddle looking through his field glasses at the guesthouse. He has left a rider behind to bring the reinforcement troops to his position.

"I don't see a soul out anywhere up there. I'd expect to see some hands somewhere this time of the day. Let's move up a little closer for a better look."

As soon as the he moves his entire scouting party up to where Josh's sentry can see them, the hand takes off running for the house. He's there and pulled inside before the officer gets his glasses out for a look.

"There's a whole bunch of them coming this way right behind me."

"Thanks, you've done a good job." Colonel Housler pats the hand on the shoulder.

"Jim! Josh! Get you're torches lit. As soon as we're able to see the devils, walk straight out there and light off those cannons. Then reload them with a shot load, and get back in here."

"The rest of our troop should be here any minute, so let's go. At a walk now, and keep your eyes open. This could be a trap," the commander instructs his men.

"There they are!" one of the hands yells from his position at a shuttered window of the guesthouse. Josh and Jim are out the door on the run. They lay their torches down on the fire holes, causing the cannons to answer their command, one at a time, close together.

Boom! Boom!

The Union troops stop and spread out.

"Damn! You were right, Major. They've been expecting us all this time," the sergeant exclaims.

"I'm not sure about that, Sergeant. If their intent is to hurt us, they would've waited until we're in their range. It seems to me these were warning shots. Besides that, I didn't see any Confederate gray on those two men."

"I'll tell you what. Get three men, then tie a white flag on the end of your rifle. Let's see if these people want to talk."

"Corporal."

"Yes, sir."

"Hold the rest of the men here until we get back."

"Yes, sir."

The sergeant follows his orders.

"Ready?"

"Let's go, at a walk. Hold that flag up where they're sure to see it, Sergeant."

The five soldiers proceed toward the guesthouse, the major and sergeant side by side in front, with the three troopers side by side following close behind, all dressed in their Union blues.

"Five of them are coming, holding up a white flag, Charles. I think, yes, they're Union soldiers, not Confederates," June announces.

"They want to talk. Help me out onto the porch somebody!" the colonel expresses urgently.

"Wave them in, Jim!" he yells.

The soldiers keep a steady pace walking toward the house. They see Jim waving his arm signaling them to keep coming. But that's just what they'd do if they were trying to lure someone into a trap.

"Keep your eyes open, men," the major orders with a low voice.

Once they see the colonel being helped out on to the porch, their fears of an ambush lessen.

"This is just a farm family trying to protect themselves," the sergeant observes.

Their horses stop ten yards from the front porch.

"What do you want here, Major?" the colonel demands.

"Are you harboring Confederate soldiers here somewhere, sir?" he answers with a question of his own.

"Hell, no. A garrison of them just took over our other home late yesterday afternoon. All our people had to come here. That's who I thought you was, coming here to try to take this place, too."

"Where did you get those cannons?" the Union officer asks.

"We got them, that's what matters. Now, I'll ask you again. What is it you want here?"

"Nothing. I had a hunter visit me last night explaining about seeing a hundred or so rebel soldiers out here. He said the first house, and you're it."

"He must not know about this house. He meant the main house, is my guess. He was talking about those that threw our people out yesterday. It's over that way—a twenty minute ride. That's where the Confederate troops are."

At the same time at the Anderson home, the two soldiers assigned to watch the Union troops report back.

"They're moving, Colonel. It looks like they're moving into a farmhouse back that way, just like we did here. We didn't wait around to see, but we heard a couple of cannons go off after we left."

"They're the point of a larger force, it seems," the colonel thinks as he rises from his chair behind a desk in the den of the Anderson home. "They, obviously, don't know we're here, so they haven't sent word to their main body as yet. I need to keep the upper hand. Our main force will be arriving in a couple of hours. Common sense tells me to eliminate as much interference as possible."

Unknown to him, a pair of eyes and ears have just arrived in the form of Lilly, watching and listening through a large round mirror on the wall of the den. She thinks it a good idea to see what's happening here before going on to the guesthouse.

"Captain!" he calls loudly.

"Sir?" he says as he hurries into the den.

"That company of Union soldiers is occupying a farmhouse between here and town. I don't want them getting wind of us and tipping our hand to their main body, which is around here close somewhere," he explains. "Are you ready to move?"

"Yes, sir."

"Good. We'll move out in five minutes. Our objective is to secure that farmhouse allowing no one to escape. With the element of surprise, we should overcome them easily."

"That's probably where the family that was here went, Colonel. There has to be a lot of civilians there," the captain explains.

"Our orders are to secure and hold a safe place for our troops. We'll respond to the resistance we get. There are Union troops at the house now. If they want a fight, I can't be concerned with civilians."

Lilly watches and listens as the colonel speaks.

"Let's move," he concludes.

In less than a minute, Lilly is peering through a mirror in the living room at the guesthouse.

"What to do? What to do?" she ponders, feeling the urgency to tell someone about the Confederate's plan.

"I gave my word I wouldn't get involved. If I try to tell someone here, they're going to ask an awful lot of questions. But I can't just let this happen."

She watches her mama, the colonel, and Selma, as they deal with the five Union soldiers out in front of the house. Her heart swells with need to hug and kiss them all.

"Who can I trust? Who can I take aside and tell them without them telling everybody else? Not Mama, she'll be too emotional. Everybody's keeping an eye on the colonel because of his injury. Belle and Alberta Mae won't know how to handle it without getting me involved. Then who's left? Mrs. Housler, Selma. She doesn't know me that well. She has to be the one, and with everybody looking out front at the soldiers, I can get to her right now."

Selma is looking through a crack in the shutter back away from the others at the door, watching her husband. She feels a soft tap on her back and turns to see. Her eyes open wide, and her mouth opens to express her surprise. But Lilly's hand covers it at the same time she puts a finger to her own lips to keep her quiet.

She takes her hand and leads her away, up the stairs, down the hallway, into a far back bedroom of the house. As soon as the door is closed, Selma speaks.

"How did you get here, Cheryl? Is everybody else here, too."

"Don't yell or anything, Mrs. Housler, you promise?" Lilly cautions.

Selma nods her head yes, keeping her eyes on her every second.

"I'll explain later, but for right now, listen. I'm Sheree, not Cheryl."

Mrs. Housler takes breath as if she's going to speak.

Lilly's finger covers the confused woman's lips.

"Ssshhhh! Listen to me, we don't have much time."

"Those Confederate soldiers over at our house are on their way over here to capture all of you. I need you to tell your husband and those Union troops so they can get ready for them."

Selma looks at this young woman in front of her as if she has lost her mind.

"How did you get here? What will I say? Why don't you tell them yourself?"

"Look, you're having trouble understanding. Can you imagine what would happen if I went down there to tell them? It would take fifteen minutes just to get people settled down." A sense of urgency is fuming inside Lilly.

"You've got to tell them now, before it's too late. Run, tell them now. We'll explain it all later. Now go."

With her head spinning, Selma runs from the bedroom, down the stairs, and into the living room, where she starts yelling.

"We're going to be attacked by the Confederate army. They're on their way here right now. We only have a few minutes to get ready. Hurry!"

Everybody hears her. Those inside turn to see what the commotion is all about when she starts pushing people aside, tearing her way through.

June tries to grab her but is unable to hold on, as she bolts onto the front porch.

"Charles, don't ask me how I know, just listen!" she pants. "That Confederate army is on their way over here from the other house. They're coming to capture us and these Union soldiers. They'll be here in a few minutes. We've got to get ready."

"What the hell are you raving about, woman?" the colonel reacts, twisting around in his chair to see his wife.

The major, taking her at her word, issues orders.

"Sergeant! Get the rest of our men in here! Now!"

"I'll explain later! I'm not sure how many there are, but they'll be here in a few minutes!" she explains.

June has followed her best friend onto the porch.

"That captain I talked to told me there was a garrison coming. How many is that?" she yells at the major.

"At least a hundred men, ma'am!" he replies without expressing concern. "You all get back inside. Let us handle this. Where in the hell are my reinforcements?" he screams to himself.

"Jim, you and Josh get that cannon back over there where it was. Careful with it now, remember, it's loaded," the colonel orders. "Selma, you and June take the rest of the women and children down to the cellar. If you're right, there's going to be one hell of a fight out here in a few minutes.

"I'll get the rest down there, but I'm staying up here to fight," Selma reacts.

"I said, get yourself down in the cellar. I can't be worrying about you and June," he demands.

"Save your breath, Charles, we're staying up here. We've earned the right. If anybody goes to the cellar, you are," June bellows back at him.

The colonel leaves it at that and turns his attention back to the major. "We're armed to the teeth. Tell me and my men what you want us to do."

"How many do you have who can handle a firearm?" the officer asks.

"Nineteen, not counting me."

"Have your men posted at the windows and doors. Anywhere they can get a clear shot. Start shooting when we do. Just make sure your people don't shoot at us. My men will handle the cannons," the Union officer advises, as his horse jitters from all the commotion. He's concerned, but he knows he has a hundred and fifty men on the way to back him up. "If I keep these Confederates busy, my reinforcements can circle them from behind. We'll have them in a crossfire," he confides to himself, knowing he could soon be overrun because of his foes' numbers.

The Confederate troops have arrived from the direction of the Anderson home and stand waiting just over a rise. The colonel and captain lie on the ground on top of the hill, with their hats off, watching the Union soldiers scatter around the house.

"It looks like he's getting ready for us, but there's no way he could know we're coming. We didn't know ourselves until a half hour ago," the colonel mentions suspiciously.

"We outnumber them by a good many. This shouldn't take too long," the captain assures.

"They've got two cannons down there. One on either end of the yard. Where in the world would they get two cannons? There's no wheels around anywhere. They've got them set up on grounded mounts."

"They're probably the same ones we saw at the other house when we first went to chase the people out," the junior officer replies.

"Are you telling me you let them take two cannons from that property back there? Two cannons they're about to use against us?" the senior officer asks with a bit of disgust.

"They had them loaded and pointed right at us, sir. Each one had a man with a torch ready to touch it off. I'd have lost half my command if I'd tried anything."

"Never crossed your mind to get them when they were leaving with their wagons, did it? They weren't pointed at you, then, were they?"

The captain has nothing to say.

"I'll take half the men and go head on at them from here. You take the other half and come at them on our left flank. Let me know when you get into position. I'll start with a real commotion. Give me thirty seconds, then charge. That should give you time to get close enough to overrun them. Knock out those cannons first. Then go after their troops. The resistance from the house can't be much. We'll deal with them last. Got it?" the head man lays out the plan.

"Yes, sir. I'll signal you when I'm ready." The captain slides back down the hill to get to his horse.

"Do you see the two of them up there on that rise, sir?" a Union corporal addresses his senior officer.

"Yeah, I see them. They're checking us out. You know, if I was them, I'd come straight at us from where they are now to draw our strength there. Then I'd use the flank coming from over there behind the barn, so we can't see them coming until the last minute. They'll try to overrun us from there."

"Sergeant! Place that cannon over there to face the barn! Snappy now, they're here!"

"Colonel Housler, can you hear me?" he continues.

"Yes, Major, I can hear you fine."

"Place as many guns as you can to face toward the barn, and get ready, they're here, just over that rise."

"We'll be ready," Charles Housler shouts back with assurance.

"Come on," the major whispers to himself from behind an overturned supply wagon.

Inside the house June and Selma act like army sergeants getting everybody ready, putting them in places with some protection, so they can see to shoot. They have twelve of their nineteen guns facing the barn. Each position inside the house has a minimum of three rifles ready to fire. Contrary to Charles's orders, enough women and older children are at hand to reload the empty guns.

The upstairs windows aren't shuttered, but are open down from the top, and up from the bottom. Lit candles setting on the windowsills will provide the fire to light fuses on glass bottles and jars filled with powder, rocks, nails, and glass. The idea is to light the fuse, wait as long as you can, then give it a heave out through the open windows at the top. Having it explode just as it hits the ground will be perfect. Those handling these deadly missiles have been trained not to drop them inside or to allow any fire near the reserves, with fuses intact, stacked nearby. Should they run short on supply, they have the hand bombs sent to them by Marty Schoener.

The lower opening of the windows will be used to rain rifle fire down on the invaders.

At his insistence, the still recuperating Mr. Housler sits on a straight chair at a window downstairs, with a handgun.

Once the attack starts, June will direct the progress downstairs, while Selma will do the same upstairs.

"Come and get it. We're ready this time," June's words are reassuring to those who hear them.

Lilly watches from beyond the reflecting glasses of the mirrors, moving from room to room. She wants to be out there with her mother, but knows it isn't possible.

Selma hasn't given Lilly another thought since she sounded the alarm. Her whole being is wrapped up in defending their position.

"I won't have to explain anything to anybody. Mrs. Housler will wonder if she actually talked to me or not," Lilly thinks as she watches the busy woman moving from post to post, checking, rechecking, to be sure everything is in place.

All is quiet for the next several minutes. All activity has ceased.

A single shot breaks the silence, an obvious signal.

A wide line of soldiers appears on the top of the rise, all at the same time. Their horses at a gallop, followed by infantrymen on foot, at a trot.

"Hold your fire until I give the signal!" The major's orders are heard inside as well as outside the house.

Closer and closer, the sound of the charging horses hooves gets louder and louder. Behind them, ground troops yelling. Their numbers, along with the noise, are intimidating.

The major raises his hand when the oncoming force is a hundred yards away.

"Get ready!" he yells. "Fire at will!"

The first volley sounds like a roll of thunder, lasting three or four seconds.

A half dozen of the horsemen fall, some with their horses.

By the time the next shot is heard from the Union soldiers, the Confederates are not more then twenty yards away. Guns begin firing irregularly but consistently all around. The Confederate ground troops are shooting back.

One of the cannons explodes shaking some of the glass windows of the house. Fifty half inch shot whizzes through the air, spreading out as they go, each seeking a target. Thuds and splats can be heard as they hit. Horses rear up and scream in pain. Soldiers tumble to the ground in agony. Ten or more lie still while the attack continues over their lifeless bodies.

Through all of this, the sound of a bugle signaling the other attack coming from beyond the barn confirms the major's worry.

Two Union men are trying to reload the cannon when the incoming horsemen use their handguns and sabers to shoot, stab, and slice them to the ground.

With the force of the frontal onslaught proving to be more than the Union troops can handle, it's apparent to the major there's no use trying to deal with the attack on his flank.

"Retreat to the house! Retreat to the house!" he yells with all his might then turns to make the dash along with his men, but something hits him in the back with a thud. It feels like he's been hit with a brick, but he's unable to get his body to react to his brain. A warm liquid comes up his throat and out over his open lips. His knees fold under his weight, causing him to fall forward toward the ground. He grits his teeth together preparing for the impact, but instead, four strong hands catch him, pull him to his feet and drag him inside the house.

"The major's been hit!" one of the men yells as they enter and lay him on the floor. More soldiers push their way through the door, causing them all to abandon the injured man for other duties.

"Okay, give them hell!" Selma yells from the upstairs. The Union troops are out of the way now, enabling them to throw their missiles. Guns are banging and popping from everywhere in the house. The sound of exploding hand bombs begins outside. There's no use of the officers shouting orders to the men, they can't hear above the noise. Besides, every man has his hands full.

About half of the major's command makes it safely into the house. The rest lie in various places outside as the battle rages on.

"We never fired the second cannon! They're trying to turn it around on us!" Colonel Housler shouts.

"Selma! Get those four out front trying to turn that cannon!" June yells up the stairs.

The Confederate soldiers are wrestling with the weight, trying to turn the cannon on its base, when two smoking fuses come hurling from the sky. One explodes about six feet off the ground, filling the area with projectiles. One second later the second bursts violently just above the cannon barrel. Four Confederate soldiers lie motionless on the ground. One lies on his stomach with the breach of the cannon barrel resting on his back, the business end pointing up and at the front porch. His gray Confederate blouse has caught fire, which laps hungrily at the fire hole. Unaware of impending doom, five Confederate soldiers rush the front door at the same time the cannon comes to life.

The muzzle spews smoke, burning powder, and hot lead with a mighty force, then the heavy loud explosion is deafening to those close by.

The half-inch shot from the barrel tears through the doorway and wall around it, fragmenting as it goes. Pieces continue like a spray through the hallway and living room, searching for something to kill. The heavy wooden door is blown completely away between the top and bottom hinges. Smoke drifts away to reveal five dead soldiers lying in a heap on the porch.

Lilly is watching from behind the mirror directly in front of the oncoming shot. She sees her mother lifted off her feet into the air to slam hard on the floor, then the mirror shatters into thousands of pieces, eliminating her view.

Frantic with fear for her mother, she loses all sense about how to move around to another mirror. Nothing seems to work.

"Settle yourself down, Lilly! Settle down!" she yells at herself in her mind. "Think! Think!"

At last, she's looking through a glass in the parlor. With no hesitation she jumps through and runs to the entry way. She finds her mama lying face down. No one can help her, they're all busy trying to survive. There's four big jagged holes ripped through the back of her mother's blouse. Blood is oozing out causing big splotches.

The sounds of the raging battle disappear from Lilly's ears.

"Oh my God, Mama," she cries, bending down to turn her over. June's stomach and chest is dripping with red running everywhere.

"Mama!" is all she can scream.

June opens her eyes wide to look straight at her daughter.

"Thank God, it's you, Sheree. I've prayed to God every day since you've been gone that I'd see you again before I die," she smiles, allowing blood to run from the corners of her mouth. She labors a raspy, quivering, short breath and lets it out, never taking her eyes off her Sheree.

"Oh no, Mama! Don't go! I love you so much! Don't go!" Lilly cries.

June smiles again and presses her lips together trying to swallow, followed with another short scratchy breath. She tries to speak, but her whole body shakes, and she lets the air out. Her eyes stay fixed on her daughter's face, as she dies in Lilly's arms.

Holding her mama in her arms, she raises her face to the sky, and lets out a moanful cry—long and hard. Although there are no tears, the sound would bring them to those who hear it, but no one does.

The number of Confederate soldiers seems endless as more storm through the now open front door. Their blazing guns soon find their marks on Jim and Josh, propelling them backward from the impact of the bullets.

Lilly lays her mother down gently, and casually walks to pick up two abandoned handguns from the floor. One in each hand, she raises them, and in spite of being hit with shot after shot from the intruders, she begins firing.

Her training at La Nesra comes to the surface. Using her thumb to cock the hammer in one hand, at the same time she pulls the trigger of the gun in her other hand, she continues swinging side to side, blazing hot lead to find targets. One hand and then the other, the pistols explode with violence. Each time, a Confederate soldier drops in his tracks.

Her eyes glazed, she doesn't seem to be aware as she continues her onslaught. The colonel of the Confederates steps in to see her blasting away. He takes aim, but is hit with a bullet from the gun of Colonel Housler. Another shot from the smoking barrel of Lilly's gun hits him between the eyes before he hits the floor.

Charles Housler lifts his gun again to thwart the efforts of a soldier taking aim at his chest and hears a click when he pulls the trigger.

"Damn!" he yells and throws the pistol at his target.

The soldier's bullet hits him squarely in the chest. Colonel Charles Housler falls with dead weight to the floor.

Lilly turns her sights on that soldier and lays him out at the colonel's feet.

Everything is in chaos . . . moving too fast. Gray and blue uniforms are everywhere.

A cry from upstairs fills the house.

"Run! Get out! It's burning! It's going to blow!"

People—Union, Confederate, and civilian, all yelling and screaming—jam the stairway, trying to leave the upstairs.

A low roar of an explosion is heard by Lilly, who now is kneeling on the floor with her mother in her arms. The roar builds to a pounding sound, and soon becomes a blast, shaking the foundations of the house.

Yells and screams from the second floor tell the world human flesh is burning. People are dying. Only those near the head of the stairs are left standing. The screams subside to a few moans, and faint calls for help.

She stands up shaking her head. The house is filling with smoke. She looks up and sees fire on the second floor burning its way through from above, lapping down under at the downstairs ceiling with a rolling flame.

A woman's ear piercing scream from upstairs hits her ears.

"Help me! I'm trapped! My leg is stuck! Help me! Somebody, please!"

As if she has been commanded to look for this soon to die soul in the smoke and heat, she moves next to the railing. Progress up the stairs is hindered by cut up, bloody, and burnt people. The few who have lived through the explosion, bump and knock against her, as they stumble down the steps. It all stops when the last one passes her by.

"Can you hear me? Where are you?" she yells from the top of the stairs. Large blazes are everywhere, and growing. A few more degrees of heat will cause a persons skin to burn and melt away.

"I'm over here! Please hurry! There's no time!" the woman screams.

The dark gray smoke is getting as thick as gravy, making it nearly impossible to breathe. The only way to get around is to feel your way with your feet, or get down and crawl to feel with your hands. Lilly lowers down where the air is better.

"I'm coming, talk, so I can follow your voice," she instructs the trapped woman.

"Over here. Over here over here," the woman says again and again and again.

The floor is covered with splintered wood, broken glass, pieces of furniture, and bodies. Lilly works her way along feeling, touching arms, faces, crawling over lifeless forms.

At last, she puts her hand on the woman's body.

"I'm so glad you found me! There's something lying across the back of my leg and I can't get it off!" the woman, lying on her stomach, says.

Lilly feels around and finds it to be a rafter from the roof. Once she moves out near the end, she raises up on her knees, reaches down to get a grip with both hands, and lifts with a grunt.

"Tell me when you're free!" she urges the woman.

"A little more and I can make it! That's it! I'm out!"

"Can you walk?"

"Yes, I think so. Get out of here fast, the cellar is filled with powder and ammunition. It's all going up when this fire reaches it."

Still working on adrenaline, Lilly takes her by the hand, pulls her through the heat and smoke, down the stairs, and out on to the porch without stopping. While they stand choking and wheezing, two Union soldiers rush to beat the flames on their burning clothes.

The fighting has stopped. The reinforcements the major was expecting arrived and have taken charge with little effort. Soldiers, both blue and gray, are sitting around together, exhausted. At the moment, no one celebrates a victory or bemoans the loss.

Once they're safely away from the house, Lilly asks the woman, "Are there people in the cellar? Are they all out of there?"

"Yes, most of the women and children were down there, but surely they're out of there by now," the shaken woman responds.

For the first time they get a good look at each other.

"Sheree, it's you. You are here. I didn't dream you up. It's me, Selma."

Lilly doesn't react except to say, "I've got to find out if those people are still in there. I'll be right back."

As she turns to leave, Selma grabs her around the waist with both arms, and hangs on.

"No, don't go back in there, it's going to explode any minute!" she yells.

Hearing that, everybody jumps to move farther away from the burning house.

"Stop fighting me, will you! I'm not going to let you kill yourself by going back into that house! Somebody help me!" Selma yells for help.

A Union soldier picks Lilly up and carries her back away from the house, with Selma following right behind.

Immediately, an explosion shakes the ground, and shoots a cloud of smoke and flame into the sky a hundred and fifty feet. Burning boards, pieces of furniture, pots, pans, smoldering clothing, body parts, and countless other items begin falling in a large circle around the now demolished house.

Everybody moves again, farther out, to avoid the rain of debris

There's nothing left of the house. Just a pile of burning wood. No one could live through the blast and the heat. Anyone not among the people here, have not survived.

Selma collects herself and looks around.

"Charles! June!" she shouts.

When there is no response, she starts running in and out through the survivors calling their names over and over.

"Charles! June! Charles! June! Charles! June!" she shouts until, finally, she comes to the realization they are not here.

Lilly follows her movements and is by her side when she stops.

"Mama and your husband are gone, Mrs. Housler. I was there, I saw it all. Mama died in my arms. Mr. Housler didn't suffer. It was quick for him."

Selma snorts out the air left in her lungs and hangs her head, shaking with tearless sobs.

"Poor John" are her first words. "What will he do? He loves her so much, what in the world will he do?"

She pauses for a few seconds.

"There's nothing left here to bury, is there? Should we look for something?" she mutters mindlessly.

The captain of the Confederate soldiers, standing close by, hears her.

"No, ma'am, you don't do that. We'll take care of all that. I want to assure you that anything and everything we find will be treated with reverence, and a proper reading will be said over them all."

"He's right, ma'am," the sergeant of the Union forces affirms. "We'll see to it."

That thought leaves Selma's mind allowing others in.

"Jim? Josh?" she says with a loud whisper. "What about Alberta Mae, and Belle? And what about Sachel?"

"I don't know about Alberta Mae, Belle, and Sachel, but I saw Jim and Josh go down," Lilly confirms.

Selma stands as if in a stupor.

"There's a tunnel down there, you know," she says without moving her eyes.

"A tunnel. Where?" the sergeant is quick to ask.

"It takes off from cellar and comes out in the barn."

"Can you show us?"

"Follow me," she orders.

A few soldiers are picking up pieces of burning debris and tossing them back toward the house in an effort to save the barn. So far, it's working.

"Over there," she commands. "Under those feed sacks, there's doors. It's under there."

Enough help has followed her to make short work of getting the doors open.

Smoke rolls out in billows, pushing everyone back. They can feel the heat as it passes.

The sergeant turns to lower himself backward down the ladder into the tunnel. It doesn't take him long to appear again with his head just above the entrance.

"Get these women out of here," he calmly instructs his men.

"What's wrong?" Selma moves toward him.

"I'm not sure, ma'am, but there's a body lying at the foot of this ladder. I can't see too good, but I think there's several more. I'll need a lantern to be sure. There's no sense in the two of you staying here and seeing this. So, get on out of here. Go back over there with the rest," he finishes, motioning with his hand.

Lilly puts her arm around and silently coaxes Selma to do as the sergeant says. After they leave the barn, he continues.

"Get that lantern," he points. "I've got a feeling there's a lot more down there." He takes the lantern and descends again. "This one here is just a kid, a teenage girl. Let's see if I can pass her up to you. I need some room to move around."

After the girl's body is removed, he bends down and enters the tunnel on his hands and knees. He does not go far.

"Damn!" he yells and backs out of the hole to stand up.

The soldiers standing above look down for an explanation.

"There's bodies all back through there. I need a volunteer to crawl back in there and see if anybody's alive. I'd do it myself, but I'm too big, can't get around, but somebody your size could," he says, and climbs up out of the entrance.

"The lantern's down there, and get me a count. How many males, how many females, how many adults, and how many children. Get started," he orders the smaller, younger soldier.

Ten minutes later, the soldier appears from the tunnel coughing and choking, his own mucus dripping from his chin.

"I went as far as I dared, Sergeant. It just got to be too hot the farther I went. I couldn't take it any more."

"Anybody alive?"

"Nobody, sir. Nobody could live down here with it sealed up that way." He climbs out of the hole and stands wiping his face with his bandanna.

"How many?"

"My count is twenty-six. Nine adult women and the rest girl children, aging from maybe three to fourteen or fifteen. There might be more, but I couldn't go any farther back in there. It looks like they couldn't get this here door open to get out, and there was no going back. I had to push some off the top of others to get past. The smoke must have got them."

"Corporal!" the sergeant addresses the soldier next to him.

"Sir?"

"I want you to put this body back down there. Then, I want you to scour the whole area around out there for bodies, and body parts. Any you find I want put down there with the rest. Make sure you don't miss anything. Understand?"

"Yes, sir."

"Now, once you're sure you've got everything, I want you to use a light charge to blow that tunnel shut, and as soon as you can, I want the same thing done on the other end. There's no sense spending a day digging a mass grave when we don't have to."

"Yes, sir."

"Any dead horses or other animals can be dragged to a low spot in the ground, then covered over with dirt. I'm leaving you with thirty men, so you should have enough help. I'll be taking the rest of the troop and the prisoners back to join up with the lieutenant on the other side of town. As soon as you get this job done here, go on over to the other farm house to see if any more of these rebels are there. If there are and you can handle it, go ahead; but if it looks like big trouble, get a message to me, and we'll come running?'

"Yes, sir, I'll probably get this end sealed up, then go on over there while the fire's burning down," the corporal begins to explain.

The sergeant interrupts, "You handle it. I'll expect you back at camp by the middle of the afternoon tomorrow, unless I hear different. And don't take any unnecessary chances. I've seen more death today than I care to for a long time to come."

Selma and Lilly watch as the sergeant approaches them.

"I'm leaving a company here to clean up, but I need to get the rest of my men back to camp. The two of you can't stay here. You can either come back to camp with us, or I can drop you off in town. It's up to you. I can't let you stay here."

Lilly doesn't want to stay here. She needs to get back to her family in Atlanta, and there's no way of doing that from here.

"Drop us off in town then," she answers for Selma.

Following procedure, the sergeant has his men check the area for any usable firearms, along with unused ammunition, and has it loaded on a wagon. Two horses have to be shot where they lie. The wounded people are loaded onto horseback, or wagons for the trip. Union soldiers, according to rank, are riding any extra horses. The rest of the Union army, a few farmhands, and Confederate prisoners walk.

Lilly has plenty of time to think during the trip into town. She will be late getting back and that will put everybody on edge. They will probably be expecting to hear everything is okay.

"How do I go about telling them? Should I take Daddy aside and tell him first? I don't know how I could do that, the rest will know something's wrong. I don't know if Mama heard me tell her I love her. If I hadn't come home when I did, I would have never seen her again. I have to spare Daddy the details of it all. He doesn't need to carry that around with him. And then there's Robert. He's sick with worry about Elizabeth now. I know Charlotte and Mama must have been close after I left. It just makes sense. Randall just lost his daddy, and now, I have to tell him about his mama."

She looks at the down trodden woman sitting astride the horse next to her.

"I really shouldn't leave Mrs. Housler. She's lost her husband and several close friends, too. She needs somebody. It's not a good idea to tell her about me right now. I need to get her settled in a good safe place so I can go."

"Falcon is probably worrying about me. He shouldn't, I can take care of myself. I miss Joie. I miss her in every way a mother can. I can't let her grow up the way I have. She has to have family around her. I've got to get all this settled before she's big enough to know." Lilly's mental conversation is broken by someone speaking.

"I'll just drop you here at the hotel, if that's okay with you?" the sergeant turns in his saddle to say.

"This will be fine," Lilly replies.

"I'll have your horses put up at the smithy's, so if you need them," he continues while they dismount.

The women step back out of the way and watch as the procession moves past. Townspeople come out of their shops to take notice as well.

After they get registered into their individual rooms, which wasn't easy because of their appearance, Lilly tries her best to get Selma to eat something. But the only thing she wants to do is lie on her bed and stare at the ceiling.

"Maybe, if I leave her alone, she'll go to sleep," she considers.

"Selma, I'm going to lie down, too. I'll be right next door if you need me for anything. Okay?"

She doesn't acknowledge hearing a thing. Lilly waits a couple of minutes then says, "I'll be right next door."

The door of her room closes with a click, then she turns to look into the mirror she'll use for transportation. Since she casts no reflection, she's unable to see herself.

"I must look a mess," she says out loud. "These clothes are burnt and covered with blood, and there's bullet holes in my shirt, but the wounds are healing. If I show up in Atlanta looking this way, I'll scare them all to death. I don't have any money, and if I try to get anything on the book, they'll ask too many questions. Hhhmmmmm.

"Selma's about my size, a bit smaller, but I should be able to fit into her clothes. They look better than mine. That's not a bad idea. If I take her clothes, she won't try to move out of her room until I get back."

She returns to Selma's room. "I'm going to get you out of these clothes and under your blankets so you can rest properly. Okay?" Lilly explains as she begins. Selma doesn't help much, but she doesn't resist.

Back in her own room, Lilly discovers that Selma is more than a little smaller than her. The clothes barely fit over her motherly chest and just-had-a-baby hips. But other than being dirty and a little burnt here and there, they will do.

She stops to think before entering the mirror.

"Am I ready to do this—will I ever be ready? Here goes."

At the end of the trip, Zola says.

This is the last time I will be here to help you, Sheree. You know everything you need to know to travel by yourself. I will no longer come to you when you call.

Lilly steps up to the white space and peers through expecting to see her family waiting. Nobody. The room is empty.

"They would have left someone here even if the rest had to leave for some reason. This must not be the right room. There's nobody in there, I'll just go through and ask someone where they are."

"Can I help you, miss?" the clerk behind the registration desks inquires.

"Yes, can you give me the number of Mr. John Anderson's room, please. He said it's 211, but there's no one there and there should be. I'm his daughter."

"Pardon me for asking, but how many of you are in that family? If my count's right you're number three, all looking alike."

Lilly doesn't respond.

"That's the right number. He must be out. Here, take this key and let yourself in. You can wait for him there." The clerk drops the key into her hand, unsure why his bit of humor wasn't appreciated.

After entering the room, she takes a better look around and finds a note lying on the bed.

"You're late, we'll be back in no more than an hour. Wait here for us."

Thirty-five minutes later, the door opens and they enter with John in the lead. It's as if they feel guilty, because nothing is said; they simply file in and quietly find a place to sit. You'd think they have already heard the bad news.

Lilly occupies the only overstuffed chair in the room. She sits somber, legs crossed, arms folded, not knowing where to begin.

"We've had word about Elizabeth, honey. It's not promising, not promising at all."

Chapter Thirty

Lilly sits motionless, without expression, hearing the news of Elizabeth. She has been wrestling with the problem of telling her remaining family about the deaths of those back home.

"My God, look at you. Are you okay?" Falcon moves to kneel down in front of his wife.

"You look like you been through a war or something. You've got blood on your hands and face, and your clothes look all burnt." He takes her hand in his.

The rest of the group stands back, watching and listening.

"I'm all right. I'm okay," she stalls, knowing her next words will bring more hell into the lives of those who hear them. "I have to tell you all, but I don't think I can. It's too much." Her words fall off at the end, and a tear from her left eye flows down over her cheek to linger on her chin.

John stoops down beside Falcon in front of his daughter.

"It's all right, honey. We're your family. Just take your time. We're here to help each other."

She leans forward and reaches out, puts one arm around Falcon's neck, the other around her daddy's, and pulls their heads to her shoulders. With a tearful sobbing, she begins.

"They're all dead. Everybody but Mrs. Housler and a few hands are all dead. The guesthouse is a pile of ashes, and they're all dead. Mama died in my arms."

"Mama!" Charlotte screams.

Lilly breaks down completely and closes her grip on her father and Falcon. The rest move in around the chair to put their arms around each other, and grieve.

After many hard questions and strained responses, she is able to pull herself together enough to explain from the beginning.

An hour passes as each individual finds their own way of handling the grief. One by one they settle down until the room is silent. Contemplation sets in while they sit wherever they have found a place, the bed, a straight chair, or the floor.

"I suppose I should go back to the farm," John poses.

"Why?" Robert asks indignantly. "There's nothing left there. There's nothing to go back to."

"Sheree says the main house is still there, son, and a few of the hands. Besides, I need to be there for your mama, and Selma," he explains.

"Mama's gone, Daddy! She's dead! Don't you understand that?" Charlotte screams and bolts through the open door into the hallway with Cheryl on her heels.

The room stays quiet for a few minutes.

"I just meant that I feel like I need to be there for some sort of service for your mother. I wasn't there for her when she died, and I need to be as close to her as I can get right now. And I need to be there to console Selma. She loves Charles, and everybody else there. You know she and your mother have been like sisters for years, and right now, she's there alone. That's all I meant," the elder Anderson relates while hanging his head, fighting to hold back his emotions.

"Mrs. Housler was asleep in her hotel room in town when I left. I should get back there before she wakes up. I'm not sure if all this has sunk in on her yet," Lilly realizes and relates.

"I'm sorry, Daddy, I know you love Mama with all your heart, and I can't imagine how you feel right now. But I can't go back right now. There's nothing I can do there, and I need to find Elizabeth," Robert informs everybody.

"You said you had news of her. What did you find out?" Lilly asks her brother.

"She was sold to a ship's captain at Charleston, three days ago. The ship's supposed to leave with the next tide, which I understand means early in the morning. I know I can't get there before it leaves, but maybe I can get on another ship headed that way," he explains, feeling helpless.

"I can," his sister offers.

"What?" Robert asks without thinking.

"I can be there long before it leaves. Maybe there's a way I can get her back," she offers again.

"But first, I have to go back home and make sure Mrs. Housler is going to be all right."

Everyone in the room looks at Lilly, knowing she can.

"You just got back, and look at you. Don't you need some rest or something?" Falcon shows concern for his wife.

"I'm okay. I don't seem to need all that much rest when I'm out of my life body. I would like to change my clothes, and maybe take some money to Mrs. Housler. She has nothing but the clothes I left there. I'm wearing hers because mine were such a mess with the blood and all." Lilly sees her husband's need for her in his eyes as she speaks.

"I'm so sorry to put you through all this, but if I don't try, and we never see Elizabeth again, I'll never forgive myself. This could be our last chance."

Falcon snaps himself into a façade to remark, "I understand, and I'd go if it was me. It's just that this is all happening so fast, and I wish I could go with you. But I know I can't, and I know you have to."

"I don't know how, but I'll make it up to you when I get back. That's a promise I'll look forward to keeping," his wife assures.

Sally appears in the doorway.

"The girls just told me. I am so, so sorry for all of you. What can I do?" she says with feeling and sincerity.

"There's not much anybody can do right now, Sally. We need some time to put our lives back together." Randy speaks for the first time, showing his maturity.

The redhead steps aside enough to allow the two girls back into the room.

"I'm sorry, Daddy, I feel worse now than before. I shouldn't have said that. Can you ever forgive me? You know I love you and wouldn't hurt you for the world. It's just that, well—" John cuts her off as Charlotte begs for his understanding.

"It's all right, honey, I know. Don't worry about it. We all hurt right now, and it's best to get it out. If you need to scream, then scream. There's nobody to blame, but this God forsaken war."

"What are we going to do?" Cheryl boldly asks.

"I'll stay here with Bob, if that's okay with you?" Randy speaks as he looks at his friend.

Bob nods yes at the same time Lilly confirms her part.

"I'm going to find Elizabeth, but first I'll check on Mrs. Housler back at the hotel."

"You all know I'm going back to the farm. That leaves the two of you. What do you want to do?" John gives his daughters room to decide for themselves.

"I think we should go home with Daddy." Charlotte looks at Cheryl as she lets her preference known.

"I agree. Things have to be right in my mind before I can go off doing anything else. We're going home with Daddy," Cheryl confirms.

Sally nods her head in agreement with everyone. "Anything I can do, just ask."

Randy stands up from his position on the floor. "There is one thing, Sally. Can you fix it so I can get into La Nesra with Falcon? I mean, I'll stay with Bob wherever he wants to, but it might be useful if I could get in and out of there."

Lilly looks at her once close friend with left over tears in her eyes. Then a small knowing smile forms on her lips.

"Oh, I see. I saw you looking Nora over last night. And Sherman took to you like ice to lemonade," she kiddingly interjects.

"You never know," Randy grins at her comment, not noticing Charlotte's questioning glance.

Everybody feels a teeny bit of comfort hearing their exchange of understanding.

"To answer your question Randy, I don't have to do anything. You can go in and out now as long as you're with Falcon, or Lilly. The same goes for you, Robert, although in your case I'd go straight to their quarters. No sense in tempting those who see you there," Sally explains with confidence.

"I wouldn't try to take anyone else right away, though," she addresses Lilly's husband. "They're not big on visitors."

Another hour passes with quiet conversation covering memories from times past to what the future might bring. Lilly feels it's time to start her journeys, but wants to stay with her family.

"I hate to ask, but I don't have any money to give to Mrs. Housler. Do any of you have any extra?" she begs.

Shortly she has more than enough to cover the cost of a few pieces of clothing, room rent, and food for at least two weeks.

"Thank you all so much, and now I have to go," she says. "I don't want to, but every minute I stay here, the less time I'll have in Charleston before the ship sails. God bless you all."

She takes Falcon in her arms and kisses him hard. After releasing their grip on each other, she moves gently away and says, "I'm going now, turn your heads and don't look."

Four steps and she's through the mirror. No one turns their head, and all watch in amazement. She's gone.

Once on the other side, Lilly remembers she can no longer summon Zola. She said she would not answer her call any more. "She said I have everything I need to do it myself, so, here goes. Think La Nesra. Think, our home at La Nesra. Concentrate, close my eyes and . . . open my eyes. There's a white square. Let's have a peek through.

"Aha! I'm home."

Lilly removes her tattered clothing and resumes her body, then wolfs some food and drink. All the while she's eating, she holds Joie and talks with Nora.

"You say he likes me?" Nora responds to Lilly's comments about Randy.

"I believe he does, and I can tell you for a fact, he's one good man."

"I never had anybody have feelings for me before. I guess I never thought anybody ever would. Well I'll be . . ." she contemplates.

"Remember, I haven't said a word to you about this. You can't let on."

"Don't you worry about that. Just pray for me that I don't get all nervous and do something stupid if he starts talking to me."

"I have to go, Nora, and I'm not sure how long I'll be gone. Promise you'll take special care of my husband and Joie." Lilly, again, doesn't want to leave.

"I promise, ma'am. You know I will. Don't you worry."

A few minutes later Lilly has passed through the mirror, leaving her husband, Joie, and her life body behind.

Something feels different this time. Urgency! She feels a sense of urgency, but from what? Where?

"I don't know what it is, but I have a feeling something's going to happen if I don't get out of here in a hurry."

She concentrates, then opens her eyes to see a white square.

"This must be my hotel room."

The feeling of urgency is stronger than ever, she quickly slides through the mirror. She's about half way when something slams her from behind knocking her the rest of the way out and onto the floor with a thud.

"What was that?" she says out loud. "That was scary! All this time, and that's the first time I've ever had a feeling like that. It's a good thing I was already leaving. What would have happened if I wasn't near a white square?"

Then she remembers Mr. Vaughn explaining the dangers on the other side of the mirror. She asked him how she would know if something was after her and he said "don't worry, you'll know." "Could this be what he meant?" she whispers to herself.

"I'm going to take a quick peek back in there. I won't go in, I'll stick my face through just far enough to see."

Carefully, cautiously, she puts her nose to the glass and pushes gently. Slowly the front of her face clears into the other side. She opens her eyes.

"Oh! My! God!" She tries to scream, but her voice is muted on that side of the mirror. Something smacks her face forcing her to fall back into the room, allowing the last half of her yell to echo off the walls.

"What was that?" She gasps for her breath. "It had a gruesome shape, that kept moving, changing, never the same! It had foot-long horns that kept moving in and out, big warts and deep seeping sores! It had bloody eyes, then it didn't have any eyes! It had long and short pointed teeth, but then it didn't have a mouth at all! Instead of a nose, it had three holes arranged in the shape of a triangle, that snorted mucus and smoke! It was all head and no body, arms, or legs, but it slapped my face, hard!

"That was absolutely the ugliest, scariest thing I've ever seen in my life!" she all but yells out loud, her heart pounding.

"Get a hold on yourself! Think this thing through! Fall back on your training! There's an explanation for it! Think!" she continues speaking out loud.

"I can't do this right now, I need to settle down! Oh Lord, I have to go back in there to get to Charleston! Will it be waiting there for me when I try to go through? What have I got myself into now? Oh Zola, I need you desperately!" Still speaking out loud, her volume increases.

"If I can stop shaking long enough, I'll check on Mrs. Housler. It will get my mind off that thing for a few minutes, then maybe I can figure something out."

Getting through the door and into the hallway makes her feel a little better. Probably because of the distance from the mirror, and knowing the door is closed behind her.

She opens the door to Selma's room and sticks her head in first to see if she's still in bed. She's not. The bed is empty, the blankets tossed aside.

She glances at a clock on the wall. "I've been gone for over four hours. She could be anywhere by this time. I'd better check at the desk, perhaps they've seen her or know where she went. Unless she put on my bloody filthy clothes, she's running around in her underwear."

The desk clerk said she came down the stairs in her underwear and went out through the front doors onto the sidewalk, then turned to the left. That's the last he's seen of her.

"Didn't you ask her where she was going dressed like that?" Lilly asks him indignantly.

"To tell you the truth, ma'am, I never have seen anything like that in my life, and the thought never crossed my mind," he answers candidly.

"How long ago?" she asks hurriedly.

"It hasn't been more than fifteen minutes."

She hustles to the wooden sidewalk and looks around carefully. No sign of her anywhere. "Now, where would she go? She knows the same people we all know. She'd probably go to someone who knows her. Doc Shaw. I'll bet her burns and such are bothering her, and she went to have him look them over."

She moves at a fast trot to the doc's office. The lights are out. No sign of movement.

Bang! Bang! Bang! She hammers on the wooden part of the door, next to the glass. A light appears from the back of the building. Shortly, she sees Doc coming dressed in his pants and an undershirt.

"What's all the commotion?" he complains as he opens the door.

"Hi, Doctor. I'm Sheree Anderson, remember me." Before he can answer, she continues, "Have you seen Selma Housler? I left her at the hotel earlier, and now I can't find her."

"Oh yes," he begins at the same time scratching his gray head. "She's over there curled up on my examination table. She came in here dressed in nothing but her underwear, shivering from the night air. She looks like hell, I'll tell you that. But she wouldn't let me touch her at all. Says she doesn't have any money. Says she just needs to be with somebody tonight. Wouldn't take my bed. I told her I'd sleep out here, but she wouldn't hear of it. I found her a blanket, and she was asleep before her head hit that pillow. Not a peep out of her since.

"What's going on? How did you get here?"

"It's a long story, Dr. Shaw. Daddy will be back from Atlanta in a few days, he can tell you anything Mrs. Housler hasn't told you already."

"Right now, though, I need a big, big favor. Will you take care of her until he and my two sisters get here. It could be two or three days. Here, take this money I brought for her. If it's not enough, you know Daddy will square up with you. Can you please? She has a room at the hotel, but doesn't have any decent clothes, and she hasn't eaten a thing for some time. I'd like to wait and take care of it all myself, but I have to be in Charleston, so I can't stay."

"Slow down young lady. I don't know what's going on, but it must be a lulu. Are you talking Charleston, South Carolina? And why doesn't she have any clothes anyway?"

"I can't talk right now. Will you help me please? Please?"

"You know I will, Sheree, but I can't wait to hear this one," he says with assurance.

During her walk back to the hotel, Lilly tries to get an understanding of the monster beyond the mirror. "If I went through a different mirror, one a distance away from the one in my room, maybe that thing wouldn't see me. Maybe I'd have enough time to get to Charleston before it finds me. How could it hurt me? We're all just souls in there. We really don't have a body like out here. It did hit me twice though, and I can't deny that. I need to talk to Zola. She can tell me what this thing is, and what I can do about it. I'll find another mirror, then I'll try to get Zola to talk to me. But where do I find a mirror? Hmmmm? There's not much open this time of night. Wait, I know, the saloon, there has to be mirrors in there."

The double doors at the entrance of the bar are swung back inside, allowing the light of many oil lamps to spill out onto the sidewalk. Lilly peers inside and notices a large chandelier, hanging in the center of the room, holding eight lamps. Off to the right three men are playing cards. On her left, two men stand together at the bar, talking, with beers in front of them. The barkeeper makes a total of six. Four empty tables with various styles of straight-back chairs scattered among them in a disorganized manner complete the furnishings. The heavy stench of stale cigar and cigarette smoke, mixed with alcohol, along with the dank odor of dirty spittoons, turns her stomach. The wooden floor is black with years of abuse from mud, dirt, and spilled drinks. Smoke rises in layers, casually, like thin clouds, seeking the heat coming off the lamps.

No one takes interest when she enters until the barkeeper motions with his finger to the two men at the bar. Then both of them turn at the same time to look in her direction. Trail weary, dirty with sweat, their manner indicates they've been here a while and have emptied many a glass.

"Evening, ma'am," the one on the right says in his deep loud voice. A put-on smile exposes yellowish teeth with several black spots near his gums. His comment gets the attention of the three playing cards, whom all look her way at the same time.

"What's a little lady like you doing in here this time of night?" the man at the bar continues.

It takes some effort, but she doesn't acknowledge his inquiry with a flurry of words aimed at embarrassing him. She looks around to locate a mirror, anywhere. There is one five-foot-wide hanging behind the bar. But it has shelves in front holding bottles and glasses. She would have to jump from the top of the bar to get through. That will not work. Wait. There's one hanging over a piano setting up against the back wall. Without warning, she moves, picking up speed as she goes. A foot on the piano stool, a strong push of her leg and through she goes, much to the bewilderment of the men watching.

"They'll be talking about that for a while" she says to herself.

"The monster isn't here. This is good," she thinks.

"I'm going to call for Zola just twice, if she doesn't come, I'm headed for Charleston."

On her second call, Zola appears. Why did you call Sheree?

"Thank you for coming, Zola. There's a terrible demon or something in here chasing me. I don't know what to do about it. Can you tell me what it is and why it's chasing me?"

Listen carefully. What you felt, and what you think you have seen, comes from your own mind. It is a sum of all your fears and desires. I have explained to you before, I am not of the appearance you see. Your mind sees me in a way you can understand. Nothing here has a form as you know it, not even yourself. There are many dangerous souls here. They thrive on the sense of fear exuded from others. That which you saw comes from your own soul. You must cleanse your mind to rid yourself of it. When you have mastered that, you will be much more capable of understanding and dispersing the rest.

"How in the world do I do that? I'm not even sure I understand what you said."

The way to eliminate a fear is to face it squarely with the knowledge that you know it for what it is. When you believe that, you can conquer it, and others who might test you. I must go.

"Thank you," Lilly thinks, but too late, Zola has left.

"Darn, I wanted to ask her how to find my way to Charleston. Up to now, I've only moved between things I'm familiar with. I've never been to Charleston, so I have no idea what to think about. Maybe it's all relative. If I just think Charleston, maybe I'll get there," she rationalizes. "Here goes."

She squeezes her eyes shut hard and says Charleston over and over in her mind.

She feels a little movement, and that hollow feeling of fear she felt before is creeping in again. "It's coming again, that thing is coming. Hurry!"

She opens her eyes to see a white square. Without hesitation she reaches for the vertical edges to get a grip to propel herself to the other side. Her legs feel odd, like something has passed completely through them as they slide through the mirror.

"Whoooeeee! That was close again. I have to work on that when I can, but one thing at a time. Where in the world am I. This is a very small room, all made of wood. The ceiling is so low, another few inches and I'd have to bend down a little to move around. This reminds me of a ship's cabin, like the ones I've read about. Someone left a lamp burning in here, so they'll probably be right back. I need to get out of here. There's a small window over there, I'll take a look outside.

"Water everywhere, I'm on a ship out in the water. I can see lights from things on shore. They're at least a hundred yards away, maybe more.

"Think, Lilly, think. Zola has told me that I know all I need to know to move around. Wait a minute. Anytime I've needed her help, she always asked me to think about my question. She could read my mind on that subject once I opened it up to her. This must work the same way. Whatever it is that guides me must read my mind, so when I think Charleston, it takes me to wherever I know I want to go.

"If that's the case, I told it to take me to Charleston, South Carolina, to a boat that is leaving with the tide in the morning, with Elizabeth on board. I could be on the same boat with her right now. One thing I know for sure, I can't stay here long. And this white shirt won't help me hide out there in the dark. I need some clothes that make me look like a sailor or something.

"There's a huge trunk over there, let's have a look. Aah—this is just what I need, and I believe they'll fit well enough. Here's a hat too. That's good. I can put my hair up under it a little. No one needs to know I'm a girl. This is too easy. If Elizabeth is here, well, it's just too easy."

She slips out of her clothes, then into these she has found, and none too soon.

"Someone's coming! Hide and take my clothes with me! Where? This small room provides no place for an adult person to conceal themselves. There's not much time! The trunk—if there's room!"

In she goes and pulls the lid down over herself. Luckily, the lid is ten inches deep, otherwise she wouldn't fit. A little clink comes faintly to her ears, but her heart is pounding so loud she pays it no mind.

"I thought I left this lamp burning. No sense wasting good oil if I'm not going to be here, now is there?" a man comments with a grouchy voice. "I'll just turn it off, and we'll be on our way to shore."

"Be quick about it then," a different man's voice instructs tersely.

She waits patiently until she hears the two leave. As soon as their voices fade, she pushes up on the lid expecting it to open. It doesn't move. Panic starts to set in as she realizes that little clink she heard was the clasp falling down over the lock loop. A second later she feels like it is getting harder and harder to breathe. "I'm locked in, the lid won't budge. There's barely enough room for me in here, leaving very little for air. Think, Lilly! Think! Settle down and think." Her muffled screams cannot be heard beyond the cabin walls.

"Maybe there's something in here I can use to pry the lid open. It's hard to move to get my arms and hands in position, but if I squeeze around, ah, there . . ." She can feel the rough edges of the lid scraping as she forces her skin to slide across it.

"Anything. Come on, anything at all."

Her right hand is wriggling its way down through the contents of the trunk. It touches something flat about ten inches long, six inches wide, and a half an inch thick, an oval shape. Because of its size, and since she can lift her elbow only so high before hitting the lid, it's difficult to maneuver it up. She has to slide it back and forth through the layers of clothing, which are compacted by her weight, moving it up a little at a time. The air is stale already. If there is any coming in anywhere, it's not enough to sustain life.

"I have to move quickly, before I pass out," she tells herself. "What if whatever this is doesn't help? I won't have time to do anything else. Maybe I should give this up and do something else. What though? There is nothing else."

She struggles for another three minutes trying desperately to pull the article to the surface. Each breath is more difficult, forcing her mouth open, and causing her to suck the bad air in.

"I can't give up. I have to do it. No one's going to help me, I have to do it on my own." Then a thought flashes through her mind. "If I die in here, someone will open this trunk and find me." She pictures a scruffy seaman putting his hands on her, dragging her body out of the trunk onto the floor. The thought makes her shiver inside. "I'm getting out of here if it's the last thing I do." At last she has the object next to her face, but there's no light to determine what it could be.

"It's smooth like a mirror. If I can turn it over, a little more. I have to push the clothing down more to get it to turn, there. Okay, let's see if I can put my finger through. Yes, yes, yes, it's a mirror," she yells joyously. With five beats of her heart she is on the other side. "Amazing. Simply and utterly amazing. Now, that was a close one."

Not wanting to dally, she tells herself, "Keep moving, that monster of a thing will be coming."

"Elizabeth. Elizabeth." She concentrates her thoughts, then opens her eyes to see a white square. Once through it, she finds herself in a cabin similar to the one she just left. The door is standing open against the wall. Out through the doorway she can see the flickering of a lanterns light as it approaches, accompanied with clomping footsteps.

"Hide. Hide again, but no trunks this time." Instead, she slips quietly behind the open door, with barely enough room to hide her existence.

"You'll not come out of here again until we're at sea. So, you might as well try to sleep. We have to lock the door you know," a pleasant but serious voice announces.

"Women," another voice says, "a woman on a ship is bad luck, you know. I fear we're in for it."

"She's the captain's problem, not ours. He's sweet on her, so it'll do us no good to complain. We're to do what we're told and hold our tongues," the first voice explains curtly.

Lilly stands behind the door, as flat against the wall as possible, and watches as a woman is shoved from behind into the cabin. Although she is unable to see, she thinks it must be Elizabeth. The woman lands on the floor in the shadows, and remains still until the door is pulled shut and locked from the outside.

Lilly stands still, holding her breath, since the closing of the door has left her exposed.

The woman on the floor stirs and starts fumbling around in the dark. When a match comes to life Lilly is looking at her back. The woman picks up a lantern and successfully sets the wick afire, then moves away from the door toward a window.

"Is this Elizabeth?" she thinks. "I'll scare her half to death if I say anything. What shall I do? She'll see me if she turns around."

"Elizabeth?" Lilly says with a questioning whisper.

The woman stops in her tracks, then turns around with a jump, swinging the lantern against the somewhat concave exterior wall with a bang. Her eyes are wide and wild with fear.

"Who the hell are you?" she yells.

"Sssssshhhhhh, I mean you no harm. Are you Elizabeth?"

The woman leans toward her, holding the lantern up high, as far out as she can, trying to get a good look at her intruder.

"Why, you're nothing but a mere child, you are. Who are you and what are you doing here? How did you get aboard this boat?" the woman finds her courage and demands.

"Ssshhhh. Please lower your voice. They'll hear you," Lilly begs.

"Them? Hell, they pay little attention to me, especially when he's off the boat. I rant all the time just to irritate the bastards.

"They've caught you, have they? They're always looking for young lasses like you. You're a looker, you are." The woman suddenly seems afraid of nothing.

Lilly ignores her questions thinking they will only lead to more.

"I can tell by your voice, you're not Elizabeth, or at least not the Elizabeth I'm looking for. Are there any other women aboard this boat?"

"None I know of, except for me. I hear, though, he's off to get one right now. They should be coming back shortly. What do you want with this Elizabeth anyhow?"

"She's my brother's bride to be. She was taken from our farm farther inland, and I've tracked her to here."

"You, a wisp of a lass like you, has come to rescue this Elizabeth from this crowd. You best have some reserves in your pocket. Must I inform you that you're locked in here with me? You've made a terrible mistake coming here. You'll suffer the same fate as your Elizabeth, if that's her name. I'll bet they can get a pretty penny for you over there, and that's what they'll do. These are not nice people lassie. They'll take what they want from you on the trip over, and then sell you off for more of the same once we get there. And that you can count on."

"Will you help me?" Lilly asks.

"Me? Me help you, you say?" the woman asks in a jeering, negative way.

"What can I do? Are you loony? There must be at least thirty of them on this boat when it's at sea. Did you not hear them when they chucked me in here? They'll not concern themselves with me until the morning, and probably not early at that. They'll busy themselves with the new one they're bringing until it's time to leave. Then they'll all get to work setting the sails and the like. By the time they remember me, locked up in here, this boat will be miles from the shore, it will. You a good swimmer, are you? Ha. Ha. Ha.

"You're stuck here, as am I. You've sealed your fate, you have, and there's naught you can do about it now."

"How long have you been here?" Lilly needs information about the boat and knows she has to start somewhere.

"Too long, lass. I've not been off this boat in two years or better. You lose track of time, you do."

"Why are you here?" she continues.

"I'm his woman, I am. As long as I give him what he needs, he'll not sell me off. He treats me like dirt, and me doing for him what I do. He keeps me locked up like an animal when we're at anchor. I've no respect for myself any longer. He passes me around to the lot of them, as well. I've had thoughts of jumping over and feeding the fish, but I've not got the nerve to do it. They never beat me, though. I'll give them that, and they see that I have what I need."

"Would you like the chance to escape from here?" Lilly takes a risk.

"Would I? You bet I would." The woman is quick to answer.

"Well, if you'll help me find Elizabeth, we'll take you with us when we go."

"Ha. Ha. Ha. Ha. You don't listen, do you? You'll never get off this boat yourself, let alone take me or this Elizabeth with you."

"If I can, will you help me? If I can't, are you any worse off than you are now?"

"I think I've lost the last bit of my mind, I have. You're serious, you are?"

Lilly nods her head yes with commitment.

"You know we'll both be tied upside down on a yard arm for doing this, don't you?" the woman warns.

"They have to catch us first," Lilly counters.

"Lassie, are you daft? I've told you. They've caught us. We're locked in here."

"You're locked in here, I'm not." Lilly stops the woman's ranting, and continues, "I'm beginning to think I've misjudged you. You talk like you're unhappy with your life here as a captive, but now I wonder. Regardless, if you help me or not, I'm here to free Elizabeth and take her home. If you won't help me, I'll leave you to your chosen fate."

"No. No. No. I'm of a mind to go with you. Please, I'll do anything I'm able to do." The woman sees Lilly's point.

"All right, that's better. Now, tell me about this boat. I need to know how it's laid out, where the crew spends most of their time while they're here, where they'll bring the new woman aboard, and the location of their armory, then . . ."

In the meantime.

Physically tired and emotionally drained, John, Charlotte, Cheryl, and Sally break up the gathering, all needing a good nights sleep. He and his two daughters plan to leave as soon as possible, headed home to pick up the pieces of a life destroyed. Sally will stay on here and continue obtaining information that can be used against the Company.

Falcon, Bob, and Randy decide they'll spend the night at La Nesra. During their ride back from town, the conversation forms around the mysterious containers. They plan to go for a look at them as soon as they check in with Nora.

The guard at the gate passes them by once he sees Falcon's ring.

"Keep the noise down so we don't wake up the children," Falcon cautions his visitors as they follow him up the stairs to his home.

He opens the door to see the place glowing from the dim light of a lamp setting on the kitchen table. Nora is seated on a straight-back chair, fiddling with a piece of material she's using to make Sherman a shirt. She raises her head to watch them enter.

"How's everything here?" Falcon asks with little more than a whisper.

"Everything's fine," she replies with a smile. "Looks like you brought company with you."

"Yeah, we decided to get the guards familiar with seeing us together. You remember Robert and Randy?"

"I surely do," she smiles and looks, giving a nod each.

Robert says, "Hello."

Randy's face brightens up. "Good evening, ma'am. You look real nice sitting there."

Robert smiles at his friend's approach.

Nora is quick to look at Randy's face and give him a complete once over without moving her eyes. Liking what she sees, she puts on her best smile.

"I thank you for that, Randy. A woman doesn't hear talk like that much around here." That came out just right. She didn't sound nervous at all.

"I'm going to check on Joie, and get the key. Then I'm going to show them the containers. There's no need for you to wait up on us," Falcon relates.

"Oh, no, I'll be up. I'm not tired, and I want to get started on this shirt. Can I fix something for you to eat when you get back?" Nora answers without taking her eyes off Randy's face.

"That would be real nice," he responds as if she spoke only to him.

Robert grins again.

Falcon looks down on his baby girl, lying, sleeping peacefully on her back in her crib. He reaches to pull her blanket up a little more over her chest. Then he moves to his bed where Lilly's life body lies. He bends down and presses his lips to hers.

"Be safe," he whispers.

"We shouldn't be more than a half hour, or so," Falcon surmises as he walks back to the others, the key to the wall door in his hand.

As the trio descends the steps headed for the back wall, Falcon explains. "We'll stay in the shadows as much as we can. No sense in bringing attention to ourselves. No talking until we get there."

They move swiftly between buildings, quietly, from shadow to shadow, until they arrive at the last building before the wall.

"See that door over there," Falcon whispers and points in the darkness. "I'll go first to get it open, then I'll motion for you to come. That way we won't all be standing around waiting."

Bob and Randy wait as he makes his way to the door, and watch for his signal. It doesn't come; instead, Falcon runs back. "It doesn't work, the lock has been changed."

Meanwhile, back at the boat sitting in the harbor at Charleston. The woman is speaking to Lilly.

"So, let me just get this straight in my mind. You're going to climb through that mirror—that mirror right there—and come out of another mirror out there somewhere. And that starts your plan to get us out of here. Saints preserve us, you're as loony as I first thought."

Lilly walks to the mirror and pushes her arm through up to her shoulder, and looks at her new acquaintance.

"Lord, save us all. What do I have here? What are you, some sort of ghost, or something?" the woman exclaims.

"Don't ask questions. Just know I can do what I say," Lilly insists. "Now, how will we know when they get here with Elizabeth?"

"We can watch out this little window here." The woman points to the small round window, the only one in the cabin. "They come and go from this side of the boat, about half way along."

"I don't know if Elizabeth can swim, which means we'll need a boat to get to shore," Lilly poses.

"You bet your life we need a boat, I don't swim either," the woman confirms.

"Is there one we can put in the water, so it'll be ready when we are?"

"There's another the size of the one they're using, but the likes of us won't be able to get it to the water. It's a big thing, it is. You'll see. I wouldn't count on that."

"Do you suppose they'll leave the one they're using in the water?"

"Yes, they will. They tow one behind this boat unless a storm comes along." The woman is gleefully encouraged.

"All right, problem solved."

"And soon enough." The woman clamors turning back from the window. "They're coming back now."

Lilly plans to keep her end of the bargain, but feels uneasy about trusting this woman she has just met.

"I could be wrong about her. She might tell them about me just to make them think more of her. It's too late now, I'll have to run the risk."

When the smaller boat bumps the side of the ship, it is easily heard in their cabin.

"Okay, I'm going," Lilly informs the woman. "I'll get the key to let you out while they're occupied getting everybody aboard. Be ready, and remember, you can't take anything with you except what you wear. We'll be moving fast, so we can't be fooling with anything to slow us down."

Lilly enters the mirror in the cabin and comes out a few seconds later through a mirror the woman has told her about in the galley. The key to the locked cabin door is hanging on a nail just where she said it would be. Then it's on to their cache of powder, shot, and ammunition just beyond the bulkhead at the end of the supply hold. She picks up a small keg of powder and a length of fuse.

"Matches, and a knife," she says to herself. "Aha, here we go. Excellent."

With the keg of powder under her left arm, matches in her pocket, and the fuse in her teeth, she climbs the ladder from the galley to the deck. As expected, all hands are gathered, watching, helping the people aboard, and moving supplies from the arriving boat. A quick peek with her head above the galleys entry confirms no one is watching.

She moves onto the deck, and around the mainmast, where she stops for a better look. Then she runs to the farthest end of the boat, places the powder keg in the stern of the second smaller boat, and opens the bunghole. Using the knife she cuts two and a half feet of fuse, then inserts three inches of it into the opening of the keg. A quick look around, and it is back to the mainmast. Stop. Check to see. All clear. A short dash and she is on the top step of the ladder leading down to into the folks hole leading to the cabin holding her new friend. She jumps backward off the third step to the floor below, and turns to run to the cabin door.

Uuummmppphh!

She runs head on into the chest of a big husky seaman. He immediately throws his arms around her and says, "And who might you be?"

His breath in Lilly's face reeks with the smell of alcohol and garlic. His body odor, a weathered face with a scruffy two-inch beard, and unruly long hair under a tattered blue cap make up his first impression.

Instinctively referring back to her training, she slams the palms of her hands together against his ears. That loosens his grip just enough to enable her to smash him between his legs with her right knee. He howls with pain. One of his hands goes to his left ear, while the other tries to cover his crotch. She is free of his grasp, and could easily get away, but she knows he will recover too soon.

She takes her right arm back, puts the weight of body behind it, and thrusts her fist into his throat just below his Adam's apple. He drops to his knees clutching his throat, then to the floor, squirming for his breath. With no time to lose, she hurries to the cabin, and with a quick turn of the key swings the door open.

"Find some rope and something to make a gag with fast!" she says louder than she should. "I had to deal with one of them here in the passageway. Did you have anything to do with him being here?"

"No, no, lass, not me, I didn't know he was there myself!"

The woman has no trouble getting rope for his hands and feet, and an old rag stuffed in his mouth, bound by a stocking wrapped around his head, completes the job.

"So far, so good," Lilly says just to be saying something.

"Lock your door so they won't know you're gone. But first, let's drag him in there."

The woman stays quiet but obeys immediately, making Lilly feel a little better about trusting her.

"Here, take these matches. I placed the powder just as we agreed. The fuse is ready. All you have to do is light it when I give you the signal, then run like the wind back to me.

"When the keg explodes, I'm hoping the whole lot of them will go running. But regardless, we have to handle those that don't. I know I can handle two, so if just three stay with Elizabeth, we'll be all right. I'm counting on you to deal with the third, so, don't let me down. Any more than that, and . . . well, I'll figure something out.

"Once we have Elizabeth free, we're into their boat and away. They'll have no other boat so we should outrun them to shore with no trouble. Let's go."

Lilly peers above the hold again, with her head just high enough to see. She motions below with her hand for the woman to follow, and moves quickly to hide behind three large crates stacked on the opposite side of the deck, directly across from the boarding party. The woman stops momentarily with her, then continues on to the farthest end of the boat. Still in her sight, she waits there for the signal, matches in hand.

It seems like it is taking forever, but Lilly waits until the first of the boarding party arrives on deck. A wave of her hand sets the woman in motion. She sees a small spiral of smoke, the fuse is lit. In a few seconds, the woman is back at her side.

They watch as more people step onto the deck. At last, two seaman climb aboard, one on either side of a woman, dragging her with them.

As if it was waiting for them to appear, the keg sounds its fury!

The shock shakes the boat violently, causing ripples in the water to scatter like a nest of frightened snakes.

Folded sails are suddenly afire, along with rigging, and the deck. The stunned crew stands and looks for a long moment.

"Fire! Fire!" someone yells. All but the two men who have their hands on the arriving woman bolt toward the explosion.

"I'll take the one on the right!" the woman exclaims, and takes off running wildly directly at him. Lilly has no choice but to follow her lead.

When the woman gets within the length of her body from her target, she leaps and flies through the air headfirst, hitting him in the midsection. He reels off balance, his hand jerks loose of its hold on the young woman's arm, and his head bounces off a piece of tackle knocking him senseless. Then he rolls backward over the sideboard and into the water below. The older woman lands on all fours on the deck.

Lilly is not so lucky. Her target draws a single shot pistol from his waistband, aims it at her rapidly approaching figure, and pulls the trigger. The bullet hits her with a thud in the upper right chest, knocking her to the side to land hard, stretched out on the deck a good three feet to the left of her target. The older woman is immediately on her feet to jump a few steps and land on his back. She throws her legs around his thighs, and starts flailing his head and neck with her fists. That gives Lilly time to collect herself and get back in the action.

She calmly walks the few feet to reach the two struggling with each other. The seaman still has the gun in his hand, waving it around, trying to hit the woman on his back. Lilly grabs, and jerks the empty firearm from his hand, and says, "Shoot me, will you!" Then, still holding the gun by the barrel, she whacks him on the head with the butt. He howls and staggers; she hits him again. This time he folds like a piece of old rope to the deck, with the woman still hanging on, thumping him from behind.

Lilly grabs her by the shoulders, and pulls her loose, they stand for a moment looking each other.

"Leave him!" she says. "Let's go!"

Lilly is the first over the side, pulling the new arrival after her. The rope ladder swings and bends, making their descent difficult and slow. As soon as her feet are in the boat, she looks up to see the woman from the cabin just starting down the third step, below her is who she believes is Elizabeth. She puts her hands up to guide her into the boat, but not soon enough. Above them both, the last of their group struggles, trying to loosen a tangled foot. She lets go with one hand from above to reach down, causing her to shift her weight. That makes the ladder jerk to the right violently, throwing the young lady below her off balance, she slams into Lilly, pushing her backward over the side of the boat into the water with a big splash. The young woman clings to the ladder with her arms above her, swinging back and forth flailing her legs, keeping the tension tight with her weight before getting a foot down onto the boat below. The woman from the cabin winces with pain from the tight rope jerking against her tangled foot.

Lilly swims her way to the stern of the boat to climb aboard, watching as the captive woman lets go of the ladder to pick up an oar. She thinks the oar will be extended to help her aboard. Instead, the frantic woman begins trying to hit her with powerful swings that smack when the wood hits the water. Her third swing glances off Lilly's shoulder, forcing her to back away from the onslaught. She treads water just out of reach, waiting for the woman from the cabin to free her foot and finish her descent.

"What the hell are you doing girl!" she yells and grabs a double handful of the young woman's hair. Then with a hard yank, she puts the oar swinging female flat on the bottom of the boat.

"You are one hard little bitch to save!" she yells again. "Now, don't you move or you'll feel the wrath of my fist! You hear me, girlie?"

Lilly chases the now floating oar, and with it in tow, swims to the stern of the boat again to climb aboard.

"Are you all right?" she asks the woman from the cabin. "How's your foot? Can you walk?"

"I'm fine, lass, don't you worry about me. What are we going to do with this one here?" she replies.

"Are you Elizabeth Sanders?" Lilly asks, standing over, dripping water on the face of the woman at her feet.

"I certainly am not. Are you responsible for that explosion on my husband's ship?"

"I see. So you're the captain's wife, aren't you?" the woman from the cabin remarks. "And I'm the Queen of England, I am."

"Are you being truthful?" Lilly asks, not wanting the answer.

"She's not his wife, dearie. He's sworn to me on his mother's name, he's not married. Whatever your game, it won't work here missy."

Lilly looks carefully at the woman's image. The reflection of the flames from the fire on board the ship bounce off the water to make flickering shadows wave across her face. She's young and beautiful with a softness in her face. Her eyes seem to burn with fear and sadness. A closer inspection of her clothes shows them to be worn and dirty.

"You're not the captain's wife, are you?" she speaks slowly and quietly.

The woman lying on the bottom of the boat shakes her head with a little, no.

"Please tell us who you are. We won't harm you."

"People have promised me that before, but after I did what they wanted, they . . . they . . . lied to me." Water glistens in her eyes.

"I'm Sheree, Robert's sister, I'm looking for his—"

The woman cuts her off.

"You're Robert's sister Sheree? The real Sheree? Please tell me you're not lying."

"I'm Sheree, and my guess is you're Elizabeth Sanders. I'm here to find you and take you home."

Elizabeth stands up and rocks the boat back and forth, trying to hug the two women. Lilly has to settle her down.

"We're not out of danger yet. We're still in the range of their rifles, so let's get this boat moving. We can talk when we're safely away."

The trio rows to a secluded inlet. They step over the bow onto the shore, then shove the boat adrift. Lilly is the first to speak.

"Well, now, we made it this far, but look at us. We're all a mess. We can't walk into town amongst other people looking like this. We need some money."

"Is that all?" the woman from the cabin smartly states. "Well, I brought mine with me, I did." She pulls on a leather thong to produce a pouch up from between her breasts and tosses it to Lilly. "There's two hundred gold in there. I've saved it over the two years they had me on that boat."

"You mean you sold yourself for it?" Elizabeth asks.

"Not on your life, lassie. They took me when they wanted, pay or not. This I got in appreciation." Lilly and Elizabeth laugh at their friend's serious answer, and soon are joined with her own.

It is quickly decided that the cabin woman will slip into an inn on the Southern edge of town and register for a room. Lilly and Elizabeth will enter up the back stairs where she will let them in.

An hour later they stand on a landing outside the upstairs entry of the inn selected. They knock quietly, and momentarily, the door opens.

"Come on in here. I've got it all fixed up. We have room 202. The man downstairs says we can go down to his kitchen and get something to eat. He's friends with the owner of a woman's store close by. It's closed for the day now, but he's going to get him to let us in there in about an hour, so we can get something decent to wear. Then in the morning, he'll see to it that we get some transportation to get us out of here."

"My word, you did all that in that short period of a time. Do you have any of your money left?" Elizabeth wonders in amazement.

"Didn't cost me a penny," she responds.

"What then?" Elizabeth pursues.

"Well, there's only room for the two of you in the double bed in that room. Me? I'll spend the rest of the night downstairs."

"You mean you—?" Elizabeth stops short.

"Don't worry your pretty little head, lass. He's young and real smart looking, he is. And he says he has a long hot bath waiting for the two of us. My lord, there's been many a time I would have traded my left arm for a long hot bath over these past two years. This one is clean-shaved and has no smell of sweat, rum, or tobacco juice."

Elizabeth looks at Lilly expecting her to somehow intervene.

Lilly rolls her eyes and shrugs her shoulders, then says.

"Let's get to the kitchen and eat. Do you suppose your friend could find a way to get a telegram off to my brother?" she addresses the woman.

"I don't know, but I'll ask. I'm betting we can work something out."

"I don't remember hearing your name. Do you have one?" Lilly asks.

"I'll tell you that if you'll tell me how you can get shot at point blank range, then get up and walk away without a scratch."

Chapter Thirty-One

Three months later.

Robert and Elizabeth were married a month after their joyous reunion at Atlanta. The wedding was conducted, at Elizabeth's request, in the orchard behind the ruins of her once happy home. She believes her parents were there.

As it all worked out at Atlanta, when Lilly learned from Falcon that the lock had been changed on the door to the secret room inside the wall, she remembered the mirror she used to travel from there was left, and was probably still lying on the floor. Her memory served well, allowing her to travel to the room to learn that all of the bodies and containers were gone. The whereabouts of their location, or who moved them is a mystery. Although, since Ty and Mr. Vaughn were the only two people aware of the discovery, it's obvious one or both of them are behind it.

Lilly, Elizabeth, and Millie have become great friends. Mildred O'Toole is the proper name of the woman rescued from the boat, at Charleston, along with Elizabeth. She came to America with her parents when she was just sixteen. Two years later her father was murdered by a stray shot during a street robbery. Her mother was unable to cope with her father's death and fell to ill health, mentally and physically. With no skills to fall back on, Millie was left to forage any way she could. It was a rough life, but she learned to survive by the use of her wits for the better part of seven years. That's when the sea captain took a fancy to her, and kidnapped her while she slept in his bed. After that, she was kept aboard ship. Since she had no place to go when Lilly set her free, it was agreed she would, at least for the time being, throw in with the Anderson group. If she has any living family, she has no idea where they are, or for that matter, any reason to try to locate them.

Randy and Nora have gotten past their shyness with each other and have become a family, although not legally married. It makes Lilly warm inside to see her childhood friend feeling so happy, so whole.

Circumstances have brought this interdependent group of young people together. Their loyalties are unspoken, but deep feelings for each other are understood and apparent. It has been agreed that they would all move back to the Anderson farm for the foreseeable future, giving themselves time to heal their emotional wounds amid family and friends.

Sally, along with Rose and Hawk, will stay on at La Nesra continuing their efforts to supply information to be used to thwart the efforts of the Company. The knowledge regarding the supposed, now missing, Herculean and death angels, has been passed along to the three of them. They will continue to monitor Tyrone Black, and Mr. Vaughn, hoping to discover which, if either, can be trusted, and the new location of the containers.

At the Anderson farm, no time has been wasted, and the efforts of the remaining family members have given results. Charlotte and Cheryl have stepped to the forefront to take charge of assembling the necessities to shelter, feed, and clothe the remainder of the families from the three farms.

Since the vast majority of the furniture from the Anderson home was destroyed in the guesthouse fire, and the belongings at the Housler farm went up in smoke, along with the home and contents of the Sanders place, there was little left to outfit the only home left standing, the Andersons' main house.

It's decided that all three farms would be put together as was discussed earlier on, with the headquarters at the Andersons home. Charlotte's and Cheryl's organizational skills put everybody to work gathering anything and everything they could use to house the entire group. While some of the shacks of the hands were not burned and were able to house them all with some crowding, crude bunks were built throughout the Anderson homestead to provide temporary resting places until proper accommodations can be arranged.

For the first few weeks, John and Selma seemed listless and somewhat removed from the group. More often than thought to be healthy, they were seen sitting for long periods of time, near each other, saying nothing, lost in blank stares. Robert suggested that they be left alone to find their own way back to the family. His wisdom was shared by all when he explained that John and Selma, both, felt deep responsibilities for what happened. John believing the new job he assumed was at the root of it all, knowing he should have been at home when this all happened. Selma sits conjuring ways she could have made more of a difference. She doesn't understand why she survived, and most of the time wishes she had died with the rest. A little at a time, they both have increased their interest in the living and are functioning better as the weeks pass.

They approached the rest of the group to relate that they needed to provide a proper resting place for those lost in the guesthouse battle and fire. So, the area of the guesthouse has been cleaned of debris and any hint of the battle waged there. That which couldn't be burned was buried.

Per Randy's instructions, the only open entry to the tunnel below, the well, was filled in and leveled with the rest of the property. A fence has been built to surround the area where the house stood, and a pad, large enough to support a monument, has been constructed. When it arrives from Baltimore, the monument will serve as a headstone and memorial for all those who gave their lives trying to preserve what was theirs. The name of each person, along with their date of birth, will be chiseled into the gleaming white marble; starting with the youngest, then continuing according to age. Out of respect for Cole and Caroline Sanders, Jacob Stoker, and the hands killed earlier, their names will be included on the monument. It seems to be a fitting tribute and remembrance for all concerned.

As the surviving elders of the three families, John and Selma eventually accepted their roles, and continue to pull all the souls together. It's a feeling of 'we know what we must do, let's get to it and get it done.' As part of the process, Marty and Rachell Schoener have arrived in preparation for a meeting, which everyone expects to be a declaration of war on the known despicable spirits infesting humanity. John and Selma have every intention of not letting them down.

Morning at the farm has brought drenching rains, eliminating the possibility of holding the meeting outside as planned. There is no one room in the house large enough to hold all those attending, so it's decided to move to the main barn. It's dry and the seating will be at least as good as outside, probably better. The women have a fire going in a cookstove at the rear of the barn, making it possible to have hot coffee to compliment several varieties of cookies, cakes, and pies.

With Marty at this side, John walks into the barn pulling a stack of papers from under his jacket. Selma, feeling the need to be a part of everything, has been keeping a watchful eye out for them. As they enter, she picks up a hammer she has placed on a makeshift table of two barrels with boards laid across them, and bangs it several times in an overzealous manner.

"Okay everybody! Finish getting your coffee and sweets and find a place to settle down! Then we'll get started! The rain on this roof is noise enough!" she says in a stern bellowing tone.

John looks at Marty, unable to control a little smile. Marty leans over to John's ear and says, "You've got to hand it to her, she has a way with people." They both laugh out loud, which seems to be contagious for it's picked up by the crowd and spreads quickly for reasons unknown, especially to Selma.

"All right, now settle down!" She bangs the hammer again.

Smiling faces do as she says. Any tension that was lurking behind those faces seems to rise, and disappear with the smoke from the cookstove.

"A good morning to you all," John begins. "It warms me inside to hear you all laugh again. And I know there are people watching from above that are happy we're getting on with our lives." Two amens are heard from the silence.

"I think you all know Marty and Rachael Schoener here." He turns to acknowledge his friends, who now are sitting on a bale of hay behind the table with Selma.

"Someone's coming, Mr. John!" A hand stationed at the open barn door exclaims.

Marty rises to accompany Mr. Anderson to the doorway.

"It's Doc Shaw."

"We're over here at the barn, Doc! Come on over!" he yells.

In a few seconds, a buggy stops just outside the barn door, then shortly Doc Shaw enters in a hurry to get out of the downpour.

"You're up and out here early this morning, Doc, is something wrong?" John's voice shows his concern.

"No, nothing's wrong. I was just awake early this morning, and have been wanting to come out to see how you all are doing. If I wait until later in the day I get tied up with other things and miss my chance. What you got going on here? Am I interrupting something?" he comments.

"You're always welcome here, Doc, you know that, but we're about to start a meeting to rededicate ourselves to our mutual cause. Your presence might be looked upon as an act of supporting us," John replies.

"I'm surprised at you. Not for saying what you just said, but for not inviting me out here today in the first place. Hell, I feel the same way you all do, so count me in. There's just one thing though, I smell coffee brewing, and I'm going to need a cup of that before I quiet down."

Selma laughs as she rises from the hay bale. "Come on, Doc, there's some goodies back here too. I'll fix you up, don't you worry about that."

Millie is sitting on a bale of hay between Charlotte and Cheryl. She wiggles her pointing finger of each hand, motioning them to bend their heads toward her.

"Who is that handsome man? He about took my breath away when he came through that door?" she whispers loudly, rolling her eyes.

Charlotte pulls back to give her an amazed 'have you lost your mind look.' She's never heard anyone refer to Doc as handsome, or show any amorous notice of him.

"Did I say something wrong?" Millie continues. "Is he single?"

"No, that's Dr. Cedrick Shaw, our family doctor. It's just that I guess I've never looked at him that way before. But now that you mention it, I can see he's not bad looking at all. He's not married. Everybody calls him Doc," Charlotte explains.

"He's a good person to have as a friend, I can tell you that firsthand," Cheryl adds.

"Will the two of you see that I am properly introduced before he leaves?" Millie pushes. "How old do you suppose he is? He certainly looks distinguished."

"I have no idea, but he's been around ever since I can remember," Charlotte answers, feeling she needs to defend Doc. "That would mean he's old enough to be my father, and probably yours too."

"I like older men, lass, but just settle yourself. I promise, I'll do him no harm." Millie senses Charlotte's feelings and ends the conversation by laying her hands on her lap and facing forward.

Charlotte looks at Cheryl and with an almost unnoticeable shrug of her shoulders, and nod of her head, dismisses the thought for now, and directs her attention to her father's voice at the front of the group.

She notices more life in his face. His smile is a little wider and his eyes have some of the, once apparent, sparkle back in them. It lightens her heart and lessens the worry she has felt since the death of her mother. "I love you, Daddy." Her lips move silently with the words, and by fate or coincidence, he is looking directly at her.

His smile gets even brighter when he looks directly into her eyes and says loudly. "I love you too, honey."

"Let's get started," John tries to settle the din of voices in the barn.

Selma rises from her seat. "Do I have to bang this hammer again?"

A roar of laughter responds along with her own, then dies off to silence.

"Our job is to do everything we can to make a place, here on these farms, for our families to grow and prosper in peace," John begins.

"It's true, we're starting all over for the second time. Right now we barely have the things we need for an existence. But we have each other, and with each other we'll build these farms back to where they were and beyond that. Things will only get better from here on. Before this meeting is over today, each and every one of you will have your chance to stand up and have your say.

"My girls, Sheree, Charlotte, and Cheryl, along with Robert, have organized all the areas of running these three farms as one. They'll explain all that as we go along.

"Selma is going to tell us how we all now own a part of this one big farm, and how it will be handed down through the years to our heirs. It's all legal. You're all a part of it, and it can't be taken away from you. She'll explain it all and give you a chance to ask the questions I'm sure you'll have.

"We'll need to hire more help to do everything that needs to be done around here. We want to hire families, people who will bring their families here to live. They won't be owners like you and me, but they'll be paid for what they do, and be treated like they belong here.

"As you know, I have the job, along with Marty and Rachell, to do everything we can to put a stop to this war. We won't pick a side and fight, but we will act to save as many lives as we can, and choose our battles to put an end to the lawlessness we have witnessed firsthand. A large group of people out there, who call themselves the Company, are trying to take away our freedoms. They want to rule over all of us like a king from long ago. They want to take away our right to own this farm, take away our right to defend ourselves, and replace that with a tyrant to reign as he sees fit. We will use every resource at hand to put down and destroy their efforts. Our ultimate goal is to disband their entire organization.

"Needless to say, we all have our hands full. We'll overcome our problems and our enemies by working hard with purpose, one day at a time. We begin anew today. We'll look back only in remembrance, and push forward not letting up with our efforts until we have satisfied our goals."

Applause and shouts in agreement resound.

"Now, let's get my daughters up here and get started with the things that are the most urgent on all our minds. Ladies." John finds a seat beside Marty and Rachell.

At the same time, at La Nesra, in Atlanta, Sally, Hawk, and Rose have developed a close mutual relationship, with the knowledge of their real purpose being kept secret, while performing their duties for the Company. Mr. Vaughn seems to be as easily accessible as before, but discovering the whereabouts of Tyrone Black has been like trying to track thin smoke in a wind.

With a trust afforded Sally from her years of faithful service to the Company, with Rose's ability to disguise herself to appear as someone else, and Hawk's ability to move quickly, effortlessly, from point to point, the trio has made inroads enabling them to secure documents and overhear conversations meant for a restricted few eyes and ears. It's become obvious that the Company's plans are to aid the efforts of the South and to impede the plans of the North.

The efforts of the trio have brought a codebook into their possession. It describes the various ways of constructing an encoded message, and the methods of translating their meanings. This book must be given to the proper officials in the North. But as any good spy knows, you can't trust just anyone. The book should be given to a proven loyalist. The best bet is to get the book to John Anderson, and do it quickly. He can move it through the proper channels securely.

At the same time, they are getting bits of possibly related information having to do with the placement of a tool or weapon of some sort. It might be a load of arms and ammunition meant for the Confederate army, but Sally's instincts tell her it's more than that. She senses it could make the difference in the outcome of the war. But what is it? Where, and when, will it materialize?

The threesome have been using the vacated home of Lilly and Falcon for their meetings. It's being kept available for the couple's visits from time to time. They are there now discussing the situation.

"We need to get better information before we do anything," Rose is saying. "Bad information is worse than none at all."

"We can do that, but it's going to take time, and by the sound of things, we don't have much of that. Besides, we need to get the codebook to Mr. Anderson," Hawk reminds everyone. "If this information is about nothing more than a shipment of guns or the like, it's important, but not enough for us to delay moving that codebook."

"Yes, you're right, Hawk, but I have this gut feeling this is something really big. I mean something that could decide the outcome of the war," Sally cautions. "If I'm right, worrying about the codebook is a waste of our time."

"There's only so much we can do. Meetings are held behind locked doors every day. One of us needs to be in there with them somehow. We need to be there without them knowing it," Rose ponders.

"That's it!" Hawk squawks.

Both women look at him wide eyed.

"Lilly. Let's get Lilly," he continues. "She can stand behind a mirror and hear everything."

"I hate to bother her right now. She's finally home with her family after years of being cooped up here. What if I'm wrong and this whole thing turns out to be nothing? I'll have brought her back without good reason." Sally backstrokes from her position.

"But what if you're right? I say, if there's a chance we can foil a Company plan to somehow place a weapon with such a consequence in the hands of the wrong people, then we have to do any and everything we can," Rose states matter-of-factly.

"I agree with Rose, Sally. We have no other choice, so, let's waste no time getting her here." Hawk supports his idea.

"I'll get a wire off to her as soon as I can get into town. I'll word it so she'll know to travel to here, her old quarters, and wait until we come to get her. Agreed?" Sally poses, expecting positive responses.

Back at the farm it's getting along toward dinner time.

"I need a break, and I'm getting hungry. Is anyone else?" Robert announces.

That's all it takes to adjourn. People are up and moving around immediately. The rain has slacked up to off and on sprinkles, but the sky is still covered with dark clouds.

Food enough for all was prepared yesterday and last evening, with the idea of having everyone eat in the front yard. But with all the water, that plan has been abandoned to one of fixing yourself a plate and finding a dry spot wherever you like. The ladies are busy in the kitchen of the main house setting out the food, plates, and utensils.

John is just finishing a glass of cool water as he sits on the edge of the front porch, using his jacket to protect his backside from the wet boards.

"Mr. Anderson, there's a lone rider coming in at a gallop. See him?" Randy points.

John is on his feet and moving out to get a better look. "Robert, go get something in your hands to show some authority. Quick now."

Everyone is still on edge when an unexpected visitor appears. The past tells them danger can be as near as that. People milling around stop in their tracks. Others come from inside the house when Robert returns with a repeating rifle in his right hand, the butt resting on the belt of his pants with the barrel pointing into the air. He takes a position on the front porch, standing at the edge with his legs apart, so as to be seen by the incoming rider.

John turns slightly to acknowledge his presence with a nod.

"Let's just see what he wants before we get off on the wrong foot," he cautions all within hearing distance. "Keep an eye out all around for any kind of movement."

The rider continues to come at a steady pace up into the yard to within fifteen yards of group. There he jumps down from his saddle, drops his reins on the ground, and walks slowly toward them.

John notices the stranger's holster is tied to his leg.

"Can I help you with something?" he asks before the man gets too close.

"This here the Anderson farm, is it?"

"That's right. What can I do for you, sir," John responds sensing the tension building in those standing around him.

"Is there a Sheree Anderson Justice hereabouts?"

"Supposing there is—what do you want with her?"

"I've brought an urgent telegram from town with instructions to give it to her and only her. I'm to wait for an answer. Is she here?"

"Randy, find Sheree and explain what we have here," John directs over his shoulder, never taking his eyes off the stranger's face.

"You folks seem a mite on edge about something. If you're worried about me, then don't be. Like I say, Virgil at the telegraph office paid me to bring this telegram out here." He reaches for the breast pocket of his chore jacket.

"Move slow if you have to move!" Robert speaks sternly, shifts his position to hold the rifle barrel with his left hand, and puts his finger on the trigger.

"We have our reasons for being careful, mister. We don't know you, so if you want us to relax our attitude, you'll take that hogleg by the butt with your thumb and forefinger, and hand it over to me," Marty says and takes a few steps toward the man raising his hand as he moves.

The man slowly follows Marty's instructions being careful not to make any unexpected moves. After the gun leaves his fingers, he reaches for his rain soaked hat to lift it with his right hand to allow him to wipe his dripping brow with the left sleeve of his jacket.

"You folks must be expecting some real trouble out here," he comments. "I'm Virgil's cousin, in town for a few days visiting. My wife and kids are over at his house right now. I'm just helping him out by bringing this telegram here to you."

Randy and Sheree appear from the house.

"I'm Sheree," she says, while moving down the porch steps.

Again the man reaches to his breast pocket to produce a folded piece of paper. He holds it out allowing her to move toward him to reach it.

"Thank you," she reacts as she unfolds the paper.

"I'm supposed to wait for your answer," he reminds everyone.

"Would you like a cup of good hot coffee, and something to eat?" Robert asks at the same time he lowers the rifle.

"Would I? You bet I would." The man breathes with relief.

"I'm Nathan. Are you Mr. Anderson?" He puts on a broad smile and sticks out his hand to John and Marty.

The group relaxes as a unit and resumes their activities.

Sheree motions to her daddy with her head to come into the house. Marty, Randall, Falcon, and Robert follow.

"I have to leave right away. They need me at La Nesra," she begins, holding the message out for all to read.

Robert takes it from her hand and reads it out loud for all.

"Urgent. Stop. Proceed to Falcon's nest and wait. Stop. Signed. Sal. Stop."

"I don't know what it's all about, but apparently, they need me for something. Sally wouldn't do this if she didn't just have to. I have to go." She looks at her husband for his approval.

He shrugs his shoulders and nods in agreement, knowing this is their life for now.

"Tell that man, there will be no reply. I'll change out of this dress and be on my way. Maybe I can be there and back before you miss me," she teases Falcon.

At La Nesra, near Atlanta, Sally is climbing the stairs to Lilly's home away from home. She has delayed her return from town by making a few purchases to be used as her reason for going, if need be. Before she reaches the landing, the door opens to allow Rose to peek out.

"She's here. She just arrived."

"You made it here a lot faster than I thought you could," Sally explains as she gives Sheree a hug. "How are you, and how's your family doing?"

"A lot better," she answers. "It's going to take some time, but everyone is going to be okay. Thanks for asking. Now, tell me what's this all about?"

The three—Sally, Rose, and Hawk—take turns showing and explaining what they know, what they suspect, their fears, and elations.

"You have no better clue as to what this might be?"

"That's all we know," the three say almost in unison.

"I need to nose around a little, then. Give me a couple of hours then let's meet back here. I'll see what I can uncover," Sheree suggests.

"That's good, but be careful. You can't let anyone see you here. They think you're back at your farm," Sally points out. "And stay behind the mirrors."

As she enters the mirror in her bedroom of her home at La Nesra, Sheree's mind is on the beastly object lurking somewhere, probably just waiting for her. She makes an effort to not let her mind focus there for too long. "Okay, let me think. Mr. Vaughn's office. Concentrate.

"Aah, there he is with his director of security. I'll need to get my ear up close to the white square to listen. Not too close, though, I don't want to show through."

Mr. Vaughn is speaking. "I can't believe he moved those bodies that quickly. He had to have help, but who? I thought I knew him, but I was wrong. And now, we have no idea where he is."

"He has to be talking about Tyrone Black," Sheree thinks to herself. "And it looks like Mr. Vaughn has taken his director of security into his confidence."

"The man has left no sign of his departure. He's left before like this to be gone for several months at a time. Perhaps he'll be back," the security officer offers.

"Yes, well, I need better information than you seem to be able to offer. I know something is about to happen, something big. I can feel it in my bones. Are you sure there's nothing out of the ordinary going on right under our noses?"

"There's no sense of me hanging around here. They don't know anything," Sheree thinks to herself. "Mr. Vaughn knows he can find Tyrone Black if he really wants to, but it would mean coming through the mirror to do it. I know he won't because he has a real fear of doing that. But I can. Here goes.

"Think, Sheree, think . . . think. I'm moving. It must be a long way off because I've never moved this fast for so long a time before. Okay, I've arrived somewhere. I'll peek through the white square."

"Oh, wow. What is this place? I've never seen anything like this before."

"It appears to be a house or something, with the walls, floor, and ceiling made of polished stone and green swirled marble. This room I'm looking into is furnished with beautiful things. Wood tables that shimmer with luster. Chairs like the ones I've seen in pictures of old castles. There's tapestries hanging here and there, and silk throws lying about. Bookshelves take up about half of that wall. There's a desk over there, facing toward me from the corner. There are no windows I can see, but there's light enough to read by. Where's it coming from? I can't tell from here. If this is just one room of a large mansion, I can't wait to see the rest of it.

"Well, no sense staying here. I need to locate Tyrone Black, and he must be here somewhere. I'll need to slip through the mirror and nose around. I know I'm taking a chance, but what else can I do. I need to know what's going on. It's so quiet in here if you dropped a penny on the floor, the echo would go on for days. There's a doorway which leads to a hallway.

"This hallway is an oval going all the way around like a porch, and must be at least a hundred and seventy-five feet long if measured across the center. Lots of doors lead off all the way along this left side. But the other side of this ten-foot-wide floor has a three-foot-high banister made of marble. The balusters are all carved with scrolls. It looks like this place is several stories high, and I'm not on the bottom floor. I'll take a look over the banister.

"Oh my. It's a long way down there. There are four of these banisters below me. That puts me on the sixth level of whatever this is, and there's, let's see, four more above me. Then, the same thing is replicated, beyond the open center, on the other side. There are five gigantic chandeliers hanging from the domed ceiling way up there.

"This place is huge. It could take me days to locate anyone in here, and I don't have that much time. There has to be a better way.

"I'll bet if I let out a scream someone would come running. But then, they'd know I'm here. Hhmmm. I'll try thinking about him like I do on the other side of the mirror. It's worth a try. Here goes.

"Think, Sheree. Tyrone Black . . . Tyrone Black . . . Tyrone . . . Ty . . ."

She hears a voice from below.

"I tell you, someone's calling me. Didn't you hear it?"

"I didn't hear a thing, Ty. Your imagination is playing tricks on you. Come on back in here, let's continue."

It was a woman's voice. I can't put my finger on it, but it seems familiar. "Don't look at me like that, I know what I heard."

Lilly is frozen in her tracks, not breathing. "He's just below me. I need to get down there. First though, I should take off my boots, then I can move around quietly on these marble floors in my stocking feet."

She sets her boots in the hallway just outside the door of the room she came from, then turns to her left and runs to find the staircase. She doubts she will ever find her way back, but just in case she does, she'll know the doorway marked by her boots is where she'll find the mirror she came through.

She slides to a stop at the top of an eight-foot-wide staircase, which spirals slightly to the right down to the next level. Her stockings are too slippery on the floors, so she removes them, and stuffs them in her pocket. Slowly, one step at a time, she begins descending the stairs. The soles of her feet let her know the marble is cold, but it's better than slipping off a step and falling to the bottom. About halfway down, she stops in her tracks.

Footsteps softly echoing from the hallway below. The closer they come the louder they get.

"What should I do? Go back up? No time! I'll squat down behind the banister and hope they don't see me." A shot of fear races through her body. She holds her breath and peers between the balusters as the footsteps come closer.

"It's a person dressed in some kind of shiny silver clothing, like a uniform, carrying a red box. It looks heavy from the way he handles it. Good, he's passing. He's not coming up here."

She watches as the person stops at a door, knocks lightly, then proceeds through. She hears that familiar voice from within the room.

"Aha! You've brought it. Thank you. That'll be all."

"That's Ty's voice!" she tells herself excitedly. "I don't know if I'm just lucky or if this type of job is always this easy."

As soon as the person in the silvery suit leaves, she is down the stairs racing through the hallway—but wait. She stops, catching her breath. "Which door is it now? They all look alike, I've lost track of which one it is, I spoke too soon. What could be behind all these doors? If I pick the wrong one, Lord only knows what I'll get myself into. Maybe if I listen at each one."

The first two reveal nothing but silence.

"I'm getting nowhere with this. I'll try the knobs, if they'll turn, I'll crack them a little, just enough to hear. I'd better start over because I think it's one of these four."

"This one's locked." She moves to the next. "So's this one." Next. "This one's turning. Carefully, slowly, quietly, now, just a little push to open it."

The door moves about an inch—then suddenly swings open rapidly pulling her arm straight out. Before she can let go, a hand grabs her wrist and pulls her into the room with a jerk. She hears the door slam shut behind her.

Trying not to fall, she stumbles forward groping for her balance. It takes only seconds to regain her composure, but before she can realize what's happening a voice comes from behind her.

"Just as I thought. I knew it had to be you, Lilly."

"Tyrone Black!" screams through her head.

"I've been expecting you," he continues. "It took a few minutes, but I finally realized it was you calling my name in an attempt to locate me."

She turns to face him. He's dressed in black, as usual, looking all pressed and neatly trimmed. At the same time her eyes glance quickly to take in the rest of the room. A thick brown carpet covers the floor leaving a three foot area around the perimeter exposing gray marble. The walls, for the most part, are adorned with tapestries, pictures, and metal configurations, meant to be art. There are no windows. The furniture is all a dark wood polished to a high luster. There are no mirrors.

"How did you know I was at the door?"

"You have a lot to learn, young lady. You see, when you called my name to find me, you revealed yourself. Since I have the same abilities as you, I can find you the same way. The difference is, I understand how to do it without your knowing."

Lilly stands still, her mind churning, calculating what to do next.

"Let me introduce you to a colleague of mine," he moves on.

She looks to her left to see a stout built man, probably in his late fifties. He's completely bald with blond bushy eyebrows. His round face appears large due to his small ears and wide thin lips. A narrow somewhat longer than normal nose, and dark blue beady eyes, give him a foreign sort of look. He's dressed in a uniform similar to the person she saw in the hallway, except his is a medium brown color. He has a pendant hanging on a chain around his neck.

"Remsar, meet Lilly from our installation La Nesra. Lilly, Remsar is the reigning official of our American forces. He's the top man with the Company in this country."

Lilly stands silent with no movement to acknowledge Remsar's presence.

"You'll recall our conversation regarding Lilly, Remsar. She's one of our brightest and talented young people rising through the ranks. Right now, though, she's going through a period where she doubts our purpose," he further explains.

"Yes, I recall," Remsar speaks in an unemotional manner, never moving the expression of his face. "Perhaps we can change her mind."

Ty elects not to pursue this area of conversation and changes the subject.

"Why are you here?"

She stands silent, motionless, sternly looking straight into his eyes.

"You might as well relax and say whatever's on your mind. You're not going anywhere, at least not until we talk about a few things. There are no mirrors in this room, so think it through, then we can get down to business." He concludes by dragging a padded straight-back chair to block the door, and sits down.

Remsar finds a seat behind the marble topped wooden desk.

After a moment of consideration, she speaks.

"What's in the red box there on the desk?"

"That's it, is it?" Ty begins. "You've got wind of something going on and you're here to find out what it is. Am I right?"

She nods affirmatively keeping a stern appearance.

"You are aware, are you not, if I explain it all to you, you'll never be allowed to leave here," he warns.

"Ty!" Remsar cautions.

"Don't worry, I know what I'm doing," he advises in response.

"You'll never let me go anyway, now, will you? So, what makes the difference?" she points out smartly.

"I'm hoping you and I can come to some sort of agreement. You have a great deal of potential for the Company, and I'd much rather have you working with us than keeping you locked up as a prisoner," he offers.

"Perhaps we should give her some time to consider her options, say thirty days in one of our cells," Remsar poses.

Ty does not respond, but sits looking at her, feeling it's time for her to decide.

"It's some choice you've given me. If I say I'll not try to escape and stay here to help you, how can you possibly believe I'll keep my word?" she asks.

"I can find you no matter where you are and deal with you as necessary. As an example, have you felt something on the other side of the mirror acting aggressively toward you? As another; the raids on your farms were staged by me. The deputy was acting on my orders."

"You mean you're responsible for all those needless deaths?" Lilly's temper begins to show.

"I suppose I am, but the deputy let things get out of hand. My instructions were that no one was to be injured. The men he hired went too far." He defends his orders.

"Then you were also behind the Confederate attack at our guesthouse!" Lilly's breath feels hot coming from her mouth.

"No, absolutely not. That was a tragic misfortune caused by the Confederates ill-fated attempt to establish an authority in an area strongly held by the Union forces. It's not our purpose to destroy and kill. If you can open your mind to take an approach of listening, learning, and understanding, you'll see that the Company is not the dastardly, unfeeling, out-to-eliminate-all-who-do-not-agree-with-it's-ideals organization you deem it to be. The Company is the redemption of all mankind."

"But why then? Why did you order the attacks in the first place?"

"I felt I needed a show of force to bring you, your family, Amber, and Sally back to our way of thinking. I had Mr. Vaughn send Sally to check on Amber, and see what she could do as a last resort before instructing the deputy to act. She failed miserably mainly because that's what she wanted all along. Her usefulness to us is near its end.

"As I said, there was to be no burning or killing of anything or anybody during the raids. I went to your farms looking for the deputy to deal with him severely, and finally caught up with him at his office in town. Your family was already there. If your father hadn't shot that misplaced servant of Satan, I would have. He deserved to die."

Under the circumstances, Lilly feels she has no other choice but to go along with Ty's wishes. "All I can say is, I'll try. That's the best I can do right now," she snaps defiantly.

"I believe that's a good place to start then," he moves forward.

"I'll excuse myself, I have other matters that need my attention," Remsar announces and walks toward the door. Ty moves over enough to let him pass through.

"I can't feel what you feel, and I have no way of knowing your thoughts, but I can assure you, I mean you no harm. However, I do have a job to do along with the responsibilities that come with it, and make no mistake, I will take care of business," the man in black explains after the door is closed.

Lilly seethes inside, but shows no signs of it. "I'll play along with him for now, but my time will come." She thinks as she listens to his self-accreditation.

"To show you that I mean what I say, I'm going to tell you about this red box. Pull that chair over here and sit down." He feels more comfortable blocking the only exit from the room.

"Now we're getting somewhere," she sighs under her breath as she pulls a chair closer to him, trying not to look too eager.

"This red box contains glass vials of bacteria. Do you know what bacteria is?"

"Germs, I suppose, or at least that's what our instructors taught us."

"That's right. This bacteria, if placed in the right places can cause those who ingest it to become violently ill. It won't kill anybody with normal health, but it can take them off their feet for four or five days. It's not contagious such as smallpox, or a plague of some kind. Only those who take the bacteria directly into their system by swallowing it will be effected. It can't be passed from one person to another either, well that is, unless one person eats another person's excrement, which isn't likely." Ty waits for a question from Lilly.

"What are you going to do with it? How much of it is in there?"

"We're going to place it in the hands of the Confederate military with instructions to strategically distribute it to the Union forces, the higher up in the ranks, the better. It makes sense that if people are ill, they won't be effective fighters, if they're able to fight at all. Then consider the care they'll need. That'll occupy more people. If used properly, and timely, there's enough in there, well . . . we think it's possible that two thirds of the Union forces could be on their backs at one time. When the Confederate's properly place it, they'll know when it's time to attack and overrun the North. It could give them a great advantage, perhaps end the war." He takes a breath.

"When? When do you plan to do it?" she quizzes.

"Right now, we're getting our people set in the right places. Of course, they're currently members of the Union forces. Some are uniformed, while others aren't. As soon as I hear everything is ready, we'll distribute the bacteria. None of these agents know why they're being set up as they are. All they know is, it's something big, and that they are to wait patiently for instructions," he explains.

"And that's why no one knows any more about it than that." She thinks.

"How long will this bacteria live? I mean, it seems to me you'll need to use it before long, or it could die right in there in those glass vials," she points out.

"You know . . . you and I would think that, but this bacteria is not from here—our world. Don't ask me how, because I'm not trained in this area, but not only will it live in the solution it's packed in indefinitely, it multiplies while it's stored. Its life span is about eight days once it's out of the containers. It takes just ten hours to manifest itself in the human body. After that there's not much a person can do until it dies off on its own." He enjoys feeling knowledgeable.

"So, if all the cooks in the Union army were to put some of this into the food they serve, anybody who eats it will get sick? Is that how it will work?"

"It's as simple as that, but not limited to food. Simply licking your finger which has some on it will do the same thing. Troops drink from canteens some of the time.

Whiskey or beer, you name it. Even a pencil held between your teeth could do it." He smiles, enjoying the possibilities.

"Will it soak through your skin if some is put on your clothing, or will one person's sweat give it to someone else if it gets in their mouth?"

"I'm not sure about the sweat, but I don't think so. It won't soak through your skin if you get it on your arm. It has to be ingested." Ty's shifting in his seat signals that question and answer time is about over.

"No one is safe then?" She gives in to the grim potential not realizing she has posed a good question.

"That's not an entirely accurate assumption." His manner tells her he thinks he's going too far divulging this highly guarded information, but his ego won't let him stop.

"There's another box, a black one that goes along with this one. It contains vials of bacteria, too, and those will destroy these here in the red box. If a person ingests some from the black box before becoming infected with those in the red box, he'll feel only a slight ailment. If he's already ill from ingesting those from the red box when he swallows those from the black box, then his recovery time will be shortened to about twenty-four hours, or so I understand."

He leans back on his chair with a glint of triumph on his face. It is not often he gets the chance to boast. He knows this plan he's working was developed by those above him, and he's no more than a pawn receiving instructions as how to carry it out. But he also knows Lilly isn't aware of that, so he's confident she thinks he's the mastermind.

She ponders for a long minute, then asks.

"What happens if some of this bacteria gets put in a stream or lake? Won't it infect all sorts of things. Won't innocent people, and a lot of animals, be infected?"

"The instructions for its use will prohibit that from happening." Ty's defiant response shows some aggravation.

"So, you were the stranger who showed up at the deputy's office with the Stokers' twin boys, aren't you?" She intentionally changes the subject.

"That's right. As I said, I had to shut him up. The man was an idiot who shouldn't have been brought into our organization in the first place. He had never seen me before, so he had not idea who I was."

Lilly sees that he's getting more and more edgy from being interrogated.

"Can I ask three last questions?"

"All right, but then, we're finished for now."

"Okay, number one, did you move the containers with the bodies from the room in the wall. You do know they're gone and the lock has been changed on the wall door, right?"

"Yes, I know, I did. I've already explained about those beings. Their existence must be preserved at any cost. I felt leaving them there with so many knowing their location was too much of a risk. I couldn't be sure when someone would slip up and let it out. So, I moved them," he confesses. "Next question."

"Daddy told me that he dug a bullet out of my horse Pooch, and that was what made him fall and throw me. He said it was something new, more advanced than he'd ever seen, and that not just anybody could have something like it. Did you have anything to do with that?"

Ty smiles and leans forward to sit upright.

"You're quite the detective, aren't you?" he answers.

"I was there all right. I'd heard all about you and your family, and frankly, I wasn't happy about the way things were being handled. After a lot of consideration, I decided the best way to put an end to a relationship of that kind before it became a thorn in my side, was to eliminate you, the motivating factor. I saw my chance when I noticed those two bumbling fools Mr. Vaughn sent to bring you to La Nesra getting into position to shoot at you. They were way out of your range with the weapons they had. I'm privy to a lot of things with my position. One of them is the armory. The rifle I had can drop a buffalo at six hundred yards. My mistake was, I didn't have the time to dismount, so I fired from my saddle. I tried to shoot at about the same time they did, but the sound of their gun startled my horse. He jerked a little and pulled my shot off. I wasn't sure if you were alive or dead until you showed up with Sally. But that's all behind us now. I still believe I was right with my thinking at the time, but now, well, I need someone like you. You're a very talented young woman, and you're smart. The Company needs more people like you, and that's the reason I'm willing to work with you."

Lilly's emotions are overwhelming, but she can't let them show. The taste of blood from biting her lip seeps through her mouth. Not uttering a sound she screams, "You pompous piece of crap! You're nothing more than a hired killer! My mother and all those others would still be alive if not for you! I'll get you, you devil! I don't know how, but I swear to God above, I'll kill you with my bare hands if I have to! I swear it!"

"Ask your third question," he continues.

"Is this really you here, or are you like me, able to move around without your body?" she asks.

No reply.

"Your heart is as cold and hard as a piece of steel, isn't it?" she pushes him.

He sits silently and looks at her. Finally, he makes a move.

"We're finished for now. Take your chair and move back over there away from the door," he instructs.

As she moves, his eyes follow. When she gets far enough away from the door, he walks to the desk, leans over a brown box, and pushes a white button.

"They'll be here in a minute to take you to a holding room. I'll have some history related to you to help explain the Company and our reasons for doing all we do. I'm suggesting you listen carefully to it. We'll talk again later. And, oh yes, you might as well relax, you'll soon see there's no escape from here. No one ever has."

It isn't long before two taps are heard before the door opens. In walks four people dressed in silver uniforms with hoods that come up over their heads and down their foreheads about half way and come to a point. They have no weapons, and their hands are down at their sides. She's unable to tell if they are male, female—or both.

Ty motions with his right hand, Take her away.

Her thoughts of breaking away disappear when two of them move to her sides and take her upper arms in a grip, like steel. Another gets in front of her and the last, behind. When they move, she moves. The guards leave her no room to maneuver, so escape is hopeless right now. They walk together to the end of the hall to stop in front of a door with no knob or hinges. The front guard slides his hand over a small box on the wall. The door rises revealing a small room. The five step inside then turn to face the open doorway. The front guard reaches out to put his finger over a hole in the metal wall, which causes the door to close from above.

"Amazing," she thinks.

The little room starts shaking, then she senses the floor is moving out from under her. As quickly as it started the sensation eases up, but in just a few seconds she senses her weight on her feet becoming more than normal. The small room stops shaking and the door slides up. They step out into a hallway. She looks up expecting to see the rows of banisters, one for each floor. Instead, she sees a dingy ceiling about eight feet high. The lighting in this hallway is almost nonexistent.

The guards are moving fast now, practically dragging their prisoner. They stop in front of a solid steel door that has no window. The front guard grabs a D-shaped handle and pulls it open, allowing them all to enter the well-lit room. Once inside, the rear guard produces a piece of something they place into her ear. It has a piece of wire running straight up over her ear to extend several inches above her head. The guards then leave the room, closing the door behind them. She hears the key turn in the lock.

She looks around to see a small marble table with a matching bench sitting at one end. And there's a little bed, not large enough for her to stretch out on. The room is clean and bright but not at all inviting. She reaches to remove the apparatus from her ear when suddenly it comes to life. A voice that sounds like it's inside her head calls her by name.

"Lilly, please do not remove the receiver from your ear. I am going to read to you. I have been instructed to supply you with information regarding the Company. Should I read too fast, too slow, or if you do not understand, please wave your hand. I will then pause to adjust or explain. Please wave your hand that you understand."

She waves her hand.

"Thank you, I shall begin."

"It is important that you have a clear understanding of the reasons for the goals of the Company. The information I am entrusting to you comes from scrolls, tablets, books, and other methods of recording and storing history in an archival manner. It is neither theory nor lore that has been set down in other rank and file. This to be deemed as authentic and factual. To preserve time it has been categorized and condensed into pods. You are listening to pod number one, the Beginning.

"They call themselves Korgots. They are here and have been here for scores of years. It is not known where they came from or to where they will go. It is heard they are leaving soon to travel back to their world, leaving behind a force to gather the riches of our world, and await their return to claim them. To them, the riches of our world are our souls, those occupying our earthly bodies. The length of the Korgot's lives are extended far beyond ours, but once their bodies have died, so has their souls. Earthly souls are born again, and again, making it their purpose to meld our civilization with theirs, creating a being that will live for hundreds of years, then to be reborn at life's end. They have determined that the souls of our world must be willing to cohabitate with theirs. The union of a being from their world and ours will not produce a living offspring if either soul does not give themselves to it freely and totally.

"It is the charge of those of their world left behind, to unite the peoples and countries of our world into one. One that will follow the teachings of a leadership promising a never-ending life. A leadership aimed at people so inured with pain and bliss, love and hate, insecurity and confidence, illness and wellness, malice and benevolence, that they will embrace, with complete faith, the promise of an eternity of peace.

"Addition to pod.

"They have departed for their world. We are told they have left hidden an unknown number of death angels to insure our world does not unite against them when they return to transport our bodies and souls. If resistance is noticed when they return, they will awaken these super beings to destroy the world, and all souls, by fire. If no resistance is noticed, willing souls will be taken aboard transports. Those unwilling souls left behind, and our world itself will be destroyed, by the same death angels, after the departure of the last transport.

"The time of their return is unknown to us.

"Addition to pod.

"Three groups of five death angels each have been discovered. With this discovery we have learned that one death angel was eliminated from each group by a force opposing the Korgot plan, and one Herculean angel has been placed in its stead. The Herculean angels are to lie in wait, to be resurrected with the death angels, to destroy them before they are able to unite their destructive powers. It is now accepted that forty death angels have been left here on earth. It is not known whether all are placed in groups of five, nor do we know if a Herculean angel was placed with each group. It is impossible to determine which of the group of five is the Herculean angel. Should an attempt be made to destroy all the angels, good and bad, it would mean we could eliminate the only protection we have against the threat of the Korgots' return. Especially if any of the death angels remain secretly hidden and undisturbed.

"To be sure, we cannot be absolutely positive that any of this information is accurate. Are these bodies those of death angels? Are there Herculean angels mixed with them? We cannot be certain these sorts of angels exist at all. The bodies we have located could be no more than those of mankind. The plan to seek the location of all death angels, and to pull them together to one location to be monitored, continues to be supported.

"Leaders of men have risen in all corners of our world. Some with powers received from those who departed for their world, some not. All are teaching hope, faith, and life everlasting. Our group of resistance is eking out advances, but it has become necessary to don the cloak of secrecy. Our cause cannot be fought openly. We are many, and we are strong, but we are vulnerable because of the overwhelming numbers against us."

Lilly paces around the small room listening through the device in her ear.

"This is the same thing I've heard already, except Ty told us back at La Nesra that these people were coming back for our natural resources, our gold, silver. Now I'm hearing that they're coming back after us, our souls. That's a big difference, and it's sounding like the Company is trying to do the right thing. I don't know. Ty is probably trying to change my mind, so this is the way he goes about it. I need some time to think," she tells herself.

"Yes, you waved your hand. Do you not understand?"

"Oh yes, I understand perfectly and it's very interesting. It's just that I'm suddenly very tired, and I'd like to lie down for a few hours. Can we stop for now and resume later?"

"I will awaken you in three hours, is that satisfactory?"

"Yes, that will be fine. Can you dim this light a little? It's glaring in here."

"Sorry, I am unable to control that function."

"Will you watch over me while I sleep?"

"Sorry, I am unable to control that function."

"What if I need you for something. How will I communicate with you?"

"I will be available again in three hours. Are we finished?"

"Yes, I believe so," she replies.

"I will awaken you in three hours."

Lilly curls up on the bed to wait five minutes . . . then.

"Hey! Are you there? Can you hear me?" she yells.

No response.

She removes the ear receiver and places it on the floor beside the bed.

"Good, I need time to think. Priorities, first things first. I need to find a way out of here, then I need to get the information about the germs to the right people in a hurry. But will they believe me? I should take some of the red box bacteria with me, and maybe some from the black box as well. I could just destroy the red box, but they would probably just produce more of it. It would delay them for a while, but that's not the best solution. The Union needs some of the bacteria so they can come up with a way to counter it if people start getting sick. Once they believe me, perhaps they can take precautions to stop the army from using it in the first place." Her mind starts churning.

"Several little problems, though. First, I need to get out of here, then I have to find the red box, because I doubt it's still in Ty's office. And, I have no idea where the black box is either. I wouldn't store them together if it were me. I'll also have to locate a mirror, and I've a feeling they could be scarce around here.

"How do I get myself into these messes. It looks like I've really done it this time. I wonder what Falcon and Joie are doing back at the farm right now. I know what Falcon would say about all of this. He'd say, 'let me think about this logically.' Hey, thank you, honey, that's exactly what I need to do."

She rolls over on her back and pulls her knees up to keep her feet on the small bed, then lays her right forearm across her eyes to block out some of the bright light.

"Let's see now, I got into this place through a mirror. I can get out the same way. No mirror in here. Hmmmm.

"Ty said he knew I was here, and he knew where I was because I thought about him. He said he knows more about it than I do, and that he could find me without me knowing it. He also said I was smart and talented.

"Hurmph. I don't even know how to tell when he's thinking about me, let alone anything else. Maybe I should start all over.

"Zola told me that I was on my own, and that I knew everything I needed to know to move around behind the mirrors. I wonder if I even need the mirrors. I wonder if I tried, could I move around like that out here. I guess anything's possible. Who would have thought I could do what I've already done?

"I'll just try to move a little bit. Let' see, from here to the table. Here goes. Shut my eyes, think the table . . . the bench, think, think. Nothing. Maybe on this side I need to see where I'm going. I'll try it with my eyes open. Here goes.

"Stare at the bench, say it. Move me to the bench. Concentrate . . . again. Move me to the bench.

"Oooohhhhhh, I'm moving. I'm there. Now, that was really strange. Okay, move back. Stare at the bed, concentrate. I did it again, this is fun."

She moves back and forth several times, playing.

"Okay, back to solving my problems. Can I move through a wall? Let's see. Nope, I must have to see wherever I want to go to.

"How can I use this to get out of here? I know, I'll ask for something and when they bring it in here, I'll move out into the hallway through the open door. I'd better make my escape on my first try, though. If I don't, they'll do something so I won't be able to try again.

"On the other hand, if I do that and I get out of here, they'll know I'm loose. Then they'll all be looking for me.

"Oh, well, that's not such a good plan. I need a way out right now. They won't be looking for me for a while. But how? Think! Think, girl! The answer must be here somewhere.

"My instructor at La Nesra taught me if I ever needed to find an escape route from a prison cell, I should look at how the necessities of life are provided to it. Those are food and water, air to breathe, and elimination of waste. The one of those that I'm not aware of is the air I breathe. There has to be air coming in here somehow, but where, I don't see how. That light is so bright I can't see past it. If I can move up there—

"Whoa! Can I stay up here? Will you look at this. It must be thirty feet up here to the ceiling. I'm way above the light, and just hanging here, holding on to this pipe of a thing going down to it. The light's so bright down there it's reflecting up here, so I can see all right. There's a big square hole in the wall over there. Let's see, I'll let go here and try to move over there. Yes, there's air moving into here from it. It's big enough for me to crawl through, but it's mighty dark in there. I'll have to feel my way along. The bottom of it feels like smooth stone. This is my chance, so here I go."

She crawls on her hands and knees into the dark opening. Soon the light from the entrance dims and disappears behind her, it's pitch black. There's plenty of room to move and enough air flowing that it causes her hair to move. After a few minutes she arrives at a shaft of the same size that goes straight up. She stands up to feel as high as she can. It's smooth on all sides, so there is no chance of climbing it. Being unable to see, she can't make herself move straight up. Back down on her hands and knees, she moves on through the continuing tunnel. Just a few yards ahead she comes upon another tunnel moving off to her right. Should she continue on or take the turn?

"I'll take the turn. I still have at least two and half hours yet before anybody checks on me. If this doesn't lead anywhere, I'll come back here and go straight," she utters softly, discovering her voice will travel in faint echoes.

As she moves carefully along, never knowing what might be beneath her hand when she places it down, another piece of her instructor's wisdom enters her mind.

"The movement of the air, it's not blowing in my face any more. It's coming from behind me. I'm on the way out." Elation moves through her body.

With a new energy, she picks up her pace. She starts sliding her knees on the smooth floor and sort of drags herself along with her arms. This way she moves at least twice as fast. Two or three minutes pass when a faint haze of light reaches her eyes, getting brighter as she moves forward. She moves even faster covering the next forty feet to stop at the unobstructed end of the tunnel, and looks down at least thirty feet to a hallway below.

"Once I get down there, I'll probably never find my way back to that cell, but I have found my way to here. I need to believe in myself more. I can do this, I know I can. Is there anyone coming down there? No, well then, here goes."

She's down to the hallway floor in the bat of an eye, still on her hands and knees. After looking around quickly for trouble, she stands to decide her direction.

"It all looks the same. It's a guess at best. My instructor told me if my choices are exactly the same, choose the one on the right. I don't know why he would say that, except it's a way to make a quick decision. Well, I'm taking his advice, he's been right so far. I was facing that wall when I got down here, so, that way would be to the right."

She passes a lot of doorways which have no knobs, just that little box on the wall beside them. She moves at a trot, passing them by.

"Those have to read something on their hands before the door opens. I'd try it but I might sound an alarm if mine doesn't work. I'd better not.

"I'm coming to the end of this hallway. There's a door on my left with a handle and a glass to see through. There's stairs in there."

Once through the door, she sees that the stairs lead up, and down.

"By the feel of that little room we were in, I'd say they brought me down, so I'm going up."

The stairs up cover half the distance and lead to a landing before turning back and up to the next floor. They are open on Lilly's right side with a stone banister and a solid polished stone baluster. As she steps up to the landing, the hallway door from above opens allowing two guards to walk across the upper staging and start down the stairs. She darts back down to the stairs, crouches down low beside the baluster, her heart in her throat.

"I've got no where to go, and I can't let them catch me. Even if I evade them, they'll sound the alarm that I'm escaping. There's nothing I can do but the worst thing I can think of; I have no choice." She analyzes her options, then waits, with chills running down her back.

When the two people coming from above step foot on the landing, she moves like a shadow. Before either can react, she's behind the one closest to her, places her left arm around his neck, places her right arm behind his neck, grips tightly with her hands and arms and gives a jerk. She hears a loud snap and feels the guard go limp in her grip. She turns to see the second fleeing back up the stairs, almost to the upper level. A quick thought to cover the distance puts her at the top of the stairs ahead of the panicking man, and is moving toward him when he sees her. Startled and disoriented, he tries to turn to run back down, but loses his balance and falls over the banister. She hears him hit with several thuds.

Knowing he must be silenced, she moves to the bottom of the lower level stairs almost instantly. He's lying on his back, upside down, at the bottom of the steps trying, but unable, to move. She bends down over his face.

"You poor devil," she whispers, standing over him. "It looks like your back is broken. I'll try to help you if you can answer my questions. Okay?'

He forces out a gurgled yes.

"I'm looking for the red box that contains the bacteria, and the black box that goes along with it. Where are they?"

His pain is apparent when he pushes to get his words out. "Third floor. Room 17."

"How do I get in there? I don't have a key," she continues relentlessly.

He moves his eyes up and down trying to look at his chest.

"Pocket," he breathes with a rasp.

She feels his shirt pocks and finds a small thin rigid piece of white material.

"This?" she questions.

The guard signals yes with his eyes, while forming the word on his lips. Then looks at her expecting her to do something to help him.

"I'm sorry, but I have to do this. I wish I didn't"

She reaches down with the first two fingers of her right hand to shove them deep into the soft spot between his collarbones at the base of his neck. He gurgles, trying to breathe, before a quick twist of her fingers ends his struggle.

She shivers all over as if coming back to her senses.

"Oh my Lord. Look at what I've done. I never thought I'd be able to do anything like this." She kneels, clasps her hands, and looks straight up.

"Oh God. Please forgive me for what I've done. I am so, so, sorry. I didn't want to do this, they left me no choice." She recites a short prayer for the fallen guards and herself, then stands to assess the situation.

"They'll find these bodies, but there's no place to hide them. I'll go up there and throw that one down these stairs to wind up here with this one. Maybe they'll think they fell down the stairs together."

After completing her task, she elects to climb the stairs to two floors above the one just ahead. When she peers through the glass she knows where she is. Once through the doorway, the rows of banisters stand proud above her. A quick count tells her she's on the third floor, just where she wants to be.

"I probably have another two hours before they find me missing, that is, if no one uses those stairs. Now, let's find this room number seventeen."

She moves quickly only to find the doors have no numbers.

"All right now, let me think. These doors are undoubtedly numbered in sequence from one end of this hall to the other. If I start at that end over there and count seventeen doors, that could be the one. The only other possibility would be to start at the other end and count from there. It has to be one of the two."

"I'll start over here, it's closer to me." She stands with her back to the banister and starts counting, pointing her finger at the first door. When her finger points at the door in front of her she starts walking as she continues to count. "Sixteen, seventeen. This is the first one." The thin piece of white material is in her hand ready to pass over the small box on the wall beside the door.

"Wait," she tells herself. "If this is the wrong door, I might set off an alarm. I'd better know where the second door is before I start. It'll save precious time if I need to move fast. I need to mark this door first. Darn it, I don't have a thing except this card, and I can't leave it here, I'll need it for the other door." She searches her pockets to find her socks. She lays one of them on the floor in front of the door, then moves silently to the other end of the hallway, far enough to begin counting the doors. When her finger points to the one closest to her, she begins walking and counting, as she did before.

"This is it, number seventeen," she finalizes.

"Since I'm here I might as well try this one first. If it doesn't work, it won't take me long to reach the other one."

Before placing the white card over the opening in the box beside the door, her right hand moves to her brow to wipe the sweat moving down from her forehead. "Oh, Lord, I hope this works." She squints her eyes, braces for the worst, and lays the card over the opening. She waits. Nothing.

"The other side of the card. I might have tried the wrong side." Again, nothing.

"Must be the other door," she thinks, and runs to the door with the sock on the floor in front of it. "I don't know for sure if that guard was lying or not.

"All right. Last chance."

As soon as the card covers the hole of the box, a distinct click resounds. The hint of a smile almost makes her lips move, and a surge of new energy shoots through her body.

Her left hand, already in place, twists and the knob turns. A little push moves the door slowly, silently opening enough to allow her head to protrude to peek inside.

"Not a soul in here." A deep breath of relief fills her lungs.

Once inside, with the door closed, she begins her quest for the red and black boxes. The room, an office, isn't all that big, and very similar to the one she was in earlier. She knows the boxes are at least a ten-inch cube, so it doesn't take her long to find herself in front of a seven-foot-tall, four-foot-wide, double-door wooden storage cabinet. The obvious keyhole tells her it is locked before she tries to open it.

"Darn. What now? Look around, Lilly, what can you use? Maybe there's something in the desk. Just this heavy letter opener. Nothing small enough to get into the keyhole.

"Think, Lilly, think," she says out loud, knowing no one can hear her.

She moves back to the cabinet, works her fingers of both hands between its back side and the wall, puts a foot against the wall, and pulls with all her might. It's heavy but it moves enough, after two attempts, for her to get behind it with the letter opener.

"If I can get this blade started between the frame and a board back here, I can pull it off and get in that way." She starts sticking and prying at a board.

"A little more, aaaahhhh, good. Now, if this letter opener doesn't break, I can pry this board loose. Okay, great, now, get my fingers in there and pull."

With a little more work she's able to remove enough boards to look inside. The various supplies, and old records, fly across the room as she pulls them out and gives them a toss. Finally, she stops, carefully reaches in and pulls out a red box. After placing it on the desk, she returns to retrieve a black one of the same size. She stands looking at the two objects of her efforts, almost disbelieving her goal has been accomplished—so far.

"Stage one complete, now I need to get out of here. I probably should take a few of these vials from each box and put the boxes back. They might not know right away that I took anything. But that will take too long, and besides, I'd probably break the glass vials if I take them out of there. No, I'm taking the boxes with me.

"Are there any mirrors in here? No such luck. I'll see if I can make it down to the second floor. If my boots are still there, I can find the room and the mirror I came through."

She stacks the black box on top of the red one and picks them up with both hands.

Just as she is ready to move, she freezes.

"Stop where you are, Lilly! There is no use going any farther! We have been watching and following your path all along!" a booming voice resounds throughout the room.

Chapter Thirty-Two

Lilly's heart stops momentarily when an amplified voice fills the room.

"Stop where you are, Lilly! There's no use going any farther! We've been watching and following your path all along!"

It is as if a blood jam has stopped her heart. She feels the force of pressure, her chest growing tighter and tighter, then with a big thump, her heart starts again. The next few seconds seem like an eternity. Her breath must have left, because she is suddenly gasping for air. Her mind races, looking for a way out, but then, out of what. There's no one else in the room. No one to fight. No one to resist.

The door opens and swings wide before she is able to pull her senses together. She now knows the feelings of vulnerability, exposure, and fear in their truest forms. Caught in the act, defenseless, helpless.

"Where were you going with those boxes?" the voice booms through the room again. "Do you have visions of giving the Union army their contents in an attempt to thwart our efforts?"

Lilly expects to see someone, anyone, standing in the doorway, but there is not. There is no threat of anything, nothing, but that voice.

"Try to feel and remember the emotions you are experiencing. Now place yourself in this setting." The voice sounds even louder. "You are standing amidst millions of people all over this earth years from now. The sky is covered with strange objects, which almost block the sun. They are everywhere. Huge round gleaming craft hovering several thousand feet above the ground. You know they have arrived to transport all of humanity from our earth to their lair of existence. You also know that they will take with them only those who have transformed themselves to accept, without question, a promise of forever lasting life in a land of never-ending bliss. Further, you know that those humans who have not conformed will be left behind and executed with the total destruction of earth.

"Then add to it the fact that you have not conformed. That you have, your whole life, resisted being herded into their way of thinking. There is no denying who you are to these invaders. They know everything about everybody on this earth. A lie will not save you, but then, you will not be given a chance to lie. Neither will you be given a chance to change your mind and conform. When they come, when they arrive, it is too late. There will be no one to fight. You can run, but to where? Why? They're not going to come looking for you. They'll be here to transport the humans already living the life they expect. They will have no use for you.

"All the pleading, begging, and self-justification will fall on deaf ears. Your family, friends, and acquaintances who have conformed will pry your clinging fingers from their skin, to take their place in line to be transported. You are hopelessly lost. There is absolutely nothing you can do to change your destiny. You are finished. Earth and life are no more. And the truth of it all is, these intruders do not want the bodies of the humans being transported. All they want are their souls."

When the echoes of the voice fade from the hollows of the room and hallways, silence prevails. She stands perfectly still, undecided about what to do next.

"Even if what you say is true, God won't let it happen!" she shouts back at the loud voice. "Our God won't let it happen!"

"God is one of the reasons it will happen. It must happen," the voice roars in response.

"Who are you?" she fires back, her courage building. "Show yourself!"

"My appearance would not be pleasing to you. I am like nothing earthlings have ever perceived. Learn to accept my voice as my presence," the voice continues.

"That's not likely, whoever you are!" she speaks indignantly.

"I am—to use a word familiar to you—an angel. I am not of this world. You may refer to me as Cycostice. I am here as a messenger from a place beyond your knowledge," the voice explains.

"Look!" she begins. "You're wasting your time with me. I'll never be able to make myself believe all this hogwash. Especially since I've seen no proof of what you're saying. As for you, well, you could be anyone. I know the Company has means to do all sorts of things. Staging your voice could be a simple matter for them. You've offered nothing but your assurances that any of what you say is true. From the information given to me before by other people, no two of you agree on it anyway."

"What would you believe?" Cycostice inquires.

"What do you mean?"

"Tell me what you will accept as proof."

Her mind runs wild. "It has to be something the Company could not expect. Something they can't produce on the spot like this. Something so outrageous they'll laugh when I tell them."

"I'm waiting, Lilly."

"My mother! Bring my mother here now! Have her tell me all you say is true!" she demands.

"Your mother is not of the living, Lilly." Cycostice is obviously informed.

"So? You asked me what it would take!" she sasses.

"Are you sure? Can you stand the pain of her presence?" Cycostice sounds concerned in a mechanical way.

She doesn't respond. "There's no possibility they can do this," she tells herself.

"You would be wrong about that," Cycostice responds to her thought.

A full minute passes in silence before Lilly feels a cool brisk wind rush from behind her through the room, pulling the door shut with a slam as it exits into the hallway.

Still holding the two boxes, she leans her right thigh against the desk, waiting, wondering what is happening. It seems to be warmer, and getting warmer still. The lights dim a bit, and a soft, subdued orange glow is noticeable in the center of the room, just in front of her. It hovers about a foot off the floor and moves a few inches from side to side, up and down. Her eyes expand in wonderment.

"What in the world?" she whispers.

The image gets brighter, more distinct, at the same time changing colors to more of a red, then to a shade of lavender. It's growing in size. Now it's more blue, and it's turning to a misty mint green. "It's so beautiful!" she exclaims.

The shape is changing, more elongated from top to bottom. It's taking a form.

"Oh my God!" she gasps, as a face and the shape of a body becomes apparent.

She stops thinking; taking in the sight is almost more than she can comprehend. The object becomes more and more focused until it becomes the perfect, airy, ghostly figure and face of her mother. Her garb is a gown of a silky, shiny, soft appearance. Its color seems to continually change from front to back in a waving pattern, all different shades of mint green. She stands upright, but her feet are above the floor.

Lilly's eyes are wide, and her mouth open; she is in a knowing stupor.

The figure floats toward her and reaches out a hand to touch her face.

"Sheree, my darling child," she hears.

"Mama! Is it really you?" she stutters. "How can I know it's really you?"

"Do you remember what I said to you the morning before your accident, as you left our front yard riding Pooch? Don't run that horse, and don't be gone too long. Do you remember? I knew you were on your way to meet Randall that morning. I had known about your friendship for some time."

Her mama's touch feels warm to her cheek. Tears roll down her face and drip off her chin.

"Do you believe it is me, Sheree?"

"Oh yes, Mama. I know it's you. I love you so much." Happy, wishful, tears flow more heavily.

"Believe the words of Cycostice, Sheree. They are the pure truth. Prepare yourself to become a force to oppose and repel the advancement of mankind toward being led by false prophets. There is but one God, though he is known by many names. Swear to me you will do as I request. The world needs you, my darling daughter." The wavering green full body halo surrounding the image grows brighter for a few seconds then settles back again.

"But, Mama, how will I know what to do? How will I know who to trust? I'm afraid! I'm all alone! I don't know for sure who I am! How can I make any difference anyhow?" she sobs.

"You are all you need to be, and you know all you will need to know. Learn to use your God-given gifts. He has His reasons for giving them to you. I must go."

"Wait!" she exclaims wildly. "Are you all right where you are? Are you happy? I need to know, I can't let go of you if I don't know."

"I am in a wonderful place where I will be when you get here. Do not fear death, my angel. Understand that what you are being asked to do will only bring you closer to me in the end. Believe that I love you and you are always with me."

The image moves close, and Lilly feels lips on hers. Then it pulls away dimming and shrinking as it goes until it fades through the same colors it arrived.

The lights in the room come on bright again.

She lets the boxes fall to the floor to put her palms to her face and bawl.

After a few emotional minutes, the voice begins again.

"Are you satisfied, Lilly?"

She reaches down, pulls her shirt tail from her waistband to wipe her face, and running nose.

"Yes, I believe I am," she concurs after taking a short jerky breath.

"I am pleased. Expect that your path will not be an easy one. You will sacrifice in many ways, but be assured you will be blessed for it," Cycostice explains.

The door opens. This time, Ty and Remsar enter as it swings.

"I need to explain a few things to you," Remsar begins without waiting.

"First of all, there's nothing in those boxes except a few small bottles filled with alcohol. There was never a plan to poison the Union troops, nor a bacteria in the first place. All of this has been staged to bring you here of your own accord. Your incarceration was necessary to let you get to know yourself—your abilities. You need to rely on your own resources and talents, and learn to understand just how far you are willing to go to do what must be done.

"The Company has known from the day your were born that you are destined to be more to this world than just another person. Cycostice has made sure of that. Up until now, you've been trained and pushed into maturity. And now, at last, you're here."

"You mean, all of this has been a put on to lure me here? Why couldn't you just tell me and bring me here? Why go through all this?"

"As I said, you needed to learn about yourself. You needed to experience all you have been through to be ready to accept what you are just now beginning to understand."

"I killed two of your guards. You know that, don't you? Was that part of my learning process too?"

"Yes, it was. As cold as it sounds, it's a small price to pay. You know now that you are capable of taking a life if necessary." Ty joins the conversation.

"I'll never kill anybody ever again, that I can assure you!" she states flatly.

"Good, that's the right attitude. But believe me, when the time comes, if it comes to that, you will," he finishes.

"You know, Lilly, from this point on, we will need you here on a full time basis. No trips home to the family," Remsar points out.

"What about my family? What will I tell them? You both know you're not well thought of at the Anderson farm," she asks, and explains.

"Tell them the truth. If they believe you, then you've made a good beginning. However, if I were you, I'd expect to be shunned by them and all your friends," he comments.

"You'll need to deal with it in your own way, but, the reality is, once you get started here, you'll probably never see them again. You'll be better off if you cut your relationships clean, and have no expectations for the future," Ty suggests sternly.

"What about my daughter and husband? Can they come here with me?"

"No! Absolutely not!" Remsar's response is exaggerated and firm. "There can be nothing to get in the way of your accomplishments."

"Go home. Take thirty days to do what you deem you must, then come back ready to get completely involved. Keep in mind, there are people out there, not unlike your father, who know about our organization. Once word gets around about who you are, some of these people will delight in taking your head to serve as proof you're dead. Just be very cautious about whom you trust," Mr. Black warns.

"I suggest you return to La Nesra, first. Have things settled there before returning to your home." The boss of the Company poses.

Lilly ponders. "I wonder? You know, Sally, Rose, and Hawk are already trained for service with the Company, and each of them has a special gift. Would it be okay if I brought them with me?"

"As we said, those decisions are yours alone. They must not be brought here to this place, however. When you get a good understanding of where you are, you'll agree, and be glad of it. No one but you should come here," Ty explains.

"Not to worry, I don't know where here is at this point," she informs them.

"Well, all right, you can leave when you're ready. We'll expect you back thirty days from today. Agreed?" Remsar advises and asks.

"Yes. I agree," she commits.

With the aid of Ty's directions to the correct room, Lilly returns quickly to her dwelling at La Nesra to find no one there. She's confident they'll return shortly, and is glad in a way to have some time alone. Time to think.

"That was Mama, I know it was. It was so good to see her again. I probably shouldn't mention her to anyone. Stirring up memories would serve no purpose. But then on the other hand, knowing she's in a good place might help them let go. Ty and Remsar are cold-blooded, unfeeling men. They didn't bat an eye at my killing those guards.

"What Cycostice did must have been true. How would they know about Randy and me otherwise?

"How much should I tell these folks here? I suppose only what they need to know. And just what is that? Oh, Lord, help me please. I'm going to mess this up, I know I am. There's so much I don't know, and I'm not sure I understand any of it.

"For one thing, I've changed sides. Sally has just changed sides in the opposite direction, so, I don't know where her thinking will be about this. Hawk and Rose will probably go along with me, not that they'll be tightly committed. My changing sides will be the single biggest problem to explain. Once I've accomplished that, I'll only have to tell these people, all of them, what I want them to know."

"Uh, oh! The steps squeaked, someone's coming! I'll step back out of sight, just in case!"

The door swings open slowly allowing light to flood in. It occurs to her that she has neglected to light a lamp. A person steps inside, but she's unable to determine who it is because of the outside glare from behind. The person shuts the door carefully, quietly, as if they don't want to be noticed, then moves in a sneaky manner to a bedroom corner, crouches down beside the dresser and waits. Since there are no walls, this whole living quarters is one large room, and if you're in the right location, you can see the whole area.

"What's going on here? I'd better stay put for the time being." Her concern is for the next people through the door.

Several minutes pass while the two wait in the semi-darkness. The person by the dresser moves to adjust positions, but Lilly doesn't dare.

The sound of footsteps, more than one person is coming up the outside steps.

The door swings open quickly and two people enter. She notices one is a woman.

"Probably Rose and Hawk," she thinks.

A lamp is lit before the door is closed.

"She should be here in a few minutes," Rose's voice explains.

"Yes, you're right. We might as well sit and relax for a few minutes," Hawk's voice agrees.

"Should I run over there screaming there's a person hiding behind the dresser, or should I let this whole thing unfold?" Lilly's heart beats faster.

Before she can reach a decision, squeaking steps announces another person about to arrive. Rose moves to the door and opens it, allowing Sally to enter.

"Good, you're both here," she says gladly. "Has she returned yet?"

"No, not yet?" Rose replies as she closes the door.

"How long has it been?" Hawk asks.

"Going on three hours. She should be back by now," Sally indicates.

Lilly glances back and forth from the hidden intruder to her three friends, ready to pounce on a seconds notice.

"What's taking her so long? She was going to Mr. Vaughn's office to listen in for a while, then, if she discovered nothing there, she was going to find Ty Black." Rose shows her concern.

"You know how she is, she gets on the other side of those mirrors and loses all her common sense. She takes too many chances?" Hawk agrees.

"Yes, you're right, she's probably gone though a mirror somewhere to search for information. That would be just like her. Sometimes she worries me to death. We all know we told her not to do that, and we agreed we'd all meet back here in two hours." Sally supports the other two.

"Did she take the codebook with her?" Hawk inquires.

"No, I have it right here." Sally reaches inside her handbag and produces a small book. "I plan to give it to her when she comes back. The faster she gets it into the hands of the Union forces the more quickly they can put it to use."

The person crouched by the dresser makes a move!

Lilly watches as the figure moves to a standing position, holds out his right arm with a gun in his hand, and announces while moving toward the trio.

"I'll take that! Just as I suspected! You're all a bunch of spies!"

Lilly now recognizes him to be Mr. Vaughn's director of security.

"Well, I've got the goods on you now. Mr. Vaughn will be pleased with this information. You'll probably hang for it, you know," he says, almost yelling, as he proceeds to grab the book from Sally's fingers, at the same time he waves the gun back and forth, pointing it from person to person.

The three are startled by his sudden appearance, catching them unaware. Sally is facing him when he comes from behind Hawk and Rose.

Without hesitation, Lilly moves effortlessly to position herself within a foot of his back. Sally sees her appear from nowhere, but manages to act as if she has not. Hawk's eyes find hers, so she glances back and forth quickly, signaling him to look behind their captor.

He immediately draws the director's attention hoping to give Lilly time to do something, anything.

"Hey, what are you doing?" he yells.

The director stops swinging the gun to point it directly at Hawk.

"Are you going to give me troub—"

His words are cut off when Lilly reaches from behind him to grab his wrist and pull it downward. The gun goes off with a 'bang' as she continues her movement to pull his arm up behind his back causing it to bend at the elbow and fold up between his shoulder blades. The bullet has gone harmlessly into the floor. It's a simple matter to jerk the firearm from his grip with her free hand. Then with one smooth motion she clobbers him on the head with it, causing him to sink to his knees, then fall in a daze flat on his face onto the rug.

"You showed up just in time!" Sally exclaims excitedly. "I'm not sure what would have happened if you hadn't."

"I've been here for a while. I saw him when he came in and hid over there. He didn't see me, so that's when I decided to wait and see what he was up to," Lilly explains.

Sally looks down at the moaning heap on the floor at their feet, and says, "What do we do with him now? He heard us talking about the codebook. We can't just let him go."

"We'll have to kill him. I know the perfect spot to hide his body. Nobody will ever find him," Rose speaks with enthusiasm.

"Good idea!" Hawk confirms, ready to take part in the process.

"Whoa. Hold on a second," Lilly pleads. "Why should we kill him? I think Mr. Vaughn will hang him for us. When I listened in a while ago, it was easy to see that this bag of trash is on Mr. Vaughn's bad side. All we have to do is turn the tables on him, and tell Mr. Vaughn he tried to sell us this codebook. From what I heard, that's all it would take to have this one swinging from a rope in the morning, for treason. There's no sense having his blood on our hands."

After a bit of discussion, all four agree that would be the right thing to do. Lilly divorces herself from the process, leaving it all up to their discretion. The prisoner is tightly bound, gagged, and deafened with cotton plugs in his ears. They place him next to the far back wall of the room, to await his disposition.

"He can't hear us now," Sally states, looking at Lilly. "How did things go for you? Did you uncover anything?"

"You won't believe what I've been through?" she starts, not knowing where she will stop, or what she will omit along the way.

"You three are people I care very much about. I hope you'll be able to understand the position I've been put in when I'm finished. Try to believe in me, and that I'm trying to do the right thing. I'm not crazy, and no one has a gun to my head forcing me to do anything. This is all by my own choosing. Trust me when I say, I need you now, and I'll need you even more to help keep me on the right path with your counsel during the hard times."

Sally, Hawk, and Rose sit, somewhat wide eyed, not knowing what's next to be heard from their friend's lips.

"Let me explain completely before you ask questions. It'll be easier that way," she begins.

At first she hunts for the right words to express feelings and paint the intended picture for their understanding. Then everything seems to fall in place. Words flow from her mouth that she has hardly had time to produce. It's as if someone, something, is helping by preselecting her course and laying out the information to support it. As she continues, her mouth moves and words come out that perfectly describe every needed detail. She feels odd because the words being used are not hers. Perhaps someone, somehow, is using her as their puppet. Time passes as she carefully lays it out.

"And that's it. That's the whole thing," she concludes.

None of the three speak. They sit and look at her face.

"Well, what are you thinking? You're making me very nervous," she clamors looking from one to the other for an indication.

"Who are you, some kind of Goddess or something?" Hawk blurts out.

"I honestly don't know, Hawk. I don't feel like it, at least, not now. I don't know."

"Are you going to tell all of this to your family?" Sally asks cautiously.

"I'm not sure, but I don't think so. See, just like now, I need your input on this sort of thing. I don't feel like I'm smart enough to decide these things."

"Wow!" Rose expresses her feelings, and moves to put her arms around her friend. "A whole new set of problems has been dumped in your lap. I'm glad it's you and not me. I can only speak for myself when I say this, but I'm with you to the end. I feel like I've always known you were meant for bigger things than this life. I love you, Lilly, ask anything of me, I'll be there for you."

Tears come easily to Lilly's eyes today and a few roll down her cheek as she pulls Rose to her shoulder and kisses her forehead. Then she turns her attention to Hawk.

"What I'm about to say will probably be a surprise to everyone, but I hope not too much of one to Rose," he says before she can speak. "I love you, Rose. I've wanted to tell you for a long time, but I've been afraid you don't feel the same way about me. I know if I don't say this now, I might not get the chance again. I want to be with you doing whatever it is that makes you happy. Lilly, I love you too, and I'll support you anyway I can. And if Rose will have me, we'll make one hell of a team." With that he moves close to put his arms around both young women.

"What are you saying . . . exactly?" Rose's face glows as she looks into Hawk's eyes and asks a serious question.

He doesn't seem to be able to speak. He tries, but nothing comes out.

"Dammit, Hawk!" Sally finally shouts and slaps his back sharply. "Ask her to marry you."

"Will you, Rose?" He blushes a bright red. "Will you marry me?"

She leans closer and adoringly caresses his face with her eyes.

"I've been wanting to kiss you since the first time I saw you." And she does, right there in Lilly's arms with him.

Sally is overcome with emotion and waddles on her knees to the group to throw her arms around everyone. She's unable to hold things back.

"Well, answer the man," she orders. "Tell him yes, you'll marry him."

Rose pulls back from Hawk and says, "I will, yes, yes, yes."

Now they're all crying, including Hawk.

After a few minutes of happy tearful chatter, they all begin to settle down, knowing there is one yet to be heard from.

Sally moves back to her seat and turns around to sit down. She feels everyone's eyes before she looks up.

"Do you really want me, too?" she asks with sincerity. "I'm older than the three of you, and, remember, Lilly, you and I haven't always seen things the same way. I have a way of speaking my mind and being a little stubborn about some things. I have a temper, too, that brings out my masculine side, and that's when I can be vulgar. If I'm asked, I'll tell the truth, whether it's liked or not, and that will go for you, too, Goddess and all. Don't make the mistake of thinking I'll change, because I won't. And don't think you'll run me off when you get upset with me, because I won't go."

Lilly rises from her seat, kneels down in front of Sally, and takes her hands.

"I've come to love you, Sally. Yes, whether you like it or not, I love you. I wish I knew myself as well as you seem to know you. Maybe with your help I'll learn how to do that. All the things you've said are just a few of the reasons I love you. Yes, I want you to be with me, with us. I need you. Will you? I have no idea where all of this will lead, but I know I'll feel a whole lot better about it with the three of you with me."

Sally agrees making it unanimous.

"Thank you, my dear friends. This has been some day so far, and I imagine it will continue when I get home, which is where I must go right now. I'll be back here in no more than thirty days." She does not dally, but leaves immediately for home.

Falcon is sitting on a straight-back chair in front of a makeshift bed where Lilly's life body peacefully lies. Joie is asleep in his arms. He has spent most of the time his wife has been gone right there, on that chair, keeping her safe. He's caught napping when she returns through the mirror.

Instead of waking him, she tiptoes to the bed and lies down to unite and become one. Then, she stirs on the bed enough to get his attention. His sleepy eyes widen when she sits up and smiles.

"Did you just get back?" He beams.

"Just now," she coos back.

"I've been worried. You've been gone longer than I thought."

She cuts him off. "Put Joie down, close the door, and come to me."

He does as she requests and lies down on the bed, on his side next to his wife. She turns toward him to start running her fingers over his face. His forehead and eyebrows, down his nose, around his eyes, traces a line around his lips, follows his jaw line up and around his ear, and finishes by running her hand through his hair.

"I love you more than I will ever be able to say," she whispers in his ear. "Don't say anything, just hold me and make love to me."

Joie's squirming and fussing awakens them both at the same time to find themselves entwined in each other's arms. She's up first to pick up her daughter and snuggle her between them in bed. Nothing's said, but Falcon knows something's going on. He'll not say anything about it, she'll tell him when she's ready, he knows that.

"Will you look at the clock. We've been asleep for over three hours. And you've been a little angel, haven't you?" She puckers her lips when she speaks to her baby.

"I'll bet you're hungry now; shall I find Nora to feed her so I can stay here with you?" she asks her husband softly.

"No, she needs her mama. You haven't had the chance to spend any time with her lately. Why don't you take care of her? And, honey, take your time, enjoy her." He feels a sorrow in his wife, and wants her to have some happiness.

"Don't worry about me, I'm not going anywhere."

"No, you're not, you beautiful man, but I am," she thinks heavily.

Roosters on the barnyard fence roust the Anderson farm just at daybreak. Lilly awakens with a ravenous urge to eat something. She recalls eating yesterday morning, but with all that went on yesterday, she didn't think to have something again.

"I'm starving," she whispers in her husband's ear. "I'm going to throw on a robe and go down to get some toast or something. I'll send Nora up after Joie, all right?"

"Okay," Flacon mutters with his face in his pillow.

The kitchen is alive with activity when she walks in. Nora is helping out, but stops when she sees her.

"I'll go take care of little Joie, ma'am," she says and speeds to carry out her promise.

"Coffee, ma'am?" A question from the cook that requires no answer. She hands a steaming mug of black coffee to Sheree.

"Miss Selma's in the dining room if you've a mind. I'll be bringing her breakfast, what can I get for you, honey?" the cook continues.

"Yes, bring me something, anything, right now, and then I'll take whatever Mrs. Housler is having as well. Thank you so much."

Sheree enters the dining room to find Selma sitting alone, sipping her coffee. She's dressed and ready for whatever the day brings. Sheree notices how beautiful she still is, and the poise she maintains. But she looks older than the last time she saw her, more starch in her skin and expression. "I know it has only been less than a day since I last saw her, but I swear she's aged five years. She looks like an aging schoolteacher sitting there," Sheree mentions to herself.

Selma smiles when she enters.

"Come sit over here, close to me. I've not had a chance to chat with you for some time. I'm real glad to have this opportunity."

Sheree would rather just sit quietly for an hour or so, drink her coffee, eat breakfast, and get cleaned up before socializing. But that's not the way it will work today.

"Yes, ma'am," she replies politely. "How've you been, Mrs. Housler?"

"I'm fine, Sheree. Now let's cut the small talk. We've got to talk fast because there's no private conversations around here any more with the way we're living. I'm sorry to be so pushy, but what the hell is going on with you, your husband, and your baby? Your mother would turn over in her grave, if she saw you running off leaving them here like you did."

Sheree pulls back in her chair from the unexpected assault.

"Whoa!" she thinks to herself. "Don't let her get you all riled up. She doesn't mean anything, it's just her way."

"Mrs. Housler, I don't think it's your place to—"

Selma cuts her off. "You don't know what goes on here when you're gone. Nora takes good care of Joie, but a baby needs her mother. And besides, she has a family of her own with Randall and Sherman. And Falcon, that poor boy is lost without you. He won't eat right, he doesn't want to talk to anybody, and I hear he never goes to bed while you're gone. He's going to worry himself to an early grave. What's so damned important that you have to up and leave that way?"

The words, she hears, burns a hole in Sheree's heart. She hangs her head to let her finish. When Selma settles down, Joie's mother gets up and heads for the door.

"Where are you going. I didn't mean to upset you," Selma calls after her.

"Well, you have, Mrs. Housler," she snaps back as she closes the sliding doors. She pushes the sleeves of her robe up on her arms as she returns to confront her accuser. "Are you sure you want to know? Because if you do, I'm going to tell you, and you'd best hold your tongue while I'm doing it. And for your information, Mama didn't turn over in her grave when she found I wasn't home with my family. She came to see me and told me I'm doing the right thing. Now are you sure you want to hear what I have to say?"

Selma sits, her mouth open, unable to speak.

Sheree lays it all out for her mother's best friend. As before, once she gets started, the words seem to flow endlessly. The only break in her dissertation is the few minutes it takes the cook to deliver their breakfasts. She's about to finish up.

"And now, I have to tell my husband, my baby, my family, and friends, that I'm leaving for good. I won't be back. I'll tell them to forget me and make a life for themselves without me. Can you imagine how I feel about that? How am I ever going to explain all this to Daddy? You know he's the head of the Sons organization, who are sworn to dismantle the Company—the very people I'm supporting. After all he's been through, and now this, I'm afraid he'll have a breakdown or something.

"But whether you think it's right, or not, I was there, I saw Mama, and I know what they're telling me is the truth. I have to do it. I have to do it for all my family and friends, and everybody else in the world. And that includes you, too, Mrs. Housler. I have to do it for all the grandchildren of our families, and all their grandchildren of the future. I haven't gone looking for this heavy responsibility, but it has certainly found me."

Tears are again flowing down her cheeks.

"It has found me, and I need all the help and understanding I can get. There's no way for you to know and believe the hurt I feel inside. I hurt because I'm leaving my whole world behind, but I also feel the pain that will be inflicted upon humanity if I don't do everything I'm capable of doing to stop this atrocity from happening. I'm not asking you to give up your world to help me. All I'm asking is for you to understand and support me. But then, I know what you've suffered over the last few months; I know the feeling of your grief. Lord knows I felt it at an early age. Maybe I have no right to ask for your support. Maybe you don't care. Well, I'm sorry if that's the way you feel, but I don't have the time, nor the strength, to drag your resentment along with me. I'm going with or without your blessing." She stops to stand behind her chair facing Mrs. Housler. "I'm finished now. You can speak."

Selma still sits with her mouth open, speechless, her breakfast sitting in front of her, getting cold. If her eyes had not been following Sheree's every move around the room, one might think she is in a coma.

Sheree waits for a response until she is satisfied there will be none, and is about to move toward the door.

"You poor, poor, thing," Selma bleats. "What have they done to you?"

Sheree cuts her off. "You haven't believed a word I've said, have you?"

"Why—that's not true, Sheree. You see, I've not forgotten the visit you made to me that black day you came to warn us about the Confederate soldiers. You pulled me from that burning trap and saved my life. You took me to town and put me to bed out of harm's way. I also know you left there to go to Atlanta to explain what happened, then you came back there to check on me before you left that same day to go to Charleston to save Elizabeth. These are all such selfless deeds that have guided all our lives and no amount of thanks can be enough. But you haven't expected anything for it, all you've ever wanted is the love and support of your family. And, may I say, you deserve it.

"I misspoke earlier. You're right, I was out of place. I apologize. Now I understand completely, and I'm begging you to let me be a part of it. I'll do anything if you'll let me. I'm not very well educated, but I'm smart, and I learn things quickly.

"I'm betting your father will blow his top at first, but when he thinks about it, he'll be ever so proud of you for what you're going to do. And don't worry about him when you leave, I'll take care of him. I'll see to it that he's not alone to sit around and grieve, and I'll make sure he eats good and gets his rest." Selma rises from her chair to take her best friend's daughter in her arms. "Your mama would very proud of you, honey," she whispers.

"She is," Sheree whispers back, laughing through her tears.

"Would you rather I explained all this to your daddy?"

"No. I have to tell Falcon first, then Daddy," she replies thoughtfully. "But listen, after I tell Falcon, I would sure feel a lot better if you could be there when I tell daddy. And then if you could sit beside me when I tell all the rest."

Dealing with Selma's onslaught brings a renewed confidence in Sheree. Maybe her family will be more understanding than she previously expected. Telling them will not be any easier, but the outcome could be a lot brighter.

Falcon is waiting in the kitchen for his wife to come out of the dining room. He puts on a cheery smile when she walks in. "My breakfast got cold in there. Do you suppose I could get another?"

"You can eat together then, I just starting to fix your husband's," the cook replies.

Not much is said about the meeting in the dining room during their breakfast together. Sheree pushes food down as if she's never going to eat again. Falcon watches and grins from time to time. As soon as their forks are placed on their empty plates, she reaches for his hand as she gets up.

"Come with me, I want to tell you about the meeting I just had."

He follows obediently, happy to be with his wife. They walk side by side, hand in hand, out past the barn to the back rails of the corral fence. Unknown to them, two pairs of eyes watch from chairs on the front porch.

They watch as Sheree turns from Falcon to face and place both arms on the top rail. After a while, she turns back to face her husband, who is now hanging his head. She takes his hands to place his arms around her waist, then moves her hand to his chin to raise his head. She puts her forehead against his. He pulls her to close, and they stand like that together.

"I wonder what's going on with those two?" John asks.

"They're in love, John, can't you tell that?" Selma smiles and murmurs fondly with a chiding manner. "They have the kind of love we had, the kind that goes on forever."

Selma keeps an eye on the couple as the day passes, expecting Sheree, at any time, to come and pull her aside, getting ready to tell her daddy. But the couple stays together at a distance from others until midafternoon.

Convinced John won't hear from Sheree today, Selma has found her way to the site where the guesthouse once stood. She stands looking at the fence and sturdy footer where the monument will be placed. Everything is soaked from the downpour yesterday, but the sun is peeking through the clouds here and there, trying to lap up the crystal-clear water from everything it touches.

"Thought we'd find you here," she hears John's voice from a distance behind her. She turns to see John walking hand in hand with Sheree.

"You've caught me, I'm afraid. Sometimes I get so lonely for him . . . it makes me feel better when I come here."

"That's what this place is all about," he soberly implies. "I'm thinking of putting a few chairs around out here. You know, nothing fancy, just something to sit on and relax with our memories. What do you think?"

"That's an excellent idea. I know I would enjoy that."

"Good," Sheree's father confirms.

"Now, why in the world did you drag me all the way out here?" He changes the subject to quiz his daughter.

"Well, Daddy, I have something to tell you, and I need you to brace yourself."

"What is it?" John's tone gets stern and serious.

The three stand in close proximity while Sheree explains. Selma, having heard it before, keeps a close eye on John. He dances from foot to foot, at times shaking his head; at others, kicking the toe of his boot into the soft ground. He says nothing until he thinks she is finished.

"Are you through?" he shouts, throwing his arms up. "What else can happen to this family to tear my heart out? What are you thinking, Sheree? You're turning your back on everybody who loves you! I don't know how you can do it! Have you forgotten that I've sworn to do everything I can to destroy the Company and everything connected with it? You and I will be enemies, fighting each other. Our family will be forced to pick sides! Can't you see that? Have you forgotten that the Company was behind the raids, and most likely the battle that killed your mother?"

She takes a breath ready to explain further, but stops when Selma raises an openhanded finger to her lips.

He continues ranting. "I know you have reason to punish me, but the rest of these people have done nothing. I just don't know how you can even consider throwing it all away. If it's about me, say so. Hell, it would be better for me to leave instead of you."

Sheree wants to speak again, but Selma's hand moves and this time she shakes her head a little no.

"Well, I'll say this! Go! Go on, if that's what you have to do, but never come back here expecting to find a father. If you leave, you're dead to me. You died when we buried that empty box. Now get out of my sight!"

Sheree can't take it any more, she turns and trots away, back toward the main house.

As soon as she's out of earshot, Selma starts working on her longtime friend.

"John, what the hell are you doing!" she yells. "I know you love that girl. I know it hurts to hear the things she says, and that you might never see her again. Well, it hurts us all. How can you possibly think she's doing this out of spite for you? Wasn't that you there this morning with me, watching when she told her husband about all of this? Didn't you see the love they have for each other. He has to give her up, too. How do you suppose he's handling it? This is something she has to do. Someone, or something, bigger than you and me, or any of us, has called on her to do it. And, John, she's going to do it with or without your blessing, because she knows there's no other way. She's already forgiven you for what you did to her. It's not a part of her anymore. Do you honestly think she could ever take up arms against you. Could you, just this one time, be wrong about something?

"You've got me riled. Are you so pigheaded that you can't see what she's saying is true? She's giving up her life to devote herself to saving the souls of this world. And what a saintly endeavor it is. She must get it from her mother because she sure as hell couldn't get it from you."

He says nothing, just stands seething.

"Oh, to hell with it!" she screams at him in an alarming volume. "You're a fool if you let her go like this. Turn around and get your ass after her, and when you run her down you tell her how much you love her, you tell her how you want to be a part of her life no matter what. You cry and tell her how much you'll miss her, and that you'll do everything you can to see that her husband is kept well, and her baby is raised right. You tell her not to worry, and then swear to it. If you let her go this way, you'll never forgive yourself. Once she's gone, there's no getting another chance. So you get going now, or so help me, John Anderson, I'm going to hurt you, and I mean hurt you badly."

He jerks his head as if awakening from a spell. Then, unexpectedly, grabs Selma, puts his arms around her, spins her around and lets her fly, before taking off at a run to catch his daughter.

He doesn't have far to go since Sheree made it just out of sight over the first rise, then fell to her knees in the mud and grass to raise her clasped hands toward the sky in prayer.

She hears him coming, yelling her name. "Sheree, honey . . . for God's sake, wait!"

"Thank you, Lord," she says out loud before turning to accept her father's arms as he slides to her on his knees, mud and muck flying everywhere.

Considering she fell flat on her back when John let go of her, Selma is not far behind. Although she tries to resist, they pull her down with them into the muddy mess.

They all sob clinging, holding on, explaining their need for each other, and swearing their support forever. After a while, the sobbing turns to weeping, the weeping turns to a playful push, the playful push turns to a handful of mud up against someone's face, and a good-natured wrestling tumble results. Shortly, all three are covered with mud and water. Laughing with exhaustion they settle down to catch their breath. Since both women teamed up against John, Selma waits for Sheree to move before she can get off his chest. His daughter just happens to glance at Selma's muddy face, catching her looking into John's eyes.

"Daddy, I don't know if either of you know it yet, but someone has their eye on you," she thinks. A warm feeling spreads through her heart, and she smiles at the sky. "Thanks, I know you've got your hand in this."

The trio trudge back to the house to be verbally greeted by fun makers everywhere they look. Things like "three little piggies been playing in the mud" and "is there anything left in that mud hole?" seem to be their favorites. It isn't often when the elders of this clan put themselves in such a position, so everyone enjoys the good-natured fun. But, it soon becomes old news, and everybody drifts away to mind their business.

John catches Robert's eye and motions him over.

He greets his father with a broad smile. "You're not going to grab me, are you, Daddy?"

"No, son, you're safe, from me anyway. I can't vouch for these two," he kids. "Listen, I want you to gather our immediate family for a little meeting right after we get cleaned up. We have some news to pass along to you all."

He looks at his father with a question on his face, expecting more of an explanation.

"We'll get into it all at one time. Right now I need to get out of these wet clothes," John advises.

"Randy, and Nora?" his son continues.

"Sure, you bet. Say in about forty-five minutes."

"You got it, Daddy, forty-five minutes in the den," he confirms.

The elder Anderson nods his head yes, and is on his way into the house. The women have already gone ahead.

"Thank you for what you did back there, Mrs. Housler. I don't know what you said but you sure changed his mind in a hurry," Sheree compliments Selma, as they climb the stairs together.

"I must admit that just for a minute back there I thought he was about to stomp me into the ground. I said some awful things to him. Well, I don't care, he made me furious and I pushed him really hard. I guess it worked," she replies. "You know come to think of it, he didn't say anything to me. Not one word."

"Hmmm, imagine that," Sheree says under her breath, as she turns into her bedroom.

The adults attending the meeting as immediate family consist of Robert, Elizabeth, Charlotte, Cheryl, Falcon, Randall, Nora, Millie, Marty and Rachell, and Doc.

Apparently Millie, somehow, convinced Doc to stay around for the rest of the day and have supper.

Sheree, Selma, and John complete the group. Others present but not counted are Sherman and baby Joie.

"Before we get started I just want to say that Selma and I already know what Sheree is about to tell you, and we've given her our total support. I'm saying this so none of you think for some reason we won't; I guess that makes sense. Well, anyway, Sheree has something to say." John feels if the rest know where he and Selma stand, they'll have no problem supporting her, too.

Sheree stands and explains it all from the beginning, hopefully for the last time. No one asks a question, or hardly moves during her presentation. She looks for emotion in their faces, but sees none.

"And that's all there is to it," she finishes. "Does anybody have anything they want to ask me. I'll answer if I can."

Falcon speaks up. "I'd like to say something, then ask a couple of questions.

She shakes her head in approval.

"You all know that my wife will be leaving me behind, too. And I know you must understand how I feel about that. I know in the deepest part of my heart that this is tearing at her as bad, or worse, than it is at me. But she has to do what she has to do, and I'm not going to try to stand in her way. She explained to me that she'll be working with a group of people we both are acquainted with in Atlanta, and from time to time, she'll be in contact with them.

"Well, honey, I want to know if it's okay with you if I join ranks with them? I won't expect any more than to be involved the same way they are."

"I never thought of that," Sheree responds, while running it through her mind. "But what about Joie? What will happen to her?"

"That brings me to my second question. Dad, Mrs. Housler . . . I'm asking you to take Joie and raise her as your own, will you?"

John and Selma look at each other with bewilderment.

They look at Falcon, then at Sheree, and then back at each other, in unison.

"I've always wanted a child, but I wasn't blessed with one of my own. I think I would like that very much. It'll put purpose back into my life. I'll do it," Selma explains and accepts the offer, then looks at John.

"If there was a way to work things out with Sheree to keep her here, I'd say no, but under the circumstances, I can see where you want to be as close to your wife as you can get; I know I would. And I can see that with you there in Atlanta you might get to see her once in a while. Come to think of it, we might get a bit of news as to how she's getting along once in a while. I know we'd all like that. So who am I to stand in the way of a woman having her first baby? I'll do it, too," he rallies cheerfully.

"Sheree?" Falcon lets his wife have the deciding vote.

"That would make me very happy, honey. I can't think of two finer parents, and who knows, like Daddy says, maybe you and I can spend some time together."

The entire crowd starts talking at once, causing the room to become loud. Sheree feels a tug at her arm. It's Randall, motioning her out of the room, to follow him into the kitchen.

"When do you have to leave?" he asks.

"Ooops! I forgot to mention that. I have to leave in twenty-nine days, starting tomorrow. Why?" she queries.

"We wanted you to be the first to know. We're going to get married. I haven't had a chance to ask her when yet, but I'd like to do it while you're here. I would never have met Nora if it hadn't been for you. One other little thing," he says leaning over closer to her ear. "We're going to have a baby."

She grabs him, pulls him off his feet, and hugs him hard. "I'm so happy for you, Randy. When are you going to tell everybody? I won't be able to keep my mouth shut, you know."

"I'm going to ask her right now, and if it's okay, we can just go ahead and tell everyone about it now."

It all happens everyone is supporting Sheree with her new undertaking, and plans for the wedding are getting under way. Although not happy about it, Mrs. Justice feels a lot more settled with leaving her husband and baby behind. As the new leaks out, a celebration is started, which eventually includes the entire population of the farm.

Sheree finds a few quiet minutes in her bedroom to kneel down beside the makeshift bed, fold her hands, and thank God for allowing things to work out the way they have. She then returns to the party to enjoy her family and friends.

The next day.

"Have you seen Daddy, Mrs. Housler?" Sheree asks as she moves from the house to the front porch, to see Selma sitting on the steps with a coffee mug in her hand. Getting to bed late last night has not prevented anyone from rising early as usual this morning.

"Yes. He, Robert, and Randall went over beyond the barn somewhere to figure out where they're going to put all these houses we're needing." She points as she speaks.

"If Falcon comes looking for me, tell him where I am, okay?"

Selma nods her head yes as she watches the young woman bounce down the steps and move at a trot for a few steps, before settling down to a swift gait in the direction of the barn.

John, Robert, and Randy are standing together as she approaches. Robert's pointing and moving his arm back and forth as he speaks.

"What are you three up to?" she asks causing them to turn at the same time.

"I'm beginning to wonder if we know. What brings you out here?" John kids, knowing she must have something on her mind.

"I'm glad I caught the three of you together, because I have some information you might be interested in having," she unintentionally teases.

"What's that?" Robert is quick to challenge. "Is there more you haven't told us?"

"No, no. Nothing like that. The people at the Company told me there's a ship on its way from Spain with its holds full of repeating rifles, ammunition, and gold, destined here for the Confederacy. It's expected to arrive within the next three or four weeks."

"Arrive where?" Randy speaks up.

"Roanoke, they say," she advises without hesitation.

"If these are the same rifles that fired that round at Pooch, then we can't let the South get their hands on them," Robert is quick to remind everyone.

"I don't know what kind of rifles they are, but there's also something called a Gatling gun coming, too."

"Ohhhoooo!" Robert sighs. "That's really not good. The Gatling gun can fire close to a hundred and fifty rounds a minute for as long as you can feed it ammunition. It's used for one thing, and that's killing a large number of people in a hurry. We can't let something like that get in the hands of the Confederacy."

"Just how sure are you about this information?" John asks.

"I can't swear it to be true, but getting it was a condition I placed on my doing what they want me to do. I believe they have too much to lose to lie to me about it," she answers as honestly as she can.

"I can't see how we can take a chance that it's not true. If that ship shows up, someone has to stop it before they get their hands on its cargo," Randy interjects firmly.

"Is there any chance you can check it out any further?" John asks his daughter again.

"No, Daddy. There's several reasons why," she begins.

"No, that's okay, I know you would if you could," he interrupts.

"Another thing, I expect you'll be receiving a copy of the south's agent's codebook before too long. You know, the one that tells how they send their messages back and forth to each other so the North can't decipher them. I would have brought it with me, but it was needed in Atlanta to take care of some unfinished business." A thought goes through her mind to tell Falcon to make sure he gets the book to John as soon as the trio in Atlanta is finished dealing with the director of security.

"Sheree, the more you talk, the more it sounds to me like we can maybe work together after all. If we can pass information back and forth, I mean, if we can trade information that won't cause us to lock horns.

"As I think about it now, it seems that maybe there are two factions working within the Company at the same time. One to save the souls of the world, then, one trying to sabotage their efforts. It makes sense, and if I'm right, you're going to find it out in a hurry." John shows his interest and a glow of excitement.

"Which would mean we can all work together at destroying the bad guys, right?" Sheree picks up on the intrigue. "You know, that would certainly explain a number of inconsistencies I been puzzled about."

"How much time do we have to get ready to disappoint those Southerners?" Robert poses to the group.

"We have to be ready to act within two weeks, I'd say. And since we don't know for sure exactly when that ship will arrive, we have to be there waiting for it." Randy gets caught up in the stimulating conversation.

"Hot damn!" Now we're getting somewhere!" her brother exclaims, with accompanying body language.

"Do you have any idea of the name of the ship?" her father asks, bringing quiet to Robert's and Randy's glee.

"They told me it's a frigate flying the colors of the Confederacy. They call it the *Savannah*."

Sheree spends as much time as possible with her husband and baby over the next several weeks. She makes it a point to make contact with each and every person on the farm. A practice that, she quickly learns, is welcomed by each, and awaited by all in their turn. She can tell by their interest in what she says, along with their easy flowing questions about life and the hereafter, that they all, each and every one, support her trying to do the right thing.

Her sisters want to know if she can tell them if they will get married and have children, kiddingly, of course. Several hands ask if she will take messages to a departed love one. One young woman, who lost her husband in the fire, wants to go with her.

Her relationship with Selma has grown quickly to one paralleling that of a mother and daughter. Although nothing is out of the ordinary, Sheree can see Selma, probably unintentionally, getting closer to John.

The wedding came off without a hitch. Marty and Rachell decided to stay for the wedding. Everyone, in one way or another, played a part. It is disclosed that the first house to be built will be for the new couple, Mr. and Mrs. Randall Stoker.

All too soon, John, Robert, Randy, Charlotte, Cheryl, and the Schoeners leave for Baltimore. Marty has been brought up to date about the incoming shipload of arms and gold. Sheree keeps her distance since she does not need to know how they will handle it.

Selma has mixed emotions when they all leave. She's sad to see them go, but with them out of the house, well . . . now she can really get something done.

The monument arrived and sets proudly on its foundation. As expected, it's a gleaming appropriate memorial. John kept his word and has had six wooden chairs placed just inside the fence.

Millie has decided to stay on at the farm to help out. Some think she has other reasons since Doc is visiting more often than before. But all are glad that she will be around to watch over Selma.

The morning of day thirty comes too soon for all those left at the Anderson farm. Selma has been trying, unsuccessfully, to hide her tears from the others. Sheree and Falcon have been standing outside saying goodbye to everyone with hugs and kisses as they pass in single file.

As they enter the house Sheree is speaking. "Honey, I know how this is going to sound, but I don't think I can stand waiting for another six hours, knowing what I have to do. It's tearing me apart inside. We've said what we need to say to each other. I'd like to go upstairs, kiss Joie, and be gone. Please let me?"

Millie and Selma watch as Falcon takes her in his arms and kisses her gently and long. When he lets go, he doesn't look back. A quick turn sends him past the two standing in the kitchen doorway, out through the screened door onto the porch, and gone.

"See you in Atlanta when you least expect me! I love you!" she yells after him.

A quick hug with Selma and Millie, then Sheree runs up the steps to kiss her baby. The two women stand at the bottom of the stairs in silence.

"Don't forget your mama, Joie. Be sure, I'll never forget you. I love you, you sweet, unknowing little angel," she whispers her last words to her daughter in her ear. She tenderly places a long kiss on her cheek then lays a gold locket and chain on her blanket. Inside is a small picture of them together.

Chapter Thirty-Three

At Baltimore, a meeting of the Sons organization is in progress, with the entire Anderson entourage present, along with Marty Schoener, and a high ranking field agent, George Foster. Their topic of discussion is southern frigate *Savannah*.

"The South will bring supplies from somewhere if they're to wage this war. Unless something changes, they don't have the ability to produce everything they need. We've been tracking their ship movements, so I can confirm that the *Savannah* left port at Charleston, along with two other cargo ships a good six months ago. Barring any unforeseen problems, your information could be accurate," the thin aging white-haired agent relates to his peers.

His heavy wool winter suit, tie, vest, and long-sleeved shirt are warm for this time of year. Beads of perspiration show on his forehead. His elbow rests on the arm of a captain's chair pushed back away from the table, allowing him to cross his legs. The pipe in his hand emits a small rippling of smoke after he puts the stem to his lips for a puff. He pulls it away to continue.

"One thing bothers me, though, I can't see them bringing those ships to Roanoke. With what they're carrying, I'd dock them at Charleston, or farther South."

"Yes, I agree," Marty chimes in. "With our capital being at Washington DC, the Union isn't taking chances. Those waters are heavily guarded. If they tried to bring a war ship like the *Savannah* in there, all hell would break loose."

John thinks as he speaks. "And I have it on good authority that she's coming, and should be here within the next ten days. The farther away they are from the front line of their forces, the longer it will take to disperse those new rifles to their troops. And with their capital moved to Richmond, those could be good reasons to bring them here."

"We can notify our people down the coast to keep an eye out for them, so if they do anchor farther South, we'll know it," Marty suggests. "In the meantime, we can get ready here as we planned."

Tap. Tap. Tap.

"See who's at the door, will you, son?"

Robert opens the door to accept a small package, wrapped in a sturdy brown paper. "Thanks." He turns, holding it in his outstretched hand. "It's addressed to you."

"I'm not expecting anything. Hardly anybody knows I'm back in town. Hold on a minute." John rips the paper to reveal a small book.

"Here's a note." He stops to read it, then looks up grinning. "Gentlemen, this is a book of the encrypted codes of the Confederate states. The note says, '*Savannah* is now known to be reporting to Charleston. As proof, enclosed is a coded message intercepted and copied from a telegram. You can use this book to decipher it for yourselves. Hope it's not too late.' And it's signed, 'I Love You All, Lilly.'"

"I'll send a rider immediately to verify whether she's arrived yet," George offers.

"We don't need to do that," Robert explains. "Not if we leave right away."

"I agree with you, son. But first, George, are we represented in Charleston? Do they have firepower available?"

"Yes, we are, but I can't vouch for what they have to fight with. We usually don't get into that," he answers.

"Well, there's not enough time to notify the Union forces. So, it looks like we'll have to go and take what we need with us."

"You said we, John. You're not going, are you?" Marty is quick to question.

"We can handle it, Daddy," Robert pipes up.

"I'm sure you can, but I'm going," John comments firmly. "I need to see what one of our groups is made of, and this is a good chance to go unannounced."

"Getting to Charleston will be as dangerous as destroying those guns once we get there. We'll be traveling right through the heart of the Confederate forces, and I don't expect they'll be naive about our movements," he says and rises from his chair.

He paces back and forth for the next minute or two.

"Marty, can you find some Confederate uniforms? Make mine a ranking officer's, and the ones for Robert and Randall, because of their age, something lesser. Say, a sergeant and a corporal. We'll dress you girls up proper, take a fancy buggy, and hide right out in plain sight. They'll be less likely to question an officer and his family protected by two soldiers."

Marty grimaces, shakes his head, and looks at George Foster for answers.

"Yes, but once you put on their uniforms you'll be considered spies if you get caught, and probably be shot in short order," he cautions.

"Well, sir, I believe that's what we'll be, and we should expect that. This is a volunteer operation, so if there's anyone here who thinks they shouldn't be part of it then speak up now. You won't be faulted for it." John waits for a few seconds.

Silence.

"All right then, here's what we'll do . . ."

When Lilly arrived at La Nesra, she found Sally, Hawk, and Rose ready and willing to act on her orders. As it worked out, the director of security admitted he had no loyalties to La Nesra and committed to work against them. He believes the codebook is being kept by Sally, Hawk, and Rose, and will be used against him if necessary.

She has explained that Falcon is on his way to join their ranks. Her instructions to them are to determine who in the Company's organization at La Nesra would support their efforts, and those who wouldn't. She agrees with her daddy's observation regarding the two elements at work within the Company's framework. It's a place to start sorting it all out.

She took the codebook with her when she left La Nesra to meet with Tyrone Black and Remsar. After a few hours of indoctrination there, she was able to get a few minutes to herself, allowing her to travel to Baltimore to deliver the book, and the updated information regarding the ship *Savannah*.

One of her first questions was, "Where is this place located and what is it called?"

"Canozira, in the center of a mountain on the southwest side of America." The location didn't help much, but the name, at least, gave her a reference point.

Another question put to Ty proved interesting. "Who are you, and where do you come from?"

Taken by surprise with the question, he asked to be given an hour to put his thoughts together in order to explain fully in an organized manner. Lilly took it as a stall tactic, but because he didn't refuse her an answer, and acted obligated to give one, she felt more in control of her destiny then ever before.

"How am I supposed to know where to begin and what to do?" Her third question drew more than expected.

She will learn while she sleeps. She was advised not to concern herself with the why's and how's of her involvement, but to relax, and take in her surroundings. Her education will begin shortly, and with it will come the understanding she seeks.

She has been assigned a dwelling with seven adequately sized rooms. One of which is occupied by her personal assistant, and another by her personal maid. She sees the need for a maid, but the personal assistant? Well, what's her purpose, what's she going to do?

Her maid brings meals on a tray from somewhere, adhering to a breakfast, dinner, supper schedule. For right now, her food is being chosen by her personal assistant, but before long Lilly will be able to order anything, anytime she wants it. Since she is outside her life body, it takes only a small amount of nourishment to keep her strong.

Her new home is comfortable with all the necessary furnishings. The walls are nicely decorated with paper and paint, but she's been told if the colors are not to her liking, they will be changed to suit her tastes.

The other rooms consist of a kitchen, which in her mind will never be used, an office—den combination place, a meeting room containing a table with a lot of chairs around it, her bedroom, and a wash room. The latter has an elimination stool that does away with deposits by the push of a large button and a gush of water. It, also, has a shower with two spigots, one for hot and one for cold water. Her bedroom has a large closet where she found everything she will need. And to her amazement, there is at least one mirror in each and every room.

It has been almost an hour since Ty asked her for time to arrange his explanation of who he is.

Tap, tap, tap. Her first visitor is at her door.

"May I come in?" Ty, dressed in his normal black garb, asks as she opens the door. His six feet four inches plus height requires him to bend down to clear his head when she motions him inside.

He follows her into the den where they sit, she on the couch, and he on a chair facing her some six feet away.

"You asked who I am, and where I'm from, I believe," he starts.

"I'm the son of Hans Briermiester. You knew my father by the name Colonel Charles Housler," he bluntly relates.

Suddenly filled with renewed interest, she shifts her position on the couch.

"How can that be? You're too old" goes through her mind.

"I can tell by your reaction, you doubt the veracity of my words. Hear me out before you jump to the wrong conclusions," he admonishes. "I am, as I said, the son of Hans Briermiester. I was taken away from my father years ago as a way for the Company to control him. He's followed their orders for years, fearing they would harm me if he didn't. He was permitted to see me once a year for a long period of time, but I changed, and the visits stopped. When I say I changed, it was due to a disease taking over my body. I'm aging more rapidly than a normal human, and if not for my ability to leave my life body, as you do yours, I could be a very old man in a few years, probably dead in five. Because life's process slows down to a near stop when we're out of our bodies, I'm looking forward to many productive years. And should a cure for my infliction be discovered along the way, well, you see what I mean. My purpose is to make sure you are fully educated and informed about your responsibilities, and future with the Company."

"But then, why—?" Lilly tries to interrupt.

He raises his hand and continues.

"Whether you believe it or not, I love my father. But he had no idea about me, I mean, not like the Company does. They arranged everything to get him indebted to them, and that gave them the perfect excuse to take me from him. You see, Lilly, I've the same abilities as you. I can move through the mirrors, change positions from one point to another with just a thought, and seem to have the strength of ten men when I need it. My mind is as sharp as a tack. The Company helped me to understand myself, and has given me a good life. I have aspirations for the future, which you'll discover as time passes. And the Company, with all its complicated faults, will be my vehicle to attain them.

"And there you have it. That's who I am," he concludes.

He then anticipates Lilly's question to start again.

"You can see why I wouldn't order a raid that might kill my own father. And certainly, I wouldn't order a military battle at a house where I know he's mending from a wound. He left this world not knowing what happened to me. I certainly didn't want that. No one here wanted to hurt him, or any of your family, at least, not after I took that shot at you. The Company's interests have been solely in you and me."

"You're the same as me?" she squeezes in a question.

"That's right. But you have abilities that I don't. You're not aware of them yet, but it won't be long. There are others here, and out there, too . . . but first." He stops himself in midsentence. "Let me explain a few things before I get everything out of its proper order.

"The battle for souls that you are about to engage, dates back to times before records or archiving information was even thought about. Any information carried on forward from those times was done by word of mouth, from one aging person to a much younger one. The older person was, and is, referred to as a 'sender,' while the younger one as a 'receiver,' It's been going on for thousands of years, the passing on of information from generation to generation."

"So, you're a sender and I'm a receiver, is that what you're saying?" she poses.

"It would seem that way, but I think probably not. If it weren't for this disease, I'd not try to pass information along to you. These receivers and senders seem to know each other when their paths cross. Until then, they lead normal lives. Once they meet though, a relationship is formed quickly, and the transfer begins."

"How do they do it?" she quizzes. "It would seem to me that it would take longer and longer each time they do it over the years."

"It's a mental process. It just happens between them. One problem with this continuing on for years and years uninterrupted, is an unplanned death of a receiver or sender. If the process has not yet taken place when one or the other meets their demise, then the information is lost. Now, since this sort of loss has happened countless times over the centuries, there have been blanks where information was missing, information needed to carry on the plan of salvation of humanity. So, something had to be supposed and entered in the blank places. Mortal men have, by necessity, determined what the information should have been, and have filled in the blanks with their, sometimes biased, thinking. Therein was the beginning of major misunderstandings of mankind as to their destiny and how they will get there. Fallible human involvement emits bias information into the track of destiny with catastrophic results. Am I confusing you?" he asks.

"Not one bit, go on," she replies hastily.

"Well, over the centuries, because of interpretations of unclear, partly factual, partly assumed information, different blocks of humanity began to separate from the mainstream and form their own expectations of the hereafter—and their plans for the best way to get there. This went on for centuries, with the meaning of words being accepted differently by the different sects back then. But as long as humanity worshipped our one true God, it was considered harmless.

"Then, however, powerful men with unlimited resources changed everything. They created other gods and began using them to fleece their followers. False prophets were mixed in among true saints, and they began vying for the lives of humanity, not for the salvation and preservation of everlasting souls, but for their own selfish personal gains."

"And that's when the people from the other world came, the Korgots. They saw the opportunity, and took it." Lilly believes she sees where he's headed.

"That's about it," Ty agrees. "They came with their advanced technology, awed and threatened humanity, and frightened the world into believing they were gods themselves. They developed a plan to guarantee the future of their own culture by mixing our everlasting souls with their long life-spanned bodies, eventually to evolve into a being with an everlasting life. They stayed here for several centuries to convince mankind that they were from a land where beings live forever, and started promising the same to any individual prepared to go with them after they left and returned with the necessary transports."

"But the truth is, all they want is our souls to make them and their whole civilization live forever. The more souls they can entice, the better their chances are of succeeding," Lilly summarizes.

Ty sees no point in agreeing with her. She understands what has happened. He sits looking at her.

"So, if I were to build on what you've just said, I would believe that not only are the plans of the Korgots here and working to gain our souls, but that groups of unscrupulous powerful people are using the same promises to attract followers to their purported religions, their sole purpose being to expand their own personal gain."

Ty smiles in agreement, then grimaces at the thought.

She takes a long look at his face, thinking.

"So, you're telling me that the Company is working against all of this. I mean, the Company is trying to do the right thing for all of life on earth. Right?"

Ty nods yes.

"But with all of this going on, how's a person to know what's right, who to trust, who to follow. Where are people to place their faith?" Her voice is more intense. Her words flow more quickly.

"Exactly," he responds.

She shakes her head quickly from side to side, as if to clear her mind. Then, she is on her feet pacing from side to side, back and forth, almost running. She stops to face him, then looking down, she speaks.

"No, no, I don't want to do this. There's smarter people than me who can do a whole lot better job. Get someone else, I can't do it. I won't do it."

Ty smiles up at her.

"Are you laughing at me?" she shouts.

"Not at all, not at all. We expected you to react this way when you realized exactly what we've been preparing you to understand. It's all part of your learning process. Actually, you've accepted this very well based against what we expected," he explains calmly.

"I don't care what you say, this is way to big for my little brain. I can't do it, not even if I want to, which I don't," she fires back.

"Yes, you can. You've already given up the life you've known since you were born. All your family and friends, even your husband and child, you've placed aside to be here. You're feeling intimidated by the vastness of it all right now. But remember, you're not alone. We have an organization unlike any other on this earth. Millions of people will react to our leadership, your leadership. Cycostice has explained that you have talents which will enable you to comprehend the root of our problems, and direct us through this maze of confusion to a final solution. Not only do you want to do it, you know deep down, you have to do it.

She stands, looking into his eyes, feeling he's right, but a hollow loneliness owns her soul at the moment. "But, I, I . . . I'm so afraid."

“Of course you are, anyone would be,” he patronizes. “I know you must feel frantically unstable and hesitant at the moment, but realize, this is the worst of it. From this point on, your confidence will grow. Your knowledge and desires will push you beyond all of this. Your greatest satisfaction will be your trust in yourself, your own abilities. Believe in yourself. Set your ego free. Start trusting your instincts. The truth is, you’re ahead of schedule for your training. You ask questions expecting honest answers. You want to know. Do you see what I mean?”

“I think I’m beginning to, but I have so many questions, uncertainties, that keep running through my mind. I’ve never been able to figure out who I am. Maybe I will now, I don’t know.”

“Give yourself time. Soon you’ll be answering your own questions. Your part in all of this will become more apparent each day,” Ty assures her.

“One more thing to keep in mind,” he points out. “Our organization has its flaws, too. People from these unwanted sects have infiltrated into the Company over the years. We’re aware of most of them and have decided not to acknowledge their presence. But we’re certain there are others we haven’t yet discovered, people we trust and rely upon. They will slit our throats in our sleep if it serves their purpose.”

“But we have our people in their organizations as well, right?” Lilly asks.

“That’s correct, we do; and unfortunately we view their lives as they do ours—expendable,” he concludes.

The next few days pass quickly for Lilly. Every minute of her time is filled with seeing and learning new things. Information flows to her from every angle, even while she sleeps. She jerked herself awake two nights ago to hear a noise that is best described as a fingernail being pulled across a blackboard. It turned out to be a method of transferring information to her, at a very high speed, when her brain is less active with other things. Those who work with the process explain that her retention is about four-fifths of that which is offered. They seem to be very pleased and said once the basics have been given, the process would be slowed to every other night, then every third night, which will continue as often as possible for a time unknown.

She spent most of her second day with Remsar, following him through the compound, as they call it. He showed her as much as they could cover that day with the promise of continuing when time allows. One place, in particular, proved to be amazing. The science and discovery area contained things so far advanced to acknowledge their existence beyond this confinement would be a disaster. As examples, but not limited to, a gun that shoots a light which can melt a rock like a block of butter three hundred feet away. It can also be used to cut shapes out of solid steel in just a few seconds, or brought to a fine point to remove a growth from the human skin, touching only the affected area. A differently tuned light can be cast upon a point a great distance away. Then, an object can be placed on what is called the beam at its origin, and it moves fast along the light to its destination. The beam can be bent to go around corners, as well as up and down to go over a hill, or any other object in its path. Another is a vehicle that can hang in midair, move up, down, and all over the place all by itself, with no means of support. They say it can fly faster than a bird, and can travel beyond the moon to another world. They are shaped sort of like an upside-down saucer with a small cup turned upside down on top. They were left here by the Korgots. She counts at least twenty-five of them, stored in rows of five, in places like small caves cut out of a solid granite wall five stories tall.

The most startling of it all, though, are the strange looking beings moving about doing various tasks. They are shorter than an average-sized grown man, and their bodies are thin with narrow shoulders. They have arms and legs long like ours, only small and thin, but then they have three long toes they can use like fingers. They have three long fingers and a thumb for hands. Their heads are round like a ball, and larger than they should be for the size of their bodies. Their chins are almost pointed, then their face widens as it goes up. A small mouth, a nose that is just two holes in their face, and two protruding black eyes the size of large apples. Their ears, like their noses, are just a hole on each side of their heads. All of them are wearing one piece, gray, skin-tight garments that cover their whole bodies except for their faces.

The presence of Remsar and Lilly does not seem to bother them, as he points and explains that they are workers left here when the Korgots went back to their own world. Their tasks are to keep their equipment in perfect working order. Of the four hundred and twenty of them left here, these forty-six are thought to be the last remaining; but no one can be sure, since there could be other clusters somewhere in the world. Our sun, daylight, and outside environment are too harsh for the survival of these beings, so this underground compound was built to suit their needs.

Remsar relates that while these creatures have brains, and live, they seem to have no soul. They crave nothing, and communicate only when absolutely necessary with each other, or in response to an inquiry or direction. They live well together causing no problems with each other, or any human being, and act abnormally docile. They, and only they, can operate the flying machines. Many of the Company's scientists have tried to no avail. The controls seem to respond only to these strange creatures' touch.

Nourishment for their bodies is supplied by a machine which accepts nothing from the workers, but produces a brown pasty substance that emits no flavor, aroma, or appeal at all to human tasters. That's all they eat—ever—and not much of that. If there is any elimination of waste, no one has seen it. There is no noticeable difference in their anatomy to define a sex, nor has an offspring ever been produced. All indicators lead the scientists to believe these beings are created, not born, and if not interfered with, will continue working—repairing themselves as needed—forever.

She is also taken back by the round balls of various sizes that glow in different colors, but are connected to nothing. The white ones give off light brighter than any lamp she has ever seen. Even the gas lights at La Nesra do not compare. The thought of the whole world being lit with them passes through her mind. The colors are mixed randomly throughout the science and discovery area. Some flash on and off while others change colors, one right after the other up to four times. It is beautiful and relaxing to her heavily weighted soul and body.

Remsar disturbs her daydream by taking her hand and leading her away from it all, back to reality. There are so many wonderful things there, too many to bring them all to mind. She tells herself she will find a way to go back again soon to learn more.

Meanwhile, back at the Virginia border, the Andersons' quiet invasion through the Confederate front lines is easier than John expects. He and Robert are dressed in Confederate gray, mounted on spirited horses, riding alongside the buggy. Randall, also in gray, is driving his two beautifully dressed young women passengers with all the pomp and circumstance possible. They travel on the main roads to appear as part of the normal traffic.

When they approach the first blockade, the Confederate soldiers take no notice of the trunks lashed to the back of their buggy, filled with everything they need to destroy the weapons aboard the *Savannah*. The return of a hand salute from John is all that is required for their safe passage into hostile territory. Now it's on to Richmond, and a train from there to Charleston.

Getting seats on the train out of Richmond is an experience. With the seats booked to capacity, the only way to get tickets is to buy them from one of the many people who has purchased them with no intention of taking the trip. The price, of course, has gone up to the point of being ridiculous. But when you need to keep moving, you pay it.

Everyone in the group has been instructed not to speak unless it's required. There's no sense taking any unnecessary chances with a slip of the tongue being overheard. Their bench-style seats face each other with enough room to accommodate them all. There are no berth cars in this train, so, they will spend another night right where they are, and arrive at Charleston around noon tomorrow. When the chatter in the car dies down, the rhythm of the wheels clacking as they bridge the gaps of the steel rails slowly lulls them, one by one, to sleep.

Charlotte is the first to stir when the taste of cigar and black coal smoke, combined with stench of wet spittoons, causes her to strangle on her own saliva. An attempt to cover her mouth to stifle her coughing so as not to awaken the others proves to do the opposite. The sudden movement brings Randall to his feet in a daze.

"I'm sorry," she whispers trying to be quiet, but several others in the car apparently were just waiting for an excuse to start talking. From there the noise keeps getting louder and louder until everyone stirs.

"What time is it?" Cheryl whispers, not wanting to move to check for herself.

"Almost six thirty." Randall looks at his pocket watch.

"I'm really hungry," Robert's first words this morning.

"We have enough salty ham, cheese, and bread left for some sandwiches," Charlotte replies while pulling a covered basket from under her seat to her lap.

"I think there's enough apple pie to go around, too." Cheryl pulls another basket into view.

"Sounds like we're all set," John announces cheerily. "Now, if we had some good hot coffee to go with it."

No sooner do the words leave his lips than the rear door of the car opens to expose a steward carrying a heavy three-gallon galvanized coffeepot.

"I've got some hot coffee in this here pot, but you gotta have your own cup so get some. It's good and fresh," he shouts and begins moving slowly down the aisle.

Everyone in the Anderson group gets their share by using the same dirty metal cups they used yesterday, and the day before. Once his cup is full of the steaming liquid, John raises his eyes to say, "Thank you, Lord, for this fine day and this coffee."

After the steward makes sure each person gets their share, he throws the little bit that is left, along with the grounds, out through an open window. Then proceeds to wipe the empty pot dry with his bandanna, puts on a big grin, and walks back through the car, passing it from side to side looking for tips. He expresses a 'thank you' for all reward.

As soon as they consume their breakfast, Robert and Randall decide to check their stowed trunks, just to be sure their munitions are safe. They've been gone for a few minutes, headed for a box car located toward the front of the train.

John notices the power of the steam engine is being throttled back. Then the brakes are applied and the traction wheels reversed to spin backward. Those in his group are fortunate to be seated, for those who are not are thrown forward violently. The train comes to a complete stop at the same time the pressure release valves give off a long loud puff of steam.

Pfffffsssssssssssssssssssssss!

"What's going on, Daddy?" Charlotte is quick to ask with a startled look, turning in her seat to look forward.

People are climbing back into their seats from the floor using loud foul language, and causing a great deal of commotion. John puts his head against the immovable window pane to look forward along the side of the short train.

"There's some Confederate troops climbing aboard a couple of cars from us. That's about all I can tell from here," he relates with concern.

"What about Robert and Randy? That's the way they went," Cheryl adds, to John's already growing worries.

"I don't know. They can take care of themselves," he answers. "Let's just keep our seats for the time being and see what's going on. Maybe they're just putting someone on or taking someone off, nothing to worry about."

Five minutes pass with no indication.

Ten minutes. People in the car are getting restless, wanting information. Two soldiers move in a hurry from the front of the car to leave through the back door. No sooner does that door close than the front one opens presenting a cavalry officer and four of his men. They are shoving and pushing Robert and Randy along with them.

The girls have turned in their seats to witness the scene.

"OhmyGod!" they say, in unison, as if it is all one word.

"Are these two yours, sir?" the officer inquires as he approaches John. "They claim they're traveling with you. Is that a fact, sir?"

John gets to his feet. "What's going on, Lieutenant?" he asks indignantly.

"We received word about a white man and a black man who killed two of our boys, took their uniforms, and are supposed to be on this train. I've got orders to take them into custody," the soldier righteously replies.

"Well, you've got the wrong two here. They're with me. But I can tell you that two soldiers just left through that door in a hurry to get somewhere. As you say, one was white and one was black. They're dressed in Confederate gray." John stands calm in his Confederate officer's uniform with his left thumb hinting the direction of the door. That's all he has to say; the soldiers release their prisoners and rush out through the back door.

Robert and Randy find their seats breathing a sigh of relief.

Shortly, the rest of the mounted troop passes their car with their horses at a run. A few minutes later shots are heard . . . four, five! Silence!

"Poor devils," John sighs. "I hated to put those troops on them, but we don't need more questions about us. I had to do it."

"Come on, engineer, get this train moving," Randall wishes out loud.

No one needs to talk about what just happened. It just hammers home how fast things can go wrong with deadly results.

The rest of the trip is uneventful. As soon as they arrive at Charleston, Robert and Randy take two of the trunks to a livery for temporary storage, while John and the women take the one with their clothes to locate accommodations. They are able to get two adjoining rooms on the second floor of a nice hotel not far from the ocean. They change their clothes while waiting for the boys.

"Get out of those uniforms," John urges as the two come through the door. "No sense pushing our luck. Did you get our trunks stored?"

"Yes, sir, we did. And we rented a carriage and team, too, just like we planned," Randy assures.

"We'll go to the dock to see if the *Savannah*'s logged in yet. If not, maybe they have some word about her," Robert comments as he pulls his boots back on.

"You two be more careful. Don't show too much interest in that boat, or someone will get suspicious," Cheryl cautions.

"What are we going to do if she's here, Daddy?" Robert continues. "What if she's unloading already?"

"Let's not waste our time figuring out something that we don't know to be true. See what you can find out, and meet us back here in no more than an hour," John replies with instructions.

"Why not meet at that little restaurant just down the street. I don't know about the rest of you, but my breakfast left me two hours ago," Cheryl points out.

"An hour then, at the restaurant, agreed?" John recaps.

While the boys are out scouting for the *Savannah*, John and the girls walk around the city streets leading to the shore, looking at the contours of the land and any areas that are secluded enough to hide them after the sun sets. They notice an inlet, several hundred yards deep, ending at a narrow that might be a creek. There's nothing built close around it, and it seems to be well protected with trees and brush.

"That's a likely spot right there." He nods the direction, not wanting to point.

"It's quite a distance, Daddy. The farther away we are, the longer we'll have to be in the water." Charlotte's observation is appreciated.

"We need a small boat of some kind. Something we can hang on to on our way out there," Cheryl offers. "And we can put our explosives in it."

"A boat might be too noticeable. What we need is a raft," John suggests.

The hour passes too quickly, but as agreed they all meet at the restaurant. After getting seated at a table in a back corner, as far removed from the crowd as possible, they put their heads together.

"It looks like we're too late. The *Savannah*'s been here for two days. They've started unloading her already. And get this, Daddy, there's two other ships that arrived at the same time she did." John's son informs everyone with a disgusted voice.

"Boy-oh-boy, this changes everything. Do we know for sure that they're unloading firearms, and the like?" John queries.

"We didn't want to look too interested, so we haven't tried to get close enough to find out," Randy offers.

"Well, there's no sense in risking lives unless we're certain. We need a better understanding of what's going on before we can plan anything. Let me think about this for a minute," the elder Anderson requests.

"Let's get some food, I'm starving," Cheryl announces, and motions to a matronly woman who appears to be taking orders from other tables.

John sits quietly thinking as the others discuss the Charleston area and wait for their food. As soon as it arrives, and the woman leaves them alone, he speaks.

"There's a lot to consider here, and I think we're going to need some help. As soon as we're finished, the boys and I can see if we can contact one or two of these agents Marty told us about. And ladies, I think it's time you earned your keep. This will be a good job for you. These Southerners won't think much of you two pretties strolling around looking at the water. Now, here's what we'll do."

At Canozira, Lilly has almost all morning to herself, giving her time to ransack her new home. The kitchen has everything anyone could ever need. One thing she finds intriguing is a box about five feet high and three feet square. When she opens it a cool soft breath of air hits her face. She lays her hand inside to discover it's really cold. There's food but no place for ice. It's not hooked to anything, just setting there. Puzzling to say the least. Satisfied that there is nothing especially good or bad within her dwelling, she plops down on a sofa, pulls a throw pillow under her head, and starts to think.

"I should know where those ten bodies are. I'll ask, but I get the feeling they're not going to tell me, not just yet anyway. Maybe I can find them myself if I think about it hard enough. I found Ty that way the last time I was here. Here goes. Nope. So much for that. I'll ask, all they can do is tell me no. Let me think, what else. I'm not happy with the way they're feeding things into my brain while I sleep. They might be turning me into something I don't want to be. I've read about that somewhere, the power of suggestion, or something. They make people do all sorts of things they never would do before they fed their brains while they're asleep. I'd like to have another talk with Cycostice. I'd like to be sure that was really Mama.

"I must not forget, I need to get back to my life body every two weeks for a few days. If I don't keep myself fed and healthy it will eventually effect me here. I miss Falcon and Joie. I wondered why we were never allowed to discuss religion amongst ourselves while we were students at La Nesra. It would make sense that if our whole goal is to be certain people worship our only real God, and not some fake one, why wouldn't they have taught us about it? They tell me everything will become clear as I go along. Is that because they'll change me to that way of thinking? It could happen without me knowing it.

"Who's a person supposed to trust? Someone told me just recently to trust my own instincts. Trust in myself. I believe it was Ty. He said I would learn to answer my own questions. What does that mean?"

"There's no way to tell day from night in here. There are no windows at all. How can they stand it in here never seeing the out-of-doors."

She hears two knocks in rapid succession at the door.

It's Remsar and Ty inviting her to go with them to the science and discovery area. They promise a surprise. She moves with them as they swiftly walk through the halls and down the steps. A wave of Remsar's hand over the box at the side of a door causes it to open.

There it is, hovering ten feet off the floor, a flying machine.

"Come on, we're going for a ride." Ty grins and takes her hand.

Remsar walks to stand in a beam of light coming from the belly of their transportation. Then, just like magic, he rises up until he's inside.

"You're next." Ty nudges her to step into the light.

"Oh my. I feel as light as a feather. I'm moving, but I don't feel like I'm going to fall. Here I go—up." Lilly's feelings change from second to second. "It's wonderful, this is scary, where are they taking me, I don't want to go."

Remsar is waiting inside the machine to take her hand and lead her away from the entry hole in the floor. Ty appears above the floor almost immediately and steps toward them as the opening closes. They sit in seats that seem to form themselves around their bodies as they sink down. Once settled, a bar with straps attached to either end swings down from above over their shoulders to latch them solidly against the back and seat. She looks around, trying to take it all in. Two of the strange beings sit side by side in similar seats five feet in front of them, at the controls. They seem to be connected to the machine by wires plugged into their ears. Little lights of every color imaginable glow or flash. Some of them flash in rows, over and over again, like they're moving. A finger of the being on the right touches a green square and the machine starts moving up. There's no noise. She can hear herself breathe.

Up, up they go, perhaps fifteen stories, then they enter a passageway just large enough to allow the machine to pass through. They seem to be picking up speed.

"We're going to bang into something." She tells herself loudly, a heartbeat away from expressing her feelings to all concerned, when the passageway widens and expands into the most beautiful starlit sky she has ever seen.

"Where are we?" she says in awe.

"We're flying above the earth. Isn't it beautiful?" Remsar answers.

"But how?" she implores.

"I'm not the one to explain it to you, but think about it. One day all of mankind will be able to do this. That is, if there is a mankind," he replies.

Lilly lets herself become a part of the experience as the machine streaks across the sky without a sound. The bright moonlight illuminates the sparkling peaks of the snow-covered mountains below, making her feel like a soaring eagle. She wishes the sensation could go on forever.

She looks down in wonderment. Her eyes widen with a short breath of amazement when the machine starts moving away from the earth at a tremendous speed, but there is no sensation of movement. If she closes her eyes to not look, it's like sitting in a chair at home.

"Open your eyes, Lilly. Look down," Remsar requests.

"Ohhh!" she exclaims.

The earth is just a ball. It looks just like the globes in school at La Nesra.

All too soon, the machine speeds down bringing the earth closer and closer, to slow down and enter a passageway. She knows the ride is over. The three disembark the machine and move to Ty's office to relate about the experience.

"What do you think?" he simply asks.

"Well, for one thing, I thought it was daytime when I left my room. And the odd thing is, I was thinking about how easy it would be to get confused like that. What time is it?" she asks.

"About four thirty in the morning," he answers.

"To answer you, I've never dreamed of anything like it. I know I'll never forget it. It was absolutely amazing. I have to know though, why did you take me there?" she continues.

"One reason is that it's a lot of fun, but we want you to understand the Company has the technology to wreak hell upon the devils of this earth, but chooses not to do so. Can you imagine the panic that would be caused by one of our machines flying over a city spewing flesh-eating rays, mutilating, and killing everything it touches. It'll be another hundred to a hundred and fifty years before humanity will be ready to fathom what you're seeing and experiencing right now. One of our goals is to give this information to our fellow man a little at a time, allowing him to get comfortable with it, to understand it, and to use it for peaceful purposes," Ty explains.

"How do you know who to give it to? What if you give it to the wrong people and they use it against other people?" Lilly is quick to understand one of the problems associated with this technology.

"Exactly," Remsar chimes in.

"If we disrupt the balance of power between different countries, sects, or clans, and if the ones with the power are governed by warlords instead of peace-loving people, well, you can imagine what would happen. And this is our lesson for today. One of our goals is to move mankind forward, advancing his knowledge about such things without allowing him to destroy himself in the process. When the Korgots come back with their transports, they will expect to find an earth occupied by unwillful lambs. Lambs that will gladly follow them without resistance.

"We might catch them by surprise and fight them off when they arrive, before they can disembark their transports. But not only will the technology they left here be required, we need to advance it, we need to multiply our might. Some of it can be mustered right here, but we know the best path would be to give it to our brothers and sisters here on earth. But we might murder each other and destroy our earth before they get here."

Lilly tilts her head down, rolls her eyes up, and looks back and forth at them without moving her head. "Look, both of you. If you think this conversation is going to change my thinking, then you've got the wrong person. This is way, way too complicated for me. Everything you're talking about will be over and done with before I figure out what I should be doing. You've got the wrong girl for this, be sure of that. Now, why don't the two of you just let me get out of here to go back to my simple life while you continue with your world saving plans. You, and the world, will be a whole lot better off for it." She speaks clearly, with feeling and certainty.

"No, Lilly, as I've said before, you're wrong. We all know it's an awesome responsibility. Hell, Remsar and I are just people. How do we know we're doing the right thing? There's others like us all over the world asking themselves the same thing. All we can do is believe in something we think is right, and fight for it. What's the alternative if we don't? We, the three of us, can live out our lives, perhaps, before the transports get here, and just leave it up to each future person to fend for themselves. But let's not forget, that will undoubtedly be the end of mankind as we know it. So, what choice do we have? We've been called upon by something bigger than ourselves to save the world, even if the people in it fight our efforts. Can we do it? Do we have the time to do it? I have days when I wonder, but the alternative always brings me back to one thing. We won't succeed if we stop trying," Remsar continues.

"To be honest, we're concerned that you might stop trying, and that's why we went for the ride. We need to convince you that what we are saying is true. We believe that you—yes, you—are meant to play a big part in our success. Will you do it alone? Of course not. It'll take all our efforts together to manage such a huge undertaking. And by all of us, I mean our entire organization of millions of people all over the world. People who will follow our lead. People who will give their lives if necessary to further our goal. But we need leaders, we need you." He telegraphs his finish by resting back in his chair.

Lilly sits with them in silence for a few minutes looking, glancing, at each other.

"I'm going to perfectly honest with you," she starts firmly. "My experience so far with life has taught me to trust no one completely. I mean, not even my own parents. I can't be sure that the people I'm closest to right now won't turn on me. This lonely feeling of continuous exposure won't let me rely on anybody's promises. I do not accept totally, anything you've said or done to be what it seems. I fear you have ways to make my mind conjure up anything you want me to believe."

The two men sit listening intently. When she stops speaking, they remain quiet, letting her have the time to think and expound her inner most thoughts.

"I don't trust you now, and I don't think I'll ever completely trust you, or anyone for that matter, ever. You've seen to that. You've made me this way, and I hate you for it. I hate my life because I don't even trust myself. How can I dedicate myself, feeling the way I do, to spend my whole life working at what seems to be an impossible undertaking. I need to find me before I do anything else."

"God bless you, Lilly," Remsar prays. "I know we've put you through a lot over your young life. And I won't try to convince you that I know how you feel inside. I can only be to you what you'll let me. May I tell you a short little story?

"There was a little boy I knew when I was young. A boy brought into this world as a product of a long line of incestuous unions. At an early age, he became aware of his ability to cause things to grow more quickly when he touched them. He soon discovered he could pick up a dying plant with his bare hands, gently clean the soil from its roots, settle it back into fresh soil, and watch it turn a radiant green again, within a few hours. He was the center of attention for many years. His skills continued to grow stronger as he aged through puberty.

"At his of age of sixteen, his mother caught an illness, which doctors at the time determined would be fatal. He loved her so much, he couldn't stand to see her withering away. And because of that, defying his father's wishes, he left their home carrying with him the pain and burden of eventually losing her. The feeling of helplessness consumed his soul. Not knowing where to find peace, nor what he would do with his life, he wandered for months, eating only what he could beg. Until one day, he came upon a young woman sitting on the steps of a large shanty out in the hills, with a baby in her arms. He stopped to ask for a bite of food and water. He soon learned the baby boy was starving since he refused to suckle his mother's breast. He took the baby from her arms, not knowing why, and cradled him in his left arm, gently touching the child's face with his fingers. When he loosened the blanket from around his shoulders and arms, the baby started fussing and soon began to cry a shrill sound. Thinking he had done something wrong, the young man passed the baby back to his mother. When she pulled him to her chest to comfort him, the infant boy started to root around, tossing his arms and head. She put her finger to his mouth and he began to suck. Needless to say, the baby started to eat. The parents declared the young man to be a saint sent to them by God to heal their son. Well, he could have no part of that since he still grieved about his dying mother. So he left, carrying with him a bag of food, and a jar of water.

"Over the next few weeks, he discovered a bird flopping on the ground with a broken wing. When he picked it up to comfort its pain, it started struggling to get free until he finally had to let it go. It flew away, up and up into the sky, as if it was never injured. Three more times, different things happened to finally convince him that he did indeed have some sort of power to heal living things. Feeling this to be true, he thought of his mother and literally ran the two hundred miles distance back to his home. His father met him at the door to explain that his mother was laid to rest three days earlier.

"When the boy related to his father what had happened, the news traveled quickly. People from all over brought their afflicted to him to be cured. Before long the numbers were so many, the father began to charge for his son's services. Over the next few months the boy watched as the riches mounted up until, one day, a man approached his father with an offer to buy the boy for a large amount of money. It took only a few minutes for them to reach an agreement. The boy was put in a cage after he was caught twice trying to escape his new owner. He was kept like an animal, his meals being slid on tin plates under the bars. He was taken out only when it was time to perform his gift on an ailing person, in front of hundreds of paying sightseers.

"One day, a man in the audience watched closely as the young man healed a poor wretch of severe back pain. He was so taken by what he saw, he purchased the boy away from a miserable existence. Then he took him to a place where the boy's talents could be put to good use in the name of humanity, a place where he was treated with the respect and dignity he deserved. A fairy tale ending to an amazing true story, you'd think. But the boy grew into a man. A man who has never been able to forgive himself for leaving his dying mother. Had he stayed, he knows he would have saved her. If he had not left, they could have spent years and years together, as a family. Perhaps there would have been another child or two. A brother or sister for a lonely yearning man. But alas, none of that was to be. The young man grew to be truly alone in this world, and to this day, he's been unable to find peace," Remsar finishes solemnly.

"That's a beautiful story." Lilly chokes back a hard swallow. "What ever happened to him? Where is he today?"

"You're looking at him," he replies peering into her eyes. "I had the opportunity and ability to save my mother, but I was too wrapped up in myself, my pain, to stay with her. When I think of how I touched that baby's jowls, it could just as easily have been my mother's. If I had stayed and nursed her, well, you see what I mean.

"I implore you, Lilly. Don't turn your back on this opportunity to use your gifts in behalf of humanity. God has a way of rewarding those who give of themselves.

"Cycostice has told you that you have talents from God. You also know there's more to learn about them, and from them. If you knowingly throw them away, don't you see? It could turn out that without your involvement, this world as you saw it earlier tonight might be a lifeless charred black ball spinning through the sky. Now suppose it happens during your lifetime. You'll not be able to go back to change it," he concludes.

"I understand what you've said, Remsar. But how can I change the way I feel? I don't know how to do that, even if I wanted to. Don't you understand?" Lilly reacts.

"Take my hand?" He reaches for hers.

She leaves her seat to kneel down in front of him and accepts his grasp.

He closes his eyes and relaxes his face.

A feeling of release begins to move over her body. A gentle, relaxing mood creeps into her mind. It seems like things are being put away in her brain, almost like straightening up a messy room. It's settling to get it all sorted out, stacked neatly, and put away.

He relaxes his grasp on her hand and lets go.

"How do you feel?" he asks.

"I feel wonderful," she says, meaning every word of it. "What did you do to me?"

Ignoring her question, he asks one of his own. "Aren't you curious as to why I haven't used my gift to heal Ty of his disease?"

"Why haven't you?" she responds soberly.

"I've tried on numerous occasions. But for whatever reason, I seem to have no effect on his problem. Because of that, I must believe my gift works at God's will, not mine. So I ask you again. How do you feel? Is it God's will to allow me to settle your mind?"

Lilly suddenly has a grasp on the meaning of what these two men have been working to help her understand. "This is astounding. I don't feel like I know any more than I did a few minutes ago, but it's like that doesn't make any difference anymore. I still have all the questions, but I'm not afraid. I'm still me. I don't feel like I've changed or anything. I just, I feel really good about myself."

"Isn't it wonderful?" Remsar resumes. "Once you begin doing this work, you will be amazed at how you feel about it. As Ty says, you'll have trying times, times when you doubt what you're doing; but you'll remember this feeling you have right now, and it will bring you back every time."

Ty speaks up.

"So, what do you say, Lilly? Are you ready to leave your doubts and concerns behind? Can you place your trust in something larger than the three of us?"

It's six thirty in the morning when John, Robert, and Randall can been seen walking abreast toward the water's edge of the Charleston, South Carolina, shore. They are to meet with an agent of the Sons organization, with hopes of getting the additional support needed to destroy three ships laden with arms and ammunition.

The task has been complicated by the fact that part of the ships cargo has already been unloaded. Charlotte and Cheryl spent yesterday afternoon, until dark, close to the docks, snooping to determine the answers to a list of questions posed by their father.

Their investigation indicated the crews unloading the ships work only during the daylight hours, from seven in the morning to seven at night. The first ship to be unloaded is the *Savannah*. When they are finished with her, the other two ships, which are presently anchored farther out, will be moved in one after the other. The *Savannah* will stand guard over the process.

Everything being unloaded is transported to the railhead, where it is eventually being loaded into waiting freight cars. Apparently, certain things have to be loaded before others, which means a great deal of the boxes have to be placed on a roof covered platform to wait their turn. The loading of the railroad cars is slow at the moment, but once all those boxes needed first are in place, it won't take long to empty the platform. It's thought that once a freight car is loaded, it will be scheduled into a train to head for a destination currently known only to ranking individuals.

Covered wagons move, slowly, heavily on a schedule of about one every hour, from the ship to the platform. The empty wagons rattle and bounce past the loaded ones on their return trip for another load. The girls reported there are many soldiers guarding the process all along their route.

The more information the Anderson group gathers, the more doubtful they are about the possibility of destroying all of the guns and ammunition. Perhaps it would be best to destroy the two loaded cargo ships anchored in the harbor, and let it go at that. Being successful at that will be a great accomplishment.

These thoughts and others occupy the minds of the three Sons patriots before they stop to knock on the door of a shop labeled simply "The Tack Shop." A few seconds pass before they hear locks being opened, then the door swings inward slowly.

"We're supposed to meet with Mosey here at six thirty," John calmly advises.

The door opens wide allowing them to enter. The only light comes though the large glass window in the front of the room, to show walls covered with all sorts of leather gear for horses and working animals. The man who opened the door points his dye stained hand, toward the back of the building. "They're back there."

John, the first of the three to reach the doorway indicated, pushes a blanket covering his entry aside, then steps through into another room. His son and Randy are right behind him with their hands on their guns.

"Which of you is Mosey?" Robert's father asks the three waiting men.

They're all dressed in a mix of jackets, striped pants, various faded colors of shirts, brown broad-brimmed hats, and tall boots, including spurs. None have seen a razor, or a bar of soap in weeks. Each has a tin cup of coffee in his hand sitting on straight-back chair.

"I'm Mosey. You John Anderson?" the one in the middle speaks up and rises to his feet to extend a hand.

"That I am. This is Robert and Randall," John replies, feeling the weight of his expectations come crashing down.

"Hear you need a little help, but if you ask me, you need a lot of it if you're thinking of taking on half the Confederate army. I don't know what we can do, but lay it out and we'll see," Mosey offers, pointing to several chairs.

John, unimpressed by what he sees, lets it pass. He needs help, and Mosey comes with a good recommendation. If he had a choice, though, he wouldn't pick these three.

"I don't know what you've heard, but we're here to destroy three shiploads of guns and ammunition. Two of the ships are anchored in the harbor and the third, the *Savannah*, is unloading at the dock." John grabs a chair, straddles it and sits looking over the back as he speaks. He continues with a brief explanation of the situation, then waits for a response.

Mosey presses his lips together hard, having just taken a swig of coffee, snorts through his nose enough to ruffle the hairs of his mustache, and moves his head to the side pushing his chin upward.

"Want some coffee, boys? There's some in that pot there on the stove. I can't guarantee how good it is, but it sure as hell's hot. There's cups over there," he offers, gesturing with his cup in hand. Then he takes on a serious look and places his attention directly on John.

"You're the boss man with the Sons, that right?" he asks.

John nods yes.

"I hear you've been away taking care of some personal things, and be sure you have our sympathies for your losses. That being the case, I don't know how up to date you might be about what we're up to here at Charleston. So, let me fill you in a bit." Mosey begins to make an impression.

"I'm the chief of operations for this part of the country. Bud and Norm, here, are part of my staff. We go by one name, it's a whole lot easier that way. There's more than a hundred and fifty of us around here, so if it's people we need, we can muster a few." He continues to impresses John, Robert, and Randall.

"What you're telling me's not exactly news. The truth is, we've been cooking up a plan, and we're about to make a move on these boats ourselves. Now, I don't know what you've got in mind for these guns and such, I mean, whether you want to keep them, or whether you want to destroy them so these Confederates can't use them?" He stops to allow John to reply to his statement.

"Honestly, the thought of keeping them never entered my mind," John begins, only to have Mosey cut him off.

"Okay then, hear me out. You might like what we're planning to do.

"You know the North is trying to put up a blockade so the South can't bring anything into Charleston by way of the sea. Right now ships can get in if they're careful, but it won't be long before it's going to get hard to do. One thing the South doesn't want is for ships to be sunk out there to block others from getting in or out. Those two anchored out a ways are flying neutral colors. They're sitting low in the water so we know they're loaded down. We believe there's some shenanigans going on, and their captains are providing a service unknown to their homelands. We think if we create enough of a ruckus here on shore, they'll try to hightail it out to some open water because they don't want word to get back that they're hauling guns for the Confederates. They've got their sails down, but their boilers are lit. They know by the time they get their anchors up they'll have enough steam to move, there's not much we can do about that. But the thing is, once they clear our outer banks, beyond the range of their shore guns, they're fair game for the Union gunboats. We've made sure they'll get a big surprise out there."

"What's going to stop the *Savannah* from escorting them out of here? Her stacks are blowing smoke, too. She's here to protect those other two, so you can bet she'll be the first thing the Union sees," Robert wonders and warns.

Mosey grins and then says, "If everything goes right, she won't be able to get away from the dock. We've had people working underwater for the last two nights removing her rudders. It's slow work, but I hear we'll finish up tonight. When they start turning that propeller, all they'll be able to do is go forward or backward; and even if there's enough wind for her sails, they'll still have the same problem, they won't be able to guide her."

John slaps his leg and yells, "Well, I'll be damned. That just might work. But how can you be sure the cargo ships will move?"

"We've got mortars that will place a few shots at them from shore. We'll try, but we don't have to hit them, just come close enough to make them believe all hell's breaking loose," Mosey answers with confidence.

"As I say, the captains won't want to lose their ships, and they know the Confederates don't want them to block the channel."

"What about what's left on the *Savannah*?" Randall wonders.

Mosey turns his head to look at him.

"We're hoping most of it will already be unloaded. But whatever's left they'll get to keep. I don't think that amount will be will make any difference in the outcome of the war."

"Yeah, I see your point," Randy continues. "But what about all that's already been unloaded. Some of it's on a platform out by the railroad tracks, and the rest is already on rail cars."

"Well, I'll admit, the rest of our plan is a little risky," he says, as if the first part of their plan is a cinch.

"After what I've just heard, I can't wait to hear the rest of it." Robert's voice is heard.

The chief of operations gets on his feet to move to the stove, adds coffee to his cup, turns to offer the pot to everyone else, returns to his seat, and begins.

"I guess the best way to put it would be, we're going to steal it. All of it, that is to say, that's on the rail cars. We all figure the Sons, namely us, can put it to good use, so why blow it up. Anything on the platform we're going to set fire to, and that should help those two cargo ships out there to decide to move."

John's opinion of Mosey and his two sidekicks has completely changed.

"Well, fellas, if you agree, here's what we're going to do."

Chapter Thirty-Four

At the Tack Shop in Charleston, John has sat patiently listening to Mosey give a sketchy description of his intricate plan. Finally, he can wait no longer.

"I can understand removing the rudders from the *Savannah*'s helm, and I can see how you might chase those ships out of the harbor. But I have some problems with your idea of stealing a train, and burning that platform right under their noses. It'll take a good half hour just to get a steam engine in there and get the cars hooked together. That is, if they're all in a row on the same track. Our idea has been to destroy everything, and keep all this firepower out of everybody's hands; not take chances that could make us fail in our attempt."

"Mr. Anderson, with all due respect to you and your men here, you need to understand something. Once this fracas is over, you and they will hustle back north to your homes all wrapped up in the safety of the whole Union army. It's different with us. We live here. The Confederates need guns real bad. Hell, they come to our homes and take any old relic they can get their hands on. Then they take it and give it to some young boy, and march him into battle with a slim chance of getting his first shot off. They've been known to ride twenty miles to get a gun that someone has rumored exists. Our people are getting so they can't hunt for food, let alone protect what's theirs from unscrupulous drifters. We need these guns. We figure it's worth the risk," Mosey counters.

"You just said they've traveled twenty miles for one gun, what do you suppose they'll do for a trainload of them. It sounds to me like you're signing death warrants for all your families. And have you considered that if you're lucky enough to get the train out of here, you still have to hide it long enough to unload it. Now, I don't know how many wagonloads it took to put those boxes on those cars, but I know it'll take just as many to empty them. What do you think these boys in gray will be doing all that time? A train is a hard thing to hide. In the first place they're big, in the second place they blow black smoke, in the third place they make a lot of noise, and last of all, they have to stay on iron rails," John fires back.

Mosey holds up his open left hand, his finger pointing toward his leader.

"I appreciate your concerns, but just let me give you some details. They won't come after us for the guns; the Union army is going to steal them. We've got enough uniforms to pull it off. As far as stealing the train goes, we've got two of our men working here in the yard. One's an engineer and the other's a fireman. No one will question a thing when they start hooking those four cars together. We won't blow up the platform until we're ready to roll.

"We're also going to set fire to several buildings close by here, and with the commotion down at the docks, they'll think we're moving the rail cars out of harms way. Now then, we'll have a man on a telegraph pole along the tracks twenty miles out. When the train passes him he'll send a message to another of our men on a pole another fifty miles farther away. There'll be enough help on this end, and the other, to remove a hundred yards of rail to keep another engine from coming from either direction. Our men on the poles will cut the telegraph wire before they climb down.

"The train will go on until it meets up with a whole passel of our people, with horses, wagons, mules, and the like. They'll empty those rail cars in a hurry, and leave in all directions. By the time the Confederates figure out what happened here and get to the train, our trail will be colder than the boiler on that engine." Mosey sits back in his chair.

"Wow," Randy blurts out. "Now that's what I call a plan."

"You might want to leave a Union hat or two lying around out there," Robert adds.

Mosey nods yes and grins.

"I've got to hand it to you, you've thought this through. What part are we going to play?" John inquires.

"Well again no disrespect, but, I don't want to be the one who gets our general and his family killed. I just can't see sending some of you home in wood boxes for your families to bury. They've been through enough. So, I'd prefer you just sit this one out on the front porch of your hotel," the chief operating officer says seriously.

"When?" John's question signals his approval of the scheme.

"Just at sundown tonight. We figure the fires will be brighter and the explosions louder the darker it gets. We'll be less of a target, and our uniforms will look better the dimmer the light, too. When we leave here, I'll pass the word to get our timing worked out." Mosey seals the pact.

The meeting breaks up in short order, so the Anderson group heads for their hotel to pick up the women, then find a restaurant for breakfast. The men relate their meeting with Mosey while they are finishing their meal, sitting at a round table.

"You're awfully quiet, Daddy," Charlotte comments.

"You sure are." Cheryl supports her sister. "What are you thinking?"

"I'm wondering if Mosey has thought anything about the *Savannah*'s cannons, and the shore batteries. I can see where their mortars can chase the two ships out and away far enough that their shore batteries are out of range, but any of them could be turned inland and rain shells down on their operation," John confides. "I didn't hear him mention them, did any of you?"

"No, but I'd bet he's thought about them. He seems to have thought about everything else," Robert explains.

"But what if he hasn't? What's on your mind, Mr. Anderson?" Randy asks.

"On second thought, I think it's best that we stay out of it now that we know Mosey and his crew are all organized and ready to move. Like Robert says, he's probably thought about it anyhow. Besides, he's right when he says our families have been through enough."

John realizes he shouldn't have said anything, and tries to discourage the direction the conversation is headed.

"How could we do it? I mean, if we had a mind to, how would we do it? Randy pushes forward.

"Well, I wouldn't worry too much about those on the *Savannah*. They can only move around so much on their deck, and they can't get that much elevation on the barrels, either. Their barrels are short, too. From where they set, I doubt they could reach the train yard with any kind of accuracy. On the other hand, the shore batteries can be turned around to fire inland. They're a whole lot bigger gun with longer barrels. Of the two, I'd say they're the ones, if any, that will give him trouble," Robert advises.

"Where are they vulnerable?" Charlotte wants to know.

"I got up close to look at the shore batteries when I was in school at Philadelphia. Shore cannons are set on a steel track laid out in a circle. That way they can be turned all the way around with no trouble at all. They have long barrels that make them more accurate at long distances, and the breeches are set to they can swing way down to push the muzzle up to seventy degrees or more. All of that gives the gunners a lot to play with when they aim it. I watched their practice and was amazed to see a good crew fire at least twice a minute, and they can close in on a target with just three or four shots.

"There's usually at least four men on each cannon. The way they do it is they swab out the barrel to clean out old used powder, then take a shell that has a bag of powder attached to it and stuff it in the muzzle, powder end first. Then they use a rammer to pack it down into the breech. There's a hole on the top of the breech called a vent, or fire hole, where they stick a knife or something down into to tear open the powder bag. A thing called a friction primer with a ring on its top is placed in the vent hole. Then they hook a lanyard, which is a hook on a piece of rope, to the ring. When they yank on the lanyard, the primer makes a spark to set off the powder," he concludes.

"Do they keep them loaded all the time, or wait until they need to shoot and load them then? Wet powder won't work." Randy's is a good question.

"They keep a plug in the barrel and vent hole to keep the weather out. In really bad weather they throw a canvas over them. I imagine they're loaded and ready to shoot all the time," Robert surmises.

"Not that we're going to, Daddy, but what would you do to make them so they couldn't use them," Charlotte urges, furthering Randy's inquiry.

"From what I hear, I guess I'd plug up the fire hole, and dump something into the barrel that would take a long time to clean out. They wouldn't take the chance of firing a cannon with a partially plugged barrel, knowing it would probably blow the breech and muzzle wide open. Honey mixed with sand and a few old rags would do the trick. They wouldn't try to fire them until they're cleaned out," her father answers.

"We can do that." Cheryl trumpets. "Let's do it."

"How are we going to do it?" Randall questions. "They're not just going to allow us to walk up and ruin their cannons."

"A diversion, we need a good diversion. But what?" Charlotte wonders.

"What do soldiers like? Wine, women, and song," Robert laughingly chimes in.

John gets up from his chair and moves toward the doorway. When he steps outside to the porch, the others get to their feet getting ready to leave with him, thinking their efforts to go after the cannons have been in vain. But, he stops, turns back, and stands there looking at them. They sit back down as he returns to put his hands on the table, motioning them to bend in close.

"Listen to what I'm saying. The soldiers guarding the cannons have guns with real bullets. This is not some piece of a storybook we're living here. If things don't go right, these Confederates won't send our bodies home in a wood box to our families like Mosey says. They'll throw us in the ocean for fish food. Are you sure you want to do this? There are no guarantees."

He takes a two-second look at each of their faces.

No responses. He takes that as a yes.

"Okay, here's what we'll do. Robert, you and Randall go on out there to get the lay of the land. We need to know how many men and cannons they have and how they're set up. Don't concern yourself with them that are out of range of the town. And we'll not worry about those that won't shoot because they can't get a target. They won't chance firing blind into the city. When you get back I want you to . . ."

At Canozira.

The loud rapping on her door disturbs Lilly's sleep. She instinctively jumps up and heads toward the noise. Staggering to keep her balance and fighting to clear her head, she pulls the door open.

"I'm sorry to disturb your rest," Ty's greeting is cheery. "But I'd like you to leave for La Nesra as soon as you can get ready. It's early, I know, but if you leave now you'll have plenty of time to work things out there with your husband and friends. Remember, we'll pick you up in the pasture to the west of La Nesra's wall at two AM. You must be there ready to board our craft. It won't wait long. That's two AM, in the pasture out beyond La Nesra's west wall. Don't be late. Oh yes, so there's no doubt later on, that's two AM Atlanta time. Got it?"

"Yes, I understand. What time is it now?"

"Two thirty in the afternoon."

"Shall I let you know when I leave?"

"No, that won't be necessary. Just be sure you're ready when your transportation gets there to bring you back," Ty repeats.

It takes about an hour for her to get ready, and make the trip through the mirrors to her previous home within the walls of La Nesra.

Sally is busy in the kitchen preparing a meal, standing with her back toward Lilly when she arrives. Trying not to startle her friend, who is holding a knife, she clears her throat.

Sally jumps a little and turns quickly. "It's you, Sheree, I'm so glad to see you. Falcon will be thrilled that you're here."

"I don't have that much time. They're sending a machine to pick me up at two in the morning. I have to return to my body and go back with them. They have a place all prepared where they can feed by life body while I'm gone and everything," Sheree blurts it all out in one breath.

"I see," Sally acknowledges. "They should all be here in a few minutes. It's my turn, and they're never late for supper. One of us is here all the time, you know, to watch over your life body while you're gone."

"Oh, I've missed you all." Sheree softens an awkward moment, and steps toward her friend with her arms open wide.

John Anderson, dressed in his Confederate officer's attire, rides alongside a carriage carrying Charlotte and Cheryl, dressed in their finest, all painted up, and smelling like a field of aromatic flowers. Robert and Randy, also dressed in Southern gray uniforms, sit up front as driver and escort. They're nearing the encampment of soldiers trusted with the care of the shore cannons.

The two young men brought back information that there were two batteries of six cannons each, separated by a fifty yard strip of flat cleared ground. The guns are all the same, and just like the ones Robert described earlier. They're being guarded by six men, three at each battery. The total number of soldiers in the camp is estimated to be at least thirty.

John had a blacksmith melt down lead bullets from their cache of ammunition to make twelve lead plugs three inches long and tapered to allow them to be inserted into the fire holes of the cannon. A couple of good hits with a sledge will cause the soft lead to expand, sealing the breech. He has also brought along an ample supply of bourbon, rum, scotch, rye, and a bag of sleeping powders he bought from a local doctor.

Robert and Randy will pass out the bottles of liquor to the soldiers, making sure each one is laced with enough of the sleeping powder to do the job. Earlier today, they located honey to mix with sand, enough to fill twelve glass canning jars; and tore up more rags than they'll need to plug the barrels of twelve cannons. These, along with the lead plugs, sledge hammers, and a supply of hand bombs, are hidden under a canvas on the back of their wagon, secured with a rope.

The suns position in the sky tells John the afternoon is wearing on, as the group moves into the camp.

Timing is critical with their plan. Too soon, and they are vulnerable if more soldiers arrive and notice the cannons have been sabotaged. Too late, and the Confederates might send a message from town to turn the cannons and shoot inland. Since there is only one way in and out of the encampment, they must avoid being trapped by getting back to town before the attack starts. It will take time for the booze and drugs to do their job.

Other concerns are nondrinkers, religion, number of soldiers, and John's biggest fear, the commanding officer of the camp.

The women start drawing the attention of the soldiers as soon as they are within earshot, squealing and yelling encouragements to the yearning men. The ensemble pulls to a stop in front of a makeshift building constructed with wood boards for walls and a canvas tent for a roof. A Confederate states flag along with the flag of South Carolina hung from the top of long poles at the entrance, make it look like the camp headquarters.

John steps down from his horse by the side of the carriage, and swaggers around to the front of the team. A young soldier at the entrance snaps himself rigid and salutes. He returns the recognition with a much less exaggerated motion.

"Your commanding officer in there?" he says sternly.

"Yessir."

"Get him," John persists coldly.

Twenty or so soldiers stand back away looking at the women and wondering what's going on.

The young guard returns through the doorway first, followed by a soldier of about the same age with sergeant stripes on his sleeves of gray.

"Can I help you, sir?" he asks as he salutes.

John again makes a saluting motion.

"You the commanding officer?" he asks grimly.

"Yes, I mean, the lieutenant went to town for supplies and left me in charge while he's gone. So, I guess so."

"Did he take anybody with him?"

"Just two of our men went with him."

"How long before he gets back?"

"Can't say for sure, could be any time now."

"Listen, I've been ordered to bring this party out here to you fellas. I've got some whiskey and women for your pleasures."

"What? You've got—you've brought what? I'm not sure—"

"You heard what I said," John confirms gruffly.

"Oh, I don't know, my lieutenant will skin me alive if he comes back here and finds us all drunk with a bunch of women. He'll have my hide," the sergeant wrings his hands at the thought.

"I'm not here to ask your permission. I've got orders from the general himself." He pulls a rumpled paper from beneath his blouse.

"Can you read, boy?"

"No, sir, I never learned it."

"See this paper here in my hand. These are his orders, and he's not used to his orders being disobeyed." John gets gruffer as he speaks.

"Now, I'm going to save your neck. You can agree to what I'm here for, or I can put you under arrest and tie you to that tree over there. Hell, I'll even smack you on the head with the butt of a rifle if it'll make you feel any better about it. Your lieutenant won't want your skin either way, but it's up to you. What's it going to be?"

"I reckon when you put it that way, it's all right with me, sir," the young man concedes.

John turns to the carriage and wagon.

"Break out the booze and women. You there, bugler, call assembly. Let's get this thing rolling."

"Sir," the sergeant begins. "I have to leave guards at the guns, and that's a fact."

"How many?" John asks insistently.

"Two at each battery."

"So be it," John agrees, and walks to the side of the carriage.

"Cheryl, you handle the four guards, send the other two back here. Remember, if you're going to drink, watch the bottles. Don't get them mixed up and wind up asleep yourself," he cautions under his breath.

"I'll handle it," Cheryl assures her father curtly.

Charlotte, Robert, and Randy all make sure each soldier is getting his fill of liquor . . . and sleeping powders.

John walks around to make sure any problems that come up are handled swiftly.

An hour passes.

The elder Anderson finds it hard to believe that all of the men accepted the liquor without question. Those still able to speak are of a much fewer number, and getting smaller as the minutes pass. Soldiers sleep where they fall.

Mr. Anderson is also keeping a watchful eye on the road coming into the camp. He doesn't want to be surprised should the Lieutenant show up from town with his men.

Cheryl sits on the ground half way between the two batteries with one remaining guard. The other three lie flat on their backs having fallen over from where they sat. She glimpses to see her daddy looking, and holds up a bottle to wave it around.

John nods yes to acknowledge seeing her. She apparently takes that as a sign to start working on the cannons. She gets up, leans over, and whacks the almost unconscious man on the head with the bottle. He falls limply to the ground.

"Looks like we're started whether we're ready or not," he tells Robert and Randy. "I think we'll be all right, the rest of these here are too woozy and interested in Charlotte to be watching us. I'll take care of things if they do. Grab your tools and let's get this over with."

The two young men, and Cheryl, make short work of hammering the lead plugs into the fire holes of the cannon, and ramming the rags, mixed with honey and sand, down the barrels to pack them in the breech.

John watches proudly as they work together in such an organized manner. Just to be sure about his own responsibilities, he has picked up two hand bombs and some matches.

Fifteen minutes pass, the job is finished and his crew has returned to the wagons.

"We're done. Let's get out of here," he orders.

With all the empty bottles and equipment packed on the carriage, and everybody aboard, he mounts up to lead the procession in a wide circular turn.

The road is nothing more than tracks worn into ruts with grass and weeds between them. Existing rocks and holes from rocks that have been removed from the path make for a bouncy, jolting ride. Most of the way the lane leads through open meadows of long grass, but in one area, about two-thirds of the way to town, it trails through a stand of large pines where just enough room for a single line of traffic has been cleared. The long gentle curve to the right somewhat follows the contour of the shore line, which is several hundred yards away. Since this stretch of road is a third of a mile long, there is no way of knowing if another vehicle is coming from the opposite direction. But apparently, it has never been a big problem due to the scarce number of travelers with wagons who use it.

The group is about halfway through the pines, with John riding several yards in front of the team pulling the carriage. He throws up his hand to signal stop when another wagon appears, coming toward them. The driver pulls the opposing team to a stop some thirty yards away.

"Whoa."

John, dressed in his Confederate officer's uniform, assesses the situation. There are three Confederate soldiers riding a freight wagon. One of them has lieutenant marked on his uniform.

"This must be the commanding officer from the battery camp. That wagon is moving heavy. They're hauling supplies," he thinks, dismounts, and looks back at Robert and Randy, both of whom have jumped down off their seats to join him.

"We can't let these three get back to that camp just yet. We're going to have to delay them until this is all over," he says softly to his two accomplices as soon as they are near enough to hear.

"I'll take the officer, you handle the two on the wagon. Follow my lead."

John turns, and the three of them walk toward the lieutenant who has also jumped down from his wagon.

"Looks like we have a little problem, sir?" the Confederate soldier confirms as he salutes his superior.

John waves his hand in response.

"More so that you might think," he replies.

"Go on over and say howdy to the boys," he instructs, and gestures to move Robert and Randall toward their wagon.

"Sir?" the lieutenant questions, not understanding his ranking officer's remark.

John pulls his handgun and levels it at his stomach. Robert and Randall, on either side of the incoming wagon now, follow his actions, and wave their weapons signaling the soldiers to get down.

"We don't want to harm any of you, but you have to be detained for a while. That means the three of you are going to be tied to some trees over there. Don't ask questions because you won't like the answers. Just do as I say," John speaks bluntly with stern firmness in his voice.

"The hell you are! Get 'em, boys!" the young officer yells, as he lunges at John, knocking his gun hand aside.

The unexpected charge causes the older Anderson to lose his balance and fall backward, hitting the ground hard with the soldier on top of him. John's instincts tell him to roll to the left before the lieutenant can establish his position. Once he's free of the man's weight, he jumps to his feet ready for a fight.

The soldier has other plans, however, and comes up with his own sidearm in hand, pointing it at John's chest not more than four feet away.

A shot rings out! John braces for the impact—nothing!

He looks up from the soldier's gun to his face to watch his eyes glaze over and his body wilt at the knees. Down he goes to lie still on the ground. The other two men, having jumped at Robert and Randall from the wagon, cease their efforts when they hear the shot. Everybody looks to see where it came from.

Charlotte is standing up, peering around the confines of the carriage.

Cheryl stands on the ground next to the wagon, feet spread apart, one just in front of the other, holding the stock of a smoking rifle against her face.

"I had to do it, Daddy! He was going to shoot you!" she screams in defense.

"Damn!" John expresses his distaste for what has just happened, then turns his attention to his fearful daughter.

"You did the right thing, Cheryl, and don't you forget it. I told him to behave and no one would get hurt. He had other ideas, and he paid the price. You saved my life, honey, and I'm grateful."

"How about the two of you?" Mr. Anderson turns to face the other soldiers.

Both men raise their hands into the air signaling surrender.

"Help me. Help me, please," a weak labored voice moans from the wounded lieutenant.

Charlotte is off the carriage kneeling down to inspect his wound. Blood gushes from his back and chest to puddle under his body. She makes a determination within a few seconds and looks up.

"Nothing we can do for him. He needs a doctor, I don't have the equipment."

"We can't take him to town," Robert interjects with certainty.

"Could he make it long enough for us to send help out here?" her father asks.

"I can't be sure. He might live an hour, maybe two or three. I don't know," she answers.

"Robert's got a good point, Mr. Anderson. If we take him to town, he'll turn against us, and if we leave him here, the first thing he'll do is let those two loose. The smart thing would be to finish him off." Randy's sudden opinion seems cruel, but honest.

"Yeah, everything considered, you're right," John agrees.

"I'm sorry as hell, lieutenant, but there's nothing I can do except give you a choice of how you die. I can either finish it now or leave you tied up here like you are with no hope." The words almost choke him as they come out.

He glances at Cheryl still standing where she was with her hands clasped to her face covering her eyes. The rifle lays at her feet.

"Tie those two up against some trees over there," her daddy instructs and motions with the back of his hand to Robert and Randy.

"What's it going to be? If you can't decide, we'll move you over there close to your friends, but we'll have to tie your hands and legs," he continues.

"No, don't leave me here like this. I'm shot up too bad. I ask one last thing of you though," he pleads.

"What's that?" John reacts.

"Have the one that shot me do it." He breathes, showing his teeth through a grimacing sweaty face.

"Well now, I don't thin—" the elder Anderson's words are cut off.

"I'll do it, if that's what he wants." Cheryl moves to pick up the rifle.

"You don't have to do this," Robert exclaims. "I'll do it. There's no need for you to carry this around with you for the rest of your life."

"Or I can do it," Randall offers.

Charlotte gets up from beside the wounded soldier, bringing his gun from the ground with her right hand.

"What's your name?" she asks calmly, softly.

"David . . . David Hampton," he answers and looks up, raising a quivering hand. "Why, you're a pretty thing. Pretty as an angel."

She slowly cocks the hammer as she points the gun at his head.

John sees the muscles in her jaws and lips tighten while she looks directly into the face of the crazed young man, the revolver jumps with a bang.

The lieutenant lies lifeless, his eyes open with a blind stare.

She lowers the gun and turns away, mumbling, "Yeah, an angel from hell."

"You'll rot in hell for this, you traitor bastards. We'll remember you and hunt you all down if it takes our whole lives," one of the Confederate men yells and spits at them.

"We're all soldiers in this stinking war, and we take no pleasure in any of this. You'd do this, or worse, if the shoe was on the other foot. Now, shut your mouth before you get some of the same." Robert explodes with anger.

Nothing more is said. The body is dragged off the road not far from the where the two soldiers are tied.

John instructs Robert to move the supply wagon as far to the right as possible, against the trees. Then they sit on top of it to use their feet against the side of the carriage to push it up and away as Randy drives it slowly past. There's a lot of wheel scraping, but with some effort their equipment finally sets clear on the town side of the blocked road.

"Now bring that supply wagon crossways in the road, do it so the team can be unhitched and brought to this side. Tie some rope to the wheels on the far side, then throw it over the top. We'll use the horses to pull it over. That'll slow them down."

With the horses and carriage back on the blacksmith's lot, and the leftover bombs and their long guns stowed away in their trunks, the Anderson group makes a deal with the smithy to purchase six horses, and gear, for two hundred dollars, Confederate, and all the unopened bottles of liquor they brought back. He'll have the animals saddled, and the trunks tied to one as fast as he can. The trunk from the hotel will be the last loaded. He expects them to be back in less than two hours.

The five head directly to their rooms to change clothes. Then they appear out on the front porch of the hotel as the last rays of the sun fade from the horizon. It's been decided that John, Charlotte, and Cheryl will watch the efforts of the Sons people at water's edge, while Robert and Randall get as close as they can to the happenings at the railroad yard. They'll meet back here after it's all over to trade tales of their experiences.

The first mortar shell explodes in the harbor sending water thirty feet into the air. The trio is off at a run toward the docks. The two young men move in the opposite direction.

Mortar shells explode one after the other, as the Andersons reach a good spot and join twenty-five other observers on the dock of a warehouse overlooking the water. Each round seems to get closer to its target.

At first, bellows of white smoke start rising from the already hot stacks of the two cargo ships. Then it changes to a thick black tube shooting up twenty feet, before it starts to spread out over the water.

"They'll have steam in no time at all now," John observes, as the mortars continue their relentless efforts.

They watch as the crew of the *Savannah* frantically rocks the frigate forward and backward with her steam-driven propeller, trying to turn her from her moorings. As expected, with no rudder to answer the helm, she wallows against the wharf.

Hands on the dock, on that side of the ship, use poles and their feet trying to push, and swing her bow seaward. It's obvious that no one has considered the use of her cannon for any reason.

"If they'd stop the propeller, and then try to push her away, they might get somewhere, but this way they're just slamming into the dock over and over again," an experienced old salt standing on the dock tells one and all.

Suddenly, the closest of the two cargo ships explodes in an upward manner causing both smoking towers to fall sideways into the water. It is supposed that a mortar shell dropped down her stack. Less than a minute later, a second and third eruption, caused by the cargo of powder and ammunition, breaks her in half. Hands jump from all sides into the water, swimming hard to get away from the fire and the hail of exploding bullets.

"Will you look at that. I thought the idea was to chase them out of the harbor, not sink them where they're anchored," Charlotte observes.

"The black smoke is so thick I can't see if the other one is moving yet or not, can you?" Cheryl adds.

"If we can't see her, then chances are neither can the mortar operators. Give it a minute or two, the smoke will clear. Maybe she'll have time to make her move," their daddy offers.

Sounds of shots and explosions are heard from behind the group gathered on the dock. All turn to see nothing but a little smoke over toward the railroad yard.

"Here we go," Charlotte tells her kin under her breath.

"There she is—she's moving." Someone yells.

Everyone turns back toward the water again to see the second cargo ship moving, under the smoke from her stacks, headed toward open water.

"She's sure blowing a lot of smoke," a male voice points out.

"Yeah, and it looks like they're trying to get her sails up, too. Another couple a hundred yards and she'll be out of their range. Five dollars says she makes it," a different voice offers. There are no takers.

Everybody turns again to look for clues to explain the cause of all the noise behind them. What sounds like small arms fire and hand bombs are now continuous. Smoke of different shades of gray and black is rising from five or six separate locations. A man dressed in a business suit appears on the dock, panting from a long run.

"Union soldiers have attacked the rail platform, blew it up, and set fire to the biggest part of that side of town!" he yells breathlessly. "Come on, they need all the help they can get." He waves his arm in a follow me fashion, but gets no volunteers.

Ten or twelve shots in quick sequence are heard.

"That has to be a Gatling gun." Cheryl identifies the source.

"Sounds like Mosey's got his hands full." John feels a bit relieved that his group is not a part of it.

"I don't hear any cannons going off over on the coast. They must all be asleep at their posts," Charlotte says loudly, amused with herself.

"Let's get back to the hotel and wait for the boys. It's all over here from what I can see," John suggests.

The three find two rockers and a straight chair on the front porch to watch the people of Charleston scamper here and there doing Lord knows what. The bells of fire equipment being moved are heard off and on, and by the looks of the smoke the whole town of Charleston will be on fire shortly.

Twenty minutes later, much of the clamor has settled. The glow of fires under the smoke light up what would normally be a black sky. But the sounds of battle are silent.

Robert and Randy appear, trotting out of the darkness. They leap up onto the porch, breathing hard with excitement.

"That was something to see," Randall gasps.

"They never did get the train," Robert says, and pauses to take a breath, giving his friend an opportunity.

"They blew up the platform and the railroad cars. They never even got the engine close to those cars." He stops to catch his breath.

"Two soldiers threw hand bombs at the engine, until one landed right in the laps of the engineer and fireman. It blew the roof clear off, and must have broke the fire box, too, because the whole thing went up spewing scalding water everywhere. They had a Gatling gun set up on the back of a wagon they brought in, too. I don't think Mosey knew about that," Robert finishes.

Calming down, Randy continues.

"I don't know what all they used to do it, but I'll bet there's not one thing anybody could use that was on that platform, or those railroad cars. The only thing left of the cars are the steel wheels, and they're sitting upside down on their carriages alongside the track, which is all twisted and broke."

"Could you tell how many of ours were killed or wounded," John asks, concerned.

"Not really. People were moving around so fast, and there wasn't any good light with all that smoke. I'd guess at least two hundred men are down though. There's people lying everywhere. If there were people close to where those bombs went off, no one will ever find a piece of them," Robert answers.

"How'd things go with the ships in the harbor?" Randy thinks to ask.

"One ship blew up and sunk where she was anchored," Charlotte explains.

"The other one finally got moving and got away," Cheryl manages to add before Charlotte.

"What about the *Savannah*?" he continues.

"Just like Mosey said," John credits the man. "She didn't move away from the dock. I think with all the trouble they were having trying to save their ship, no one on board knows yet about all the rest of what was going on. They didn't fire a shot."

"And there was no sign of shooting from the coast batteries, either." Charlotte shakes her head and smiles.

"We'd better get our things together and get out of here before someone starts putting things together. I'd say let's catch a train, but from what I hear, they might not be running for a while." John grins, gets up, and enters the hotel, followed by his motley crew.

It's getting late at La Nesra. Sheree, Falcon, Sally, Hawk, and Rose are sitting around the supper table with their dirty dishes still sitting unattended. A single lantern—the only light in the large open room—hangs in the center of the table to illuminate the immediate area, casting eerie moving shadows on the floor, furniture, and walls. Their conversation has moved from thoughtful serious considerations to laughter, while they attempt to crowd as much as they can into the short time they have together. Before long, the three left for two hours, giving Sheree and Falcon time to be alone together.

All the necessary explanations have been aired out and heartfelt good-byes, once again, expressed. Sheree has invited them all to accompany her when she leaves, as long as they remain back, out of sight of the approaching craft. All four are skeptical about what they will see.

"Someone check the time," Sheree suggests.

"It's one on the nose," Sally replies, holding her arm closer to the lantern.

"I don't have long now. I don't want to be late. I'd rather be early."

"We'll leave in a few minutes then," Sally decides. "It'll take some time to get there, too."

They walk close together, whispering back and forth, through the compound yard, out through the front guard gate, then turn right to follow the wall to its end. At the corner they turn right again, and walk along the wall about a hundred feet.

"This will be a good place for you to stay. The shadow of the wall will keep you hidden, and it will be far enough away they won't detect you with their equipment," Sheree explains, then gives each a hug and kiss on the cheek. She lingers with Falcon in a long, loving, embrace, then kisses him hard on the lips, and turns away.

She walks forty or fifty yards out into the field and stands ready.

Four pairs of eyes watch expectantly, able to vaguely make out her form, from the blackness of their position.

They wait. They wait.

"Do you see anything?" Rose asks. "What time is it now?"

"It's time; should be any minute now," Falcon answers anxiously.

"I think that star is moving, see it?" Sally points, her arm and finger.

"It's moving fast, getting bigger as it comes," Falcon expresses with anticipation.

One instant the object is moving at a tremendous speed toward the field, the next it has stopped, hovering above the ground. A colored light appears from the bottom of the craft allowing the group to see Sheree's silhouette moving toward it. She's in the light, she's moving up into the machine. The light ceases; the craft remains still for a few seconds, then—as fast as it came—it's gone.

"Can you believe it? I wouldn't unless I saw it with my own eyes," Hawk exclaims.

"I saw it, but I'm sure not going to tell anybody about it. Who would believe me?" Rose answers in awe.

"Let's get back before someone gets suspicious," Sally says, and moves away from the rest.

"You know I support everything Sheree's doing, but I have to say, I've a feeling there's more going on then she knows about. I pray for her every day. May God protect and be with you, Sheree," her husband whispers, while his eyes search the sky with the hope of one last glimpse of her presence.

A year passes while Lilly continues to be inundated with information. It comes from everywhere; books, lectures, hands-on experience, and a system of brainwave osmosis during her sleep. It's constant, it's consistent, it's effective. She's understanding more and more of her power, her keen mind, her never lacking energy, and the reasons for the position she is training to fulfill. She's not seen her life body since her trip back from La Nesra. The weeks slip by in the form of days.

"Lilly, the time has come for you to venture out of the comfort of these walls, to experience what you've learned, and to discover firsthand your importance to mankind." Ty speaks during an informal setting over breakfast, along with Remsar.

"A group of powerful men from all over the world are meeting in the morning to discuss, among other things, you. Oh, they don't know you the way we know you, they only know that you exist. They meet once a year to decide a course of action to be taken concerning the most important, pressing problems of the world. No trivial matters are brought to this meeting. Only those deemed potentially ruinous or constructive to our world will be entertained. The decisions made will impact all of mankind, for all attending will take with them their agreed-upon plan for the following year. Their plan to further the cause of being ready when the Korgots return to earth. These are the wealthiest, most influential, and probably least-known men of our world. They call themselves the World Alliance."

"We are known there by Urlee Oldspahr. Unknown to them, he represents our interests and brings back the details of their agreements," Remsar interjects.

"Urlee Oldspahr has requested your presence there," Ty continues. "We agreed, but only if you can remain anonymous, and only for the time they spend discussing you."

"Yes, we think it will be a good experience for you, but why give them reason to include you in their thinking," Remsar adds. "These people reign without conscience, they can be very dangerous. They answer to no one but themselves."

Lilly feels she's finally being accepted. They are actually divulging information detrimental to their entire operation.

"To accommodate our requirements, he's given us coordinates to put you in a secure area to witness the meeting. Their agenda is laid out carefully, so you'll arrive at the specified time. You'll use your movement through the mirrors to the exact location," Ty explains.

"How should I prepare?" she wonders.

"You are prepared. We believe this meeting will give you the proof, the confirmation, you've been looking for. You'll be there to listen and understand, that's all," he finishes.

"Now, when that part is finished, you are to return here immediately. Do not remain too long. You'll be safe enough for a short period of time, but as you can imagine, their security is intense. Get back here as soon as you can," Remsar specifies strongly.

Ty hands her a piece of paper.

"These are the coordinates. Memorize them now."

She looks at the paper for a few seconds, then hands it back to him.

"Are you all set?" Remsar asks.

She nods yes.

"Good, leave here at four in the morning. We'll be waiting to hear your report when you get back," he concludes.

Lilly is up at two thirty to be sure she has plenty of time to get ready. Her personal maid and assistant tend to her needs quickly giving her forty-five minutes to spare.

"Maybe I should leave a little early. It wouldn't hurt to be a little early now, would it?" she thinks. "What if I have a problem finding this place. A few extra minutes could still get me there on time."

She goes to her bedroom, closes the door, and slides through her floor length mirror hanging on the wall. Once on the other side, her mind turns to recalling the coordinates, and begins to run them over and over.

Her concentration is broken by the feeling of someone—something—at her back. Cautiously turning, suspended in midair, she sees Zola.

"You startled me." Her thoughts transfer to her acquaintance.

"I can warn you just once, they are near. Leave this place. Leave it now, and for all time. They are here to find and destroy you. Hear and heed me." Zola's words go through Lilly's mind.

"What—? Who—? Why?" she emits, in rapid succession.

Zola turns to quickly disappear.

Before she has time to think, she senses another presence coming closer and closer.

"Do not be alarmed by Zola's fears," a male voice echoes in her head. "We will protect you from any who wish you harm."

"Who are you? I can't see you?"

"We will travel with you to keep you safe."

Lilly's mind is spinning. "I don't need any help. This is supposed to be a secret meeting I'm headed for. I can't let these things in here know where I'm going."

"We'll travel with you to protect you." The voice resounds again.

"Not this time you won't," she mouths, and dives back through the mirror to her bedroom.

"What will I do now? They'll probably be waiting if I go back in there. Hhmmmm. I need a different mirror, one at a different location. But where?"

"I know . . . but I'll have to take a mirror with me."

She races out through the bedroom door, grabs a two-foot oblong mirror off the living room wall, and runs to the area where the flying machines await.

Not knowing whether they will permit it or not, she asks a guard if someone will take her for a ride. She is known by most here now, having been seen with Remsar and Ty. The guard gestures to one of the pilots of the crafts, and soon she's on her way into the sky.

She taps the pilot on the shoulder, waves her hand goodbye, then places the mirror on the floor and jumps through. She has prepared herself to concentrate on the coordinates quickly, not allowing anything to distract her mind.

"Something is coming at me very fast. Hurry now, think, think!" She's moving, faster and faster, several seconds pass! She stops!

"It's still coming after me! There's a white spot! I'm going through, there, I made it."

"What is this place?" She gets to her feet from the floor where she landed.

She looks around, turning slowly, trying to discern her whereabouts. The mirror she came through hangs on the wall four feet off the floor.

"I'm closed in on three sides. There's a short wall on the fourth with a light glowing beyond it. I'll take a little peek." She moves, carefully placing her feet as she goes.

A first glance over the wall reveals a circular room, fifty feet in diameter, containing an immensely large round table with the seats on the outside of the rim. The table itself is about four feet wide all the way around, with a large open area in the center, making it twenty feet across. Beyond the seats, an aisle goes all the way around the outside. Then, pews are tiered steeply upward, with five rows staggered back from each other, each of which protects their occupants with heavy railings. There are lights dropping from the ceiling on gold-colored chains, down ten feet below Lilly's perch. Their reflectors force the light mostly downward to flood the area brightly.

"No one can see me from down there with those lights in their eyes," she considers.

A longer second look reveals a man in each seat at the table. She thinks it convenient that there is no room for additional seats, and that all are filled. This could have been some sort of battle arena a long time ago. The voices of the men can be heard distinctly throughout, but they are all in different tongues. One might speak English, while another responds in French.

"How do they ever understand each other like this?" she asks herself. "Do they all speak and understand the various languages, not likely."

Then she spies an earpiece lying on a chair near the wall. She puts it in her ear, sits on the chair, and listens. No matter who's speaking, it's coming out in English to her. Somehow, whatever language is being spoken is translated into the receiver's tongue automatically.

"This must be tied in with Urlee Oldspahr. Why else would this one be in English?" she surmises.

"That brings us to the matter of the liberator," one of them says, then she settles down to listen, questioning, who is the liberator?

"Our last meeting a year ago confirmed to us that the liberator exists, and is here on earth being prepared. Is there anything new to discuss?"

She stands up and leans over the wall a little to see who's talking. It's a man with a bald head, except for a ring of gray hair over the tops of his ears running all way around the back.

"There's word it's a woman," another voice is heard. "A young woman with all sorts of powers being coveted and trained by the Company."

"Do we know if she has the angels?" the first voice rings out.

"I've been informed that the angels were located by the Company, but they disappeared again. Whether the Company has hidden them again, I'm afraid I don't know. It would make sense for them to keep them close at hand, so when the time comes, she'll be right there to deal with them," a third man comments.

"It's certain that we don't have them then. Am I correct?" the first voice asks.

"We have no information to that effect?" a different person speaks.

"I've information from reliable sources that this woman is ready to begin a crusade. Her mission will be to discredit and deface all attempts at religion, except that of the Company and her own. With the powers she reportedly has, she will, most likely, launch a crusade with acts of mystical behavior to assemble a group of disciples—disciples of diverse sects already amounting to legions of followers. That will impact our ability to be ready when the Korgots get here." Yet another voice is heard.

"Let's get back to the facts before we try to provide a solution to this questionable problem." The first voice to be heard announces. "Let's hear what our accomplishments were this time last year."

"Last year, the reports from all twenty-five venues of the world averaged less than thirty out of a hundred people would be ready if the Korgots appeared then. I've just received the numbers for this year, and will need time to insure their accuracy, but it appears we're about thirty-one out of a hundred this year. Obviously, we've made progress when you think of the numbers involved. One more person out of every one hundred people in this world amounts to a sizable amount. But it's not nearly enough to be ready. With our standards in mind, we'll need seventy out of every one hundred people. We've a long way to go." A report from their records keeper seems to support action.

"We cannot afford to give the liberator a free hand to expand the efforts of the Company. Our covert resources must be doubled and redoubled if necessary, to find and destroy this woman." Yet another opinion, this one more concerned.

The room resounds with many voices all adding their thoughts at the same time.

Lilly peers over the edge of the short wall to see the gray-haired man raise both his arms to settle the disruption. At this point, there is no doubt in her mind—they are talking about her.

"What are we saying, gentlemen? What course of action is required?" He escalates the conversation.

"She must be stopped now." The response is supported with a volley of agreements in various languages.

"We all agree with that, but how, to what extent?" The apparent leader tries to organize their thinking.

"Destroy her by any means necessary." Heavy words are heard above all others.

"Are you saying we should authorize her annihilation?"

"May I stop you all for a moment?" A gruff base voice settles the noise.

"I'm not sure you all realize what we're faced with," he continues. "As your duly-appointed commander of world security, I can tell you this woman is not your ordinary female. Among other things, she has the ability to live outside her body. The Company, if they're smart, has her flesh and blood body hidden away somewhere. Heavily guarded, she could be anywhere, perhaps along with the angels we so desperately seek. Her image, outside of her body, looks as real as you or me, but if she stood here in front of us right now, a knife through her heart would do her no permanent harm. You can't kill that which is not truly living in the first place."

"Are you saying she's invincible?" A good question from the group.

"What I'm saying is that if you're going to murder her, you first have to find her real body. Other than that, the only thing you'll be able to do is capture and detain her out of body self," he advises.

"Are you saying she's a ghost?" Another voice is heard through the ear pieces.

"In a sense, but when you see her, you'll never know it by her looks and touch."

"What's your recommendation?" the leader of the group asks of the commander.

"I support the premise of murder, if we can locate her body, but I imagine we'll find her out of body self long before that. She can be restrained, she's not able to pass through walls. So, in lieu of murder, we can lock her up. Her body will lie dormant until her out of body soul returns. Either way, she'll be unable to fulfill her prophecy. We can continue our search for the angels, and if we're fortunate enough to find her with them—well, you see what I mean."

Before anyone else can speak, the commander continues.

"I've already authorized the organization of four teams. Each team has five highly-trained men. They will work separately from each other, each using any resource available to locate and identify our target. Once we know who she is and where she is, we'll combine these forces to trap and contain her. It shouldn't take long, perhaps, sixty days. I plan to offer a large reward to the first team to find and identify her, then a much larger one for the entire group when we have her in chains. With your support, I'll set it all in motion," he finishes.

"Would it be possible to keep us informed with your progress?" Urlee Oldspahr asks, trying to be in a position to warn the Company of upcoming events.

"I will do my best to keep each of you informed as to our success on a monthly basis. However, the details of our operations must be kept covert. You all understand, I'm sure," the commander responds.

Lilly shrinks inside, realizing the plan she has just heard is a plot against her. Simply put, people are being paid to do away with her in any way they can. Twenty heavily-trained armed men will begin looking for her by the end of the day today.

"They obviously think I'm a big threat to their being ready for the Korgots when they arrive. I had no idea that people consider me that way. They don't know me. How can they feel that way when they don't even know who I am?" She tries to accept what she's heard. She turns her attention back to the meeting to hear them move on to another area of discussion.

"I'd better be more careful when I travel around. It could be anybody looking for me. How will I ever be able to talk to people about what to believe if I can't feel safe?

"Remsar and Ty were right to send me here. I'm glad they did, because now I know for sure what they're saying is true. I'd better get out of here and get back to Canozira before something happens."

She hesitates before slipping through the mirror. "I have to keep moving once I'm in there. I don't want whatever it is in there to find me again."

As soon as she's completely through her entryway, before she can attempt to move, a closeness surrounds her; something is holding her still.

"What th—?" she exclaims in her mind.

"Fear not, Sheree. No harm will come to you." She hears in her mind's ear.

It's as if she's in a barrel of tight air, causing a grip that's so tight she's unable to bat her eyeslahes. She would not have a sense of movement if not for a fast approaching dark cavelike spot in front of her. Closer, closer! "I'm going to hit it!" she screams inside.

It's a black hole leading somewhere.

"I'm inside something, still moving, toward that light over there. It's getting bigger, like I'm in a tunnel and that's the way out. The light is so bright; I need to close my eyes, but I can't. Oh, this hurts my eyes. Almost there, I'm in the light. It's not so bright now, my eyes must have adjusted to it. Still moving. The light is fading a little. It's like I'm coming out of a fog, or a cloud. It's getting thinner. I can see faint colors. The sky, the beautiful blue sky. I'm stopping."

"Look down, Sheree." The voice rings in her head as the grip around her lessens.

"What is that?" she thinks, as she scans a massive, desolate, black, hellish-looking ball of something.

"It is your world of the future."

Chapter Thirty-Five

The words "it is your world" echo through Lilly's head as she winces from the sight of the black, desolate, life-barren, crusted ball below her.

"It is within you to change its destiny."

The grip on her body tightens, and her trip is reversed back to where she started.

Once she's released from the invisible hold, it takes only seconds to reach the safety of her dwellings at Canozira.

"What was that?" she pants, listening to her heart thump. "Whatever it was, it convinced me. There's no way that Remsar, Ty, or anyone else would stage all of this just to prove their point, even if they could. It's all true! I must believe it! And I don't know how, but I have to save the world!"

The words come out of her mouth, getting louder and louder as she speaks. They bounce off the walls of her bedroom to slam back into her head with a sobering, upsetting effect. She feels sick to her stomach.

"I have to find Remsar and Ty!" she shouts, and dashes out into the hallway.

It takes a few minutes for her to locate them both and explain what has taken place. "I saw it with my own eyes! It was horrible!" She remembers the burnt earth.

"I don't know who or what it was that took you there, but believe me when I say we had nothing at all to do with it," Remsar assures her. "We felt the meeting would convince you of our sincerity."

"There are things on the other side of that mirror that terrify me. Zola warned me not to come back. I sensed she fears for my life. I don't want to ever go back in there." She's unable to control her shaking hands as she exclaims.

"You're convinced, then. You believe us?" Ty keeps the moment rolling.

"Oh, yes. I believe. But what can I do? I'm really frightened of this whole thing," she continues, pacing back and forth.

They look at each other in agreement.

"You're ready for your final state of training. It takes about two days. You'll be connected to a few wires and sleep while you lie on a comfortable table. When you awake, you'll feel like a new person. All your fears and inhibitions will be gone," Ty advises.

"And you will be prepared for the assignment you were born to inherit. You will be unstoppable. You'll see." Remsar's excitement makes him quiver.

"Are you ready?" he continues.

"Are you talking about my flesh and blood body when you say you're going to hook me up to something?" she needs to know.

"Yes, once your body is properly indoctrinated, your out-of-body self will be the same. Come now, let's get started. We've all waited a long time for this moment." Remsar takes her hand in his, gesturing with his other to move.

"Come with us, Ty. This is a great day."

Lilly resumes her life body when it is brought to her, then slides into a deep, restful, almost comalike sleep, aware of everything, realizing nothing. Dreams come and go quickly, appearing as flashes of memory and hope, moving to yearnings and strengths, followed by satisfaction and bliss.

She feels annoyed, something is shaking, stop it. Leave me alone.

"Stop it, dammit!" she hears her voice scream, bringing her to consciousness.

"There there, dear, you're all right." A soft female voice accompanies a warm hand touching her face.

"Where am I?" Her first conscious words since she was put to sleep have her looking for a position to defend.

"You're waking up from a nice long nap. You're in our hospital where you've been for the last two days. Don't worry you're completely safe here. I'm your nurse. I've been with you for the last six hours to take care of you while you wake up. Can I get you anything?"

"Water. I'd like some water."

"Certainly, here you are. Try to raise yourself up so you don't spill it all over yourself. Let me help you." The nurse tries to put her arm under her back to help.

"Get out of the way, I don't need your help." The words are Lilly's but come out differently than intended. She sits up and gulps the glass of water.

"More," she blurts, and shoves the empty container out to her helper.

The nurse fumbles, the glass starts to fall, but Lilly's hand moves with a blur to grab it and push it back into her grip. The woman in white makes an effort not to show her amazement, settles herself, refills the glass with water, and hands it back.

This time she drinks slowly, taking time to breathe between swallows. She consumes another half glass of the soothing liquid.

"I'm sorry for being short with you. I feel like the whole world has done something to put me in a bad mood, but I don't know what. This isn't like me at all," Lilly says, lowering the glass to her lap.

"Don't worry about it, honey. I've been told to expect exaggerated attitudes, which will pass within a few hours. Your moods might change abruptly too, so that's why I'm here, to help you through it. You'll begin to feel like your old self again in a few hours," the nurse explains. "Now, if you like, lie back down and sleep. I'll awaken you again in about an hour. It's all part of the process."

"Yes, I think I will."

Lilly has lost all track of time. Her nurse has aroused her from a sound sleep more than several times, only to talk with her for a few minutes, and suggest she go back to sleep.

Later.

Her eyes pop open, she's totally awake, her eyes flick in all directions, but the rest of her body lies completely still. Instantly, Lilly recalls who she is, where she is, the reasons, and the rest of her life.

"I'm so comfortable I might never move again. I feel really good, I must have needed a rest," she thinks. "I'm hungry enough to eat a cow, hooves and all."

"Nurse," she says, and turns to locate her whereabouts.

"Good morning." Ty all but sings out. He and Remsar are sitting on two chairs about five feet away.

All of the wires that were connected to her in various places, including her head, are gone. The nurse is nowhere in sight. Her mind is clear and sharp. The unexpected sight of the two men is instantly processed without surprise.

"Is it over?" she inquires.

"Yes, it is. You are now equipped with everything you'll ever need," Ty explains cheerfully.

"I don't feel different. I mean, I don't feel smarter or stronger or anything."

"Oh, we know, but you will. Let's give you a little test just to show you what we mean. See the table there?" Remsar points his finger at a small table supporting a tray with a pitcher of water and two glasses, setting against the wall, eight feet away.

"Tell yourself you want that table to move to your bedside."

She looks at the table and back at Remsar.

"Table, come to me," she says in her mind.

The table moves effortlessly, without making a sound, to her side.

"Now, tell the pitcher to pour some water into a glass. Be specific. Look at the object you're addressing."

"Pitcher, pour some water into that nearest glass."

The pitcher rises, tilts, and begins pouring, and pouring, and pouring. The water is about to spill over the rim.

"Tell it to stop," he orders.

"Stop." Lilly orders in her mind.

The pitcher tilts back and sets itself back on the tray.

"You will need to remember to be as explicit as you can, otherwise, well, you saw that your thoughts, your wishes, will be followed exactly. You must be specific." He makes a point.

"Wow," she expresses with delight. "But how?"

"The power of your brain has been released. The human brain has an enormous ability that is normally never used, mainly due to the individual's lack of motivation, or knowledge of how to tap into it. Centuries of teachings and various methods of discouragement have created layers of resistance into our minds, making it almost impossible for us to reach our true mental capacity. Yours is an exception." Ty begins to openly examine the facts.

"The single and most restricting thing is denial. You, as do we all, possess from birth this ravenous need to be normal, to be accepted, to be like everyone else. We are taught to be compliant with what we see in those around us. We learn to limit our abilities to coincide with the rest of our world. To do otherwise makes us an outcast, an odd person. He put you here to carry out His mission. We have volumes of information concerning your arrival, your young life, and the training required as you matured. Each step has been carefully calculated and followed. We had to wait until you accepted your role," he concludes.

"And that is to save the people of the world," she says with determination.

"Exactly."

The next several months allow Lilly the time and space to discover and accept her new powers. Ty and Remsar encourage her to venture farther and farther into her abilities, but at the same time labor to get her to exercise self-control, to channel her strengths toward the needs of her mission; to not allow herself to get caught up in disagreements or meaningless disputes that will have little or no effect on her destiny. They teach her to use her wisdom before she releases her powers. Her maturity is reaching scores of years beyond her age, and becoming more so every day. Her energy pushes her on with an urgency surpassing all those around her. She requires little sleep, eats only when she's hungry, seeks out solutions to problems before they come up, thrives with diplomacy, and seems to love it all. Seers say she has a glow about her that is unmistakably angelic.

"I need to see the death angels you're guarding," she asks Ty in the form of a statement.

"Why?"

"I feel I need to confirm their existence. It will be my responsibility to watch over them, so I need to know where they are. Please show me now."

"I'll need to consult with Remsar before—" he starts, but is cut off by her voice.

"Will it be necessary for me to locate them myself? I would rather you take me there now, but if you believe there are reasons I shouldn't know where they are, then tell me." She gently warns him.

Ty's face turns red thinking he's riled her temper. He sees for the first time how she is able to kindly insist that her wants be satisfied.

"I'm waiting," she urges.

"You misunderstand, Lilly, I have no objection revealing the location of the angels. My concern is for the security of your body. I believe the safest place for the angels would be the best for your life body, too. But if for some reason, our enemies locate the angels, and found you there with them, it would be a simple thing to control you. As you know, if your life body—or your out of body spirit—is not shielded completely with steel or something just as dense, a mirror placed in front of your flesh and blood face will bring your spirit back to it immediately. Then as long as the mirror is in front of your face, your out of body self is trapped inside. Perhaps a better choice would be to place your body at a different location, away from the angels?"

"Thank you, Ty, I understand your concern, but I must know where they all are kept, and have immediate access if I choose," she responds, thinking her body will be shielded wherever it's kept. "Now, please take me there," she insists.

"Yes, absolutely." He turns and walks briskly away with her on his heels.

Down below the lowest level accessible by any of the workers or staff of Canozira is a labyrinth of various-shaped rooms. Some have three walls, others four, five, or six. Hallways, running in random directions determined by the various-configured walls, turn left and right with others leading off them. It's laid out to confuse those not familiar with its design.

"A person who doesn't know their way around down here could be lost forever," she thinks, as Ty twists and turns through the maze, until finally they arrive at a door. He uses a key to enter the room. It's brightly lit to display the ten containers, each holding one angel. She walks between them looking down at their still figures.

"This place is totally secure. No one will find them here," he brags.

"If I can find them, so can someone else," Lilly counters. "I would like you to provide me with a key, and arrange for my passage into here at my discretion. I must protect them at all costs," she informs her mentor.

'That's fine, as soon as we return upstairs," he replies agreeably.

"Now, please take me to where your life body is kept," she calmly requests.

"No, absolutely not. You have no need to know. Even Remsar doesn't know the whereabouts of my life body. Apparently, he doesn't need to know, why do you?" His temper surfaces and his face turns red again.

"I've asked you nicely, Ty. Now, take me there before I lose my patience," she asserts firmly.

"Never!" he exclaims and turns to leave the room.

With no more effort than a glare, Lilly looks at him. He raises a foot off the floor then flies backward into a wall and hangs there unable to move, struggling to no avail.

"I'll return in forty-eight hours to see if you've changed your mind," she says with a bit of a smirk about her face, and starts to leave the room closing the door behind her, when she hears.

"Stop! I'll take you there."

She follows him to the lift where they enter and start moving up, passing floor after floor, to the very top of the structure. They exit into a hallway to approach a door guarded by a sentry on either side. His hand passes over a small box and the door slides open to the left. They walk through to see another closed door in a short hallway. A wave of his hand over the small box causes the door to open upward exposing a room brightly lit by the sun. She looks up to see a ceiling of glass.

"I like the sun, so I had the ceiling built to open for a number of hours during the day. At night it closes. I've never liked being in the dark all the time," he points out.

She looks down to see a container in the center of the room, with wires running into it from a box with flashing lights. There's a fountain in the corner with water spilling over a two-foot-high spillway to splash and gurgle into a large bowl of stones and pebbles below.

"I think the tranquillity of this room is good for my life body as it rests here," he adds.

"You've certainly taken good care of yourself." She notices to herself. "Ty, I want no one to have access to this room but me—and that includes you."

"Why? I don't understand." He is obviously stunned with her words.

"I need to feel sure that the man who tried to murder me several years ago doesn't get the urge again. You've been telling me for quite a while now to trust you. Well, it's your turn now. Trust me. Perhaps I'll get a good feeling about you and change my mind." She stares directly into his eyes as she speaks.

"Yes, I see. I'll tend to it at the same time I tend to your wishes about the room below." He agrees in the most subservient manner he can muster.

A month passes while she learns more and more about herself, and her newly-gained freedom to do as she sees fit. She, Ty, and Remsar are just finishing breakfast.

"I'm going back to La Nesra for a week." She announces. "I have business to take care of there and I'd like to see my husband. Is that okay with you?" She looks first at Ty, and then Remsar.

"That's a wonderful idea. When you return we'll be ready for you to start amassing and leading our followers. Fifty thousand or more people will be waiting for us in Italy. After that the word will get around quickly. We'll move on throughout Italy, then Spain, France, and all the rest. This is truly exciting, our day has finally come," Remsar happily agrees.

"Ty?" she asks.

He shrugs his shoulders, nods his head yes, and pushes his arms out away from each other turning his palms up, insinuating it makes no difference whether he agrees or not.

Lilly arrives at La Nesra at one in the morning as planned. All is quiet as she stands at the foot of their bed looking down at her husband lying on his back sleeping peacefully. She moves around to sit carefully at his side, then bends down to put her lips gently against his. He doesn't stir. She does it again, this time a little heavier, a little longer. He moves and bats his eyeslahes open, then sits up with a jerk when he realizes there is a person in front of him.

"Sheree?" he exclaims.

"Yes, it's me," she answers cheerily, backing out of the way of his movement.

"It is, it is you." He opens his arms and pulls her to him hard.

Their lips find each other's face and neck as they frantically clench and caress. They linger in each other's arms, creating a softness to mold them into one.

After a minute or so, she pushes slowly away.

"I'll be here for a whole week, honey, and we can spend all of it together. But right now there's something we have to do," she explains.

"What?" Falcon wonders.

“I’ve brought a few things with me. Only, I left them on three flying machines which are up there, out of sight, waiting for my signal to land.” Sitting in the darkness on the bed beside her husband, she points up.

“What did you bring?” He asks trying to understand at the same time.

“You know those containers containing the death angels we found in the wall, the ones that disappeared right after we found them? I have all ten of them right up there. We need to get Sally, Hawk, and Rose here as soon as possible to decide where we’ll hide them.” She informs her man.

She moves out of the way allowing Falcon to get to his feet. “Let me slip on some clothes and I’ll have them here in fifteen minutes. How long do we have?” he questions.

“I promised I would be no more than two hours,” she answers.

“But how?” He wants to know.

“I’ll explain it all later. There’s a whole lot more, but right now we need to get this done. Hurry!” she urges.

Twenty minutes later, after greetings with hugs and kisses, the group is assembled at the kitchen table where Sheree is finishing up a brief explanation.

“So, we need a place where we can hide them temporarily. Then, after I leave, I want you to move them again, anywhere, so I won’t know where they are. It has to be a place that’s completely surrounded by steel or some other metal. They can’t be traced that way. After that, do not reveal the whereabouts of them to anyone but me, and then be sure it’s really me. They have ways of doing all sorts of things, so you have to be certain it’s me.” She pauses.

“Sounds to me like we need a password or something,” Rose poses.

Hawk follows up. “It’ll have to be something that no one would think of?”

“They know you very well, Sheree. It can’t have anything to do with you,” Falcon interjects. “It could be a phrase.”

“Hey, I know.” Sally beams. “It’s perfect. I didn’t realize until I—well listen, if you turn the name La Nesra around backward, it’s A-R-S-E-N-A-L. It spells *arsenal.* What if we come up with a phrase like, ‘I’ve come for the arsenal’? Then whenever we talk among ourselves, we can refer to the containers as the arsenal, and no one will think a thing about it.”

“Perfect.” They all agree.

“We need to hurry.” Sheree spurs on. “We have about an hour and twenty minutes to signal the flying machines. Where can we hide the ‘arsenal’ for now?”

“How about putting them back in the wall where we found them in the first place?” Hawk ponders.

“No honey, that won’t work. We have to move them again. How would we ever get them in and out of there without someone asking what we’re doing. Besides, too many people know about it,” Rose reminds her husband.

“It has to be somewhere other than here at La Nesra then,” Falcon points out.

“I have an idea, but it might be a little too risky,” Sally begins and gets everyone’s attention.

The looks on their faces ask "what" without saying a word.

"There's a livery in Atlanta that Robert and Randy used when they were here to rescue you, Sheree. You know, when they took Cheryl instead of you. Anyway, I've come to know Smitty and his son Luke, who own and operate it. We can trust them completely, and there's room enough to hide the arsenal in their barn."

They all look at each other back and forth.

"You've done it again, Sally." They extend their congratulations.

"Wait! Won't they have a lot of questions when they see the containers, and let's not forget the boxes with the wires and lights." Falcon makes a good point.

"I had a shelf put underneath each container so the black boxes would fit there. Then I had them all wrapped up in canvas just before we left. The only thing they'll be able to see are the wheels of the carts they're on," his wife is quick to explain.

"Any other questions or suggestions?"

"Good that's settled, now let's get to town quickly. We can just make it." Lilly moves from the table as she speaks.

Once out of sight and sound of La Nesra, the group pushes the horses they acquired from the stable to a gallop. The guard at the gate hardly noticed them leaving. It takes the better part of forty-five minutes for them to cover the few miles to Atlanta, leaving them a scant fifteen to make the arrangements and signal the craft above.

"Let me go in first. I'll roust them out and tell them what we need to do. I won't tell them the whole story, just enough to let them know this is top secret, and that we'll move them within the next ten days or so." Sally explains and runs into the large barn behind the blacksmith shop and corral.

She appears back outside in a few minutes with Smitty and Luke at her side. They are still in their long johns and barefooted.

"Bring them on," Sally orders. "No time for introductions right now."

"Now you two get ready to see something you'll never be able to say anything about to anyone," she warns the livery owners.

Standing in the darkness behind the barn in a large open area away from the livestock and the eyes of the townsmen, Sheree raises her hands toward the sky. She closes her eyes to concentrate. Those watching see a glimmer of light extend out beyond her fingers to dance as if it's alive, then dim and die.

In a few seconds, the first flying machine swoops in to hover above the ground. A pale light appears underneath, and soon four containers are on the ground, then it's gone.

"Start moving these out of the way, another load will be here in a few seconds. There will be just three on each of the next two machines," Lilly orders and explains.

The next few minutes pass like a blur as two more machines zoom in one at a time to unload. There is a lot of amazement, but no talking between those receiving the merchandise of undisclosed nature. Smitty and Luke keep looking over their shoulders as they move the cargo, watching the craft come and go. Another fifteen minutes and the containers are hidden inside the barn under a mountain of hay and straw bales.

It's not daylight yet when the five arrive back at La Nesra to collapse onto the sofas and chairs. Someone suggests they're hungry, which starts Sally and Rose working in the kitchen making an early breakfast. The conversation turns to Lilly, and why she's here, other than to bring the containers.

"When I get back, the first thing we'll do is go out and practice our ways of convincing people of our purpose. Then after we feel we're ready, we're going to be out of the country for a few months. We're going to Europe, where I'll begin God's work converting as many as I can to follow his teachings. They tell me there will be at least fifty thousand people at our first gathering in Italy. From there we'll travel all over, bringing as many people together as possible. I've gone through a lot recently; I'm totally convinced that our race will not survive in the future if I don't act soon. I must spread the wisdom of those before me to each and every human being on earth. I must amass them all together to thwart the efforts of those who want to rob us of our souls. You've seen the flying machines, but you have yet to be made aware of my powers. Ty and Remsar believe most of the people I speak to will follow my teachings readily when they witness my abilities. Here, I'll give you a quick example of what I'm talking about. Brace yourself, honey," she continues.

Falcon is sitting on an overstuffed chair with his right leg lying across his left knee. To his surprise, he begins to rise while not changing the position of his body. Up and up he goes until his head nearly touches the ceiling. He stops to just hang there.

"This is scary, Lilly, get me down, please," he begs.

She settles him gently back into his chair. "I can start fires with my finger—watch." She points at a cold candle some six feet away setting on a table. The wick begins to smoke then bursts into a glowing ball of flame.

"I remember everything I see, everything I do, everything I hear. I've learned to communicate with the strange beings at Canozira. I use my mind, not my mouth. They understand me and I understand them. It seems I never really need to eat or sleep when I'm out of my life body, at least not the way normal people do. I feel strong. I've never felt better in my whole life, and I have a meaningful purpose to devote myself to. I'm told I'll develop other powers as I go along. But right now, I have no idea of what they'll be. I'm anxious of most new things, but I don't seem to fear anything." She looks at each of her friends faces as she speaks. "Enough of this scary stuff. What have you all been doing?" She changes the subject.

"You're not scaring us, Lilly," Falcon speaks up. "It's just listening to you makes us feel like our lives are so small—you seem larger than life. You seem to be part of something that we'll never truly understand, and yet you're still my wonderful wife, and our friend. It's a lot to deal with."

"Where do you go when you're not here?" Sally asks.

"It's a place called Canozira. It's where all of the bigwigs of the Company come to when they're not out doing Lord knows what. Here, I've written down its location with its coordinates. Keep this somewhere safe, so if it ever becomes necessary to find me, you'll have a place to start. It's in the center of a mountain in the southwest territory. I come and go through tunnels in our flying machines, so I have no idea about how to get there on a horse or anything. They don't welcome outsiders there, so if you come, be careful. They can be a dangerous bunch. They're the law there, if there is such a thing, so if you get caught they answer only to their own conscience about how you're treated."

"What about you? Do they treat you that way, too?" Hawk asks.

"Actually, they treat me as if they're afraid of me, or maybe they just don't want to see me get upset toward them," she responds honestly.

"You're not a prisoner then?" Rose continues the questioning.

"No, or at least I don't feel that I am. I didn't ask, I told them I was coming here."

The rest of her visit is filled with loving her husband, getting reacquainted with her friends, and gathering information about baby Joie, and everybody back on the farm. Some time is also spent visiting with Mr. Vaughn, and his director of security.

All seems well enough to satisfy her yearnings for a while. But when it's time to go it never gets any easier. She leaves at two in the morning on a gleaming flying machine streaking toward the stars.

"She's gone. Who knows when we'll ever see her again." Falcon hangs his head and digs the toe of his boot into the ground.

"I know it doesn't help you any, but we all feel the same way." Rose offers some comfort. "We'll miss her together, and we'll all be here when she comes back."

"Let's not spend too much time feeling sorry for ourselves. We have a problem to work out. Where in the world are we going to hide the arsenal, and how are we going to move it when we do? We told Smitty and Luke we'd move it within ten days. That gives us just three to go," Sally reminds everyone while they are walking back into the confines of the walls of La Nesra.

"I don't know where to move them, but I've been thinking, and I might know how we can do it," Hawk presents.

"Just how is that?" his wife insists, as if she knows his thoughts are child's play.

"Treat them like they're dead soldiers. There are dead soldier's bodies being transported on the trains all the time anymore. We can just drape a Confederate flag over them, and take them about anywhere on a train. I hear they do it for nothing as long as there's room, so it won't cost us a dime," He offers.

"He's right. That's a good idea, Hawk. And the North and South even allow the dead to be transferred back and forth across their lines. Just one little problem, take them where?" Falcon supports his friend, thinks for a few seconds, then continues. "I wonder if there's somewhere on the Anderson farm we could put them."

"We don't have time to figure that out. Although, what do you suppose the Andersons would say if we just showed up dragging the arsenal along behind us?" Sally adds jokingly.

"I can tell you if we did, they're the kind of people who would do whatever they could to help us, and you can bank on that. When I think about it, once they help us hide them, they would work to keep the arsenal secure, too. It'll take some planning, but I think we're on to something here. I think we should do it." Falcon convinces himself, and hopefully the others.

"I don't know if I agree with the idea of passing our responsibility off on to someone else. We promised Lilly we would find a place for them. She thinks only we will know where they are. If we get the Andersons and their people involved, you see what I mean," Sally asserts.

"I agree with Sally. And another thing, is it a good idea to put all ten of the containers at risk at the same time? I mean, maybe we should split them up. If we put all ten on the train and one is discovered, they're all gone. How could we ever explain that to Lilly?" Rose throws an additional stone into the gears of the plan.

"You know, I imagine Smitty and Luke have smuggled all sorts of things in and out of Atlanta. Let's ask them before we go off and do something we'll regret. Personally, I'd rather have them all together where the four of us can keep watch," Sally suggests.

First light finds the foursome dismounting their horses at the back entrance of the livery barn. Smitty and Luke are just finishing their breakfast of biscuits and gravy.

"You folks are up mighty early this morning. Something must be going on," the elder of the two speaks, amusing himself.

"You're right about that, Smitty," Hawk talks for them all. "We need your advice."

"Oh, oh. The last time anybody asked for my advice, he wanted to know if I wanted him to cut off one of my fingers, or one of my toes," he jokingly replies.

"What did you say?" Rose asks without thinking.

"Well, I just told him that my advice was for him to walk away, or my son Luke, who was standing just out of his sight, would blow his head off." He smiles as he speaks.

"So, what happened? Did you blow his head off?" Hawk can't wait to hear the answer.

"How the hell could I? I wasn't even there at the time." Luke shakes his head. "He just bluffed the man."

"What did he do?" Rose again pushes the story forward.

Smitty points and wiggles his ten toes, then holds up eight fingers, two thumbs, and laughs.

"The last I ever seen of him was his back going out that door."

Everybody laughs, but Smitty is the loudest and longest.

"The advice we need is how to get these boxes out of your way. We thought about putting them on a train and take them north but we're not all settled on it. Do you have any ideas as to how we could do it?" Falcon explains, trying not to give too much information.

"We thought we would treat them like dead soldiers' bodies and drape a flag over them," Rose adds.

"I don't know if I'd do that. I get all sorts of stories from people that come in here. Twice over this last month people have come to me to buy wagons and horses to haul their kin back home when the soldiers made them take the coffins off the train since they needed the room for troops and equipment. These boxes here take up an awful lot of room," he relates seriously. "I like your idea about the flags and all, though."

"Which direction you figuring on taking them?" he continues.

No one speaks.

"Now, look. You all come in here asking me these questions when these boxes are close enough for me to spit on, and now you're afraid I'll tell somebody where you're taking them. Listen to an old man and listen good. You can't go through life never trusting anybody. People need people, and right now you need me." His words hit home with the group as he moves on. "Did I ask you what's in those boxes? Did I ask where that flying machine came from that brought them here? And now I've got those boxes right here under my nose. I'm trying to say that I'm your friend, and neither Luke, nor me, are going to do anything to hurt you. Can't you see that?"

Sally speaks for the foursome. "Yes, Smitty, we certainly do, and we appreciate what you've done already. The truth is there's some pretty serious stuff in those boxes, and we promised we'd take care of them, and put them somewhere safe. We're thinking of taking them north to the Anderson farm, but that's a long way to go, and we have no idea how we'll get them there." She turns to aim her words at the rest of her group. "Smitty's hit the nail on the head. We can't do this by ourselves. Rose, you and I have to go along with the guys on this one, and let them work it out."

She turns back to Smitty.

"We'd rather not split them up if we don't have to."

"Good, don't you worry, you're secret's safe with Luke and me," the aging black man begins, and shakes his head gently up and down yes. Now, I was thinking there might be a way, that is, if you're not in too big a hurry to get there, and we'd have to take the wheels off them boxes too. We might just put them on the railroad after all," he ponders.

"What?" all five listening say at about the same time.

"It's a different kind of railroad." Smitty lays out an idea that seems to agree with everyone. He finishes up by saying, "So, you all agree then?"

Affirmative remarks are heard from all, including Luke.

"Good, then you go back and do what you need to get ready to go, and Luke and me, we'll take care of things here. You just be back here the day after tomorrow just after dark, and we'll get started."

Sally, Falcon, Rose, and Hawk meet with Mr. Vaughn shortly after their return to La Nesra. They tell him they will be gone for a while visiting friends and family, but they should be back in no more than sixty days. They said they are going by horseback, so they are taking four good animals and a wagon from the stable. All feel as though he didn't believe them, but he did bid them well on their trip. It's agreed to keep a watchful eye out for someone following their progress. The rest of the time before their departure is spent packing clothes and making plans, until at last, it's time to leave.

Smitty and Luke have the business closed up for the day, and are waiting in the barn with two saddled horses, when they arrive.

"Where's the boxes and wagons?" Falcon says, concerned that he doesn't see them anywhere.

"Luke and me and three drivers took them, along with the wagons and horses, to some close friends of ours' place last night. We thought it would be better to leave from there than here. That many wagons and people leaving all at once would cause too much of a commotion. This way we just left about a half hour apart and no one thought a thing about it.

"Let's get moving. Luke and me have to be back here in time to open up in the morning, and the Sorrels are hard people to get away from once you get there."

"Sorrels? Aren't those the people that helped Robert and Randy when they were here to get Sheree?" Sally recalls Cheryl's recount of their trip.

"That's right," Luke breaks his silence. "They've got everything ready for us when we get there. And you might know, Mrs. Sorrels won't let us get away before she feeds us all more then we can hold."

The wagon carrying the clothing and supplies, with Sally and Rose riding, alongside the four horsemen come to a stop in front of the home of Mr. and Mrs. Sorrels. It's dark, but five wagons, each loaded with two boxes covered with Confederate flags can be seen by the light of a nearby fire, with at least fifteen black men, women and children sitting in a circle keeping warm in the cool night air. The warm orange and yellow light of the flames casts shadows and flickering light to illuminate the area. Teams stand hitched, ready to roll.

Mr. and Mrs. Sorrels come out of the house to greet the new arrivals, then lead them inside to—of course—eat. Conversation is rampant during the meal, and while the dishes are being cleared their hosts recall all of the years they have worked moving slaves along the underground railroad. They estimate thousands have passed through their house and barn.

"You, young folk, keep in mind on this trip that you're all kin, and you're taking your dead home to bury. These people out here are your slaves that you brought along to help. Smitty, Luke, and us have put all kinds of supplies on the wagons, so you should have enough for everybody on your trip. Smitty's right you know, you can get your boxes where you want them to go, and at the same time we can move these families out there to freedom in the North." Mr. Sorrels gets up and walks around the table to a roll top desk as he speaks. "You'll be a little slower moving along, but just bear with it, you'll get there safe and sound."

He takes a large brown envelope from a drawer and turns around. "Which of you is the ramrod of this outfit?" he asks.

"Sally's the oldest," Hawk is quick to announce.

"Thanks a lot, you'll pay for that later." She acts as if she is miffed, but not so anyone would believe it.

"You might as well give it to me, since I'm also the smartest of the bunch." She holds out her hand to accept the package. "What's in here, anyway?"

"Just some papers telling our people out there what to do when they get into Union territory. You might have to read it to them. We'd give it to them, but if they got caught with it they'd hang for sure."

"I understand, and we'll take good care of things for them," Sally confirms for the group.

"You should get going now. It's almost midnight and those teams have been standing a long time. Try to keep moving, the speed don't matter, just keep moving until early tomorrow afternoon. Then make camp and get some rest. Like Mr. Sorrels says, you won't move as fast with all these people and wagons, but just keep going. And listen, keep all your guns out of sight. Most of these soldiers around here will cut a man's throat to get his gun," Smitty advises and cautions.

Mrs. Sorrels leaves through the back door to get the people from around the fire, and put those they can onto the wagons. The children are hoisted and tucked away into any space available, then the driver sits on the seat. Two older women are accommodated with a ride on the back of Sally and Rose's wagon. The rest walk alongside.

The adults will take turns riding the wagons, then once daylight comes, the children will be turned loose to keep up. They'll stop midmorning for a late breakfast which will hold them until supper. Good-byes are a big thing with the Sorrels, especially the missus. She has to hug and kiss each and every one of the travelers.

Their journey begins.

The caravan is able to move along more quickly once they reach a northbound road. The boxes take up a lot of room, but they are not all that heavy. With that and the smoother surface, everybody can ride. The plan is to cover as close to forty miles a day as they can.

Smitty brought along four extra horses, so along with the two Falcon and Hawk are riding, they will be able to rest their teams on a rotating basis. They'll buy what feed they need along the way. Take good care of the horses and keep everybody healthy. That's everyone's job, and they do it without being told. No matter how big or small the problem or worry, the whole troop is there for each other.

"You know, these are nice people, Rose," Sally mentions as they bounce on the seat of the wagon. "I remember Sheree and Falcon saying the Andersons were looking for people to take up residence with them. I wonder if these folks would want to stay there."

"I wouldn't say anything to them until you ask the Andersons. You don't want to get their hopes up only to find out there's no room for them there," Rose wisely advises. "It's a good idea, though."

"Speaking of good people," she continues. "What about Smitty and Luke—and let's not forget Mr. and Mrs. Sorrels."

"You're right. I guess we just bring out the best in people," Sally pokes fun.

The road is hard, and the days are long. Trying to cover forty miles is taxing on the people, animals, and equipment. Repairing tack and greasing axles are daily chores for the men. Feeding and brushing the horses, preparing meals, and keeping the youngsters alive, busy the women and older children.

Some stretches of road are crowded for miles with traffic moving in both directions. Soldiers, at times, move like they're late for something, passing slower moving wagons by going off the road, kicking up dust to settle on everything, making the air hard to breathe. Bandannas tied over people's noses and mouths are a common sight.

And it is hot.

Nobody pays attention to a caravan of wagons hauling corpses. In fact, oncoming vehicles have the tendency to pull over farther, and sometimes stop, to let them pass.

On the eighteenth day, at noon, the lead wagon pulls into the front yard of the Anderson home with the other five strung out behind.

One of the Andersons' hands has already entered the house to announce the incoming travelers. Selma is the first to appear on the front porch and slowly steps down shading her eyes to see who it is.

The only two people who know the way to the Anderson farm are Falcon and Sally, so they're riding the lead wagon. But their broad-rim hats, traveling garb, and the bright sun make it difficult to see who they are.

"Who is it?" Charlotte quizzes, as she steps out on to the porch with Cheryl and Millie on her heels. It's an unexpected sight to see all these wagons.

Selma doesn't reply, but continues walking, noticing the boxes and Confederate flags.

"Mrs. Housler! It's us, Falcon and Sally!" he yells as he jumps down from the wagon.

"What in the world—?" she says without thinking.

Charlotte, Cheryl, and Millie have caught up and are at her side.

All excited that the trip is over and seeing four good friends, Sally, dressed like a man, squeals and runs to greet them with frantic hugs and kisses.

After introductions and a brief explanation of their purpose are made, they settle into the kitchen for coffee and further conversation.

The black travelers are immediately warmly welcomed by the hands, wives, and children. This is an occasion for them since visitors are scarce out here on the farm.

"Where's Joie? I can't wait to see her," Falcon asks.

"She's with Elizabeth, Nora, and Sherman. They're all putting up a barn over at Der Bote," Cheryl replies. "There's not enough room in the two we have here, I guess. They say they have to build another one over at the Sanders' place, too. John's home for a while, so he, Robert, Randall, and several hands are all over there, too," Selma adds.

"Well, if you ladies can get along without us for a while, Hawk and I need to ride on over there and talk to them about these boxes," Falcon suggests. "And I'd really like to see Joie."

"Go then. We'll be just fine. You just bring them all back in time for supper," Charlotte chimes in.

Falcon and Hawk get two fresh horses as recommended by the driver of the farm, and make their way to the area where the main house of Der Bote once stood. As they ride up they can see the skeleton of a big barn taking shape on the foundation of where the old one once stood.

Randall spots them first and alerts the others. He remembers Falcon and Hawk very well and recognizes them at a distance. He, John, and Robert stand together near the structure awaiting their visitors' arrival.

Once their feet hit the ground the two are affably greeted with handshakes and hugs.

"Where's Joie?" Falcon asks bluntly, excited to see her.

"They wandered off over in that direction a few minutes ago." Robert points with his finger, his elbow bent. "Before you go chasing off after them, what brings you here? I know you didn't come all this way just to visit."

Falcon and Hawk explain the entire situation as briefly as possible, at the same time keeping an eye out for Elizabeth, Nora, Sherman, and Joie.

"So, we need a secure place to keep these boxes," John states, using the word we to include himself and the rest.

"Yessir, we do. And wherever it is, it needs to be all lined with metal, like steel. That way they can't be tracked by anybody," Hawk adds to the problem.

"Another thing, may I call you Dad?" Obviously, Falcon has thought about it and waits for an answer.

"I'd like that, son."

"Well, Dad, there's more. We've got eighteen slaves—men, women, and children with us that we brought from Georgia. We used each other as cover to get here with the boxes, and they're looking for their freedom. Is there any chance they could stay here with you and help work your farm, at least for a while?"

"I don't see why not. What do you think?" John looks at Robert and Randall.

"We can use the help, Daddy," Robert agrees.

"He's right, sir," Randall, always ready to show his respect for John, confirms the decision.

"They won't be owners like the rest, but they'll earn and be paid a wage." Robert is quick to explain.

"That will be just fine, but they won't expect any more than bed and board, so you don't have to do all that," Falcon points out.

"Yes we do. There's no slaves on this farm. Everybody works at it, and gets paid for what they do. That's the way it is. Even the two of you," Randall speaks firmly. "That is, if you want the job."

"We've never had a paying job before. You can count me in, just tell me what to do." Hawk's enthusiasm blossoms.

Falcon shakes his head and grins in agreement.

"That's good, we'll handle all that later when we get back to the house. Right now, we need to figure out what to do with those boxes." The elder Anderson settles the matter.

"You know, luck would have it we're just now building this barn. Maybe there's a way we can make a place for those boxes while we're at it," He continues. "The thing is, this farm will probably be one of the first places they'll look for them. That means we have to be a bit smarter than they are. I mean, if we just board off an area and line it with steel, they'll find it in no time. We have to come up with something they won't think of, or a place they will walk right past when they see it."

"What if we dig a hole and put the barn floor over it?" Randall suggests.

"It's going to need to be something where we can get at them ourselves in a hurry if we have to. You never know, we might have to move them," Robert wisely advises.

"You know where we could put them? The perfect place just came to me—the smoke house. It's just over there beyond the rise, and it's plenty big enough. All we'd have to do is line it with something. Right now it's lined with bricks," Randall strongly suggests.

Everyone agrees.

"Where are they now?" John asks.

"When we left the house, they were setting on five wagons in your front yard." Hawk's words sound anxious.

"We'd better get back and get them into the big barn until we can get the smoke house ready. We don't need some drifter going by and spreading it all over town." Robert picks up on the urgency of the matter.

"Then let's go." Randall turns to head for his horse.

"Do you all mind if I stay here to see Joie when they get back. They'll want to know where you went anyway, so one of us should stay," Falcon volunteers.

"Good idea," John concurs. "Come on back to the house when they get here. We'll start on the smoke house tomorrow."

Elizabeth, Nora, Sherman, and Joie come strolling in at Der Bote about thirty minutes after all have left but Falcon. He's had time to talk with the hands and get a good look at the beginnings of the barn.

His daughter is shy from his attention and touch, but he's thrilled to see her wobble, walk, and move around. He mentions that he sees Sheree in her. They comment that she's a very smart little girl, and predict her to be a scholar.

Then it is back to the Anderson homestead.

It doesn't take long to run the wagons through the big barn and unload two boxes off each one. They set them off in one corner and pile bales of hay up high enough that they can't be seen.

John has Sally call all the traveling slaves together for the purpose of asking them what they want to do from here. She produces the envelope given to her by Mr. Sorrels, and reads from the pages within.

They have two practical choices. One being, to follow the instructions in the envelope: to locate specific people at certain towns and to follow them to freedom in the northeast. Or the second, to remain here on the farm to work and be paid as hands.

When asked to be heard, they all, to the person, elected to remain on the farm.

After that's decided, the once-slaves, now free men and women, are courted away by the hands and the families of the farm to find places for them to stay until proper quarters can be made.

The rest of the afternoon, during supper, and for an hour afterward, is filled with trading information back and forth, getting caught up. The subject of Sheree pops up again and again with various questions about the last time she visited La Nesra, how she looked and felt, what she's doing, and her whereabouts. It's all answered openly and honestly to the close-knit family and friends. They receive the information as true, but do not understand how it's possible.

After reporting in at Canozira, Lilly spent the first week studying a script. It tells her what she's going to say and how she will act while doing it. It tells her how she will levitate people in her audience, people that have been put there who are expecting it to happen.

When she questioned the reason for pretending the person doesn't know about it, she's told that to move an unsuspecting person off their feet and into the air could cause an adverse reaction from the crowd. It's explained that it makes no difference who the person is, only that it's happening, and it's not a trick. At different times she's to levitate herself and move about, move objects out over the masses for them to touch, ask some to hold up personal items then take them from their hands, and move them through the air to her hands on the stage. And to light fires from a distance. Remsar will practice his gift of healing several times during the meeting, as well.

The words of the presentation have been carefully chosen, and put together to make each statement concise and powerful. Questions, such as, are you truly on the right path to everlasting life? Will you be left behind when our Lord and Savior comes? Are you ready to watch the loved ones in your life suffer the consequences of your allowing them to ignore the truth? Do you believe judgment day is coming? Can you see by the demonstration here today that all things are possible? It's all free today, but can you imagine the price you'll pay for not joining the effort for the salvation of mankind? You say you don't think it's possible to destroy the whole world, all at one time, do you?

At this point, Lilly will ask all to stand back from a five foot cube of solid marble setting on a platform of steel in the center of the crowd. As people have arrived before the meeting started, they are urged to inspect it to prove it's genuine. They will watch as she reaches her arms, and causes the marble to catch fire at the top, a fire so hot that it melts the marble causing it to run down the sides and drip to the ground where it will cool to hard marble again.

Those attending will be asked to carry what they have seen with them, to pass it on to others, telling them the truth about the end of the world and everlasting life. Telling them the woman on the stage is an angel sent to warn every human on earth that judgment day is coming. Telling them that this is a last effort to get people to conform and be ready.

The whole presentation takes almost two hours. At first, Lilly feels like it's too long, too shocking and frightful, but the more she reads it, the more she feels the sense of urgency it portrays. Soon, she gives herself to it; she feels the momentous, consequential responsibility of being the tool of God.

"I must do it. It feels right. It is right. Help me, Lord, to do thy will." She stands up from her sofa, throws the script in the air, and yells in prayer.

Everybody is settling down for the night at the Anderson farm. Selma and John have found their way to the front porch, as they have been doing lately, for a nightcap of brandy.

"Why didn't you tell those poor people today what would have happened if they followed the instructions in that envelope?" Selma's question is not a criticism. She just doesn't understand the omission.

"Why—they made the right decision," John replies knowingly. "Do they need to know that in most of the years past when men, women, and children came through here headed for freedom, that they would walk into the waiting arms of traitors? That they would be sold off for profit, then be shipped back South to slave traders where their families were split up, auctioned off, and sent Lord knows where? Sometimes I think the colonel confessed too much to us. Hell, I don't know, maybe it somehow made it easier for him to live with it. But to answer your question, I just felt like they would feel better about themselves if they made the decision. You know, make a decision like they're free to do whatever they think's right."

"You wouldn't have let them follow those instructions then?" she pursues.

"No, I couldn't let that happen."

"I don't mean for this to feel like an inquisition, but have you mentioned to Falcon or Sally about what you were told when you stopped in Baltimore on your way home," she wonders.

"No, I haven't, at least not yet. And don't worry about asking questions. I need that to keep my balance," he replies calmly.

"Are you going to?" she presses.

"I'm not sure if what I was told is true. And I sure would hate to upset everything for no reason," he explains.

"What if you don't tell them and it turns out there is something to it?" Selma doesn't let up. "Shouldn't they be the ones to decide?"

"Now, you've got me there. But listen, they're going to be here for six weeks or so. Let me see what else I can find out before I open a can of spoiled worms."

They sit in silence in the dark for a few minutes, him on his straight chair, her in her rocker, sipping their brandy and enjoying the evening together.

"I love you more every day I'm with you, John," she announces softly, intimately.

He reaches across the short distance between their chairs to put his hand on hers.

"You know I feel the same way about you. A man would be a fool not to love a woman like you. It's getting so I don't want to be away more than a few hours at a time. But it's still too soon. I keep wondering, just like now, what they're doing, and what do they think about us," John's words are not new to her ears.

"I don't mean to pressure you—Lord knows I'll wait—but you know, June and I were real close. And I know, if she could, she'd walk right up and say to us that we belong together. They would both want us to have any happiness we can find.

"We've been blessed with a beautiful little girl to raise. I want to be her mother and you her father, is that wrong?" She hangs her head to suppress a tear forming in her eye and the lump in her throat. She's not normally like this and doesn't understand her own feelings tonight, let alone why she's expressing them this way.

He chuckles a little.

"Hell, I'm old enough to be her grandfather, and as a matter of fact, I am her grandfather."

Selma can't help but laugh along with him.

"Promise me something. Don't go out and find someone younger and leave me."

"I'll do better than that. I promise that when I'm ready, I'll sweep you off your feet and marry you. My mind has to be right, though, or I don't think we'd be happy for long. I don't want to hurt you, honey; you've been hurt enough," he assures.

"Did you just call me honey?"

He looks to see her smiling face, her eyes sparkling in the darkness with pools of tears. They sit in silence again, holding hands, thinking their own thoughts.

A flying machine delivers Remsar, Ty, and Lilly, during the night, to a large town on the west coast of America. They are expecting a crowd of several thousand people to attend their first public appearance. People from the Company have it all set up to take place at ten this morning. Everything is ready.

"I'm a little nervous," Lilly comments, as they make their way to the hotel where rooms have been reserved for the next three days.

"Don't worry, that will all pass once we get started. I think we all have a bit of the jitters," Remsar commiserates.

"Try to get a few hours rest. It'll make you feel better," Ty piles on.

"Me? Sleep? Not tonight," she says under her breath.

Morning comes, and the sun rises steadily to make the time nine forty-five when they arrive at the outdoor stage. All personnel are ready, and the presentation is about to begin. Lilly wipes her sweaty palms on her gown, then looks to see if she made a spot.

A band starts playing a rousing church hymn to start things moving. Then a man she has never seen before takes center stage to introduce everyone.

It's her turn, she hears her name, she feels herself walking out on to the stage, her head down. The crowd's roar causes her to look.

"I've never seen thousands of people all in one place like this before. I can't recall what I'm supposed to say."

Without warning, an unexpected explosion behind her makes everybody jump and turn with confusion. There's thick smoke, with the smell and taste of oil, everywhere. Strong hands grab her arms, and before she can pull loose, a bag is put over her head. Then something like a net, made out of wire, slips over her head, over her shoulders, down over her hips, and is cinched tightly against the calves of her legs. She tries to move but it's useless.

Somebody lifts her like a feather and moves quickly off the stage. She hears Remsar and Ty shouting her name, trying to find her.

By the squeaking noises she knows she's now in a carriage and moving away from the area in a hurry.

Chapter Thirty-Six

"What the hell just happened? Where is she?" Ty yells to anyone who will listen, waving his arms as if to brush away the throat-and-eye-burning fog.

The incoming breeze from the ocean casually takes the smoke with it, allowing those on and near the stage to clear their lungs. Coughing and gagging accompanies tear-flushed eyes and running noses.

"She's gone! They've taken her!" Remsar determines loudly.

"Did anyone see who took her, and which way they went?" he bellows over the noise of the loud mumbling crowd.

"If you mean that woman in the white dress, they loaded her into a carriage, and lit out over that way," a woman farther back from the stage screams and points her finger.

"Ty! Get some men on horseback and get after them immediately!" he shouts orders, feeling helpless.

Mr. Black is swiftly ushered to a horse where he and ten security guards mount to give chase.

"I'll bring her back! Count on it!" he hollers as he leaves.

After the horses leave their sight, Remsar, along with several ranking Company officials begin to stare each other down. He's thinking, trying to put it all together. They're thinking, what went wrong, expecting the worst.

"The people who did this had to be part of your security force. There was no one else close enough to this stage to work that fast. It had to be your own people. Get all of your men together—right now. Those missing from your ranks are the culprits," the Company's high level officer speaks first.

"Yes, I agree, but remember, about half of our men left with Ty," the head man on the west coast replies. "I'm not sure we can name them all."

"For God's sake, man, try! Do something! Do you know the seriousness of what just happened here? The one person on this earth who could turn the tide of our path to destruction has just been kidnapped from right under our noses," the senior officer of the Company howls.

The older man bows his head slightly, holds out the palms of his hands a foot from his waist, then, looking down, grimaces with the burden of fault.

"I mean no disrespect, but what else can we do for the moment? Ty and my men are in pursuit of those dastardly villains. May we take a few minutes to determine the best use of our time while we wait for their return?" he begs calmly.

"Such as?" Remsar challenges harshly.

"If our men catch up to them our problems have been simplified. We determine who the guilty devils are and hang them. On the other hand, suppose they don't catch them? My first thought is they'll hole up here in town, for a while at least. There are thousands of places to hide. I don't think they'll take the chance of being caught out in the open outside of town. You and I both know who's behind this. They infiltrate us the same way we put our people in amongst them. And it's common knowledge among those who need to know, there's money on her head, dead or alive. This was very well planned and executed, which makes me believe their escape will be orchestrated the same way. With this line of thinking, our best bet would be to seal off every avenue of departure from the city, then start a systematic search of the entire area, street by street, building by building," the elder dignitary relates.

"That could take days," Remsar says indignantly.

"If you have a better idea, I'm listening. But if you don't, the longer we wait the less our chances are of trapping them."

"I agree. Let's get it done."

"You heard the man. Don, call out all your men and get them organized. And while you're at it, get the local law involved. That way whatever we do will be legal. Let's get this town shut down," the west coast Company official exclaims.

Ty's sidekick stands, his hands to his sides, at the center of the stage watching the Company's men, and the crowd disperse. He shakes his head slightly and thinks.

"What a way to start. It won't be as easy to bring people together again, especially here. But on the other hand, if we play our cards right, we can use this to our advantage. First things first, though. Let's look at the facts. We know Lilly's captors are undoubtedly one of the teams from the World Alliance. They don't know her, or what she's actually capable of doing, but they've probably constrained her in a way they think will limit her powers. They might not know to shield her with metal when they hide, so if nothing else, we can bring her back to her life body with a mirror in front of her face."

The carriage containing Lilly and two of her kidnappers moves through the city streets following the horses' thundering hooves. With a person on either side of her, she's thrown into them when the vehicle slides around sharp turns, left and right. They have her pinned against the seat with their shoulders, keeping her from being tossed forward and back. Amazingly, she feels quite calm. A bag over her head and face, then a tight strong netting down over her body almost to her ankles have her a bit bewildered, but she's not panicked at all. The bouncing and jostling keeps her off balance making any attempt to free herself impossible. Knowing an opportunity will come, she decides to let things settle down.

"I wonder what was in this bag before me. Whew, I hope they take it off before too long. It's stinky, hot, and stuffy; not real easy to breathe," she says to herself.

Then as quickly as it started, the carriage slows and comes to a stop.

"Get her inside!" someone shouts.

She's pushed and pulled off the seat and out through the door. A strong pair of arms lift her off the ground, then she feels herself being drooped over a shoulder to be carried away. A few steps up, a step or two, then a door opens, and they move inside.

"Take her upstairs. He's up there." She hears a woman's voice.

They move up the stairs, through a short hallway, and a turn to the left.

"Lay her on the bed for now," a male says.

"I'm not sure if your name is Lilly or Sheree, young lady, but if you give me your word you'll stay calm and quiet, I'll get that bag off our head. What do you say?"

"Please do." She answers quietly, politely, her voice somewhat muffled.

The net is loosened at the top and spread out over her shoulders, then the bag over her head is pulled up and off.

"That's a lot better," she says taking a long breath of clean fresh air. "Thank you. What about the rest, can you take this off of me."

"Not just now."

"Why did you abduct me, what are your intentions?" She forges forward.

"I hear you're worth a lot of money, dead or alive. My plan is simple. I know the people with you there on the stage want you back and will probably pay a fortune, but I also have good word that another bunch wants their hands on you, too. Now, that makes for good competition. The highest bidder shall have you for their own," the man explains.

Lilly looks him over as he speaks.

"No sense in trying to figure me out. I'm nobody you or anybody else around here knows. And once I get the money, no one around here will ever see me again," he flatly states.

"What makes you think anyone will give you money for me? I'm just another actress trying to find her way through life. I don't know who you think I am, but you've made a big mistake. You've got the wrong woman."

"Well, we'll see about that. Now listen to me, you just be a good girl and no harm will come to you. This shouldn't take more than a few days, a week at the most. If it turns out that you're worth nothing, then I'll let you go. But I'm betting I can get enough money to set me up for the rest of my life."

Lilly's mind is jumping from one point of view to another determining her best course of action. She knows Ty and Remsar will come looking for her, but does she want to be rescued right away? This might be a good opportunity to do some snooping around without their knowing it.

"If I escape from these people, what can they do? They're in no position to tell anybody about it," she tells herself. "Ty and the rest will look for me for a few days, then give up and go back to Canozira."

"Sir, if you let me go now, I won't tell anybody who you are, but if I have to escape on my own, I might have to hurt you, and I don't want to do that."

"Ha ha ha!" He laughs. "So you're going to hurt me, are you? Not wrapped up like that, you're not."

"Come closer, I want to tell you something and I don't want the others to hear. Come on, don't be afraid. As you say, how can I hurt you," she implores.

"You must think I'm stupid. I'm as close to you as I'm going to get. I hear you've got some sort of powers, and that's why they want you so bad. But, I can tell you this,

I'm not taking that net off you. It's made of strong steel wire, and you're not likely to get out of it on your own."

"Well, then, you can't say I didn't try to be nice," she declares firmly as the door slams shut on its own, sealing them in the room.

The man's eyes get big with astonishment, then flit back and forth at her and the door. His first thought is to run and open it again. But to his further amazement, a stick cane leaning against a corner on the opposite side of the room rises and moves toward him, blunt end first, faster and faster as it comes. He stands in awe as it takes the aim of a musket ball directly at his forehead.

Whop! The sound of a ripe pumpkin being hit with a stick resounds from the walls.

He falls back and slides down the wall to sit on the floor, his legs spread out straight, his hands lying limply at his side. The cane drops to the floor with a *klunk.*

It takes her a few minutes to wriggle out of the netting, but soon, Lilly stands looking down at her would-be captor. "How will you ever explain this to your cohorts?" She smiles and slides through the full-length mirror standing on the floor in its swivel frame on the other side of the bed.

Once on the other side, she sets her mind on Canozira and moves as expected toward her destination. All along the way she feels as if something, or somebody, is hanging on to her. It's not like a grip, it doesn't slow her down, it's not threatening, it is just there.

Soon, she sees the white square and slides through into her bedroom. Once inside she turns to look back at the mirror to catch a glimpse of a partial face peeking through. It pulls away, back behind the glass, and is gone before she can get her head through for a better look.

"Someone, or something, has followed me here, but, who? They must be lurking around in there just waiting for me to enter. I have to believe they're part of the group the World Alliance has sent after me. Who else would it be? At this point, not too many people know about me," she surmises for a minute, then lets it go to put her attention elsewhere.

Back at the Anderson farm the planned work is moving along. With a good many of the hands pitching in, it took just one good day's work to hide the arsenal along with their accompanying boxes, still covered with the canvas. They lined the smokehouse with metal roofing material in double layers over the existing bricks. It's a tight fit, but they're able to get all ten boxes inside. They change the securing device of the door to a clasp and padlock, then with that in place, the entry and the smokestack are concealed with a pile of dead brush.

Few people know of the existence of the smokehouse, so no one will expect it to be there. They all feel the boxes are safe.

Today, everyone—except those needed for daily chores and those concealing the boxes—have worked at erecting the new barn. It's been a long day of labor, but they can see the results of their toil. It's good work; good for their aching souls.

Supper has been over for an hour, and the hands, with everyone attending, have built a large fire out behind the main barn not far from the house. They have music to accommodate singing and dancing, which can be easily heard by those on the front porch and steps of the Anderson home. It's sort of a welcome get-together for the new families that accompanied the arsenal from Atlanta. The whole Anderson bunch have found their way to the porch sitting wherever they can get comfortable to listen to the poor man's gala.

"That sure sounds good, doesn't it? It's been too long since I've heard it," Robert reminisces, his back against a post as he sits with one leg bent, his foot on the porch, and the other placed on the top step. Elizabeth, snuggled between his legs, is leaning back, resting on his chest.

John and Selma occupy their usual chairs side by side, while Charlotte, Cheryl, and Millie sit abreast in a newly installed porch swing. Sally has pulled a chair from the dining room to sit on John's right, to look down on Rose and Hawk, who have their arms around each other, perched on the edge of the porch with their legs hanging over. Falcon, Joie, Randall, Nora, and Sherman are holding hands in a circle in the yard, dancing around and around to the music for everyone's entertainment.

Life seems as it should be for a change.

Sally reaches to place her hand on John's, resting on the arm of his chair.

"You are making a good life for a lot of people here. May God bless you for what you're doing." She puts feeling into the words.

"It's the people themselves that make it what it is," he comments, not bothering to pull his hand away. "This place would be nothing without everybody here, and that includes you. It's just as much yours as it is mine, and that makes us all grateful for each other."

Selma can't help noticing that Sally leaves her hand on John's. Before she can reconsider and stop herself, she takes his other hand and pulls it over to the arm of her chair where she embraces it between hers.

"This would be a good time to tell everyone about what you heard at the Sons headquarters. They're all here," she says, loud enough for all to hear.

"I don't know, Selma. Like I said before, I'm not certain if any of it's true, and for that matter, what we think we know is sketchy. I don't want to get people riled for no reason." With that, he pulls both of his hands away from the women.

Her words will not be disregarded by the rest of the group. They all want to know and urge John to relate whatever he has to them.

"All right, but remember, don't take this as gospel. Just put it in your mind to think on," he begins. "It seems that a couple of our agents at the Company have came across some sort of document, or book, that could be interpreted to mean a whole different future for our Sheree than she's told us."

Those adults in the yard move to the edge of the porch.

"How's that?" Falcon asks.

"Well, it doesn't name her exactly, but it pretty much describes her to a tee. And as I said, we don't have enough information to draw any firm conclusions, but if what they say is true, Sheree is on the wrong side of what she thinks is right."

"What?" One word describes the outburst of the entire group.

"To put it in a few words, she could be the one who is supposed to wake up the arsenal we have here, and get them going to destroy the world."

Everyone is adamant with their remarks claiming it to be impossible.

"I feel the same way you do," he continues. "But I keep coming back to one thing, the Company. Some powerful men in this county have told me that the Company is doing the devil's work, and they are willing to spend a great deal of their money to stop them. Maybe they know more than they told me. Maybe they expect me to find things out for myself. I don't know, but I can't turn against Sheree, my own flesh and blood, again. I just got her back from a big mistake I made a long time ago," he explains to everyone, and grinds his teeth together.

"What can we do then? We should be able to do something," Millie interjects. "Shouldn't we at least try to tell Sheree what we know?"

"I don't think we should get her all upset over this unless we're sure of what we're talking about. Besides, I hate to be the one to say it, but we have to consider that she might already know, and is going ahead with it anyway, for whatever reason," Cheryl bravely points out.

"She's right. We shouldn't tell her anything until we know for sure one way or the other. I know my wife, and she wouldn't be part of anything like that. That being said, she might do it without knowing about it. She's counting on the four of us—Sally, Hawk, Rose, and me—to do what we can to keep her informed and safe on our side of things. She said so when she left her body with us back when this all started. We have to do what we can, and I'm the man to do it." Falcon commits himself to the task.

"Just one thing." He looks hard at John and then the rest of the group. "Are you all ready to do whatever it takes, if I find out it's true?"

"We'll have to, son, but we have to have positive proof. I'll put some pressure on the right people on my end of it, too. Let's all hope there's nothing more to it," John agrees.

Canozira is a big place to find something when you don't know what you're looking for. Lilly is secure with her thinking that she has a few days to look around without the threat of Remsar and Ty getting suspicious. There are others, though, with eyes and ears just the same, so she cannot go ransacking through the entire place. She should take her time, and snoop methodically, casually. Where to start?

"I'm glad I moved the death angels when I did. They might catch me, but they'll never find them, not even if they have a way to read my mind. I honestly do not know where they are. For once, I feel like I did the right thing," she tells herself.

"I don't think Remsar's or Ty's office would be the place to start looking. They are both cunning enough to know that would be the first place anybody would look for information.

"But where? Where would I put something I would never want anyone to find? To be more specific, where would I put something that I did not want Remsar or Ty to find? I would put it where neither of them would think to look, in their office, or their living quarters. Well now, that could mean if there is something either of them do not want me to see, it might be right here in my quarters. I can ransack here all I want. My two helpers were reassigned to other duties while I was to be gone."

For the next fifteen minutes she takes her time to consider and look in all the places she might hide something. She has just finished removing all the drawers from the desk in her den to look beneath them, nothing. Her eyes scour other objects looking for any sort of a hint screaming, "hiding place."

On her way from the den, headed for the kitchen, a small table gets her attention. The top measures close to four feet long and less than a foot wide. It sets against the back, its top almost level with the sofa. A large oblong doily beneath a wooden bowl containing carvings of colorful wooden fruit, sets centered as a decoration. Each exposed six-inch side supporting the top has a drawer-front façade, giving it a look of places to keep small things. She knows they are fake fronts because she tried to open them shortly after she got here over a year ago. At the time, she even stooped down to look under to be sure there were no drawers there. But what if? A drawer three or four inches deep could fit there. She stoops down and puts her finger up underneath, against the side, then slides it up until it touches the underside of the top. She marks the distance on her finger with her thumb and pulls it out to lay it against the outside. There's a difference of at least two inches. It takes only a few seconds to remove the bowl and doily, and turn the table upside down. Carefully, slowly, her fingers move around the edge of the underside, her watchful eyes searching for a clue. Nothing.

"Oh well, on to other possibilities," she murmurs, and grabs a leg to move the table a little so she can set it right side up.

Click.

The sound is unexpected and makes her think she broke the leg, but as she moves to get a different grip, she notices the back—the side with no drawer facade normally toward the sofa—has moved about a quarter of an inch away from the leg.

She looks at the other end, it is the same way. Excitement builds within her. She moves to position herself square to the table, grips both ends of the back with her fingers, and pulls. It moves stubbornly, but with a few yanks it slides completely out. It's a drawer, but it seems to have a lid. There's a groove all around the inside upper edges with a thin piece of wood slid into it, like a drawer bottom might be. Her hands tremble a little when she turns the drawer around enabling her to slide the piece of wood outward. As it moves, it begins to expose a crudely bound volume of something.

The book measures eight inches wide by twelve inches tall and two inches thick. It appears to be very old. She sits still, with reverence, to take in the moment and appearance of the ancient volume. Then carefully, she lifts the book from its concealment to place it on the rug. She can hardly wait to read the words on the first page, which looks a lot newer than the rest.

"Hello, Lilly. When you find this book, you will have proven to yourself that we are keeping nothing from you, that all we have said is true and accurate. It contains original information to support our claims with dates and names. The author writes of two powerful organizations on this earth. One being the Company, our group, and the other the group you witnessed at the meeting, the World Alliance." He gets into significant detail as he describes the old, complicated, covert struggle between them. "Pay special attention to the period of time it covers, and weigh this view against what you know the situation to be today. Take your time and digest the contents entirely. When you're finished, please bring the volume to either Ty or me. You understand it's a treasure that belongs in our archives. Signed, Remsar," Lilly reads out loud.

"How did they know I would be looking for something? And how did they know I'd find it here? They must know me better than I thought. Do you suppose they staged this whole kidnapping knowing I'd come back here? Or, maybe this has been here a long time, and they've been waiting for me to find it. A lot of questions without answers, as usual.

"They must believe this book will finally convince me I'm doing the right thing. Otherwise they wouldn't let me read it. I'm beginning to understand one thing for sure. I have to pick a side, or take a position soon. This bouncing back and forth isn't good. I have to make a final decision and stick with it. I need to commit one way or the other and get into the fight. So far, I've just been accepting anything that comes my way, drifting this way and that, depending on the suggestions of others. It's time to plant my feet and let my views and passions be known. Let them be known in ways that can't be misunderstood." She speaks out loud as if talking back to Remsar's note.

"I'll read this book, and then I'll do what I need to do. No more little miss nice girl. No more pushing me around. No more training. I'm tired of being everybody's puppet. The world is going to see me as I am, like it or not."

Meanwhile.

The Andersons' extended family decided to sleep on their decision to ferret out factual information regarding Lilly before taking action. It's midmorning when they convene again. They're all gathered in the den.

"Any additional thoughts before we firm things up?" John brings things to order.

"I'd like to say something." Everybody turns to look at Randall.

"You all know I think the world of Sheree, I have for years. I wouldn't do anything that would cause her harm, and you know that, too. But I think the way we're going about this is all wrong. I have a feeling it'll take too long to uncover whatever it is we're looking for. It's going to be too late to do her any good. We don't know where she is or have any idea about how to find her. We can't send up smoke signals or beat a drum to let her know. I think this is urgent. We need to find her right away and warn her of what we suspect. Let her decide what to do with whatever information we can give her. I think the first thing we should do is locate her."

Everyone is frozen by his unexpected outburst. It started out calm, almost timid, then gained momentum, and finished with a loud voice, making demands.

For a minute or two the room stays quiet.

Randy feels he might have overstepped his bounds. His head turns from side to side, as his eyes move from face to face, looking for a hint of support.

"He's right," Falcon speaks. "It could take a month to come up with proof enough to be absolutely sure."

"Do you mean to tell me that we have no way, no idea, of how to contact Sheree?" Selma asks with disbelief.

"I'm afraid so," Sally admits. "We've talked about it with her, but she's said more than once, there is no way to do it. She gave us some coordinates of the place she was going to the last time she was here. It's somewhere in the southwest territory. A place called Canozira."

"A lot of good that'll do us. What do we know about coordinates? Don't they deal with the sea? Ships and things I mean," Charlotte infers.

"You forget I spent a few years on the sea, Missy. I learned a lot about navigation and such. Just give me the right maps, a sextant, a few clear dark nights, and a compass. If the coordinates are accurate, and given the time, I can put us in her underwear with her." Millie surprises everyone with her choice of words, causing a sprinkling of chuckles within the gathering.

"Do you mean you can mark a map where the coordinates are and we can go there to find her?" Selma gets back in the conversation.

"It's not quite that easy. We'll mark a map all right, to get us in the general vicinity, then zero in by taking new readings every day, and use the compass until we get to the exact meeting of the numbers of the coordinates. If the numbers are right they'll be in degrees, minutes, and compass directions. I'll have to go along on the search to make the calculations," Millie continues.

"Dad?" Robert asks his father, out of respect.

"I see Randall's point. Let's find her." A loud mingling of voices support John's words.

He waves his arms up and down to settle the noise. "Let's get this organized and move with it. Falcon, I think you should head it up." He hands the leadership to his daughter's husband.

"Since we're all familiar with the Company, Rose, Hawk, and I should go for sure. Millie, we'll definitely need you, and Cheryl, you can pass for Sheree if need be. Sally, we'll need you back at La Nesra. Dad, we need you to get more information through your office. That leaves Robert and Randy," he concludes.

"They should come with me," Sally offers.

"What about the four of us?" Elizabeth points to Selma, Charlotte, and Nora. "Isn't there something we can do? We seem to be left out."

"Come with me to Baltimore. I can use all the help I can get." John extends an invitation.

"What about the children?" Randy asks.

"There's plenty of help here to take care of them. We won't be missed for a few days," Charlotte explains.

"I'll stay," Selma decides. "Someone has to run these farms, and take care of our baby. Besides, I don't mind at all. If I'm never involved in any more battles, that will be fine with me. So, go on, do what needs to be done, and don't worry about things here."

"I'll stay with you, ma'am. I won't be any use to anybody in Baltimore. This farm and these children are all I know," Nora confides.

"It looks like it's you, Beth, and me, then Daddy." Charlotte smiles at the opportunity.

"On second thought, I think I can be more of a help here with Selma and Nora. I would rather stay with them," Beth decides. "I don't know, but in my mind, it seems every time Selma gets left alone things happen. I'll feel better knowing what's going on here."

"I'll feel better too, honey. I mean, with the three of you watching out for each other I won't worry as much," Robert confesses and supports her decision.

"Where are we going to get everything you need, Millie. I doubt you'll find them around here anywhere. And what about Doc? What's he going to say about all of this. Will he let you go?" Robert poses with a grin.

"Me? Let me go? I'm still my own woman, I am. I've got him twisted around my little finger. He'll not forbid me anything. He might grouse a bit, but I'll get my way. Aaahh, you're just joshing me, aren't you? Ha ha ha." Her face beams and her eyes sparkle when she realizes his intent.

"I'll probably need to go to a larger city to find a sextant, the maps, and the like. That will take four or five days. Knowing that, we won't be able to leave here for at least a week," she continues. "It could take a month to get deep into the southwest territory, probably six weeks. Is that going to do us any good," the once seagoing lassie asks.

"Well, the rest of us can get started right away. That'll give us time to see what more we can find out. We'll try to stay in touch with your group by using the telegraph, although, I'm not sure how far into the territory it goes right now." Robert tries to further organize the effort.

"I think it's the best we can do, so we just have to work with it. At least we'll be a whole lot closer to finding her than if we wait," Randy explains. "We should all work at what we're doing with vigor. The faster we can make things happen, the better off Sheree will be."

On the west coast, Remsar and Ty are getting impatient. It's been more than twenty-four hours with no word of Lilly. They are sitting in the lobby of their hotel awaiting word from their people.

Breaking a period of silence, Ty speaks.

"What would she do if she had a chance to escape those devils? Would she come here, back to us?"

"That's a good question." Remsar takes notice. "When I think about it, unless they take every precaution, they won't hold her captive long. She would go home, back to Canozira?"

"Then what are we doing sitting around here. That's where we should be. But just in case she does come back here, we can leave word with these people to send her home. Let's get moving," Ty offers, for Remsar's agreement.

At Canozira, Lilly has not put the book down since she found it. It takes time to read and understand the meaning of the language from so long ago. She soon realizes that some of the passages can be understood differently, perhaps not as intended by their author. She has walked around her quarters, reading out loud at times, to better understand the exact meaning. While at other times, she has clutched the closed book to her chest, holding her place with a finger between the pages, and paced back and forth, thinking. Not once has she stopped reading, or had any urge to lay the book down. The passing of time is the farthest thing from her mind.

She pauses for a moment after reading the last few words scribed on the last page of the ancient paper. A stare, like a daze, comes over her face as she sits alone in her quarters. Unknowingly, her hands carefully close the book and let it rest on her lap. Fifteen minutes pass, then, as if awakening from a good sleep, she stirs with a new energy.

"So that's it. That's what this is all about. Everything they have told me so far is true, but it's only part of the truth. The Korgots are coming back all right, but someone knows when. Their planet comes close enough for them to travel here every so many years. They have passed this way many times over the years, but so far, when they attempt to pass through a tear they have made in the lining of our dimension, they have been repelled by our people. When they come back—if they break through—they'll activate the arsenal. Each time they come, they get stronger, which means our defenses have to get stronger, too.

"The book infers our Maker will cause to be born, a person whom will have all the powers necessary to repel and destroy whatever the intruders bring to the opening in the lining. This person will sleep between the times of the attacks, and be held as a sentinel to be awakened when needed.

"That sure sounds like me all right. So it makes sense that if the bad people get me and keep me locked away somehow, I won't be able to protect us. And if they kill me—well, I can't let that happen.

"I don't know why Remsar and Ty couldn't just tell me this whole story. Probably because they believe I wouldn't go along with being stored away like a rag doll until someone deems it's time to wake me up to do their bidding.

"I'm in the way of the World Alliance. If they eliminate me, they'll have the advantage. What would happen if those who are hunting me, suddenly became hunted by me?

"The book doesn't dwell on it, but it seems the World Alliance is working to control the wealth of the world. Then, when the time is right, they plan to sell our souls—along with the riches they have amassed—to the intruders for the price of everlasting lives for themselves.

"I've done the right thing by hiding the arsenal and putting my life body, and Ty's, in there with them. Only I know where I put the two death angels I took away from the original ten."

"Oh, goodness," she yawns. "I'm feeling a little weary. I'll rest for a few hours before deciding how I'll proceed from here."

She retires to her bedroom to lie across the bed and quickly finds a restless sleep, unaware when someone silently enters her quarters to stand at the doorway for a long minute, then withdraw with the same catlike stealth.

"Just as we thought, Ty, she's sound asleep on her bed. No sense bothering her right now. We'll let her get some rest before we get the details of what happened. I'm relieved now that I know she's safe," Remsar advises.

"Yes, I suppose that's best. She needs the time to settle down after all she's been through. I have to say, though, I feel the urgency to know about those people that kidnapped her. The sooner we know, the more likely we are to catch them," Ty agrees yet remains antsy.

"I know, I feel the same way. Look here, she found the book; and if I know her, she's been up most of the night reading. We'll wait two hours before we awaken her. Agreed?" Remsar points out and asks.

Another hour passes while Lilly lies motionless in her room, her head lying on her right cheek. Her right arm is at her side, her left up near her face and bent to lie just above head. A close look at her face reveals her closed eyelids rapidly twitching and moving from the activity of her eyeballs, rolling and flitting beneath.

Visions of monsters clawing at the other side of what might be a blanket protecting her from their vicious thirst for her blood run through her dreaming mind. Their long, sharp claws will eventually tear their way through the weakening material, allowing them access to their prey. Her heart speeds up, when her breath gets short and heavy in anticipation of the sight of them. Yet she sleeps.

Light from the other room enters through the open door, and fades into darkness inside her bedroom. Two dark figures come from the other side of the mirror to go undetected, except for the slight wisp of air caused by their movement; one toward her on the bed, the other through the open doorway. Only seconds pass before the figure reappears, to be seen sliding the book Lilly found into a large leather pouch, which it straps to its back. A clenched fist with a thumb pointed upward signals them both to take action, as if it has been planned and practiced to perfection.

One of the figures gently takes her left forearm and moves it to the center of her back, at the same time pulling her right arm to meet it. While a heavy twine is wrapped repeatedly around her wrists, the second figure gently pushes her chin down to open her mouth. Then a ball of cotton, covered with cloth, is pushed inside and a long bandage is wrapped twice around her neck and jaws. The wrapping continues up her face, exposing her nose, to be wrapped three times around her eyes. At the same time, her knees are bent allowing the twine confining her wrists to be tied off, extended, wrapped several times around her ankles, and tied off again.

Lilly struggles to wake up, believing the monsters have succeeded, mauling their way through the protective shield. In her dream, her screams are muffled by the lack of air. She has no strength, no power to fight back.

When the two figures effortlessly pick her up from the bed, her eyes pop open beneath the blindfold. A split second passes before she realizes what's happening. Her stomach and back muscles react, pushing and pulling her body violently back and forth, twisting and turning. She's unable to form words to scream because of the cotton ball, but scream she does, hearing it only through the hollows of her own ears.

The figures move her easily across the floor and through the mirror leaving no evidence of their presence behind.

Time passes.

"It's been over two hours," Ty prods Remsar with his words.

"I see it is," he replies as he puts his pocket watch away. "Let's go."

The pair stand in the hallway, knocking on the door for a few minutes thinking it is the proper thing to do. But when there is no response, Remsar produces a key allowing them to enter.

"She isn't here," Ty points out indignantly.

"I can see that," Remsar replies grimly. "Relax, she has to be around here somewhere. We'll wait for her right here."

After waiting until they can stand it no more, a search is made of the Canozira compound. There is no sign of Lilly.

"The only explanation is she left through the mirror. We've checked, no one has seen her. You were the last," Ty sums up.

"There's just three places where she might have gone. I suggest you travel immediately to La Nesra, and if no luck there, to her family's farm," Remsar advises.

"In the meantime, I'll go back to the west coast. I feel sure we'll find her. But we'll report back here in three days, with or without her."

Not knowing what to expect, Ty travels via a flying machine. If by chance Lilly has resumed her body, he'll need it to get her back to Canozira, since she won't be able to move through the mirrors.

He rousts Mr. Vaughn out of a good sleep.

"Where is everybody? Have you seen Lilly?"

"No, I haven't seen Lilly for some time. The others are on a holiday at the Anderson farm. What's going on? Is something wrong? What time is it?" Mr. Vaughn moves to a nightstand in his bedroom to splash some water into his face from a wash bowl. He turns to face Ty as he dries with a towel.

"She's missing?"

"Who's missing? Lilly?"

"Yes, one minute she was asleep on her bed at Canozira, and the next, she's gone. She was kidnapped off the stage on the west coast, but she must have escaped her captors since we found her the next day at Canozira. We think she has to be here or at her family's farm. Remsar is on the west coast looking for her."

"Well, if she's here, I sure don't know about it. It won't hurt to check though. Come on, we'll get over to her quarters. It's a place to start," Mr. Vaughn scurries.

After exhausting the probabilities and possibilities of her presence at La Nesra and coming up with nothing, Ty leaves at two in the morning for the Anderson Farm.

Mr. Vaughn will wire him if anything changes at Atlanta.

So as not to create too much of a stir at the farm by having the flying machine land there, Ty decides to show up in town and rent a horse to get to the Andersons' place. It's the middle of the morning of the second day by the time he gets there.

Elizabeth spots him from her seat on the front porch, and moves to the front door to call inside for Selma. "Someone's coming. A lone rider, I can't tell from here who it is."

Selma hurries from the kitchen to the front porch, at the same time Ty slows his horse to a walk as he enters their front yard. Instinct puts a rifle in her hands as she goes out the door.

"Morning," Ty calls out from the distance of fifty yards.

The women do not respond, but his voice gets the attention of two hands at the barn, who start moseying shoulder to shoulder toward the house, keeping their eyes on the stranger.

"Don't be alarmed," he calls out, assessing the situation. "I just need some information. Can I come closer so we can talk?"

"Come ahead. Keep your hands where I can seem them," Selma orders calmly, firmly.

"Thank you, ma'am. My name is Tyrone Black. May I ask yours?" he speaks as he nears the porch.

"Tyrone Black, I've heard your name. It's burnt into my mind. You're my dead husband's son, aren't you? You shot Sheree's horse out from under her, almost killing her, didn't you?" she replies, ignoring his question.

"You must be Selma," he says with a grin, as if he has heard nothing she said.

"That's right. What brings you here?" she asks, never changing the expression of firmness on her face. Elizabeth stands quietly at her right shoulder.

Ty surveys the vanishing prominence of his position when the two hands move within an arms distance of his back. His reins are in one hand, but his other hangs just inches from the butt of one of his two handguns, which are in holsters tied down to his legs. Trying to defuse a tense moment, he tosses his reins at the hitching rail so they wrap around on their own. Then, he puts both his hands on the rail and steps backward to lean toward it to put some weight on his arms. A gesture that he feels will put everyone at ease.

"Your hands can take my guns, if you've a mind," he says. "But if you look, you can see the hammers are still looped to the holsters."

"Your being Charles's son means little to me. My notion is that you are the one man responsible for the raids on our farms that murdered some very dear friends of mine. If I knew for sure, I'd kill you where you stand. Now, speak your piece, Mr. Black," Selma scorns.

Hearing Selma's words enrages Elizabeth to move to the screen door, reach inside the house to produce a shotgun, and return to stand four feet from her friend's shoulder.

"Move away from him," she instructs the hands and motions with the barrel of the gun. "It's you that's responsible for the killing of my mother and father, and all our hands then." The young woman glares and cocks both hammers back with her thumb.

"Whoa! Hold on, you two!" Ty's voice escalates, but he doesn't move a muscle.

"All I want is to know if you've seen Lilly over the last two or three days. It's important."

"No, she hasn't been here. Why?" Selma answers.

"Is my whole group from La Nesra still here? I understand from the people back there that they came here for a visit a few weeks ago. You know—Falcon, Sally, Hawk, and Rose."

"They were here, but they left yesterday for Atlanta. You must have passed each other without knowing it," Elizabeth explains.

"Why are you here looking for Sheree?" Selma asks again.

"Honestly, Selma, she's missing. We don't know where she is, and we're worried about her." Ty figures he might as well be honest about it.

"Well, she's not here. Is there a message, in case she shows up?"

"Just tell her I was here and ask her to contact me right away. It's for her own safety. Some people with bad intentions are searching for her. I need to get her back so I can protect her from them."

"Is that it?" she bluntly asks.

"Yes, I believe it is," he concludes.

"Good day, Mr. Black." Selma turns into the house leaving Elizabeth and the two hands to watch him leave.

On the west coast, Remsar is meeting with the Company's people in the area.

"So call off the search. Unless these locals found a way to track her back to Canozira, she's no longer in their hands," he explains, as soon as the group comes together.

"Yes, we know." A response comes from a younger agent. "We have the four in custody who kidnapped her from the stage. It seems she brained one of them while being covered with a wire net and a bag over her head, then made her escape from a locked room without anyone seeing her go. They left the carriage and their sweating horses stand out in front of the house where they took her. Not too smart, the lot of them. Word worked its way back to us and we arrested them all. They were after any ransom money they could get for her, nothing else. Now they all believe she's a demon of some sort."

"Good work, men. I appreciate it. The problem is, she's missing again. She returned to Canozira; I saw her myself. Then two hours later, she vanished, nowhere to be found. I need all of you to put your ears to the ground, do whatever it takes to get a clue as to where she is."

"What exactly do you want us to do?" an elder agent poses.

"Put pressure on the known agents for the World Alliance. Stay after them, cause them problems. Push them hard to see if we can flush out something," Remsar answers.

"But we need to be careful with that. We don't want them to know who we are," the elder continues.

"Believe me, they already know who you are," Remsar counters. "Stick close to them. Don't let them out of your sight. Let them see you the first thing every morning and the last thing every night. Do you get the idea? Also, alert as many of our covert agents as possible, asking them to keep a watchful eye out for a hint of Lilly's whereabouts."

As agreed, Remsar and Ty meet at Canozira on the third day after the incident.

"Nothing! We have nothing, we know nothing!" Ty rants.

"We must give it time. Let our sources do their work. What else can we do?" Remsar's question is like a statement requiring no answer.

"I've asked Mr. Vaughn to let me know the minute our people arrive at La Nesra from the Anderson farm. I'll see what I can pry out of them. I certainly didn't get much from my visit with my father's wife. She's one tough woman. She and a younger one held me at gunpoint all the time I was there," he explains.

"Do you think Lilly was, or had been there?" Remsar asks.

"No, I don't, but I thought it strange that none of their men were around at the time. I'm not sure what that means, but for some reason these two women were left alone out there in the middle of nowhere. Have you ever had a feeling there's something going on, but you just can't put your finger on it?" Ty's questions produce no answers.

"Let's get with our agents in the area and have them nose around. Who knows, we might come up with something. Anything will be more than we have now."

Sally, Robert, and Randy arrive at La Nesra in the middle of the afternoon to be presented with a note by the guard as they enter. Sally puts it in her bag to read after they take their horses to the livery, and tote their belongings upstairs to the vacant quarters of Falcon and Lilly.

"Let's see what we have here. Aaah, Mr. Vaughn wants to see us as soon as we arrive." Sally reveals the contents of the note.

"Shall we go?" The three look at each other and head for the door.

Mr. Vaughn explains the mystery of the missing Lilly, and asks if the trio has any information he can pass on to Ty. Sally speaks for the group.

"Mr. Vaughn, we talked about you quite a bit on our way here from the farm. Can we trust you? I mean, if something happened, and you had to protect and support us regardless of the consequences, would you do it? Can you keep a secret between the four of us?"

"No, don't expect me to turn against an organization that has kept me from poverty all these years. I thought I could, but I realize now, I can't. I'm too old to change my ways. Do not tell me anything I can use against you. That's my advice to you," he replies without hesitation.

"Even if it effects every human being on earth?" Randy chimes in.

"I don't know you well, young man. Aren't you two the ones who came to free Lilly a good while ago?" Mr. Vaughn points at Robert as he speaks. "What would I be doing trying to save the world at my age?"

"It sounds to me like you've sort-of given up on life, Mr. Vaughn. In the first place, you're not that old. In the second place, I know a lot of that spunk you had back before you located your body is still in you. And finally, we aren't going to ask you to go against the Company. All we want is some information that we think you can help us get." Robert reasons.

"You want me to be your spy, is that right. boy." the old man interjects, cutting to the point.

"No, not exactly, Mr. Vaughn," Sally begins again. "I'm going to take a chance and let you in on some information we came across."

He sits quietly showing little or no interest.

"We have heard that Lilly will be working to help enslave and destroy all the people on earth instead of saving them, as she's been told. We believe there's a book, or a document of some kind, here at La Nesra that will prove or disprove that. All we need from you is your help to locate it, or turn your head while we search for it. That's all."

"Who gave you this information?" he asks.

"My father," Robert is quick to reply. "We're hoping the information isn't true. But if it is, we believe Lilly should know. We know she'll not want to be a party to it."

"Yes, I see. What makes you think I won't turn the lot of you over to Ty? He was here and gave me instructions to let him know when you arrive. He wouldn't waste any time dealing with a traitor and two of her comrades." The dedicated Company man comments.

"For one thing, Mr. Vaughn, if it weren't for Lilly, you'd still be looking for the body you occupy right now. Would Ty have done the same thing? You know, he moved all of the angels without saying a word to any of us, including you. How many years did you say you looked for your body? Would he have led you to your body, or would he have moved it along with the others. Think about it for a minute. Has Ty ever said anything to you about leading the life on this earth down a road to destruction? Has he made any mention of a plan to save you from it? What if the information we received is correct?" Sally pauses for a few seconds for effect. "Wouldn't you like to know for sure? If you are unable to bring yourself to help us, then at least allow us access to the archive of records here at La Nesra," she finishes.

H shifts his position, then rises from his chair a little to reach his pipe and tobacco. He sits back down, leans back, and puts the pipe into the pouch to begin scooping tobacco into the bowl with one finger. After packing it solidly, he puts the stem in his mouth, folds the pouch and lays it on the desk, and pulls a match from his vest pocket. A quick scrape of his thumbnail sets it ablaze. He holds the fire to the rim of the bowl and sucks on the stem until smoke encircles his head. As it drifts up and away, he removes the pipe from his mouth.

"You won't find anything like that in the archives." His words of this nature are not expected. "I've made it my business to get a look at everything in there. There's nothing like that or even a hint of it. If there is such a thing around here, it would have to be in Ty's office, or perhaps his quarters. Now, because of what this is, I'll take a look and see if I can find something. But I'll only show it to you if it deals directly with the information you've received. If it works out that there's nothing, this conversation never took place. Understood?

"Meet me here tomorrow at two in the afternoon."

Falcon's group of five, including himself, decided to travel with John and Charlotte to Baltimore, then head west via train from there. It was reasoned it will save time, plus allow a place for them to leave their horses and gear, which otherwise they would have to sell, or give away. It took Millie half a day to locate the equipment and maps she needs for their venture. It's packed away safely in a wooden crate since she will not require it for some time. They intend to travel as far as possible by railroad and stage coach, then horseback and pack mules. Millie will begin her calculations to pinpoint their destination when she gets closer, having already determined the general area by using a map. They figure it will take the better part of three weeks, with the problems the war is causing all forms of transportation.

Remsar and Ty have all but turned on each other because of their frustration with losing Lilly. They sit in Ty's office at Canozira seeking solace from each other.

"We have botched things very badly. We should have placed more guards around her. I should have stayed in her room until she woke up. I lost her not once, but twice," Remsar laments.

"Yes, you should have, and I should have not have waited with you. I should have went there immediately as I knew to do. We're both responsible for this, there's no denying it. We'll have to answer to the directors for it sooner or later. Our one way out of this mess is to find her before they convene, but at this point, where do we begin." Ty bemoans the inevitable.

"Let's start at the beginning and determine what we know," Remsar begins.

"First, she was kidnapped by several bungling fools who thought they could sell her back to us. Next, we find her here, asleep on her bed. She has found the book, as we have been expecting her to do for some time, and obviously read it. Then, within a two-hour-period of time, she disappears without a trace, along with the book. No one here saw her come or go, and no one at La Nesra or the Andersons' farm has either. Is there anything I've missed."

"No, that sums it up," Ty concurs.

"All right, now, as far as I have been able to discern at this point, one of two things has happened. She's gone off on her own to either find us, or to start her own campaign. We've been right on track with our understanding of her reactions to various things to this point. Knowing that, I don't think she's out there looking for us, I believe she would have stayed here to continue our work, particularly after reading the book. What do you think?" Remsar pauses looking for support.

"Yes, I agree," Ty offers.

"Good. Now, suppose—just suppose—those bungling fools had a job to do and did it magnificently. Those who planned it knew they'd never get her out of the city. Her escape from them was planned to perfection. When she left, they had one of their own ready to follow her. That's the only way they could have found her here. Never has anyone been able to track us to one of our portals and enter our compound. They used her to find us, then came through our mirror and took her back. Not only do they have her, they now know where to find us."

Ty interrupts him.

"By 'they' you mean . . . ?"

"Isn't it obvious? The World Alliance."

"If you're right, we're at a tremendous risk right now!" Ty exclaims. "Damn, can this get any worse?"

"Settle yourself. We'll raise our shields. No one will get through, but then, we can't either, at least not through the mirrors. That means if Lilly escapes again, she'll not be able to come back here," Remsar points out.

"We have to assume you're right. So, before you raise the shields, let me pack a few things and leave for La Nesra. I'll get them prepared in case she shows up there," Ty urges.

"That's a good idea, but before you go, let's get a look at the death angels. I have a bad feeling about all of this. I'll have the shields raised now, but we can lower them long enough for you to leave when you're ready."

The two men walk swiftly through the maze of short hallways in the extreme lower level of the compound. The door opens exposing the room where Ty has kept the angels since he moved them from La Nesra.

Both stand agape at the doorway of the empty room.

Chapter Thirty-Seven

"She's taken the angels. No one else knew they were here," Ty explains angrily, as he stands next to Remsar in the doorway of the empty room.

"But why?" Remsar counters in amazement.

"Control—she wants to control everything. I didn't think she would go this far, though," Ty responds.

"What do you suppose she's done with them? Where would she put them?"

"They could be right here under our noses. She forced me to take her to the room where my life body is kept, then proceeded to make it accessible only to her. They could be there, but if they are, we'll never be able to get to them. The room is impregnable, I saw to that." He continues to explain.

Being outwitted by the young woman, and now having to admit it to his superior, makes him feel vulnerable. His self-image as a tough, cunning leader of men is threatened, causing a familiar need to kill something to surge through his veins.

"Well, there's no sense in wasting our time with that then. I don't know how she did it, but could she possibly have moved them from here to La Nesra, or another area? Perhaps her family's farm?" Remsar will not let himself pursue Ty to verbally assault him for his obvious blunders.

"You're going to La Nesra anyway to see if she's been there, so why don't you look for the angels there first, then if you find nothing, go on to the Anderson farm."

"I don't think it's a good idea for anyone from here to go to their farm right now. I know if I show up again, there will be bloodshed. It's not that I mind that, but I might have to kill them all; and until we find the angels, that's probably not the best thing to do. I'll search La Nesra, and if I discover anything, I'll let you know immediately. If you haven't heard from me by tomorrow evening, assume I've found nothing," Ty suggests.

"Our best bet is to find Lilly. She can lead us to the angels and save a lot of time. If we determine they're hidden on the Anderson farm, well, then I think we need to bring them back here, regardless of what it takes," he concludes.

"She escaped from captors before," Remsar recalls. "She's very resourceful. I have to believe she'll come back here if at all possible. I'll wait for word from you before I attempt anything. That will give her time to work her way free from them."

"One other thing comes to mind. While I'm getting prepared to leave, why don't you check the transportation logs of our flying machines? See if, by chance, Lilly has used one of them without our knowledge," Ty suggests.

Meanwhile, at La Nesra.

Mr. Vaughn has searched Ty's office for anything to prove or disprove the suspicions of Sally, Robert, and Randall. Not needing the wrath he'll receive if he's caught, he takes great pains to look everywhere, then put everything back the way it was. It takes the better part of an hour. When he finds nothing, his next move is to his boss's living quarters.

Getting blamed for searching Ty's office is a bad thing, but getting caught inside his living quarters could mean the gallows. A lock pick and the thin blade of a knife are his tools as the older man kneels in the hallway, his brow wet with sweat, working to open the lock on the door of Ty's residence before someone comes along.

"Come on, come on." He tells himself over and over.

"Damn!" He hears footsteps coming up the stairs just fifty feet away.

He's on his feet and moving the opposite way through the hall, not daring to look back over his shoulder to see who it is.

"I'll come back later this evening when there are fewer people around. It's too risky right now," he vows to himself.

Sally, Robert, and Randall are keeping themselves out of sight at Falcon's residence within the La Nesra compound. It's giving them time to rest from their trip and carefully plan their next move. They sit together in the living room area of the abode.

"If Mr. Vaughn finds what we're looking for, this could be a lot easier than I ever imagined," Sally relates with a positive attitude.

"Do you suppose we can trust him? Will he bring whatever he finds to us? He doesn't seem to care much for Bob and me," Randy notices.

"I don't imagine he has many allies around here. Besides, Sally reminded him of how he got his body back after so many years of searching. From that standpoint, he probably will. But on the other hand, the way he talked, I don't think he wants to draw too much attention to himself. If he thinks he can get his hands on something to use as barter, something to protect and further himself with Ty, he'll probably use it for that, and blame us for coming here to find it. I'm not sure what he'll do, but you can bet he's thought about it," Robert warns.

"I think we have to proceed believing he'll try to get rid of us if he can gain from it. We need to be just as crafty. We need a way to make him think we'll turn the tables on him if he tries. Let's not forget, he has no idea his director of security is loyal to us, not the Company," Sally points out.

"Another thought to add to it all, Mr. Anderson has an agent or two running around here somewhere. How else did this information get back to him in the first place?" Randy's words are a statement formed as a question.

"This could be a race to see who gets to these documents first. He might not find anything even if it does exist. You know, when this is over, we should write a book about it," Robert muses kiddingly.

"No one would believe it. Would you, if you hadn't lived it?" Sally quells his thinking.

"Let's get our heads together and see if we can come up with something to deal with all of these possibilities. We need to be ready, no matter what," Randy implores.

It is a quarter past eleven in the evening.

Mr. Vaughn makes his way cautiously through the building to once again find the door to Ty's living quarters. The hallways and stairwells are vacant of people, making it necessary for him to walk on the balls of his feet to suppress the clicking of his heels on the marble floors. He has brought a small candled lamp along to light, once he gets ready to work on the lock.

He's ready, down on his knees in the darkness, strike a match, light the wick . . . there. He sets the lamp on the floor in front of the door, off to the side enough to allow him to work without getting burned by the rising heat. The glow of the small light flickers softly, illuminating the door knob and lock, as well as his hands and face. He is a perfect picture of a sneaky thief at work.

He silently works his lock pick and knife back and forth, up and down.

Click, click.

"Aha," he whispers to himself.

He pushes the door open, pockets his pick and knife, picks up the candle, enters the room, and turns to face the door as he gently shuts it.

He turns, with every intent of using his candle to locate the nearest gas light, when out of the darkness—

"It took you long enough to get in here!" a loud gruff voice booms and fills his ears. Terror races through his body as if a lightning bolt has struck. He freezes in his tracks, not breathing, waiting for something to happen. From beyond the light extended by the candle, a match fizzes and comes to life. A hand reaches to a gas light on the wall. The hissing sound of escaping gas for a second, then a *plip*, and brightness fills the room

There stands Ty, putting the match to his lips. His quick breath extinguishes the flame. Sitting on a chair a few feet away is the director of security.

"You have anything to say to explain what you're doing here, breaking into my quarters?" Ty speaks firmly with no expression.

The older man tries to keep himself standing by stiffening his weakened knees. Knowing there is no defense for what he has done, his mind churns rapidly trying to get organized for the onslaught about to begin. He grits his teeth to hold his tongue.

"Do those two from the Anderson farm and Sally have anything to do with this?" Ty's voice is no less insistent.

Mr. Vaughn has nothing to say.

"I could have you shot for this. You know that, don't you? No one would blame me if I did? Aren't you going to say anything in your own defense?"

Silence.

"Well, I don't know what the hell's going on around here, but I intend to find out. Since you have nothing to say, I'll tell you a thing or two. You're under arrest. When we're through, the director here will put you in chains in the bowels of this building, just like you've imprisoned many before you. There you'll stay with no food, no water, nothing, until you get your tongue back. Don't think your friends will come to help you. I have guards in place at their quarters, so they'll not leave there either, until I'm satisfied with some answers.

"Mr. Vaughn, you're leaving me no choice. Lilly is missing, a rare book of great importance to our cause is missing, the death angels are missing, and I have no solid explanations for any of it. This entire compound is locked up tight, and will be kept that way until I get to the bottom of this," Ty orders and explains his frustration.

Mr. Vaughn finds his voice.

"Ty . . . can we speak privately?"

He considers his options. "I don't know what you have to say that can't be said here and now in present company, but if it will help shed some light. Give us a few minutes, Director, wait outside."

The door closes and Ty looks at Mr. Vaughn in a questioning manner.

"Sally came back from her trip to the Anderson farm, bringing Robert and Randy with her. They immediately pulled me aside and asked if I would help them find a book, or manuscript, reportedly here somewhere."

"Didn't Falcon, Hawk, and Rose come back with her?" Ty interrupts.

"No sign of them yet."

"Go ahead," he urges.

"John Anderson led them to believe the purpose of the Company is to support the eventual entrapment of our souls here on earth with the aid of Lilly. According to them, Lilly is to revive the death angels and lead them, which is against everything that I have been told is holy. I'm certain what they're looking for isn't in our library archives. So, I thought it could be in your office or quarters. I searched your office and found nothing, and that's what I came here to do," Mr. Vaughn confesses.

"Did they say anything about the angels or their whereabouts?" Ty questions.

"Not a word, but keep in mind, I didn't ask." The older man feels more comfortable now that they are talking.

"You must have their trust, otherwise, they wouldn't have brought this to you, now would they?" The tall man dressed in his usual black garb suggests. "Well, sir, I believe you. I think you've told me everything since you included your search of my office. You were seen entering and leaving there earlier today, so I already knew about it. I thought these quarters could be next on your list, and that's why the director and I decided to wait for you.

"Here's a piece of information you don't have. Lilly signed out three flying machines from Canozira one evening for several hours. The destination of all three was the coordinates of Atlanta, Georgia. That's when she moved the angels, I'd bet on it. But, where in Atlanta? I could put together a search party, but I can't be sure they're still there; besides, Atlanta is a large area with countless places to conceal those boxes. Considering that they may not still be in Atlanta, the only two places she would be likely to take them would be here or the Anderson farm. Are you certain she hasn't somehow found a way to get them in here without your knowing it."

"I don't see how. The guards would have reported it."

Ty thinks for a minute, knowing he moved them through the gate past the guards when he took them to Canozira. He made sure the guards were told to say nothing of it, and any record of it was destroyed.

"Well, before I go off on a goose chase, I'd like to know what your three friends know. This where you come in. Instead of putting you in prison, I have a job for you. And if you handle it properly, I'll forget these infractions completely. But if you go against me, I'll see that you never see the light of day for the rest of your miserable life. Understand?"

"Yes, I understand, what do you want me to do?"

Ty walks to the door, opens it, and motions the director to enter.

The clamor of a group of heavy footed people coming up the outside stairway, then the commotion of opening the door and entering their quarters, awakens Sally, Robert and Randy.

It's dark in this large living area with no walls to separate the rooms, but it's apparent from the light coming through the open door—someone is here with a purpose.

Robert lights a lamp.

The director, with two guards, stands holding Mr. Vaughn's arms behind him.

"What's going on?" Sally quickly slides her robe over her arms, wraps it around her body, and ties the belt, as she moves toward them.

Her two friends are right behind her tugging and pulling up their pants.

"You're all under arrest, including your comrade here," the director announces, then pushes Mr. Vaughn forward, causing him to fall to the floor.

"He'll explain. Don't try to leave these premises, or you will be shot," he concludes, then leaves with the two guards.

Young Mr. Anderson moves to close the door behind them.

"What's going on?" Sally asks, giving Mr. Vaughn a hand up to his feet.

"They were waiting for me when I broke into Ty's quarters. They made me tell them everything. We can't leave here, except to do absolutely necessary things. And then, a guard will accompany us wherever we go," he explains briefly.

"What are they going to do with us?" Randy asks, wide-eyed.

"I don't know, they didn't say. Apparently, Lilly's not the only missing item. Some sort of valuable book, and the death angels, have disappeared. He's also wondering where Falcon, Hawk, and Rose are. Do you know about any of this?" he asks and pauses.

Before anyone can respond, the door suddenly swings open back against the wall with a bang. The director and the two guards have returned. He points to Sally and motions her to follow him, leaving the guards in the room. She follows down the stairs where he stops and turns to face her.

"Ty has placed him here to spy on the lot of you. He's doing it to save his own skin."

"Thanks," she acknowledges, then returns to the apartment. After the guards leave, she offers an explanation.

"He tried to bribe me to give him information about all of you. I turned him down." She's concerned that Robert or Randy will unknowingly say the wrong thing.

"To answer your question, we left Falcon, Hawk, and Rose back at the farm. They wanted to stay and help with the raising of a new barn. I imagine they'll be here in a couple of weeks or so. Do you suppose the missing book is the one we're looking for? And what do you mean, the death angels are missing?"

"I'm only repeating what Ty told me. I don't have the details," he replies.

Robert senses immediately what Sally is doing and nudges Randy's shoulder before he speaks. "I don't know what good keeping us locked up will do them. We can't tell them something, we don't know."

A month passes.

Nothing has changed at La Nesra. Ty has no additional information, and his four prisoners still have nothing to say. The days have passed slowly while they all wait for something to happen, a break. There is no word of Lilly.

John Anderson sent several telegrams in attempt to contact the threesome at La Nesra, but he's received word back that they could not be delivered due to tight security at the gate. He's now working through the Sons to determine the situation inside their walls.

It's been a peaceful month at the Anderson farm. The new barn is finished and another has been started on the Sanders' place. Selma, Elizabeth, and Nora miss their men, but they're busy, and that helps.

The trip into the southwest territory has been uneventful, but trying at times, for the small band of well doers making their way to Canozira. Falcon, Hawk, Rose, Cheryl, and Millie are travel weary. The taste of trail dust, the grit of sand, along with the smell of horse sweat and manure, is getting old. The weather is dry, hot, and water is scarce. It seems they travel miles and miles every day, then wake up in the morning to see the same landscape, never any closer to permanent landmarks than they were the day before.

Millie is sure she knows where they're going, but it was agreed, after getting advise from several local people, to hire a guide to get them across this barren land, mainly because of the need for water. He's an old Indian by the name of Sancho who speaks enough English and Spanish to get by. He keeps a wad of tobacco in his mouth continually, refusing to spit it out when he eats. His teeth are stained, hiding their decay to a degree. The juice from his chew causes him to strangle and gag on a regular basis, and small streams of juice-laden saliva trickle from the corners of his mouth, down over his chin, to drip on his shirt. His clothes are as old and dirty as the horse blanket he sleeps under at night. He's skinny and bony, but as wiry as they come. His friendly open mouth smile would be a welcome sight if not for his appearance and body odor. The group is glad to have him along, as he proves his worth every day by leading them to water—and out of the way of roaming bandits. His demands for doing the job are quite simple. He has been promised a steady supply of tobacco, keep for him and his horse, and four bits a day, that is, every day out and every day back.

The nights are cool enough for a fire to feel good, and the skies are filled with stars. Millie works every night, sometimes during the wee hours, making calculations to lead them onward.

The days give them spectacular vistas when they enter and begin their climb through mountain passages. Working their way up and over peaks, then down the other side only to be confronted by an even higher peak to be mastered, takes time and effort. Sancho finds trails to give them the footing they need to keep moving. This evening, Millie makes the awaited announcement.

"We'll be there tomorrow."

Once he sees where they're headed, Sancho informs everyone he will take them to the edge of the snow-peaked-mountains base, but can go no farther. He claims the gods live there, and bad things happen to anyone getting too close. To prove it, he has invited them all to stay awake tonight to see them. He says they will come out of the mountain and fly around, looking for anybody they can find to scoop up and take away. There will be no fire after dark tonight. It is far too dangerous. It's shortly after midnight when he points upward toward the mountain peak. "There—see it?"

Falcon, Hawk, and Rose have a good idea of what he's talking about, but hesitate to say anything. Millie and Cheryl are intrigued by the small fireflylike images emerging from the mountain to fly round and round, then zip off into nowhere in different directions. Things settle down for a while, then—all of a sudden—they're back. They move round and round a few times before disappearing back into the mountain, where they came from.

"Did you see that, didja?" Millie exclaims.

"I sure did," Cheryl confirms.

"It's all part of why we're going there," Rose reminds them.

Sancho is quick to remind them all he's not going that far.

Some of the group will sleep this night, others will not. They break camp at first light to begin their final day of travel. About three in the afternoon, their guide stops. When the rest catch up and gather around, they see all sorts of baskets, flowers, beaded bracelets, necklaces, and food at various stages of decay, neatly arranged on the ground, obviously left by someone.

"These offerings are left by the people who live here to thank the gods for not taking their souls. This is as close as anyone can go, to go farther is forbidden. So I must turn back. Pay me now. I don't like being here too long."

Rose begins to untie one of the packs on a horse to get the money.

"Can you tell us—do you know of a way up there?" Falcon asks the guide.

"I was up there halfway once during the day. They don't come out during the day. If you head toward that rock with two peaks and follow the tree line, you can get to where I was, but from there, I don't know."

"That's a start, Sancho. Thanks for what you've done for us," Hawk expresses.

Rose passes money to the Indian, then he takes his horse by the reins and turns to go back down the mountain, asking for nothing else.

"Don't you want some supplies and water to take with you?" Falcon speaks up.

"No. I'll be fine. Be careful with your supplies. You'll need all of them before you get out of here. Hear me. You'll not be able to take your animals much farther. You should set them free. Other animals will kill them for food if you leave them tied. Choose carefully what you will carry with you. If you are loaded too heavy, the climb will tire you too soon. Remember too, the higher you go, the harder it is to breathe." Sancho is soon out of their sight, leaving them to cope for themselves.

"I don't think we would have made it this far without him," Cheryl comments.

"For sure he saved us a lot of time. We didn't have to retrace our tracks and start over at all. We would have been all over this mountain trying to get to here," Hawk agrees.

"I wonder what our chances are of finding our way back," Millie speaks up. "My equipment is too heavy to carry with us. I'll have to leave it here."

"There will be plenty of time to fret about that after we find Sheree," Falcon reminds them all. "Right now we should get moving. We still have a few hours of daylight left. Let's see if we can make it to those two tall rocks up there before dark."

"It's not that I think we're doing anything wrong, but it occurs to me that the entrance to this place could be anywhere. I mean, do we really know what good it's going to do us to get way up there," Rose poses.

"That's a good point, honey, but where do we start looking. This is a big mountain, and the only thing we know for sure is those things come out of it up there somewhere. Unless we come up with a better idea between here and there, our best bet is to get as close as we can, and try to get in where they come and go." Her husband reasons.

"He's right, Rose, it's the smart thing to do. We could spend days looking. If there is an entrance down here somewhere, you can bet it's well hidden," Falcon agrees.

"It's settled then, let's get moving," Millie urges.

About an hour before dark, they settle in under the overhang of a large rock for the night. They figure being protected from above and their back side is the best they can do. Their journey up to this point has been a rigorous one to be sure. Twisting and turning through thick brush, scaling smaller boulders, sometimes on their hands and knees, always going up.

Sancho is right, the air is thinner, and a lot cooler. They decide to build a small fire to get warm and prepare some hot food before dark, feeling they will not have a chance after tonight. They brought a four-day supply of food, mostly jerky, hard biscuits, and water. Tonight their meal is hot beans, bacon, skillet bread, and steaming coffee. They eat heartily, then cover the remaining embers of the fire with dirt.

After stowing their provisions back against the rock behind them, they wrap themselves in blankets and huddle together to keep warm, and wait. They are a lot closer tonight, and should get a better look at where the flying machines are coming from. The rock over their heads will keep them out of sight and undetected by the pilots, they hope.

Believing the flying machines will not start moving around before midnight, it's decided they will trade off standing guard for the next few hours. That way they will feel safe when they sleep, and be secure in the fact they will not sleep through the flying objects display. To do that would mean another day could be added to their climb. There can be absolutely no talking or noise of any kind.

As hard as they try, no one can get to sleep. Rose, their first sentry for the evening, keeps ssshhhushing them when they move around trying to get comfortable. Finally, one at a time they sit up, wide awake, wrapped in their blankets—watching, silently waiting.

Shortly after midnight the activity starts. This time the size of the objects can be more closely determined by Cheryl and Millie who have not seen them before.

"Glory be, they're a lot bigger than I thought," Millie whispers.

"Everybody, see if you can get a fix on the spot they come from. Then watch to see if they go back inside the same way," Falcon softly alerts his peers.

Suddenly, without warning, one of the machines streaks toward them, stops not more than two hundred feet away, and hovers some fifty feet above the slanted terrain. A beam of bright green light appears from its bottom and starts moving across the ground directly toward them. There's nowhere for them to go, nowhere to hide.

"Don't move," Hawk instructs, concerned someone will run. Like frightened rabbits they freeze, afraid to breathe.

The light continues to come until the boulder they are hiding under is completely exposed. They cower in the shadow of their cover.

The machine sinks lower in the air and moves closer until the beam is focused directly on them. It stays motionless for a full minute, then the light moves quickly over the ground, back toward the machine, and goes out. It then reappears directly on them to do the same thing again . . . , again . . . , and again.

"I think they want us to follow the light to their machine. What do you think?" Cheryl notices nervously, barely whispering, her lips not moving.

"Yes, I agree. And I think we should do it quickly. It's hard to tell what they'll do if we don't," Falcon determines.

"Let's go!" Hawk says out loud.

"What about all our gear?" Millie wonders.

"Leave it. I doubt we'll have a use for it where we're going." Rose makes sense.

Even so, Falcon and Hawk pick up their handguns and stick them in their belts. Seeing that, the women do likewise.

"Ready? Let's go," Cheryl commands.

As they start to move toward the machine, the green light follows them to light the way. When they get near a foreign-looking figure with big eyes drifts down to the ground in a soft light. It directs them, one at a time, to enter the light with him. They do, and they are then gently lifted up into the flying machine. When the last soul is aboard and seated, it soars into the sky with the same speed it arrived, taking aim at a dim light on the wall of the mountain.

The five passengers do not move a muscle except for their eyes. Hearts are pounding and breathing is rapid, but they're not being threatened or harmed in any way. If it were not for the fear of the unknown sticking in their throats, they would notice the beauty and serenity of their trip. The flying machine enters the mountain through a tunnel to stop at the arrival station. There, it parks and disembarks its passengers. The two strange beings walk together to face Cheryl, bend a little at the waist, and bow their heads. Then they move away.

"They must think I'm Lilly. They think I'm Lilly. They think I'm Lilly," she says in quick succession.

"Saints preserve us. I thought we'd all be dead by now," Millie exclaims. "But I think you're right, lass. Otherwise, they would treat us like prisoners."

"Well, it makes sense. You look just like her. They brought you home, and we came along for the ride." Rose moves excitedly to Cheryl to give her a big hug.

"We're inside, can you believe it? I would have never thought of trying to get them to see you as Lilly. The good Lord is with us tonight. Thank you, Lord," Hawk cheers.

Falcon is more reserved. His logical mind sees their good fortune fading if anyone other than these creatures spots them standing around. "Move normally, but let's get out of here. They believe you're Lilly right now, but that could all change in a hurry. Come on, let's go. You lead the way, Cheryl, it'll look better that way," he instructs his friends.

"Lead the way to where?" she counters.

"Turn around and head for the door you see straight ahead of you," Falcon directs. "Keep your heads still and move along at a normal pace. We don't want them to think we're a bunch of tourists."

When Cheryl approaches the door, it opens automatically. As soon as the last person is through, it closes behind them. They are in a hallway with a flight of stairs up, and a flight of stairs down, on their right.

"Now what? We've never discussed what we'd do when we got in here. I guess this is the bridge we thought we would cross when we got to it," Rose comments seriously.

"I recall Lilly saying she went through a door near the stairs, and was able to see all the different levels. She mentioned the third and fifth floors. But we don't know if we need to go up or down until we determine what floor we're on. This first door, here on the left, let's see where it leads," Falcon surmises.

It opens easily allowing them to move through, then closes automatically behind them. The sight of long balconies, one after the other, up and up, down and down, takes a minute to be absorbed.

"It's beautiful, isn't it?" Millie sighs.

"This is it. This is what Lilly spoke about. Let's see, count the floors below us and we can tell what level we're on." Falcon moves to the edge of the open side of the hallway to lean over and look down.

"Good God, man. Get back. You'll fall over." Hawk, using a burst of speed, leaps to grab his friend by the shirt.

"I wouldn't fall too far. There's just one floor below us. That means we should be on the second floor. We need to go up one. Come on, let's get back to the steps."

Falcon turns away from the edge and walks quickly to the door. There is no knob or handle. He studies for a second, then waves his hand over the little box on the side. The door does not open. He starts to do it again, but Cheryl grabs his arm.

"No, don't. Lilly told us she had to hold her hand over a lighted ball somewhere in this building before hers would open these doors. She also said if two tries were made by someone not authorized, it would signal the guards."

"We won't need those stairs out there anyway," Hawk reports from his position near the banisters edge. "There's stairs over there, at the end of this hallway."

"Wait," Rose requests.

"Are we sure what we're looking for is on the next floor up, or should we check this one first? Look, we have to pass all these doors to get to the steps anyway. Shouldn't we check them as we go? These appear to have regular knobs on them."

She makes sense, so they check the doors as they move down the hallway. Every one is locked.

They climb the marble stairway to the next floor to find every door locked, as they were on the floor below.

"We need a better plan. It could be that all the doors on all these levels are locked all the time," Millie suggests, panting a little. "I'm a mite larger than the likes of you four. If I have to climb all these stairs, I'll be exhausted before I get to the top. There must be a better way."

"I see your point, Millie, but seeking out someone to ask directions might not be in our best interest," Rose chimes in kiddingly.

Cheryl offers the obvious. "I don't know, but perhaps we should do just that. The pilots on the aircraft think I'm Lilly, isn't it possible others will, too. Let's find somebody. You all stay out of sight and I'll ask."

"Who? We haven't seen a living thing since we left the aircraft area," Hawk reminds her.

"We'll wait. Someone has to come through one of these doors sooner or later. You all go sit on the stairs, I'll wander back and forth for a while. Let's see what happens," Cheryl commands with confidence.

Twenty minutes pass as she paces, at times, dragging her hand across the top of the banister as she moves along. "Let's give it a few more minutes," she calls rather loudly to her cohorts.

Time passes.

She's about to give up, and turns to walk to the head of the stairs when a noise from behind stops her in her tracks.

"Lilly . . . is that you?" She turns quickly, her eyes flashing here and there, looking for the origin of the voice. She spots a partly bald gray-headed man closing a door behind him, looking straight at her about fifty feet away.

"Where in the world have you been? You've had us all very concerned." He moves closer as he speaks, his voice filled with compassion.

She notices him tilting his head from side to side, and squinting his eyes trying to see more clearly as he approaches.

"Ah, oh, this doesn't look good," flashes through her mind.

"Wait a minute—you look a lot like Lilly, but you're not her, are you? Who are you, and what are you doing here?" His voice moves from one of wonderment to demanding an answer.

"I'm Lilly, I've changed a little since we last saw each other," she stutters. "You know, my hair, and my clothes."

"Don't give me that hogwash. You look enough like her to be her twin, but you're not Lilly. Now answer my questions, or I'll have to call security. Who are you, and what are you doing here? How did you get in here?"

Cheryl feels it is pointless to try to carry this charade any further. At the same time, the effects of exposure and vulnerability allow inadequacy to set in. She needs help.

Her four sidekicks have heard everything, and are cautiously trying to get a glimpse of the man whose voice echoes through the compound.

She steps backward making it look like she is about to turn and run, causing the man to come at her more aggressively. She stops when she's able to see her friends, all sitting, hiding behind the banister, then gives a wave of her arm, signaling them to come to her aide.

The four of them rise and run up the few steps, thinking the worst.

The man stops in his tracks, raises his wrist close to his mouth and says, almost shouting.

"Security! Level E immediately! Intruders! Imminent danger!"

The four surround Lilly and quickly survey the situation.

"Take him," Falcon orders, his gun in his hand, shielding Cheryl.

The others surround the man before he realizes what's happening. He raises his hands over his head not wanting to escalate matters any more than they are.

"Don't hurt me! Just tell me what you want!" The man urgently surrenders.

"We're not going to hurt anybody unless we have to," Hawk assures their prisoner.

"I'm Lilly's husband. We want to speak with her for a few minutes, that's all. This is her sister Cheryl, and three of our friends." Falcon informs the man.

"You're Falcon?" the man asks in surprise.

"That's right."

"And you—you're her twin sister, our Amber?"

"Yes, I am."

"Whooeee! You don't know how glad I am to hear that," the man says in relief and lowers his arms.

The next few seconds is filled with confusion as no less than fifteen security guards appear from the floor below, to circle and train their weapons on the intruders.

All five fill their hands with a gun, hammers back.

"Stop! Stop!" the gray-haired man yells. "Everybody, lower your guns."

After looking each other over carefully, both sides cautiously ease their weapons down and relax.

"Thank you for your fast response, but I can see now that these people are our friends." The man dismisses his security people.

"My name is Remsar," he says as the heavily armed group disperses. "Come with me please, here, to my office."

"I'm sorry to put you through that, but I had no idea who you were. I hope you understand. How did you get in here anyway?" He continues into his office and sits behind his desk. He motions the rest to relax on the other chairs, and for Millie to shut the door.

"Let's just say it wasn't easy," Falcon answers. "We didn't think you would welcome us, besides, we have no idea of the location of the front door."

"I see, I believe you, but I'm not able to grant your wish to speak with Lilly. Obviously, you haven't heard, she isn't here. She disappeared about six weeks ago, and as yet, we've not been able to locate her. May I ask, what is so desperately important to bring you here at such a great risk? Perhaps I can help you," Remsar addresses the entire group.

"Are we prisoners?" Hawk barks, ignoring the question.

"If you mean, can you leave when you want—you're not a prisoner. If you mean, can you search our facility for Lilly, well then, I'm sorry, but I cannot allow that. But believe me as I believe you, if I knew where she is, I wouldn't stand in your way at all. She can come and go as she pleases. She can see who she wants to see, with no interference from anyone. When I say we're gravely concerned about her safety, I mean it in the strongest sense. There are many people in this world who will harm her." Remsar tells the truth, and realizes if these people have any information about the angels, the only way he will get it is through cooperation, not force.

"What can we do to help find her?" Cheryl asks.

Her inquiry leads the Company official to fully explain the events leading up to Lilly's kidnapping, her escape, and her disappearance from her quarters.

"So, you see, presently, I'm at a loss to know what anybody can do. The world is a big place, and once she passes through a mirror, she can be anywhere in a few seconds," he finishes.

"May we see her quarters?" Falcon asks, thinking he'll feel closer to his wife there.

"Certainly, but I doubt it will offer you much. It's more of a working home than a family-homey place. We'll go there in a few minutes.

"Aaa, may I ask the names of your three friends," he asks politely.

"I'm sorry," Falcon leads off. "This is Hawk and his wife Rose. We're friends from La Nesra. And this is Millie O'Toole, our friend from the Anderson farm."

"Are you the Rose I've heard about? Are you able to change your appearance at will to resemble someone else?" he inquires unexpectedly.

Her eyes widen at the attention and recognition.

"Yes."

"And you're Hawk, the fastest man alive." The Company chief grins as he speaks.

Hawk nods his head. "Yep."

"And what is your forte, Millie?"

"Awww, they brought me along for the rough stuff. You know, to break some bones, or cut off a finger or toe, if it comes to it, that sort of thing. Ha! Ha! Ha!" She laughs and points her finger at Remsar. He picks up on her jest and laughs with her.

"Actually, I'm sort of the navigator of the bunch. I spent some time asea and learned a bit about it from the best teachers there are. Tars are a rowdy bunch, but they do know the ways of the big water, and taught me a lot about people in the process." She goes on more than she should.

"You've all given me something to think about. Let's walk up to Lilly's quarters while I run it through my mind," Remsar suggests and leads the way.

He doesn't say much and pays little attention to the back-and-forth conversation among the five with him. The lift that takes them up six floors amazes them.

His key turns, and with the twist of the knob, he pushes the door open, then motions, inviting everyone to enter.

His mind is somewhere else and it's apparent to the visitors.

Falcon waves his hand in front of their host's eyes. "Hey, are you in there?" he kids.

The older man's senses bring his attention to the present. "Sorry, help yourselves. Look around all you like. When you're finished come in here and take a seat. I have an idea that might have some merit."

The search party does exactly that. When they finish looking, they're sure there is no clue to Lilly's whereabouts in these quarters. In fact, just as he said, there's nothing to prove she has ever been here.

"What's your idea?" Hawk is first to ask as they gather to listen.

"We must all agree that no matter what our differences might be, one thing we have in common is Lilly's whereabouts and safety. Am I right? And we must all believe she is still alive?"

Affirmative responses.

"It will take longer than some of us can tolerate to locate her the way things are right now. We need to shake things up. We need to add some confusion to her abductor's plan. We need them to believe they might have the wrong woman."

"How can we do that? We don't know who, or where they are," Rose interrupts.

"Let him continue. He's headed somewhere," Falcon responds.

"Well, it occurs to me that I have two potential Lillys here in this room with me right now. If we make a few changes in their appearance, no one will know the difference. I'm referring you to Rose, with your abilities, and, of course, you Cheryl. We can make Lilly appear in two different places at the same time. We can make it seem as though you have her powers.

"With Hawk's speed, we can make objects seem to move from one place to another by themselves. Everyone in this compound will believe Lilly has returned."

"Okay, I can see where you're headed, but remember, Cheryl tried to imitate Sheree and failed at the attempt once already. Even if we put that aside, what good is it to us if we can pull it off.?" Falcon reasons.

"I can assure you, her captors have spies here amongst us. They'll get the word back to wherever she's being held. If we can give them reason to believe they don't have the right person, they'll have to come to take a look for themselves." Remsar makes his point.

"And we'll be ready for them when they get here," Millie cheers the idea.

"It might take quite a while for all this to work, wouldn't you say?" Cheryl poses.

"It will take the time it takes. Although I doubt it will take all that long, especially, if Lilly hasn't given herself away to them. She's been trained to deny, deny, deny, if she's caught. Our charade could add immensely to her credibility with them."

"How will we set up security? I mean, we got in here. This is a big place?"

"How can we possibly sort out who's supposed to be here or not?

"Haven't the guards already seen you two? Didn't you identify yourselves to them? They know who you are."

"So these villains come here, and we catch them. Then what? We still won't know any more than we do right now."

"Questions. Questions. These are all good questions. I didn't say I have all the answers right now. But keep thinking—write them down so we'll overlook nothing. We'll find answers and solutions to all our problems as we go along."

"From your response, I believe you're all behind the idea. Am I right?" Remsar urges a positive response.

Meanwhile, on the east coast.

John Anderson and his daughter Charlotte have spent weeks digging through piles of paper with bits of information from their agents in the field, putting pressure through the proper channels for more. Their successes have been small, and the task seemingly has no end. They sit in the kitchen of the small home they have rented in Baltimore, discussing the situation. John has decided to go home for a two or three week visit, leaving Charlotte to continue the search for information regarding Sheree's purpose with the Company.

"I know you feel like you're deserting me, Daddy, but I think you need to take a break and go home. A few weeks away from here will give you a whole different outlook."

"I don't like the idea of you here alone with all this responsibility," he counters.

"Mr. Schoener is here, and what about all the other people, they'll still be here. If anything happens, someone will protect me from what ever it is. Go on," she continues.

Tap. Tap. Tap.

Charlotte rises to answer the knock on their door.

"Morning, Charlotte, has John left yet?" Marty Schoener asks earnestly.

"No, he's in the kitchen. Come on in. Would you like a cup of coffee?"

"Coffee sounds good, thanks."

"Morning, John, I'm glad you're still here. We finally have some news," Marty begins, as he sits at the table. Charlotte places a mug of steaming liquid in front of him.

"The reason we've heard nothing from La Nesra for so long is that the gates have been locked for security reasons. No one has been able to get in or out, and that includes our people there. But our agent in Atlanta has been able to connect with one of our people inside the walls and came up with some interesting news. Listen to this.

"First of all, Sally, Robert, Randy, and a fellow named Vaughn are all under guard—restricted to their quarters—have been for a month. Do you remember a fellow named Tyrone Black? He's the stranger at the sheriff's office that day you shot the deputy," he asks John.

"Yes, he's also Charles Housler's son," John reminds everyone.

"I remember him, too," Charlotte adds.

"Well, he's the honcho giving the orders. Word is he's going to keep them prisoner until he locates the death angels, which apparently have been missing for some time. He believes they know where they are. Our people on the inside are concerned he'll act irrationally and hurt someone if he doesn't learn something before long."

"They think he might torture them?" Charlotte's temper takes over.

"That, or—I really hate to say this—he might use someone close to them to make them talk."

"Someone like Selma, or Elizabeth, at the farm," John stirs.

"Or your baby granddaughter," John's next in command contends.

John's brow wrinkles at the suggestion. "Our agent is part of their security there, isn't he? This is good information, is it not?" he implores.

"He's their director of security. He wouldn't pass this along unless he thought there's good reason," Marty assures.

"Damn! He could have someone on their way to the farm right now, or for that matter, they could already be there." Joie's Grandfather sinks in his chair.

"There's more," the early morning messenger continues.

"Regarding Sheree's efforts for the Company and the proof we're looking for." John's good friend pulls some papers from his breast pocket. "These are hand written copies of a few pages that have been cut out of a book. They found them at La Nesra, but there's no sign of the book they came from. They couldn't remove the actual pages from where they found them, so they copied everything over onto these here. I've gone over them briefly, and I have to say, they're inconclusive. I can see where it could be construed that Sheree is what they say, but without the rest of the book, to me, these prove nothing."

"Let me see." Charlotte takes the pages from him. "This is some other kind of language. What is it? I can make out some of the words, but some of them . . . ?"

"English has changed a great deal over the years. If you take your time, you'll be able to get the idea from them. If you look you'll notice they're numbered at the bottom. The numbers skip around making it apparent the pages have been removed from various places throughout a book. One thing we know for sure is, these are the pages that started our search for the truth in the first place," he finishes by picking up his cup for a sip.

"In any case, I have a strong need to get to the farm now. Do you mind if I take these with me?" John determines and takes the pages from Charlotte.

"Want me to go with you?" Marty offers.

"I think the best place for you right now is here. But thanks, I appreciate the offer."

"Why not take a few of our men with you. It won't hurt us here at all, and I'd be a whole lot more comfortable about it. You don't know what you might get into." John's second in command persists.

"I don't think—" He's interrupted by his daughter's loud voice.

"Dammit, Daddy, don't be so bullheaded. People worry about you, can't you see that. Now, you take Mr. Schoener up on his offer and thank him for it, or, so help me, I'll go with you, and it won't be a pleasant trip."

"I can have them here in thirty minutes," Marty adds.

John nods his head yes, but he doesn't want any fuss made over him.

"I'll take two. Will that make you both happy?"

"I'll be back in thirty minutes. They'll be ready to move when we get here." Marty gets up from the table and leaves before anybody can say any more about it.

"Let's get a look at these pages while we're waiting." Charlotte gets her daddy's mind off what just happened.

Thirty minutes pass quickly.

Rap. Rap. Rap.

"That must be Marty, back already. Give me a hug, honey. I'll send a telegram if there's any problems at the farm. If I don't, everything's all right."

"Okay, you be careful. Tell everybody I miss them, and I love them," she calls, as he walks through the front door.

He stops in his tracks on the front porch. "Didn't I say two, or have I forgotten how to count." Charlotte hears him say, then moves to a window to look out. There's Mr. Schoener and four other men.

"They come in a set of four, and I didn't want to break them up."

While this is going on at Canozira and Baltimore, the four being held prisoner at La Nesra are getting antsy. They have been under guard for over thirty days now. Ty opens the door to their quarters without knocking to find them sitting at the table eating their noon meal. He's dressed in black, as usual, but is not wearing his ever-present guns and holsters. He enters and saunters toward the table.

"I'm going to try to talk some sense into your heads. I know you don't want to be treated this way, and I don't like doing it. But I need some information. All you have to do is tell me everything you know about Lilly's disappearance, and the whereabouts of the angels. Tell me that and you're free." He comes right to the point.

Mr. Vaughn's eyes flit around to each of his fellow prisoners. Inside his body he feels an energy building. He's not sure what, but something is about to happen, and for once, he has done his part, and is ready for retribution.

"I can't wait any longer. If I leave this room empty-handed, the first thing I'm going to do is go to Atlanta and visit a few of your friends. I'll start with the father and son at the livery. Oh, I see by your faces, you didn't think I knew about them. I can be very persuasive when I have to be. You see, I don't need them. I can be as insistent as necessary, and if they don't tell me about the craft coming from the sky carrying a certain cargo of boxes, then I'll move on to another of your friends. Get the picture."

Sally looks at Robert and Randy, then back at Ty.

"Those people can't tell you something they don't know. You'll probably kill them, and they won't be able to stop you, unless they lie. I know I'd lie if you hurt me."

"Are you saying you know something they don't?" Ty insists.

"I'm saying, how can anyone answer a question when they don't have the information? I don't have the information you're looking for, so I'm sitting here in prison. I've been here over a month. I'll tell you a lie if you promise to set me free." Her tone is arrogant and teasing.

"Shut your smart mouth!" he shouts. "After Atlanta, I plan to take a trip to the Anderson farm. I'll continue my questioning there. If I get nothing from the adults, I'll bring a few of the children back here, and let you watch when I question them."

"You wouldn't do that. What are you, some kind of animal? You don't have the brains of an imbecile," she sasses. "Did you hear me? You're an idiot! You're a fool!" she shouts.

He storms at her with a vicious look on his face.

"I'll shut your filthy mouth for good!" he yells and grabs her by the arms to fling her in the air across the room.

He turns toward her, his face red and twisted, snarling through his teeth, and runs at her again. Furniture, anything in his way goes flying aside or crashes under the weight of his heavy legs.

"You don't know me! Nobody knows me!" he continues to scream at the top of his lungs.

Sally is in a daze trying to find a way to defend herself when he pounces on her again. He picks her up by the front of her dress with his left hand. Then, the fist of his right hand slams into her jaw just below her eye. Unconscious, she drops like a dead weight, her head smashes into the carpet with a loud thud.

Robert and Randy both reach him at the same time, but too late to stop the first fist. They wrestle him to the floor, and hold him down. Still he continues to scream.

"You people are the imbeciles of the world! You're all stupid to think you can outwit me! I'll show you all! One day I'll rule this world! Then you'll all come begging for my favors! My father will be proud of me then! He'll wish he had stood up for me, and took care of me when I was small! He'll be sorry he let them take me away!"

His screaming settles when the guards appear to pull the two young men off him. He collects himself, runs his hands over his face and through his hair, then turns to face the two men.

"You tell that crazy bitch she just moved things up a notch. Forget Atlanta, I'm going to the farm first. Did you hear me?"

Unexpected by all, Sally's voice is heard.

"I heard you," she says scornfully. "I don't want you to hurt those children, so I'll show you where the death angels are. But you have to take me with you—me, Robert and Randy."

Ty snorts a short chuckle. "See what I mean, you're all alike. You fool with me, you'll find out what pain is all about. Then all you want is for it to stop. You'll do anything to get it to stop—anything. Do you know the difference between you and me? I don't care about the pain. You can cut my leg off with a dull knife, it makes no difference to me. I've learned to not let pain overcome my will to succeed. That's why I'll never fail, and that's why I'll lead the world one day. I'll send you all to hell if that's what it takes. I'll give you a day to lick your wounds. We'll leave the day after tomorrow. The three of you, four guards, and me."

"And you, old man." He points to Mr. Vaughn. "I'll deal with you when we get back."

With that he barges through the door, bounces off the left side of the jam, and stumbles heavily down the steps.

Mr. Vaughn moves to the doorway to see if he's gone and not lingering just outside. "He's an animal of the worse kind. If I was younger I'd split his head with something. You shouldn't have talked to him that way, Sally—now look what he's done to you," he clamors

Sally gets to her knees, then with a struggle, forces herself to her feet. "When are you going to wake up? Can't you see? Don't you have any pride left? He treats you like dirt on his boots. If I ever met a living puppet in my life, it's you. You're not like him—you could never be like him. Deep inside you're a decent human being, but, you try to be tough and mean to please him. Why?"

"To stay alive, that's why," he cuts her off and retorts quickly.

"After all these years, if I tried to change, I'd have to kill him—or he'd kill me. You saw him a few minutes ago. A wild man crazed with frustration. Get a look in a mirror, look at what he did to your face. Think of how little it took for him to lose control. He's worse than this when he gets really angry. You're a fool for provoking him."

"I did what needed to be done. Listen to me. We all know you're his spy. You've already proven to us that you can't be trusted. I don't know what he meant about dealing with you when he gets back, but I expect it won't be anything pleasant. One thing's for sure, if he decides to kill you there's no one to stop him. And here's the sad part of it all, I know you'll be here. You'll take whatever he dishes out. One day you'll be put in a box, and stuffed into the ground. There'll be no marker for your name. Whatever legacy you have will be buried with you, and forgotten when the last shovel of dirt hits your grave." Sally boldly continues to bash the once-respected, now-downtrodden man.

"Let me clean my face a little, then I need to talk to you two," she tells the two men who pulled Ty off her, then moves toward her sleeping area.

Her two friends stand looking at each other not knowing what to say. Mr. Vaughn moves to the farthest corner he can find, dragging a straight chair with him, and there he sits, elbows on his knees, head in his hands, facing the wall.

Sally returns in a few minutes to huddle with her comrades at the opposite side of the large room.

"Keep your voices down. That was more brutal than I expected, but I had to do something to get us out of here. We stand a good chance of getting away from him outside these walls, and that was the only way I could think of to do it," she confides.

"I'll say it was brutal," Randy sympathizes.

"Are you going to be all right?" Robert shows his concern.

"I will, once the swelling goes down." She smiles carefully, and chuckles softly. "He was going to the farm with or without us, so at least we have a chance to stop him. We'll watch for our opening, then do what needs to be done. Agreed?"

"What about him?" Randy points over his shoulder at Mr. Vaughn.

"Let him work out his own problems. We won't be welcome here after this, so, there's not much we can do anyhow," she states confidently.

The following day passes peacefully. Mr. Vaughn is nowhere to be seen. But, the threesome noticed Ty walking past their quarters in the early afternoon.

They're up and ready to move out before daylight the next morning, bringing everything they need with them. They'll not be back here regardless of what happens. A guard trounces up the steps just at daybreak to announce their departure. Their baggage and supplies are loaded and tied down on to one of the several packhorses.

"Looks like we're going all the way by horseback," Robert mumbles to Randy.

"Yeah. Looks that way," he replies without his lips moving.

"Look over there." Sally nods her head in the direction.

There sits Mr. Vaughn on horseback trying his best not to look at them. There are Ty, three guards, and him. It appears Ty has traded one of the four guards he talked about for the long-time Company servant. No greetings are traded this morning. As soon as the supplies are secured, everybody mounts and moves out with Mr. Black at the lead.

John Anderson, with his four guards, moves along steadily with their horses at a trot. They're traveling light allowing them to move across country. This way, verses using rail to get closer before using horses, will cut at least a day and a half off the their trek. He has plenty of time to think.

"It won't be long now. Maybe I'll be able to get his rock out of the pit of my stomach once I'm home and know everything's all right." His memory of past events creeps in, keeping his nerves on edge. "Almost everybody at the farm knows by now where the boxes are hidden. I couldn't blame any of them for telling if it meant harm would come to one of their children. Aaah, everything's probably all right. I'm spooking myself for no good reason." His mind turns it over and over.

"What I should probably do is move the arsenal somewhere else. Somewhere only I know about. That way they would have to get it out of me. But what would they do to our people then, if they couldn't find their death angels? Is it worth it? On the one hand, some of our people, or their children, could get hurt. Word from Marty is that it could be Joie. Selma would die protecting that child. Then there's Elizabeth, Nora, and Sherman.

Robert and Randall, she would never forgive me if anything happened to them." He's unaware of things around him, his horse plods along, following the two men in front.

"On the other hand, if the arsenal is what they say it is, the rest of the world could be a whole lot worse off a few years down the road. I promised a lot of people I would hide and protect those boxes until I heard otherwise from them," he ponders.

"Lord . . ." He raises his head toward the sky. "I could use your help right now. What should I do? Is it right to put all this on one man?" No sooner do his soft words escape his lips than an echo goes through his head.

"You know what you must do. It will be the right decision."

Selma and Elizabeth are in the coop near the main barn, gathering eggs and feeding chickens when five men are spotted coming over the rise toward the homestead.

"Riders coming, Miss Elizabeth!" a nearby hand speaks loudly.

The leader of the men on horseback urges his horse ahead when he sees the two women coming out the door.

"It's John! He's home," Selma yells for all to hear. Charlotte has sent a wire from Baltimore letting her know he's on his way.

After greeting each other with handshakes, hugs, and appropriate kisses all around, the new arrivals are moved to the kitchen for a good hot cup of coffee and a slab of pie. The conversation surrounds family and farm matters. Elizabeth and Nora make sure his guards have accommodations, and begin a quick tour of the area, leaving Selma and John to themselves.

"Tyrone Black was here," she calmly relates.

John's head snaps up from his coffee mug to look her in the eyes.

"Relax, he barely got off his horse. We were never in any danger. He wanted to know if we had seen Sheree, said she is missing and they have no idea where she might be. I told him we haven't seen her, and that the rest of the people from La Nesra were on their way back to Atlanta. He got on his horse and left."

"What else did he say?"

"Not much, thanked us and left. He wasn't here ten minutes. We weren't at all hospitable, though. Elizabeth and I met him out front before he got down, her with a shotgun and me with a rifle. Two of our hands walked up behind him, close enough to get their hands on him if need be. Haven't seen or heard from him since."

"Thank God for that. You did the right thing by showing him you're not afraid to face what comes. He'll remember that." John needlessly supports her actions.

He fills her in on the information Marty related before he left Baltimore for home.

"So, as you can see, he's holding them prisoners and then, to make a threat toward Joie, he's coming to the end of his choices. He'll be back, frustrated, looking for the arsenal, and Sheree—or a fight."

"Well, all I can say is, if he's looking for a fight, we'll give him one," she exclaims when she hears Joie's name. "I guess that's why you brought help?" Her statement accents into a question.

He nods yes, not mentioning they were forced upon him.

"Did he say anything about the arsenal?" he asks.

"No, not a word."

"That means he's not sure they're here, but sooner or later our people will have to lead him here. Sally's been their agent for years, and if it's one thing you teach your agents it's when you're taken prisoner, get outside of your constraints any way you can. In her case, she'll probably get them to bring her and our two boys, out from behind those walls at La Nesra. She knows they'll have to get out in the open if they're going to escape." John educates his close female friend.

"More coffee?" she offers.

"A half a cup," he responds, as she caresses his hand before taking his mug.

"You know, Selma, I've been thinking about you a lot lately." His words, spoken toward her back as she leaves to get his coffee, cause her to stop and turn. She freezes with a feeling if she moves he will not continue. He looks from her face to his folded hands on the table, as if thinking, but inside he knows what he wants to say. It's just that he doesn't want to see her hurt any more in her life, and getting close to him could do just that.

The silence is killing her, she wants to move toward him, but that might push him the wrong way. It's best to give him whatever time he needs. Don't move. Don't say anything.

"Well, I've been thinking," he finally divulges. "I'm not getting any younger, and we're both lonely . . ." He stops again.

She can't take it any more, a quick move puts her on her knees, sitting on her heels at his side. She pulls at his arm to make him turn to face her. Not knowing what else to do, she lays her head on his thigh.

He puts one of his hands on her hair, the other gently on her cheek.

"Say it, John. Say it," she begs in her mind.

"It's getting so I think a lot about you and me together. Me touching you, holding you. I lie awake at night thinking how it would be—you and me together," he whispers.

She raises her face to him.

"Oh, John, me too."

"The thing is, are you sure it's what you want? With everything that's going on, are you sure you want to get yourself that close to anyone right now? After all you've been through? Something could happen and cause you to get hurt all over again."

"You and I both have been through a lot these last few years, and we can't change any of it. We'll carry those precious memories to our graves, never forgetting. But I'd rather have those memories than nothing at all, and I wouldn't have them if I hadn't lived through it. You and I can make memories, too. We can have whatever's left of our lives to build on what we have now. There were no guarantees back then, and there's none now, but that's no reason to stop living. You and me together, that's a good reason to start living again," she softly reasons.

She sees water pooling in his eyes, causing hers to do the same.

"Dammit, John." She throws caution to the wind and rises to sit on his lap, putting her face just inches from his. "Don't you love me? If you do, kiss me. Kiss me now."

An urgent tickling feeling starts in his stomach and races through his body. A feeling he has not had since the last time he made love to his darling June. Selma is in his arms—he's kissing her.

Kissing John in this way is everything Selma thought it would be. It makes her whole body weaken and takes her breath away. She lets go of the fear of losing him and sinks deeper into his arms. Slowly, softly, with the slightest whimper, she surrenders to his mounting needs.

He feels her nestling closer and closer, her breasts pressing against his chest. The urge moving through his body becomes more and more difficult to control. He puts his arm around her back, placing his hand on her trim waist. His other arm moves under her legs, behind her knees. He lifts; she moves up seeming as light as a feather. He's on his feet, out of the kitchen to the stairs, up the steps, lips against lips, kissing harder and harder, into the main bedroom. He kicks the door with the heel of his boot to slam it shut, then lays her gently on the bed.

"Are you sure?" he breathes, as they pull away just enough to take a breath.

"I'm sure."

Elizabeth, Joie, Nora, Sherman, and baby Randy Junior, along with the farm's two foremen are at the breakfast table when John and Selma appear.

"Sleep good you two?" Beth asks cheerfully.

"I'll say," Selma replies and exhibits a quick wink.

John smiles, a little bashful.

Knowing how her close friend feels about John, Elizabeth can't hold back. She's up from the table and runs to give her, and him, a big hug. "It's about time you two figured out something the rest of us have known for a long time. We saw the door shut, so we kept the children down here," she continues quietly so the youngsters won't hear.

"Anybody hungry?" Nora offers, knowing the response.

"I could eat a bear, fur coat and all." The smiling John is quick to answer, and moves ahead toward the table.

Elizabeth holds Selma back a little to whisper in her ear. "Did he ask you?"

"First things first, one thing at a time," she replies in her ear.

Others at the table move over to allow the couple to sit together. Both are relieved that the present family approves of their decision.

A hearty breakfast is enjoyed by all, while their conversation encompasses daily life and concerns around the farm. It's not long before those with chores and responsibilities leave the table, taking the children with them, leaving the new couple alone.

An empty cup clicks when it settles onto the saucer from John's hand.

"There's a few things I need to attend to for a couple of days, honey," he addresses his newly acclaimed love. "I'd rather not say what they are right now, mainly because knowing might bring a lot of trouble down on you, and for security reasons. But I'll be gone for a couple of days."

Selma is still floating from last night. She can hardly believe everything she has prayed for has come about. “The guards are going with you, right?” she wonders.

“No, that’s just it—I need to do this alone.”

“You go do what you need to and come home to me safely.” She rises from her seat to plant a little kiss her man’s cheek, not wanting to create a fuss. But she understands now, more than ever before, John is known for his effort with the Sons. There is many a man out there that would like to get him in their sights, especially the loyalists of the Company.

In the meantime, Tyrone Black’s group plods toward the Anderson farm.

Ty has elected to make the trip by horseback, not wanting to give his prisoners the opportunity of having a lot of people around to help in their escape. Nobody says much. Each rider is left to their own thoughts, at least until they settle down for the night. Then a few things are said by necessity, but there’s nothing jovial about it. The prisoners are kept away from each other as much as possible, especially at night, giving them no chance to arrange a plan, let alone an escape. Leg irons with long chains connect them each to a guard’s leg before they settle down, complicating any attempt to run. The three lie in wait for their captors to make a mistake. They would rather slip away at night, but it appears the daylight hours will be their only chance.

Sally’s face is black and blue, her eye swollen shut. It must be painful, but she doesn’t let it show. She has her hair pulled over that side of her face to keep it shaded from the sun. She continues to think. “Maybe we should work to give just one of us a chance to escape. If two of us distract our jailers for a few seconds, one of us might get away. But who? Certainly not me, I’d be lost in these woods forever. Robert probably has more savvy to travel by himself, mainly the direction to go, more so than Randy.” She tries to logically work out a plan. “I need a few minutes with them to coordinate. That means I have to get Ty to put us together and make it his idea, or make it look natural, not planned.”

The string of horses and their loads move at a quick trot, one trailing after the other across a valley of wild wheat.

Sally, riding third in line behind Ty and Mr. Vaughn, begins to sway more and more on her saddle. Robert, next in line, sees she’s going to fall from her horse, and kicks his horse’s sides. The suddenness of the movement gets Randy’s attention, as well as the three guards, who spur their horses to thwart a possible attempt to escape.

She leaves her saddle on the left side, her arms flailing limply at nothing, making no attempt to break her fall, to hit the ground on her side more toward her back. The impact forces air from her lungs though her vocal chords to make an involuntary noise.

“Uuuhhh!”

Robert is off his horse and to her side within a few seconds with Randy right behind him. He bends down and lifts her to a sitting position with his left arm behind her back, her head stretching her neck backward. He puts his right arm around to hold her up until he can slide his forearm up her back to bring her face up close to his.

"Get ready to make a break for it. The first chance we get where there's some cover for you to get away, Randy and I will get their attention. I'll put my arm up, when I take it down, make your move. Get to the farm and tell them," she whispers as if these words are her last.

Randy is at their side now.

"Did you hear that?" he quickly asks his lifelong friend.

"No."

"You two are going to draw their attention so I can get away. I'll head for the farm. Figure out what you're going to do, then wait for her to raise her arm up over her head, move when she takes it down," Robert says softly, swiftly, with one breath.

"Got it," he acknowledges just before Ty and one of the guards pull him away.

"She must be hurt more than we thought," young Mr. Anderson suggests. "That hit you gave her must have rattled her brain or something."

Ty stoops down beside the pair.

"How bad is it, Sally?" he asks with disgust.

She turns her face toward him rolling her eyes and squinting like she's unable to focus her vision. "I'm okay, I just got real dizzy for a minute. I need some cool water to wipe my face." She struggles to reply.

"Can you travel?" he urges, with no emotion for her condition.

"I think so. Just give me a few minutes."

"Help her up," he orders the guard and Robert.

"Let her be—I'll get her," Robert snaps. "You've got to stop doing this or you're going to kill yourself." He manages to say under his breath as he lifts her to her feet.

"Your job is to get away, don't worry about me," she murmurs back.

He gets a canteen from her horse, wets a kerchief and hands it to her. She carefully, gently, wipes her tender face. Then he lifts her up to mount her horse.

Another few miles pass before Sally notices a spot ahead that might work with her plan. The trail narrows with a big boulder on the right side and a drop off of some fifteen feet on the left.

"I'll wait until Robert and I clear the narrow part, then I'll run straight at the two ahead of me. That way, Randy can bottle up the three guards behind him. Robert can squeeze by on the left."

As she passes the large rock, she turns in her saddle to see the young Mr. Anderson directly behind her, as if he has read her mind.

A hand in the air, a quick hard kick at her horse's sides, her arm comes down, and she's moving directly at Mr. Vaughn.

Her horse's shoulder hits his left leg before he has a chance to think. His horse whinnies and rears up to its right, almost losing its feet, throwing him into the air.

She continues toward Ty, he's turning his horse to look back. Her horse hits his broadside at the left front shoulder, the unexpected force pushes it sideways, off its feet, causing it to fall on its side.

She feels the wind off Robert as he whizzes past the confusion, catching a glimpse of him bent over close to his horse's neck, slapping the reins at its hindquarters.

Fortunately for Ty, he's thrown clear of his falling horse. Men have been killed beneath their fallen animals.

Her mount is out of control. It knows this is not a normal thing to do, and wants to get away from it in the worst of ways. She tries to rein him in but he's having no part of that. He tears out at full speed, chasing after Robert.

Amidst all of this, Randy has created his own diversion. He catches the guards unaware when he turns back to dash directly at them. Two of them react with their horses to tumble down the embankment, and the third's frightened animal rears up to put its rider into the air, before turning and running back the way it came.

When Randy spins back to see both his friends make their getaway, he notices Ty, along with Mr. Vaughn, on the ground, and decides he's not being left behind. His heels find their mark on his horse. He feels the power as the animal's loins tense, then air hits his face and hat as he streaks past the last threat to stop him.

During the time this is happening, Remsar has decided he needs Ty back at Canozira. He realizes if he is successful and attracts Lilly's abductors with his two make believe models of her, he will need someone to backtrack them through the mirror.

He normally doesn't take on a mission such as this himself, but because of the circumstances, he rides a flying machine to La Nesra during the night to get his cohort and take him back to Canozira.

"Are you sure they went to the Anderson's farm?" he questions the director of security, feeling disappointment.

"Yes, sir, I am. He believes the death angels are hidden there somewhere."

"Well, we need him at Canozira. He can do that another time. I'm going there to find him, but if something happens he comes back here before I see him, explain, and tell him to wait here for me. It won't take long for me to get there and back."

Chapter Thirty-Eight

He has not looked back since he escaped.

A mile or so behind, he left two of his friends while he tries to distance himself from Ty, Mr. Vaughn, and their guards. His horse's mouth is wide open, his tongue hanging out, dangling, several inches below his chin. The white lather forming on the sorrel hair of his chest and shoulders, and heavy panting, tells Robert he will not be able to push his animal this hard much longer. He turns on his saddle to glance back over his left shoulder. There's a lone horse and rider, keeping pace but not gaining. He turns to face front, then he swings around again for a second look. "It's Sally!" he yells out loud. He looks back beyond her to see no one.

His horse slows when he tugs gently on the reins and comes to a stop, waiting for his friend to catch up. Still caught up in the moment, his steed prances around excitedly, while being controlled by the reins. It takes only moments for Sally to arrive and pull her horse to a stop beside him, both look back from where they came.

"What happened?" he says with wonderment.

"I'm not to sure. My horse got a mind of his own and bolted. When I realized I could get away, I just kept on coming," she exclaims panting, more loudly than needed.

"Randy?" One word with the proper accent is all that is needed.

"I don't know, I didn't think to see." She hates to admit.

"Uh, oh, here they come! I see one of them!" she continues, and pulls her reins to head her horse away from the incoming threat.

"Wait! That looks like—! It is! That's Randy! He made it! Hot damn, he made it!" Robert shouts.

In the course of everything that has happened, and the bleak outlook of what might come, Remsar, waiting for darkness so he can travel to the Anderson farm, takes a long look at his position. He changes his clothes to blend with the garb of the area of the country. "I don't know what I'm going to find when I get there. Ty's the only one who knows who I am. The only thing either of us wants is information about Lilly and the angels. I hope he hasn't already confronted them with hostility. The smell of bull shit attracts more flies than the stench of burnt gunpowder any day," he muses looking at himself in a full length mirror, feeling confident.

Time passes.

John opens the screen door leading into the kitchen at the Andersons' farm calling out a cheery "I'm home!"

Selma is the first to meet him at the doorway from the kitchen to the hallway. She flings herself at him with a tight hug and kiss.

"I'm glad you're home safe and sound," she says quietly, still in his arms.

"You're all I've thought about since I've been gone. I couldn't wait to get back," he breathes in her ear.

Elizabeth and Nora appear with a gray-headed, well-dressed man close behind them. They both give him a welcome home hug, then turn to see Selma standing beside the stranger.

"John, I want you to meet the Reverend George Remsar. Reverend, let me introduce my dearest friend, John Anderson." She beams, being careful not to appear to assume too much about their love relationship.

John smiles and puts his hand in that of the Reverend's.

"Don't misunderstand my interest, may I call you John?" The clergyman is the first to speak.

John nods his head yes.

"But unless these old eyes misinform me, you appear to be more than just good friends. Am I right?"

John and Selma chuckle at the same time.

"You can," he replies. "Fact is, I love this woman with all my heart, and she says she feels the same about me."

Unable to stop herself, Selma grabs her man again and gives him another kiss, right there in front of the professed servant of God.

"What brings you way out here, Reverend?" he inquires, when Selma relaxes and pulls away.

"He's looking for a good place to start a church," Nora speaks up, sort of surprising everyone.

"Yes, he wondered in here yesterday, on foot, with no more than the clothes on his back. He didn't want to intrude but we insisted he stay here for the night," Elizabeth explains.

"I would hope so," John agrees. "How did you get yourself into a fix like this?"

"Well, as I explained to the ladies, I was confronted two days ago by several men who apparently needed everything I had worse than I. I didn't resist them, and they didn't hurt me. After they left, I started walking until I saw smoke over the horizon, which turned out to be your hands burning off brush. They directed me here to your home. I certainly do appreciate your hospitality. I'd like to repay you somehow, but, obviously, at the moment, other than my bible—which they let me keep—I don't have much in the way of material things," Reverend Remsar relates in a sober, humble manner.

"Don't worry about it. You're welcome here as long as you want to stay." Nora puts her hand on his shoulder and extends an invitation.

"She's right, Reverend, we'd like that. Besides, you might have more to offer than you think." John catches Selma's eye and winks.

For a moment, she doesn't know what to think, then it hits home.

"A-a-a-a-a-are you saying what I think you're saying?" she stutters cautiously.

"It looks like I am—if you'll have me." He grins and removes all doubt from her mind.

"Yes! Yes! Yes!" she screams and leaps into his arms almost knocking him backward. "I'll marry you. I'll marry you today."

Elizabeth and Nora run to the happy pair for a group hug and congratulatory comments.

"You're not serious about today, are you?" Elizabeth questions Selma.

"I don't know, why not?"

"Because we're going to do this right, that's why. Let's see . . . Saturday is a good day to get married. That's three days from now. How's that?" Robert's wife continues. "That will give us time to make all the arrangements."

"Whoa! What arrangements? I don't want this to be a gala. I want a simple ceremony, and become John's wife. Do you agree, honey?" she explains and asks her betrothed.

"Whatever you want, that'll be fine with me. Can you stay with us that long, Reverend?" he confirms, and checks the minister's plans.

"I have no place to be in particular. It would be my pleasure," he answers.

Plans move forward for the wedding on Saturday. Consideration is given to the absent children, Robert, Sheree, Charlotte, and Cheryl, as well as Randy, but in the end it's decided to go ahead, since there is no way of knowing when they will all be home together.

Time moves on.

It's the afternoon before the day of matrimony. Saturday will be a holiday for everyone on the farm. Only those chores absolutely necessary will be tended to by the hands, which they figure take a few hours if everybody pitches in.

John and Selma have been into town several times for various reasons. They have invited a few friends, mainly Doc Shaw to the one-thirty-in-the-afternoon event.

She bought a new dress, while her new husband-to-be took care of business at the mayor's office, and the telegraph station.

They, and the reverend, are just getting back from their—hopefully—last trip in to pick up essentials for the expected feast being prepared. The surrey stops with a squeak of leather harnesses at the hitching rail in front of the main house. It's close to three o'clock.

Nora and Elizabeth storm through the screen door slamming it into the front of the house. They jump from the porch and race to the wagon before either John or Selma can get to the ground. Together they shout.

"We have a surprise for you, and you'll never guess what it is!"

"Oh, my dear, I don't know! What is it?" Selma bounces back in defense of the onslaught.

Just then, Robert and Randy appear from within the house, with Sally and Nora close behind.

"They just got home about a half hour ago," Nora informs the happy couple.

"I heard you all were being held under guard at La Nesra?" John's statement turns into a question.

"It's a long story. I'll give you all the details later," Robert explains, as he watches Mr. Remsar get out of the surrey and walk toward them.

"Everybody, this is the Reverend George Remsar. He's staying with us for a few days, and will officiate our wedding. Reverend, this is my son, Robert, my adopted son, Randall, and our good friend, Sally.

Sally's is the last hand George Remsar shakes. She smiles politely and comments, "Have we met before somewhere?"

Remsar is a little taken back. He knows they have never met, but he has heard the name Sally from Ty on several occasions. Sally from La Nesra, along with Robert and Randy, it's her all right. But where are Ty and Mr. Vaughn? These people standing here are supposed to be prisoners.

"I don't think so, my dear. I'd remember a lovely young woman like you. Anyway, I'm not from around here—just passing through," he adds pleasantly

"Yes, I'm sure you're right, although your name sounds familiar to me for some reason," she concludes and puts it out of her mind.

It would seem to most folks, with all that has happened, there would be a bit of melancholy hanging over the heads of the about to be married couple. But the Reverend and everyone on the farm have knelt in prayer for those gone and those lost, which has lifted everybody's spirit and attitude. Having a man of the cloth staying here is good for all their souls.

"This evening, this evening meal before our wedding vows tomorrow, is special to Selma and me." John Anderson stands at the end of the dining room table with his fiancee seated at his side, glass in hand, to give a toast.

"We both want to thank you all for the love and comfort you've showed and given us since we lost Charles and June. You've never swayed from it, even when I've been down and blue, and not very sociable."

"Me too," Selma speaks and raises her glass.

"And now, with your support, as we begin the rest of our journey through life as husband and wife. Well, we both just want you to know how much we love each and every one of you. We don't know if we would have made it without you here for us. So, this toast is to you, the most wonderful people on earth. Thank you very, very much."

He raises his glass to his lips, and the rest of the table stands with applause.

Before the applause subsides, the household cook enters the dining room.

"One of the hands needs to see you right away, Mr. Anderson. He's out there in the kitchen."

John moves without hesitation to the kitchen. He's gone for just a few minutes to return with the hand at his side, and to the shock of the entire room says.

"Reverend—we have to impose upon your services. His wife was carrying a large knife at the same time she was moving a basket of potatoes into their kitchen. She fell, and has stuck the knife completely through her chest. She's dying and he begs you to be at her side."

"Certainly! Take me to her immediately," he announces loudly.

The hand's shanty is some one thousand yards away from the main house. Everyone runs with him the entire distance to the small three room structure of wood. Reverend Remsar enters the kitchen through the back door to see this poor man's wife lying mortally wounded on the floor, on her side in a puddle of blood, still conscious.

Everybody gathers around leaving plenty of room for him to do what needs to be done.

He kneels to slide his arms under her side to lift her to a leaning, sitting position. "Stand back!" he orders, then takes the knife by the handle and pulls it out of her with a jerk. Blood squirts from the wound and sprays all over the place from the dripping knife blade. He immediately places one of his hands over the entry wound on her chest and the other over the exit wound on her back. Then, he pushes hard with both hands, grits his jaws together, squints his closed eyes, and lets out a howl like no one here has ever heard in their life.

He holds this pose for a full two minutes, then carefully begins to let up on the pressure. He continues until he's able to take his hands away from the wound completely. He motions for the husband of the injured woman to come to her side.

"Take your wife, clean her up, and put her somewhere she can rest for a few days. Feed her good. She'll be weak from the loss of blood for several weeks, but she'll live."

The hand does as he's told and picks her up in his arms not knowing what to expect. The blood has stopped pouring out. She's wake and lucid.

"I'm all right, he's saved my life. Dear Lord, he has saved me," she sobs to her husband.

"Are you saying she's going to be okay?" Sally's skeptical words are on everybody's mind.

"She'll be fine. Here, let me show you." Remsar motions Sally to come and look at the wounds as he opens the woman's clothing enough to see.

"The marks are still there, but they're both sealed like they're healed together," she announces loud enough for all those waiting outside to hear.

"It's a miracle!" is heard from someone.

"You healed her, Reverend. God bless you," the husband cries, standing there with his bloody wife in his arms.

"Not me, my son. God has healed her. I'm merely his pawn." The Reverend Remsar takes no credit for what has just happened.

Later, after everything settles down, the group returns to their meal, still in a state of awe at what they all witnessed to be true. Voices are buzzing around the table.

The edge of a spoon against a crystal glass gets everyone's attention.

This time Selma is standing with a glass of wine in her hand.

"I guess I've seen it all now. I now know, as do we all, without a doubt there is a God up there, and for what he has blessed us with tonight, we will all be forever grateful. It was He who brought Reverend Remsar to us out of nowhere, and fixed it so he would stay, to be here tonight. The reverend refers with humility to himself as a pawn of God. That might be, but tonight he saved one of our own, and I know we would all like to repay him in kind. Right now, though, as a beginning, let's all raise our glasses to the Reverend George Remsar, a saint among men."

The rest of the evening proves to be relaxing and fulfilling for all those attending. With hopes of getting a good night's rest in preparation for a busy day tomorrow, the festivities break up at a reasonable hour.

The Reverend Remsar excuses himself, by announcing he wants to check on the hand's wounded wife before he retires, just to be on the safe side. His concern is understood, and appreciated.

He knocks lightly at the door of the shanty he visited just a few hours earlier. The sound is not familiar to those living within because rarely does anyone, other than their peers, venture their way at this time of night, and they all have a 'walk in' relationship.

A child, obviously a son, about ten years old appears to cup his hands around his face and press them against the screen to look into the darkness.

"I'm Reverend Remsar—I was here earlier to help with your mama. Is your daddy here?"

"Yessir," the boy answers politely, and pushes the door out to allow entry.

"Daddy! The reverend's here," he loudly announces throughout the small home.

"I just came by to see how your wife is doing," Remsar suggests when the hand appears from the bedroom.

"She's doing just fine, sir, thanks to you. She's awful weak, but she says she feels okay." He is glad to report.

"That's good to hear, really good news." The professed minister observes with a smile. He pauses for a few seconds, then continues.

"You know, earlier today when I was here, you said if there was anything you could do for me, well, perhaps there is."

"Oh, yessir. Anything, you just ask me. We don't have much, but you're welcome to any of it we have." The hand beams at the opportunity not knowing what to expect, but without reservation.

"Aww. No, no, I just wonder if you could answer a question for me, that's all."

The hand has no idea where the reverend is headed. He stands silently waiting, looking at the shoes of his visitor.

"Have you seen any big boxes arrive here at the farm recently? There might be ten or twelve of them?" Remsar waits for an answer.

The husband fidgets with his hands, and shifts his weight back and forth on his feet.

"Don't make me talk about that. Please, sir, I swore to God I wouldn't."

"Telling me won't break your promise. I am a man of God, am I not? You saw what I can do. Your wife is alive right now because of me. When the boxes came here, did you hear them being called angels? Don't you think God would want you to tell me about his angels?"

"Yessir, I hear what you're saying," the farm worker replies nervously, feeling threatened. "But I just can't do it; I promised you see."

"Well, I can assure you, what you say to me will never be heard outside the walls of this room. I don't like putting it this way, but since I've no other choice. You don't want things to change for your wife, do you? Sometimes if I get upset, the good things I have done change. They turn back to what they were before. Now, I know you don't want that to happen, and I wouldn't like you to lose her just because of this. Do you understand?"

"Yessir." The hands face turns forlorn. He knows what he has to do, but his guts are wrenching. "All I know is, they came in here on some wagons, and we put them in the old smokehouse over at Der Bote. That's all I know, sir."

"Der Bote? Where's that?" Remsar chases his response.

"The next farm over that way." The trembling man points.

"Thank you. No one will ever know about this talk," the Reverend assures.

"No one but me, sir. I know, and that's bad enough. I just let all my friends down, and now I can't be trusted. I can't even trust myself."

Everybody's up early in anticipation of the wedding this afternoon. Selma has kept to her room, so as not to be seen by John. Her breakfast is delivered on a tray, while all her wishes are carried out by those around her.

John spent the night downstairs on a couch. His idea, not hers.

Doc has arrived early, looking for a hearty meal. Attitudes are bright and cheery as the final preparations funnel together. This is a day meant for relaxation and fellowship.

The time finally arrives.

Everyone at the farm is present, except the wounded woman and her husband, to witness the union of the elders of this expanded family. Everything is perfect, just as planned. The ceremony is small and short, and the declaration of 'man and wife' signals the start of their day-long imbibements of liquor, food, and music. After enjoying a plate of food and a good stiff drink, Remsar approaches the happy couple with a hug and handshake of congratulations.

"Would you mind if I borrow one of your horses and take a short ride. You know, we of our profession like a bit of solitude on occasion," he requests of his hosts.

"Not at all. Hold on, I'll get a hand to saddle one up for you," John gladly offers.

As soon as he is out of sight of the farm house, Remsar turns his horse to circle back directly toward town.

The streets are bustling with people when he arrives in town. It being Saturday, the day most folks come into town for supplies knowing others will do the same, giving them a chance to talk and catch up. He heads directly to the hotel, dismounts, ties his reins to the rail, takes two steps up to the wooden sidewalk, and walks inside.

"I'm looking for a tall man, probably dressed all in black. Is he staying here with you while he's in town?" he asks the desk clerk, not knowing what name Ty might be using. He knows he's in town because he saw him yesterday when he was here with John and Selma. They tacitly acknowledged each other at the time, so he knows his cohort is expecting him.

"Yes, he's here, room 211 up the stairs. He said you'd be coming. Go on up."

Remsar nods his head 'thanks,' and proceeds up the steps.

A light *tap, tap* is all it takes for the door marked 211 to open. He enters and closes it behind him.

"Took you long enough to get here," are Ty's first words.

"Yes well, you'll be glad of it when you hear what I've learned. The angels are beings kept in a smokehouse at a farm called Der Bote."

"That's my father's farm," Ty says with excitement. "I know exactly where that smokehouse is. Who told you? Are you sure?"

"One of the people who put them there told me. It's a long story for another time. But I'm certain that's where they are," Remsar assures.

"I'll get my men together and get over there after them right away," the tall man says, anxious to get moving.

"Wait a minute, I don't want to create a big scene out there right now. I've got them all trusting me without reservation. I want to find out if they know anything about Lilly before I show my hand. Since you know where they are, here's what I think you should do."

The two men spend the next fifteen minutes masterminding their next moves and trading experiences that have brought them together here in this room, in this hotel. Ty is amazed to hear about the search party's arrival at Canozira, and scoffs at Remsar's plan to flush out Lilly's captors. Remsar leaves the hotel first to go back to the farm. Ty waits ten minutes, then rounds up Mr. Vaughn and the three guards. They head to the livery for the horses and equipment they will need to haul the boxes.

Over the time it takes for the wedding and Remsar's trip to town and back, the farmhand frets about telling the secret he has sworn to keep. He finally finds his way to his wife and sits on the bed beside her. "I made a big mistake," he confesses. "I told the reverend about the boxes and where they are. I ache all over from it."

"I heard what happened. What else could you do? Anybody would have done the same thing. Don't worry about it. It probably won't make any difference anyway," she soothes and supports her husband.

"I've got a real bad feeling about it, honey. I've got to tell what I did," he bravely speaks up. "What do you think they'll do to me?"

"Don't do it. Your name probably won't ever come into it. But if it comes to that, tell them then. They won't do any more to you then than they will now. Honey, we just got here. We just started making a good life. You don't want to mess it all up, I know you don't," she begs in a weakened voice.

"I have to. I just have to, and I wanted to let you know before I did it in case something happens and I—and I don't come back." He begins to cry.

"Just wait a while then. Give them a chance to get the wedding over with, and get past their food and things. Wait a few hours longer," she pleads, thinking he might reconsider.

"Okay, I'll wait until sundown, but then, I have to tell." He rises and turns for the kitchen to prepare something to eat for his temporarily bedfast wife and their hungry children.

Remsar returns to the farm unnoticed by anyone. He rides into the barn, then pulls off the saddle and blanket to place them on a nearby rack. After leading the horse into an empty stall, he removes the bridle and hangs it on the nail provided on the post next to the door. He closes, latches the door, and turns to go outside, thinking he will casually drift back into the activities of the party. A figure appears in the doorway, causing him to jerk to a stop.

"I'm sorry if I surprised you, Reverend," Sally apologizes as a matter of courtesy, the several drinks she has taken shows in the manner of her speech.

"I'm sure I know you from somewhere, but I just can't put my finger on it. Have you worked with the Company, or somehow been associated with them?"

"Hello, Sally. No, that's all right. I wasn't expecting to meet anybody, and you startled me. You know, I've thought about it since you mentioned it before, and I have to say, you must be thinking of someone else. Someone I remind you of perhaps. I don't know anything about the Company you mention." He walks to her, takes her elbow, and leads her back to the festivities without saying anything more.

The gala continues while a group of five men with three wagons circle the Anderson farm, out of sight and earshot. Their destination: Der Bote. The thought of finding the death angels builds within Ty with each turn of the wheels. Mr. Vaughn sits at his side, leading the procession with their horses at a gallop. It won't be long now.

The farmhand wanting to tell John what he has done moves closer and closer, working his way through the happy voices and clamor. He wants to avoid the reverend, and yet somehow get Mr. Anderson's attention.

"There's Sherman, Nora's son. I'll have him tell Mr. Anderson to meet me. Meet me where? The barn, I can get into the barn with no one seeing me." He touches the boy's arm to get his attention, then puts his head next to the young man's ear.

Sherman trots across the yard toward John and Selma. The hand watches as Sherman interrupts their conversation to pass on the message. Then, he turns and moves to the barn. There he waits, cowering behind a large barrel, not daring to look to see if John is coming. The stress causes him to sweat and pant. His mouth is dry and nasty tasting.

Shortly, John enters the barn glancing around as he moves. The hand appears from behind the barrel, approaching cautiously.

"Is something wrong with your wife?" John inquires, concerned.

"No, sir. It's not that, Mr. Anderson. I have to tell you something. Please don't hurt me. I'll leave if you want me to, but I have to take care of my family, and if you hurt me I won't be able to," the trembling man begs.

"What? I'm not going to hurt you. What's the matter? Settle yourself down, you can tell me." John squats down to meet the man at his level since the hand is now on his knees crying. John places his hand on his shoulder.

"I've done something bad, Mr. Anderson. I told the reverend where we hid those boxes. I had to, he was going to hurt my family. He said he would make my wife worse, so she would die if I didn't, and I know he can do it. I'm sorry I let everybody down. Don't hurt me," he sobs.

"I see. There now, you've done the right thing by telling me," John begins soberly, patting the man's shoulder. "Nobody's going to hurt you. I want to thank you for being brave and coming here to tell me. Now, you go back home and take care of your wife and family. Don't worry yourself about those boxes. I'll take care of things from here."

The elder Anderson leaves the barn first, after advising the hand to wait five minutes before heading home. He walks into the mix of people speaking with a few as he moves along, his direction however, is to his son Robert.

After a few words, Robert moves casually to Randy, as his father locates Sally. They all come together at the edge of the front porch steps to stand in a closed circle. It takes just a minute for the situation to be explained to the group.

"It's obvious our reverend is here on a mission to confiscate the arsenal. And since we know he went for a ride earlier, he probably met with Ty Black. That means Ty is probably at Der Bote right now breaking the lock off the smokehouse door," John is quick to point out.

"What should we do?" Randall is first to speak, ready to take action.

"I knew that man was up to no good. I even talked to him a few minutes ago about it," Sally offers for no reason, other than to get it off her chest.

"Assuming what Daddy says is true, we're probably too late to keep Ty away from the arsenal. So let's think this through for a minute." Robert's maturity shows. "Since our Mr. Remsar is still with us, there's something more he wants. And that must be Sheree. Let's not forget, too, we have a team that has to be close to their compound at Canozira by now. Maybe we should play along for a while to see what he does. We can send a couple of hands out to see what's going on at Der Bote and report back here. It's your call. But I think the first thing we should do is break up this party just in case trouble starts. We need to be careful not to tip our hand in doing it though."

"Randy, go and get a couple of hands on their way. They had better go on foot since we don't want our preacher friend alerted to anything. Pick a couple of good runners."

"Sally, let's you and I start closing this shindig down. Just tell a few of them the truth without mentioning the reverend, and spread the word to start drifting away," Robert supposes, as he passes out assignments.

"Now, Daddy, you have a whole different set of problems to deal with: how to tell your new wife, or wait, maybe I misspoke. Is she—or not. Is this guy really a minister?" he continues with a big grin, as he jests with his father.

"Yeah, I know, the thought has already crossed my mind. She deserves this day where she's the center of it all, and I hate for it to end all wrong. Besides, as you say, we're not sure if it's legal or not. I believe I'll wait to tell her when we know for sure." He grins back at his son.

"So, I suppose you'll come up with a reason to sleep on the couch, or maybe out in the barn, right." His son continues to push, a bigger grin on his face.

"Not a chance of that happening. If I don't want to tip her off that something's going on, I have to follow through as a husband." John sticks out his hand for a quick shake from his oldest child.

John takes the good-natured barbing as he should, but he cannot help recalling that his son had a big crush on Selma a few years ago. It's true he and Elizabeth are happily married, and Robert has already explained that those feelings for his new stepmother are long since gone. Still, he has had her in his arms in a romantic way more than once, and that's not going to change or go away. It makes him a wee bit uncomfortable to banter on the subject, and he wonders why his son would do it in the first place. Regardless, he knows what he has to do, he can't start off their marriage with a lie.

"Selma, honey, let's you and me leave these young pups to their fun and find someplace where we can be alone?"

"It's early, John, how's that going to look?"

"Well, we're newlyweds. They're going to think we want to be alone, and from there, who knows—who cares," he states very-matter-of-factly.

He takes her hand, and leads her into the house, then upstairs to the bedroom. Before she can say a word, he starts.

"We have a little trouble brewing. Ty Black and his band are probably at Der Bote right now loading the arsenal onto wagons. Our Reverend Remsar is the one that put him up to it."

"What are you talking about? Are you sure?"

John explains the whole story as he knows it.

"What about you and me?" she asks, believing she knows the answer.

He takes her in his arms and relieves her mind when he says, "Isn't this dress tight and confining, Mrs. Anderson? I think you should get out of it and get comfortable. In fact, I'll help you."

Robert, Sally, and Randall take turns standing vigil the rest of the night. Everybody but the new couple—and the reverend—have been alerted to sleep with their guns, just in case. Dawn comes as peacefully as the night has passed. The cool morning air smells fresh, full of good things for the soul.

In the meantime.

The plan out west at Canozira is coming together. Rose and Cheryl have kept themselves out of sight, but Falcon, Hawk, and Millie have had the run of the place.

They have asked a lot of questions to which candid responses have been given. The three of them are known throughout the compound now, and have no trouble going anywhere they want, except for several tight security areas. The five easterners have occupied Lilly's quarters since their arrival, and are sitting in the room where she found the book hidden in the secret drawer of the sofa table.

"Should we get started?" Rose asks. Remsar has been gone for a while and they're not sure when he might be back. When he left to get Ty at La Nesra, he said it would take no more than two days.

"I don't know. This sitting around is starting to wear on me. I feel like we should be doing something, too. I mean, that's why we came here in the first place." Falcon's words don't answer the question, but do relate his feelings.

"Just suppose I start showing myself as Lilly. If I don't get too close, you know, so I don't have to speak, what could it hurt?" Cheryl poses.

"The thing is, will it bring someone or something down on us that we're not able to deal with? If, as Remsar says, word gets back to Lilly's captors, and if they do come here looking, what are we to do? No, I think we should wait just as we are." Millie adds her opinion.

"Millie's right with what she's said, and we know from our scouting around in here, there's little else we can do." Hawk adds his consideration.

"Perhaps we should go looking for him. Cheryl got us in here in by being Lilly. Can we leave and come back the same way? Maybe we can get back to La Nesra by using one of their machines," Rose challenges the group.

"Now there's an idea." Hawk reaches to pat his wife on the head. "Someone should stay here though. Just in case Remsar returns and wonders where we are."

"No. We stay together. If one goes, we all go. If one stays, we all stay. We're already missing two people, Lilly and Remsar. We don't need to be looking for anyone else. We can leave a message here somewhere saying we went to La Nesra, and will be back as soon as we can." Millie puts her foot down fearing she might be the one chosen to stay here alone.

Falcon rises from his chair to walk around the room, his mind churning. "What good is it going to do us to go to La Nesra? We've spent our lives there. I'm skeptical about Remsar's plan to find Sheree, and I'm not at all convinced we'd find her, even if we're able to bait her captors to send someone here. I think our job here is done."

"We might have a chance right now to leave, but that could change. Look around, all Remsar or Ty needs to do is say the word and we're prisoners. It occurs to me that we should leave, but not to go to La Nesra. If we can get a ride on one of their machines, lets go back to the farm. We need to find another way to locate Sheree, this is leading us nowhere, but, at least now, we know." His logic sets their thinking straight.

They all concur and start planning ways to communicate and convince the strange people to pilot them to the Anderson farm. If all goes well, they hope to leave tonight.

Back east, Robert is meeting with his father to relay information from their two scouts they sent to Der Bote last night.

"Our hands said the wagons were just leaving when they arrived. They couldn't get close enough in the dark to see what was loaded, but after Ty and his men left, they checked the smokehouse. The lock was broken off and it was empty. It looks like they got what they came for."

"It sure looks that way. Can you think of a reason we shouldn't deal with our impostor? Your new stepmother knows all about it, and for now, she's holding her temper. But if he provokes her somehow, well, you know how she is."

"The only consideration we have at this point is Sheree, and since he doesn't know any more than we do about her, I say let's get him." Robert is adamant.

They locate Randall before attempting to approach the Reverend George Remsar, then proceed into the house together to carry out their mission. It's quickly determined that Mr. Remsar has left. A trip to the barn tells them he took a horse, and left before dawn this morning.

"We must have spooked him somehow?" John surmises as they walk toward the house.

"Yep, I imagine so. He's probably met up with Ty Black by now." Randall adds it all together.

"Are we going to chase after them?" Robert inquires as they turn into the house.

"I'm all for letting them go. I'd like to see this farm settle down and get peaceful for a while. Maybe it can now." His father's reply comes as a bit of a surprise to the two young men.

"Riders coming!" a hand, working on a fence a hundred yards away, yells.

The trio turns to see a group of horses on the horizon headed toward them.

"You boys grab some iron and get back here," the older Anderson orders grimly, not raising his voice.

The two head for the house on the run. Selma and Elizabeth hear the commotion and wonder what's going on. When Robert and Randall come back through the door carrying rifles, the women are right behind them with guns of their own. They stay on the porch while the men continue on their way to John's side. Robert tosses his daddy a long gun as the intruders get close enough to be identified.

"It's Ty and Remsar. There's six of them total." Randall notices and chambers a bullet in his rifle.

John glances over his shoulder at the two women standing ready to back up their men. The farmhand in the field took off, running to bring more help from the rest of the hands. When the riders pull to a stop about thirty yards away, Ty and Remsar dismount and approach the armed defenders.

John, Robert, and Randall see seven hands, bearing their weapons, closing from across the field. Farther out behind them are five more.

"John," Remsar greets the senior Anderson. "Do you remember Ty Black?"

"I've met him before." The memory of the man's speed with a handgun goes through his mind.

"You must think we're a couple of fools," Ty challenges.

"Why's that?"

"You knew the angels weren't there at Der Bote. You sent us on a goose chase."

"I didn't send you anywhere. What's this about angels?" He plays with his accusers mind.

"Don't hand us that, the fact is Sally, Falcon, Hawk, and Rose brought them here. Your hand admitted it to me yesterday. Up to now, we've played along, but my patience is wearing thin," Remsar states.

"Tell me where they are and no one will get hurt. Otherwise, whatever happens is on your hands, not mine." Ty's voice gets louder the longer he speaks.

"Somebody is giving you bad information, Mr. Black. But I'll give you a few words of advice. Look around. If you reach for a gun, the first shot from three of us is going into your chest. If you're smart, you'll leave while you can. Otherwise, we'll bury you here."

"We're not here to shoot anybody," Remsar interrupts. "All we want is what's rightfully ours. We'll leave now, but we'll be back tomorrow with wagons to get the angels. Keep this in mind, sir, we have your daughter and four of her friends being held prisoner. Starting at noon tomorrow, we'll kill one of them, and then one every hour after that until you tell us where the angels are. Got it? We'll be back at noon tomorrow. Come on—lets go," he orders Ty.

Nothing more is said until the offending men are out of sight.

"We have a serious problem unless one of you knows where the arsenal is. Maybe I'll ride over there to see for myself. Yes, sir, a very serious problem," Randall reiterates.

"Do you know anything about this, Daddy?" Robert recalls his father has been gone somewhere, by himself, for several days.

"All I know is what you know. I'm as puzzled about it as you are." John pauses in thought. "How can we give them something we don't have? They must be telling the truth about capturing all five of our people. Otherwise, I don't know how they would be aware of them being out there. We'd better use the time we have figuring out a way to handle them before they can kill our friends."

"I agree, but give Randy and me time to take a quick trip over to Der Bote. I'm like him, I'd like to see for myself," John's son concludes, and leaves with his longtime friend, headed for the barn.

Selma and Elizabeth wait on the porch for John to get closer.

"Where are they going?" the younger woman asks.

"Der Bote, they want to see for themselves that the arsenal is gone."

"Do you think they actually have our people captive?" The older woman wants to know.

"I don't see how else he would know they're even out there. I don't know how they're going to kill them off one at a time from here though." John's thinking has progressed.

"Yes, I see what you mean. He's either brought them here somehow, or he plans to murder them all either way," Beth calculates.

"We won't go wrong if we believe the worst," Selma reluctantly admits.

The bunch from the Company rides toward town.

"Those people hate you with a passion, Ty. They'll kill you if you give them the chance," Remsar warns his comrade.

"I know. Do you remember I told you there would be blood spilled if I came back here? Now you've seen what I mean firsthand. The last laugh will be mine, though. They can shoot this body, beat it, and bury it, but they don't know I'm just like their daughter, Sheree. I'm out of my body, making it impossible for them to snuff my life. They have to find my life body to get rid of me.

"Ha. Ha. Ha," he retorts.

"Don't get too big for your britches. You have no idea where your real body is being stored. Lilly, however, knows, and should something happen to her family with you to blame, I wonder what she might do if she got wind of it," the gray-haired leader of the Company chides.

They ride silently for a few minutes.

"Regarding the five prisoners at Canozira, I won't be able to get back there until early in the morning. I ordered a craft to be in this area looking for my signal every morning at two. That should still give me plenty of time to get there and back. I'd appreciate you coming with me, Ty, just in case they give me trouble on the way here," Remsar explains to his cohort.

"Mr. Vaughn, I want you to round up as many men as you can to help us tomorrow. Make sure they know how to handle a gun. You'll probably have to pay them, so work it out. Get as many as twenty-five," Ty orders.

"I don't think that farm worker lied to me about the angels being there at that smokehouse. He really thought that's where they were," the reverend impersonator thinks out loud.

"You can bet on it," the man in black agrees. "The entrance was all covered with brush and there was a sturdy lock on a steel door. Nobody does that to an empty smokehouse. They were there, which means they're still around here somewhere."

Shortly after the midnight hour, anyone watching the heavens for miles around the farm could see a tiny star glimmer, brighter and brighter. A star growing larger and larger until it turns into a streak of light moving at a tremendous speed. It appears to be falling, to eventually crash into the earth. But once it disappears from sight behind the horizon, it slows to hover just above the ground, behind the rise, out of sight of the Anderson home.

Five figures appear in a strange green light from its underbelly. As soon as the figures move into the darkness, the craft moves up and away, gaining speed to penetrate the dark sky as quickly as it came.

The only sounds are the heavy feet of the figures moving through grass and weeds until they reach the summit of the rise. They stop momentarily to survey the house and surrounding area. Then they move on, getting closer and closer to . . .

"Stop! Stop right where you are and don't move!" a man shouts.

They stop.

His loud voice stirs others from their sleep, but mainly it alerts other guards also on duty tonight. Men with lanterns move from various directions to encircle the figures.

"Don't shoot. We're friends of the Anderson family," a self-appointed spokeswoman announces.

"Is that you, Millie?" one of the guards questions.

"It's me all right, and I've brought all your friends back with me as well. You all remember Cheryl and Rose, and this is Falcon, and Hawk."

"Sure, we remember, how could we forget. Sorry for the welcome. We had some trouble here yesterday afternoon, and we thought it might come back in the black of night. I sure am glad it you instead of them. Come to the house, everybody will be real glad to know you're here."

It doesn't take long for the entire farm to awaken, especially when the word is spread that the prisoners the man spoke of yesterday afternoon somehow are free, and here safely. It takes the better part of an hour for the new arrivals to explain all that's happened to them, and then for the farm people to explain what all has been going on here.

Questions are fired from all directions, and answered, as they linger on the porch and surrounding area. Everybody gets to hear everything firsthand as they should. If these families are going to fight a bloody battle, they should know why. As the conversation turns redundant, the hands and their families drift away, knowing the sun will come up in just a few short hours. Soon, only those living in the main house, and their newly arrived guests remain. They all go indoors.

"Are you all serious when you say you don't know where the arsenal has been taken?" Cheryl asks innocently, thinking now that they are alone the truth will come out.

"All we know at the moment is they're gone. We can be sure the Company doesn't have them after this afternoon," Robert affirms.

"If anyone here moved them they aren't owning up to it. Randy and I rode over to Der Bote for a look, but it was just as they said this afternoon. There's nothing to give us a clue as to what might have happened, or for that matter, how long ago.

"It's been a trying day people. Let's use the rest of the night to try and get some sleep. This new day promises to be a dandy," Selma suggests as she motions Elizabeth to help with arrangements for their additional guests.

Almost as if it is planned, Remsar and Ty arrive at their pickup point just as the lights go out at the main house, not a mile away. If everything goes as planned, their craft will arrive in about ten minutes. "There it is," Ty hears his partner by necessity say. They are on their way to Canozira to bring the waiting visitors back east to barter their lives for the missing angels.

They learn their supposed prisoners are gone.

"What do you mean they're not here? Where are they?" the head of the Company yells and rants.

"The travel log shows they were dropped off not far from where you were just picked up, sir," an officer of their guard reports.

While Remsar screams and raves about how this has been the worst time of his life, Ty hangs his head and chuckles through his nose at the turn of events over the last couple of months.

"What would make you think you should allow them to take one of our crafts and leave?" his superior speaks; the guard trembles.

"Lilly made the request, sir. She's always been permitted to travel as she wishes. You left no orders to the contrary. How was I to know you didn't want them to leave?"

"You might as well settle down. It's just another mistake you and I have made in a series of them lately. The question is, what do we do now?" Ty interrupts with the truth of the matter, not wanting to spend any more time here than necessary. "Are you sure it was Lilly who made the arrangements. How many people left here together?"

"Five—according to the log, sir."

He looks at Remsar. They surmise from the number it was Cheryl, pretending to be Lilly, and that Lilly has not yet returned.

"You're dismissed," he tells the guard.

"I don't see any sense in going back to the Anderson farm right now. Unless we find a way to put pressure on them, all we'll do is get some good men killed. I need to get back to stop Mr. Vaughn from recruiting those men, though. Wait a minute, that gives me an idea. If you agree, here's what we'll do . . ." Ty's eyes sparkle as he lays out a plan.

Remsar decides his place is at Canozira, reasoning he should be there in case Lilly appears. Ty will return to the farm to set their plan in motion.

Someone pounding at his door stirs Ty from a deep sleep, at the hotel in town.

"Yes." he says in a loud grumpy voice.

"You wanted to be woke up at sunrise. Well, it's sunrise."

It's mid-morning at the farm on this overcast, humid, rainy day. The work goes on, regardless of the weather. Horses, cattle, and chickens need to be fed, not to mention the children. Cows need to be milked, stalls cleaned, eggs fetched, gardens weeded, maintenance done to the building and fences, and all the family's needs, such as baking, sewing, clothes washing and ironing; the list goes on and on.

Even as these hard working people toil, they know a fight is likely, and there will be family and friends hurt from it, maybe killed. Most of them, however, trust their lives to those people more suited when it comes to planning a defense. But when the time comes, they will be there, ready to do their part. Their guns are out of sight, but not far from where they're working.

"Someone's coming!" a sentry yells for all to hear.

Robert and Randy come running out of the barn to see a lone figure walking beside his horse, seemingly in no hurry at all. He's dressed in a suit rather than the normal working man's clothes. A dark narrow brim hat is pulled down on his forehead, shading his eyes. When the man sees them, he raises his free hand over his head with his elbow bent and keeps it there.

Elizabeth pushes the front door screen partly open, allowing her to step her right foot on the porch, and bend around to take a look, not wanting to go out onto the wet surface.

As the man gets closer, more farm people appear, some wearing rain protection, others carrying guns.

"It's Mr. Vaughn," Sally calls out.

"Don't shoot!" he responds loud enough for all those he sees to hear.

Robert walks to meet him, keeping a keen eye on his hands.

"What are you doing here? Did your bosses send you? I guess you know by now that your prisoners have escaped, and are home safe and sound."

"No—I didn't know that, and no one sent me, I'm here on my own. Can I talk with the man in charge?" the older man queries.

"Are the rest just over the rise there waiting for you to draw us off, so they can swarm in all over us?" Robert's insistent.

"I'm here alone. If anybody's out there, I don't know anything about it. I left town early this morning. None of them saw me leave. Reach over here and take my gun, I mean no harm to anyone. I'd like to speak to Mr. Anderson, I guess."

Robert takes the man's gun from its holster, and waves with it in his hand for him to follow.

"This is Mr. Vaughn, from La Nesra in Atlanta. Says he wants to talk to you," he explains as they approach his father.

"Sally, Falcon, Rose, and Hawk all know me from La Nesra, and I'm sure you've heard my name many times before. I've been acquainted with your daughters, Sheree and Amber, for a long long time, too. I've done some things over my life that I'm not proud of, and I suppose you've heard about a lot of them. I can't imagine what your opinion of me could be. But some recent events have made me reconsider my life, and what I'm doing with it. I have no family that I know of, and I'm getting old. What I'm trying to get around to say is, I'd like to throw in with you and your family." He raises his right hand as if to stifle any disparaging remarks. "I know what you must be thinking—who am I to come here like this after all that's happened? What gall I must have to think you'd ever trust me enough to believe what I say.

"I can only ask you to listen to Sally, Hawk, and Rose when they tell you what the Company thinks of me these days. Ty Black is in town right now knowing I've ran out on him. If he sees me, he won't ask any questions, he'll kill me on the spot—if I don't kill him first.

"Mr. Anderson, I need another start in life. I'm as loyal as a person can be, but I can't go along with the Company any more. So I'm asking you to take me in. I know a lot about the Company, I've worked there most of my life. Anything I know is yours for the asking. I'll stand with you and fight them starting right now, if you'll let me." The man humbles himself in front of all watching.

"Don't trust a word he says. He's a liar, and the worst kind of devil, just like the rest of them, he is," Millie shouts, from the corner of the house.

The loud din of voices supporting her words settles after a few moments.

John waves his arms to get quiet. He wants to befriend the ranking official of the Company. This could be the step forward the SONS organization needs to begin dismantling their threat to society. But it's not in anybody's best interest to accept him for what he says. It's too dangerous.

"You're asking a lot of people to put their lives on the line by taking you in. To us, you're the enemy. I'm not in a position to grant your request right now. We all need time to think, so here's what I'll do. We'll lock you up and keep you isolated for a couple of weeks. You'll have no contact with anyone but me, Robert, or Randall. If after that we've not uncovered anything to the contrary to what you've said, we'll consider your proposal. But if we find anything to make us believe you're here on behalf of your two friends, you're a dead man. Got it?" John lays it out very plainly, very firmly. He continues.

"There's one other option I'll give you for the next thirty seconds. Get on your horse and get the hell out of here as fast as you can."

Mr. Vaughn hands the reins of his horse to Robert, tacitly saying.

"I'm here to stay."

Ten days pass with no word of Ty and his bunch. Mr. Vaughn has been accommodated with a room at the back of the main barn. He's been no trouble, whatsoever. The only people he sees or speaks with are John, Robert, and Randy. They chat with him about various things, as they take care for his daily needs. He has four more days to go.

It's the afternoon about an hour after their noon meal. The sun is hot, but it's cool in the shade. Selma walks toward John as he works trying to get a blade loose from its place on a plow, to heat and straighten it.

"Have you seen Joie?" she asks, squinting her eyes, holding her right hand up toward the sun, with her left lifting the front of her dress to keep from stumbling.

"No, I've been busy here though, haven't been looking," he responds.

"Well, I can't find her anywhere. The girls are all here, they haven't seen her since dinner, either. I'm beginning to scare myself. Will you help me find her?"

"You bet, honey. She's probably just wondered off somewhere following one of the children. She can't have gotten too far. We'll find her," he assures his new wife.

A quick check here and there produces nothing. He sends her back into the house to have the women check thoroughly to see if the young girl is hiding, playing a game or something. Meanwhile, he rounds up a couple of hands to help him search. Their little granddaughter, Sheree and Falcon's daughter, is nowhere to be found.

Within thirty minutes everyone on the farm is searching for her. Falcon has men out looking a half mile from the house. Selma is in tears thinking of her dear little one all alone—lost—wondering why her mama doesn't come and get her.

Another hour of hunting, looking everywhere a small child could be—nothing. Falcon and the searchers have all returned empty handed.

At this point, Selma is beside herself; it's taking all of the younger women to keep her from going out of her mind. Her wailing and sobbing is causing some of the other women to join in as they surround her trying to give comfort in any way they can. She keeps repeating over and over.

"What kind of mother am I?" Then she goes on to add all sorts of self-degrading phrases. "God blesses me with a beautiful little girl, and I don't know how to take care of her. I don't deserve to have a child. I should have paid more attention to her. It's all my fault she's gone. If she's hurt, I'll kill myself." All the while she is sobbing, her whole body jerking, writhing in self-brought pain.

Not being able to find his daughter is frustrating, and to hear Selma cry in pain is more than Falcon can stand. Robert sees him running to the barn. He heads him off to catch him by the arm just before he goes through the door.

"Where are you going?" he insists.

"I'm going to beat it out of him, that's where I'm going." His eyes are large and wild looking.

"Noooo, you're not! I can't let you do that! He's been locked up all this time, how could he have done anything with Joie!" he scolds, as Falcon jerks his arm away and continues inside.

Not knowing what else to do, young Mr. Anderson tackles the raging man and brings him to his knees on the dirt floor. He tries to grab his arms and pin him down, but it's more of a job than he thought it might be.

"You're a real handful," he says loudly, trying to catch Falcon's battling arms. "Randy, if you can hear me, get in here—I need help!"

In a moment, Randy and one of the hands join him to pin the out-of-control father to the floor.

"Settle down! Settle down! We'll work our way through this together. We won't stop until we find her. If we find out Mr. Vaughn has any part in it, he'll pay for it. I promise you that," Randy says loud enough for the struggling man to hear, not thinking of the man behind the locked door a few feet away.

Joie's father eventually tires himself out, being no match for the three men.

"If we let you up will you behave?" Robert worries.

"Yeah, I'm okay now. I just lost my mind for a minute there. I'm sorry to cause the three of you trouble. You did the right thing holding me down the way you did." It's his way of saying there will be no hard feelings about what has happened.

"Can we ask Vaughn if he knows anything about Joie?" he begs.

"Sure, I'll open the door, but you stay back here with Randy, all right?"

The door of the cell opens to present Mr. Vaughn standing wide eyed . . . with the appearance of a man about to be shot.

Chapter Thirty-Nine

"Don't shoot me. Please!" Mr. Vaughn pleads, as he stands defenseless—a prisoner—in the small room at the rear of main barn.

"My little daughter is missing, you bastard. If I find out you've had anything to do with it, I'll hold your head while Selma cuts your throat. Do you hear me?" Falcon shouts at the older man.

"I am truly sorry to hear about your daughter, but think clearly for a moment. Why would I come here voluntarily, to turn myself over to you, then do something you that would cause you to kill me? I've been locked in this miserable little room for almost two weeks. Until just a few minutes ago, I didn't know there's a problem." He defends himself, and continues, "Joie—Joie is Lilly's child, is she not?"

"That's right," the seething father answers. Robert and Randy are standing ready to grab him if he starts toward their prisoner.

"I remember when she was born. You need to remember, too. I'm the one who approved your marriage. I made sure your daughter's birth was well tended to. I set you up with a nice place to live, even gave you a maid to help out. Nora—I believe is her name. I saw her out there when I arrived. She has a son—aaahhh, Sherman, I think."

Mr. Vaughn goes on and on about how he did not try to stop them when they escaped from La Nesra to come here to the farm, and about how he accepted them back at La Nesra after that. "I wasn't supposed to come here with Ty and his henchmen. But I couldn't take it any more. So I decided I'd make the trip, and wait for the right time to get away. I even did my part to help the three of them escape on the way here. If you let me out of here long enough to go inside and sit down with you, I'll tell you some things about me. Some things I know you'll be interested to hear."

Robert looks at Falcon. "What do we have to lose?"

"I don't know, nothing I guess. You should get Selma ready beforehand, though, because she's in a real mean mood right now," he reluctantly agrees.

Once inside with listeners all around him, Mr. Vaughn surveys their situation.

"First of all, if Ty has taken Joie, he won't hurt her. That would only cause you to never tell him where the angels are hidden. No, sir, if he has her, you'll be hearing from him. He'll want to negotiate a trade, Joie for the angels."

"But Joie needs a woman to care for her. She's just a little girl," Selma points out.

"Be assured, she'll have the best of care. I know how worried you are about her safety, so when I say this, don't think for a minute that I don't," he spurs on. "If he has her, she won't be around here for long. He'll have her transported to a place you'll never find. That's when he'll contact you, when she's completely out of your grasp."

"Oh Lord," Selma sighs. Millie, standing behind the grandmother's chair, squeezes her shoulders with understanding. Cheryl and Nora sit on their heels on either side.

"All right, that makes sense to me, now what's your part in this?" John insists.

"I think if you do not intend to give him the angels, then we must find Joie, and do it quickly," Mr. Vaughn divulges.

"How can we give him something we don't have. Honestly, we don't know where those angels are," Randy speaks, caught up in the moment.

"At the risk of turning all of you more against me, I must say, someone here in this room knows where those boxes are located. And if I believe that, so does Ty Black. That's the reason we must find the child, find her before he's certain you're not going to give him what he wants. If he convinces himself you'll never give those boxes up, I hesitate to think what he's capable of doing. As you all know, he has access to the flying craft from Canozira. Since they usually fly only at night, and since your granddaughter came up missing just a few hours ago, she's probably still in this area."

"He's right, Dad. They only fly at night, and no matter where they are they always go back to Canozira before daylight. Ty has to have a predetermined spot picked out for them to swoop in from Canozira and load up. A certain spot and a specific time after midnight, most likely," Falcon adds.

"That's midnight tonight." Mr. Vaughn is quick to show the urgency of action.

"That doesn't give us much time, does it?" Cheryl bites her tongue after letting these words slip out. "I'm sorry." she quickly adds.

Selma ignores her slip of the tongue. "What are you suggesting?" she dares their prisoner.

"I believe I might be able to help you. Let me nose around and see what I can find out. If I can get an idea of where the pickup spot is, we can get there a little early and foil their plans."

"Oh! Now I see your plan. We're supposed to let you go so you can run off to your comrades. You must think we're stupid. You're not going anywhere until we find Joie. You get that mindset and we'll get along. You don't, and we won't" Randall is the first to say what they all believe.

"We can do both, Randy," the once Company man continues. "You see, I possess the same power that your friend Lilly has. I can climb out of my body and move around just as you see me here. I'll leave this body here with you, then I'll go searching. You can be sure I'll be back that way. How's that?"

"His body was missing for years and years, and he just recently got it back. He swore then he would never leave it again, so, I don't think he'll take a chance of getting caught outside like that ever again. He knows the one way he'll die while he's out of his body is for us to destroy his real one. We'll have him over a barrel," Sally testifies.

Mr. Vaughn throws his arms and hands out, palms up, indicating, she's right. "All I ask is a decent safe place to leave my life body."

"Can you work your way through the mirrors just like Miss Lilly?" Nora asks.

"Yes, I can. In fact, that's how I'll make the time to do what needs to be done. I think Ty will have Joie inside somewhere. I'm a little rusty after all these years, but I should be able to find her," he informs confidently.

"Then you'll bring her back here?" Nora pushes onward.

"Probably not—you see I'm not able to bring a living creature back through the mirror. And if I try to break her free from them, I'll probably fail at the attempt. Are you aware that Ty Black has the ability of moving outside his body too? He can chase me through the mirrors, so I don't dare take the chance of getting caught. If they catch me, then what hope do we have of foiling their plan? No, our best bet is for me to overhear enough to determine where the pickup point is located. Then we can take the necessary manpower with us to get her back. They have to be at the pick up site a little early for their departure, the flying craft won't wait around if they aren't ready. We'll get them before the craft gets there."

As they should, all heads and eyes turn to John. He rises and paces back and forth, thinking, then turns to face the longtime Company man. "Why don't you locate where she is right now, then come back here and tell us. We'll go to get her before they leave for the landing site."

"If it can be done that way, of course, that's what we'll do. But I have to make that decision there, on the spot, when I find her. But if I believe we're better off waiting until later, I don't want a lot of squabbling about it. That's why I didn't mention that possibility in the first place," Mr. Vaughn says bluntly, with no regard for their feelings.

"It looks like we're covered then. I can't see what else we can do. There's not enough time to travel overland and search everywhere ourselves. And since we'll have the upper hand, I think it's worth a try. That is, if you all agree," John decides out loud.

After leaving his life body in a nice, but small, place in the attic, Mr. Vaughn asks for a picture of Joie. He studies it for several minutes before handing in back. Then, he steps through the floor length mirror in the bedroom of the Anderson home.

For a moment, he pauses, collecting his thoughts. He remembers his past and the terrible forces that chased him for years. He has sworn he would never again appear in this dimension. His senses are on edge.

"I must be wary of my surroundings, but I have to do this," he tells himself firmly, then starts to concentrate on the small child's face, and her name, Joie Justice. Harder and harder he concentrates. He begins to move, faster and faster. A few seconds pass as he swiftly covers a distance. He stops near a white square of incoming light. As he moves closer and tilts his ear to hear, a voice is apparent, that of a female talking softly.

The angle of the mirror is not providing the view of the room he needs to see her or to whom she is speaking. He decides to take a quick look and pushes his head through.

The woman has her back to him, sitting on the floor. In front of her is a child, they are playing with something he's unable to see. The child looks directly at him, points her right forefinger, and begins to pucker. He pulls back as the woman turns.

He watches as the woman comes into his view, looking for the cause of the young girl's actions. She looks all around, including several times at the mirror. Since she doesn't call for assistance from anyone, he feels she did not see him.

"That's her all right. I need to find another mirror to get out of here and determine where we are. There are several white spots I can see from here. I'll check them out. The first two tell him no more than he already knows, but the third pays off.

"How original, Ty, you've got her in a room at our hotel in town." The mirror he's looking through hangs in the lobby of the hotel.

"If I knew the exact room?" He runs it through his mind. "Aahh, I'd better not, if I get caught, the Andersons will never get her back. I'll check out the rest of these portals; maybe one of them will give me more information. If it comes to it, I'll have a few of the Andersons' men wait and follow them when they leave here for the departure site."

"But I'd rather be there waiting for them. I'm confident he won't have an army with him, because he doesn't want any more than necessary to see the flying craft. In fact, as I think about it, he won't want anyone to see it.

"Tyrone Black, Tyrone Black," he thinks, and visualizes the man. He moves a short distance to another white square. There on the other side of the mirror sits Ty and the three guards he brought from La Nesra.

"Someone's looking for me from the other side?" Ty thinks, questioning his feelings. "It has to be Lilly, or Mr. Vaughn. I'm guessing the former. You're right on time, young lady. You're probably spying from just inside the mirror there on the wall. But I don't want these guards to see that, now do I?" The man in black studies his choices.

"As I said earlier, we'll all leave here at midnight. That will give us plenty of time to meet with the rest of our men. I'll feel a lot better when we join our reinforcements. I see no need to go over our plan again, but just to appease me, do you all know what you're supposed to do?" Ty questions his comrades.

Heads nod all around confirm they understand, as Mr. Vaughn watches and listens.

"Okay, go about your business, and be ready in the lobby a little before midnight. We have plenty of hired guards to keep things secure until then." Ty grins to himself as he speaks.

They all leave the room, leaving it empty and silent when the door closes. Mr. Vaughn steps carefully through the mirror, moving cautiously to the window.

"We're on the second floor. Makes sense." He moves to the door and opens it a crack to peer into the hallway.

"Room number twenty-six. There's six men on chairs that I can see from here. She must be on this floor, but which room. The guards are strung out all along the length of the hallway, there's no way to tell." He waits thirty minutes, keeping an eye on the happenings through his view from the ajar door.

"Aaah! Nothing. I'm wasting my time. I might as well go back to let them know the little I've discovered. It's something, I guess, at least more than we knew when I got here." He vacates the room through the mirror.

Once back at the Anderson farm, Mr. Vaughn explains all he has witnessed and adds his thinking as he finishes.

"Without more definite information, about the only thing we can do is get as close to the hotel as possible, and watch both of the exits. As I said before, I think Ty will wind up by himself with your child. We need to be ready when that happens."

"With the six guards I counted in the hallway, the three he brought with him, and Ty himself, that makes ten armed men. If we try to rush them, there will be gunplay, and I don't like the odds, someone will be killed. He has to get away alone to meet the aircraft, so we should wait until he pulls away from the rest. Once he's by himself, out of earshot from the others, we'll get the child. Agreed?"

"What if he hurts her when we jump him?" Selma has a good point.

"Honey, we have to wait and see the situation. We won't take any more chances than we have to. Keep in mind, if he hurts her he loses his grip on us. If it comes to it, he'll probably let her go to draw us off, to protect himself," John offers.

All eleven of them leave for town in time to be there an hour before midnight. They slip in a few at a time, moving along the backs of the buildings facing the main street. They go in the back door of Doc's office to watch the entrance of the hotel through the front window. With the lights off, the curtains are pulled back giving them a good view without the danger of being seen. Robert and Elizabeth volunteer to watch the back door, so, they separate from the rest to work their way around to be there before midnight.

There is practically no one to be seen anywhere in town except—wait a minute, there comes a woman and man with a small child about the size of Joie. They're going into the hotel. Before long, here comes another, and in a few minutes another, and another.

"What the hell is going on?" John's mind is racing. "He's got something up his sleeve."

The answer comes at midnight.

Out of the hotel onto the sidewalk comes a man dressed in black and a woman with a small child. He waits until his horse is brought to him by two armed guards. He mounts, then the child is lifted up to him. Then, before they leave, another man dressed in black appears on the porch, with a woman and a small child, and the same process starts again.

"They're making us split up. There's no way of telling which ones are Ty and Joie. We have to follow them all," Cheryl correctly explains.

"Take Falcon and get going," he orders.

"Rose, Hawk, you're next up. Be careful; make sure it's Joie before you do anything, and don't take chances that will get you hurt."

The same thing happens again, this time with Randy and Nora on their tail. Selma runs to get Robert and Elizabeth from across the street just in time for them to start trailing after the next man in black, two guards, and child.

That leaves John, Selma, Doc, and Mr. Vaughn still watching the hotel from Doc's office.

"This is driving me crazy. I want to be out there, knowing what's going on. Why are we waiting here?" Selma urges with impatience.

"We don't know that they have moved Joie yet, honey. Four young children were taken in there earlier and only four have left so far. Each of them had two guards, so if Mr. Vaughn's numbers are right, that means there's at least one guard left, maybe it's Ty Black, and our Joie," her husband reasons.

"Don't forget those four men who went in there with those women." She squirms with pent up aggression and fires back. "How can you be sure she's still in there."

"The women didn't leave, they stayed here and went back inside," Mr. Vaughn adds information. "The men, in all probability, haven't left either."

"It looks like it's anybody's guess." Selma snorts a sigh.

"That's why he's doing it this way, to create enough confusion to throw us off. I could be wrong, but I think Joie is still in there. I say let's wait it out." John takes a position.

"Why don't you see what you can find out?" Selma addresses Mr. Vaughn.

"That's a very good idea, I wish I had thought of it," He comments. "I can tell you if she's still here in just a few minutes."

He moves without hesitation to a large oval mirror in Doc's living quarters. Once on the other side, he concentrates on her name.

"Joie—Joie Justice. Joie Justice," he concentrates.

Nothing. He doesn't move.

"Ty Black. Ty Black." He concentrates on Ty's face and name.

Nothing.

"Something's not right. He concentrates on the image of the hotel lobby and begins to move. A white square appears enabling him to peer through into the room.

It is empty. No one there but the desk clerk.

Without drawing attention from the clerk, he exits the mirror and scoots up the stairs. No guards. The four men and women along with Ty Black are nowhere to be seen.

There seems to be no reason for secrecy at this point so he trots down the stairs to confer with the desk clerk, then out onto the front porch and motions for those watching to come running.

He explains that their prey has apparently left the premises, and that all the others left through the rear door a few minutes ago.

"If you're right, at least we have them all being tailed, but I still can't lose this feeling that Ty wasn't one of them. He could be one of those who slipped out the back way. If you all want to do anything different, go right ahead, but I have to follow my nose. If he went out the back, I'll find him." John holds on to his belief.

"I'll get a lantern from my office, John. If he went that way we'll need the light to pick up his tracks. There's no sense in us trying to catch up with those who have already left. Let's stick together," Doc speaks his mind, then trots off the get the lantern.

It's difficult for them to determine much from the tracks behind the hotel. Horse traffic and all those people leaving give a mix even the best of trackers couldn't separate.

"What do we do now? Which way do we go?" Selma asks in desperation.

"You think he's still in there hiding, waiting for us to leave?" Doc poses.

“My God, that’s it, Doc. That devil outfoxed us. He’s not been in the hotel since we got here. He left earlier. This thing with the four children has all been an act to draw our attention, giving him all the time he needs to get away.”

“Damn! Damn! Damn! How could I have been so gullible?” John beats himself up. “I’m so sorry, Selma. It just never occurred to me.” He hangs his head in disbelief.

“I know, you’ve done everything possible. You’re not the only one to take part in this mess. None of us thought about his leaving early. You’ve done all you can.” She puts her arm around his waist and gives a gentle squeeze.

“I suppose it’s still possible that one of the four who left here was him. If that’s the case, where should we be—here, or at the farm?” The choice suggested by Mr. Vaughn.

“If we’re done here, I’d just as soon go home.” John’s wife takes his drooping chin and pulls it toward her face, questioning.

After the trip home, and a pot of coffee, a weary John, Selma, and Mr. Vaughn find there’s little to talk about except the missing child.

One by one, their pairs of trackers start reporting to claim no success. While three of the four got close enough to make a positive identification without making contact, only Robert and Elizabeth had to get the drop on their assignment before they could be sure it wasn’t Ty Black. They all sit around with their heads in their hands, searching their minds for another avenue of hope. It seems nothing more can be done until Ty contacts them to negotiate a trade.

John and Selma retire to their bedroom, not to sleep, just to be alone, together. They lie on top of the bedspread, side by side, holding hands, looking at the ceiling.

“Poor Falcon. He’s all alone with this, at least we have each other,” she comments with a tone of consolation.

John knows what she means, but instead of concurring, he keeps his thoughts on his wife. “I can’t find the right words to say how sorry I am that things worked out this way. I wish I could take the hurt away from you somehow.” His words are accented with feeling.

“I know you would, honey, but you can’t put all the blame on yourself. I’m the one who let them steal her away in the first place. I know if there is any way you could change things, you would.” She tries to lessen his feeling of guilt.

He grits his teeth, swallows hard, and gently grips her hand, as if to say “if only you knew.” She takes his gesture as thanks for what she said.

A few hours earlier at Canozira.

“No luck with getting the angels yet, but here she is, just as I planned. We can use her to get anything we want,” Ty reports.

“What about Mr. Vaughn?” Remsar wonders.

“It worked like a charm. He’s there with them now. They have no idea.”

“Excellent, just excellent. I still believe he’ll do us more good than kidnapping their child. I mean, if Lilly has been in contact with them, or if she does, he’ll be right there. Are we set up to communicate with him?" The head of the Company needs to be brought up to date.

"Our craft will be in position to receive his signal every third day starting today. If he learns anything, they'll bring him here at once," the man in black gladly speaks of his success.

"Can we depend on him?" Remsar's question is a good one.

"Don't worry, he's a whipped man. He'll do exactly as I tell him," he assures with complete confidence.

Time passes with silence since everybody drifted off to their rooms for the rest of the night at the Anderson farm. It's shortly after dawn when a pair of eyes looks down at John and Selma lying on their bed, fully clothed, hand in hand, asleep. The eyes are drawn to the wedding bands on their fingers. After a moment, they move out into the hallway, and proceed to open the doors, peering into each room, only to close them again and move on. The eyes linger when the door opens on the smallest bedroom, the one farthest down the hallway. They enter, close the door, and move toward the bed. A hand moves carefully down to cover the mouth of the sleeping person.

"Falcon, sssshhhh." The awakening, startled man jerks, trying to breathe.

His eyes strain to see in the dim light.

"Cheryl? What is it?" He sits up instantly, expecting the worst.

"No—it's me, Sheree, honey."

"Oh, Sheree, thank God you're here," he says louder than she would prefer, and grabs her into his arms. "I've missed you so much, my heart aches all the time."

"Me too, darling. If we're quiet, we can have some time alone before the others start moving around. Okay?" she purrs close to his ear.

The two young married people lie and love together until they are sure everyone in the house is up and about, before making their appearance downstairs. Falcon is the first to enter the dining room.

"You'll never guess who came to me in my dreams last night." He beams a big broad smile. Conversation stops when everyone looks at him with questioning eyes.

"My beautiful, wonderful wife."

His announcement is followed by her move to his side with a voiced, 'ta da.'

The commotion goes on for fifteen minutes with as many tears as hugs, as the family greets another of their own, who has been absent too long. Her arrival has given a much needed lift to the spirits of one and all, even Mr. Vaughn. Sheree is not surprised to see him here at the farm, since her husband has already disclosed the details of the kidnapping of their daughter. The chatter continues with questions and answers all around. Sheree has trouble giving everyone attention at the same time.

"So, how did you escape?" Mr. Vaughn booms, naturally curious.

"I didn't. The truth is, they let me go." She answers without any explanation and resumes her conversation with her new stepmother.

"But why?" he further requests loudly, as if demanding an answer ahead of everyone else.

"Mr. Vaughn, you might be here with my family's approval, and that's okay, but you don't have my approval, yet. I just arrived here this morning, and there are things my family and I need to talk about before I put any trust in you at all. Is that plain enough?" she responds, almost attacking him.

Feeling rejected, he cowers where he sits.

"I was going to wait a while, but since you brought it up—I'd appreciate you leaving the house for a few hours this morning. As I said, I want to meet with my family, and well, you're not invited," she finishes bluntly.

The entire table of people, including Mr. Vaughn, are somewhat shocked at the take-control attitude of their once-polite, not-so-nearly-abrasive daughter, sibling, and friend.

Falcon is unable to control himself. He begins clapping, slowly at first, then faster and faster. It spurs the rest of the family to join in applauding her audacity and confidence. Mr. Vaughn rises from his seat and slides the chair back to the table. He turns and walks out of the room.

John makes a move to catch up to him before he gets out of the house. "Don't take that the wrong way. My extended family just needs to hear that kind of confidence right now. I'm sure that applause wasn't meant to hurt you, it was meant for her."

"I was there, Mr. Anderson, I know the meaning of the whole conversation and the applause. I also know your daughter. I'd be lying if I said it didn't hurt a bit, but I have to earn my way into your trust—all of you. That's the way it should be. She just let me know where she stands, and I respect that." The once head tutor at La Nesra explains.

"That's good to hear. Why don't you take a buggy into town for a while? You can follow up a little to see if anything has changed from what we knew last night. And you can let Doc know Sheree's home," John offers.

"I believe I'll do that. Thanks." He pats his host's shoulder.

John waits a few minutes then walks out front and motions for a hand to join him. "Our guest is headed to town for a while. Give him what he needs in the way of a horse and buggy, and let me know when he's gone. Pass the word around, if anybody sees him come back, let me know right away."

"Yessir, I will," the hand assures.

"I'll be in the house," Mr. Anderson advises.

He walks back inside to the dining room to see everybody excitedly talking at once. When they see him enter the din dwindles to quiet.

"I'll get word when he's gone to town for the day," he informs the group. "I've got the hands watching for him if he comes back before we expect him to, so we can relax."

"Let's get some fresh coffee in here and we'll get started," he requests.

After the word of Mr. Vaughn's exit from the farm arrives, the coffee is on the table, and relief has been achieved for those who need it, the dining room chairs are once again occupied with the Anderson blood and adopted family.

"I suppose I should go first and start at the beginning," Sheree suggests, looking around the table at all her loved ones, feeling a bit of pride at being one of them.

"I can't explain in words how good it is to be here with all of you, so I'll just say—I love you all very much, and I hope we're never separated this way again. When I was abducted from Canozira, I was taken to a place in the mountains in Europe. It was different than Canozira, but much the same. It has flying machines and all the futuristic things, just like the Company's headquarters. I was isolated for quite a while. I'm not sure how long, I sort of lost track. I was never mistreated, and was taken care of very well. I knew I was a prisoner, but other than that, I was fine. I was never given a remote chance of escaping. These people knew exactly what they were doing.

"One morning, a person came to talk with me. She said after I dozed off naturally, they put me in a deep sleep several times, to enable them to examine me. Of course, they learned I was my out of my life body right away, and determined that I was not the person they so badly wanted to capture after all. They told me a book I had been reading just before they came to get me, caught their interests, and they confiscated it. I have to say, when I read the book it reinforced what I already knew about me helping the rest of the world to survive. But the old language was new to me and I had to fill in a lot of places on my own to understand it.

"This woman took a lot of time to be sure I understood what she was saying. She said they felt the same way I did about the language, but they went a step further and discovered the book is written in code. It's hard to explain, but the words are mixed together in a certain way, then there's a repetitive sequence like take two letters in a row, then skip the next three, like that. She had the book with her and showed me how it worked.

"The thing is, when you do it that way, you soon find out there are some pages missing, and those pages are needed to get the complete understanding of who I really am, and what I'm meant to do in life. One thing they determined from it, though, is that I am not a danger to them or their objectives to save mankind. I couldn't believe what they said, but they had a complete translation made of the book, and they let me read it. I could compare their translation to the book itself anytime I wanted.

"It's true, can you believe it? All this time, all these feelings I've had about me helping to save all of mankind, isn't true, or at least not in the sense I was told. They say they believe I have a part to play in all of it, but it has little, if anything, to do with me dealing with the death angels."

John sits calmly, but impatiently, while he listens to his daughter explain it all. Everyone at the table cringes at the thought of something from another world attempting to break through our sky, and invade our planet every so many years. She tells it all, on and on, until her family feels fulfilled when she finishes.

"So they let me go after feeling I knew all about it. They know I'm no threat to them, and now, I know it, too."

"Can you hold on right there for a few minutes? There's something I need to do," her daddy asks, and leaves the room. She's still answering questions about her story when he returns to her side.

"Could these be the missing pages from that book?" he wonders as he hands her the twenty or so pages of hand written scribbles given to him by Marty Schoener, at Baltimore.

She takes them from his hand carefully and studies the top page for less than a minute. "They could be. They're written the same way, only the book was printed very neatly. These are somebody's sloppy handwriting. Where did you get these?"

"These are copies of the originals. The real ones are somewhere at La Nesra. One of our agents discovered them and made these," he says with confidence.

"May I take these to a quiet place and work with them for a while. I hope I remember enough to decipher them from the code they used. Time will tell, I guess. Can we adjourn for a couple of hours and meet back here then?" she entreats.

"Good idea. Back here in two hours everyone," he announces.

Sheree pours over the pages, making notes as she goes through the stack. A knock on the door of Falcon's room drags her from her cell of concentration.

"It's Selma, you've been up here almost three hours. Do you need a break?"

She opens the door to her stepmother, and stands, looking at her with loving eyes.

"I've not had a chance to tell you how happy I am for you and Daddy. And if you don't know it already—I love you." She takes Selma in her arms for a long gentle hug.

"Would it be okay if I call you Mom?" she says in her daddy's wife's ear.

"Oh Sheree, I'd love that. I've always wanted a family, and that would make this one perfect," her new mother answers with tear filled eyes.

After another few seconds of clinging to each other, Sheree moves away to collect, and put in order, the numerous papers lying here and there throughout the room. "Okay, Mom, I'm ready," she announces with a teethy smile.

While Selma is getting everyone back to the dining room, Sheree snacks on a sandwich and a glass of iced tea at the kitchen table. It seems she missed dinner, so, this will tide her over until supper. At least, that's her instructions from her new mom.

At last, everybody is present and can hardly wait for a report.

"I'll say this first, I'm not sure of the complete accuracy of my translation of these pages, but I am almost certain they are the ones missing from the book. I'm also surprised to learn what I have discovered, and I fear the consequences of its meaning."

Not knowing what to expect, those at the table wait with hungry expectation of her next words.

"Among other things, I find that I definitely was not put here to save the world. The pages reveal that there is a person, a person marked by six freckles or moles arranged in a circle somewhere on their body. I don't have them."

"I can testify to that," Falcon declares knowingly.

Everybody laughs at his candor.

"The thing is, I know someone who has those marks." She stops for a few seconds. "It's Joie. She has them up under her right arm, six of them in a circle about an inch across."

Mixed voices erupt around the table.

"There's more—and all of it not good," Sheree says, and swallows hard. "If what I think is true, she's not here to save the world. She's here to awaken the arsenal the next time the Korgots come from that other world. It could mean the end of our civilization, and my child will make it all possible. It even mentions a woman being raped and producing the devil's baby. That has to be me. Apparently, I'm here to give her life, and Joie—that sweet little innocent girl—is the devil's child." She stops to collect herself.

"That can't be true." Selma stands and defies what she has heard. "That little girl could never grow into something like that. Yes, it's true, I've seen those six little freckles in a circle, but what does that prove? There's probably hundreds of people in the world with a circle like that. It doesn't prove a thing."

"I hope you're right, Mom. But that's not what I believe as I stand here right now. It all makes perfect sense. Keep in mind, when I say she's the devil's child, I mean she's part of a very long-term scheme set up when the Korgots left centuries ago. She's not inhuman. I have certain powers, but I'm not inhuman. She's flesh of my loins. But she has an inborn duty she must act out sometime during her life. Nothing will change her. She will do what she knows she must."

"Let's assume for a minute that it's all true. Where does that leave us?" Cheryl jumps ahead of their emotions.

"For one thing, we should ask ourselves, who all is aware of what we know? Does Ty Black know about this? Is that the real reason for kidnapping our little Joie?" Millie queries.

"May I say something?" Sally interjects. "I recall Ty saying, when he lost his mind for a few minutes at La Nesra, that he would rule the world one day. Am I being too presumptuous to think the originals of these lost pages have been in his possession for some time? Does he know most of it, but just not know it's Joie he's looking for? Perhaps his interpretation makes him still think it's you, Sheree. My point is that since he has Joie, will he see the circle and put it all together?"

"Do the people who just let you go know anything about this?" Randall narrows it down.

"I don't think so. They know the pages are missing and would like to get their hands on them, but I doubt they know about Joie. They would have said something."

"I know I'm probably not as in tune with this as the rest of you," Nora explains herself up front. "But does it say anywhere in there how or when she'll be able to bring those angels to life? Like how old does she have to be, or something?"

"That part isn't clear to me, but it seems all she needs to do is touch them."

"So she touches them, what happens then?" Elizabeth pushes forward.

"They will do whatever it is they're meant to do."

"And nobody can stop them." Rose and Hawk prove their thoughts are together.

"Let me play the part of the eternal optimist." Robert is heard from. "If Joie's destiny is as you say, at least we know it now. Who's to say her fate can't be changed long before it comes to that. Another thing, even after she comes to realize what she has to do, first she has to find the arsenal. That might not be an easy task. We don't know where those boxes are right now ourselves. What I'm saying is, let's get our priorities straight before we get all worked up over this."

"Robert's right. We should think on all of this, then plan out what we need to do, and how to go about doing it." His wife supports his wisdom.

"I agree with that, but what do you think about me turning these pages over to the people I just left? They can have an accurate translation in a few days. Maybe we can throw in together, making our solution easier," Sheree asks the group.

"I guess I feel about them like you do about Mr. Vaughn." Randall surprises everyone with his candidness again.

"What if I bring them here for you to see and talk with," she continues.

"It would be a start, but I don't think we should turn anything over to them unless we all agree." Cheryl lends her vote in the favor of Randall's thinking.

"One last thing before we break this up. What are we going to do about getting Joie back?" Selma insists.

"I can tell you right now, if she's at Canozira, it will be next to impossible. The place is a fortress. From what we saw, the only way in or out is with the use of those flying machines. Cheryl got us out of there by impersonating you, Sheree, and I imagine they've taken steps to stop that sort of thing." Millie paints a dismal picture.

"Yes, I know. And if I was them, that's where I'd take her. Right now I doubt Remsar and Ty know I'm back. If Mr. Vaughn is still loyal to the Company, Ty has him set up to make contact somehow, probably with a craft coming to check on him every so often. How else could he pass along information? So, depending on their schedule, I could have several days before he tells them about me," Sheree starts to think out loud. "He wants us to trust him. So if I approach him with a plan to get Joie back, I could insist he prove his loyalty by telling us how he will keep in contact with Canozira. Then knowing when it will arrive, I could include the craft into our plan."

"Another condition could be that he has to leave his real body here, as he did before. That way we'll always have some control over him," Selma adds.

"Do you plan to go to Canozira with him? Won't that put you in danger as well? Then they will have both Joie and you," Randall warns.

"I don't think I have a choice. I could go through the mirrors by myself, but I can't bring Joie back that way. We need one of their flying crafts to do that, and that means I must work with him. Sending him to do the job on his own is expecting a lot. And if anything goes wrong, Joie might need my protection. I'll speak with him and see how much he resists telling me about his whole arrangement with Ty. Maybe then I can get a better feeling about him," Sheree explains her dilemma. "But as it is right now, I believe I'm our best chance at getting Joie back."

"Excuse me!" a familiar assertive voice echoes through the room.

All heads and eyes turn toward the interruption to see a dark skinned, black-haired beauty standing in the doorway. It's Charlotte, grinning from ear to ear. A rousing welcome bursts forth and continues while everyone gets their chance to greet the third female of the Anderson quintuplets.

"What are you doing here?" Selma's question brings order to the noisy chatter.

"I've brought urgent news. Daddy, you know those pages you brought with you? Well, listen to this. Our agent at La Nesra discovered this code book—and tells how to decipher all of those confusing words. It makes them easy to understand, and, boy, are you in for some big surprises," Charlotte spews, eagerly holding a thin book out for all to see.

"I wasn't expecting to see you here, Sheree," she continues. "I'm thrilled that you are, particularly since all of this directly involves you and Joie."

"Mr. Anderson!" a voice from behind Charlotte is heard.

"Mr. Vaughn is coming back up the road."

"Okay, thanks!" John replies. "Keep him outside for a while. I'll let you know when we're ready for him."

Information is quickly traded back and forth bringing Charlotte up to date. Everyone is eager to speak to a fresh ear. They find that Sheree's translation of the pages is for the most part accurate when connected with the information she brought from the time spent with her captors.

"I'm afraid I eavesdropped for a few minutes before I announced my arrival. I'm glad I did because it gave me an insight about your discussion." Charlotte is about to add her opinion. "I understand your strong needs to get Joie back right away, but that might not be the thing to do. It seems obvious to me that she won't be able to activate the arsenal for an unknown number of years down the road. If you go after her right now, they'll be on guard, expecting you to try to get her back. Let things settle down for a while, give yourselves a chance to take your emotions out of the mix. As time passes, they'll let down their defenses more and more. Go after Joie when they least expect it."

The next ten minutes of hearing one opinion after another produces little. Finally, it's agreed to wait a few days before trying to settle on any one approach to the problem.

Charlotte has one last point to make.

"If Mr. Vaughn is still working for the Company, why not use his eagerness to pass on information to your advantage. For example, tell him you give in, tell him you know the location of the arsenal, but you won't make a trade until Joie's back here safe with you."

"Not taking anything away from you, Charlotte, but I'm sure we've all thought of doing just that. I'm concerned that getting tricky could cost us lives, lives that none of us want to give up. We've seen a lifetime of that already," her daddy reminds.

"I know." His daughter acknowledges with humility. "One last thing, then I'll shut up. Does anyone in this room know where the arsenal is hidden? I don't think it's important for all of us to know where, but I think we all should take special care of that person."

No response.

Although the entire family yearns to take action to get Joie back with them, several days—then several weeks—pass with no word from the kidnappers. No one has mentioned a meeting to lay out a strategy, or to talk about a plan. To say life on the farm is going on as it should would assume too much.

Mr. Vaughn has fallen into their way of life. He has taken over some of the lighter duties, freeing up the younger men for the more strenuous work. He's jovial and more than willing to do his part. He thoroughly enjoys the family meals where he blends well with the bonds among people who truly care.

"I know it's not my place to say this, Lilly . . . err, I mean, Sheree," he mentions, as they unexpectedly linger at the breakfast table after all others have left. "But when are we going to do something about Joie?"

"In good time . . . in good time." She passes on the subject.

"Look, if you're waiting for me to make a move of some kind, we could be waiting for a long time, because all I truly want is what I already have, a life here with all of you." His comment sets the stage.

"It's true, I guess, at least for me. What I need are some truthful answers from you.?" she speaks honestly.

"Okay." Nothing further needs to be said on his part.

"You and I have a long history, Mr. Vaughn. I've seen you at work. I've personal knowledge of you manipulating circumstances to enhance your own gain. I'm suspicious of you for that. Also, I am not naive about your relationship with Ty Black. I believe you and he have a plan worked out where you have the ability to communicate on a regular basis. Just knowing that will never allow me to trust you. It would be like giving a known thief a key to a room full of gold. As soon as my back is turned, all or part of the gold would be missing." She challenges him to respond.

"I wish there was a way you could see into my mind, but you can't. All I can do is be completely honest with you. I can't erase all those years at La Nesra. I was doing my job. I was being loyal to a cause, the cause of a Company that took me in, sheltered me, and gave me a life, such as it was. But time has changed things. You weren't there to see how Ty treated me just before we left La Nesra to come here. He humiliated me in front of everybody."

Sheree cuts him off. "He beat Sally, too, and that was part of her plan to escape. So that doesn't prove anything to me."

"Yes, I can see your point, but regardless, I decided that very day I was going to do anything I could to destroy him—him and his quest to rule the world. He's an extremely dangerous man. He's convinced he's meant to rule this world one day. He must be stopped by any means. I didn't know anything about him taking Joie. He asked me to come here to make friends with all of you to get information, but what he didn't know was, he gave me the perfect method to leave his grasp permanently. It's true about his wanting me to communicate with him. He said there would be a craft on watch for my signal at one in the morning every third day from the day he left, whenever that was. I suppose he might still think I'm doing what he asked, I don't know. I've lost track of the days, so I have no idea when a craft is supposed to be near.

"He told me to line up a bunch of gun—carrying killers to come out here, too. I made no attempt to do that, so I imagine he has his doubts about my loyalties. But all of that was before he took Joie. You remember I told you about people looking for me on the other side of the mirror, and I couldn't go back there again." He continues to make his case. "I went in there to try to get Joie back. It didn't work out, but I tried. Odd thing though, it almost seemed like Ty was expecting me."

"If you used him to get near to where they were keeping Joie, then he knew someone was in the area," Sheree offers. "You saw her then?" she asks.

"Yes, but there was nothing I could do. There was a woman with her, with six guards in the hallway of the hotel. I moved around trying to get a better advantage. That's when I saw Ty. You're probably right, because I used his name to find him."

"Unless he saw you, he couldn't be sure who was trying to locate him. Did he see you?" Joie's mother proceeds.

"No, I'm sure he didn't."

"You haven't contacted him since then?"

"No. Absolutely not."

"That's interesting, you know, there's a possibility. Mr. Black might have thought I was there because he wasn't expecting you. He still believes my family knew where I was after I was kidnapped, which you know, they didn't."

"If he thinks that, then he's waiting for me to confirm it." Mr. Vaughn gets her point, then sees a little further. "Oh no, no, no. I'm not going—I'm not."

"Not the real you, he won't be expecting you to be out of your body," she says.

"I'll listen to what you have in mind, but I'm making no promises." Her past tutor at La Nesra agrees.

They lean their heads together and converse at a near whisper.

"So, you see, that way I'll be able to go with you, and we'll have a way out if all goes wrong," she purports.

"If I do this, will it square me with you? Will you believe me then?" he barters.

"It will, if you don't turn me in while we're there," she accepts the tender.

"What about your family?"

"We're not going to tell them. I don't want to get their hopes up for nothing."

"I think you believe they'll be against our going. Am I right?"

"That, too."

The first thing Mr. Vaughn has to do is determine the day the craft will be checking for a signal, if in fact, they still do. He takes a calendar and starting from the day Ty left, he counts off every third day. As luck would have it, the craft would be due tonight.

Ten minutes before one in the morning finds the two of them signaling across the sky with a lantern sporting a large reflector. Back and forth, up and down, slowly toward the western horizon. Right on the hour a star begins to move, getting larger and closer. Sheree hides, outside of their detection range, and lays an oval mirror on the ground.

Mr. Vaughn carries a large carpet bag. Once aboard, the pilots motion for him to get seated behind them. Then while they are busy with the controls, he opens the bag, removes a good-sized mirror and lays it on the floor behind the empty seat beside him. As they streak away into the sky, Sheree quietly appears from the mirror. She lifts the door to a storage hatch she found on a previous trip, grabs the mirror, climbs inside, lays a facecloth she has brought along on the floor over the latch, and closes the door down over herself.

The experience is exhilarating for the aging man, his first at flying high above the earth. He repeats over and over "amazing, just amazing."

After the craft reaches Canozira, settles at its docking station, empties the two pilots, and the man carrying the carpet bag, Sheree opens the cargo hatch and begins to move, working her way to the exit, leaving the mirror behind. Since the bottom of the craft never touches down, she holds on to the edges and bends down to put her head below the opening for a quick look. She wriggles her way through feet first and hangs by her arms to get as close to the floor as possible, then lets go. A careful survey of her surroundings says no one has seen her. A thought moves her instantly to the door leading into the compound of Canozira. "Here goes," she thinks loudly, then a wave of her hand opens the door. A wave of her arm in the doorway and it closes again.

"Wheee. They haven't changed anything yet, that's good. I can bring Joie through here easily," she confirms. "Mr. Vaughn is probably on his way to Remsar's office to talk. He knows what to do if there's trouble. Now, to find Joie."

She moves from point to point, making her way to her quarters. It's a place to start. Her key still fits the lock, she's inside. A fast search reveals nothing. Her daughter isn't here, but where?

"I don't want to go through the mirror and search that way. Ty might sense I'm here. And there's no future in running all over the place either. If anyone sees me, trouble will start." After a minute of weighing her options she decides it's worth the risk and walks to the bedroom. "Whoa, there's no mirror." Her voice hits her ears.

A room by room glance proves there are no mirrors anywhere in her quarters.

"This doesn't look good. I'd better get out of here while I can." Her thinking changes from finding her captive daughter to self-preservation.

"She isn't here, Lilly!" a deep voice booms off the walls. "And there's only one way out of here for you." She recognizes Ty's voice. "You continue to underestimate me, and that's a big mistake on your part. You can try to escape, but it'll do you no good. Guards are outside your door with orders to bring you to me one way or another. They're armed with the needed equipment and instructions to use it if you resist. I'll see you in a few minutes." His voice falls silent.

Knowing she has little choice for the moment, Lilly opens the door and accepts the guard escort to Remsar's office. They take up a position on each side of the door as she enters.

"Ha! Gotcha!" Ty beams as he moves toward her a few steps. "When are you going to understand and accept you are no match for me? This has worked out just as I told Remsar it would. Now I have you, your daughter, and your cohort, Mr. Vaughn, to negotiate with. It's just a matter of time and I'll have the angels again."

Lilly glances around the room, no mirrors. She acknowledges her past tutor with a quick look into his eyes.

"Why are you treating me this way? Of course I'm looking for my daughter, but I don't deserve this. What's changed? Don't we still have a job to do? Am I not still a part of it? Where did you get the idea I'm competing with you?" she fires questions at Remsar and Ty, hoping her cohort hasn't given her away.

Ty shakes his head with a tacit no.

"Here you stand with your buddy, on a mission to grab your child and run, and you have the nerve to challenge our reasons for detaining you."

"I'm not here with him," she insists coldly. "I knew he would come here sooner or later, so I waited until he made his move. I wanted to see if I could verify a few things before you found out I was here. I figured he would draw your attention while I did it, that's all. Now, let me remind you of something Mr. Black. I moved the angels in the first place to keep them from you, and I moved them again for the same reason. I know where they are. Keep in mind, also, I have your life body tucked away where you'll never find it. Don't worry though, it's being protected. The only thing is, if I don't check in on a regular basis, you know, to show I'm all right, who knows what might happen.

"And now, to use your phrase, you have the nerve to stand there and tell me I'm a prisoner, along with Mr. Vaughn, and my daughter. I think you need to reconsider your position." She spits venom with the accuracy of a viper.

Ty looks at Mr. Vaughn.

"I didn't know she was here until she came through the door. I came here to tell you she was at the farm. Remember?" The double agent defends himself with an answer to a question not asked.

"Bring Joie to me right now and I'll let this all pass as bad judgment in the course of all that's gone on. Otherwise, what am I to think?" Lilly continues.

Mr. Vaughn feels proud of his student of many years. He doubts she knows where the angels are, but admires her bluff.

Remsar holds his tongue, waiting to see where this is headed.

"Why did you go to the farm instead of coming here, and what did you come here to sneak around and confirm?" Ty insists.

"I went to the farm to try to sort things out in my mind. That book you forced me to find made me think about a lot of things. Finally, I decided I'd come back here to get it, and read it again. I want to see if I can clear up a lot of questions. Add to that, the kidnapping of my baby girl. Those are the reasons I'm here."

"The book isn't here. Whoever took you took it with them, or that's what we think anyway. You didn't bring the book back with you then?" The man in black bounces back with a fact that lends Lilly to believe she is starting to make sense to him.

"No, didn't I just tell you I came here looking for the book?" she sasses.

"Did you notice there are pages missing from the book?" he points out, passing on a chance to guff her back.

"I didn't, but that's probably why I couldn't make total sense of it. Do you have the missing pages? If I could see them maybe that would answer my questions." She stops, hardly able to wait for an answer.

"No, I've been searching for them for years. I wonder if they still exist." He pauses thinking, then continues. "Tell me where the angels and my body are, and you'll have your daughter," he bargains.

Lilly accepts his answer concerning the missing pages as an honest one, knowing his ego wouldn't let him lie about it. "Absolutely not. You give me Joie, then, when she's safe back home, I'll give you the angels or your body back, one or the other." She glares.

"Wait. Wait. Wait," Remsar joins the conversation. "Let a cooler head prevail here. You both are forgetting that we're all trying to accomplish the same thing. With you back, Lilly, nothing here has actually changed from before you left. It's true we don't know where the angels are, but then, they were already gone before we missed them, we just didn't know it. I'd like to get the three of us back to where we were, all of us working toward the same goal.

"We have Joie, and you have the angels, as well as Ty's body. It's a standoff. Let's leave it that way for a while. After cooling down for a few weeks, maybe we can work out our differences," he mediates.

Lilly and Ty stare at each other for a moment.

"I'll agree to that with two conditions. One, Mr. Vaughn goes back to the farm as one of you, and is allowed to continue to report in to me. And two, this 'cooling off period' lasts for no more than sixty days. After that, I'll work this out my own way," the Company henchman offers.

"First I get to see Joie to make sure she's all right," the young girl's mother wages.

"No. I'm not asking to see proof that you have the angels and my body, and that they're all right."

"Okay. Agreed," Lilly concedes. "I have a number of things to wrap up back at the farm, so people won't worry about me. I'd like to do that before I return here to pick up where we left off. I just need a few days," she informs the group.

"That's fine. I'd like to spend a few hours with Mr. Vaughn before he goes back. Can you find your way back on your own?" Remsar agrees and requests.

"You know I can. I'll see you again in three or four days." She leaves the room.

"Let her go," Ty orders as she passes the guards in the hallway.

Lilly is not happy with the way things have turned out, but she at least knows she will be back in a few days. With her full privileges, she will be able to search Canozira for her daughter. Mr. Vaughn will be out of danger then, too. Perhaps all of this is for the best.

It is just another workday on the farm, breakfast is an hour after daybreak. The aroma of hot coffee, sizzling bacon, and browning biscuits, fills the main house.

Mr. Vaughn joins the family at the table expecting to see everyone. He arrived back from Canozira about two hours before dawn. He notices an empty chair. Who's missing? He doesn't want to be the one to ask, so he watches and waits.

"Isn't Sheree coming down for breakfast this morning?" Charlotte inquires.

The din of chatter falls off a little as all expect a response from Falcon.

"Uuuuhhhh, she won't be here for breakfast. She isn't here." He accommodates their curiosity.

Mr. Vaughn's heart skips a beat.

"Where is she?" Selma asks. "Is she all right?"

"I'm not supposed to say anything, but she left last night for Canozira with Mr. Vaughn to find Joie. She hasn't returned yet," he confesses.

Conversation stops, then every head at the table turns to look at their mistrusted guest.

"Oh no. Don't blame me for this. I don't know where she is. The last I saw of her was in Remsar's office early this morning," he retorts, then goes on to fully explain the circumstances of his being here without Sheree.

"That's really odd," John jumps in. "A person would think she'd come back here with any news before romping off somewhere else."

"Before she left, she told me to expect her back before dawn, and that if she wasn't, something went wrong," Falcon explains further.

"I'm telling you the entire truth. She was fine the last time I saw her. She made an agreement with Remsar and Ty, and was headed back here. I swear to all of you, that's the way it was. I'm supposed to meet one of their flying machines every six days, just in case they need me for something. I can ask them about her then, but I don't believe they've done anything. They have too much to lose." The previously loyal pawn of the Company looks down at the food on his plate, and suddenly loses his appetite.

"Let's not get too excited for now. She'll probably be home shortly," her daddy speaks wishfully to calm a building furor.

On the morning of the seventh day, when Sheree still has not come home, the family is anxious to hear about Mr. Vaughn's meeting with the craft from Canozira.

"Ty came to speak to me. He's as surprised she isn't here, as we are. He came to find out why she hasn't returned to Canozira as she said she would."

"Do you believe him? Could he be hiding her, trying to pull a fast one on us?" Randall is skeptical.

"Yes, I believe him. He didn't ask for anything, or make any demands. He just got back aboard the craft and flew away."

Another two weeks pass with no evidence of Sheree. Life goes on by necessity, and this isn't the first time she has been missing for months at a time. They all miss seeing Joie and her antics, but they feel they know where she is, and is being treated well.

John has decided to return to Baltimore, and has wired Marty Schoener the date of his arrival. His four guards ride with him as they leave early this morning.

"Be careful." These are the last words they hear from Selma as they move out.

The first day of their horseback ride is quiet and calm. John's mind is mostly on things back at the farm, including his new wife, Sheree, and Joie. They bed down shortly after supper so they can get an early start in the morning. Any other time, their stops would be planned at a village or town where accommodations are available, but he wants to get to Baltimore faster, so he elects to take the shorter routes and sleep on the ground.

Times passes.

It is the last morning of their trip. They should make Baltimore in the late afternoon if they stay at it. John's mindset has changed from the farm to what he expects to find when he gets to his office. He and his guards have become goods friends. They all have kin in and around Baltimore, so they are just as anxious to get this trip behind them as is he.

Their horses are picking their way across a rocky slope, when John feels something hit his arm hard just above his right elbow. The sound 'thud' enters his ears just before he feels the left quarter of his head tear away, and his body lurch to the left as he starts to leave his saddle. He strains his eyes, trying to stop the darkness from closing in—dimming to nothing.

Time passes.

"If it isn't Marty and Rachell Schoener," Selma exclaims to the household as she greets her unannounced friends at the front door.

"What in the world brings the both of you all the way out here . . ." Her voice trails off at the end, when her mind catches up to the possible reality of this unexpected visit.

"Can we gather the family around?" Rachell asks solemnly.

"What's the matter? Is it John? Oh my God, is he hurt?" she questions, getting no answers until the family members close at hand are present.

Marty, with tears rolling down his face, relates the ambush of John and his four guards. John was killed instantly, along with three of the guards. The fourth lived long enough to tell what happened. He continues for those still able to listen.

"The bastards shot them from behind the rocks. They didn't have a chance at such a close range. Their bodies were searched, and anything of value was taken, along with their horses and supplies. With the hard surface they were on, there was no tracks to tell which way they went. No clue of who they are at all. When John didn't arrive as I expected he would, I sent a couple of men to look for them. It took two days. We had to bury them where we found them, you understand that. There was no other choice."

"I'm sorry Selma, I couldn't bring him home." Marty breaks down completely.

Randall and Nora leave the house to explain to the rest of the farm folk.

Two weeks later, midmorning on the front porch of the main house.

"Can I get you a nice cup of hot tea, Selma?" Rachell asks. Marty left for Baltimore, but she couldn't go and leave her long-time friend in this state of mind.

"I need to do something, Rachell," she responds without paying mind to her question. "I need to bury something of John's out at our family graveyard. Just about everybody who ever meant anything at all to him is there. I've got this feeling he'll never rest where he is, maybe he'll come home if I do." A short thinking pause.

"And then maybe I can visit him there," she yearns.

Rachell kneels to clasp her hands on those lying on the grieving woman's lap.

"Of course, we'll do that. Tell me what you have in mind, I'll get a hand and the family, we'll all do it together."

"No, I'd like to do it, just you and me. John didn't have many material things that he cared too much about. He cared more for people. You know he gave up the sole ownership of his farm, and divided it up amongst all those that work here. He made sure they all got a fair share and a chance for a good life.

"I'd like to take that old tattered sweater he liked to wear all the time, and put it in a nice box of some kind. I want to get a picture of everybody here on the farm and put it in a box with the arms of that sweater wrapped around it, and bury it as close to June as we can.

"Before we were married, I told June I'd take care of him, and one day bring him home to her." She stops and looks up at her friend with sad questioning eyes.

"Yes, honey, that sounds like a perfect thing to do." Rachell's tears roll down her cheeks and drip off her chin.

Selma shakes her head slightly, gives a slight hint of a smile and says, "Yes, that's what we'll do. He'll like that."

Chapter Forty

Years and years have passed since John's death. There has been no word of Sheree or her daughter Joie.

Selma Housler Anderson gave up on life after her late husband's murder. She lost her will to go on, and died of a broken heart less than three years later. Her name is chiseled into the magnificent marble monument alongside that of her good friend June, and their mutual husband John. She had requested to be cremated with an early picture of the four of them, John, June, Charles, and herself, dressed in their finest, attending a rare gala at Der Bote. She asked that her ashes be buried there in a small wooden box. Her wishes were granted.

Sally went back to La Nesra to try to pick up the pieces of what was left of an earlier life, and to make an effort to locate Sheree and Joie. With the absences of Ty Black and Mr. Vaughn, new people were assigned to facilitate and manage the compound. After a few years, she moved to Atlanta to open a saloon. Before long, folks at the farm received word that she married a Frenchman and was leaving the country.

The Company eventually abandoned the aging La Nesra entirely, leaving it open to looters and destruction. People feared the presence of the empty buildings, until one day many explosions leveled everything, except the massive surrounding walls. All of the doors and gates were removed. The hidden room inside the rear wall was never discovered or mentioned.

Randall, Nora, Sherman, and Randy Junior moved to Washington DC to allow him to further his career as a lawyer. She resisted steadfastly at first, but when she realized he was going with or without her, she accepted her destiny with open arms. With the war over and the slaves emancipated, times were changing. Randall caught the calling of freedom for all men, and knew the nation's capital city was where he needed to be. Letters moved between the Randall Stoker family and the Anderson farm with regularity, as well as occasional visits back and forth.

Dr. Cedrick Shaw and Mildred O'Toole at last discovered their true feelings for each other, and the inconvenience of living apart. They married and had a child. They lived in town where Doc continued his practice. She became an apprentice dressmaker, and later on, took over the shop where she worked. They were a regular sight at the Anderson farm.

After John's death, and the end of the war, the funding of the Sons organization dwindled. It wasn't long before Marty Schoener turned the entire organization over to a United States government agency. He and his wife Rachell returned to Memphis, where they lived out their lives. They stayed in touch with those at the Anderson farm, as well.

Remsar, the head of the Company organization in North America, passed away, leaving a vacancy which was quickly filled by Ty Black. He elected to close the operation at La Nesra, to manage the Company from their stronghold at Canozira. He continues to look for his life body, the missing angels, and Lilly. His only interest in the farm is the location of the angels. He hangs on to the belief that Mr. Vaughn will one day obtain information regarding their location. With his life body being nurtured by a box with flashing lights, his aging process is slowed to practically nothing.

Mr. Vaughn remains at the farm with his newfound family. Because of his age, he has elected to stay out of his carefully concealed life body as much as possible. Unlike the others, he's not connected to a life sustaining box, which means he must revisit himself regularly to nourish and exercise his human flesh. And that he does, once every three months to remain for a complete week. The location of his life body is known only to him. His days, his own to do with whatever he sees fit, find him laboring at farm work. It gives him a sense of satisfaction. But his true passion is finding Sheree, Joie, and the death angels, not necessarily in that order. He knows he can keep this up for quite some time, but it will not last forever. After all, his life body is already old itself. That urgency pushes him to follow the slightest sign of a lead, thus far, to a dead end. He has no idea where any of the three lost quarries are, but he knows a volume of places they are not.

Robert and Elizabeth built a house of their own on a section of the farm, about a half a mile from the main house. As they were an intricate part of the management of the farm, one of them was at the Anderson homestead almost every day. They made sure their three children had no part in the hunt for their aunt, cousin, or missing boxes.

Cheryl and Charlotte, two fine-looking women, never married. They both claimed they just never came across a man they felt that way about. Suitors visited from time to time, but nothing ever came of it. Their time was spent running the farm, which grew over the years with several purchases of parcels next to their existing land, making it the largest in the county.

After John and Selma were gone, Falcon couldn't find a reason to stay at the farm. He said he just couldn't stand living there like that, knowing his wife and child were out there somewhere, needing him. He left and never returned or communicated with the family again. They all felt he would die out there, alone, searching, pining for the sight and touch of his beloved Sheree and Joie.

Hawk and Rose grew restless feeling they needed to see some of the world. Their young lives kept them at La Nesra, so now that they are free of that—unencumbered—why not travel. They worked the farm for a few years and saved their money. Then one day, it was time to leave. After promising to write and stay in touch, they took two good riding horses and two packhorses loaded with everything they could carry, signed over their share of the farm to the remaining full blood Anderson children—including Sheree—and took off to discover a new life. The last news of them was from out west, where they had joined a traveling carnival. Hawk's ability with speed and Rose's ability to change her appearance fit right in with the road show. They said they were enjoying life as themselves. They were, in their words, "working their way around the world."

Many years pass.

As anyone would expect, time has caught up with the remaining founders of the Anderson farm. Their names and faces, for the most part, are just memories to a new, sometimes twice-removed, generation of fresh, energetic, mechanized-minded business men and women. The farm flourishes in the hands of these children and grandchildren of those tough, determined souls who received shares when the Anderson, Housler, and Sanders land were united into one, then divided among all those living there. As a shrine to their ancestors, the marble monument holding their names has been kept as it was in the beginning. The area has been enlarged to accept many more graves of those whose names have been chiseled on the marker. It's tended to regularly, to keep the grass trimmed and green. The wooden fence has been replaced by a five-foot-high white wrought-iron one with an eight-foot-tall, double wide gate at the front. The hands of two cast iron angels come together at the top when it is closed. The original six chairs put there by John and Selma are long since gone, but four white wrought-iron chairs take their place in the exact same spot. Visitors bring cushions and sit, remembering those who have gone before them. It's a place of prayer and peace.

It is now the first part of May, 1947.

The screeching sound of a large heavy door with metal wheels on the top and bottom, rolling on rusty rails, breaks the silence of the desert in New Mexico. A group of ten men and women enter this huge warehouse that once was an airplane hanger. They are all dressed in the uniform of the day.

"All right, now, we've divided this area up into ten sections, one for each of us. You have a copy of the floor plan, and your name is penciled in on the area you are to search. The crate we're looking for is ten feet, by ten feet, by ten feet, so it should be easy to spot. It was put here years ago along with all this other stuff that nobody knew what to do with. It will be marked like it says there on your paper. "Top secret, do not open under any circumstances." It will have these numbers, one of one, USG3300-3377869-1865-Level-9. Got it?" a man with stripes on his sleeves explains.

"Yes, sir," each of the others answers.

"Take your time and look thoroughly. Yell out when you find it," he barks.

They all stand for a few seconds determining which way to go.

"This could take all day, sir," one of them speaks to his superior officer.

"That's why there are ten of us, soldier. Let's get cracking. We've got till noon to find it. The colonel will be here then."

"What's in the darned thing?" Another searcher wants to know.

"I couldn't tell you if I knew, which I don't. Now get to work."

And hour passes.

"Hey—I think this is it!" a voice rings out from the back of the building.

The officer climbs over several crates to get a look at the markings on a huge wooden box. He stoops to follow with his finger as she calls out the numbers.

"This is it," he clamors and stands up.

Everybody looks around trying to determine the easiest way to move it outside.

"We're going to have to move a lot of stuff, sir," one of the men observes.

"Yeah, I know. That's one reason why nothing's where it supposed to be in here. Over the years, whenever anybody dug something out, they just put things back any way they'd fit. What a mess. One good thing though, no matter what we do, we can't mix it up any worse."

"We'll be better off to take it out the back end here. Look around for some floor jacks." He orders two of his people. "While you're doing that, we'll open the back door. We'll bring that overhead hoist around here and get it hooked up. Then we'll pick it up enough to let the truck back under it." Their leader lays out the plan.

With just three more crates to move, they notice a military officer's car pull up out front. The leader of the workers moves quickly to receive its occupant. He gets to the opening car door before anybody can get out. "Sir, if you like, it would be better to go around to the back side. We're almost ready. Is the truck coming?"

"It should be here in a few minutes. Any problems?" He hears a voice from inside the car.

"No, sir. It took a little bit to locate it, but so far, no problems."

"That's good. Stay here, the truck will be here shortly. You can direct it around back."

"Yes, sir," the subordinate officer responds.

It's not long before the large crate is loaded and chained down to the wooden bed. The officer's car leaves with the truck trailing not far behind.

"I wonder what's in there that's so important, and where they're taking it," a soldier asks thoughtlessly.

"We'll never know soldier." An honest answer from his ranking officer.

The crate arrives at its destination as planned. A group of ranking military officers, including doctors and nurses, wait impatiently as it is carefully opened. At last, a whole side section is removed and slid away, exposing the contents. They all stand motionless for a long fifteen seconds, taking in the many metal tanks, glass vials, glass tubing, and a special bed, all bolted and clamped into place. On the bed, lying on her back, is a young adult female with a leather mask covering most of her face.

"Ready?" A doctor in a white apron gets set for action.

"This will be a miracle if she's still alive after all this time," a nurse comments, as they move toward the open crate.

"Get all of this apparatus out of the way. Once we start it won't do her any good anyway," the doctor speaks again.

A crew of six medical people work in unison to loosen the clamps on the bed, and clear a way for it to be moved out into the room. It takes fifteen minutes, but once accomplished, a doctor leans over and listens to her chest with a stethoscope.

"Sssshhhh!" he calls for quiet to stop his cohorts from moving around.

He listens carefully for a minute, moving the scope around from place to place on her chest.

"I can't detect a heartbeat, but I think I heard several breathing sounds. Let's try to wake her up. Get a needle in her arm," he orders calmly.

A glass bottle full of liquid, connected to a rubber hose, held high over the bed, is hooked to a needle inserted into the vein of the unaware woman.

"Give it fifteen minutes, we'll know by then."

Ten minutes later.

The woman makes an involuntary move of lurching up several inches off the bed, and begins sucking for air with her mouth wide open.

"Hhhhhuuuuuuuuuuuuuhhh!"

The gasping sound of air moving through a small raspy opening fills the room.

"She's alive." Several of the spectators cheer at the same time.

"We're not out of the woods yet," the doctor cautions. "It's a damn good start, though. Keep your fingers crossed. She should open her eyes in a few minutes."

Per his prediction, the young woman's eyes snap open wide with excitement. She moves nothing but her eyes to look around the room several times.

"Where am I?" Her first words come out strained to a loud whisper.

"Don't be afraid," the doctor soothes. "You're safe. You're in no danger at all."

"Where am I?" she insists more sternly.

"You are in a military hospital in the state of New Mexico, in the good old United States of America," He answers happily. "How do you feel?"

"I'm not sure, can I sit up?"

"Sure, let us lift you. No sense in taking a chance of you hurting yourself now."

Three nurses carefully raise her to a sitting position, then at her request they swing her body allowing her legs to hang down over the side of the bed.

"Oh, that feels so good," she coos.

"Do you know your name?" the doctor inquires softly.

"What's going on here? Is there something I should know?" the woman urges.

"What's the last thing you remember?" the medical man persists.

"I was on my way home from Canozira after a meeting with Remsar, Ty, and Mr. Vaughn. Why? Something's wrong, isn't it?" She shows signs of becoming upset.

"No, no. Nothing's wrong. Relax, take a few deep breaths. I'll explain it all to you, but first let me check you over to make sure you're okay." He puts his hand on her shoulder beside her face.

She knocks it away.

"Who are you? Who are all these people? I want some answers, and I want them now, or you'll get to know who I am quicker than you expect." She slides off the bed onto the floor, preparing for a fight.

Everybody steps back away, giving her room to settle down. A man in a military suit with braid on his coat, steps forward slightly.

"I'm General Mandassa. We just woke you up from a long, long sleep.

"Believe me when I say the year is 1947. Records indicate you were captured back in the middle 1860s and put to sleep. The description we have of you, and who you are, seems almost unbelievable. You should be well over a hundred years old. Our knowledge of your existence is one of national importance. You have been located and resurrected by the order of the president himself. He thinks you might have reservations trusting us, so he's sent a person to explain it all. The president believes you'll understand after you meet the ambassador. He's waiting just outside. Shall I bring him in?"

"I suppose?" she agrees, not knowing what to expect.

"Come in please, sir." A nurse opens the door and speaks into a hallway.

Through the doorway comes an old, very well groomed, balding gray-haired black man. His white teeth gleam from beneath the smile on his dark lips. He walks slowly, carefully supporting his balance with a sturdy cane.

"Remember me?" He teases with a bit of quiver in his aging raspy voice.

She pulls back away slightly and grimaces her lips. "No, I don't know you."

"You look me over real close now, you hear?" the old man instructs.

She watches him walk several steps closer, and notices a little limp. A quick glance at his feet shows one foot turns, more than usual, in toward the other one. She studies his face carefully, squinting her eyes. "No, it can't be. Randy, is that you?"

"That's right, Sheree. How did you know me, by my handsome boyish looks?" He jests with a laugh.

She hurries to give him a big hug and kiss, being careful not to knock him down. "What happened? Look at me, then look at you. I've missed something somewhere." Her wit and humor are showing.

"It's been over ninety years since you and I met in the afternoons by that old willow on your daddy's farm. Those memories of how we loved each other back then will never leave my mind—mainly because I still do. People say I should have been dead twenty years ago. I tell them all that I'm not leaving this earth until I've found you and Joie. You, on the other hand, have been asleep in that box a good part of that time. You haven't aged at all. Just look at you, as beautiful as ever, so young."

"What about Falcon and my family? What about Joie? What about Nora, and your family?" she presses for answers.

"It's a long story, honey. We'll get together and take all the time we need to answer all your questions. But for now, let me just say this. Time has moved on without you."

"You're an ambassador for the president of the United States?" she asks him.

"Well, sort of. Actually, I'm a lawyer. I've done my best to further the cause of the poor man. By using the money I've made adjudicating, I've been able to lobby in the government at Washington DC. It's got so everybody knows me. I've asked so many questions of so many people through my efforts to find you until, not too long ago, the government asked me why? I told them, figuring they'd lock me in the loony bin, but, instead they said they needed my help. One thing and another, and here I am."

"You're a judge, then?"

"Yes, that's surprising, isn't it? Who would have thought." He answers with humility, looking his age of one hundred and four.

She offers a sweet admiring smile of approval and nods her head knowingly, never taking her eyes away from his. "I am thrilled to see you, Randy, when can you start bringing me up to date?" She continues to show her immediate need to know everything.

"These folks are going to need to work with you for a day or two, so they know you're okay. They want to start feeding you and make sure you're healthy, then they'll dress you up in today's clothes so you can move around outside. I'll be back then," he assures.

"You'd better be. Don't go off and leave me, you're probably the only person I know on this whole earth."

"I'll be here, don't you worry about that. Oh my, where's my mind? They want me to ask—are we looking at your real-life body?"

"That's a good question," she acknowledges. "May I have that mirror over there?" She directs the general.

Then, with a look at Randy she asks, "Is it okay for me to do this?"

"Yes, they all know everything I know. It will be fine."

She has the officer hold the mirror in front of her by its edges, and to everyone's amazement, pushes her hand and arm through it.

Sheree bounces back quickly from years of no activity. Her insatiable appetite for information is driving her caregivers to their wit's ends. They decide after two days to let her have her way, and give her walking papers for the military base. She wants to be taken to see Randy, first thing.

The trip to the officer's club to meet her friend proves exciting. All the motorized vehicles, airplanes, and war machines are new to her eyes. She has learned earlier in life the potential for such things, so she understands and accepts them without question.

Randy is sitting in a red leather chair at a small table, in the corner of the main room of the officer's club. It's carpeted wall to wall with beautiful dark wood furniture. Sofas and chairs abound in this obviously masculine—driven decor. It is beautiful.

He struggles to his feet when he sees her coming. A gentle, meaningful hug, and they sit facing each other across the table. A waiter approaches. "Can I get you something, ma'am?"

Sheree looks at her friend with questioning eyes.

"Coffee for our lady," He orders. The waiter leaves them alone.

The next six hours pass without notice to Sheree. Randy answers all her questions slowly, thoroughly. They enjoy a meal together, never getting away from, or losing track of their conversation. Finally, she notices how tired he's beginning to look.

"I'm sorry. I'm getting tired from being up so long. I could use a nap. Can we do this again tomorrow?" she offers.

"Yes, good idea. We can both use a bit of rest. Back here, tomorrow, same time?"

Sheree collects her sense of time by meeting with Randy over the next few days. It all comes together, until now.

"So, the United States government captured me when I was on my way home from Canozira on the other side of the mirror. They sedated me and kept me in that crate all these years. What's going on, how did you find me? What do they want with me now, all of a sudden?" Her questions continue to flow easily.

"As I understand it now, your daddy and the Sons organization wasn't the secret from the United States government we thought it was. In fact, the government was using them as a pawn. The legislation couldn't get the money together to finance a venture like the Sons. So money was siphoned off legally to certain companies and individuals, then passed on to the Sons. The Federal government knew all along about the Company's operations at Canozira and La Nesra. They also knew about the twenty-five men who made up the World Alliance. They knew about the spacecraft, they knew about the Korgots—everything. They knew about you, and finally, Joie. They captured you to keep you out of harm's way until you were needed to stave off the Korgots and stop Joie." The centurion lays it all out.

"Took them long enough." Sheree pouts.

"They lost you, almost forgot about you, is more to the truth," he proceeds. "They didn't pay much attention to me, until their scientific people figured out the Korgots are coming back for another attempt during the first few days of July. After stewing on it for several months, someone mentioned my name. I told my story, then they rummaged through old files and found what they were looking for—information about you and where you were. The rest you know up to now. They're terribly concerned that we will not be able to repel the Korgot devils another time. They say they have to believe that Joie will be in place to release the arsenal," he finishes.

"You mean, they found the arsenal, they know where it is?" she pursues.

"They don't know where the arsenal is, but they have to think the Company or the World Alliance does. Our government doesn't know where Joie is right now, either, or so they say," he casts his suspicions.

"You think they aren't being honest then?" She needs clarification.

"I don't know. You realize that Joie is eighty-six years old now. Unless she's like you, she shouldn't be too hard to handle these days.

"I do know they need me to help feed their information to you. They think you'll accept what I say as gospel, whereas, it would take a lot longer without me." He relates his feelings to let her know his concerns.

"What do you suppose they want me to do?" she wonders.

"They haven't said yet?" he answers curtly.

"You say Mr. Vaughn is still around back at the farm?" Her thinking swings.

"As far as I know, he is. He's like you, you know, he's not aging either." Randy fills her ears with what she wants to hear.

"And you're sure no one has heard from Ty Black?" She's fairly confident Ty has never located his real body.

"No, the last we know for sure is what you found out when you and Mr. Vaughn went to Canozira. Everybody knows about Joie now, and what she's here for. It didn't surprise anyone when I told them." He tries not to omit any bit of information.

"I think I'll make a visit to the farm. I need to speak with my old friend, Mr. Vaughn, and I'd like to see everything again. Do you suppose they'll try to stop me?" she asks.

"I don't know, perhaps you should tell them first."

"Yes, I'll to that. We'll see if I'm a prisoner here or what," she schemes.

She relates her wishes to travel to the farm to General Mandassa. He readily agrees, but asks her to delay her trip for a few days. He wants her to meet with him and his staff to be thoroughly briefed on the current situation. She agrees, this is one meeting she does not want to miss.

It takes the general a day to gather his staff around him, and another day to bring everyone up to date. So the meeting is scheduled the morning of the third day. After everything is considered, and rehashed, the meeting breaks up at two forty-five in the afternoon. Sheree is preparing to leave in the morning.

A light rap on the door of her quarters brings her to open it.

"General Mandassa, I wasn't expecting to see you again today. I'm just getting ready to leave for the farm." She greets her visitor.

"Yes, I know, that's why I'm here," he explains.

"Is something wrong?" She feels a little defensive.

"Oh no, I had some thoughts about your travel arrangements, that's all," he offers.

"Oh?" Here it comes, she thinks.

"Were you planning to move through the mirrors? If so, I would rather you didn't. Now, hear me out." He stalls her response. "I would like to keep your part in this a secret as long as possible. If you move through the mirrors, it will probably tip our hand. We'll fly you there. It won't take that much longer, and you'll make an old general happy," he insists without making it seem that way.

She considers his proposal for a few seconds.

"That will be fine, General. When can I leave?"

"Just one more thing," he adds. "I'd like you to take a companion with you. A woman moving around alone out there might draw closer attention from the unsavorable side of our society."

"I can take care of myself, General," she answers defiantly.

"I know you can, but the way you'll do it will be in the newspapers the next day. I'll assign a female staff member to you. Her orders will be to watch your back, that's all."

Thinking about the problems it could cause if she refuses, she decides to accept his terms. But she believes there is more to it than that. He probably wants assurances of her return to New Mexico. They will leave for the farm shortly after daybreak tomorrow.

The general's aircraft of choice is a four-passenger single-wing reconnaissance plane with two hungry engines. The noise is horrendous and the seating is miserable. It takes the biggest part of the day, and three fuel stops before the plane finally circles the main house of the farm to land on a flat field about a quarter of a mile away. Their arrival and landing brings everyone on the farm running.

By now, Sheree is not well known by the hands and managers of the farm. A quick introduction of herself, her companion, and the pilot gets them a ride on a wagon that brought a load of people to see the airplane. Before long they are at the main house greeting the people currently living there, none of whom she has ever met. Everybody is gracious and willing to accept her verbal credentials as a long lost relative of the Anderson family. They stare at her because she talks of times back beyond her age appearance. After waiting what she thinks is the proper amount of time, she asks for Mr. Vaughn.

"Does Mr. Vaughn still live here?"

"He lives here on the farm, but we hardly ever see him. He built a small house about a half a mile over that way," one of her once-removed nephews points. "If you want, I can have one of our men take you over there."

"I don't want to put you to any trouble," she says humbly.

"No trouble at all. In fact, he can stay until you're ready to come back. Please accept our hospitality, and stay here with us while you're visiting. I know everyone will want to meet you. They'll want to know all about you," he offers.

"To tell you the truth, Mr. Vaughn and I have known each other for years, and we have some unfinished business. Thank you for your kindness, but I think we'd better plan on spending most of our time there with him. If you can give us some directions, I'm sure we can find it on our own. We need to stretch our legs anyway after that airplane ride most of the day." She sidesteps his offer, not wanting any more people than necessary getting too close to their mission. Besides, once her nephew tells her where the house is located, she'll remember it well, this farm was home at one time.

Sheree and her companion, Lieutenant Corry Ferrel, dressed in civilian clothes, find Mr. Vaughn at home. He lives in a three-room house with no utilities or facilities. His water comes from a well, and for lights, he still burns kerosene lanterns. The wooden boards of the house are all darkly weathered from lack of paint, and the metal roof is the color of rust. There is no defined yard around the dwelling. Weeds and thorn bushes reseed themselves and grow at will. A small barn with enough room for four horses and a wagon sums up the structures nearby. He comes out of the house to find out who's coming to bother him this time of the day.

"He hasn't changed much," Sheree says to herself, as they get closer to the house.

"What do you want?" he yells when they are fifty yards away.

"Mr. Vaughn, it's me, Sheree Anderson," she yells back.

He motions with his arm for them to keep coming, and sits on a rickety chair to await their arrival. As they get closer he leans forward to get a better look. By now, the sun is going down and shadows are edging in.

"Well I'll be—it is you. Sheree Anderson, you look just like I remember, you haven't changed a bit," he exclaims as if he's found a long lost friend.

"Neither have you, Mr. Vaughn. I want you to meet my friend Corry."

Sheree does not, but Corry presents her hand for a shake. He takes it and looks her over as they greet each other.

Corry is a stalky built brunette, with straight hair touching her shoulders. She's five feet six inches tall and weighs one hundred forty-five pounds. She has dark piercing eyes under her heavy eyebrows. Her nose and mouth are almost manly when accented by her square jaws and short neck. She looks and presents herself as a scrapy individual. She squeezes his hand firmly to let him know.

"I need to talk with you, can we go in?" Sheree asks.

"Sure, it's a mess though. I don't get many callers out here," he replies and turns to go back inside the small house. "I'd offer you something to eat or drink but I don't keep much here. It spoils and gets stale if I do. Make some room somewhere and sit down. Make yourselves at home," he offers generously.

"If I can find anything, do you mind if I whip up something to eat? I know I could stand something. Is the water any good?" Corry surprises them both with her forwardness.

"Is she like this all the time?" He laughs and asks anyone who will answer.

"Go right ahead. As I said, make yourself at home. And the water's good and sweet. It comes from an underground spring, so, it's nice and cool when you get it fresh. That's one reason I built this place here."

Corry gets busy, trying to get out of their way. "Oh, one more thing, then I promise I won't ask for anything else," she calls before going out the door with a bucket to get water. "Do you have room to put us up for the night. We have nowhere to stay."

He looks at her back as she leaves, then turns to Sheree. "That one tells it like it is, doesn't she?" Then he yells after her, "I've got the room but you'll have to make up the accommodations, and mind you, the bed is mine!"

"I'm sorry, I had no idea she was going to act this way," Sheree apologizes.

"That's all right, I like her. Can she cook?"

"I don't know, I just met her this morning."

"Sheree . . ." He gets serious suddenly. "I can't tell you how many prayers I've said asking the Lord to bring you back here. I was beginning to think the worst."

"I'm glad I'm back. I've spent several days with Randy Stoker, and he's brought me up to date with things. Let me fill you in with some information I think you will find interesting," she begins.

Two hours pass as they talk back and forth. Corry serves up some delicious fried potatoes and onions, with freshly baked biscuits, a jar of apple butter, and a pitcher of water. Afterward, she finds several comforters and makes up a bed for two on a rug in the room next to that of Mr. Vaughn's. It's been a long day for all three; they tire out early.

"Thanks, Corry, for all the work you did this evening," Sheree mentions as she lies down on her half of the bed made by her friend.

"I told General Mandassa I'd take good care of you, ma'am. And that's what I intend to do. Now get yourself some sleep, I'll be right here if you need me for anything."

Sheree feels free and safe for the first time in, well, she cannot remember when.

It is almost eight o'clock when Mr. Vaughn stirs and awakens the rest of the house. It is a lot later than any of them are accustomed to sleeping.

"I saw you have chickens when we got here yesterday. Where do they roost and nest?" Corry asks.

"There's a lean-to on the back of the barn. I rigged up some poles and a few boxes back there," he replies.

“Do you ever gather any eggs?” she follows up.

“Nah, I don’t pay much attention to them.” He refers to the chickens.

“What do you eat, man? How do you live?” She seems concerned.

“It doesn’t take much for me to get along. Go on out there and see what you can find, but be careful of the roosters. They can get excited sometimes when you start scaring the hens,” he calls after her as she leaves the house.

While Corry is egg hunting and their host is washing up, Sheree works at cleaning off the kitchen table and buffet hutch. She sees there are no clean dishes for breakfast, and discovers a bag of coffee in a glass jar under a pile of what appears to be scrapbook papers. She locates a small tub and pours in some water. The hard remains of an open box of soap powders require the use of a knife to separate enough to wash the dishes. The lumps of soap don’t dissolve easily in cold water, but she puts the dishes in the tub anyway.

“I found seven eggs—probably could find more but those roosters are real pests. This will be enough for the three of us. I was planning to mix them all up with the leftovers from last night, if that sounds okay with you?” Corry explains.

“That sounds fine to me,” Mr. Vaughn calls from his bedroom.

They sit at the kitchen table with plates of steaming food and freshly brewed coffee. Nothing has been said for a few minutes as they savor Corry’s cooking.

“If there’s somewhere I can make some purchases, I’ll stock up on a few things so we don’t have to eat potatoes at every meal.” She informs her two diners. “Do you have a car? I don’t see one,” she continues.

“No, no use for one.” His response is short and final.

It’s decided they will hook two horses to a wagon he has in the barn for a trip to town. If possible, they’ll rent a car for the duration of their visit. The conversation turns toward the reason for their trip.

“As I said last night, the government is expecting another attempt by the Korgots sometime during the first two weeks of July. They think, after all this time, it’s almost certain that the Company, and the World Alliance, know about Joie. The government has these huge lasers spread out all of the country to help fight off the intruders. They have so many because they can’t be sure exactly where these aliens will attempt to break through. They rightfully believe they’ll have their hands full repelling them, and are fearful that Joie will start an upheaval at the same time. They think if she’s able to locate and activate the arsenal, it would require more military to deter them than the world has available.”

“Yes, it seems that it’s all coming to a head.” He feels the gravity of the problem.

“I, personally, don’t think the Company knows what Ty’s ambitions are. If I’m right, the Company will use their spacecraft to help fight the Korgots. I know the World Alliance has spacecraft, too, and will probably do the same thing. I have to believe the World Alliance also has lasers standing by, but I’m not sure about the Company,” Sheree continues, thinking out loud.

“I think you’re right about Ty. His plan is to rule the world, and the one way he might pull it off, is to be the man left standing after the fighting is all over.” Mr. Vaughn shares her opinions.

"Well then, it seems simple to me," Corry interjects with an attitude that surprises the others.

Sheree and Mr. Vaughn turn their eyes to the lieutenant as if to say, what?"

She looks at them as if to say, you really don't know? "It occurs to me from everything you said last night, and here this morning, that there are many factors you aren't sure of, or know at all. You don't know where the arsenal, or the death angels, are located. You don't know this Ty Black's plan, and most importantly, you don't know if your daughter Joie is still in their hands, or still alive for that matter. Am I correct?" She waits for a response which is not forthcoming.

"Lure them here. Lure them here before the aliens can start their attack. You said yourself, those death angels disappeared from a place close to here. It would be believable for you to find them here. Get that information to Mr. Black, and I'll bet one, or both, of them will come running. We can be ready and pounce on them when they get here," she finishes, then adds. "We learned in strategy class that a good unexpected offense is sometimes more effective than an expected defensive build-up."

"Go on," Sheree urges.

"Well, ma'am, they can't be sure about you. I believe you don't know where the angels are, but, they can't disregard the possibility that you do know. Nor do they know whether you're even still able to be involved in all of this." Her thinking strikes home.

"Ty Black is a cunning ruthless man. To underestimate him would be a big mistake. He's a man who would shoot you from behind as quickly as facing you. He has no conscience," Mr. Vaughn's volunteers.

"We don't know Joie. We wouldn't know her to see her. We don't know what powers she might have either; although, if she's still alive and young enough to be a threat to us, she must have something.

"I'm saying, what you're suggesting could be a very dangerous thing to do. If they find a way to eliminate us, what chance does that give the rest of the world?" he warns.

"What she says sounds like a good idea, but there are no assurances we can even get them here, let alone overcome them when they do. I do believe, though, we can't fight something we can't see or get our hands on. If you have another thought about it, I'd like to hear it." Sheree expresses her position.

"How will we know when they get here?" he counters.

"They'll find us. What other choice do they have?" Corry grins with satisfaction.

"Why do I do this?" the older man ponders. "If I had stayed in my life body, like I probably should have, I'd be dead and not have to worry about any of it."

"Where is your life body?" Joie's mother asks.

"I might ask you the same thing," he challenges.

"But that's the thing, Mr. Vaughn. I don't know where my life body is, really. You can relate to that, I know, yours was missing for years and years," she reminds him.

"There's a difference, mine was taken from me, you stored yours somewhere on your own. So, don't tell me you don't know," he defiantly insists.

"I'm glad I was briefed on all of this beforehand. If I hadn't been, I'd sign you both up for the mental hospital." Corry is amused at their argument.

"When I say this, it will be the first time since I did what I did," Sheree begins. "I hid my body, along with Ty Black's, where I thought they would never be found. A place where, if they were found, they would be in a position to do the most good for mankind. I hid them with the angels. I hid them along with the arsenal. I took two of the death angels and left them in a room at Canozira. So you see, if Ty and Joie get the upper hand and find the arsenal, she will probably destroy the two of us when she makes the discovery."

"It hasn't turned out as you figured it would, has it? And with the way things are, you've left two angels right under their noses. They probably have them and are just waiting for the attack to begin," the elder of the three points out.

"The turn of events surprises me. I thought at the time that Daddy had something to do with moving the arsenal, but now that he's gone, unless he's told someone, we might never know where they are. The truth is, I didn't know they were hidden in the smokehouse in the first place," she speaks candidly.

"I don't know why I'm doing this, but I believe you, Sheree. My life body is concealed in a nice chamber beneath these floor boards. Now, we both know, so what's your point?" He bickers.

"Maybe we should encourage them to search for the arsenal for a while before we pounce. If we could find it, and at the same time disarm Joie, this whole mess would take on a different appearance. Without her, those two angels I left at Canozira are worthless to them," Sheree offers.

"Ma'am, I agree with you. If we're going to do it, let's do it right," Corry encourages.

"Mr. Vaughn?" Sheree polls her previous tutor.

"Oh, what the hell. Let's do it," he exasperates.

"Good. The first thing is to invite our enemies into our web of conspiracy." Corry sneers as she speaks.

"I think I can get that job done through General Mandassa. Don't worry, it will be given to one of the Company's agents in our midst. We just need to determine how to word it."

"If we're to keep me out of the mix, then you'll have to be the bait, my good man." Sheree reaches to pat Mr. Vaughn on the shoulder.

"Figures," he snorts.

"If we like, we can leave right away on the airplane that brought us. We can get back to the base and have this whole thing in motion within the next couple of days," the lieutenant mentions with the slightest hint of urgency.

"Yes, great idea. General Mandassa should know what we're doing anyway," the young Anderson ancestor agrees.

"Mr. Vaughn, we'll be back within a week. Put on your thinking cap and come up with a good plan for when they arrive." She knows what he's capable of doing.

Two weeks later, an airplane circles the Anderson farm and lands in the same field as before. After working their way through the crowd of greeters, Sheree and Corry hustle to Mr. Vaughn's small, ratty, house.

He sees them coming and walks toward them sporting a big smile.

"I was beginning to think you two ran out on me," he yells before they can get close enough to make out what he's saying.

"What took so long?" he says as they get near, both panting from the hike.

"A lot of different things. First, we had to convince the general to do what we wanted. Then the content of the message had to be just perfect, and then they wanted to send a bunch of soldiers to help us out," Corry relates while Sheree catches her breath.

"But we're all set now. The message was passed along sometime earlier today."

"Come on in the house. You're going to be surprised. I went to town and loaded up on things. And I found a car I could get from a fellow at a gas station, so it's behind the house. I didn't think I'd make it here in one piece with it though. I hope one of you knows how to operate it."

Sheree looks at Corry with a startled look on her face.

"Yes, yes. I can drive," she answers hurriedly.

While Corry is banging pots and pans, Mr. Vaughn and Sheree sit at the kitchen table talking.

"The opinions of the government boys are that Ty and Joie will wait until it's almost time for the Korgots to start their attack before they show themselves here. It makes sense when you think about it. They come here, show their might and muscle, and activate the angels. The general thinks we should expect them no sooner than three or four days before they believe the attack will start." Sheree expresses the military's opinions.

"How long does one of these Korgot attacks last?" Mr. Vaughn must have something in mind.

"None have ever lasted more than one night, starting a couple of hours after dark," the woman across the table from him relates.

"How will we, or Ty and Joie, know when it starts? If it starts on the west coast, how will any of us know?" he persists.

"All I can tell you is what they tell me—the weather will change abruptly and there could be lights in the sky," she explains. "Did you do what I asked and put your mind to work figuring out what we'll do when they get here?"

"Yes, and I had plenty of time, if you get my drift." Mr. Vaughn explains what their plan should be to eliminate the threat of the arsenal once and for all. His plan does not include the two left at Canozira. "It isn't that complicated when you think about it. First, we separate Ty and Joie. They'll be easier to deal with individually. Then, we'll do them in at the same time. That way one will not be able to summon the aid of the other."

"Let's not forget, we can't just eliminate Ty. He's out of his life body. The best we can do is to incapacitate him by putting him to sleep or something. And we don't know about Joie," Sheree accurately points out.

A pause.

"Well, go on, how do we do that then?" Corry urges impatiently.

Mr. Vaughn continues, "We can't take them to the arsenal because we don't know where they are, but if we . . ."

He explains his plan in detail. The women have their doubts, but then, what else can they do. All three wholeheartedly agree to make any adjustments they can come up with between now and when their adversaries arrive.

At Canozira.

Ty and Joie have become close friends over the years. He looks about the same as always, wearing black most of the time. He's aged a little because of the disease his real body fights.

She has some of her mother's features, but overall, she more closely resembles her father. They have known about her circle of six marks for years. She, with his help, has discovered her many gifts of abilities not common to mankind. She's able to move through mirrors, move objects and herself around instantly, and heal herself from wounds, just like her mother. Her senses are keen and as sharp as a razors edge. She doubts things in life, but one thing she knows emphatically. Her mission is to arouse the angels when the Korgots return. Then she will sit at the side of the conquering tyrant, as his wife and commander, as they continue to discover, vanquish, and pillage the lands of life forms throughout the many dimensions they are able to travel.

Ty understands that even he cannot stand in her way. They have conspired to allow him to rule a vast galaxy as his own, a reward for helping her throughout the years. She, however, has no intention of keeping their bargain. While he—never trusting anybody but himself—hosts a growing feeling of skepticism of her sincerity.

"Listen to this," he says as he walks into her living quarters with a piece of paper in his hand. The same quarters her mother occupied at one time. "This is a message just decoded from one of our agents in New Mexico. 'Ty, the boxes and their contents have arrived intact. Expect your arrival at the farm immediately. Signed, Vaughn.' Do you know what this means? He's found the angels, Joie. He's found them." His excitement grows.

"Let me see." She grabs the paper and scans over it. "It certainly seems that way. Well, well, this is working out just perfectly. We can be ready when the attack starts. Our time is here, and I'm ready," she boasts loudly.

"A lot of time has lapsed since I've heard from Mr. Vaughn. Do you suppose he's up to something? He's had plenty of time to change his loyalties," Ty contemplates. "It seems perfectly timed on his part. I mean, coinciding with the Korgots arrival. Another consideration is my life body. I'm not sure Lilly's there with him, but if we eliminate her, I might never locate it."

"Stop your worrying. Two things: firstly, unless he's worked at staying connected somehow, he doesn't know about the attack. And secondly, what do we care? If he's located the angels, we'll take them; if he hasn't, we'll snuff his measly existence for causing us the trouble. As for my mother, if she's there, we'll subdue her and make her tell us where your body is concealed," she blurts with bold confidence, having no real interest in his problems. "When shall we go?"

"Our best estimate is the attack will come on the fourth or fifth evening of July. I don't want to be here when the attack starts anyway, so we'll plan to be at the farm on the second. That should give us time to be cautious, and still get to the angels. In the meantime, I'll get word to our agents in the area to check on Mr. Vaughn's activities. Who knows what we might come up with."

About thirty days later.

"I have word from one of our agents at the Anderson farm." Ty approaches Joie in the hallway outside his office at Canozira.

She follows him into his office and takes a seat across from his desk.

"An airplane was seen landing and taking off from a field there, at least twice four to six weeks ago. The passengers were two women, one of them claiming to be related to some of their people. They, apparently, met with Mr. Vaughn shortly after their arrival, both times. Since then they've kept pretty much to themselves, moving around in an old jalopy to do day to day errands," he reports.

"We could take this to mean my mother has made it home, and together with Mr. Vaughn have discovered the angels. I have no idea who the other woman could be. The timing's right," she suggests.

"Yes, I agree with your thinking. If anyone knows where those angels are, it's Lilly. If we assume Mr. Vaughn is still on our team, his report of this activity would prove it." He shores up her assumptions, then continues. "Let's alter our plan to arrive there at four in the morning on the fourth of July. We could have everything settled and be ready to react if the attack starts that night."

"That will work well. Once I get access to the angels, we can relax and wait for our friends' long anticipated arrival." She presses her lips together, then pushes them out as she runs her tongue along the crease on the inside.

July third finds Sheree, Mr. Vaughn, and Corry watching the midnight sky expecting to see a moving star.

"If they're coming it's going to have to be soon. This whole thing could be over within the next couple or three days," he affirms his cohorts' thinking. "You two get some sleep. I'll stand watch. If anything happens, I'll wake you immediately," Corry insists. She napped earlier, knowing her responsibilities will keep her up this night.

Her two friends retire to the house feeling comfortable with their sentry on duty. She watches the lights inside dim and go out, then moves a wooden straight-back chair into the shadow of the house to wait, her eyes scanning the sky.

One o'clock comes and goes. Two o'clock. She's up off the chair moving around, restless. Three o'clock.

"It looks like another uneventful night," she tells herself.

Four o'clock in the morning, July fourth.

"Sheree says they should be here by now if they're coming. Oh, my neck is stiff from looking up so much. If nothing happens by five o'clock, I'll call it a night," she mutters softly, wanting the company of her own voice.

"Wait . . . a . . . minute . . . there's something happening. It's just like they said, that thing just swooped to the ground over beyond that hill. They said to wait for it to leave, then wake them. That way they'll know it wasn't something falling to the earth."

A few minutes pass, then. "There it goes." She speeds into the dark house.

"Sheree, they're here," she says with a normal voice, and shakes the sleeping woman's shoulder.

"They're here?" Mr. Vaughn's voice is heard from the other room.

"How long ago?" Sheree's eyes pop open to make her fully alert.

"Just now. That flying saucer thing came and went just as fast as you said. That was something to see." Corry's voice relates her excitement.

"Are you sure all the mirrors have been removed from the house?" Sheree wants reassurances.

"Like I said, there was only two. We wrapped them up in potato sacks, and put them in the barn." The once Company man is certain.

"That's great, we won't be getting any surprise visits. Now all we can do is sit and wait," she acknowledges.

"I'm starving," Corry announces. "Anybody want some cold coffee and left over chicken."

"All you think about is eating, woman," Mr. Vaughn criticizes.

"When I get nervous, all I want to do is eat," she explains and heads for the food.

The sun comes up, and the morning drags on with no sign of Joie and Ty. While her two friends remain at the house, Corry takes the rented car and drives around for an hour, hoping to get a sight of something. She finds nothing out of the ordinary.

"Maybe we should go into town looking for them," she says when she returns to the house, anxious to get this whole thing over with.

"I think that would be a mistake. Make them come to us." The older, more experienced, Mr. Vaughn,is absolute.

"I agree, let's not get in too big of a hurry, stick with our plan," Sheree supports.

Meanwhile, earlier in the day.

Although it seems to Corry that the spaceship lands just over the hill from the house, it actually sets down less than a half a mile from town. Ty and Joie hoof it the rest of the way, and settle themselves at an all-night bar and grill.

The town is decorated; celebrating the festivities of the Fourth of July. Banners are stretched across the main street, light posts are wrapped with cloth of red, white, and blue, and a platform is built jutting out beyond the sidewalk in the center of town.

The visitors from Canozira order breakfast, and wait for the town to come alive. As soon as a few people begin to walk past the window by their table, Joie looks at Ty. He nods yes.

"I'll be right back," she assures.

Out onto the sidewalk and up the street to the hotel she moves, glancing around quickly to see if she is drawing any attention. Everybody she passes makes good morning gestures, but no one takes special notice.

"This is good, there are going to be a lot of people in town today. New faces are expected, so they will not suspect us at all," she thinks and feels a little tickle of excitement. She pushes the door open and walks to the front desk of the hotel, sporting a big smile.

"Morning, can I help you?" the clerk inquires.

"Yes, I hope so. Do you have a room available for tonight and tomorrow night?"

"Yes, ma'am, I have several, but they'll fill up fast, being the holiday and all."

"Do you have one on the back of the building, preferably upstairs."

"Yep, actually I have two on the second floor."

"May I see them?" She notes his expression changes to question her request.

"Oh, the room isn't for me. My brother's coming, and he's asked me to secure a room. He's particular, so if I could glance at them, I'd feel better about it."

"Sure, sure, I understand. Take these keys and look them over."

Joie walks up the stairs to the second floor. It takes just a few minutes before she's back at the desk. "I'll take this one." She hands the key to the clerk. "If I pay for it now, will you hold it for him?"

"That would be fine. How will I know him? He has to register before I can give him a key. What time do you figure he'll be here?"

She hands him a piece of paper. "This is his name. He'll arrive later this afternoon, or early this evening. I can depend on you holding it for him?"

"Ma'am, the rent on the room is paid for two nights. If he doesn't show up, it'll set empty for two nights."

"Thank you, you're very kind." She turns and leaves.

Ty looks up as she enters the bar and grill.

"Problems?" he asks as she sits down.

"Everything went fine. We're all set there. Now, how do we get out to the farm."

"I just bought a car from the grill cook." He dangles the keys from his fingers. "He said there's no vehicles around here to rent, but he had a car he'd sell me. Then, if I want to bring it back, he'll keep half the money and give the rest back." Ty grins as he speaks.

They leave the bar on their way to get their car when Joie says.

"It won't surprise me to find out the angels are somewhere here in town. I can't explain it, but I have this feeling; I could almost reach out and touch them."

It's early afternoon before they near the small house belonging to Mr. Vaughn. Their newly purchased relic of a car sets idling roughly as they walk ahead to look over the next hill.

"That must be it. It sure isn't much, is it?" Joie shakes her head.

Sheree, Mr. Vaughn, and Corry, all standing outside the house, see the car coming.

"I wouldn't expect them to arrive in a car. I mean, they came here in a spaceship." Corry doubts it's Ty and Joie.

"Who else could it be. Nobody ever comes out here except the two of you, and now them." Mr. Vaughn's terse comment signals her to be quiet.

The coupe rolls to a stop some fifty yards away, the doors open and its occupants get out.

"Well, well, hello, Lilly. I wasn't sure if you'd be part of this or not. I can't say I'm surprised you're here." Ty opens the conversation. He nods in acknowledgment of Mr. Vaughn.

"Remember me, Joie?" Sheree questions her daughter, knowing it must be her.

"No, but I know you from your picture in this locket. It doesn't do you justice."

"No pun intended, I'm sure. You said 'justice,' our last name." Her mother explains, suddenly feeling a connection to her daughter.

"There's no sense fooling around, let's get to it. Mr. Vaughn, I've received word to the effect that you know where the angels are located, and have invited me here to get them. Is that accurate?" The man in black cuts to the matter at hand.

"That's right. Sheree led me to them. She knows where your life body is, too." He takes several steps toward his one time boss.

That signals them all to move toward each other to eliminate the shouting back and forth.

"So, take us to them," Ty orders.

"It's not that easy. Put yourself in our shoes for a minute. It's been a long time since my days with you and Remsar at Canozira. I know my feelings about how things were back then have been tested again and again, and that makes me wonder about yours. Let's not kid ourselves, we both know about Joie and her purpose. And we both know about the attack expected within the next few days. Before we lead you anywhere, we need some assurances about what's going to happen to us once you get everything you want. Right now, our world has the ability to repel the Korgots as we have many times before. But if we let Joie get her hands on those angels, well, it's a whole different story. So, what's in it for us?" Sheree bargains.

"My, you have changed, Lilly. You know, in the back of my mind I've always known your biggest concern is self-preservation, but this? You're willing to barter away all of the souls on earth for the right deal for the three of you? It's hard for me to believe that. I'd sooner believe you lured us here to put an end to us," he responds knowingly, his eyes watching for a telltale sign in the faces of his opposers.

"You're forgetting me. I've been loyal to you all these years, so when I say this, think about it real hard. If we were of a mind to destroy you, we could have done it already. Sheree knows where your life body is. If she does away with it, you're history. We also know where the angels are, and if we destroy them, Joie's threat is gone. Things change, people change. What's in it for us?" Mr. Vaughn righteously proclaims.

Joie looks at Ty. "He's right, you know."

"What is it exactly that you want?" Mr. Black seems to want to work out a deal.

"We have a list of five thousand names, including ours. These lives and souls are to be spared, and the earth is to be left inhabitable. To make it more palatable for your conquering Korgot friends, leave us here for several centuries, then come back and gather more souls for your purposes, again leaving enough for our race to continue. It could go on for all time," he answers.

Corry, standing, dressed in her military best, acts as if she represents at least five thousand people.

"You have said you wanted to rule the world, well, here's your chance. And with you in control of your own life body again, you could do it for a long, long time." Sheree teases his ego.

"And the two of you go on forever, too," he adds.

"How about you? Do you have the gift, too?" he addresses Corry.

"Look, I'm nobody right now. But I will be somebody when we put this deal together. The life I have left will be a whole lot longer and better than what I'm looking at right now," she says convincingly.

"All right, how do we do this?" Ty agrees.

The three look at Joie awaiting her approval.

"Me? Yes, of course." She seals the deal.

"First of all, when is your spacecraft due? Is it tonight or when? I assume you'll want to take the angels, and your life body, with you?" Sheree starts setting the hooks of their plan.

"Yes, that's right, they'll be here at one in the morning, every morning, until we summon them to land," he divulges.

"That's what we thought. So, tonight is the night to get this all done," Joie's mother continues. "We'll wait until after dark, when the celebration in town gets in full swing, so nobody will notice."

"I've already reserved a room at the hotel in town. We feel the same way. I didn't want to draw any attention so I left word that my brother would arrive and register for it. It's all paid for. Here, this is the name I gave him." Joie volunteers and passes a piece of paper to Mr. Vaughn.

"Good, I'm not sure why you thought to do so, but we can use it while we're waiting to move all those boxes to the spacecraft pickup sight," he confirms as he reads the name on the paper.

"They're in town then? I knew it!" Joie's eagerness builds.

"Mr. Vaughn will go into town right away to make a few arrangements. He can ride back with you, Joie. Let him register and get a key to the room. Then, you slip past the clerk and join him there. Ty, you stay here with Corry and me. We'll get your life body and take it to the pickup spot. She can stay there while you and I get to town to help with the rest. Once we're all there we can use both cars to move the boxes. How's that?"

"Five trips and we'll be finished." Ty does the math. "Let's do it."

"Just one more time, you both agree to our terms as we explained them?" Sheree checks one last time for appearances.

"Ty? Joie?" she asks.

"Yes, definitely." They acknowledge

"I'll get my things together and be with you in a few minutes, Joie," Mr. Vaughn advises and turns to go into the house.

Ty, Sheree, and Corry watch as the black sedan leaves for town. After the car drifts over the first rise, they go inside the small house to wait until the sun starts to set. Corry fixes an early supper while they talk, recalling memories of years gone by. As he begins to relax, trusting them more and more, they move around the house doing this and that, until he seems at ease. Then they break out a bottle of laced bourbon and encourage him to drink what he wants. He resists at first, but with a little coaxing, he agrees to a small drink. When the meal is ready, they sit at the table enjoying steaks and fried potatoes, and a bit more bourbon.

Afterward, they make sure he sits in the only overstuffed chair available, to rest. Little by little, he droops and drops off to sleep.

"Boy, it took enough of that stuff to knock him out," Corry exclaims.

"Ssshhh. Not too loud, you might wake him up," Sheree warns. "Get that rope, we'll tie him up good and tight."

After laying him on the floor, they tie his hands behind him, and bend his legs up and bind them together. Then, they wrap a strip of white muslin around his head over his mouth and knot it on the backside of his neck.

"There, that should hold him," Sheree says, feeling a job well done. "Listen, I'm concerned about Mr. Vaughn. I don't like the idea of Joie already having a room set up at the hotel. They must have a plan of their own," she relates. "I'd like to take a peek through the mirror at that hotel room. Will you be okay for a half-hour by yourself with him?" She motions toward Ty, lying helpless on the floor, sound asleep.

"I'll be okay. What can he do if he wakes up?" she encourages Sheree to go.

"If he does, and starts anything, hit him hard on the head with something. Got it?" Cory hears her last bit of instructions.

Sheree leaves the house for the barn, then unwraps one of the two mirrors stored there. She leans it against a stall door, and slips through.

Mr. Vaughn is sitting quietly, contemplating, in the hotel room when Sheree looks from behind the mirror. Joie is nowhere to be seen. She clears her throat as she moves to enter, so as not to startle him. He raises his head and turns a little to greet her.

"Where is she?"

"She's not here, yet. I'm beginning to wonder about her." He worries. "What are you doing here so soon?" The older man senses something is wrong.

"Everything's fine at the house. We've got him down, bound, and gagged."

Tap. Tap. Tap.

"That must be her now. Get out of here, I'll see you later as planned?" Mr. Vaughn whispers as he stands up ready for action.

Sheree slides through the mirror and emerges in the barn, close to Mr. Vaughn's home. A flickering of light through the cracks in the boards causes her to run outside.

"Oh my God!" she gasps when she sees the little house almost completely ablaze.

“Corry! Corry!” she screams as loud as she can, making the back of her throat feel like it’s coming loose.

“I’m trapped! I can’t get out! Help me!” a bloodcurdling yell comes from inside the burning inferno.

Sheree doesn’t stop to think of the danger. She runs and jumps through the open front door into the burning house.

Chapter Forty-One

Mr. Vaughn watches Sheree disappear through the mirror, collects himself together, then turns to walk to the door. He puts on a smile as he turns the knob.

"Good, it's you. Did anyone see you come up here?" He begins his charade.

"I don't think so. There's so much going on out there, I think a cannon could go off and nobody would notice. Are you okay, you look uncomfortable?" Sheree's young adult daughter shows her intuitiveness.

"I'm fine. Just a little warm, that's all," he assures her.

He motions her to sit on a chair in front of the vanity and mirror. It's been moved away from the dresser enough to allow a person to walk behind it, and turned to face the door. He sits on the edge of the bed facing her.

The conversation over the next several minutes deals with her questions about her mother's past and family. He's glad they have something to talk about, otherwise, this would be work—making small talk while he waits. The minutes pass like hours.

"Would you like a glass of wine?" he asks. At the same time, he moves to the towels lying beside a washbowl. He picks one up and wipes the sweat from his brow.

"No, I'd better not. I have a feeling I'm going to be very busy tonight. Are the angels close by? I have this really strong sense that I can almost reach out and touch them, You can tell me now, it's almost time to take me to them anyway," she urges, anxious. "Are you sure you're okay? Your shirt is wet with perspiration," she asks again.

Before he can answer, her face changes expressions. He watches as she falls into a trancelike stare. Her eyes roll up to where he can no longer see the pupils; she has a gaunt appearance, her complexion fades to a ghostly hue. A wave of his hand gets no reaction at all. He's ready to take advantage of her state and tie her up, when she snaps out of it, shaking her head like a dog shaking off water.

"They're here. The invasion is about to begin." She glares at him with the devil in her eyes, and the face of death.

"How do you know that?" he reacts, a tingling of fear slides down his back.

"They're here! I want to know where the angels are now!" she growls with a loud whisper, a hiss in her voice.

"No, it's not time yet. We have to wait until it's time," he says nervously, feeling very uncomfortable. He fidgets, water is rolling down his face, dripping off his nose and chin, sweat runs down his back. "Something's wrong. I'm not sick, but I'm burning up. I have to find Sheree, she should have been here by now."

"Hey! You!" Joie yells with a banshee howl. "I told you to take me to the angels now. You don't want to make me angry!"

Her eyes have changed. The part that's usually white has turned a bright yellow, and her pupils, a burning orange. Their stare follows him as he moves around the room, she never moves her head.

He's not sure if this hideous female transforming in front of him is causing his distress, or if it is because Sheree has not shown up as planned. He's getting warmer. He needs to remove part of his clothing. "I have to do something before she turns into a monster that wants to kill me," he urges himself.

"You're making me angry. You don't want to make me angry. Take me to those angels, NOW!" she shouts.

He walks around as her devilish eyes follow him with a burning stare. This time he continues to go around behind her. She doesn't try to turn.

"Get out here where I can see you!" she demands.

Not knowing how she will react, he bends down from behind, then with one motion he slides his arm around her neck so his elbow is under her chin, his other hand past the back of her neck to grab his biceps. He grabs his other biceps with his hand coming around her neck and squeezes. She gasps for breath and starts to rise from the chair, her feet off the floor, lifting him with her. Just before his feet leave the floor he gives a mighty shift toward her right front and jerks her neck to the side.

Crack! Her eyes fix and stare straight ahead, as she sinks back onto the chair hanging limp in his grip.

"I didn't want to break your neck, but you gave me no choice," he says to her lifeless body, then lifts her from the chair and lays her on the bed.

"I'm burning up. I have to get back to the farm and see what's going on."

Through the mirror he moves with caution. With little effort, he finds his way to the mirror in the small barn outside his home. When he steps outside, he can't believe his eyes, His house is burning, falling in on itself.

"That's why I'm so hot. My life body is down under the floor, all that heat. I don't see them anywhere." He calls out their names as he walks around the roaring fire.

"Ty! Sheree! Corry!" he yells several times. "The car is still here. Where could they be? How did this fire get started?" He tries to understand.

"If they're in there . . ." He stops at the thought, and looks up at the sky as if to say a prayer.

"Lightning, a lot of it. Look at those streaks. They're all over the sky. But there's no clouds, and there isn't any thunder. It has to be the attack of those Korgots. It's started just like she said it would. Those streaks must be the lasers.

"Sheree, where are you? You'd know what to do, I don't," he pleads.

"What should I do, what should I do?" His mind spins. "Get back to the hotel and make sure Joie doesn't somehow make it to those angels, wherever they are." He decides and runs for the mirror in the barn.

When he emerges in the hotel room, his first thought is to tie the apparently lifeless body to the bedstead. He can tear up a sheet and tie her arms and legs to the headboard and footboard, But when he checks to see if she's still in the state she was when he left, he sees she has changed. Her face is almost skeletal. Her arms and legs are skinny and bony. It's like she's wasting away.

"I can't stand to see you this way, and I can't touch you to tie you up." He turns his head, then grabs the bedspread and pulls it out from under her to cover her body.

"I'll just sit right here on this chair until dawn. The attack should be over by then. I'll be here in case she recovers and tries to get up. I can't take a chance she'll locate those angels. She said they're near here somewhere." He's used to talking to himself at this point. It seems ordinary. "Another thing, if Sheree wasn't in the fire back at the house, she'll come here looking for me. This is good, I'll wait right here." His ramblings are not heard beyond the walls of the room due to the noise from the festivities outside.

Dawn comes slowly this day, the noise outside eventually fades as the night wears on. Then it's so quiet, the lack of noise is deafening to the one remaining man on earth who knows the actual facts of the angels, the Korgots, and the covert fight among three major powers of the world.

He has been staring at the same dirty spot on the wall for the past three hours, lost in thought, expecting the door to come crashing down any minute, followed by strange-looking beings from another world.

Daylight coming through the only window in the room finally causes him to stir. "We're still here. Thank God, we must have repelled them again." He turns to look at the bed, she's still there, her feet exposed from beneath the bedspread. He moves carefully toward her, not wanting to see what she has turned into overnight. He pulls her shoes off, throws them on the floor, then looks at her feet.

They look normal. He raises the bedspread to look down at the young woman lying partly on her side and stomach. She's changed back, no longer that thing he saw last night. He puts his hand on her temple to feel for a heartbeat—nothing. In fact, she's stone cold to his touch.

"She's dead, I think she's really dead. She must have come here in her life body thinking that's what it would take to wake up the angels," he reasons.

"My life body must have survived the fire, I'm still here," he realizes.

"I could leave and let them find her, I suppose. But what about Sheree and Ty? They wouldn't die if they were in the fire, but Corry would. And let's not forget, the desk clerk saw me and could point me out. I'd better stay and straighten this mess out."

"Will I say I killed her? What else could I say, I'm here with her dead body? Will they believe me when I explain what happened? I have to tell them. Someone here has to be told what I know. Someone has to know about the Korgots and the angels, there's no one else to do it. Those angels must be here in town somewhere, and if I know that, so will Ty—if he's still alive. It's a fantastic story, though. Will these people be able to accept what I'm saying? The only reason I believe it, is because I've lived it. I have to tell them, even if it means they hang me for murdering her. I have to tell them." Mr. Vaughn runs the pros and cons through his mind over and over again until, at last, he knows what he has to do.

A telephone rings on the other side of town.

"Hello, police department." A long pause. "Hold on, I'll get the chief."

"This is a guy named Leon, says he needs to talk to you right away."

"This is Chief Turner. What can I do for you, Leon?"

Epilogue

The conversation, from Chapter One of this book, picks up where it left off at the Bartlett Hotel, in Bartlettsville.

Sheriff Collins is coming down the stairs, two at a time, wondering what all the commotion is about.

"What the hell is going on?" he yells.

"Marc says he's found some bodies in the basement," Doc Edwards, the county coroner, explains briefly.

"Let's take a look," Durrell Turner, chief of police at Bartlettsville, starts to move toward the basement door.

He's the first of the three law enforcement officers to step down off the ladder to the lower floor. They quickly follow. The air is cool, damp, with a musky smell. Along with the poor light, it feels like a grave at dusk.

"Here, I've got a match or two." The sheriff wipes the tip of one across the hip of his trousers.

DT is quick to follow suit.

"There's ten of them all right. What are these boxes attached to them? There's lights dancing all over the place," Marc says, amazed.

"Doc!" the sheriff yells up the steps. "You'd better get down here. It looks like we're going to be here all day."

Before Doc can make a move toward the cellar door, Jefferson Bartlett lays his hand on his longtime friend's shoulder.

"Wait here, Doc. Let me get those boys up here."

"Come on up out of there, I have to talk to the lot of you," he informs the three officers.

When they are upstairs in the hallway, he shuts the cellar door and locks it with a key on a ring he carries, then waves his hand for them to follow to the lobby.

People are peering out through slightly cracked doors of their rooms as they pass.

"Vern, shut the front door and lock it, we're closed."

"Gentlemen, will you all please follow me to my office." He leads them to the back of the hotel on the first floor.

"Find a place to sit, this could take some time," he graciously invites the group.

Situated behind his desk, he offers them each a cigar, lights one himself, and turns sourly serious.

"I'm about to tell you a story that you'll not believe. It's going to strain your common sense and test your fortitude. But understand this, I believe it. I believe it because it has been passed down to me by generations of my ancestors. The proof of this story you have seen in the cellar. I've dreaded this day all my life."

He begins by relating the content of a meeting his namesake ancestor, Jefferson Lee Bartlett, had with Earl Gray, the mayor of Bartlettsville, and John Anderson, many years ago.

"Mr. Anderson, apparently desperate, without many options, asked the other two men to conceal these bodies, called the arsenal, and charged them with their safety. He explained to them that the future of the human race depended on them. They understood that the task they accepted would be for the rest of their lives, and those of their heirs, for time unknown."

The story continues keeping the men occupied until mid-afternoon. When he finishes, they, to the man, are in awe. Coincidentally, Vern opens the door at this point, and pokes his head in.

"You might want to turn your radio on and listen to what happened last night."

Mr. Bartlett turns around and does just that.

Through the static and whining they hear another story.

"The sky was filled last night with bright lights zooming from earth toward the skies across the United States. Reports of the sightings of flying saucers proved to be true this morning, when two were found crashed into the ground in New Mexico. People have reported seeing strange-colored beings, with large black eyes, staggering from the wreckage. The sky over New Mexico is said to have opened up, like a surgeons blade had been at work, exposing an army of intruders. The flying saucers, twenty or more of them, attacked the invaders in a heroic battle. Bright lights from all over the world, lasers—they have called them—fired at the break in the sky, trying to thwart the attackers. It has not been confirmed, but it has been said the flying saucers that crashed were hit by the light lasers from earth. The battle began shortly after dark and ensued until the enemy was turned back at three o'clock this morning. Reports have casualties here on earth at more than two hundred. The number of military aircraft lost, close to one hundred. It's not known at this time, at this station, what or who it was. But, whatever it was has been turned away. The sky has healed itself, and all is calm in the New Mexico skies this afternoon. The military quickly sealed off the areas involved, allowing no entry.

"We've been asked to make this announcement.

"'Stay calm. We are in no danger. The world is united for the safety of mankind. Stay tuned, we will keep you informed.'"

The four men look at each other in disbelief.

"I saw those flashes in the sky last night, but I thought it was part of somebody's fireworks display." Marc is first to speak.

"Well, that seals it. How can you not believe me now?" Mr. Bartlett hammers his point home. "I believe those two people, in that room upstairs last night, were seeking the arsenal, and if they had found it, the outcome of that attack could have been catastrophic. What other explanation is there? They both disappeared from right under our noses. They had to use that mirror in the room."

The three listeners shake their heads in agreement.

"I regret to inform you all—now that you know—you have the same responsibility I've had my entire life. These bodies, the arsenal, are our problem, and it's a big one. We must believe that our visitors from last night will be back. They'll not stop until they get what they want. Then, the next time the sky opens up," he pauses for a few seconds, "I can't let myself think about it."

"How are we going to be able to keep the arsenal a secret? Half the town knows about them by now." Sheriff Collins brings up a good point.

"He's right. Word of this will spread like a prairie fire, and that will bring all the wrong people right to us," Chief Turner interjects.

"And the walls have ears and eyes. They could be watching us right now." Doc Edwards points to the mirror on the wall.

The End